EVERYONE JUST...STAY CALM

"You *bastard!*"

The words w_____—his face's impact ha_____ any favors and his fa_____ ex-gendarme had ro_____ Hamby and Omikado were tall_____ came up on one knee, and the hand which had worn the knuckledusters was wrapped around the butt of a pulser.

"I'm gonna—"

CRRAAAACCCK!

Karlstad's head exploded as the heavy bullet flung him backward and he hit the floor, sliding across it down a sludge of blood and brain matter.

The sound of the shot was like being hit across both ears with the flat of a shovel. Hamby staggered, his eyes going wide as he saw the heavy, old-fashioned automatic pistol in Eileanóra Allenby's hand. His brain was still trying to catch up when another voice shouted.

"Put it down and—!"

CRRAAAACCCK!

Hamby's head whipped around just in time to see Leroy Sexton stumble backward, dropping the sidearm he'd yanked from its holster while Omikado was ranting. The corporal's hands rose to his chest and he looked down, expression incredulous, as he saw the blood. Then he looked back up, his eyes meeting Eileanóra's pitiless gaze, and sagged to his knees. He stayed there for a moment, eyes locked with hers, then thudded the rest of the way to the floor.

Hamby stared at him, then froze as something very cold and razor-sharp touched his throat.

"Seems to me you'd best keep your hands where I can see 'em, Josh."

IN THIS SERIES BY DAVID WEBER

HONOR HARRINGTON

EDITED BY DAVID WEBER

MANTICORE ASCENDANT

THE STAR KINGDOM

To purchase these and all other Baen Book titles in e-book format, please go to www.baen.com.

SHADOW OF VICTORY

DAVID WEBER

SHADOW OF VICTORY

This is a work of fiction. All the characters and events portrayed in this book are fictional, and any resemblance to real people or incidents is purely coincidental.

Copyright © 2016 by Words of Weber, Inc.

All rights reserved, including the right to reproduce this book or portions thereof in any form.

A Baen Books Original

Baen Publishing Enterprises
P.O. Box 1403
Riverdale, NY 10471
www.baen.com

ISBN: 978-1-4814-8288-2

Cover art by David Mattingly

First Baen mass market paperback printing, December 2017
Second Baen mass market paperback printing, July 2019

Library of Congress Control Number: 2016042002

Distributed by Simon & Schuster
1230 Avenue of the Americas
New York, NY 10020

Pages by Joy Freeman (www.pagesbyjoy.com)
Printed in the United States of America

SHADOW OF
VICTORY

FEBRUARY 1921 POST DIASPORA

"I'm a very inventive fellow. With enough time, I can get to *anyone*."

—Captain Damien Harahap,
Solarian League Gendarmerie

✦ Chapter One

BRANDON GRANT HAD NO IDEA how many people he'd killed.

For that matter, he couldn't recall how many planets he'd killed people *on*. It wasn't the sort of thought that crossed his mind. Besides, he'd have needed a pretty sizable folder just to store the data, assuming he'd ever been stupid enough to write it down in the first place.

Still, this was about as far from home as he'd ever operated, and he wondered—vaguely—why these particular kills were so important. And why this one had to look like a common mugging gone wrong. The other one had been much more straightforward, and she'd been a far more prominent target to begin with, but the employer's local agent hadn't quibbled about the obvious ambush his second team had arranged for her. It was true that she was rather more visible than Grant's current target, since she worked in uniform and operated openly out of Gendarmerie HQ here in Pine Mountain, whereas the man he was about to kill didn't. If things worked right, any investigators would buy the announcement from the McIntosh Popular Front claiming responsibility for the first hit, although the MPF was going to be astounded to hear about it. So why not let the same "murderous terrorists" deal with *this* guy, as well? Maybe they just didn't want two obvious assassinations taking off people who had a close professional link? But that struck him as pretty silly. If they died so close together—within less than two hours of each other, for God's sake!—it was still going to ring alarm bells for anyone inclined to be suspicious in the first case. Or maybe this guy's cover was so deep that no one else would know he was connected to the Gendarmerie at all, far less to his uniformed associate?

He shrugged mentally at the thought. He was accustomed to making targeted murder look like something else whenever needed, and his employer's reasons for wanting someone dead were none of his business. If this was the way the people paying the freight wanted it, this was how he'd do it, but it would have been so much simpler to simply walk up behind the target, shoot him in the back of the head, and keep right on walking. It was amazing how easy that was, even with all the modern surveillance and security systems in play, if one simply thought ahead a bit and kept his nerve. But, no. *This* one couldn't be an obvious hit, for whatever reason. A scrap of an ancient poem wandered through his mind, and he snorted in amusement. It truly wasn't his "to wonder why." In point of fact, his employer paid him extraordinarily well not to wonder, but simply "to do or die."

Of course, in Grant's case, he did the doing and someone else did the dying.

He kept his eyes on his uni-link display's current pornographic feature, smiling faintly as he recalled the distasteful looks that feature had drawn from the handful of passersby who'd happened to glance at it. He didn't really blame them; it was as energetic—and loud—as it was in bad taste. That was why he'd chosen it and disabled the privacy function to make sure it could be seen and heard by anyone unfortunate enough to enter his orbit. Anyone dressed like him, leaning against a wall and watching that sort of "entertainment" might be many things, but he certainly wasn't one of the best paid assassins of the explored galaxy.

He did glance up—once—to check the positions of his team, although he was confident they were where they were supposed to be. He'd brought two of them—Markus Bochart and Franz Gillespie—from Old Earth when his employer deployed them to the Madras Sector. They'd worked with him several times before, and he knew he could count on their expertise. The other two were local recruits, but they'd worked out well so far. In fact, he rather regretted the fact that he'd have to eliminate them as one last housekeeping chore before he left the sector. Good help could be hard to find, yet he was unlikely to be operating out this way again anytime soon, and his employer, who liked loose ends even less than he did, had been very specific about that.

All four of them were in position, dressed—like him—in cheap, gaudy clothes in the orange, black, and green colors of the Tremont Towers Dragons, one of Pine Mountain's less fastidious street gangs. That was a minor risk, since the Dragons were less than popular with the local authorities for a host of good reasons, and it was always possible the five of them would draw the attention of the Pine Mountain Police. That was unlikely as long as they simply floated the street, however. Here in the sector capital officers had more important things to do than move along loiterers—even members of the TTD—unless those loiterers made a nuisance of themselves. Besides, it would actually help if some cop had made note of their presence and recalled it later. It would help steer any inquiries in the proper direction, and he hid a smile as he considered how energetically the Dragons were likely to find themselves interrogated if their target was truly important enough to justify all this elaborate deniability rigmarole.

A soft chime sounded in his earbug.

He kept his eyes on the uni-link for another ten seconds, then keyed it off, and shoved himself away from the wall he'd been so assiduously propping up for the last hour or so. He stretched, made deliberate—and obvious—eye contact with his henchmen, and then ambled away up the sidewalk. He smiled as Bochart pried himself away from the light standard *he'd* been holding up and paused to make a mock grab at a passing pedestrian's shoulder bag, then laughed mockingly as she snatched it protectively away. It was a nice touch, one that the local surveillance cameras must have caught but obviously not a serious attempted robbery which might have prompted an immediate response. When the chip was examined later, though, it would show that the "Dragons" had been in a mood to make trouble before they encountered the unfortunate victim of the mugging-to-be.

Ahead of him, the soon-to-be-dead-man came around

the corner and started down the block, and Grant's predator eyes narrowed ever so slightly.

The most extraordinary thing about the man coming towards them was how outstandingly ordinary he looked. Medium height, medium build, medium complexion, medium brown hair . . . there was absolutely nothing about him to catch someone's attention or attract anyone's notice or cause even the most suspicious to file him away in memory. Indeed, he was even more ordinary looking than he'd seemed in the imagery Grant had studied when the assignment landed in his inbox. People didn't get that ordinary without working at it—hard—as Brandon Grant knew better than most, and he'd warned his assistants against automatically accepting the inoffensive harmlessness the other man projected so skillfully.

✧   ✧   ✧

Damien Harahap was an unhappy man.

Partly that was because he disliked failure, no matter who might have employed him at the moment, and failures didn't come much more spectacular than the ones he'd enjoyed on the planets of Montana and Kornati. He didn't know—and might never know—exactly how the wheels had come off, but the news out of the Talbott Sector made it abundantly clear they had. Something had certainly inspired a Manticoran captain to take a scratch-built squadron to Monica and trash the entire system, despite the distinct possibility that his actions would provoke a shooting incident with the Solarian League Navy. Right off the top of his head, Harahap couldn't think of many reasons for a sane human being to do anything of the sort. In fact, the one that came most readily to mind was the discovery

that somebody had been providing the Monica System
Navy with first-line Solarian warships at the same time
somebody else had been fueling and feeding terrorist
movements designed to destabilize local governments
which were in the process of seeking admission to the
Star Kingdom of Manticore in places like Montana and
Split. Only a complete idiot would have assumed there
was no connection between those two happenstances,
and there were very few complete idiots in the Royal
Manticoran Navy. The RMN wasn't exactly noted for
timidity, either, and Harahap could understand how
a Manticoran officer might feel a tad . . . irked by
something like that.

The problem it posed for him was whether or not
the Manties would be able to track his handiwork
back to the Solarian League Gendarmerie. Not that
the Gendarmerie had had anything to do with it . . .
officially. Unfortunately, Damien Harahap was a captain
in the Gendarmerie, and Manticore might find it a bit
difficult to believe he'd been operating independently.
Especially since he hadn't been, however carefully
Ulrike Eichbauer had stressed the fact that he was
being given "leave time" in order to assist his current
private enterprise employers on his own centicredit.

Which was another reason for his current unhappiness. Major Eichbauer understood plausible deniability
as well as the next covert operator, but *she* was the
one who'd sent *him* the coded request to meet her
at Urrezko Koilara. He'd half expected the summons,
knowing Eichbauer. She wasn't the sort to leave one
of her people twisting in the wind, but she was also
unlikely to call him in for any sort of official meeting
until she knew whether or not his recent activities were

going to splatter all over the Gendarmerie. Urrezko Koilara was a small, out-of-the way restaurant specializing in Old Earth's Iberian cuisine. It wasn't going to be found on any gourmand's guide to the galaxy, but the food was on the high side of decent and its owner had been one of Eichbauer's best confidential informants before her promotion to major took her off the streets and into an office job. Which made it an ideal place for a quiet, off-the-books meet.

But Eichbauer hadn't been there. Worse, the owner hadn't even glanced in Harahap's direction when he arrived. Either no one had told her Eichbauer intended to meet one of her people in her restaurant, or else someone had paid her to pretend no one had. Given the faint frown of baffled memory the woman had bestowed upon him when he asked to speak to the manager and complimented her on the quality of the food, Harahap was inclined towards the former explanation. If the supposed meeting had been some sort of set up, she would have greeted him with bland innocence, not with the expression of someone trying to remember where she'd seen him before. He was accustomed to not being remembered, since it was one of his primary stocks in trade, but some trace of memory had obviously been working in there, and there wouldn't have been if she'd been briefed in preparation for some kind of operation.

So what had happened to Eichbauer? She knew how to get in touch with him to cancel the meet, and she hadn't. But he was positive the original message had come from her; among other things, no one else knew the code phrase, since he'd selected it randomly himself better than three T-years ago. It

was remotely possible she'd decided he needed to be
tidied up before any more fecal matter hit the rotary
air impeller, but there were a dozen other ways she
could have gone about that. Besides, if she'd wanted
him removed from the equation, there *would* have
been someone waiting for him at the restaurant. On
the other hand, it was hard to imagine what could
have prevented a Gendarmerie major—and Brigadier
Francisca Yucel's chief intelligence officer, at that!—
from keeping an appointment *she'd* made.

It was all very worrisome, although no one could
have guessed that from his carefree expression as he
enjoyed the early afternoon sunlight. There had to be
an explanation. The problem was that it could very
well be an explanation for which he didn't much care,
and those sorts of explanations could be...messy.

Brandon Grant's two local employees sauntered past
the oncoming target without, Grant noted approvingly,
giving him so much as a glance. They were behind
him, now, and Markus Bochart opened the gambit by
stepping into the target's path with exactly the right
ganger swagger. His left hand rose, three middle
fingers bladed together for a contemptuous thrust to
the target's sternum, while his right hand slid inside
his own unsealed jacket.

It was so satisfying when everything went according
to plan, Grant thought. In another three seconds...

"Hey, null jet! Let's see your wal—"

Although he might be a Gendarmerie captain,
Harahap's assignments had always kept him well clear
of the Madras Sector's capital planet. His weren't the

sort of talents which would have found their best and highest use on a planet like Meyers or in a city like Pine Mountain, and anonymity was one of his most important stocks in trade. That was one of the reasons Eichbauer had been careful to keep him buried in the boonies and as far out of any potential public spotlights as possible.

As a result, he was less familiar with the capital's gangs than he might have been somewhere else, but he recognized ganger colors when he saw them. Nothing had screamed overt warning to him, but the ingrained situational awareness born of thirty years of fieldwork had kept an eye on the quintet sauntering arrogantly toward him. He'd noticed peripherally when the first two stepped past him, and he knew exactly where they were. It was the trio still coming towards him that held his attention, however. There was something just a little off about them, something he couldn't have quite put a finger on if anyone had asked him to describe it.

Under other circumstances, he would have donned his nervous-mouse citizen's mask and stepped back timidly when the arrogant tough jabbed him in the chest. He would even have brought out the extra wallet he carried specifically to hand over to demanding police officers and surrendered it with proper, cringing terror. But the *other* hand—the one sliding inside the loose jacket—rang all sorts of alarms.

"Hey, null jet!" the ganger snarled scornfully. "Let's see your wal—"

✧   ✧   ✧

Brandon Grant's eyes widened as the target's right arm flashed out with serpent quickness. It darted inside Bochart's left arm, slammed into the inside of his forearm, and swept the entire arm out and to the side. Then it snaked around and its hand locked on the inside of Bochart's elbow. A sudden twist, and Bochart grimaced in anguish, his knees trying to buckle with the sudden, totally unexpected pain as the steely fingers drilling into his elbow found exactly the nerve points they'd sought.

But Markus Bochart was a professional. The pain didn't keep his right hand from finding the haft of the vibro blade scabbarded under his jacket. The plan hadn't called for it to come out so quickly—not until the belligerent ganger's temper had exploded when his victim proved insufficiently pliant. He didn't much care about plans at the moment, though. The speed and brutal efficiency of his victim's response told him that despite Grant's admonition, their target's unprepossessing appearance had lulled him into a grievous misjudgment.

His hand came out of his jacket…and he discovered just how grievous that misjudgment had truly been.

Despite his inner alarm system, Harahap hadn't really expected a lethal weapon out of a ganger. Not that quickly. But there were certain advantages to spending thirty odd T-years in unsavory places doing unsavory things. He spun on the ball of his right foot, turning his back to the other without releasing his elbow lock. His spine rammed against the considerably taller man's chest, pinning his right hand against his torso and inside his jacket, and his own right arm shot up with piledriver force. The heel of his hand slammed into Bochart's jaw, shattering it and snapping his head back viciously.

That sledgehammer hand continued its upward thrust, and Harahap's forearm snaked around the back of Bochart's neck. His arm locked, his spine bent, and the heel of his right foot smashed into his would-be killer's right kneecap as he jerked forward and down.

❖   ❖   ❖

Grant's surprise became shocked disbelief. Bochart's nascent scream as his kneecap splintered ended before it was well begun in the sharp, clear crack of a breaking neck and his body flew forward over the target's back. The vibro blade fell from his nerveless hand as he hit the sidewalk, whining as its blade sank effortlessly into the obsidian-tough ceramacrete before the auto cutoff killed it, and the man who was supposed to be already dying spun into Franz Gillespie like an outstandingly ordinary cyclone.

Gillespie saw him coming and his own vibro blade cleared his jacket with a lethal, ugly whine. That was as far as it got, though, before Harahap was upon him. One hand, far stronger than it looked, locked on the wrist of his knife hand. The other hand darted up, wrapped its fingers in his hair, and yanked his face down to meet a rising kneecap. Bone crunched, blood splattered, and Harahap pivoted, turning in place and yanking the half-blind, three quarters-stunned Gillespie past him.

The killer from Old Terra stumbled forward, directly into the nearer of the two locals, and both of them went down in a tangle of flailing limbs.

The second local gaped in astonishment as the neatly planned ambush disintegrated. He was still gaping when Harahap swept into him and a bladed hand crushed his larynx like a mallet. He reeled backward, hands clutching at his ruined windpipe, and Harahap twisted back towards his fallen partner.

Gillespie had risen to one knee, one hand clutching his demolished, broken face, trying to clear the blood from his eyes, while his other hand swept the ceramacrete, searching for his dropped vibro blade. The other local rolled to his feet with commendable quickness . . . only to meet the heel of Harahap's shoe before he was fully upright. It crashed into his solar plexus, doubling him up, sending him back to his knees, and the gendarme captain brought the point of his elbow down on the nape of his neck like an ax.

✧   ✧   ✧

It took Brandon Grant almost point-six seconds to reach his decision.

Fuck the plan!

His hand came out of his own jacket—and not with another ganger's vibro blade—as the second Meyerite went down with a sodden thud. The pulser snapped up. It found its target, and his finger started to squeeze.

✧   ✧   ✧

Harahap spun from the bloody-faced "ganger" still trying to find his feet as a burst of pulser darts shrieked past him. That hissing, hypervelocity scream was the sort of sound no one in his line of work was ever likely to mistake for anything else, and his eyes widened as the fifth and final ganger's chest exploded in a vapor cloud of blood and shredded tissue.

The corpse was still falling and Harahap's brain was still trying to catch up with his trained instincts when the same pulser fired again. This time it was only a single dart, not a burst, and Franz Gillespie went down again.

"I think you'd better come with me, Captain Harahap," a voice said far too calmly, and Harahap looked up from the five sprawled corpses.

"Pine Mountain's finest will be along shortly," the fair-haired, gray-eyed man he'd never seen before in his life pointed out as he slid his weapon back into the concealment of his tailored tunic, "and I imagine they'll have all sorts of questions you'd really rather not answer. I know I'd rather not, anyway. So . . ."

He half-bowed from the waist, flourishing one hand elegantly in an "after you" gesture, and pointed up the street.

❖   ❖   ❖

"So perhaps you'd like to explain what the hell that was all about?" Harahap asked just a bit acidly fifteen minutes later.

The private air car his unknown rescuer had tucked away in an underground parking garage five minutes' walk from the aborted ambush's site sped swiftly through the Meyers sky. Under other circumstances, he might have been concerned about a police pursuit, but some strange malady had overtaken the security cameras covering the entire floor on which the air car had been parked. Somehow he hadn't been as surprised as perhaps he should have been to see the blinking "disabled" lights.

At the moment, he sat in the front passenger seat, one hand inside his own tunic with its fingers curled around the comfort of a pulser butt. Not that he wasn't grateful for his rescue, of course.

"That, I'm very much afraid, Captain," the pilot said calmly, never looking away from his HUD, although he had to be aware of the weapon fifty centimeters from his ribcage, "was an attempt to tidy up loose ends. I'm sure you're aware of how the process works."

"And just what might make me a 'loose end'?"

"Your recent Talbott activities. You know—the ones in places like Montana, Kornati, Mainwaring. *Those* activities."

"Suppose I told you I don't have any idea what you're talking about?"

"Well, in that case, I imagine I'd have to conclude that at least one of us was an idiot. Or that he believed the *other* one was an idiot, anyway." He smiled, turning to look at Harahap for the first time, and shook his head. "Since I know neither of us fit that description, I'm sure you don't think I happened along by sheer coincidence."

"No, I don't," Harahap conceded. "On the other hand, I'm still waiting to find out why you *did* happen along."

"Ms. Anisimovna asked me to keep an eye on you," the pilot said, and despite himself, Harahap's nostrils flared.

"And why might Ms. Anisimovna have asked you to do that?" he asked after a moment.

"Because you needed looking after?" the other suggested with a broader smile, and—despite himself—Harahap felt himself smile back.

"Under the circumstances, I'll give you that one," he said. "But I'd still like to know what the hell is going on before you land this air car somewhere I might not like. So while I'm suitably grateful and all, maybe you'd better explain things in a little more depth."

"If you like," the other agreed. He locked the autopilot stud, putting the air car on its current flight plan, and slid his chair back from the console so he could turn it to face Harahap fully.

"First, my name is Rufino Chernyshev." He saw the look in Harahap's eyes and chuckled. "No, really it is! It's not the one on my pilot's license, of course, but since I'm inclined to hope we'll wind up on the same team, I don't really mind sharing it with you."

Harahap nodded affably, although he could think of another reason Chernyshev might be willing to share his real name. After all, he'd have a hard time passing it along to anyone else if he ended up dead.

"The really, really short version of 'what the hell is going on,' is that the operation for which Major Eichbauer was kind enough to lend you to Ms. Anisimovna and her associates has misfired pretty spectacularly. It's likely the fallout's going to get a lot worse before it gets any better, and at least some of those associates of hers are worried about getting their fingers burned. One of them decided to cut any strings that might lead back to his involvement. Ms. Anisimovna was afraid he might do that, which is why she asked me to look after you. Unfortunately," Chernyshev's expression tightened for a moment, "I wasn't able to get to Major Eichbauer in time."

"Ulrike's dead?" Harahap's voice was flat, almost disinterested, and his eyes showed no emotion at all, which anyone who knew him well would have recognized as a very bad sign.

"I'm afraid so." Chernyshev shook his head. "I took out the team that killed her, but I got there a second or two too late. She was still alive, but she was going quickly and she knew it. She'd been on her way to your meeting, and the last thing she ever did was to tell me where that meeting was." He met Harahap's gaze levelly. "That's the only reason I was able to get to *you* in time, Captain. Friends like that are worth having."

"Yes, they are," Harahap agreed. "And that's why you're going to tell me who ordered these hits."

"You're a resourceful man, Captain, but I doubt even you could get to him, especially if he knows you're still alive. On the other hand, I represent an organization which almost certainly *can* get to him . . . when the time is right."

"And this organization of yours sent you to rescue me out of pure altruism, I suppose?"

"Hardly!" Chernyshev snorted. "No, it sent me to rescue you because you're a very valuable asset. You demonstrated that in Talbott, and the people I work for were impressed by your talents. I expect they'd like you to continue to work for them."

"But you're not sure about that."

"Things have moved rather more swiftly than anyone expected when they handed me this assignment, Captain. I'm going to have to park you in a safe house until my instructions get updated."

"What if I don't want to be parked?" Harahap drew the pulser from his tunic and twitched its muzzle like a pointer. "I *am* a captain in the Gendarmerie, after all. Now that I know someone's put a hit out on me, I'm sure I can manage to come in out of the cold in one piece."

"Assuming your superiors aren't as interested in cutting those threads as the person who sent those killers after you. Think about it. Major Eichbauer and you could have led the trail of breadcrumbs right back to Brigadier Yucel if someone made it worth your time, and there's likely to be plenty of official disfavor to go around when Old Chicago starts untangling what's happened out here. Do you really want to take a chance that Yucel wouldn't see the upside of your permanent disappearance?"

"Point," Harahap said after a moment. "On the other hand, Ms. Anisimovna could see the same thing."

"She could," Chernyshev agreed. "But our organization still wants what it wanted before, and we're pretty sure what happened in Talbott wasn't your fault. So why should Ms. Anisimovna throw away such a sharp, useful tool? Especially"—he smiled a bit thinly—"when the tool in question has nowhere else to go?"

Harahap bared his teeth in what was nominally a smile, but Chernyshev had a point. In fact, he had a very good point. Still...

"All right," he said after thirty seconds, setting the pulser's safety and sliding it back into the shoulder holster under his tunic. "All right, you've made your point, and you're probably right. So take me to this safe house of yours. But first, tell me this. Who did order the hit? I may not be able to get to him *now*, but I'm a very inventive fellow. With enough time, I can get to *anyone*."

"I believe you could, Captain Harahap," Chernyshev agreed, head cocked to one side, his expression almost quizzical. "At the moment, all I can tell you is who I suspect was behind it. It might have been any one of several people, and it's going to take a while to confirm exactly which one it is. I'll be very surprised if it turns out to be someone else, though."

"So will I," Harahap said honestly. He recognized another consummate professional when he saw one.

"Well, bearing that caveat in mind, I'm reasonably certain it was Volkhart Kalokainos." Chernyshev shrugged. "Kalokainos Shipping's been just a little too openly involved in trying to break the Manties' kneecaps for a long, long time now, and he's invested just a bit too deeply in some operations which could cause him considerable embarrassment if they were brought to the League's official attention. They could also cause. the *League*—or the people who run it, anyway—considerable embarrassment, and Kolokoltsov and the others would throw him to the wolves in a heartbeat to prevent that. Besides, Kalokainos has more than enough enemies among the other transstellars. They'd make it worth Kolokoltsov's while to hammer him on any pretext that offered."

"And Jessyk and Manpower don't have any enemies, I suppose?"

"Of course they do, but they aren't Solly-based, either. The League doesn't really have a hammer to bring down on them—not legally, anyway. The only people *they* have to worry about at the moment live in star nations that begin with the letter 'M,' Captain."

"I imagine they do," Harahap acknowledged after a moment and sat back in his seat. "All right, Mr. Chernyshev. Take me to this safe house of yours."

"Already on our way, Captain." Chernyshev smiled broadly. "And, please, call me Rufino. I suspect we'll be working closely with one another."

MARCH 1921 POST DIASPORA

"Dust off your researching skills, Professor. Figure out where we can buy what I need to rip the throat out of my best friend's political monument."

—Tomasz Szponder,
Krucjata Wolonści Myśli

✦ Chapter Two

"IT'S YOUR MOVE, EDYTA," the blond, blue-eyed girl said, tapping the portable chess set squeezed into the armrest space between her seat and the next. "You *do* plan to move sometime today, don't you?"

"Of course I do!" Edyta Sowczyk, four centimeters shorter, with dark eyes and bright chestnut hair, tore her attention away from the window beside her. "But there's plenty of time for *that!* I want to see the spaceport!"

Karolina Kreft sighed and shook her head with an air of martyrdom. It wasn't a very convincing sigh, all things considered. At fifteen, she was barely a year older than Edyta, and she rather suspected that her younger friend was quite a bit smarter than she was. Not that Karolina was a dummy, by any means. She wouldn't have been invited on this special tour of the spaceport if she hadn't been in the top two or three percent of her class. But Edyta had been accelerated a full year ahead of her age-mates, and she was *still* in the top two or three percent of their class.

She also regularly beat Karolina's socks off at chess . . . when she could keep her mind on the game, anyway. And that, little though Karolina cared to admit it, was one reason she wanted Edyta to go ahead and move *now*. The trap she'd set for her opponent's queen's knight wasn't something Edyta was likely to miss under normal circumstances. Under *these* circumstances, though . . .

"We'll get to the spaceport when we get to the spaceport," she said. "In the meantime, let's go ahead and try to finish up this game."

"Oh, all right."

Edyta flounced around in her seat—she was small-boned and petite enough she actually had space to do that, despite how tightly packed the airbus was—and looked down at the chessboard. She reached out impatiently, then paused, fingertips millimeters away from her king's bishop. She stayed that way for a moment, then withdrew her hand and settled back in her seat.

"That was sneaky, Karolina," she said, toying with one of her pigtails' cheap but pretty green ribbons. The holo pattern printed on it flashed in the sunlight, and she tilted her head to one side, considering the board. "If I didn't know better, I'd think you're trying to pick on my poor little knight."

"Who, me?" Karolina tried her very best to sound innocent, not that she expected Edyta to buy it for a moment.

"Unless it was someone else who moved your queen," Edyta said almost absently, her eyes very thoughtful. Then she reached out again, not for the bishop this time, but for her king's knight, and Karolina puffed her lips in frustration as her trap fell apart.

✧　　✧　　✧

"How much longer, Andrzej?"

Lukrecja Wolińska had to raise her voice to be heard over the excited chatter of more than a hundred kids.

The high school teacher sat directly behind the airbus driver. As one of the four chaperones attached to the tour group, she had the luxury of an empty seat beside her at the moment, since her seatmate, Roman Sowiński, was currently somewhere back along the crowded central aisle attempting to quell some of that chatter. His mission reminded Lukrecja of an Old Earth king named Canute, and he was welcome to it.

Lukrecja's real job would start once they got the bus on the ground, and she felt more than a little trepidation as she contemplated it. All the kids on the tour were *good* kids, but they'd also been born and raised in the Projects. They were about to have the chance to peer, however briefly, through a window into the sort of opulent lifestyle they and their parents could scarcely even imagine. And it was going to be up to her to make sure they behaved themselves while they did that peering.

The good news was that any kid from the Projects understood on an almost cellular level that there were different sorts of rules for different sorts of people. They knew the families of the *Oligarchia* came from a world totally unlike their own, and they also knew there were . . . consequences to arousing an *oligarcha's* ire. She could depend on them to be on their very best behavior. The problem was that the rules of behavior they'd been taught might not be adequate for today's expedition.

Oh, stop worrying! she told herself, looking over her shoulder and smiling as she saw Edyta Sowczyk's head bent over the chessboard between her and Karolina Kreft. They were two of the brightest spots in her teacher's life, and she knew both of them—especially Edyta—could scarcely wait. In a sense, both of them had grown up in the spaceport's shadow, since their parents worked—when they could find work—for the Stowarzyszenie Eksporterów Owoców Morza, which dominated the spaceport's business. Then again, that was true one way or another of a lot of people in the Projects.

"Not much farther, Ms. Wolińska," Andrzej Bicukowski, the airbus driver said, raising his own voice but never looking away from his HUD, "but there's a traffic jam in the regular approach lanes." He tapped the earbug tied into the Lądowisko Air Traffic net. "Sounds like a pair of air lorries tangled, and then a limo ran into them. ATC's closed down the South Approach to a single lane. Don't imagine anybody's moving very fast along it, either, and this beast is a bit big to be threading any needles, so I've filed a diversion from our original route. It'll bring us in from the east side of the port, over the SEOM warehouses along the river." He grimaced. "It's less scenic, but it'll get your kids on the ground a lot quicker."

"Quicker is good," Lukrecja said with feeling, as the background chatter reached a new decibel level. "Quicker is *very* good."

Bicukowski chuckled and the airbus turned into one of the tertiary approach lanes along the outer ring route.

✧　　✧　　✧

"What the fuck does that idiot think he's doing?" Wiktoria Lewandowska growled.

She stood in the Stowarzyszenie Eksporterów Owoców Morza's main shipping and traffic control room glowering over one of the duty controller's shoulders at the display. The orange icon moving across it showed no transponder code. That was true for quite a few of the icons on his display at the moment, probably because the air traffic crews and their computers were still trying to sort out the confusion of the worst midair collision in the last five or ten years. It wasn't too surprising their systems were hiccupping, given the fact that a badly damaged air taxi had spun out of the fireball and impacted directly atop an automated air traffic relay station. But none of the other blank icons were intruding on *her* airspace. Oh, sure, the route along which it was headed was technically in a public transit lane, but it cut directly through SEOM's airspace. Public or not, that air *belonged* to SEOM, and everybody damned well knew it!

"Probably another lorry trying to avoid that pileup on the South Approach, Ma'am," the controller replied, putting her own thoughts into words. "Hard to be sure, of course. ATC's being even slower than usual updating the feeds. Probably too busy trying to sort out the mess."

"Well I don't give a damn how busy Traffic Control is!" Lewandowska snapped. "That's *our* airspace, and I'm sick and tired of having frigging gypsies drift through it anytime they damn well please!"

The controller considered—briefly—pointing out that there weren't that many gypsy air lorries working the spaceport these days. The big transport lines had frozen them out again, and it was going to be months, at least, before they started getting a toe back into those particular waters. God only knew what they'd find to survive on in the meantime. In fact, quite a few of them probably wouldn't survive at all. That always happened when the big boys shut down their access again. But it wasn't his business to tell Wiktoria Lewandowska anything she didn't want to hear.

"Tell him to clear our space right damned now," she commanded.

"Already tried, Ma'am. He's not answering on any of the standard freight channels."

"He's not?" Lewandowska turned her eyes from the display to glare at the unfortunate controller. "Why the hell not?"

"I don't know, Ma'am," the controller replied, very carefully not adding *How the hell am I* supposed *to know?* to his answer.

"Well, we'll just see about *that!*" Lewandowska stepped back and keyed her personal com. "Give me Perimeter One," she said.

✧   ✧   ✧

Andrzej Bicukowski frowned and killed another fifty kilometers per hour of airspeed. It wasn't unheard of for Lądowisko Air Traffic Control to get behind in the outlying sectors of the system capital, but it was unusual for them to drop the ball this close in to the heart of the city. Especially this close to the spaceport. The *oligarchowie* didn't like it when their flight plans got screwed up, but it looked like that pileup on the South Approach must be even worse than he'd thought it was. Over a dozen emergency vehicles were headed into it now, and it sounded as if the automated system had gone on the fritz again. Every professional driver and pilot in Lądowisko knew the entire system needed to be replaced, but convincing the people who controlled the credit flow to spend the necessary money wasn't the easiest thing in the world.

"Lądowisko Spaceport Control," he said into his mike again, hoping like hell there might be at least one human backing up the automatics. "Marianna Tours One-Zero-Niner requests copy confirmation of flight plan update. Repeat, Marianna Tours One-Zero-Niner requests copy confirmation of flight plan update."

He sat back, the fingers of one hand drumming lightly on the control column, then growled a mild obscenity under his breath as a red icon pulsed in his HUD.

Great! Not enough they won't talk to me, but now the transponder's gone down! What a time for the update feeds to shut down!

He slowed the airbus still further, going to Visual Flight Rules. Fortunately, visibility was excellent.

❖   ❖   ❖

"Yes, Control," Kazimierz Łukaszewski said. "Perimeter One copies."

He punched the button, dropping his orbiting air car out of automatic and checked his displays. There it was. The fat-assed orange icon lumbering across SEOM's private airspace wasn't even trying to clear the perimeter quickly. It was just ambling right through the middle of the airspace SEOM paid perfectly good money for. Ms. Lewandowska was right. It was about damned time the gypsies learned their lesson.

❖   ❖   ❖

Lieutenant Ludwik Kezczyński of the Siły Zbrojne Włocławka growled in disgust and came around for another circle of the spaceport. He'd just completed a four-hour training mission, and he was more than ready to put his sting ship back on the ground and hand it over to the ground crew. Not only had it been boring as hell, but he had a hot date waiting, and Pelagia wasn't the sort who cared to be kept waiting by a mere lieutenant in the planetary armed forces. He didn't think she'd be impressed when he said "I *tried*, Honey!"

He checked his display, and his ill temper eased just a bit as he realized the pileup was even worse than he'd thought it was. There were over a dozen vehicles involved, they'd landed all over the ground traffic lanes, some of them in bits and pieces, and at least three of them—not to mention what looked like a couple of ground lorries—were on fire. No wonder ATC was tearing its hair while it tried to sort out the mess. And they weren't going to get that done anytime soon, either. It looked like Pelagia was just going to have to—

His train of thought hiccuped as he noticed the icon swooping down from the north-northeast at a dangerous rate of speed. It was the sort of maneuver a trained military pilot noticed, and he punched a command into his sensor suite, then frowned. The transponder said it was a civilian air car, all right, but its emission signature matched that of a Skrzydło Jastrząb forward reconnaissance vehicle, which mounted a pair of thirty-millimeter pulse cannon and provision for up to six underwing missiles. What the hell was it doing screaming down like a bat out of hell that way?!

"Lądowisko Spaceport Control, Stingship Alpha-Five-Charlie requests priority direct link to civilian air car Oscar-Mike-Sierra-Echo-Seven-One!"

❖   ❖   ❖

Kazimierz Łukaszewski's lips drew back in an antici-
patory smile as the icon swelled rapidly in the center
of his display. It still wasn't flashing a transponder,
and he checked his approach angle carefully. Perfect.
He was coming in from the land side of the Szeroka
Rzeka estuary. His little demonstration would have
plenty of deep, empty water in which to land.

"Alpha-Five-Charlie, Lądowisko Spaceport Control."
The voice in Lieutenant Kezczyński's earbug sounded
more than a little harried. "Trying to get you that link,
but things are a little confused just now."

"Lądowisko Control, Alpha-Five-Charlie copies, but
you'd better expedite. I don't know what this idiot
thinks he's doing, but—"

Łukaszewski was old-school. Or he liked to think
of himself that way, anyhow. What he really wished
was that he'd been born on Old Earth back when
aircraft were made of canvas and wire and the only
fire control they had was the human eye. It had taken
men to fly those contraptions!

Under the circumstances, he decided, he could
allow himself a small treat, and he disengaged the
fire control computer and activated the manual trigger
button on his flight column.

A proximity alarm screamed, and Andrzej Bicukowski
stared in horror at the projected flight paths on his
short-scan radar. There was no time to ask ATC what
was happening. There wasn't even time to hit the
seatbelt warning sign.

He slammed the throttle wide open and heaved

the huge airbus around to port, circling across the
estuary in a frantic effort to avoid the midair collision.

"Oh, Christ—*no!*"

Lieutenant Kezczyński's face went white as the
airbus in the Marianna Tours livery turned sharply
left, away from the oncoming "civilian" air car. He
understood instantly what the bus driver was doing,
and why. And under normal circumstances, it would
have been the right thing to do.

Today, it was exactly the *wrong* thing.

"Oh, *shit!*" Kazimierz Łukaszewski screamed. He
tried—he really *tried*—to get his finger off the trigger,
but it was a lifetime—a *hundred* lifetimes—too late.

The airbus swerving to avoid a midair collision with
his air car flew straight into the "warning burst" of
pulser fire and disintegrated in a blinding ball of flame.

✧ Chapter Three

"SO THE INQUIRY'S OFFICIALLY OVER?"

"Yes, yes it is, Tomasz. It hasn't been announced yet, but my office's seen a preliminary draft." Szymon Ziomkowski sighed from the other side of the table's snowy linen cloth and shook his head, his expression unhappy. He picked up his vodka glass and sipped, then set it back down and gazed down into it. "A sad business. Very sad," he said.

"Yes, I'm sure it was." Tomasz Szponder leaned back in his chair and gazed at the younger man. "And did the inquiry reach any conclusions about how it happened?"

"Just one of those unfortunate things no one could've seen coming," Ziomkowski replied. "Apparently the airbus driver wasn't paying attention to the guard frequency. He flew right into the port's restricted airspace despite repeated warnings, and you know how sensitive the SZW's been about security since that business last year with the lunatic air limo driver."

"I see."

Szponder sipped his own vodka and let his gaze sweep the enormous dining room on the top floor of the Hotel Włodzimierz Ziomkowski. He remembered when it had been the Hotel Orle Gniazdo, the Eagle's Nest Hotel. But that was before it had been renamed for Szymon's uncle five T-years earlier. No one called it the Orle Gniazdo anymore.

Not when anyone else might hear them, anyway.

"Has Ludwika officially signed off on the report?" he asked after a moment.

"Not really her job, is it?" Ziomkowski looked up from his vodka glass. "She's the SZW's commanding general, Tomasz. I'm sure someone at a lower level— probably Pawlikowski—will issue the final approval on it. Or whatever they call it in the military. In fact, I suppose there's something official in the military chain of command about that. Not really my area, I'm afraid."

"No, of course it isn't." Szponder smiled and flicked his fingers in a "not that important" gesture, then raised the same hand to signal for the waiter. "I understand the *ruskie pierogi* is supposed to be especially good today," he said. "I thought we might start with that and the *krupnik*. What would you choose for the main course?"

❖   ❖   ❖

"Ordering sooner than I expected," Wincenty Małakowski observed.

"You should pay more attention to the itinerary updates." Grzegorz Zieliński's tone was gently chiding. "Mr. Szponder is a busy man today. That speech of his at the hospital got moved up."

"And even the Przewodniczący has to accommodate his schedule to Mr. Szponder?" Małakowski asked dryly.

"He doesn't *have* to, Wincenty. He simply chooses to. It's all about respect." Zieliński shook his head. "You younger people have no respect for tradition. Mr. Szponder's known the Przewodniczący since he was a teenager. He's almost another uncle."

"I know. I know!" Małakowski waved his hand in a gesture that mingled acknowledgment and apology. "And I suppose if anyone in the Party's got a right to a little extra consideration from the Przewodniczący, it's Mr. Szponder."

"Probably some truth in that, too," Zieliński agreed. "And if they're ordering now, then you and I should probably get our order in, as well."

"Good idea." Małakowski nodded and reached out to key the menu, but his eyes were still on the two men at the table in the private alcove. "Wonder what they're talking about?"

"None of our business," Zieliński replied, looking at the menu display himself.

"Probably not," Małakowski conceded.

Zieliński only made a vague sound of agreement as he paged through the menu, although both of them knew that wasn't strictly true. As hand-picked agents of the Departament Ochrony Przewodniczącego, the Chairman Protection Department, they weren't supposed to be blind to the political implications of any of the Chairman's interactions with anyone. And as Małakowski understood perfectly well, their status as sworn officers of the Biuro Bezpieczeństwa i Prawdy, the Bureau of Security and Truth, meant they had responsibilities to Justyna Pokriefke, who headed that bureau. Responsibilities which sometimes—more often than Zieliński would have preferred, really—bore precious little resemblance to the *official* description of their duties.

He finished placing his order and looked up from the menu's display, trained eyes circling the dining room, picking up the other DOP agents strategically stationed to cover every entry and exit. There'd been a time when that sort of security would have been considered overkill. Zieliński remembered watching Włodzimierz Ziomkowski waving back his personal bodyguards—all three or four of them—so that he could wade straight into huge, wildly enthusiastic crowds to shake hands, slap backs, kiss babies, and bend over to present a private ear to some party member with a private message or request.

He missed those days.

"Status check," he murmured, and nodded ever so slightly in approval as the responses came back over his earbug.

He didn't really think there were any active plots to assassinate Przewodniczący Ziomkowski, but he was nowhere as certain of that as he'd like to be, and that incident with the airbus might have some nasty repercussions down the road. A tour airbus loaded with school students wasn't supposed to be shot down in a midair explosion by a military sting ship. Over eighty dead—that was the final death toll, but whatever the official 'faxes might have to say, and whatever open chatter there might be on the electronic channels, he knew there were rumors the government was actually understating the casualties. He didn't think they were; surely no one could've gotten more than eighty or ninety, max, onto an airbus. But the truth was that he wasn't *certain* the official number was accurate, and those rumors were taking on an ugly tone. One that was actually directed at Ziomkowski himself for a change.

So, yes, it was possible that this time all the elaborate security might find itself necessary.

He watched the Chairman and his guest's appetizers arrive, then glanced up as another server reached across his shoulder to set his own plate in front of him. He murmured his thanks and reached for his napkin-wrapped silverware.

"Better dig in," he advised Małakowski. "If Mr. Szponder makes his schedule and the Przewodniczący decides to walk him out to the garage again, you don't have long."

"I know."

Małakowski reached for his own fork, and Zieliński's eyes drifted back to the brown-haired, square-faced man sitting across the table from Ziomkowski.

Tomasz Szponder was a good twelve or thirteen centimeters shorter than the Chairman, but then again, Ziomkowski was a very tall man. Szponder was also over thirty T-years older than the Chairman, and he'd been one of Włodzimierz Ziomkowski's graduate students ten years before Szymon Ziomkowski was ever born. He was also a member in good standing of the *Oligarchia*, the group of incredibly wealthy families who totally dominated the Włocławek System's economy. There'd been a time when Tomasz Szponder had been something close to a personal friend of Grzegorz Zieliński, as well, but that, too, had been a long time ago. Back in the heady early days of the *Agitacja*, when they'd both been enthusiastic members of the newly organized

Ruch Odnowy Narodowej. Back before the National Redemption Movement had succeeded in its goal of winning the political power to implement its reforms through the ballot box.

These days, Szponder had settled back into the familiar comfort of his role as an *oligarcha* and Grzegorz Zieliński had settled back into *his* familiar role as someone who protected the *Oligarchia*. There were times, in the privacy of his mind, when he allowed himself to be disappointed in Szponder, but at least he wasn't one of the *łowcy trufli*, the "truffle hunters." It was a nickname bestowed—not approvingly—on Włocławek's oligarchs as an allusion to the Old Earth swine which had been imported to Włocławek T-centuries ago by the original colonists. The Włocławek *trufla* was a native fungus with a musky, fruity and yet simultaneously astringent flavor that was almost addictive, not the transplant of the same name, but Old Earth hogs were just as good at rooting it out with their snouts.

Of course, Szponder didn't really need to go hunting for money. Not that he turned up his nose when it came his way—and it came his way a *lot*, given his Party connections—but he came from old money, as well, one of the founding families of the *Oligarchia*. That was one of the things which had made him so useful to the RON, and he'd contributed a great deal to the Party's coffers in the early days. Hadn't demanded it back later, either. Then again, demanding anything back from the Party was a bad idea, whoever you were. And he could probably afford to write it off as a good investment, anyway, given how many opportunities came the way of the *Trzystu*, the Three Hundred. There were actually quite a few less than three hundred of them these days, but they were the remaining members of the RON's original central committee. Instead of the gorgeous holographic badges issued to newer members with higher Party numbers, the survivors of that committee still wore the battered, enameled lapel pins which had been all it could afford those days. Which made it even sadder that so many of them had—

Zieliński gave himself an internal shake. Yes, Szponder had dived back into his role as one of Włocławek's elite like a *ryby grzmot* into water. And, yes, he was richer—a *lot* richer—than ever as a result. But he also continued to contribute generously to charities, like his work with the Siostry Ubogich, the Sisters of the Poor, who'd founded and continued to staff the Szpital Marii Urbańskiej in downtown Lądowisko. The hospital's campuses were located in the poorest sections of the capital city, and the Szponder family had been associated with it for over two hundred T-years.

He was also the owner of the *Lądowisko Gazety i Kurier*, the capital city's most widely followed newsfax. He'd bought the 'fax for the Party back in the early days and built it into the most influential news channel on the planet, but he was far less active in terms of setting editorial policy than he'd been back in those heady days. These days it was wiser to let the Party control things like that, although Szponder did like to keep his hand in with his street reporters. Zieliński didn't like to think about how often those newsies picked up on something important even more quickly than the BBP or BDK, and Szponder made a habit of passing those tidbits along to Pokriefke and Teofil Strenk whenever they came his way.

And then there was Wydawnictwo Zielone Wzgórza. No one knew why Szponder had named his publishing house that—there were no "green hills" anywhere near its inner-city location—and he only smiled at some private joke when anyone asked him about it. But "Green Hills Publishing" distributed thousands of copies of old-fashioned hardcopy books, as well as electronic ones, to the kids of working-class families all over the star system, especially in the Projects here in the capital. That kept him in better odor than the rest of the *Oligarchia* with the less fortunate citizenry.

Which wasn't saying one hell of a lot.

Be fair, Grzegorz, he told himself. *It's not what you wanted. It's probably not what he wanted, come to that. And you're just as bad as he is, in your own way. "Going along to get along," that's what it's called. And it's not like it should really be such a big surprise. It's the way things always work in the end, isn't it? It's just that you hoped for so much more once upon a time. But "happily ever after" is something that only happens in fairytales.*

❖   ❖   ❖

"I'm telling you that Teofil isn't going to be happy with Pawlikowski's report." Justyna Pokriefke's tone was as sour as her expression. "And neither are the troublemakers. Especially not after that bastard hacked the ATC. If we're not careful about this, Agnieszka, we could be looking at an . . . unfortunate turn of events, let's say."

"You worry too much," Agnieszka Krzywicka said, sitting back behind the hectare and a half or so of polished desk in her enormous office. "And Teofil can be as unhappy as he wants. He knows which side of the bread his butter's on, and if we have to remind him of that, I'm sure we can find an appropriate technique."

Pokriefke didn't quite glare at her, but then, *no one* glared at Krzywicka if they knew what was good for them. Not even the Minister Bezpieczeństwa i Prawdy. The BBP was the most feared institution on Włocławek, and Pokriefke had headed it for the last fifteen T-years. That made her a very dangerous person. Despite which, Krzywicka, whose title was simply Pierwszy Sekretarz Partii—Party First Secretary—and who had no official position in government at all, was far more dangerous. Szymon Ziomkowski might get to claim the title of Przewodniczący Partii and play with all the pretty toys of office, but Krzywicka had very quietly become the true power behind the throne even before Szymon's uncle's death. Behind her back, she had another title—Pierwszy Aparatczyk, First Apparatchik—the most powerful of the innumerable bureaucrats who administered the Party, and through it the government. The Izba Deputowanych, the nominal republic's nominal representative assembly met regularly in its magnificent chamber where it nominally transacted the Republic's business. But no one was eligible for election as a deputy unless he or she was a member in good standing of the Party, and Krzywicka was the keeper of the Party's portals. No one in the entire Republika Włocławek went anywhere, worked anywhere, *dreamed* anywhere without the approval of the Sekretariat Partii. The diminutive Krzywicka (she wasn't quite a hundred and forty-seven centimeters tall) effectively controlled that secretariat, and the political graveyards of Włocławek—not to mention a few *real* graveyards—were littered with people who'd challenged—or *seemed* to challenge—her authority.

None of which meant she was made of armorplast, although there were times she seemed unaware of that fact.

"I'm not saying Teofil will cross us or officially question the inquiry's findings," the commander of Włocławek's secret police told her now. "I'm saying he won't be happy with it, and there's a difference between not *questioning* the findings and supporting them with a straight face."

"Are you suggesting there's anything questionable about them?" Krzywicka smiled archly, and Pokriefke snorted.

"For God's sake, Agnieszka, everybody with a working brain knows it's a whitewash." She carefully omitted the word "another" in front of "whitewash," but she knew Krzywicka heard it anyway. "That airbus driver never had a clue he was in restricted airspace. For that matter, he *wasn't*—not legally, anyway—and by now, thanks to that air-traffic hack, at least two thirds of Lądowisko knows there was no warning at all. By the end of next week, two thirds of the *planet* will know! I told you even before the hack that it would be a whole lot smarter to just admit Lewandowska screwed up and throw her to the wolves. God knows she deserves it! I *still* think that's the smart move, especially now that the cat's out of the bag on the gray web. But once this inquiry's report's been made official, there won't be any way in hell we can do it later."

"Oh? And do *you* want to explain to Hieronim why his cousin is facing one hundred and twenty-three counts of reckless homicide?"

Krzywicka tipped farther back in her chair and raised her eyebrows as she steepled her fingers across her chest, and Pokriefke felt her jaw tighten.

Of course she didn't want to be the one to tell Hieronim Mazur anything of the sort! Krzywicka might be the most powerful person in Włocławek's government, but as the head of the Stowarzysze-nie Eksporterów Owoców Morza, Mazur was the most powerful person on Włocławek... period. The "Seafood Exporters' Association's" name was even more innocuous—and misleading—than many another Włocławekan institution's title, but it was the true stronghold of the *Oligarchia*. It was just over three hundred T-years old, and despite its name it actually represented a broadly diversified alliance of fishing interests, bankers, industrial magnates, and interstellar shipping houses.

And Wiktoria Lewandowska, the head of Mazur's personal security—*and* the SEOM's in-house security forces—also happened to be Hieronim's third cousin. That would have been enough to inspire any self-respecting *oligarcha* to quash any investigation into her actions, and the fact that Mazur knew he could count on her to follow any instruction he gave without questioning it or even thinking about it—assuming she *could* think, which seemed even more doubtful than usual, given recent events—only made him even more... disinclined to permit anything like an honest inquiry. He certainly wasn't going to allow anything that concluded she had not, in fact, warned the air-bus before she ordered her people to shoot it out of the sky. And especially not when it had been in a public transit lane across privately owned airspace rather than in the closed spaceport airspace cited in the soon-to-be completed inquiry.

Which also just happened to conclude that it had been an SZW sting ship covering the air above the Lądowisko spaceport which had fired the fatal shot rather than the SEOM *private security* air car two a half kilometers *outside* the spaceport's eastern perimeter.

Of course, it *also* didn't mention what had happened to that air car ten seconds later, did it? That sting ship pilot had better be thanking his lucky stars Mazur was more interested in keeping the heat off Lewandowska than in hammering him. Bringing that lieutenant up on charges for shooting the bastard who'd pulled the trigger out of the sky would risk opening the entire can of worms to public scrutiny, and they couldn't have *that*, could they? No, no. Best to handle this discreetly and quietly, one hand washing the other, as always.

But this one's different, Pokriefke thought bitterly. *This time it's kids who got killed. Maybe just a load of kids from the Projects, but still kids, damn it! People're willing to accept a lot—or to at least keep their heads down, their mouths shut, and their opinions to themselves—but this one's different. There's a lot of anger out there already, and there's going to be more. Especially when people start comparing the official conclusions to that bootleg copy of the air-traffic transcript. And wouldn't I love to know how the hell that got out!*

She thought about saying that out loud, but not very hard. She hadn't headed Biuro Bezpieczeństwa i Prawdy for so long without learning how the game was played. And she *really* didn't want Krzywicka or Mazur to ask her how the files in question had been hacked.

Technically, security for those files belonged to the Policja Federalna under the umbrella of Teofil Strenk's Wydział Kryminalno-Dochodzeniowy, the Criminal Investigation Department. But the Policja Federalna had never had custody of the files in question, and the last thing Pokriefke wanted was to give the KOD an opportunity to go poking around inside *her* files, instead. Once upon a time she'd been Strenk's junior partner and protégée in the Wydział Kryminalno-Dochodzeniowy. She knew exactly what he thought of what she'd done with her life since then, and the thought of how an investigation under his aegis might play out was enough to make her stomach hurt.

Besides, it wasn't as if any further protest on her part was going to make a difference in the end. Mazur had already decided how it was going to play out, and Krzywicka wasn't going to argue with him over something as unimportant as an airbus load of dead kids when none of them had been hers.

✧   ✧   ✧

"God, it's good to be home," Tomasz Szponder said, dropping into the worn leather chair in the tiny office at 7707 Bulwar Heinleina. Its old-fashioned springs creaked as he leaned back and ran his fingers through his brown hair, and he puffed his lips and exhaled noisily. "The food's always good, but it tasted like sawdust today."

He shook his head, and pointed at the equally aged chair on the far side of the desk.

"Sit," he said, and Jarosław Kotarski settled into the indicated chair a bit more gingerly than Szponder had flopped into his. Partly that was because Kotarski was a considerably larger man, with limited faith in the chair's physical integrity. It might also have been due to his awareness that the chair in question was over three T-centuries old and had once sat in the office of the very first Prezydent of the Republika Włocławek. As a former professor of Włocławekan History at Uniwersytet Mikołaja Kopernika he had rather more respect for the chair's lineage than Prezydent Tomasz Szponder's namesake seemed to feel.

Or perhaps not. Even after all these years, there were parts of the current Tomasz Szponder which had never been shared with anyone except, possibly, his wife, Grażyna.

"Why do I think it took more than just the food to spoil your dinner?" Kotarski asked as Szponder opened a refrigerated desk drawer and extracted two frosted glasses and a bottle of vodka.

"Because you know me so well?" he suggested as he uncapped the bottle and poured. "Or is it because I'm such a transparent fellow?"

"'Transparent' isn't the very first word that comes to mind when I think of you...thank God." Kotarski accepted one of the glasses and raised it in a brief, silent toast, then threw back its contents and slapped the glass back down on the desk. "So! Aside from indigestion, how did it go?"

"About the way we expected." Szponder massaged his temples wearily. "I talked to Szymon—uselessly, of course. It was like talking to Krzywicka's sock puppet!"

"That's not really fair, you know, Tomasz. I know how frustrating it is, and he's certainly not the man Włodzimierz was. But then," Kotarski smiled sadly, "*Włodzimierz* wasn't the man he used to be by the end, was he?"

"No." Szponder sighed, lowering his hands to his chair arms. "No, he wasn't."

"Did you get a chance to talk to any of the others?"

"I managed to 'bump into' Teofil in the lobby, but I wouldn't say we really had a chance to 'talk' about it. From his expression when I took the opportunity to drop a cautionary word in his ear about the rumors I'd heard from the street, though, he's not very pleased with where this is headed. I took the opportunity to drop in on Justyna and Bjørn while I was at the Kancelaria Partii, too. I don't think either of them was exactly overjoyed to see me, but they were civil enough. And I don't know about Bjørn, but Justyna is obviously worried about *something*. At the moment, I only see one real candidate for what that something might be."

"Kudzinowski *isn't* worried about it? That's interesting," Kotarski said. "I'd've thought it would be more on his plate than Pokriefke's right now."

"Apparently he doesn't think so," Szponder said sourly and poured more vodka.

Kotarski nodded, but his eyes were thoughtful. Bjørn Kudzinowski headed the Komisja Wolności i Sprawiedliwości Społecznej, the Commission for Freedom and Social Justice, which was the most powerful non-police agency in the Republic. The combined functions of the old ministries of industry, labor, and commerce had been folded into his commission, and the airbus school tours were part of a KWSS outreach program. One would have thought ...

"I wonder how much hand he had behind the scenes in crafting Krzywicka's and Sosabowska's response to this," he murmured out loud.

"I don't think Sosabowska wants to come within a thousand kilometers of 'this,'" Szponder said, recapping the vodka bottle. "As Szymon pointed out, the actual inquiry's being conducted by the Inspektorat Sił Zbrojnych. That's Brigadier Pawlikowski's shop, and he's a hard-core career officer. Unfortunately, that means he'll sign whatever he's told to sign, whether he agrees with it or not. I'm pretty damn sure he doesn't, but he's got a wife and kids of his own. And, after all, it's not like his objecting to it would change anything, would it?" He shook his head unhappily and sipped vodka. "He'll sign off on this one, too, and that insulates Sosabowska from the entire mess. I doubt she could do anything about it if she wanted to, but this gets her off the hook so she doesn't even have to try. And," he added grudgingly, "it does get her pilot out of the line of fire, too. That young man did exactly what *I*'d've done in his place. I'm just as happy he's not going to stand trial for it in the end."

"They can't really think this is all just going to . . . go away, can they?"

"I don't think they *care* whether or not it goes away." Szponder set his glass very precisely in the center of his blotter, formed his index fingers and thumbs into a triangle around its base, and stared down into it for several seconds, like an oracle consulting his crystal ball. Then he looked back up. "I think they think it doesn't *matter* how the man or woman in the street reacts to this—or to anything else, anymore. They're that far gone, Jarosław."

"Damn." The single word came out with sorrow, not surprise, and Kotarski drew a deep breath, then shook his head.

"It's not like we haven't seen this coming, Tomasz," he said. "There was a reason you set up the Krucjata—yes, and gave me a job after the University threw me out on my ass."

"I know. It's just that…that it *hurt* so much, sitting there across from Szymon this evening. He looks so much like Włodzimierz, and he was totally oblivious to any reason he ought to be doing something about this. That's the worst part of it, Jarosław. I think he's *genuinely* oblivious to it, not just closing his eyes and pretending he doesn't see, like the rest of the *aparatczyków*. He's that far removed from everything his uncle ever tried to accomplish. You know as well as I do that even at the very end Włodzimierz would *never* have stood by and watched the Party sweep more than a hundred dead kids under the carpet! Never!"

"Probably not," Kotarski agreed, although deep inside he wasn't so sure. He'd known Ziomkowski even longer than Szponder had, and he *wanted* to agree. But by the end, the man who'd created the Ruch Odnowy Narodowej had been so thoroughly captured by the system—and been so tired and worn out—he might, indeed, have let this pass. Yet perhaps he wouldn't have, either, and one of Tomasz Szponder's greatest strengths was his loyalty. It would have been not just unrealistic but cruel to argue with him about a friend so many years dead.

"Unfortunately," he said aloud, "we have to deal with Szymon—or, rather, with Krzywicka and Mazur—not Włodzimierz. And from what you're saying, that situation's about to get a whole lot uglier. If they're willing to ignore something like this, it's only a matter of time until they ignore something even worse. And from what we're hearing from the lower level cells, there's enough anger building over this one for genuine disturbances. Tomek and I went over the latest reports while you were not enjoying dinner, and it's pretty clear there's a lot of pressure building out there. We could see riots coming out of the Projects . . . and that doesn't even count *our* people's reaction."

"Wonderful."

Szponder stood and crossed to the small office's single window and gazed down on the street so far below. It looked so calm and peaceful at the moment, but it wasn't hard for him to imagine a very different scene. He'd seen street carnage enough when he, Włodzimierz Ziomkowski, and the idealistic college students who'd provided so much of the National Renewal Movement's initial fiery enthusiasm had assailed the corruption of the old Republic.

Much as he'd loved Ziomkowski, he'd have shot him dead in the street himself if he'd even suspected then what the RON would become in the end.

"It's going to be bloodier than the *Agitacja* ever was," he said softly, leaning his forehead against the crystoplast. "The BBP and the KWSS are a hell of a lot more deeply embedded than the old police and security services were. And more ruthless. And the *Oligarchia*'s learned its lesson, too. If they'd been willing to resort to the sort of tactics Pokriefke and Krzywicka are willing to embrace, we'd never have seen the Party legalized in the first place. They won't make that mistake a second time."

"Of course they won't, and you knew that from the beginning. That's why we're organized the way we are.

The question is whether or not the time's come for us to get more... proactive."

Szponder nodded against the window, his eyes closed, because Kotarski was right. He would so much have preferred to be able to agitate for new elections the way he and Włodzimierz had agitated so many years before, but he'd known long before Włodzimierz's death that that wasn't going to happen a second time. That was why he'd started building the Krucjata Wolności Myśli, the Free Thought Crusade, three T-years before Ziomkowski's final stroke. He hadn't taken that step lightly, but he'd taken it with his eyes wide open. And he'd known then that it had never been a question of whether or not the time *would* come, only a question of when.

"We're not ready yet." He turned from the window to face the man he'd recruited as the Krucjata's intellectual leader and raised one hand as he saw the protest forming in Kotarski's eyes. "I don't mean our people aren't ready, don't know what we're going to ask of them, Jarosław. I mean we're *physically* not ready. We've done—you've done—an outstanding job of building the willingness, the discipline we'll need, but we don't have the *tools*. And, frankly, I'm afraid it's going to be a lot harder to get those tools into our people's hands than I'd thought it would be. Pokriefke and her people—and Mazur's people, for that matter—have made it a hell of a lot harder to smuggle anything in or out of the system. Getting *weapons* past them will be what Tomek would call a copper-plated bitch."

"We've already stockpiled quite a few weapons," Kotarski protested, and Szponder snorted.

"'Quite a few' isn't remotely like 'enough,' Jarosław. Especially not when our 'stockpiles' consist of obsolete pre-*Agitacja* pulse rifles and less than two thousand civilian firearms. For a riot or a revolt, that might be plenty. But aren't you the one who used to teach students the difference between 'revolts' and 'revolutions'?"

"Yes, I am. And you're right."

"Exactly. Revolutions are revolts that *succeed* and revolts are the ones where everybody dies, instead. I'm not going to be a party to that, Jarosław, but I hadn't expected this airbus business, so I never imagined something like this might come along so soon. I've been moving funds out-system a little bit at a time, but I don't have remotely enough out there to buy the kind of firepower we're going to need. Worse, I don't have any idea how to get weapons on-planet even after I find someone to sell them to us!" He smiled thinly. "So dust off your researching skills, Professor. Figure out where we can buy what I need to rip the throat out of my best friend's political monument."

Chapter Four

VICE ADMIRAL QUENTIN O'MALLEY was several centimeters shorter than Captain Aivars Terekhov, but broad shouldered and muscular. His dark hair was cropped short, and his brown eyes looked out from under bushy, aggressive eyebrows on either side of a strong, straight blade of a nose. He looked like the bruising rugby player he'd been at Saganami Island, but his voice was a surprisingly smooth tenor.

He'd already greeted Terekhov and Commander Ginger Lewis, and Lieutenant Guthrie Bagwell,—*Hexapuma*'s chief engineer (and acting XO) and electronic warfare officer, respectively—when they arrived aboard his flagship, *Black Rose*. Now he rose courteously as Rear Admiral Augustus Khumalo entered the briefing room with Vincenzo Terwilliger, *Black Rose*'s commander, trailed by Khumalo's flag captain, Victoria Saunders, and Commander Ambrose Chandler and Commander Loretta Shoupe, his intelligence officer and chief of staff, respectively.

"Thank you for coming, Admiral," he said, and Khumalo nodded.

"Pleased to be aboard, Admiral O'Malley," he replied, shaking the vice admiral's hand briefly but firmly. Then he turned to the single civilian who'd been seated at the conference table and extended his hand to her, as well. "Ms. Corvisart," he said.

"Admiral," she responded as her slim hand almost disappeared in his grip. She was a smallish woman, who looked even smaller beside Khumalo.

"Please, be seated, everyone," O'Malley invited. He waited until everyone else had settled into his or her chair before sitting himself, then looked around at the attentive faces.

"I believe, Ms. Corvisart, that as the direct representative of Her Majesty and the Foreign Office, you're the logical person to chair this meeting," he said, raising one eyebrow at Khumalo. The circumstances were just a little complicated, because while O'Malley was senior to Khumalo, Khumalo was the Talbott Station Commander and—technically—O'Malley's task force came under Baroness Medusa, the Talbott Sector Governor, and thus Talbott Station's command authority. So when wearing his Talbott Station hat and acting as Medusa's senior naval officer within the Talbott Sector, *Khumalo* was senior, and it wasn't entirely clear—yet—which hat was on whose head here in Monica.

"I concur entirely," Khumalo said a bit more ponderously, and Corvisart inclined her head for just a moment. Then she leaned forward in her chair and folded her hands before her on the table.

"Thank you, Admiral O'Malley. And thank you, Admiral Khumalo. I realize that, as you say, I'm here as the direct *civilian* representative of Her Majesty's Government. Under the strict rubric of my instructions, I'm also the senior representative of the Star Kingdom. However, let's not play any games here. Admiral Khumalo, in my opinion, your and Captain Terekhov's actions—and Monican involvement in the effort to destabilize Kornati and Montana—make this an extension of your command area. As such, I believe you're Her Majesty's proper representative. I realize I'm cutting a bit of a Gordian knot here, but I think leaving you as our formal representative will capitalize on the fact that you've already been acting in that capacity and also, insulate you, Admiral O'Malley," she looked at the vice admiral, "from the political side and allow you to concentrate on the military aspects of our situation." She waited until O'Malley had nodded in agreement, then looked back at Khumalo. "And while I'm on the subject, Admiral Khumalo, I'd like to take this opportunity to state my full and unqualified approval for the actions you and, especially, Captain Terekhov have taken in Monica."

Some of the uniformed shoulders around that table relaxed ever so slightly, and she smiled faintly.

"I'm sure all of you realize there will be a formal board of inquiry in the fullness of time. Having read your reports and reviewed the preliminary take from your intelligence officers and the summaries Commander Bonifacio here"—she nodded her head in the direction of O'Malley's chief of staff, Blake Bonifacio—"has put together for me, I don't think you need to have any qualms about that board's conclusions. For my part, I intend to conduct myself as if those conclusions had already been rendered and your actions approved at the highest level. I'm fairly certain"—her smile turned almost impish—"I won't be sticking my neck out too far when I do."

She paused for a moment, then sat back in her chair.

"I'm scheduled for my first face-to-face with President Tyler tomorrow morning. Before I meet with him, I'd like an opportunity to discuss several of the points in the intelligence packet Captain Terekhov and Commander Chandler have assembled for me. I think your work's been commendably clear and unambiguous, given the short timeframe and how little access planet-side you've had, gentlemen, but I want every round in the magazine before I sit down with these people." This time her smile was thin and extremely cold. "I don't know if you're familiar with an ancient gambler's maxim the Foreign Office is rather fond of, Commander Chandler, but I suspect *you* know the one I'm talking about, Captain Terekhov?"

She arched one eyebrow across the table, and Terekhov nodded.

"I imagine you're referring to the one about suckers and even breaks, Ma'am?"

"Indeed I am. Anyone stupid enough to sign off for even a tenth of what it looks like Tyler bought into in this case certainly qualifies as a 'sucker,' and after the price your people paid derailing this plot, the only break I'm interested in giving him would occur somewhere around the C4 vertebra. It's entirely possible we'll wind up cutting some sort of deal with him in the end, little as any of us might like that prospect, on the theory that he was only a front man. I have a strong suspicion that you and Commander Chandler are correct about that, too, in which case we have bigger fish to fry than one more tinpot dictator. But I have no intention of letting him get away scot free. There *will* be a reckoning for the good president, and I guarantee you he'll give us everything we want before I sign off on any proposed settlement with him."

She held Terekhov's eyes for a heartbeat, then switched her gaze to Khumalo. Both officers looked back levelly, and she gave them a crisp nod, almost like a formal oath. Then she tapped the display in front of her, bringing it online.

"First, Captain Terekhov, I'd appreciate it if you could run back down the chain of events that brought the freighter *Marianne*—or *Golden Butterfly*—to your attention. I want to be particularly clear on its role in running arms to that butcher Nordbrandt and how that led you to Monica in the first place. I think I have the sequence of events clear, but I want to be certain of that before I confront Tyler with Captain Binyan's testimony and the documentation from his computers. After that, Commander Chandler," she shifted her attention to Khumalo's intelligence officer, "I'd like you to run down your findings from the *Indefatigables* you've examined at Eroica Station. I'm not a naval officer, and I'm not technically trained myself, so I want you to put it into layman's terms for me, as well as you can. In particular, I want you to be conversant with every detail that proves they came direct from the Solarian Navy and that Technodyne connived with the SLN's own in-house inspectors to make that happen. I want to be able to rattle off those details with so much assurance he doesn't even *think* about the possibility that I don't know exactly what I'm talking about. I'd also like to ask your electronic warfare officer, Captain Terekhov—Lieutenant Bagwell, I believe?"

She raised her eyebrows again. Terekhov nodded

to the lieutenant seated to his left, and she turned her attention to him.

"I find myself actually almost understanding nearly fifteen percent of your report, Lieutenant," she said wryly. "Given my total ineptitude for things military, that says quite a bit for the clarity with which you set forth your conclusions. Nonetheless, I'd like you to try to simplify that even more for me after we've heard from Commander Chandler. And, if Captain Terekhov can spare you, I'd like for you to accompany me to my initial meeting with President Tyler. I want you along to give me the nod if he or any of his navy people who may be present start trying to hand me any horse shit."

Several surprised chuckles greeted her last two words, and Bagwell nodded with a smile. Then she switched her attention back to his superiors, and her expression turned rather more serious.

"Given the somewhat . . . irregular nature of the Navy's presence here in Monica, I think it would be best if Admiral Khumalo accompanied me as the senior naval representative at the table. As I say, that will leave you free to continue implementing your people's control of the entire system infrastructure, Admiral O'Malley, with a degree of insulation from the political side of things. Frankly, Captain Terekhov, I'd really like to have you present, particularly in light of your own Foreign Office experience. Under the circumstances, though, I think it might be more, um, tactful to keep you and the senior Monican leadership as far apart as possible for the next little bit. Although, if they should be foolish enough to turn intractable, I have every intention of flourishing you over their heads. If there's one officer who terrifies the entire Monican Navy, it's probably you. For now, I'm prepared to try the silk glove approach, but if I need a knuckleduster to tuck inside it, that's you."

"Understood, Ma'am," Terekhov said after a moment. It was only the briefest of hesitations, but Corvisart heard it anyway. She raised an eyebrow at him, and he shrugged ever so slightly.

"Frankly, Ma'am, I'm fully occupied right now trying to put *Hexapuma* back together. Captain Kurtz and *Ericsson*'s people are accomplishing more than I would have believed they could, but she's a long way from ready to head home. If you need me dirtside, I'll make myself available, of course. But the truth is, I've seen more than enough of Monica from orbit. I don't feel the least bit slighted to not be at the table with you. In fact, it's probably a good idea to keep me as far away from those people as you can." Those blue eyes went cold and bleak. "I might find it a bit difficult to remain . . . civil."

"I understand, Captain. I don't have anything remotely like your personal history here, and it's going to be difficult for *me* to remain—civil, I believe you said? However, I do have one bit of news that might make you feel a little better about what's going to happen to the people *behind* this."

"News, Ma'am?" Terekhov asked when she paused, and she chuckled nastily.

"When we left Manticore, we did it in company with a transport—chartered by the Crown—stuffed to the bulkheads with newsies. All sorts of newsies. In fact, at least seventy-five percent of them are *Solarian* newsies. This will be one of the most public—and most broadly publi*cized*—inquiries in galactic history, Captain. It's going to hit every news channel in the Solarian League, not just the Star Kingdom, and I intend to see to it that the Solly coverage comes from Solly reporters. No one's going to be able to brush off those reports as partisan Manticoran reportage, and I can already tell there'll be more than enough blood in the water to provoke a very satisfactory feeding frenzy over *this* one. I promise you, Captain Terekhov: the people who thought they could hide in the shadows while they hired someone else to slip the knife into your people's back are about to find out just how spectacularly wrong they were."

❖   ❖   ❖

Damien Harahap looked up from his book reader as Rufino Chernyshev knocked courteously on the frame of the open door. While Harahap would never have called his current surroundings palatial, they were certainly much more comfortable than many he'd endured in the course of his career. And they had the inestimable advantage of being, so far as he could tell, completely off the Gendarmerie's radar.

Of course there were two sides to that particular advantage. If not even his employers could find him, then it was unlikely the people who'd murdered Ulrike Eichbauer and ordered his own death could find him, either. That was the good part. The *bad* part was that if *Chernyshev's* employers decided he was a liability rather than an asset, they'd find it remarkably easy to complete his traceless disappearance.

At least he'd had a chance to catch up on his reading in the last month or so, especially since Chernyshev had "requested" he remain off the net while they awaited instructions. Under the circumstances, it had seemed wiser to accede to the "request" gracefully. Besides, he'd been much too far behind on his history readings.

"Mind if I disturb you for a minute?" Chernyshev asked now, and Harahap gave him a crooked smile.

"My time is yours, Rufino," he said, sweeping one hand around his small room's plainly furnished comfort.

"Well, yes, but there *are* courtesies between professionals," Chernyshev replied, stepping fully into the room. "I know this hasn't been especially easy for you, and the truth is I'm grateful you've taken it as well as you have."

"Would it have done me much good to take it any other way?"

"We both know keeping someone like you locked down against his will can get . . . complicated, Damien. I'm just saying that I appreciate your taking a professional attitude towards all of this."

"You're welcome," Harahap said, touched—despite himself—by Chernyshev's apparent sincerity. "I do hope you're not soft-soaping me to sugarcoat some nasty bit of news, though?"

"No, no. Nothing like that! In fact, I've just heard back from my superiors. They're very happy you've managed to stay alive—with, of course, my modest assistance. On the other hand, they're sorry to hear about Major Eichbauer. My impression is that they'd really hoped to convince both of you to come to work for them. As it is, they've instructed me to ask you if *you'd* be prepared to accept an offer of employment."

"Doing what, precisely?" Harahap leaned back in his chair. He wasn't in the strongest bargaining position imaginable, but still . . .

"I don't have a lot of details about that," Chernyshev admitted. "My guess would be that they'd want you to continue doing essentially what you were doing in the Talbott Sector. I'd suspect they have a somewhat… broader canvas in mind, you understand, but all of that's just my best guess. I'm sure they'll explain everything to you when we get there."

"And 'there,' presumably, is someplace other than Pine Mountain?"

"I think you can safely assume there's a small interstellar cruise involved in the employment offer," Chernyshev told him with a slight smile.

Harahap nodded slowly, his expression thoughtful. With all due modesty, he was one of the best at what he'd been "doing in the Talbott Sector," but he'd had the advantage of years of familiarity with the area. If Chernyshev's reference to broader canvases meant what he suspected it did, he'd be operating outside that comfort zone. On the other hand, it *was* what he did best. And he had the oddest suspicion that turning down the new career opportunity would not be the very smartest decision he'd ever made.

Besides, what else was he going to do with himself? The people who'd hired his services in the Talbott Sector were among the wealthiest individuals in the explored galaxy. Not very nice people, perhaps, but filthy, obscenely rich. If he was looking at a mandatory shift to the private sector, it made sense to find the employers with the deepest pockets when he did.

"I see," he said, laying the book reader on his small desk and pushing back his chair to stand. "When do we leave?"

APRIL 1921 POST DIASPORA

"I wonder sometimes what we did to piss God off. We probably could have *handled* just the damned bugs!"

—Adam Šiml, Prezident,
Sdružení Sokol Chotěboř

✦ Chapter Five

THE FIFTEEN-YEAR-OLD DOUBLED OVER with a harsh, explosive grunt as the riot baton's head rammed into his belly like a hammer. His mouth opened, but no sound came out. Not immediately. He just stood there, both hands grasping at the anguish while his shocked diaphragm tried to suck in enough air for a cry of pain.

It hadn't gotten that far when the same truncheon hammered the back of his neck and clubbed him to his knees.

The Chotěbořian Public Safety Force trooper never even blinked as he used his armorplast shield to smash the fallen boy to one side. He was already choosing his next target as the CPSF waded into the crowd of "anarchist terrorists and hardened professional agitators" half-filling the enormous square called Náměstí Žlutých Růží at the heart of the city of Velehrad.

The high school and college students who'd flooded the capital with such high hopes saw the Safeties coming, but there was no way for anyone in the demonstration's leading edge to get out of the way. The crowd behind them was too dense. They were trapped between their fellow protesters and the oncoming riot police. Most of them dropped the placards demanding new elections—or the armloads of yellow roses—they'd been carrying and raised empty hands above their heads. Here and there a handful flung themselves at the riot-armored troopers instead of trying to surrender, but the options they'd chosen made no difference in the end. The Safeties had their orders, and neural stun batons and old-fashioned nightsticks rose and fell with vicious, well-drilled efficiency.

Many of the newer victims did have time to scream as they were smashed to the street, and few of the CPSF troopers made any effort to avoid trampling them under their heavy boots. Indeed, more than one Safety took time to kick a fallen demonstrator squarely in the mouth in passing.

The demonstration's rear ranks began to shred as the young people in them realized what was happening. Students scattered in all directions, but dozens—scores—were as unable to get out of the way as the lead ranks had been. They were grist for the mill, and the Safeties harvested them ruthlessly.

"Make examples," their CO had told them, and the Chotěbořian Public Safety Force was nothing if not good at following its orders.

✧　　✧　　✧

The soccer ball sliced towards the upper corner of the goal, but the leaping, fully extended keeper just managed to get a hand on it. She dragged it down and in, wrapping both arms around it and taking it with her as she hit the ground on a shoulder, then rolled back up on her knees with it clasped protectively in both arms.

Applause and whistles of appreciation spattered from the thinly populated stands, and the tallish, fair-haired man nodded in approval. Despite the nod, however, his attention was elsewhere, and he turned from the football pitch to frown at the brown-haired, still taller man standing beside him.

"I can't believe even Siminetti was *that* stupid," he said quietly, careful to keep his face turned towards the solid ceramacrete wall behind his companion. There were no security systems mounted to cover this particular spot, which wasn't exactly an accident. He'd made certain of that when the stadium was last refurbished and he had the entire structure carefully and very, very unobtrusively checked on a regular basis to make sure things stayed that way. That didn't mean mobile platforms couldn't be watching it, however.

"What kind of idiot doesn't understand the kind of resentment that putting over sixty unarmed students— some of them barely fourteen years old, for God's sake!—into hospital and another eleven into the morgue is going to generate?!" he continued, his tone harsh with a bitter anger which burned only hotter because iron control kept it so low.

"That's assuming he's worried about resentment, Adam," the other man pointed out, equally quietly. "Frankly, I don't think he is."

"Well he damned well ought to be!"

"You think that; I think that; and the kids who were in the square think that. I'm inclined to doubt Cabrnoch, Kápička, or Verner share our view. After all, there're plenty of more Safeties where that crew came from if things should happen to flare up. And I don't doubt Sabatino's prepared to throw in enough kickbacks to pay for a few thousand—or a few hundred thousand—more if he has to."

Adam Šiml muttered something unprintable under his breath and glared at his friend, but Zdeněk Vilušínský had known Šiml for the better part of a T-century. He knew what that glare was really directed at, so he only waited patiently for his boyhood friend to work his way through it.

Šiml turned away, staring back out across the football field while he did that working. He knew Vilušínský as well as Vilušínský knew him, which meant he also knew his old friend understood exactly what was going on in his brain at the moment. None of which did a great deal to slake his seething fury at what had happened in Náměstí Žlutých Růží.

"Plaza of Yellow Roses." That was what the square's name meant in the language of Chotěboř's original settlers. That language had been largely supplanted by Standard English in everyday life in the three centuries since the founding, of course. For that matter, only about a third of the Kumang System's initial colonists had been native Czech-speakers. It happened that the Šiml family had been part of that third. In fact, it "happened" that one of the leaders of that first wave of settlers, and one of the men who'd crafted the Chotěbořian Constitution, had also been named Adam Šiml.

Not that the current head of the family, such as it was and what remained of it, was in a position to say much about how that constitution had been shredded. Not if he wanted to stay out of Vězení Horský Vrchol, anyway, and he had far too many things to do for that, no matter how spectacular the view might be from its mountaintop perch.

Besides, it was far from certain he'd ever make it to the Safety Force's main detention facility. In the last few T-years, prisoners had started quietly and tracelessly dropping off the lists of the incarcerated. They hadn't been released, hadn't died (officially at least), and they sure as hell hadn't *escaped*. They'd simply...disappeared.

He reminded himself of that—firmly—as the rage flowed through him, but it wasn't easy. Not when he thought about Náměstí Žlutých Růží.

The yellow rose in question was a native flower, not the Old Earth version, with blossoms the size of a large man's hand, a gorgeous sapphire-blue throat, and brilliant yellow petals tipped in blood-red crimson. It was spectacular, and it had been chosen as the emblem of Chotěboř, as a symbol of renewal, freedom, and self-rule, by the original Adam Šiml and the friends, neighbors, and fellow employees of the Creswell Combine he'd helped convince to cash in their equity in the huge corporation and find a new home far, far away from the Calpurnia System and the growing power of the Solarian transstellars. To build a home those transstellars' tendrils had not yet penetrated, one far enough from the League that it would have time to create—and maintain—a democracy that meant something and had the strength to resist the sort of exploitation the Creswell Combine had represented. That was what the youthful demonstrators in Náměstí Žlutých Růží had wanted to remind every Chotěbořan about...and everyone could see how well that had worked out.

"They can't keep a lid on this forever, Zdeněk," he said harshly, once he was confident he had his anger mostly under control. "They just can't."

"Until someone repeals the state of emergency, they damned well *can*," Vilušínský said bluntly, "and you know it."

"Hruška never meant that to last this long!" Šiml snapped.

"Then he frigging well should've included a sunset clause when he issued the decree." Vilušínský turned his head to spit on the ceramacrete floor. "Not that Cabrnoch and Žďárská—or Siminetti!—would've paid much attention to it if he had."

Šiml glared at him for a moment, but then his shoulders slumped and he nodded wearily. He'd been there—in fact, he'd been a member of President Roman Hruška's cabinet—when the initial decree was issued. Even then, he'd seen where it was likely to end, and his protests were one of the reasons Minister of Public Safety Jan Cabrnoch's chief of staff, Zuzana Žďárská, had made it so abundantly (if privately) clear that his services as Minister of Agriculture were no longer required. It would undoubtedly be wise of him to seek a new career in the private sector, under the circumstances. And if he was unwilling to take her friendly hint, more . . . strenuous methods of persuasion would be found.

Which was why he'd been a very poorly paid professor of agronomy at Eduard Beneš University for the last fifteen T-years.

"I wonder sometimes what we did to piss God off," he said finally. His voice was heavy, his expression tired. "We probably could have *handled* just the damned bugs!"

"Probably. No," Vilušínský shook his head, "we *did* handle the *komáři* in the end. Whatever else, you have to give Cabrnoch at least that much. That targeted nanotech was a brilliant move, and he did find a way to get it built."

"Sure he did. And it was based on the R and D *my* people did—them and Public Health! Do you think anyone remembers that? And how did he *pay* for it?"

"I didn't say he came up with the solution, and I didn't say it came cheap. But if you'd asked most of our fellow citizens at the time whether it was worth it, you know damn well what they would've said! For that matter, they *did* say it."

"But it opened the door to Frogmore-Wellington and Iwahara!" Šiml protested.

"So? You expected people with dying kids to think that was a bad exchange? Especially after Reichart got done with us?"

Vilušínský shook his head again, but his expression had turned gentle, and he reached out to lay one hand almost apologetically on his friend's arm. Adam Šiml had lost his wife, Kristýna Šimlová Louthanová, his teenaged son, and both of his infant daughters to the *komáři*. If anyone on Chotěboř could understand the point Vilušínský had just made, it was Šiml, yet his own devastating grief only fanned his fury when he thought of how the world his wife and children would never see again had been betrayed by its own elected leaders.

Chotěboř had scarcely been on the cutting edge of technology. It was too far from the heart of the Solarian League for that. But it had possessed at least a decent medical establishment, and it had been native Chotěbořian researchers—*his* team, although he'd been given his walking papers before the solution was announced—who'd come up with the targeted nanotech to deal with the *komár hnědý rybniční*, the ubiquitous "nuisance" insect pest which had mutated into such a deadly disease vector. Yet the Chotěbořans had been unable to produce it locally, thanks to Ismail Reichart's raiders.

Reichart had seen his opportunity in the midst of Chotěboř's preoccupation with the *komáři*, not that Kumang Astro Control would have been much of an obstacle to him at the best of times, and his fleet of renegade mercenaries had hit the star system like a hammer. They'd left Chotěboř itself relatively unscathed—they'd had no desire to encounter the *komár* on its own ground—but they'd looted and stripped every bit of the system's painfully built up industrial infrastructure. They'd taken even the planetary power sats, driving Chotěboř back onto surface-generated power, with all the crippling limitations that had implied, until it could somehow cobble up replacements . . . once Reichart finally deigned to depart with his loot.

Leaving Chotěboř totally unable to implement the solution to its desperate health crisis out of its own resources.

And that was why President Hruška, at the instigation of newly elected Vice President Cabrnoch, had taken the only option he'd seen and petitioned the Solarian League's Office of Frontier Security for aid. Which OFS had provided . . . under its customary terms.

Which was how Chotěboř had effectively completely lost control of the resources of its own star system.

Under pressure from Frontier Security to "maximize income generation potential" for the system's people, Hruška had issued yet another decree, setting aside the constitutional prohibitions designed to prevent outside exploitation of the system. He'd had no constitutional authority to do anything of the sort, but the Nejvyšší soud, Chotěboř's supreme court, had flatly refused to take up the single lawsuit challenging his actions. Šiml had known every man and woman who'd joined to file that suit, although he hadn't been formally associated with it. He'd wanted to be, but he'd been in too much public disfavor at the moment, scapegoated with responsibility for failing to solve the crisis himself by Cabrnoch and Žďárská. At the same time, he had to acknowledge Vilušínský's point. However people might feel about it *now*, at the time Hruška's actions had been supported by a huge majority of Chotěbořans.

Of course, quite a few of them—and their children— were suffering a severe case of buyer's remorse these days.

In return for a sizable down payment—and it *had* been sizable, by Chotěbořian standards, Šiml conceded—in a deal brokered by the "disinterested" facilitators of OFS, Frogmore-Wellington Aeronautics and Iwahara Interstellar had received two hundred-T-year leases, with an option to renew, on virtually all of Kumang's deep-space resources. That infusion of cash, coupled with OFS technical assistance, had permitted the final design and fabrication of the anti-*komár* nanotech which had reduced the threat from the status of a deadly plague to a simply serious health threat which could be controlled, if not eradicated, by the prophylactic measures already in place.

And all it had cost was debt peonage for the entire star system.

As part of the articles of agreement Hruška had signed, OFS had undertaken the "reclamation" of the infrastructure ravaged by Reichart's attack. It had been rebuilt to something approximating its pre-raid level, and as part of the reclamation, OFS had assumed administrative responsibility for it. As soon as Chotěboř managed to pay off the loans the League had extended to it through OFS, ownership of that infrastructure would, naturally, revert to Chotěboř. In the meantime, though, OFS would be required to charge a "reasonable fee" to defray its operational costs in Kumang. The last time Šiml had seen an accounting of the debt, interest, those "reasonable fees," and penalties for chronically late payments on it had increased the original amount by approximately two hundred and ten percent.

And the payments were *always* late, since there was never enough cash flow to make them. Despite Frogmore-Wellington's and Iwahara's down payment, the ongoing annual income from the leases was a pittance, and because both transstellars saw Kumang as a long-term investment that wouldn't require developing for at least another fifty or sixty T-years, they were in no hurry to spend any development money until they were good and ready. The Chotěbořans themselves couldn't capitalize on the abundant potentials of their own star system in order to generate the income to pay off their debts because, effectively, they didn't *own* those potentials anymore, and Luis Verner, the current OFS governor—although, of course, his official title was only "System Administrator"—was fine with that. In fact, he'd gone out of his way to quash any

Chotěbořian efforts to exploit the fragments of their star's resources they still owned.

Šiml wasn't certain if that was simply part of OFS' policy to ensure none of their peons ever got out of debt or because it was in line with Frogmore-Wellington's and Iwahara's policies, and it didn't really matter. What mattered was that by now *President* Cabrnoch and his entire administration were firmly in the pocket of OFS and Kumang's absentee landlords. Cabrnoch really didn't have a choice, in a lot of ways. The sheen had started coming off his public image over the last decade or so, when Chotěboř had time to catch its breath and realize just how much of its inheritance had been traded away. By now, he had nowhere to go if he tried to buck his out-system patrons, and he clearly didn't *intend* to go anywhere.

Hruška had remained in office up until seven T-years ago, although he'd become steadily less and less relevant. By the time he'd actually died—of natural causes, as far as Šiml could tell—his vice president had been the system's effective dictator for almost ten T-years. After Hruška's death, there hadn't been even the pretense of a new election. Cabrnoch had simply assumed the office, at which point a great many Chotěbořans had realized the constitution was no longer simply dying, but dead. And that was when the trouble truly began.

"All right, Zdeněk. You're right about that. You always have been, whether I like it or not. But this time around, Siminetti and the Safeties have crossed a line. You know as well as I do how *our* people will react to this; God only knows what's going to come out of the rest of the planet's woodwork!"

"And *you're* probably right about that," Vilušínský

agreed. "So I think it'd be a really good idea to get the word out to our cell leaders that they need to sit on anything hasty."

"Already in the pipeline," Šiml said. Then he snorted. "Unfortunately, I think Jiskra may have been a bit too apt when we chose the name."

It was Vilušínský's turn to snort. Šiml had suggested Jiskra—"Spark" in Czech—as the name for their organization for a lot of reasons, including his love of history. As far as Vilušínský had been concerned, the notion of striking sparks made it the perfect choice. But Šiml was right about the ... feistiness of their *jiskry*. Those "sparks" would be only too ready to go looking for tinder after today's incident.

"That's not a bad thing, in most ways," he pointed out. "You're right about the need to sit on them at the moment, but it's about damned time we started actively transitioning into changing our stance, Adam. You know it is."

"I do." Šiml's face tightened. "I'd hoped we could do more to prepare the ground by nonviolent means, though. And at the moment, I'm afraid we're just a little short of the tools to do anything else."

"Then we'd better start finding someone who can provide them," Vilušínský said grimly. "And in the meantime, we'd better hope to hell none of our people who were involved in the demonstration point the Safeties in Jiskra's direction under interrogation."

❖   ❖   ❖

"Satisfactory," Karl-Heinz Sabatino said, rotating his brandy snifter under his nose while he inhaled its bouquet. "What's that old saying about a gram of prevention being worth a kilo of cure, Luis?"

"You really think it'll be effective?" System Administrator Luis Verner sat back in the floating armchair in Sabatino's luxuriously appointed office with his own brandy snifter. It was a sinfully comfortable chair, but his expression was less than happy.

"I do." Sabatino sipped, then lowered the glass and shrugged. "I'm not at all sure it's the *best* solution, you understand, and I've never cared for Cabrnoch's tactics. But the last thing we need is for these proles to decide to jump on the same bandwagon as those idiots in the Talbott Sector. Whatever I think of his methods, they'll think twice about pressuring him in that direction now."

"Holowach thinks it might have the opposite effect," Verner said, his eyes worried. "According to his reports, there's an element on Chotěbor that sees those rioters as martyrs."

Sabatino grimaced. Technically, he had no official standing in Kumang's governance. In fact, however, as the local CEO for both Frogmore-Wellington Astronautics and Iwahara Interstellar, he was what he liked to think of as the king frog in a small pond. Or perhaps that wasn't the best analogy. He seemed to recall fragments of an ancient fairytale from his childhood on the farming planet of Fattoria. Something about King Log and King Stork.

What mattered was that he was the current Chotěbořian government's paymaster. What amounted to petty cash for a transstellar like Frogmore-Wellington or Iwahara was more than enough to make a neobarb dictator like Cabrnoch and the key members of his regime indecently wealthy by local standards. Unlike many of his fellows, Sabatino had no problem calling that what it was—graft and bribery—although he was careful to avoid those terms in discussions with Verner. There were certain words which cut too close to the system administrator's own relationship with Sabatino.

The truth was the truth, however, and whatever terminology they might use, Verner knew exactly whose hand held his leash. It was unfortunate no one would ever be tempted to call the system administrator the sharpest stylus in the box, but Sabatino could work with that. In fact, there were advantages to having someone who was inclined to take orders first and think about them later.

It was rather more unfortunate, in some ways, that the Gendarmerie had stuck Verner with Major Jacob Holowach. Holowach had no more official jurisdiction on Chotěboř itself than Verner did, but he commanded the Gendarmerie-staffed System Security Force which was responsible for the police function in the OFS-managed orbital and deep-space infrastructure. And whatever his official status vis-à-vis Chotěboř, he and his senior analyst, Captain Heather Price, were the lens through which official intelligence estimates arrived in Verner's inbox. All of which would have been perfectly fine if Holowach had been more receptive to the customary inducements of his position. It was just Sabatino's luck to get stuck with an idealistic idiot in what otherwise was a highly satisfactory assignment.

And to have the damned Manticorans less than sixty-four light-years away, assuming the Talbott annexation went through and the Montana System ratified it. The last thing he needed was for the Chotěbořans to catch the same sort of lunacy, he thought grumpily.

It wasn't that he would have blamed them on

any personal level. In their position, he would have wanted the same things himself, and he wasn't happy about the number of people who'd been hurt in the recent...unpleasantness. Those numbers were extraordinarily low compared to what happened in other star systems, but this wasn't "other star systems." This was the system *he* was responsible for managing, and the fewer people who got hurt along the way, the better, from his perspective. Not that he thought he could do his job without *anyone* getting hurt. The galaxy didn't work that way.

Which was why it was so important to discourage any Chotěbořian tendency to emulate Talbott. The home office would be extraordinarily unhappy if they suddenly found themselves dealing with the Manties, who had a well-deserved reputation for keeping transstellars cut down to size, in rather sharp contrast to their customary comfortable relationships with the Office of Frontier Security.

"Holowach always sees bogeymen under the couch, Luis," he said, sweeping his brandy in a dismissive wave that expressed rather more confidence about that than he actually felt. "Besides, wasn't he the one that warned you the Talbotters' example was spreading to Kumang?"

Verner nodded, although that wasn't exactly what Holowach and Price had told him. It was close enough, though, and he wondered uneasily if Holowach's warnings that there was more going on under the Chotěbořian surface than the Cabrnoch Administration knew (or was prepared to admit, anyway) might not be rather more accurate than Sabatino was willing to acknowledge. The truth was that Verner much preferred the CEO's analysis. The notion that the rumbles of discontent making their way through the population of Chotěboř represented the first ripples of a generalized, still unfocused discontent was far more comforting than the idea that any sort of organized reform movement might be ticking away under the surface.

Besides, the system administrator reminded himself, *it's not like even Holowach or Price have any evidence of that kind of organization! If they did, that would be different. As it is . . .*

Sabatino watched Verner's face for a moment, then took another sip of brandy to hide an incipient frown. From the system administrator's expression, it would appear that this time Holowach had succeeded in shaking his superior's confidence. Well, it was hardly surprising he'd made the effort. Sabatino's own sources made it clear Holowach had strongly opposed the crackdown in Náměstí Žlutých Růží. Given that, of course he'd be pouring all kinds of alarmist reports into Verner's ear after the fact.

Especially when at least some of them were almost certainly accurate.

"In my opinion," he said, lowering the snifter, "Holowach's an alarmist, and the sooner you can get rid of him, the better. *However*," he drew the word out, "it's possible—*remotely* possible, I suppose—that he might have a point about how some of the more . . . civically active Chotěbořans may react to this. So maybe we need to be a little prophylactic."

"Prophylactic?"

"It probably wouldn't hurt to find a vaccine against that sort of infection," Sabatino said, rather pleased with the analogy, actually, given Kumang's history.

"Something that can pour oil on the waters," he continued, mixing metaphors mercilessly.

"What sort of something did you have in mind, Karl-Heinz?" Verner sounded a bit cautious, and Sabatino smiled.

"What we need is a local mouthpiece to soothe any tendencies towards...hastiness on these people's' part. Let's face it, Luis—from their perspective, they really do have quite a lot to be unhappy about. In fact, if I could find a way to...improve the situation locally, I'd do it. Unfortunately, the home office won't let me change the economic playing ground. But if I can't do that, we need to find someone who can convince these people—really *convince* them, I mean—that they're being listened to and that what *can* be done *will* be done. Someone from outside the government but with the stature to be listened to. To convince them he has a real chance to deliver on answers to at least some of their grievances."

"And should I assume you have someone in mind?"

"Actually, I was thinking about Šiml."

"*Šiml?*" Verner blinked in astonishment. "Karl-Heinz, he hates our guts. That's one of the few things Holowach and your people agree on!"

"That's not exactly true."

Sabatino shook his head, stood and set his glass on the end table, and crossed to stand looking out of his two hundredth-floor office window at the night-struck city of Velehrad's sparkling strands of lights.

"He hates Cabrnoch and the rest of Cabrnoch's crowd with a pure and blinding passion, all right. I'll give you that. And he's probably no fonder of you or me than he has to be. But do you *really* think he went back to his family's damned Sokol to be apolitical?" The CEO snorted. "Please, Luis! He may have been only the Minister of Agriculture when the shit hit the fan, and he doesn't have a pot to piss in, financially. But with his family name, he had to have his eyes set on exactly the office Cabrnoch ended up in. And I guarantee that the way Cabrnoch kicked his ass out of government—and blamed him for the delay in dealing with the *komáři*, to boot—didn't do one damned thing to make him any happier. There's no way in the universe a man like that could see a 'sports association' as anything but an eventual political platform!"

"But he's always insisted Sokol remain a nonpolitical, nonpartisan organization," Verner pointed out. "For that matter, his family's been adamant about that from the very beginning. If he starts straying from that line, it's likely to cost him a lot of the popularity he's regained over the last couple of decades."

There was, Sabatino acknowledged privately, at least a bit of truth to that. The original Adam Šiml had singlehandedly founded the Sdružení Sokol Chotěboř, the Falcon Association of Chotěboř, even before the colonists had departed Calpurnia en route to Kumang. It had been part of his determination to rebuild and sustain his Czech heritage, and he'd modeled it on an ancient, third-century Ante Diaspora sports association which had also been called Sokol.

There'd been differences, of course. Šiml's Sokol had also been intended as a nationalist organization as well as a sports association, but there'd been no pressure for it to become a *political* organization like its original model. Its purpose had been to remind the descendants of the Czech lands of who they were and where they'd come from, not to promote the re-emergence of Czech ethnicity and culture from the empire which had engulfed those lands back on Old Terra. The fact that it would contribute to its members' health along the way was almost icing on the cake in its founder's view. Highly *desirable* icing, but almost incidental to its other functions.

Like the original Sokol, Šiml's had emphasized gymnastics, but it had branched out into all other areas of sport, including—or perhaps especially, given Chotěbořans' passion for football—soccer. Membership had fallen over the years, though a surprising percentage of Chotěbořian parents had continued to enroll their children, at least. At one time, almost eighty percent of all Chotěbořans had been *sokoli*. By the time the *komár* turned deadly, that had fallen to perhaps fifteen or twenty percent, but Sokol had been a tower of strength during the plague years. It was a system-wide organization, outside government, which had responded with generosity and incredible effort, and many of its members had died helping others. That had earned it tremendous respect and a powerful upsurge in enrollments—*adult* enrollments, not just those of children and adolescents. And when its founder's descendant was hounded out of office, with his family's already faltering fortune decimated by the way he'd personally thrown everything he owned into trying to mitigate the consequences of the *komáři*, the governing board had invited him, the present-day Adam Šiml, to accept the *předsednictví* of his ancestor's creation.

It had been more than just a gesture of gratitude to a man or to a family name. The stipend which came with the president's office wasn't enormous, but it had at least prevented him from starving until he finally managed to land his teaching position at the university. And he'd repaid the governing board by throwing all of his energy into rebuilding Sokol into what his many-times-great-grandfather had intended it to be: an organization which guarded Chotěboř's sense of identity and trained and educated its sons and daughters—morally, as well as physically—without pounding them with any party line. That political neutrality, eschewing any partisan position, was fundamental to all Sokol had become, and it was more valuable to those parents now than it had ever been before. It was a refuge not only from the remorseless indoctrination which was part of every schoolchild's daily life but also from the increasing bitterness and even outright despair which had enveloped so many of Chotěboř's adults.

And the fact that it didn't preach any competing *political* indoctrination was also the only reason it survived as a legally tolerated organization. Well, that and the fact that President Cabrnoch was himself a fanatic footballer.

"I mean," Verner went on, "Sokol has to be the most apolitical organization on the entire planet. Even if he wanted to change that—even if he *could* change it—don't you think it would be hard to turn that around? I mean to turn it into any sort of effective political machine quickly enough to keep Cabrnoch and Kápička—or at least Siminetti—from cracking down on it long before he could complete the transition?"

"Of course it would." Sabatino snorted and turned from the window to face his guest. "I'm not saying it would *work*, Luis; I'm simply saying it's obviously what he has in mind. And I'm sure he doesn't expect to be able to do anything with it tomorrow or the day after. But that's what he's working for in the long term, I'm sure of it. And that means that however much he may—how did you put it? 'hate our guts'?—he'd see the advantage in garnering our support. He'd have to recognize how much good we could do him if he agrees to scratch our back. Which is why it's about time I made a significant philanthropic donation to his sports association." The CEO smiled. "In fact, I should have done it long ago. I mean, how much worthier a cause could there be than an association which helps people stay fit and active?"

"I don't know, Karl-Heinz." Verner plucked thoughtfully at his lower lip.

"Do you really think he's going to turn up his nose if I offer to put, say, a half million credits into Sokol's bank account?" Sabatino laughed derisively. "Of course he isn't! Hell, I'll make it a *full* million—even two or three, if that's what it takes. I'll even throw in a half dozen, brand new soccer stadiums! For that matter," his cynical expression eased for a moment, "that would probably be worth doing in its own right. It's not like I don't have the spending authorization to 'invest in local infrastructure,' and it certainly couldn't make people like me or my bosses any *less*!"

He sipped more brandy, then looked back up at his guest, and the cynicism was back in his smile.

"But the point is that I'm sure he'll convince himself there are all kinds of good reasons—ways he can use those funds against Cabrnoch, maybe even against *us*—when he starts thinking about any offer I make him. And I'm telling you the man has political ambitions of his own. He'll play ball with us, whether or not he intends to stay on the team in the end, as long as it offers him a way to begin building a solider powerbase against Cabrnoch. And when you come down to it, I don't really care what happens to Cabrnoch or Juránek or any of the others. Given how universally detested they are, Šiml might actually be a better front man for us with the Chotěbořans, when you think about it. The fact that everyone knows he was effectively forced out of government would actually work for him these days, as unpopular as Cabrnoch and Kápička have made themselves the last few years. It's been long enough people've forgotten how pissed off they were at him for not solving the emergency, just like they've forgotten how grateful to Cabrnoch they felt at the time, and it's never a bad thing to have another arrow in the quiver. So it's past time we saw about putting Šiml in our pocket as an insurance policy, and that shouldn't be too hard. Once he takes our money, once he accepts our support, we'll own him just as surely as we do Cabrnoch."

Sabatino turned back to the window, gazing out into the darkness as he considered the possibilities.

"I should've thought of this before," he said, half to Verner and half to himself. "The home office wouldn't like it a bit if the locals decided to jump on the Talbotters' bandwagon. But when you come down to it, providing them with *domestic* political reform might be the best way to stave off serious agitation for the same sort of arrangement Talbott's trying to strike with the Manties. If they think they're getting a government that will keep us in our place they'll be a lot less likely to take to the streets—or start looking for some other star nation to take them over lock, stock, and barrel—now won't they?"

"It's just that we don't want you to promise *we'll* be the ones helping them."

—Isabel Bardasano,
Jessyk Combine
Board of Directors

Chapter Six

THE SECURITY MEN IN the office foyer weren't exactly unobtrusive. Then again, they weren't supposed to be, Damien Harahap reflected as he followed Rufino Chernyshev across the luxuriously furnished waiting room. Almost every room he'd encountered since arriving on Mesa seemed to fit that description—"luxuriously furnished"—which struck him as a good sign where matters of future remuneration were concerned. On the other hand, he'd always hated the lavish working spaces with which senior Gendarmerie officers surrounded themselves. Not only was it ostentatious as hell, but the shells of luxury and self-indulgence seemed to lead directly to atrophy of the neural synapses.

The tall, very broad shouldered (and very obvious) bodyguard standing beside the door looked anything but ceremonial, however. In fact, he looked like a very tough and competent customer, and he gave them a very careful once over, despite the fact that he and Chernyshev obviously knew one another well. For that matter, they looked an awful lot like brothers.

Which, given Mesa and Manpower's attitudes towards genetic modification, clones, and cloning, they very probably were.

"She's expecting us," Chernyshev said, and the other man nodded.

"I know." His evaluating gaze lingered on Harahap for a few seconds, then he nodded ever so slightly. "Go on in."

"Thanks."

Chernyshev nodded and pressed the door button, then gestured for Harahap to precede him. Harahap took the hint and stepped through it, projecting his very best air of confidence.

He felt one eyebrow try to rise as he saw the woman seated behind the office's desk. Because it was a very well-trained eyebrow it did nothing of the sort, of course, but he found himself engaged in some rapid reevaluation of what he'd thought he knew. He'd expected Aldona Anisimovna, who'd taken the lead in the project to destabilize the Manticoran annexation of the Talbott Sector. Instead, he found himself looking at Isabel Bardasano, the wildly tattooed and body-pierced cadet member of the Jessyk Combine's board who'd clearly been riding backup as Anisimovna's *assistant* during their meetings in the Madras Sector.

"Good afternoon, Mr. Harahap," she said. "Please, have a seat."

She indicated one of the chairs in front of her desk, and Harahap obeyed the polite command. The chair was quite comfortable, but the slight angularity of the sensor plates in its arms and back were a dead giveaway to someone with his experience. They weren't quite as good as a full-bore lie detector, but they'd give Bardasano very accurate reports on pulse rate, respiration, and all of those other physical telltales.

Fortunately, after thirty years in the trade, his body was accustomed to responding the way he told it to.

"First, I'm glad Rufino was able to get to you before the assassins did," she said after he'd settled into place. "I'm sorry we didn't get to Major Eichbauer in time, as well. Based on what I saw of her—and you—in Pine Mountain, I think the two of you would've made a very effective team working for us."

"I'm sorry you couldn't get to her in time, too," Harahap replied, feeling a flicker of respect for her refusal to pretend Ulrike's death was some great personal loss to her. That was good. He preferred working with professionals.

"I imagine Rufino's given you at least some idea of what we have in mind," she continued. "On the other hand, knowing Rufino, I'm certain he didn't tell you exactly what we're thinking. And, yes, he knows a lot more about our eventual plans than I'm sure he's indicated to you. In fact, one of the things he's been doing for the last couple of months is evaluating how effective *he* thinks you could be. Understand, the ultimate decision on whether or not to offer you this...position lies with me, but it's always a good idea to have a second opinion, a sort of crosscheck bearing, I suppose."

"I understand," Harahap said when she paused. He didn't ask what was likely to happen if Bardasano decided the "position" *shouldn't* be offered to him. He was pretty sure he already knew that answer... and that he wouldn't like it very much.

"Basically," Bardasano continued, "what we have in mind is to include you in something we call Operation

Janus. As you've no doubt realized, I'm rather more than just a junior member of the Jessyk board. In fact, I represent a sizable consortium of transstellars, all of whose current operations are being cramped by Manticoran intransigence. And, as I'm sure you'll understand from our previous arrangement, several of those transstellars have their headquarters right here on Mesa. They really don't want Manticore any closer to them than they can help. That's what our op in the Talbott Sector was trying to prevent, and it showed a certain promise, even if it failed in the end. Your own work in that regard was exemplary, however, and we believe you might be able to help us with a similar operation on a somewhat . . . grander scale."

"Grander scale?" he repeated, this time allowing that wigglesome eyebrow to rise. He would have thought attempting to destabilize the governments of half a dozen star systems was sufficiently ambitious for most transstellars. If Bardasano had something *bigger* in mind . . .

"Yes." She tipped back her chair and crossed her legs. "In a lot of ways, you could think of what you were doing in Talbott as a sort of trial exercise. The object there was to prevent the annexation entirely, if we could, but that situation came at us too quickly for the kind of planning we like to devote to that sort of thing. Because of the surprise quotient, we were never really confident we could pull it together in time. No one blames you for what happened on Montana and Kornati, because that's exactly the sort of thing that happens when you rush this sort of operation."

He nodded thoughtfully. She was certainly right about that!

"At the same time we were putting that phase of Operation Janus into play, however, we were also standing up several other aspects of the op. One side is purely military, and your particular skill set wouldn't be very useful there. The other side, though, would be right up your alley, I think."

She gazed at him, her expression about as emotional as an AI, but he only sat squarely in his chair and returned her gaze levelly. After a moment, she nodded, as if in satisfaction, and continued.

"What I'm about to tell you is, obviously, very classified in my employers' view of the universe. You do understand what would happen if those employers—or I—should come to the conclusion that having shared this information with you had turned out to be a bad idea?"

"I think I have some small idea, yes," Harahap said dryly, and she chuckled.

"Rufino said you were a professional." She smiled briefly, then her nostrils flared as she inhaled deeply.

"Essentially, my employers are worried the Manties won't stop at the Talbott frontier. According to their sources, Manticore intends to keep nibbling at the Verge, encouraging other star systems to follow Talbott's example. I'm sure you know even better than I how little love is lost between them and OFS and the League in general. We think—or, rather, my employers think—the worst thing we could do would be to allow the Manties to consolidate in Talbott and simultaneously build up a glacis of local star systems that are . . . favorably inclined towards them outside that sector. The best solution, in our eyes, is to nip the entire thing in the bud by encouraging the League to express its disapproval of the Manties' ambitions here in the Verge."

Harahap nodded again, his expression intent. If Bardasano's unnamed employers actually believed they could maneuver the Solarian League into quashing Manticoran expansion they were very ambitious, indeed. On the face of it, the entire notion was ridiculous, but Harahap was well accustomed to looking beneath the face of things. And he understood better than most the degree to which money talked with OFS bureaucrats and even permanent undersecretaries in the League government. On the other hand, even the most readily bought-and-paid-for bureaucrat needed at least a minimal fig leaf if the newsies came sniffing around his actions.

"As you'll appreciate better than most, Mr. Harahap, there are always tensions bubbling away out in the Verge, and OFS hasn't made itself beloved by the locals. Even leaving Frontier Security completely out of the equation, there are also plenty of star systems where resentment of and hatred for purely local regimes are driving dangerous levels of internal unrest. In other words, Verge systems are a continual hotbed of serious, semiserious, *barely* serious, and outright lunatic fringe resistance and reform movements. You were recently in contact with some examples of that on Montana and Kornati, I believe."

"That's certainly the way to describe Nordbrandt," Harahap agreed with a thin smile. "It might be a bit overstated in Westman's case, however." He shrugged. "He was definitely dead serious, and I don't think anyone could reasonably describe him as a lunatic."

Bardasano appeared to consider that for a moment,

then nodded, as if conceding the point, before she continued.

"Well, what this phase of Operation Janus is designed to do is to locate and identify as many of those movements as possible. We want to encourage them, to give them confidence and provide them with weapons and training."

She paused, and Harahap allowed himself to frown ever so slightly.

"Excuse me," he said into the pause, as he was fairly certain he was expected to say, "but if the idea's to keep the Manties pruned back, why would you want to encourage resistance movements that can only undermine local regimes on the Talbott frontier? Wouldn't that actually provide Manticore with an incentive to expand beyond those frontiers on the theory that the locals will greet them with welcoming arms?"

"That would be what one would expect to happen, wouldn't it?" Bardasano agreed, allowing her chair to swing slowly from side to side as she nodded, but there was something almost bright and . . . sparkly in those computer-gray eyes of hers. Something that was clearly amused by his question.

"For example," she continued with a smile, "if you were still in the Gendarmerie's employ and you learned someone was promising aid to the enemies of local regimes which were allied with the League, or even to enemies of local OFS system administrators and governors, how would you react to that?"

"I'd do my best to stop it," Harahap replied obediently. "I'd try to infiltrate and shut down the resistance movements themselves; I'd do my best to interdict any weapons shipments; and I'd exert however much political influence and/or military power it took to convince whoever it was that it was a really bad idea to piss off the League."

"That's pretty much what *I'd* do, as well," Bardasano agreed. "And that would be especially true if the people providing those weapons were prepared to provide actual outside military support when the moment came. Naval support sufficient, say, to interdict the systems involved and preclude OFS administrators from whistling up Frontier Fleet to deal with the situation."

"Assuming the people in question were stupid enough to make any promises of outside military assistance, the League would probably react . . . forcefully," Harahap said slowly. "It's one thing to provide encouragement; it's another to provide not only weapons but actual naval support."

"Precisely." Bardasano nodded and leaned forward. "I realize we couldn't expect you to continue operating in Talbott, under the circumstances. And I also realize you have less . . . call it 'situational awareness' of local systems' dissatisfaction *outside* Talbott. But what you *do* have, I think, is an eye and a feel for this sort of thing. We've identified several star systems with the potential to provide the kind of distraction we need for both Manticore and the League. We have our own people on the ground in many of those systems—transstellars like the ones I represent *always* have people on the ground, after all. We're tapped deeply enough into the Gendarmerie and OFS to have access to their internal reports on events and attitudes in those systems, as well, and I venture to say our analysts are more honest in evaluating those reports. I'm sure you've had more than enough experience with the way rising bureaucratic seniority leads to an ever-increasing ability to see what you *want* to see in intelligence from the field."

Harahap snorted. One of the things he'd most liked about Ulrike Eichbauer was that she hadn't had that tendency. He couldn't possibly have counted the number of superiors he'd had over the years who *did* have it. Who'd rejected his analyses, his warnings, because those warnings clashed with their view of how the galaxy worked, especially in *their* bailiwick. And who'd then proceeded to blame him and his fellow field agents when the very things about which he'd warned them came to pass. So, yes, it was not only possible but highly probable that Bardasano's "employers" would get more benefit out of Gendarmerie field agents' reports than the Gendarmerie itself ever would.

"What I want you to do, at least as a start, is to evaluate *our* interpretation of that data. I mean we want you there, in-system, on the ground, checking actual attitudes against our analysis. And, probably, we'll also be asking you to make initial contact with some of those dissatisfied elements. Much as you did with Agnes Nordbrandt and Stephen Westman, in fact."

"I see." Harahap considered that, then shrugged. "It doesn't sound very different from what I was doing for Ulrike. Except that, as you say, I'll be well outside my regular stamping ground. With all due modesty, I'm one of the best at that sort of business, but it would be unrealistic to assume I'd be able to blend into the background equally well in star systems I've never even visited before."

"That's understood." Bardasano nodded again. "Unfortunately, we don't have anybody who that wouldn't be true of, and our estimate is that you'd be better at coping with the potential difficulties than most."

"So I assume I'd be provided with the information I'd need. Or, at least, the information *you* think I'd need." He showed his teeth briefly. "That's not always the same thing."

"In that case, what information would you require?"

"Oh, I'd want to see your analysts' take, of course. But I'd also like access to the raw data itself. The ability to draw my own conclusions based on the original source material."

"There's likely to be quite a lot of that," she pointed out, and he chuckled.

"I'm a fast study, Ms. Bardasano. I've had to be. And even if I can't review *all* the raw data, any of it I *can* get through would help my feel for the situation. It certainly couldn't hurt, anyway. And to be totally honest, sometimes the simple confidence that I've gotten my head wrapped as thoroughly as possible around the data helps me carry through something like this. I may not always be right in my analyses, but I am more often than not. And the fact that I *think* I'm right lets me move a lot more confidently. The amount of assurance I can project has a direct bearing on how readily I can get someone like Nordbrandt or Westman to accept that I'm who I say I am and trust me. As far as they trust *anyone*, at least."

"I see." She considered him thoughtfully, then nodded. "Fine. I don't see any problem, as long as the data's properly secured while it's in your possession."

"I don't think there'd be any worries there," Harahap said confidently.

"So you're prepared to take the assignment?"

He considered that question very carefully. The one thing of which he was totally confident was that she wasn't telling him everything. In fact, it was unlikely she was telling him more than a third or a quarter of the truth. In her place, *he* certainly wouldn't have trusted a newly recruited field agent with the full knowledge of for whom or to precisely what end he was working. By the same token, she clearly understood that for an operation to succeed, the operators in question had to have the tools they needed. And as all those luxuriously appointed offices and suites here on Mesa indicated, it looked like there'd be some nice perks to the job, at least.

I wonder who she's really working for? he mused. *It may be Jessyk, and I'm sure it's Manpower, but who else is involved? I doubt it's Kalokainos at this point—not if he's really the one who tried to have Ulrike and me murdered. But it could be. God only knows the alliances between transstellars are about as durable as an ice cube in sunlight!*

"So you want me to evaluate your analyses, run down any local resistance leaders I can, evaluate how likely they are to succeed with suitable outside help, and promise them your 'employers' will provide that help?"

"Almost, Mr. Harahap. *Almost*. Except for that last bit."

"About providing help?" Harahap frowned. "Forgive me, but I thought that was an integral part of what you had in mind."

"Oh, it is!" This time Bardasano's smile could have shamed a shark. "It's just that we don't want you to promise *we'll* be the ones helping them."

Chapter Seven

Society in every state is a blessing, but Government, even in its best state, is but a necessary evil; in its worst state an intolerable one: for when we suffer, or are exposed to the same miseries *by a Government*, which we might expect in a country *without Government*, our calamity is heightened by reflecting that we furnish the means by which we suffer. Government, like dress, is the badge of lost innocence; the palaces of kings are built upon the ruins of the bowers of paradise. For were the impulses of conscience clear, uniform and irresistibly obeyed, man would need no other lawgivers; but that not being the case, he finds it necessary to surrender up a part of his property to furnish means for the protection of the rest; and this he is induced to do by the same prudence which in every other case advises him, out of two evils, to

choose the least. Wherefore, security being
the true design of and end of government,
it unanswerably follows that whatever form
thereof appears most likely to ensure it
to us, with the least expense and greatest
benefit, is preferable to all others.

INDIANA GRAHAM SAT BACK in the tattered, worn
out chair, looking down at the even more worn, old-
fashioned hardcopy book, and his eyes burned. It
wasn't the first time, or the second, or even the
hundredth he'd opened *Yumashev's Great Thinkers
of Political Freedom*, and it wouldn't be the last. He
still remembered the first time his father had handed
him a copy of *Common Sense*. He'd been only—what?
eleven?—at the time. Something like that. And its
archaic language—Standard English had changed a lot
in the last couple of thousand T-years—had been a
challenge, even with a good dictionary program. But
he'd persevered, partly because he'd known it was
important to his father and partly because he'd already
acquired his father's interest in history, although it
had never been the passion it was for Bruce Graham
until the last few years.

Of course, a lot of things had changed in the last
few years.

He grimaced at the thought and closed the book.
Then he climbed out of his chair—carefully, wary of
its increasing senility—and crossed to the bookcase in
the barren little apartment's even tinier bedroom. He
slipped the thick volume (its plastic pages were thin,
but Thomas Paine wasn't the only subversive who
inhabited *Yumashev's*) into its slot and stood gazing

down at it for a moment. Given its content, it probably wasn't a wonderful idea to leave it in plain sight that way. On the other hand, the scags weren't very likely to see it unless they decided to come calling, in which case it wouldn't matter how carefully he'd tried to conceal it. For that matter, it was unlikely a typical stalwart of the Seraphim System Security Police would have the least damned idea who Thomas Paine, Jean-Jacques Rousseau, John Locke, Thomas Jefferson, Edmund Burke, Hannah Arendt, Judith Shklar, Jeremiah Towanda, or Henrietta MacIntyre had been. And given the SSSP's general reading skills, he probably wouldn't be able to read the titles off the book spines, anyway.

He wasn't sure Anderson Bligh, the Seraphim System Minister of Education, had gotten around to formally banning Paine. Education—which, under the McCready Administration, also served as Seraphim's propaganda bureau and thought police in general—wasn't in the habit of listing the names of banned authors. Those who'd come under the displeasure of Bligh or President McCready simply disappeared from booksellers' catalogs without fuss or fanfare. After all, if they told their citizens who'd been banned, they'd also point any of those citizens who might feel a modicum of discontent toward the very writers they most wanted to silence. He did know both Jefferson and Shklar had been on the last list Frieda Simmons, the assistant head librarian at the Cherubim Public Library's main branch, had shown him, though. And if Paine hadn't been added to the list yet, it could only be because none of Education's apparatchiks had ever heard of him. As soon as one of them did, he was gone. If *anyone* was going to be banned by the Seraphim System government as a dangerous rabble rouser, Paine was certainly that anyone.

And it would scarcely be the *first* time he'd enjoyed that honor, over the centuries.

Indy stood back and ran a fingertip across the spines of the books keeping *Great Thinkers of Political Freedom* company. Perhaps a quarter of them had been his father's, all he'd managed to salvage from the elder Graham's library after the scags trashed it on the day they arrested him. He'd had less than half an hour to do the salvaging before his sister, his mother, and he had been thrown out on the street. It appeared Bruce Graham, despite having made every payment at least two weeks early ever since Indy could remember, had been over a year in arrears on his mortgage... according to the lien-holder's books. And since the scags had flushed his bank accounts and seized his bank records, there'd been no way for Treysa Graham to prove otherwise. Not that it would've mattered if she could have. The lien-holder in question, First People's Bank of Cherubim, was owned by a crony of Economy Minister Trish Mansell, so the ledger was going to say whatever Mansell thought it should say. Besides, when Tillman O'Sullivan and the SSSP decided to turn someone into a "teaching moment," they didn't fool around about it.

The rest of his bookshelf's contents had come from Frieda. Technically, they were all stolen, but he was fine with that. In fact, he was part of what Frieda called her "off-site stacks." Once upon a time, before the Seraphim System had been ingested by Krestor Interstellar and Mendoza of Córdoba—back when it had possessed a government that could actually be voted out of office—its library system had been remarkably well stocked for such a galactic backwater. And not just with electronic copies. The historical collection of the main library here in the capital still contained priceless hardcopies from Seraphim's earliest settlement and a surprising number from other star systems, some quite distant, as well. God only knew how they'd drifted ashore in *Seraphim* of all damned places, yet there they were.

A great many of those documents were no longer available to the public, since they contained the sorts of things of which the government disapproved, but they were still there. So far, at least. And there were still thousands of hardcopy volumes—like *Great Thinkers of Political Freedom*, although few of the others were quite so fraught with unacceptable concepts—on the shelves.

There were fewer than there had been, though, because hardcopies were more vulnerable than electronic ones. When the Ministry of Education decided someone needed banning, its agents descended upon the catalogs of every library on the planet, and the condemned books promptly found their way into reclamation hoppers. It was even easier to purge libraries' electronic databases, but it had also been easier for people like Frieda to smuggle out electronic books and stash them away in very small, very well hidden holes before Education got to them. Photons packed tighter than printed pages, when all was said, and she could carry an entire library in her hip pocket.

In addition to Education's depredations, however, the library's hardcover collection had also been depleted by Frieda's determination to save as many endangered titles as possible. She and Bruce and Treysa Graham had been friends since grade school, and Indy remembered sitting up with hot chocolate, listening while Bruce and Frieda discussed history, politics, and the way Seraphim had slithered down the Solly python's gullet. So he'd been a natural choice when Frieda started looking for depositories for her beloved books.

He snorted at the thought, then looked at the flashy uni-link on his wrist and muttered a curse. He was running ten minutes late. If he didn't get a move on, he was going to miss lunch with Mackenzie. That was never a good idea...and especially not today.

He patted the bookcase with a proprietary, friendly hand and headed for the door.

Dad would be pissed if he knew about Frieda and me, he thought with a smile that mingled bitterness and amusement as he started down the narrow stairs (the elevator hadn't worked in over six weeks) through the miasma of cooking, overripe garbage, and other best-left-undefined scents. *The last thing he'd want is to have me sitting here with a bookcase full of subversives! But that's too bad. If he didn't want me reading them—and thinking about them—he shouldn't have introduced me to them in the first place.*

He reached the street just as one of the capital's battered but punctual trams heaved into sight. He climbed aboard, presented his uni-link's transponder pass to the scanner, and found a seat as the tram rumbled off.

He wondered, sometimes, if his father would have chosen *not* to introduce him to Paine, and all the authors he'd read since, if he'd known what was coming. He might have, actually. Bruce Graham loved his children, and that love was the reason he'd led Indy and Mackenzie into forbidden intellectual territory. He'd been determined they'd grow up knowing the things the Seraphim educational system was specifically designed to prevent them from thinking about because he'd wanted them to be more than good little helots obeying their corporate masters. But that had been before his own arrest and incarceration in Terrabore Prison, and he was also fiercely protective. These days, that love of his expressed itself in an almost desperate determination to keep Indiana and Mackenzie—and especially—Treysa out of that same grim, gray confinement.

Indy felt his eyes burn again, and his fist clenched on his seat's armrest as he gazed out the tram's open window at the passing street. The liquid whistles of robins (who bore very little resemblance to the Old Terran original) burbled happily to one another on tree branches and apartment ledges. It was a warm, late summer day—the sort that would have seen his family at the beach, soaking up sun before autumn put an end to such trips, when he was a boy. But instead of a daytrip to the ocean, he'd spent yesterday at Terrabore, for the one-hour, once-a-month visit with his father the scags allowed him, and he'd felt his lips go white as Bruce Graham hobbled into the cubicle on the other side of the thick crystoplast. His father was barely fifty years old, but he'd moved like a man twice that age...without prolong. His left arm had been supported by a sling, and there'd been ugly bruises down the right side of his face. The bright orange prison coverall had prevented Indy from seeing anything else, but just from watching his father walk, he'd known what he would have seen without that concealment.

He'd also known better than to ask what had happened. It wasn't the first beating Bruce Graham had received since he'd been arrested, although this one looked worse than any of the others had been. Besides, if Indy *had* asked him, Bruce would simply have replied with one of the only two acceptable answers: "I fell," or "I got between two of the other inmates who don't like each other much."

And then he would have given Indy "the Look." It was the Look that said, "Don't push it." The Look that said "Let it go, Son." And the Look that said, above all, "Don't do anything stupid."

He'd grown accustomed to that Look, Indy had. He knew exactly what it meant, why he saw it. In their very last conversation before Bruce's sentencing, he'd told Indy—ordered, *begged* Indy—to stay as far away as possible from anything which might draw the scags' attention. There'd been a time when Bruce Graham had believed it was possible for someone to scratch up a little capital, actually create his own small business—even on Seraphim—and hope to build a better future. Even that it might have been remotely possible to gradually win back a little of the political freedom Jacqueline McCready and her transstellar masters had stolen from Seraphim's citizens. But he'd learned better, and whatever he might have been willing to risk for himself, he was unwilling for his son and daughter to risk. And the children of a convicted "enemy of the people" were bound to be carefully scrutinized by the SSSP.

And because Indy knew how much his father loved

him, he'd promised no one in the entire system could be more apolitical than he intended to become. It hadn't been simply for the scag microphones he'd known were recording the conversation, either. It had been for the father he loved just as fiercely as Bruce loved him . . . but he hadn't meant it. He hadn't meant it then, and he didn't mean it now. There were some things he simply couldn't do, even for his father, and keeping that promise was one of them.

He *had* tried, though. He truly had, mostly because his mother had begged him to, as well. But he'd already known he wouldn't succeed—not in the long run.

The tram finally rattled up to Indy's destination and he got off, turning left to walk the two remaining blocks to The Soup Spoon. It was a small, family-run restaurant which somehow managed to keep its doors open, and if it might lack a little something in ambience, the quality of the food more than made up for it.

"Indy!" Alecta Yearman greeted him as the door closed behind him. "You're late! Max has been here almost twenty minutes."

"Don't fib to me, Naak," he said, using the pet name her adoptive parents had bestowed upon her when she was only eight. "I'm almost exactly on time, and my sister's never been *early* in her life! She may—*may*—have been here an entire whopping *five* minutes. And that's being generous."

"Well, maybe it just seems longer when you're waiting for one of your favorite customers." Alecta rose on her toes to peck him on the cheek. "Go on back. She's holding down your regular table. I'll be along to take your order in a minute."

"Thanks." Indy gave her a brief, one-armed hug and made his way through the always-crowded front dining room to the corner table in the smaller back room.

As he came out of the arch, the young woman waiting for him glanced up from her book reader with a resigned expression. She looked remarkably like Indy, not surprisingly, and she'd spent the last twenty-odd years putting up with her older brother.

"You're late," she observed, and he chuckled.

"Not very. Besides, if I'd been *early*, you wouldn't have had anything to complain about. Think how much you would've hated that!"

Mackenzie Graham's severe expression wavered, despite her best efforts, and her eyes twinkled as she shook her head and pointed at the slightly unsteady chair on the other side of the table.

"Sit," she commanded, and Indy obeyed with a suitably meek expression which fooled neither of them.

Mackenzie was better dressed than her brother, which was a necessity, given her occupation. Hers was a more sober wardrobe, however, without the garish colors Indy's rather different occupation favored.

Treysa Graham had left Cherubim years ago. The wife of an enemy of the people was both utterly unemployable and automatically denied any form of public assistance. She was fortunate her sister and brother-in-law had taken over the family farm after her parents' death. At least she had a roof over her head and food on the table, which was more than many a Seraphimian might have said. And if it was much harder for her to make her own single monthly trip to Terrabore from the country, her self-exile from the capital also kept her out of the scags' line of sight.

Besides, SSSP didn't much care about people hiding out in the country. It was possible subversives and enemies of the people hidden in the towns and cities they worried about. Which was a bit short sighted of them, when one thought about it.

Treysa would have been happier if Indy and Mackenzie had joined her, but she'd given up trying to convince them. Partly because she knew just how stubborn they were, but even more, Indy suspected, because she'd guessed what they were up to. They'd both worked hard to keep her uninvolved in anything that might bring official attention her way, but she was a very smart woman...and she was still the woman who'd married Bruce Graham. However frightened she might be on their behalf, she understood that there were some lines, some principles, that simply couldn't be abandoned without a fight.

That was the real reason Indy and Mackenzie had stayed in the capital. And it was also the reason Indy had become a street hand. It wasn't the sort of profession Bruce Graham had hoped for for his children, but it was one of the few open to a convicted criminal's son, and it lent itself well to certain...other ends.

Mackenzie, on the other hand, had avoided the worst consequences of official displeasure because she was a highly skilled IT professional. Those were too rare on Seraphim for anyone to worry too much about her father's criminal history. Even better, from the authorities' perspective, a third of her clients were subsidiaries of one of the transstellars who effectively owned the Seraphim System, and most of the other two-thirds were either "independents" who were actually fronts for Krestor or Mendoza bureaucrats, their oligarch hangers-on, or McCready Administration apparatchiks. Whatever might have been true of her father—and possibly her brother—Mackenzie had clearly learned her lesson.

Indy, however, was a street hand, one of the quasi-legitimate, not-quite-outlawed brokers of the graymarket. Almost anything was available through the graymarket, if you knew the right hand and had enough money or something sufficiently valuable to trade in kind.

In a lot of ways, McCready, O'Sullivan, and Helena Hashimoto would have loved to shut down the graymarket. Unfortunately, it had become an essential part of the Seraphim economy. Shutting it down might have diverted a few more centicreds into the bank accounts of the transstellars and the pockets of their cronies, but it also might prove the final straw for Seraphimians in general. As it was, the authorities were perfectly happy to see marginalized elements—elements like Indy Graham, who knew the ice underfoot was always thin—filling that role, since they had to know what would happen to them if they ever got out of line or became sufficiently irritating to their betters.

It wasn't much of a living, although Indy did rather better at it than Internal Revenue realized. It really wasn't that hard for a street hand, especially one with a sister who knew computers better than ninety percent of the government's IT so-called experts.

That, too, was one reason his current occupation was so well-suited to his ultimate ends.

"Have you ordered?" he asked now, and Mackenzie shook her head.

"Given that I was waiting for you and that you

have the time sense of a torpid rock, I figured I'd wait until I saw the whites of your eyes. That way my plate wouldn't be either empty or frozen solid by the time you got here."

"There you go again, maligning my character without a single shred of physical evidence to back up your baseless allegations."

"Really?" Mackenzie tilted her head, favoring him with a thoughtful expression. "You may be right. Why don't we ask Alecta for *her* opinion? Or maybe we could get Thai Grandpa to give us the benefit of his observations? He's back in the kitchen this afternoon, you know."

"No, no!" Indy said loftily. "There's no need to drag them into this. I'm far too considerate to impose on them that way."

"*Sure* you are." Mackenzie rolled her eyes, and Indy chuckled. But then he laid down the old-fashioned printed menu, folded his hands on it, and there was absolutely no humor in his eyes as he gazed at her across the table.

"I saw Dad yesterday. He looked like he'd been run over by a ground car."

Mackenzie's matching eyes went dark, and her expression tightened.

"What happened?" she asked.

"You think I expected him to tell me that in a Terrabore visitor's cube?" Indy shook his head. "Besides, I didn't need him to. It was the worst it's been, Max. I don't know how much more of it he can take."

"Damn." The single word came out softly, bitterly, from a young woman who seldom swore. Her eyes dropped to her own menu, but they didn't see it.

Those eyes were looking at something else, something far away, and they were bitter.

"I think it's time, Kenzie," he said even more softly. "Mom's safe with Aunt Sarah and Uncle Thad, and Dad's already in prison. How much worse can it get?"

"You know exactly how much worse it can get," she replied, raising her eyes to his face. "And you know exactly what Dad would say if he even *thought* we were thinking about something like that."

"Dad's not in position to say anything to us," Indy said bitterly. "He won't be for at least another thirty-five years, and that assumes he *lives* that long. You know how likely that is in Terrabore."

"Is that why you want to push ahead? To get Dad out?"

"You know there's more to it. I won't pretend seeing him yesterday, realizing how badly they beat the crap out of him again, isn't a factor in my thinking, but there's *always* been more to it than that. And we haven't been setting up the cells just to let them sit there."

Mackenzie bit her lip. She wanted to argue with him—she'd always been the cautious one, the one who'd spent her time hauling Indy out of one scrape or another, despite the difference in their ages, for as long as she could remember—but she couldn't. She'd known where he was headed from the outset, and she'd been with him every step of the way. And she agreed with him, really. Agreed with him absolutely. It was just such a big step from simply organizing to doing something... more active.

"You know what'll happen to all of us if the scags realize what's going on," she said. "Are you really ready for that?"

"I don't want to be overdramatic, Kenzie, but remember what Jefferson said about 'the tree of liberty.' I don't want to shed any more blood than I have to—not even tyrants' blood, much less patriots'—but it's gone too far to end any other way. And then there's Burke. You know how Dad always loved him."

"'The only thing necessary for the triumph of evil is for good men to do nothing,'" Mackenzie quoted softly, and Indy nodded.

"I can't do nothing anymore, Kenzie. I just can't. And neither can you, can you?"

She looked down at her menu once more for fifteen or twenty seconds, then back up at him and shook her head.

"No, Indy," she said very, very quietly. "I can't."

✦ Chapter Eight

"OH-HO! *This* IS INTERESTING, SIR."

Lieutenant Brandon Stiller looked down at the pair of uniformed legs visible—from ankles to just above the knee—protruding out of the guts of the fire control console.

"And what would 'this' be, Maggie?" he inquired. "It's just a bit hard to see down inside there with you at the moment."

"Oops. Sorry about that, Sir," CPO Magdalena Grigoriv said. Her voice was rather muffled, but clear enough. "Just a sec."

In fact, it was rather less than the specified second when the display on Stiller's tablet flicked to life with the imagery from the visual pick up mounted beside the lamp on Grigoriv's headset. He looked at it for a moment or two, rubbing his chin as he frowned thoughtfully, then shrugged.

"I give," he said. "Other than another chunk of molycirc, I still don't know what 'this' is. Any hints?"

"What this is, Sir, unless I'm badly mistaken, is a secondary backup of the tac log."

"Is it now?" Stiller's expression was suddenly intent. "I didn't know they had one of those aboard these ships."

"Yes, Sir. Gets more interesting every day, doesn't it? But look here."

Grigoriv's hand entered the field of view, indicating a pair of connectors. It was a slender, fine boned hand, since she was barely a hundred and sixty centimeters tall, which was one of the reasons she was the one exploring the innards of the consoles on the command deck of MSN *Remorseless* (until recently BC-1003 *Incomparable*, late of the Solarian League Navy). Not only was Stiller an officer (if a rather junior one), but he was also twenty-five centimeters taller than she was and considerably broader. Of course, the fact that she'd demonstrated the best intuitive feel for the . . . idiosyncrasies of Solarian tech had more than a little to do with why she'd drawn the assignment, too. It would appear that for any possible technological issue there was a right solution, a wrong solution, and a *Solly* solution. There were times when Stiller had no idea what could have inspired the SLN to adopt the one they had.

"This one"—the fingernail on the index finger tapping the connector on the right had acquired more than a little dirt—"goes straight to the TO's station, and this one here"—she tapped the second connector—"goes to the feed from CIC. But there's no connector to anywhere else. It accepts input from both those sources, and it can *output* to the tactical officer's station, but it's pretty clearly a standalone data storage unit."

"My, my, my," Stiller murmured. "I wonder if they wiped this one, too? Assuming they knew about it, of course."

"One way to find out, Sir." Grigoriv's other hand

appeared in the field of view. Nimble fingers quickly attached a probe to the memory unit's diagnostic panel, and she snorted. "Dunno exactly what's in here, Sir, but there's a lot of it! I mean, a whole big lot."

"Well, in that case, Maggie, I suppose we ought to see about encouraging it to tell us about itself. Wouldn't you agree?"

"Copy that, Sir!"

❖   ❖   ❖

"That was . . . careless of them," Augustus Khumalo said as the intelligence summary ended. "I assume Admiral O'Malley and Ms. Corvisart already have copies of this?"

"Yes, Sir." Commander Chandler nodded. "I've distributed it to everyone on the authorized list."

"And all of this was in it?" Khumalo flicked a finger at the display in front of him, which currently displayed only the wallpaper of HMS *Hercules*. It was a purely rhetorical question, as his satisfied smile made clear, but Chandler nodded again.

"We downloaded through the TO's station before we actually pulled the unit. I don't think the Monicans realized they'd given us the complete access codes."

"I think it's more likely Captain Kurtz's theory is correct, Sir," Aivars Terekhov said.

He and Ginger Lewis had come aboard *Hercules* as Khumalo's dinner guests just before Chandler delivered his latest intelligence prize. Now the admiral crooked an eyebrow at him, and Terekhov shrugged.

"I think she's right, Sir. They didn't know it was there any more than we did. If they'd known, they would've scrubbed it before we got hold of it."

Khumalo nodded. The Monicans had used the

interval between Terekhov's destruction of their operational battlecruisers and his own arrival in-system to delete all manner of incriminating files. Unfortunately for them, the Manticoran cyber forensics teams had managed to recover a great many intact computer cores from the shattered military component of Eroica Station. But this was the first complete and undamaged download from one of the ex-Solarian battlecruisers' log systems to fall into their hands. And, having scanned the output Chandler had already worked through, the admiral understood exactly why they'd scrubbed everything else they could get their hands on.

"I can understand the Monicans not realizing it was there," he said after a moment. "But *Technodyne* must have known about it!"

"They *should've* known about it," Terekhov agreed. "On the other hand, Technodyne's an enormous operation, Sir, and all this was completely 'black.' I'd bet they compartmentalized like crazy when they set it up, and we've all seen examples of what can happen when someone does that. How many times has that kind of thing bitten *us* on the ass against the Peeps?"

"You're thinking someone didn't get the word about where these ships were going, so that someone didn't bother to mention the backup to anyone else?"

"Something like that. Then again, they may have known about it all along and just not told Monica because they didn't care. They never thought we'd get our hands on these ships, Sir. They worried about changing emission signatures and cosmetic changes to weapons and sensor suites to disguise them on external scans, but they never expected our techs to actually take their hardware apart!"

"I suppose that's true," Khumalo said, forbearing to point out that any such expectations would have been amply justified if not for a certain Aivars Terekhov. "I imagine Ms. Corvisart and the Foreign Office will be very happy to get their hands on this, though."

He tapped the display at his elbow, and Terekhov nodded. The download from the backup log covered every stage of *Incomparable*'s transformation into *Remorseless*. It was a complete record of the modifications to the ship's systems, which had captured Technodyne technicians not only making modifications themselves but also running sims and instructing Monican personnel in the operation and maintenance of top-secret Solarian League Navy hardware. Worse, it had captured Technodyne supervisors discussing how the ships had been diverted to Monica's use. Since that included specific mention of the Solarian League inspectors who'd signed off on the ships' complete demolition by the reclamation crews, it was a particularly damning bit of evidence in the case Amandine Corvisart was building against Technodyne and the League in general.

"The newsies will salivate the instant they see it," the admiral predicted, and Terekhov nodded once more.

"Did Stiller and Grigoriv document every stage of this, Ambrose?" the captain asked.

"Every bit of it," Chandler confirmed. "Our crews are documenting *everything*, but as soon as Stiller realized what Grigoriv had turned up he brought in one of the Solly observers, as well."

"Now *that* was a smart move," Commander Lewis said. "Technodyne's going to scream we fabricated all of it, but that's going to be a harder sell with one of

Ms. Corvisart's pet newsies validating where we found it and how we downloaded its contents."

"Never underestimate the power of money and corruption when it comes to the Solarian League legal system, Ginger," Terekhov advised. "Of course, the court of public opinion's a different venue. It probably will do some good there."

"And it might do some good right here in Monica, too," Khumalo pointed out. "However, I suspect dinner is about to be served. Before we sit down to it, Aivars, how are *Hexapuma*'s repairs coming?"

"Quite well, considering." Terekhov waved in Lewis' direction. "Ginger and her people are just about completely exhausted by now, but with Captain Kurtz's people's assistance, we should be ready to hyper out within a couple of weeks."

"That's a remarkable achievement," Khumalo said sincerely, with an approving nod for Lewis. "I wouldn't have believed *anyone* could put her back together when I first saw your damage report!"

"I'm not sure I would've argued with you, Sir," Terekhov said. "Ginger never doubted, though."

"I wouldn't go quite that far, Sir." Lewis shook her head. "It was more a case of my not daring to tell *you* I cherished any doubts about my own peerless ability to glue the bits and pieces back into place."

"Well, whatever you may've thought at the time, Commander, you've amply justified Captain Terekhov's confidence in you since. In fact—"

A soft chime interrupted the admiral, and he checked his personal chrono.

"All right. Shop talk is now officially suspended until after dinner." He slid back his float chair and stood. "If you'll all come with me, I think the cooks have put together something fairly palatable."

✧   ✧   ✧

"No, Mister President." Amandine Corvisart's tone might be courteous, but it was also decidedly cool and about as far from affable as it was possible for a voice to be. "I'm afraid that point is not negotiable."

Roberto Tyler stared at her across his desk, then glanced at the other two men seated in his private office.

Admiral Gregoire Bourmont wouldn't meet his eyes, not that the president was especially surprised by that. Bourmont was a broken man, devastated on a personal as well as a professional level by the crushing defeat—the outright *destruction*—of his entire navy by what he'd since discovered was a scratch-built squadron composed primarily of *second line* Manticoran warships. He seemed like a man trapped in a nightmare from which he couldn't awaken, and Tyler doubted that was going to change anytime soon...if ever.

Alfonso Higgins, the Republic of Monica's chief of intelligence, was still functional, however, and he *did* meet his president's gaze. In fact, he shrugged ever so slightly, and Tyler's jaw tightened. Higgins had minced no bones about his conclusion that they had no choice but to accept the deal—*any* deal—Manticore was willing to offer at this point. His own intelligence reports and analyses made it abundantly clear that Tyler's presidency hung by the proverbial thread. The Monican electorate understood exactly how the Republic's political system worked, and by and large they'd been willing to accept that for the last several decades. Even more importantly, his fellow kleptocrats had stood firmly behind him as long as his policies continued to bring in the Solarian cash they needed to grease the wheels of their personal fortunes. But that was before Tyler had involved their star nation in one of the most colossal debacles—if not simply *the* most colossal debacle—in its history. Very few of those kleptocratic friends of his were all that fond of him at the moment. And if the Star Empire of Manticore so much as whispered the possibility of incorporating Monica into the newly annexed Talbott Sector into that electorate's ear, any plebiscite would approve the notion by an overwhelming majority.

No doubt it would, Tyler thought resentfully, returning his attention to Corvisart. *But the damned Manties have to watch their asses, too. Frontier Security may be willing to swallow a lot after how spectacularly Anisimovna and her frigging friends have screwed the pooch, but the outright forcible annexation—plebiscite or no plebiscite—of a League ally would be really pushing things. In fact, the Sollies might actually want the Manties to try it! If they can turn this into some sort of raw territorial grab on the Manties' part they may be able to shout loud enough about that to keep their public from paying any attention to the evidence.*

Personally, Tyler doubted OFS or its friends—and especially Technodyne—had a hope in hell of pulling that off. Fortunately for him, Manticore seemed unwilling to take that chance. Which, now that Tyler thought about it, might be wise of them, considering the general credulity of the Solly man in the street.

"Ms. Corvisart," he said as reasonably as he could, "you've already acquired more than enough physical and documentary evidence to support or disprove your version of what happened here. Obviously, there's nothing anyone in the Republic of Monica can do to prevent you from doing whatever you wish to do with that evidence. But surely you understand that a sovereign star nation can't simply hand over its own raw diplomatic correspondence and intelligence data. There are some records whose confidentiality simply have to be preserved if a star nation hopes to have any credibility at all in sensitive interstellar negotiations. No one would just roll over and give you that sort of access! It's out of the question!"

"Under normal circumstances, perhaps," Corvisart said implacably. "The circumstances aren't normal, however, Sir. In fact, they're decidedly *abnormal*, and I'm afraid you and I both know how they came to be that way. The evidence we already possess was acquired by force of arms. In other words, it's our legitimate prize by right of capture and, as you say, we can do whatever we wish with it. There are inevitably going to be those in the League who discount that evidence as fabricated by the Star Empire for some nefarious purpose of our own, however. That's going to happen whatever else happens, and you know it as well as we do. But the Star Empire intends to make it as difficult as possible even for someone like Malachai Abruzzi to say that with a straight face. That brings us back to the point of today's conversation, and, Mister President, without wishing to be unpleasant about this, you're not really in the best position to tell us what's acceptable and unacceptable at the moment."

Tyler felt his face darken with anger, but he bit down on the furious response boiling behind his teeth. Corvisart had made her position amply clear. Either he handed over the records—*all* the records—she'd demanded, or else she, Augustus Khumalo, and Quentin O'Malley completely disarmed the Monican Navy, Army, and Internal Security Force. They probably wouldn't be able to get *all* of those weapons out of Monican hands, especially the ISF's small arms, but they'd be able to get enough to guarantee the overthrow of his presidency. The consequences of that would be highly unpleasant—probably fatal—for a significant percentage of the Tyler family and its supporters.

But if he caved to their demands, gave them what they wanted, Corvisart was prepared to sign a nonaggression pact between the Republic of Monica and the Star Empire of Manticore. What was left of his battered armed forces would remain intact and under his command, although he'd still have to deal with some highly restive elements within them, and the Republic would be left in one piece. In fact, she was prepared to sweeten the deal by offering to include Monica in the domestic trade zone being established in Talbott, which would make his currently unhappy kleptocrats almost as happy as if his effort to seize the Lynx Terminus had succeeded. The regime's survival would remain problematic, perhaps, but by Alfonso Higgins' calculations, the odds would be heavily in Tyler's favor.

Domestically, at least. When the Solarian League finally got around to pulverizing Manticore for its effrontery, OFS might have a page or two in its plans for the client regime which had turned upon it.

But that will be then, *and this is* now, *isn't it?* Tyler thought. *There's a certain . . . immediacy to the situation, and this bitch's made it abundantly clear that she doesn't plan to wait around forever. Time to crap or get off the pot, Roberto. Besides, it's not like I owe those OFS or Technodyne bastards a damned thing after the shit pot they've landed me in!*

"Very well, Ms. Corvisart. Understand that we are complying only under protest, but the records you demand will be made available to you."

"Under the conditions specified?" Corvisart pressed, and his eyes flashed.

It wasn't enough for her that his IT people hand over the documents. Oh, no! Her people had to have access to his central filing systems to extract the information themselves, making any redaction impossible. God only knew what else they might find while they were about it, either! And she'd have her damned representatives of the Solarian League press with her techs the whole way.

It was intolerable, and he hovered on the very brink of telling her exactly that. But then his nostrils flared, and he nodded.

"Under the conditions specified," he grated, and Corvisart nodded as if she hadn't just performed a double orchiectomy upon him.

"Thank you, Mister President," she said courteously. "Commander Chandler and Commander Bonifacio will be in touch before the end of business today to arrange the details."

"'Cept there's also that bit in the Constitution 'bout property rights and trespassers and how a woman's got the right to defend her property against 'em, 'specially after she's already warned 'em they'd best get. Right this minute, I've got a real itch to exercise my constitutional freedoms. So I think it'd be a real good idea if the sergeant here escorted Mr. Omikado off the premises. Be a whole lot easier if there aren't any more bodies to drag out on the porch."

—Eileanóra Allenby,
Owner, Whitewater
Hollow Outfitters,
Swallow System

Chapter Nine

"WE SHOULD MAKE HALKIRK ORBIT in another ninety minutes, Mr. Brown."

"Thank you, Captain," Damien Harahap said, not looking up from his cabin's workstation display. "Let me know as soon as I'm cleared to go planet-side, please."

"Of course, Mr. Brown."

The intercom went dead, and Harahap shook his head, his expression wry. He'd had more aliases than he could possibly count in his career. Some had been more imaginative than others, and he had a greater fondness for some, but few had been as...bland as "Mister Brown." It was certainly serviceable, and he heartily approved of not letting anyone know anything he or she didn't absolutely *have* to know, but still...

He put that thought away and turned his full attention back to the display. It no longer featured the reams of data he'd studied on the three T-week voyage from Mesa. Instead, it showed a spectacular vista of the Loomis System's twin inhabited planets—brown-and-tan

Halkirk and gorgeous sapphire Thurso—and floating head shots of both the people he intended to meet on Halkirk and the ones he intended to avoid at all costs.

There was really only one of them he absolutely had to avoid: Lieutenant Ottomar Touchette, Solarian Gendarmerie. Not only was Touchette the senior intelligence officer assigned to Loomis, he'd also worked with Harahap in the Madras Sector less than five T-years ago. Fortunately, according to the confidential Frontier Security files Bardasano had provided, Touchette wasn't in particularly good odor with Nyatui Zagorski, the local transstellar's rep. Probably because of Touchette's habit of providing good, honest analysis... whether it said what his superiors wanted it to say or not. From Zagorski's record, the last thing he wanted was honest analysis of Loomisian public opinion and its possible ramifications.

From Harahap's new perspective, that was all to the good. Loomis was close enough to the Madras Sector for him to have been at least generally aware of what was happening in the system even before Major Eichbauer seconded him to Bardasano and Anisimovna for the Talbott operation. He hadn't realized then quite how bad things were getting, however, which promised fertile ground for Operation Janus. Of course, it remained to see whether it was fertile enough.

❖   ❖   ❖

"And where do you think *you're* going, Innis MacLay?" Maggie MacLay demanded, propping her hands on her hips and tilting her head back to glare up at him better. "I've a list of chores for you a meter long!"

"Ah, now!" Innis smiled down at his wife, then scooped her up and kissed her soundly. "It's not like I'll be gone forever, *Rùnag*. And you know I'll get right on that list the instant I walk back in the door."

"And if you do, I'll want to know where *my* husband is and what you did with him!" Maggie said, swatting him across the top of his head. "There's a reason that list's a meter long, you know."

"And what would that be?" Innis set her back on the floor and tucked an arm around her. He was a tallish fellow, very nearly two meters tall, and she was more than thirty centimeters shorter than him.

"Well, let's just say that *last* week it was only two thirds of a meter long. And the week before that it was only a *third* of a meter. Are we seeing a pattern here?"

"That you're a bit OCD about adding to lists?" Innis asked innocently.

"That's one possible explanation. On the other hand, if this list isn't shorter by the end of the weekend, there will be sanctions." She batted her eyelashes at him and rolled her hips. "*Painful* sanctions."

"In that case, I'll make this as quick as I can!"

"That would be wise of you," she told him, and rose on tiptoe to kiss his cheek before he headed out the door.

He smiled to himself as he crossed the modest house's front yard with its brilliant flower garden and headed for the ground car parked at the curb. That house was a sign of just how light Halkirk's population remained, even now, and of its modest tech base. Most places, the citizenry would have been packed into towering spires of ceramacrete to utilize limited space most efficiently, but even though Conerock was a major regional administrative center, it retained a broad belt of suburbs dominated by individual family-sized units. Innis was more than glad it was, although he had to agree that there were probably certain advantages—in theory, at least—to apartment towers... assuming Halkirk had possessed the technology and industry to build them. For one thing, a tower had a much smaller footprint for the same population. For another, he supposed it would be convenient to live only thirty or forty floors up or down from his place of employment. Except, of course, that *his* "place of employment" was out in the midst of the continent of Stronsay's hushed, green forests.

And except for the fact that you were brought up wanting at least a little space to call your own, he reflected as he unlocked the ground car's door. *And not just a light well inside a tower, either. Real space, with real green in it. And bless Maggie and the kids' green thumbs for all those flowers!*

He smiled again at that thought, but this smile was fleeting. If SEIU had its way, he and a quarter or so of Halkirk's population were going to be out of a job within ten T-years—fifteen at the most. He was more than a little ashamed it had taken that to get him to wake up and smell the coffee, but his eyes were open now. Which was the real reason he was headed for Fingal's Tavern this clear, cool Saturday morning. Not for the pint and darts he'd told Maggie about, either.

He started the engine and pulled away from the curb, wondering exactly what Tad was going to tell him.

❖   ❖   ❖

"Come in, please, Mr. Henry," the dark-haired and dark-complexioned woman said, rising behind her desk and extending her hand in greeting as the receptionist ushered Damien Harahap into her office.

"Good afternoon, Ms. MacRuer," replied, taking the proffered hand and gripping it firmly. "I'm glad you were able to see me on such short notice."

"Well, I have to admit I was a bit puzzled by your call." Nessa MacRuer sank back into her desk chair as Harahap seated himself in one of the comfortable but old-fashioned chairs in front of it. "MacNish, Tonnochy, and Duncannon is one of Elgin's older law partnerships, but I'm a bit perplexed by just how it is we can help you."

"I can't say I'm hugely surprised by that." Harahap smiled pleasantly. "It's been my experience, though, that the fastest way to accomplish something is to go directly to the person you need to talk to. Or, in this case, one of that person's closer associates."

MacRuer tilted her chair back slightly and raised one eyebrow. She was a striking woman, Harahap thought, especially here on Halkirk, which had one of the less genetically diverse planetary populations. There was clearly a lot of Old Earth Asian genetic material in Ms. MacRuer, and he wondered if her exotic—by local standards—appearance had been a factor in her professional success. The odds were good that it had. On the other hand, that same exoticness was likely to be just a bit of a handicap in her current unofficial and very quiet avocation.

"Really?" She cocked her head to one side. "My understanding is that you're in Loomis as a silver oak purchaser for"—she let him see her checking a memo on her display—"the Hauptman Cartel. That's a Manticoran firm, isn't it?"

"Yes, it is." Harahap nodded. "And I realize I'm a bit far from home, but let's face it, you don't find silver oak growing on just any planet."

"No." For just a moment, something bitter might have flashed in the depths of MacRuer's tone, but if it had, she controlled quickly. "No," she went on more pleasantly, "silver oak really is Loomis' main claim to fame, I suppose."

"And well it should be," Harahap said, and meant every word of it. The dense-grained, gorgeously patterned and colored wood was incredibly beautiful, which explained the staggering prices it commanded from Core World sculptors and interior decorators. "I have to say I understand why the market is prepared to snap up every square meter of it it can get!"

"Yes, it is." This time the bitterness was more pronounced, and her smile looked a little forced. "But, as I say, I'm not quite clear on how our firm can serve you. MacNish, Tonnochy, and Duncannon specializes in real estate law and transactions, not the commodity market. Besides, if you're in the market for silver oak, you'd really need to speak to the Cooperative."

"I understand that." Harahap acknowledged, then opened his slim briefcase in his lap and arched an eyebrow of his own. "Perhaps it would move things along a bit if I showed you what I have in mind?"

"If you'd like to." MacRuer sounded a little puzzled, but she nodded.

"Thank you," Harahap said, and extracted a compact electronic unit. He leaned forward to lay it on the corner of MacRuer's desk, and her almond eyes went wide as he pressed a stud and a green light flashed.

"There. Now we can talk," he said, and hid an inward smile as MacRuer darted a quick, nervous look around her office. Her body language seemed to put physical distance between them without ever actually moving. That was good; he'd hoped she'd recognize the unit.

"May I ask what that is?" she said after a moment, although her assumed ignorance fooled neither of them, and this time he allowed his smile to show.

"It's only a privacy unit, Ms. MacRuer," he replied. "Of course, it's an *off-world* privacy unit, and I suppose it's remotely possible I failed to register it with the local authorities when I landed. Is that a problem, do you suppose?"

His gaze held hers very levelly across her desk. To her credit, she neither swallowed nervously nor wiped sweat from her forehead, but he could see the intense thoughts churning away behind her eyes. Loomis was one of the star systems whose law codes required all anti-surveillance devices to be registered with their security forces. Quite a few systems, especially in the Shell and Verge, had regulations like that, although most Core World populations refused to tolerate them. On the other hand, only a minority of the systems which did have them were quite as ferocious as Loomis in enforcing them.

"Actually," she said after a moment, "it could be quite a significant problem. As an officer of the court, I'm obligated to report any unlicensed privacy units, and I'm afraid the penalties for possessing one are quite severe. Especially for *off-world* units."

"I'm not surprised." Harahap set his briefcase on the floor beside his chair and leaned back, crossing his legs. "I'm sure Ms. MacQuarie and the UPS get nervous when there's no software backdoor to let them listen in on a conversation anyway. Oppressive regimes tend to be fussy that way."

"I'm afraid this conversation is over, Mr. Henry," MacRuer said. "As I just pointed out, as an attorney I'm an officer of the court. Not only am I obligated to report your unit, but I feel I should also point out to you that there are limits to acceptable criticism of our star system's government."

"And I'm sure Ms. MacLean and Ms. MacFadzean would never dream of transgressing those limits," he said calmly, and watched her nostrils flare as those two names hit home. "Otherwise, as an officer of the court in good standing, I'm equally sure you would have reported them to the authorities long ago."

"I don't think I'm acquainted with either of those people," she said.

"A word of professional advice, Ms. MacRuer. When someone walks into your office and hits you cold by mentioning the names of your coconspirators against the government, the shortest response is usually the safest one. Too many syllables tend to indicate nervousness. And it's *never* a good idea to deny you know someone when the local authorities already know you've met with them. Next time, I'd recommend just saying 'Who?' and leaving it up to the other fellow to steer the conversation into something which will incriminate you properly."

She sat very still for several seconds, then sat back and crossed her own legs.

"Who are you, really?" she asked.

"A Manticoran representative. And I really am here about the silver oak. Just not in quite the way you may have assumed."

"If you expect me to say anything that could incriminate me or implicate me in any sort of wrongdoing, I'm afraid you'll be disappointed." She smiled brightly. "I have no idea what sort of fanciful flight of imagination may have brought you to *my* office, of all places on Halkirk, but I assure you that MacNish, Tonnochy, and Duncannon maintain an excellent relationship with Treasury, Security, and the rest of the Administration."

"And very useful that is for you, too," he agreed. "On the other hand, you might want to be a little careful. Lieutenant Touchette picked up on the meeting you had with MacLean several months ago—right after she resigned her parliamentary seat in protest. I don't *think* he's mentioned it to Macquarie or MacCrimmon, and I imagine you can cover yourself by creating a document file about a land purchase. She's certainly well-off enough to make that work. But I'd go ahead and get started on the paper trail now, if I were you. When you have to rush something like that at the last minute, you're likely to miss some small detail, and that's all the forensics people really need to pull it apart."

He paused, and the silence stretched out for several seconds, thin and brittle, while he wondered which way she was going to jump. Then, finally, she inhaled deeply.

"I do know both of the people you mentioned," she said. "I'm sure you'll appreciate, however, that admitting I know them—in fact, that Erin MacFadzean's been a personal friend for many years—could be . . . professionally detrimental, let's say, given their rather extreme political views."

"Oh, come now, Ms. MacRuer! *Their* rather extreme political views?" he shook his head chidingly. "I don't think Lieutenant Touchette realized that what he was seeing was a planning session of the Loomis Reform Party's provisional wing. I'm not sure about that, though," he added in a thoughtful tone. "From everything I can see, Touchette's not one of President MacMinn's greater admirers. And I'm fairly confident he thinks Zagorski is as stupid as he is greedy. So it's possible he *did* realize that and just chose not to pass it along to them. I don't think you can count on his not passing along evidence of additional unexplained meetings. And OFS didn't assign Frinkelo Osborne as a 'trade attaché' in the Solly Legation here in Elgin because he was stupid, either."

"All right." MacRuer let her chair come forward and planted both hands on her desk. "You've said enough to convince me that if you're working for MacQuarie the Uppies will be breaking down my door sometime soon. But that's about all I have to say to you. I won't even *ask* about a warrant. We both know how pointless that would be."

"The UPS does have a habit of writing its warrants after the fact, doesn't it?" Harahap said. "I wonder why they continue to bother with that particular legal fig leaf."

MacRuer said nothing, only looked at him, and he snorted gently.

"Relax, Ms. MacRuer. I'm not an Uppy, and I have no intention of entrapping you in anything. In fact, after we finish our conversation, I'm going to leave your office, go back to the spaceport, and take a shuttle right back up to my ship. I'll be in-system for another three or four days. If at the end of that time, you decide—or Ms. MacLean or Ms. MacFadzean decide—that you want to talk a little more before I leave the system, I'll be available."

"And just what sort of 'conversation' do you have in mind?" she asked.

"It happens," he said, "that I really am a representative of a Manticoran concern which is very interested in the situation here in Loomis. I did tell a little white lie when I told you I was here for the Hauptman Cartel, however. What I actually represent is a certain rather low-visibility agency with security concerns of its own. In particular, the Star Kingdom—I'm sorry, I keep forgetting officially we're the Star *Empire* now—is more than a little nervous about the Solarian attitude towards our recent annexation of the Talbott Sector, particularly after that unfortunate business in Monica. Now, I realize you're not going to ask any leading questions that I could use to incriminate you in the People's Court, so I'll just chatter away about why that brings me to Loomis.

"You see, Ms. MacRuer, we'd really like Frontier Security and Frontier Fleet to have something besides us to worry about. That's our nasty, calculating motive for talking to you. On the more altruistic front, we really do disapprove of people like Star Enterprise Initiatives Unlimited." He grimaced as he rolled out the name. "You may not realize just how much the Star Kingdom frowns on the kind of slash-and-burn exploitation people like Zagorski specialize in. Your silver oak is a priceless resource, and not just for your system, but his get-rich-quick strategies are going to burn through your entire supply of mature silver oak in less than fifteen T-years, and we both know it takes an absolute minimum of *thirty-five* T-years to replace a stand. That sort of thinking is stupid on a galactic scale, and what it's going to do to your economy in the long run is a lot worse than just stupid!

"I'm not going to pretend we're on some sort of crusade to heal all the galaxy's ills, because, frankly, all the galaxy's ills aren't our responsibility. But in this instance, we see the opportunity to kill two birds with one stone. If we can identify people who are . . . unhappy, let's say, with the status quo in their home star systems and might be thinking about doing something about that—people like those here in Loomis—we see every advantage to us in supporting their efforts. Obviously, we don't want to get a reputation for encouraging people to do stupid things, so I'm not prepared to offer you and the Provos any sort of blank check. But if I can satisfy my superiors that you have a genuine organization and a genuine plan—one that can succeed and that would make things *better*, not worse, in Loomis—I think you could count on not just financial support and shipments of weapons, but also our best effort to keep Frontier Fleet from interfering, as well."

Despite an excellent poker face, MacRuer's eyes had widened while he was speaking. Now he smiled at her again.

"I think that's more than enough on that front for this first meeting," he told her. "This is a dance I've been to more than once, and I know how the steps go, but your people are doing all of this for the first time. You're going to have to go home and talk to your leadership. Frankly, I think you need to take your time and do that right. And I'm sure you wouldn't have gotten this far if you didn't have at least some contacts in UPS, so you need to use them to make sure I actually have a ship in orbit and actually leave. Most local agents provocateur don't spend their time sailing around between star systems," he pointed out drolly, and despite her tension, she chuckled. Then his expression turned serious once more.

"I would appreciate your getting back to me before I leave in at least one respect. Travel time is a copperplated bitch in organizing something like this on an interstellar basis, so I need to know whether your people are sufficiently serious to make it worth our while for me to come back again. I'm perfectly willing to do that if you *are* serious, but if you aren't—or if you simply don't want to trust the first stranger to come blowing in your door—and, frankly, I wouldn't blame you if you don't—then we need to concentrate our available resources on other star systems who are more prepared to let us work with them. I'm not saying I want any detailed commitments from you at this time. To be honest, I'd be leery about the viability of any sort of strategy you could put together that quickly. But if Ms. MacLean and Ms. MacFadzean *are* interested, I can arrange my schedule to get back here and confer with you. Or, at least, I can arrange for one of my associates to do that. And I'd arrange contact codes before I left."

He held her gaze for several seconds longer, then reached out to the privacy unit once more.

"As I say, I think that's probably enough for a first meeting, especially a cold first meeting," he said. "And in response to something you asked about earlier, I have an excellent cover for any future contact between you and me or one of my associates. In fact, we should probably go about setting that up, shouldn't we?"

He pressed the stud again, deactivating the unit, and tucked it leisurely back into his briefcase. Then he took a note board from the same briefcase and flipped it open.

"Actually," he said brightly as the display came alive, "the Hauptman Cartel's considering investing in direct shipment of both silver oak and seafood from Loomis, now that the Star Empire's expanding into the Talbott area. Before, you were much too far away for practical shipping considerations. Now, that situation may be changing, given the existence of the Lynx Terminus, and Mr. Hauptman is very interested in acquiring his own orbital warehousing facilities here in Loomis. I've done a little research, and I've discovered that your firm represents SEIU in most of its orbital leasing and sales agreements, so it seemed to me that you were the logical people to approach. If you'll open a folder, I'll send over the specs on what we're looking for. Then you and I probably need to discuss availability and price ranges. For starters, the Cartel is thinking in terms of an investment of no more than, say, fifteen or twenty million Manticoran dollars. That would be about sixty to seventy million of your credits, if I have the exchange rate right. Assuming Mr. Hauptman's hopes work out, we'd be increasing that to—"

✧ Chapter Ten

"EXCUSE ME, MAJOR. I'VE GOT something here I think you should see."

Major Braxton Reizinger, Solarian Gendarmerie, looked up from his routine paperwork with a certain degree of trepidation as Master Sergeant Sheila Roskilly walked into his office. Without, he noticed with an even greater degree of trepidation, any announcement from his office clerk or so much as a knock on his office door.

Those were bad signs, but he made himself frown reprovingly at her.

"Master Sergeant, haven't you and I spoken about that thing called 'proper channels'?"

"Yes, Sir. I think we have," Roskilly agreed.

"I thought we had. So I assume there's a reason you aren't using them...again?"

"Crap gets lost going through 'channels,' Sir," she said simply, and he sighed.

The hell of it is that she's right, he reflected. *Shouldn't be that way, but she and I both know it is. And the fact that she's old enough to be my grandmother—and that she's been doing her job since well before I was born—probably has something to do with her... insistence.*

And the fact that she hadn't liked much of what she'd seen doing that job for the last, oh, thirty or forty T-years had something to do with it, as well.

"Then I suppose you'd better come in," he said. "Oh! You *are* in, Master Sergeant aren't you?"

"Guess I am, Sir," she acknowledged, finally cracking a small smile, and he smiled back. There might have been more than a trace of resignation in his own smile, but there was genuine humor as well.

That humor faded quickly, however. Major Reizinger headed the Verge Desk in the Solarian Gendarmerie's Operations Division, and OpsDiv was in charge of intelligence analysis for the Gendarmerie's field operations. In theory, that meant everything the SG had: intervention battalions, gendarmes assigned to standard police duties in OFS-administered star systems, gendarmes assigned to customs operations, and on and on and on. Unfortunately, the Gendarmes had far too many duties and far too many people assigned to far too many places for OpsDiv to actually *analyze* more than a tiny fraction of the data coming at it. That was the main reason so much analysis devolved on local SG commands... and why so much of the analysis those local commands performed never made it into OpsDiv's central files. There was simply too much of it.

Reizinger's boss, Lieutenant Colonel Weng Zhinghwan, who commanded OpsDiv, concentrated on cataloguing and categorizing the data stream so that she could steer it appropriately, and he had to admit she had a good sense of who needed to see what. She was also intelligent—not brilliant, in his opinion, but *critically* intelligent, which was unfortunately rare in the Gendarmerie's upper echelons—and she tried to be honest, at least with herself and her most trusted people. All in all, he'd worked for infinitely worse superiors.

Unfortunately, like anyone who'd risen to her level, she also recognized the danger of being too honest when reporting to certain of her own superiors. Worse still, Brigadier Noritoshi Väinölä, who headed SG Intelligence Command, had a well-deserved reputation for sitting on (or even rejecting outright) any analysis which might conflict with the current mission priorities of General Toinette Mabley, CO of the entire Gendarmerie. Which was one reason Major Reizinger was less than delighted to see Master Sergeant Roskilly in his office this bright, sunny morning.

"All right, Sheila. Tell me what it is *this* time," he said stoically.

"Yes, Sir. I've been looking at this for a while, actually. It started about the time the Manties discovered that Lynx Terminus of theirs. May've started a little earlier, to be honest, but that's the earliest I've found any sign of it."

Reizinger winced. Nothing to come across the Verge Desk was likely to be good news if the newly renamed Star Empire of Manticore was involved, and Brigadier Väinölä had already made it clear that the less he heard about the expletive-deleted Manties, the better he'd like it.

"And just what have the Manties been up to now?" he asked cautiously.

"Not sure it's actually the *Manties*, Sir, but somebody's sure as hell up to something. Don't have a ton of corroborating evidence yet, but let me show you what I do have so far...."

◇　　◇　　◇

"So what do *you* make of Reizinger's report?" Weng Zhing-hwan asked, spooning sugar into her cup of tea.

Despite her family name, Weng had very fair hair, bright blue eyes, and a pale complexion. She was also thirteen centimeters taller than the woman sitting on the far side of the table. The table in question was in a privacy booth in The Golden Olive, a restaurant in Old Chicago noted for its security and discretion. Weng and her companion had been meeting there very quietly for the past two or three T-years. It was safer to use The Golden Olive than the Gendarmerie's canteen or some other "official" venue, for a lot of reasons. There was no legal reason they couldn't have met openly, but neither of them could have counted all of the other considerations which made that... inadvisable.

"I think it's a good thing your master sergeant never got a commission," Lupe Blanton replied. Blanton commanded the OFS Intelligence Branch's first section, which was tasked with the analysis of non-Solarian political and military entities. She had jet black hair, a very dark complexion, and bright silver eyes, legacy of a great-grandmother's taste in genetic modification. "If she'd ever been commissioned, she'd've been canned decades ago. Either that, or she'd've been promoted until her brain ossified properly."

"That's not a very flattering portrait of our esteemed superiors," Weng pointed out mildly.

"Reality has a nasty habit of not being flattering," Blanton replied, and Weng snorted in agreement.

She finished stirring her tea, set her spoon down on the saucer, and sipped appreciatively. Then she cupped the teacup in both hands, gazing across at Blanton through the wisp of steam.

"So, having made our opinion of the upper echelons of our respective organizations clear, what *do* you think about it?"

"She may be seeing ghosts," Blanton said after a moment. "On the other hand, she may not be, too. Especially if the Manties' version of what happened in Monica is as accurate as I'm afraid it is."

"Really?" Weng tilted her head thoughtfully. "I have to admit they're doing a masterful job of massacring Technodyne, and I imagine there are going to be some red faces over at Navy over those battlecruisers that somehow didn't get scrapped even after the inspectors signed off that they had been. I gather from your tone that there's even more and worse, though?"

"I don't know if they're going to push it, but I'm pretty sure Verrocchio and Hongbo were in it up to their eyebrows," Blanton said grimly. "Mind you, none of this is coming over *my* desk, but I know Rajmund well enough to recognize obfuscation when I see it."

"'Obfuscation,'" Weng repeated with a smile.

"Improving my vocabulary." Blanton picked up the vodka martini she preferred to her companion's hot tea and sipped. "You've got to admit it's a lot politer than the nouns I usually use in his case."

"True," Weng said judiciously. "Very true."

Rajmund Nyhus headed OFS Intelligence's Section Two, tasked with analysis of *internal* threats to

Frontier Security's operations. There was a certain tension between Section One and Section Two, since OFS classified non-Solarian citizens (and all other non-Solarian entities) in systems it controlled or administered as "internal" to those systems, which led to all sorts of turf wars. It was also why things tended to get dropped when they had to be passed back and forth between the two sections. The fact that Nyhus' position put him deeply in bed with every corrupt transstellar in existence didn't help. And the fact that Section Two was also supposed to be the OFS' watchdog on its own governors and administrators only made bad worse—*much* worse—in Lupe Blanton's considered opinion.

"I get copied on all of his reports to Ukhtomskoy," she said now. Adão Ukhtomskoy was her direct superior, CO of Office of Frontier Security Intelligence Branch, which made him the OFS' equivalent of Brigadier Väinölä. "God knows there're so many CYA memos and reports flowing through the system no one could possibly keep up with all of them, but I try to keep at least one eye on Rajmund's contributions. Helps a lot when I'm trying to figure out what he's covering up this week."

"And this week he's covering for Verrocchio and Hongbo, you think?"

"Them and/or whoever the hell was working Talbott." Blanton nodded. "I'll be astonished if Francisca Yucel wasn't involved, too."

"I think she probably was," Weng confirmed rather grimly. "We've lost at least two of her better subordinates, anyway, and she's always been one who likes to tie up loose ends. We don't have any hard evidence she was involved, of course, but I've kicked it over to Gaddis at CID."

Blanton frowned. That was playing pretty damned hardball, even for someone who'd been willing to set up the entire anti-Manty operation in the first place. But if Weng was bringing it to the attention of the SG's Criminal Investigation Division she obviously *thought* Yucel had been involved, evidence or no evidence.

"'Lost' as in eliminated?" she asked, just to be sure.

"One of them, yes. We've got confirmation on that. The other one just vanished." Weng shrugged. "From what I can see in their jackets, they were both two of our better people. Privately, I'm hoping Harahap—he's the one who vanished—saw which way the wind was blowing and just got out from under. He seems to've been a damned competent sort, so if he did, I'm pretty sure he landed on his feet somewhere else, and more power to him."

"Are you getting as bad a feeling about this as I am?" Blanton asked after a moment, and the gendarme shrugged again.

"I'm not getting any *good* feelings about it, anyway. The thing that really bothers me is that we don't know—especially if you're right about Verrocchio and Hongbo, and I'm pretty sure you are—exactly who the hell is using who. The Manties' version makes a lot of sense, frankly. But if they're right, then we're even more screwed in the Verge than we thought we were."

"Ever the mistress of understatement, I see," Blanton said dryly.

"Which brings us back to my troublemaking master sergeant," Weng pointed out. "Not to mention the question of just what I do with her suspicions."

"Um."

Blanton sipped her martini, silver eyes intent.

"I hate to say it, but she's pulled together some things *my* people should've seen, as well," she said finally. "I want to have some of those people who should already have seen those things take a look at her analysis of them, but this wouldn't be the first time Roskilly's bird-dogged something we missed. The most interesting thing to me is the timing. If there really has been an upsurge in domestic unrest in the Verge, and if someone from the outside really *is* helping it along, then who the hell is it? It's too broadly shotgunned to be one transstellar—or even a group of them—trying to turf out competition."

"We've both seen transstellars try some pretty raw stuff, Lupe," Weng pointed out. "And there are definite resonances here with what the Manties claim Manpower and Technodyne were up to in Talbott."

"But Roskilly's pointing at incidents that go all the way from the Madras Sector to the *Maya* Sector," Blanton protested. "That's almost twelve hundred light-years, Zhing-hwan!"

"And some of them may be—probably are—false positives, too," Weng responded. "Roskilly's got good instincts, and so does Reizinger. That's why I put him on the Verge Desk. But they can see correlations that don't exist, just like anyone else, and God knows there are enough people in the Verge with totally legitimate complaints. People like that don't really need much outside provocation to get . . . rowdy. I think the two of them are onto something, or I wouldn't've invited you to lunch to talk about it, but that doesn't mean I'm ready to buy into some kind of galaxy-wide conspiracy."

"Even if it's not that widespread, it's still bigger than anything private enterprise's tried yet," Blanton said. "I could do without all the crap Frontier Security gets involved in, but it would take somebody with the kind of reach *we* have to screw with this many different star systems. We're talking about another star nation here, Zhing-hwan!"

"Don't go saying that anywhere Rajmund can hear you." Weng shook her head sourly. "I hear he's already arguing Manticore 'provoked' any transstellars, Solarian or otherwise, who might—*might*—have been involved in Talbott. I don't want to speak ill of your superior, Lupe. God knows I realize how distasteful you must find any criticism of him. But if he simply *had* to find a cesspool to climb into, couldn't he at least have avoided Manpower?"

"Lots of money and power at the bottom of that particular sewer," Blanton replied cynically. "I don't doubt he'd point the finger straight at the Manties, though. You're right about that. And the truth is that you and I can't take this anywhere yet. All we have is speculation and Master Sergeant Roskilly's instincts. To be honest, we don't even have any substantial straws in the wind yet!"

"It's not just Roskilly's instincts this time, Lupe." Weng set down her teacup and leaned forward. Her expression serious. "I've got a really bad feeling. And not just about the possibility that someone's deliberately making the situation in the Verge worse. There's something in the air. Something bad."

Their eyes met across the table, and, after a moment, Blanton nodded. The two of them were uniquely placed to see just how corrupt the system they served had become. They were just as well placed to see how deeply resentful the star systems being abused by it were, and that was enough to make anyone with a functioning brain nervous. People had a tendency, Blanton knew, to assume that the way things were at any given time were the way they'd always be, but that wasn't true. "Things" changed, and when too many people got hurt too badly things could change in a vast hurry... even when something as huge and powerful as the Solarian League tried to keep them from changing.

At the very least, the situation's gotten bad enough that private enterprise can co-opt OFS and the Gendarmerie for purposes of its own, she thought grimly. *If it's actually another star nation, instead, that may be even worse. They'd have to be doing it for a reason, and I doubt it would be anything the League liked. On the other hand, how much worse could it be? If whoever's behind this really can pull the puppet strings on Frontier Security and the Gendarmes this way, what else can they do?*

"You know," she said slowly, "I just had a thought. Doesn't the Navy have some sort of large-scale training operation going on out in the Madras Sector?"

"Don't even go there," Weng said after a long, still moment.

"I'm just saying—"

"Lupe, you're talking about maybe fifty *ships of the wall*. And Crandall's *Battle* Fleet, not Frontier Fleet. Technodyne might have hooks into her, but even if they have an in with *her*, are you seriously suggesting someone could steer a task force *that* size into doing her dirty work?"

"I'm just saying it's a very...interesting coincidence that there just *happens* to be a Navy task force that big and that powerful already that close to Monica. Especially since it's been at least a T-century since that many of Battle Fleet's capital ships lumbered all the way out to the Verge. Probably longer than that, now that I think about it. You don't find that interesting?"

"If it's *not* a coincidence, then 'interesting' is definitely not the adjective *I'd* choose," Weng said. "I think I'd probably go with 'terrifying'...if the entire possibility weren't so totally absurd, that is."

"Oh, of course. *Totally* absurd. The only thing it could be," Blanton agreed and finished off her remaining martini in a single gulp.

Chapter Eleven

"WE'RE TRYING TO BE REASONABLE, here, Ms. Allenby," Adam Omikado said. "Surely there's some way we can work this out."

"Best way to work it out would be for you to get the hell out of my place and get back in your air car," Eileanóra Allenby told him flatly. "You got nothing I want, and I've got nothing you want, and you'd best take my word on that. Believe me, you *don't* want what I've got for you."

Omikado's expression tightened and for just a moment something ugly looked out of his hazel eyes. He started to speak sharply, then made himself stop and draw a deep breath. Sheila Hampton had warned him Allenby— *any* of the Allenbys, for that matter—was likely to be . . . unreasonable. He just hadn't realized *how* unreasonable until he walked into Whitewater Hollow Outfitters. Just who the hell did this crone think she was to talk to *him* that way?!

Unfortunately, explaining the reality of their relative positions as frankly as he wanted to was unlikely to accomplish his mission.

"I understand you're upset, and I don't blame you," he said instead. "I wish it was possible to undo what happened. But it isn't, and it's been seven T-years. And even though we weren't actually involved in the incident, I know Tallulah offered Ms. Allenby's husband a very generous settlement, in addition to the one your own Congress offered him immediately after it occurred."

"The 'incident' you're talking about was the murder of a member of my family." If possible, the woman's voice was even flatter—and much harder—than it had been. "There's no 'generous settlement' going to make up for that. I don't know what people're like where *you* come from, Mr. Omikado, but 'round here, we don't set money prices on the people we love."

"I'm not trying to suggest any amount of money could bring Ms. Allenby back. And I'm certainly not trying to dismiss the pain and grief you and every member of her family must have felt. I'm pointing out that my company's done everything in its power to make whatever compensation *can* be made for that tragedy, even recognizing that it's impossible to make *full* compensation. And, with all due respect, Ms. Allenby, you're holding Tallulah Corporation responsible for something that was none of its doing. That was a Protection Force missile, not anything fired by Tallulah or any of its employees."

The eyes of the fair-haired sergeant in the uniform of the Swallow System Protection Force standing behind Omikado rolled ever so slightly.

Way to go, asshole, Sergeant Hamby thought, even as he warned himself to keep his expression under control . . . at least while a Tallulah executive was anywhere in the vicinity. *Your momma ever teach you how to pour piss out of a boot? Just wondering, 'cause it sure doesn't sound like it. You aren't doing any of us any damned favors lecturing her like she was too stupid to understand what happened! You're talking to an Allenby, dumbass. They don't much cotton to lectures or people who tell 'em what they should be thinking, 'specially when everybody on the damned planet knows what really happened. I'd think even a Solly could figure that out if he tried hard. And if you've gotta be too stupid to come in outa the snow, least you could do is to not aim the old biddy my way!*

"'Scuse me, but that was your precious high and mighty Mr. Parkman's air car, wasn't it?" Eileanóra asked sarcastically, as if she'd been listening to Hamby's thoughts. "Traipsing around in public airspace with all those damned armed air cars keeping it company, if I recall rightly. Well, last time I looked nobody'd died and made him God! She had every right to use that same airspace, and there wouldn't't'a been any missiles in it if the damned TSE hadn't insisted he needed all that extra 'security.'"

She glared at the tall—very tall—dark-haired man in the uniform of Tallulah Security Enterprises standing at Omikado's right shoulder, who scowled contemptuously back down at her. At just over 198 centimeters, Robert Karlstad was forty centimeters taller than she was, which didn't seem to faze her at all.

And she had a point, Hamby thought, glancing at his partner, Corporal Leroy Sexton. Sexton had always been more comfortable running Tallulah's errands than Hamby was, but even the corporal looked like he agreed with Eileanóra on that one. *Hamby* sure

as hell did...and he understood exactly why TSE
was even more hated than his own SPF. The Tallulah
Corporation effectively owned most of the Swallow System, thanks to its cozy, mutually lucrative relationship
with President Rosa Shuman and her administration.
Theoretically, Tallulah Security Enterprises, its wholly
owned subsidiary, was responsible only for internal
security in Tallulah's facilities. In fact, it operated
as Tallulah's private army, going wherever the hell it
pleased and doing whatever the hell it wanted, under
cover of a special agreement with the Shuman Administration which gave its personnel what amounted to
diplomatic immunity.

It also had a habit of arrogantly demanding special
additional security whenever it felt like it, and it had
done just that in the case of Alton Parkman's hunting
expedition seven and a half years ago. It was at least
remotely possible there'd been a genuine threat to Parkman's safety—God knew he was about as unpopular in
Swallow as a man could get, and Swallowans could be a
fractious lot, especially the ones like Eileanóra and her
relatives, who lived up in the high hollows. But it was
one hell of a lot more likely, in Josh Hamby's opinion,
that Parkman's ego had been the real reason. Most of
Tallulah's upper echelon management simply had to
flaunt their importance at every opportunity. Like the
current pain in the ass trying to browbeat a fifty-year-
old widow into submission.

"I wasn't in Swallow when that happened." Omikado's
tone was that of a man whose patience was wearing
thin. "My understanding is that our security people had
credible evidence of a threat to Mr. Parkman's life. I'm
sure if they hadn't, they wouldn't have requested the

additional security. But that doesn't change my point, Ms. Allenby. Whatever might have been requested, it was the Protection Force that actually deployed those missiles to cover his route."

Which was true, as far as it went, Hamby reflected, although it overlooked the minor fact that it was a member of Parkman's personal security detail who'd identified a battered air van returning from a doctor's house call as a threat and demanded that it be kept clear. That couldn't absolve the terminally stupid SPF trooper who'd actually launched the shoulder-fired SAM at Sandra Allenby of responsibility, and Hamby had shed no tears when one of the far-flung Allenby Clan caught up with him in a dark alley and squared that particular account. But it never would've happened if the Protection Force had been left to its own devices. And the SPF wouldn't have been there in the first place without Tallulah.

He glanced at Sexton again, and the corporal's eyes looked as unhappy as his own. Well, he'd never thought Leroy was the sharpest stylus in the box, and he knew damned well the corporal was actively on Tallulah's payroll, as well as the SPF's, but even he had a brain that worked occasionally...which was more than Hamby could say for their current charges. Omikado had been in-system for less than a local week, and he obviously hadn't bothered to learn a solitary damned thing about the locals since he'd gotten there. That was bad enough, but the truth was that Karlstad worried Hamby more at the moment. Omikado was a pissant desk jockey, the kind that just couldn't believe the rest of the universe wasn't as impressed with him as *he* was. He clearly didn't understand a thing about the woman he was talking to. If he had, he'd've been out the door already, given that his balls were so small it would take a microscope to find them.

Karlstad, though . . .

Hamby didn't know as much as he wished he did about "Call me Buddy" Karlstad, but he didn't much like what he *did* know. The man was ex-Solarian Gendarmerie, and Hamby had seen entirely too many of them working for Tallulah. Most of them had at least figured out they no longer had the Solarian League in their back pocket, but Karlstad looked like one of the ones who still thought he was serving in an intervention battalion, and his expression was ugly as Eileanóra shook her head sharply.

"You don't seem to understand, Mr. Omikado," she said then. "I don't rightly care who actually fired the missile. And I'm not interested in any 'generous' compensation to me or to my cousin. For that matter, I'm not much interested in *you*. But none of that really matters just now, 'cause the bottom line is, I'm gonna do business with whoever I want to do business with, and I *don't* want to do business with *you*."

You stupid old bitch, Omikado thought venomously. He knew she was actually barely four T-years older than he was, but the weathered face and silvering hair of someone who'd never received prolong looked far older to someone who had. *Tallulah could buy and sell you—hell, I could buy and sell you, myself—out of petty cash!*

He made himself draw another deep breath and force down his searing anger. It was hard. He loathed uppity neobarbs like Eileanóra Allenby. He'd been born, raised, and educated on Old Terra itself, and dealing with jumped up, ignorant, penniless, squatters on worthless dirt-ball planets who thought they were his equal was the next best thing to intolerable. He was willing to admit, at least intellectually, that that was a weakness. If he expected to advance to upper-echelon management for Tallulah or any other Solarian transstellar, he had to learn to pretend he respected trash like Allenby. That was one of the reasons he'd been sent out here—to learn to do that pretending.

This is all Uncle Levi's fault, he thought bitterly. *Getting me sent out to the armpit of the galaxy as some kind of* favor. *"Needs seasoning" is it? Him and his damned old boys' network! And that's exactly why Hampton* picked *me for this. I frigging well know it is!*

"A simple matter that needs the attention of someone from Management." That was how Sheila Hampton, Alton Parkman's chief of staff, had described it. The fact that she and his Uncle Levi had gone to school together clearly had nothing to do with *him* being selected for it. Of course not!

He glanced around Allenby's "office," looking for something to distract himself while he wrestled with his resentful anger. Unfortunately, it only made him even more aware of just how unbelievably arrogant Allenby—like every other citizen of Swallow he'd met—really was. And how little their circumstances merited that attitude of theirs. The office had to be a couple of hundred T-years old, and its exposed overhead beams and the well-worn, hand-hewn wooden planks of the floor weren't the affectation, the deliberate archaism, they would have been on any civilized planet. They were the best this godforsaken world could do, and she was just the sort of neobarb you'd expect to find in this weatherbeaten, ready-to-collapse-under-its-own-weight hunting lodge, festooned with near-elk antlers and stuffed snow bear heads. Not only that, but it was Whitewater Hollow's outer, *public* office. She'd refused even to invite him into her private office... assuming an ignorant, dried up old bitch like her *had* a private office!

His lip curled as he lowered his eyes from the snarling snow bear trophies, and he felt a fresh stab of anger as his gaze crossed that of the man standing behind Eileanóra Allenby. Murdoch Allenby's hair was the same chestnut shade as his mother's, albeit without the silver threaded through hers, and his eyes were the same flinty shade of blue. He was only twenty-eight, but he was very nearly as tall as Karlstad. For that matter, his shoulders were actually broader than the ex-gendarme's, and it was obvious the two of them had hated one another on sight. In fact, the cold, biting contempt rolling off of the young man seemed to infuriate Karlstad almost as much as his mother's attitude infuriated Omikado.

"No one is asking you to do business with me, Ms. Allenby," he said once he was fairly sure he had his temper under control. "But it's very inconvenient for Tallulah employees who never did a single thing to you or your family. And I hate to point this out, but it's costing *you* a lot of money."

"My business if I don't want your money," she said, chin jutting stubbornly.

"But this foolish embargo, this...*vendetta* of yours, is costing other people, as well, Ms. Allenby," he pointed out. "Every time you turn down a charter just because it would contain a Tallulah executive or because it might have been put together by our Tourism Division, you deprive your neighbors of the income they'd derive from it. Is that fair to them?"

"Haven't heard any of 'em complain," she said shortly, and glanced at the white-haired fellow leaning nonchalantly against the counter behind her visitors. "You hear anybody complaining, Roarke?"

"Not so's you'd notice, Eileanóra," he replied calmly, then squirted a jet of tobacco juice into the battered spittoon beside the counter. "'Pears to me they think it's up to you who you charter out to."

"You see?" she looked back at Omikado.

"But this is *stupid!* Can't you see—" he started, then made himself stop.

He hadn't thought her eyes could get any colder, but they managed, and he cursed himself for that momentary lapse of control.

But it really is *so frigging stupid that I even have to waste time on this,* he thought bitterly. Yet it didn't matter how amply she deserved for him to flay her verbally; what mattered was that it wasn't helping his case. Hampton had made that clear, too.

Over the last thirty T-years, Whitewater Hollow Outfitters had earned a reputation as *the* best hunting guides in the Cripple Mountains. Eileanóra and her now-deceased husband Jordan had known the mountains within five hundred kilometers of Whitewater Hollow like the palms of their own hands. By all reports, Murdoch Allenby had inherited that same familiarity, and WHO had been as zealous about protecting the environment as its guides had been about finding the best game for its clients. Despite which, Eileanóra's decision to sever all ties with Tallulah Travel Interstellar and blacklist anyone directly affiliated with the transstellar had seemed like a minor annoyance—infuriating and insulting, but still minor—at the time.

Unfortunately, it hadn't been.

Being cut off from the sort of expertise that resulted in record-book trophies had been enough to irritate a huge slice of Tallulah's management people who fancied themselves as big game hunters. They were accustomed to being deferred to by their inferiors, not slapped in the face by one of those inferiors' contempt. That would have been bad enough, but the problem had gone well beyond any purely personal outrage, because Swallow's mountains were highly touted destinations for jaded Solly travellers.

It was bad enough that Eileanóra refused to book any Tallulah Travel Interstellar charters, since Whitewater Hollow commanded the best approaches to Broken Back Mountain, the fifth highest peak on any planet colonized by humanity. Whitewater Hollow Outfitters had a system-wide reputation as the best known and most highly rated source of guides for people who wanted to explore the Cripple Mountains. Indeed, that reputation extended far beyond the Swallow System hyper limit to organizations like Safaris Interstellar, the Solarian League's preeminent organization for hunters and campers. But her refusal had at least been endurable, since WHO had represented only one source of guides, however towering its reputation. Now, though, more and more other guides and outfitters had begun to follow her example, and it was starting to spread into other areas of tourism, as well.

That was the real danger, Omikado thought. For all its power here in Swallow, Tallulah wasn't one of the Solarian League's giants, and TTI's tourist-driven revenues represented a nice chunk of the corporation's cash flow. Not enough for its loss to be *crippling*, by any means, but enough to represent a significant downtick if the current trend lines persisted. Whether she realized it or not, this vindictive old bitch had stumbled onto something that could genuinely hurt Tallulah's bottom line, especially if all her friends and neighbors decided to jump onto the shuttle with her. It looked more and more like that was exactly what was about to happen, and the home office wasn't going to be happy with Alton Parkman if it did. And, far more to the point, *Alton Parkman* wouldn't be happy with the messenger his chief of staff had sent out to stop it.

"Excuse me. I apologize for my tone," he muttered...sounding about as apologetic as he actually felt. Then he exhaled sharply and shook his head. "It's just that it seems so pointless to see you cutting off your own nose to spite your face this way. Especially when it's affecting more people than just you."

"Don't want your apologies any more'n I want your money," Eileanóra Allenby said bluntly. "What I *want* is for you to be gone."

"Well that's just too bad," he heard himself say sharply. "I don't really like *being* here, to be honest. Unfortunately, until you're willing to see reason, I'm afraid you're going to go right on being pestered by people like me."

"Not if those 'people like you' know what's good for 'em, I won't," she said grimly. "And for now, I think you'd best be leaving."

"Not until you *listen* to me," he said. "I know you're a stubborn woman—God knows you've shown that clearly enough—but *I* can be stubborn, too, and it's simply foolish for you—"

"Maybe you didn't hear my mother." Murdoch Allenby's tone lowered the ambient temperature by at least fifteen degrees. "She asked you to leave."

"And *I* said—"

"'Pears you don't hear too good," Allenby cut him off. "And being's how I'm a tad less polite—and a *lot* less patient—than she is, I'll just put it in words even a pissant educated man like yourself can understand. Get your ass the hell outta here."

"Watch your mouth, boy!" Karlstad barked. "It's going to get you in a *lot* of trouble!"

"Now, everybody just calm down," Hamby jumped in. "Ms. Allenby, Murdoch, I know you're riled, and maybe you've got a right to be. But this whole thing's getting out of hand. Nobody wants to come in here and pick any fights, but it does seem to me Mr. Omikado's been as reasonable as he could be in explaining his position."

"Don't need it 'explained,'" Eileanóra said. "Nothing new in a single thing he's said. I wasn't interested last time they sent somebody t' say it, and I'm not interested this time. So it'd be best if he stopped wasting his time and mine."

"But it wouldn't *be* a waste of time, if—" Omikado began.

Will you please *just shut the hell up*, Hamby thought as loudly as possible in the Old Terran's direction. *I'm trying to do you a favor and get you out of here before it goes any farther south! Anybody with the IQ of a rock would see you're just pissing her off more, and I'll be damned if she hasn't got every right to be pissed off!*

"Up to us how we use our time." Murdoch Allenby's flat, contemptuous tone cut across Omikado's higher-pitched voice. "So get your fat ass out that door 'fore I put a boot in it!"

"I warned you about that mouth, you son of a bitch!" Karlstad snarled, and a fist which had somehow acquired a set of knuckledusters came out of his tunic pocket.

These neobarbs obviously needed a lesson, and "Buddy" Karlstad was just the man to provide it. In fact, he'd been looking forward to it. And this prick and his damned mother had been running off at the mouth long enough. If he needed someone to teach him better, Karlstad was happy to oblige. And if his *mother* wanted a little of the same, he'd oblige *her*, too!

His fist shot forward, and he bared his teeth in a hungry smile. The one thing he'd hated about leaving the Gendarmerie was the way it had taken him off the street and the neural baton out of his hand. That was what he'd lived for, if he was going to be honest, and he'd never met the neobarb he couldn't break across one knee. Working "corporate security" paid a hell of a lot better, but now he always had to remember he "represented the firm" when some bastard mouthed off. Only this time was different. He knew that, and his mouth had watered as he read the special authority TSE had been issued in Swallow. *This* time he could put the son of a bitch down—*permanently*, if he had to—and walk away clean.

That thought filled him as he anticipated the familiar bone-crunching impact and Allenby's scream of agony. It was better than—

His eyes widened as his short, vicious punch shot straight past its target. Allenby couldn't possibly have seen it coming, and he didn't even seem to move, yet his head wove just far enough to the side. And then *his* hand snaked up. It gripped Karlstad's wrist and the hard-driven punch stopped dead. Karlstad had never imagined anyone could just pluck his fist out of the air, and his eyes began to widen in surprise.

Unfortunately, he had a few *other* surprises coming, because Murdoch Allenby was a Cripple Mountain boy, and Cripple Mountain boys took to knuckle-and-skull fighting like fish to water or Sollies to credits. Murdoch had had his first fight before he was five. His father had seen to it that he'd never lost one, either, and he'd worked the high hollows since he was fourteen. A man built a certain amount of muscle doing that, and ogre wolves and snow bears were hard teachers. A man who went hunting them had best have his wits—and his reflexes—around him if he wanted to come home with the arms and legs he'd had when he left. He didn't know who this Solly bastard was used to beating down, but he wouldn't've lasted ten minutes in one of the deep hollow gathers. In fact...

Steel-like fingers locked tight, digging in painfully. Then he jerked, and Karlstad stumbled forward, off-balance and astonished by the speed of Allenby's reactions. And by his strength. The hand on his wrist was like a bear trap, and—

Allenby's *right* hand came up in a perfectly timed uppercut that started somewhere around his own belt buckle and ended on Robert Karlstad's chin. The ex-gendarme's head snapped back, his eyes glazed, and his knees buckled, but Allenby wasn't done. He used his grip on the other man's wrist to spin Karlstad around like a dancing partner, then levered it straight up to bend the other man over sharply, and his heavy boot came off the floor. Its toe caught Karlstad directly in the seat of his pants, and the bodyguard flew forward. He crashed down on his face, flattening his nose on the wooden floorboards, and the knuckledusters bounced off of his right hand and skittered across the floor.

Omikado stared at Allenby in horror, unable to believe even one of these backwater primitives had actually offered physical violence in *his* presence.

"'Pears I've already kicked one ass," the Swallowan observed flatly, looking back at him with icy contempt. "Am I gonna have to kick 'nother one?"

"Now, just simmer down, Murdoch!" Hamby said. Allenby switched his fiery blue glare to the Protection Force sergeant, and Hamby shook his head quickly. "Not saying you didn't have the right when the man came out with those knucks! Just saying this whole thing's getting outta hand, and—"

"What are you *talking* about?!" Omikado demanded. "Didn't you just see this thug *assault* Mr. Karlstad? *Arrest* him!"

"Now, you hold on a minute, too, Mr. Omikado," Hamby said in a rather more placating voice. "Looked to me like Mr. Allenby here was protecting himself. Didn't see any knucks on *his* hand, anyway."

Omikado stared at him.

"What the hell does *that* matter?! We pay your people enough to protect our people from this kind of thing! So arrest him and charge him—*now!*"

Hamby flushed in mingled anger and shame. Anger at Omikado for making it worse when it was *his* bodyguard who was at fault. And shame because what Omikado had just said was nothing but the truth.

And how the hell do I handle this *one?* the sergeant wondered bitterly. *Because the truth is, Murdoch's absolutely in the right; but if I say that, all hell's gonna be out for noon with Tallulah! But we've already got one shit storm coming out of the Cripples over Sandra. I try to take in one of their boys just for defending himself on his own property, and hell won't hold what'll come down from the hollows! Last thing I need is to go back to the office and—*

"You fucking *bastard!*"

The words were more than a little indistinct—his face's impact hadn't done Karlstad's lips and teeth any favors and his face was a mask of blood—but the ex-gendarme had rolled onto his side while Hamby and Omikado were talking. Now he came up on one knee, and the hand which had worn the knuckledusters was wrapped around the butt of a pulser.

"I'm gonna—"

CRRAAAACCCK!

Karlstad's head exploded as the heavy bullet flung him backward and he hit the floor, sliding across it down a sludge of blood and brain matter.

The sound of the shot was like being hit across both ears with the flat of a shovel. Hamby staggered, his eyes going wide as he saw the heavy, old-fashioned automatic pistol in Eileanóra Allenby's hand. His brain was still trying to catch up when another voice shouted.

"Put it down and—!"

CRRAAAACCCK!

Hamby's head whipped around just in time to see Leroy Sexton stumble backward, dropping the sidearm he'd yanked from its holster while Omikado was ranting. The corporal's hands rose to his chest and he looked down, expression incredulous, as he saw the blood. Then he looked back up, his eyes meeting Eileanóra's pitiless gaze, and sagged to his knees. He stayed there for a moment, eyes locked with hers, then thudded the rest of the way to the floor.

Hamby stared at him, then froze as something very cold and razor-sharp touched his throat.

"Seems to me you'd best keep your hands where I can see 'em, Josh," Roarke Mullarkey's conversational tone sounded tinny and faint through the ringing in Hamby's ears, and the knife in the older man's hand—the Cripple Mountains guide's knife, thirty-two centimeters of old-fashioned steel keen enough to slice the wind—rested against Hamby's windpipe like a lethal feather. "Know you're a scabby for Tallulah, but I grew up with your daddy. It'd really pain me to cut your throat."

The sergeant raised both hands slowly, and Mullarkey nodded.

"That's a good boy," he said, reaching out and tugging the pulser from the sergeant's holster. Then he lowered the knife and stepped back. He sheathed the blade one-handed, then ejected the pulser's magazine and power pack and handed the useless weapon back.

"I can't believe you're just going to stand there and—!" Omikado started.

"Mister, I'd shut my mouth, was I you, while you're still standing." Mullarkey's tone was more than a little exasperated. "You're the one brought this, and I hate to tell you, but even us backwoods folks know to set up security in our own offices. Got every bit of this on record, including all the times you were told to go and didn't. And I'm pretty sure we got good footage of this idiot of yours bringing out his artillery.

As for the other idiot," he glanced down at Sexton, "he should'a known better'n to be drawing when guns was already out, an' ever'body knows he wasn't doin' it as a law officer." The old man sent another jet of tobacco juice into the spittoon. "Man plays the scabby fer someone who's already broke the law at least twicet, he's gotta take his chances like anybody else. That there was as clear a case of self-defense as I've seen in a long time, and whatever they may'a done to the Constitution down Capistrano way, up here 'n the Cripples a man—or a woman's—still got a right to defend himself, even against a scabby who does something really, really dumb."

Omikado stared at him in disbelief, his face pale, and the old man shook his head. Then he looked at his employer.

"Eileanora? You got anything to add?"

"Think you just about summed it up, Roarke," she said, and Hamby felt a sinking sensation as he realized her pistol was not only still out, it was lined directly up with Omikado's head . . . with a tiny trail of propellant smoke still wisping from the barrel. "'Cept there's also that bit in the Constitution 'bout property rights an' trespassers an' how a woman's got the right to defend her property against 'em, 'specially after she's already warned 'em they'd best get. Right this minute, I've got a real itch to exercise my constitutional freedoms. So I think it'd be a real good idea if the sergeant here escorted Mr. Omikado off the premises. Be a whole lot easier if there aren't any more bodies to drag out on the porch."

Her icy gaze flicked sideways to capture Hamby's eyes.

"That sound reasonable to you, Sergeant?" she asked.

"Yes, Ma'am," he said, holstering the empty pulser and then being very, very careful to keep his hand nowhere near it.

"Yes, Ma'am. Sounds *real* reasonable to me."

JULY 1921 ANTE DIASPORA

"I'll kill him. I won't even need a pulser. He's a dead man as soon as he comes in reach."

—Sinead Patricia O'Daley Terekhov

✦ Chapter Twelve

"NOW, ANSTEN. THE FIRST THING I want the yard dogs to do is—"

"The *first* thing, Skipper," Ansten FitzGerald interrupted, "is for you to get into your dress uniform and get your posterior into a pinnace headed dirtside."

Commander FitzGerald was still a bit short of anything Terekhov would have considered fully recovered from his wounds, but he'd returned to duty as *Hexapuma*'s executive officer, letting Ginger Lewis revert to her position as engineering officer. She'd been happy to surrender the responsibility to him—splitting her duties between XO and overseeing such massive repairs had been exhausting—and he'd dived back into his role with all his accustomed efficiency. Terekhov had been glad to see that, and not just for professional reasons. FitzGerald had become more than just a smoothly functioning XO.

Just at the moment, though, what the captain felt was intense exasperation.

"I know time's tight, Ansten," he said a bit testily.

"But we still don't even have her docked. For that matter, we don't even have a schedule for when a berth will come open! They were *supposed* to have one waiting for us, but there's been some kind of FUBAR—as usual—and that makes it even more important that we lock down as many details as possible right now."

"Skipper, Ginger and I have this one. You've told us exactly what needs doing; we've got all your memos; we've got copies of all your message traffic and correspondence with *Hephaestus*; and I promise we'll check off every box just as soon as the tugs get here. What *you* don't have is time to dillydally."

"*Dillydally*?" Terekhov repeated in the tone of a man who couldn't quite believe what he'd just heard.

"That was Chief Agnelli's term, I believe." FitzGerald smiled at him. "And while I realize you're a captain, and so—obviously—not afraid of any chief steward ever born, *I'm* a mere commander. I don't want to think about what she'll do to me if you aren't into that uniform and off this ship in plenty of time."

He was smiling, but he was also serious. And he also had a point, Terekhov realized when he glanced at the chronometer. They'd been supposed to be berthed at *Hephaestus* by now, and they weren't. That would make the shuttle flight at least ninety minutes longer, and *that* meant they really were cutting it close. And FitzGerald was also right that this was one schedule he couldn't afford to bobble. But *Hexapuma* was *his* ship, *his* responsibility, and—

And you have perfectly capable subordinates—God knows they've proved that *several times over! Ginger practically rebuilt Engineering by hand just to get her home, for God's sake! I think you could* probably *trust her and Ansten not to break her again while you're away!*

And if you can't, it's no one's fault but your own.

"All right," he said. "All right!" He threw up his hands. "Tell Joanna to lay out my uniform because I'm on my way."

"Skipper, I hope you realize just how pointless that message would be. She's the one who told me she had it laid out fifteen minutes ago...about the time she 'suggested' I not let you dawdle up here. That was just before she used 'dillydally' on me."

"Have you managed to find my wife, Amal?" Terekhov asked over his personal com as he half-trotted into the boat bay gallery.

"No, Sir. I'm afraid we haven't," Commander Nagchaudhuri replied apologetically. "We've tried all the combinations you gave us, Skipper, and all we've gotten is her voicemail."

Terekhov scowled. Sinead Patricia O'Daley Terekhov was a daughter of two of the oldest naval dynasties in the RMN. She was also a cousin of the present Duke of Winterfall, and her ancestors had been commanding Queen's ships—and serving in sensitive Foreign Office positions, come to that—for the better part of a T-century before the very first Terekhov's shuttle ever touched down in Landing. She understood the realities of a naval career, and the one thing she'd never done, in the almost half-century of their marriage, was fail to answer her com within thirty seconds when she expected him to screen her. And she'd known exactly when *Hexapuma* was due back. For that matter, unless he missed his guess, *Hexapuma*'s and *Warlock*'s greeting from Home Fleet had been broadcast over the entire star system! So where *was* she?

"Keep trying," he said as the flight engineer beckoned courteously but peremptorily from the inboard end of the boarding tube. "Put her through to me aboard the pinnace the instant you reach her."

"Yes, Sir. Of course!"

Terekhov signed off and hurried towards the personnel tube. The flight engineer stood aside to let him dive headfirst into the tube's zero-gravity, then followed. He was on Terekhov's heels when the captain caught the grab bar and swung feet-first into the pinnace's internal gravity, and as Terekhov headed for his seat, the engineer sealed the hatch and checked the telltales.

"Good seal!" he announced to the flight deck.

"Copy good seal," the response came back, and the seatbelt signal flashed on the forward bulkhead.

Terekhov settled into place and looked out the port to watch the umbilicals disengage in spurts of vapor, retracting smoothly in the boat bay's vacuum. The docking arms unlocked, maneuvering thrusters flared, and the boat bay bulkhead's ranging lines slid vertically upward as the pilot eased the pinnace out of the bay. It was smoothly done, Terekhov noticed, and made a mental note to compliment the lieutenant when they landed, but it was a distracted sort of note.

Where are *you, Sinead?* he worried, turning his attention to the bulkhead display as *Hexapuma*'s huge bulk and the distant, gleaming mote of *Hephaestus* dwindled behind them. *And why the* hell *aren't you answering the damned com?!*

❖   ❖   ❖

She sat one of the VIP concourse's almost sinfully comfortable float chairs, right inside the arrival gate, and her nimble fingers were busy with her pad and stylus. They almost always were when she waited. At least a dozen art critics would have been astonished—possibly even outraged—to discover that one of the Star Kingdom's more acclaimed artists saw her paintings mainly as ways to keep herself occupied when she needed distracting.

It was very quiet in the superb soundproofing, and she supposed she was glad for that. A little bustle and flurry might have helped pass the time, but the newsies had been damnably persistent ever since word of Monica broke. That had eased a bit over the last month or two, as other stories filled the 'faxes, but with *Hexapuma* and *Warlock*'s arrival in-system, that was likely to change, so she'd been grateful when the respectful young lieutenant suggested—

"*Aivars!*"

❖   ❖   ❖

His wife's stylus and pad went flying the instant the lift car doors opened, and as he watched the pad hit the floor with a sharp, crunching sound, a corner of Aivars Terekhov's mind found time to hope she'd saved her latest creation before she demolished it.

And then she was in his arms, slender and graceful, warm and soft, so heart-stoppingly beautiful his eyes burned and his vision blurred, and he forgot all about broken pads. He forgot about *everything* as he crushed her in his embrace and buried his face in the sweet-smelling silk of her feathery red hair.

"Oh, *Aivars*," she whispered, and turned her face up to his. Her lips were soft and sweet, and he drank the fire of her kiss deep for endless seconds while her arms locked around him like iron.

But then, finally, he made himself step back slightly, easing the grip which had threatened to break ribs, and drew a deep breath of badly needed oxygen.

"And why"—despite himself, the first two words came out husky—"aren't you answering your com, young lady?"

Her lips twitched at the long-standing joke—she was all of eleven hours, twelve minutes, and nine-teen seconds younger than he—but her expression was puzzled.

"Answering my com? Aivars, I've been sitting here *waiting* for you to screen for over two hours!"

"What?" Terekhov frowned. "I've been trying to reach you ever since we tied into *Hephaestus'* communications system!"

"You've *what?*" She blinked up at him. "That's ridicu—"

She stopped, green eyes narrowing, and lifted her wrist. She tapped a quick diagnostic inquiry into her uni-link, and those green eyes narrowed still further.

"I'll kill him," she said in a conversational tone. "I won't even need a pulser. He's a dead man as soon as he comes in reach."

Terekhov's eyebrows arched, but then his expression changed and his own eyes narrowed.

"Charlie?"

"*Charlie,*" she confirmed grimly. "Unless you know someone else who could've hacked into my personal account and put your information on the blocked contacts list? Or let me rephrase that. Unless you know someone else who would've thought it was a *good idea* to hack into my personal account and put your name on the blocked contacts list on today of all days?"

"Not right off the top of my head, no." His voice was suspiciously unsteady, and she glared up at him, as if daring him to laugh. But that was the sort of mistake no good tactician was likely to make.

The Honorable Charles Travis O'Daley—Charlie, to his friends and long-suffering family—was fifteen T-years younger than Sinead and universally regarded as a wealthy, overbred, conspicuously idle layabout who amused himself playing at the Foreign Office job he'd acquired solely through family connections. It certainly couldn't have been because of competence, at any rate! Everyone knew that.

Or *almost* everyone, at any rate. Terekhov was one of a select few who knew Charlie O'Daley was a very tough customer, indeed, and that his Foreign Office position was pure window dressing. Charlie could have had a brilliant diplomatic career if he'd wanted it, but that might have been inconvenient for one of the Special Intelligence Service's more accomplished field operatives. It would never have done for his cover to get in the way of what he actually did.

He did have an occasionally—no, permanently—dubious sense of humor, however, not to mention access to SIS' cyber specialists, most of whom owed him favors for one disreputable reason or another. And given that combination, it was no wonder Sinead's suspicions had instantly—

"Did I just hear my name taken in vain?" a pleasant baritone drawled, and Sinead whirled as a well-groomed gentleman in formal court attire, with hair exactly the same dark red as her own, strode into the VIP lounge.

"You are *so* going to die, Charles Travis O'Daley!"

"Now, now. None of that!" he admonished, reaching past her to extend his hand to Terekhov. His grip was hard and strong, at sharp odds with the foppish appearance he took such pains to project, and his green eyes were warm. But then they swiveled back to his irate sister and he released Terekhov's hand to wave an admonishing index finger in her direction.

"If you and Aivars had been able t' screen each other, we'd *never*'ve gotten you off the com in time for his appointment," he informed her in the maddening, aristocratic drawl that was totally absent in her own speech. "And if you'd spent all that time *talkin'* to him, there wouldn't be time for him t' muss you properly in the limo on the way t' the Palace. Now, I ask you, in the view of any reasonable person, how else could a lovin' brother determined t' look after his sister's best interests have responded t' a situation like that?"

Despite herself, she giggled, although she also shook a fist under his nose. He looked down at it, eyes crossing, and her giggle became a spurt of laughter.

"All right, so you're not going to die—*this* time! But you do remember the consequences the *last* time something like this happened, don't you?"

"Such a petty, vindictive attitude," he sighed. "Alas! It's ever my fate t' be maligned and abused. However, I'm accustomed to it. I'm sure I shall bear up with all my customary nobility when that small-minded moment arrives."

He elevated his nose with an audible sniff, and she punched him none too lightly in the chest.

"Brutal woman," he said, smiling as he rubbed the spot. But then his expression turned a bit more serious.

"Really, Sinead. If you want a few minutes—*private* minutes—before they drag him off t' the reception, you'd better grab them in the limo on the way there. I've already told the driver when you need t' arrive, and he's ready t' circle until then." He reached out and touched her cheek lightly. "That's the only place you're goin' t' get him to yourself, away from newsies, court functionaries, and—God help him—Her Majesty, any time in the next, oh, five or six days. And that's assumin' they don't have somethin' *else* planned for him, as well."

He glanced over her head at his brother-in-law and something tingled inside Terekhov. Their eyes met, ever so briefly, and then Terekhov nodded.

"He's probably right," he said, wrapping one arm around her shoulders.

"Oh, I'm *sure* he's right." She gazed at her brother with a fulminating eye. "He's *always* right. It's the only reason he's still alive!"

"Maybe," Terekhov acknowledged. "Doesn't change his point, though."

"No, it doesn't," O'Daley agreed pleasantly. "And times a-wasting."

"All right," Sinead said. "I'll let you live. I may not even trip you down two or three flights of stairs. *This* time."

"You're so good t' me." He smiled and leaned down to kiss her on the cheek. "Now go, you two! And try not t' look too disheveled when you finally get t' the Palace. Mind you, I'll be disappointed if you don't look at least a *little* disheveled, Sinead, but it *is* a formal audience with the Queen, after all."

Chapter Thirteen

Well, that was certainly a waste of time, Damien Harahap reflected as he completed his final editing pass and closed the file on his terminal.

It was a good report, concisely written and tightly reasoned, if he did say so himself. Unfortunately, the "revolutionaries" of Any Port had proved just as unsuitable as he'd expected them to.

He sat back for a moment, considering his conclusions, wondering if his expectations had colored his ultimate judgment. It was possible, he supposed... but not likely. He'd been doing this too long from the other side of the hill to let himself indulge in that kind of dangerous crap.

Besides, it's not like Operation Janus needs every star system on the list to go up in flames. As many as possible, sure. But even Manpower's resources have to be limited, ultimately. They can't do everything they'd like to do and there has to be a limit on how many lunatics even they can support, if only because of logistics. So it's at least as important to eliminate bad risks as it is to identify good... investment prospects.

It was to be hoped Isabel Bardasano saw things that way. He thought she would, but he'd also decided it was more important to give her his very best work than the work she perhaps wanted. That was why competent superiors wanted competent subordinates, and the fact that OFS—even the Gendarmerie—seemed to have forgotten that explained a great deal, in his opinion.

He shrugged. Either way, Any Port was a bust. Better to tell her that up front, whatever she wanted to hear, than to spin some song and dance about the wonderful opportunity it represented only to have that come home to haunt him later.

He punched up the next system on his list, and smiled with considerably better cheer as he tabbed through the files to the one on Somerton Spaceways. He didn't really need to revisit it—they were less than three days out now, and he'd had ample time to go digest the files during the trip from Any Port—but professionalism was a hard habit to break. And the professional in him was *very* happy with the quality of his background brief on the Mobius System . . . especially since at least two thirds of the data in those files came from Trifecta Corporation sources rather than from OFS or the Gendarmerie.

He'd never met Esteban Gibson, head of Trifecta's Mobius System internal security, but the man was a retired Gendarmerie brigadier, with *lots* of contacts. He was also a firm believer in the iron fist; he'd come up through the intervention battalions, and he'd never met a problem he couldn't solve with enough night-sticks . . . or pulser darts. Despite that, he wasn't stupid, and he was obviously far better tapped in than most to what was happening in Mobius. He'd identified several threats none of the League's official intelligence services seemed to have noticed—or reported, at least—and his data suggested at least three possible contacts Harahap was certain weren't on OFS' screens at all.

Too bad no one else in the system's capable of the same kind of analysis, Harahap thought cynically. *Xydis seems reasonably competent for a senior OFS officer, I suppose. But that's a pretty damned low bar, and the Gendarmerie's even more useless. Hell, they don't even have an intel detachment anywhere in the entire frigging system! Not My Job Syndrome again, I guess.* He'd always hated that attitude when he was in the field, but it was only too common out here in the Verge, which was enough to drive any semi-competent person into a frothing fury. *Not that I should be complaining too loudly, under the circumstances. Stupid is good from my perspective, and so is the fact that no one in Trifecta realizes Gibson's selling his data to their competition. Or what he thinks is their competition, anyway.*

He shook his head. Normally, he was a great fan of the KISS principle, especially when his own neck was involved, but sometimes he just had to stand back in admiration for a particularly artful triple or quadruple cross. In this case, Gibson was convinced he was dealing with Kalokainos Interstellar, which was engineering a takeover in Mobius in cooperation with Kellerman, Kinross, & Watts of Terra. Bardasano even had an actual Kalokainos mid-level manager (who genuinely thought he was working with KK&W) on her payroll, and he'd convinced Gibson the new management would keep him on—with a substantial raise—after the dust settled. All he had to do was provide the sort of inside information someone like Harahap needed and then stay out of

the way while that someone made use of it. No doubt
Gibson had socked away incriminating recordings of his
discussions with the go-between. His was not a trusting nature, or he wouldn't have survived as long as he
had. It wouldn't do him any good in the end, since his
true employers couldn't have cared less if he tried to
implicate Kalokainos in return for a lighter sentence,
but considering what had almost happened on Myers,
Harahap hoped he'd have a chance to use them.

*Now, now, Damien. That would be the cherry on
top, but for now, you have more fundamental things
to worry about. Focus!*

He took a sip from the coffee mug at his elbow,
arranged himself comfortably, and opened the first
folder.

✧   ✧   ✧

"God, he gets more smug-looking every year, doesn't
he?" Kayleigh Blanchard sounded disgusted, and
Michael Breitbach turned to follow her gaze out the
rather dingy apartment's window.

The enormous permanent hologram of President
Svein Lombroso towered over Freedom Park, the
ten-hectare green belt around the Presidential Palace.
The same stern-jawed face looked out from the sides
of at least a third of the city of Landing's buildings,
but the holo took pride of pace, dwarfing the most
heroically scaled statues pre-Diaspora humanity had
ever dreamed of creating, and it had just undergone
its once-a-quarter update. It was almost half the height
of the White Whore—otherwise known as Trifecta
Tower—which dominated downtown Landing. Lombroso
would undoubtedly have liked it to be even taller, but
a hundred and twelve stories was probably enough,

even for his ego, and it might have been...tactless to overshadow his corporate patrons' headquarters.

"He does look smugger than usual, doesn't he?" Breitbach agreed. "I trust you're not going around making that observation to anyone else, though?"

"I even know how to seal my own shoes, Michael," she replied scathingly.

"That was in the nature of irony," he said. "You're familiar with the concept?"

The look she gave him was even more scathing, and he chuckled. Blanchard was taller than he was, with dark hair and eyes, and even tougher than her obviously muscular physique implied. She was also a licensed private investigator, and those were rare on the planet Mobius. Just getting a PI's license and—especially—the concealed carry permit that came with it in the first place required connections in the right places and more than a little juice with the local bureaucracy, but keeping both of those—and staying out of prison—depended in no small part on watching her mouth. There was no telling when an unfortunate remark might reach Olivia Yardley or Friedmann Mátáys' ears, and they kept a closer eye on people with official licenses to meddle.

They also required periodic reports of suspicious or "disloyal" behavior. He knew how much Blanchard hated making those reports—especially accurate ones—but they underscored her own loyalty for the benefit of the regime's security organs, and that was a significant part of what made her so valuable.

"Yes, I'm familiar with the concept, Michael," she told him after a moment. "I just wish to hell I knew what he was up to this time around. God knows he's only about a tenth as smart as he thinks he is, but I get nervous when he starts doing things that look exceptionally stupid even for him."

"I'm inclined to think it's Guernicke's brainstorm. Or maybe Frolov's."

"I don't think too much of either of *their* IQs, either, but are they really dim enough to support something like this?"

"Well, whether it was their idea or not, you know they must've signed off on it for our good friend Svein to run with it this way," he pointed out. "I didn't say it was a *good* brainstorm; only that it had to have the executive suite's okay."

"I only wish we knew why anybody on the inside of the SUPP would think this was even a *half* good idea," she fretted. "Why should a covey of Party hacks decide to hold elections for the first time in almost forty years?"

"According to my sources," Breitbach said, and she knew he wasn't going to tell her who those sources were, "it's been suggested—apparently based on a report from Trifecta's security people—that a 'free and open election' which happened to return an overwhelming majority for Lombroso would go a long way towards quieting our more restive fellow citizens."

Blanchard made a gagging sound, and Breitbach smiled thinly.

"We both know what the vote count's going to be," he agreed. "But let's face it. It's unlikely to make things a lot *worse* from Lombroso's perspective, and if nothing else, anyone who tries to organize an opposition vote will paste great big targets on their backs for Yardley and Mátáys. I don't know about Yardley, but Mátáys is actually smart enough to wait until a few months after the vote before he starts disappearing the new entries on his list of troublemakers."

Blanchard frowned as she realized he had a point. But then, Michael Breitbach usually had a point. That was one reason his Mobius Liberation Front had survived when so many other resistance movements had disappeared into Yellow Rock Prison or one of the reeducation camps . . . or simply disappeared. He was a thoughtful, insightful man and he'd devoted plenty of research to the question of how a revolutionary built his movement and succeeded. The MLF, unlike most of its predecessors, used a tight cell system, and Breitbach was ruthless about maintaining security. That was Blanchard's responsibility, really, and if she didn't like some of the things it required of her, she liked the thought of a cell with a view—or an unmarked grave somewhere—even less.

"Okay," she said after a moment, "I can see that. But they're still taking a hell of a risk, Michael. Sure, it may work out that way, and I'm sure it will provide Lombroso and System Unity with at least a fresh paper mandate, whatever else happens. But an awful lot of people are going to recognize that it's a put-up job. You know how much trust they put in the official news channels already. Just pumping out the Party line and telling everyone how well the elections are going is bound to convince those people exactly the reverse is happening."

"Unfortunately, I'm not sure there are as many of 'those people' left as you think there are," Breitbach said glumly. "By this time, almost half the theoretical electorate's never lived under any other system. Just how critical *can* their thinking be with that background? You *know* what the education system's pumped out since Lombroso's 'reforms' went into place. Hell, you know even better than I do; it had already been coopted before you were out of high school yourself! And even if any large chunk of the population does see what's really happening, so what? Like I say, it's not going to make Lombroso any less popular with the people who already hate him."

"No, but if it gets out of hand, leads to actual demonstrations that end up going off the rails—"

She broke off, shaking her head unhappily, and he nodded.

Svein Lombroso's System Unity and Progress Party had seized power forty-eight T-years ago, following the disastrous Crash of '73, in an election overseen by no less a paragon of impartiality than the Office of Frontier Security when it rallied to Mobius' rescue. At the time, some had claimed Trifecta had deliberately engineered the massive economic collapse that wiped out more than half of the star system's net worth in less than five months to drive down the cost of its ongoing takeover of the Mobian economy. Arrant anti-social, disloyal fabrication and vilification by the criminal element, of course, but it *had* been said.

Of course, most who'd said it had quietly changed their minds or faced the stern justice of the special courts set up to deal with the corrupt local plutocrats whose unbridled greed had *really* caused the collapse. All with scrupulous observance of the defendants' legal rights, as OFS had solemnly attested when the families of some of those sentenced appealed to it.

That had been in the early days, before OFS,

satisfied the fiscal chaos had been sorted out, officially withdrew from the system. The OFS Commission on Mobian Affairs had been discreetly disbanded in 1879, four months *before* the SUPP formally suspended elections. That was when Lombroso's first—and, under the constitution, only—presidential term had been slated to end. In light of the massive majority which had elected him in the first place, and the unfinished nature of the SUPP's "reform platform," however, he'd clearly had no choice but to *temporarily* suspend the constitution's term limits. Obviously, he'd step down as soon as he was confident all the reforms were solidly in place, and submit his actions to the judgment of the electorate.

It was possible that at least three or four particularly credulous twelve-year-olds had actually believed that. Unlikely, but possible.

That hadn't mattered a great deal, though, since he'd also had Trifecta's solid backing. And Trifecta had already been the Mobius System's single largest employer and investor. Thirty-five percent of the system's total workforce had been direct or indirect Trifecta employees even before the crash. Now that percentage was well over *eighty*-five, and Trifecta had finished demolishing every hope of competition for its control of the system and its economy.

Breitbach was an urban planner by profession, and he'd been better placed than most to see what that meant. His employer, City Solutions, Incorporated, had been a relatively small, privately owned outfit at the time SUPP came to power. Within five years, its original founding partners had been frozen out and President Lombroso's second cousin, Jesper Lombroso, had become CEO, majority stockholder, and effective owner. At which time City Solutions had expanded by over five thousand percent as orders and projects came flooding in.

Financially, Breitbach couldn't complain about what that had meant. Back in 1879 he'd been a very junior employee, fresh out of college and full of idealism. Now he was a very well paid department head in the biggest firm of its kind in the entire star system . . . and a member in good standing—*very* good standing—of the System Unity and Progress Party. He was also perfectly placed to know that somewhere around two thirds of the firm's fees went straight into the pockets of Jesper and his cronies rather than into paying for the projects they were supposed to cover.

Not that he meant to say a single word about that, although he'd allowed Caleb Turner to compromise his computer access codes.

Turner was one of the better cyber security people on Mobius, who did a lot of consulting with the Landing City Police Department. That was how Turner knew Blanchard, who'd been a sergeant in the LCPD's homicide department until the criminal investigation side of the force had been downsized eighteen years ago in favor of beefing up Colonel Grigori Petulengro's Security and Intelligence Branch. They'd worked together on several occasions and become personal friends, and he hadn't been quite as discreet with her as he'd thought. He still didn't know Blanchard was the one who'd arranged his recruitment into the MLF, though, nor did he have the least idea that *she* was a member.

He also did some consulting for City Solutions,

which was how he'd come to know Breitbach, as well. Turner didn't much like or trust him, given Breitbach's lucrative position and fervent support of the regime, but he'd been more than willing to... acquire access to Breitbach's codes when the engineer carelessly left them lying about unencrypted. He'd recognized their value instantly, just as Breitbach had intended, and he'd used them to hack into the Presidential Guard's files for the MLF by going through City Solutions' interface with the Department of Housing and Urban Planning.

If anyone in the PG or over at DHUP discovered the hack, the consequences for Turner would be most unpleasant. Breitbach, on the other hand, might get a slap on the wrist for allowing his credentials to be compromised, but he was too well covered within the Party to worry about much more than that. He hadn't liked treating Turner as an expendable cat's-paw, and Blanchard knew he'd agonize internally if anything happened to the other man. That hadn't kept him from doing it, anyway... which was why someday the MLF might actually succeed where every other resistance and reform movement of the last half T-century had failed.

"Wasn't Joseph supposed to be here already?" she asked, deliberately changing the subject, and Breitbach nodded.

"He was. You know Joseph, though. If he said he'll be here, he'll be here. He just... marches to another drum where *timing* is concerned."

This time she chuckled. Joseph Landrum was the head of one of the MLF's alpha-level cells, but it was larger than almost any of the organization's other cells and, unlike the other alphas, it was *completely* compartmentalized, with no subordinate cells below it. Outside its own members, only Breitbach and Blanchard even knew it existed, much less who was in it, because he and his people were simply too valuable to even risk compromising.

Landrum was an executive in Somerton Spaceways, an intra-system cargo line owned—inevitably—by yet another clutch of Trifecta flunkies. Somerton did a *lot* of business for Trifecta, and although none of its vessels were hyper-capable, its activities were closely integrated with Trifecta's interstellar operations. That gave Landrum a wide range of contacts with freight agents, pursers, purchasing agents, and starship personnel, with all sorts of useful implications for the MLF. Still, Breitbach had a point. Landrum was a very smart man, intensely organized professionally, but outside the calendar kept for him by his secretary, he'd probably never been on time in his entire life.

"Do you have any idea what he wants to talk about?" she asked.

"Of course not," Breitbach said, giving her a chiding look, and she snorted in acknowledgment.

All of them knew better than to say anything important over a com or in any office, whether it belonged to the SUPP or not. The Communications Security Act had exterminated the last tattered shreds of privacy thirty-five T-years ago. Of course, the CSA had only regularized something which had been going on for years, and every Mobian routinely assumed any public venue was thoroughly bugged by the regime's security services. Or by Trifecta's internal security people, on retainer to the Presidential Guard or the MSP, more often than not. Finding places that weren't bugged for face-to-face conversations—the only safe sort of conversations—was a nontrivial task, but it wasn't impossible. Especially not for someone like Breitbach, who had access to the records on so many of the regime's failed housing projects. He'd compiled a list of suitable sites long ago and each alpha-level cell had its own dedicated set, with identifying code words for each.

"He'll be along when he gets here," he said now. "And, fortunately..."

He reached into a pocket, and Blanchard groaned only half-humorously as he produced the deck of cards.

"Oh, come on, Kayleigh! You know it'll help pass the time. Besides—"

Fortunately for Blanchard, someone knocked on the apartment's door at that very moment. She recognized the light, apparently patternless series of knocks instantly, but that didn't keep her hand from sliding to the pulser holstered under her jacket. She had no illusions about her ability to stand off a Presidential Guard SWAT team, but she could at least guarantee neither she nor Breitbach would be available for interrogation.

Breitbach gave her a crooked smile which understood exactly what she was thinking and stepped past her to open the door.

"Joseph," he said dryly. "How nice of you to drop by. Eventually."

"Yeah, sure." The man who stepped into the wretched little apartment's front room was even shorter than Breitbach, and his bright brown eyes darted around the apartment. They settled on Blanchard, and he nodded in greeting.

"Still complaining about my scheduling, Kayleigh?"

"Always, Joseph." She took her hand from the pulser butt with a smile. "God forbid you ever actually get somewhere on time. I'm pretty sure that'll trigger the energy death of the universe."

"Touché," he conceded with a chuckle. "But we can't all be OCD about things like that."

"That's CDO," she told him with a straight face. "At least get it in the right alphabetical order."

He grinned appreciatively, but then his expression sobered and he turned back to Breitbach.

"I'm sorry to've dragged you out here on so little notice, Michael, but I think this may be important. In fact, it could be *very* important. Of course, it could also be a trap, which is why I was even later than usual today. I took five different tubes and spent two hours window shopping in every mall in Landing to shake any tail."

"Really?" Breitbach gestured for Landrum to follow him into the apartment's kitchen, which had no windows or exterior walls, and pointed at the rickety-looking chairs around the small table. "In that case, you'd better tell me what this is all about."

"What it's all about," Landrum said, settling cautiously into one of the chairs, "is that I got a very unexpected contact. A fellow turned up in my office, completely out of the blue. He says he's an independent analyst surveying systems out this way for the Hauptman Cartel, out of Manticore. He may really be Manticoran, too, but he sure isn't surveying economic prospects."

"No?" Breitbach leaned back in a chair on the far side of the table and arched his eyebrows.

"No. And I really think you should give some consideration to meeting with him. Or at least authorizing *me* to meet with him for you. It's pretty obvious he already knows a lot more than I'd like him to about what *I'm* up to, but there's no sign he knows a thing about you, and I'd just as soon keep it that way. Still, if he's legitimate, he could be the answer to at least half our more pressing problems."

"In what way?" Breitbach's eyebrows came back down, the eyes below them suddenly very intent, and Landrum shrugged.

"Let me lay it out for you the way 'Mister Dabilenaren' laid it out for me, and then you can make up your own mind. First—"

Chapter Fourteen

"IT'S GOOD TO SEE THE SKIPPER back home," Ginger Lewis said as she and Ansten FitzGerald found themselves in a quiet corner of the spacious ballroom in the Landing townhouse. That townhouse, known as Three Oaks in honor of the Old Earth oak trees which had been planted on its grounds within the first decade after the shuttle Jason touched down (and which were green and standing to this day), had been a wedding present from Sinead Terekhov's father and mother.

"Yes, it is," FitzGerald agreed. "And it's not exactly a hovel, either, is it?" he added.

He swept the flute of champagne in his right hand in a slight arc, taking in the entire ballroom which had been transformed into a banquet hall for the evening, and Ginger had to agree he had a point. The Terekhovs weren't exactly paupers, but Sinead Patricia O'Daley's family had been around a long, long time. During that time, it had long since passed from the "not-exactly-paupers" into the "next-best-thing-to-stinking-rich" category. And that, she conceded, was saying quite a bit, given Manticoran standards for wealth.

The ballroom, for example, measured the next best thing to forty meters on a side, and Three Oaks was located less than four kilometers from Mount Royal Palace on one of the most expensive parcels of real estate in the entire Manticoran Binary System. She didn't even want to think what the townhouse's beautifully landscaped, modest little six-hectare lot was worth on a square-meter basis. As for the house itself—!

She sipped from the champagne in her own hand and watched Aivars and Sinead Terekhov circulating gracefully through the throng. The dinner party had been Sinead's idea. Ginger was pretty sure it had, anyway. And it constituted a significant sacrifice on her part, too. They'd arrived in system only late the previous afternoon, and the captain had been whisked straight off to Mount Royal Palace for a special audience with the Queen. Then there'd been the state banquet—and the endless speeches—afterward. They couldn't possibly have gotten home before the wee hours of the morning! After all that, she wondered, how many women who so obviously loved their husbands would have given up their second night after his return from a year-long deployment for a chance to meet his officers and senior enlisted?

I'm astonished she didn't just drag him off to bed and keep him there for at least a week, she thought with an inner grin. *Don't think she'd have gotten much resistance from* him *for that notion, either! Just look at the way they're glued to each other's sides. But if she's faking all this happiness to see us, she's an even better actor than she is a painter!*

"No, not a hovel," she acknowledged. "But I can't think of anyone who's done more to deserve it."

"No argument from me," FitzGerald said. "No argument at all."

✦   ✦   ✦

"You have a wonderful crew, darling," Sinead Terekhov said when his subordinates granted her and her husband a fleeting eye of calm. "And I especially like young Helen ... and Ginger." He looked down at her, and she laid her left hand on his elbow. "She reminds me quite a bit of Nast'ka."

"And me, of course," he agreed quietly, covering her hand with his own. "They're both quite extraordinary young women on their own, though."

"Oh, I've already realized that." She raised the empty champagne flute in her right hand, catching the eye of a liveried server, and smiled up at him. Perhaps there were shadows behind those eyes, but the hand on his arm squeezed gently. "And I doubt I could ever tell them, and all the rest of your people, how grateful I am to them for bringing you home to me," she said very softly.

"Best crew God ever gave a captain," Terekhov said, his smile only slightly crooked. "I guess you've heard me say that a time or two, but every time it's been the truth. At least this time I brought more of *them* home, too."

Her hand tightened on his elbow, and he made his smile relax. Then he bent to brush a kiss across her lips.

"Sorry," he said. "And I really am in a lot better place than I was after Hyacinth, sweetheart. It's just ... hard. When I look at them, I can't help thinking about all the faces I won't be seeing again." He shook his head. "I really wish you could've known Ragnhild

Pavletic, for example." Sadness touched his eyes. "She was special. But then, they were all special."

Sinead started to reply, then stopped herself. The server had arrived, standing one diplomatic meter away until Sinead handed her the empty flute. The woman offered a refill, but Sinead shook her head with a smile. She watched the other woman filter away through the crowd with the seeming effortlessness of her profession, then looked back up at her husband.

"I know they were. I viewed every one of your letters about them at least half a dozen times, Aivars. And I only have to look at *these* people—" the hand which had held her champagne swept a brief arc "—to know how special *they* are. How could their shipmates have been anything else? Did you think someone who was born an O'Daley wouldn't recognize that?"

"You know, I knew there was a reason I fell in love with you. Other than your good looks, money, and decadent aristocratic sensuality, that is."

"'Decadent aristocratic sensuality,' is it?" She gave a delighted gurgle of laughter and her eyes sparkled, shadows banished. "This from the spacer who only comes planet-side once a year...unless it's raining! Just where did you think all of that 'decadent sensuality' comes from, stranger? The heart isn't the only thing absence makes grow fonder!"

"Odd." He rubbed his chin, squinting his eyes in contemplation. "I never really thought *absence* had that much to do with it. Unless memory fails, back when I was a Foreign Office wonk with an office three doors down from your brother's—you remember, back when I came home every single night?—there was the time you'd spent the entire day at Genevieve's and gotten your hands on that pheremone-laced perfume. Not to mention that teeny tiny, lacy little—"

"Oh, shut up!" She smacked him across the chest. "You know perfectly well that was our *anniversary!* And don't pretend you weren't just as enthusiastic when there weren't any *pheremones* involved!"

"Excuse me, young lady, but I never implied for an instant that I wasn't just as decadently sensual. I only said that was one of the things that attracted me to you in the first place. Well, that and the fact that you're as smart and talented as you are beautiful."

"No wonder you were so successful on the diplomatic circuit!"

"No, not really. I was never able to tell straight-faced lies. It's much easier when you can fall back on just telling the truth."

He captured the slender hand which had smacked his chest and carried it to his lips. He pressed a quick kiss to its back, smiled deep into her eyes for a moment, then thought about how very much he loved her as he looked back out across the ballroom.

He would never in a million years have asked her to sacrifice his second night home to anything except the two of them, but she'd insisted. For that matter, she'd started planning it the moment the Navy gave her a definite arrival time for the ship.

The rush to assume command and get *Hexapuma* deployed on such short notice had prevented Sinead from hosting the traditional pre-deployment party, and she'd hated that. As the daughter of generations of naval officers, she understood the responsibilities of a Queen's officer's spouse only too well. Civilians generally failed to understand that for any married naval officer, his or her career was a partnership. That was true for any officer, but especially for any *commanding* officer. A captain wasn't responsible solely for the men and women under her command. She was responsible for their *families*, as well. And because she—or, in Aivars' case, *he*—couldn't be there to tackle those other responsibilities, she had to rely on someone else, which was where her spouse came into it.

Sinead had never had time to meet the families of *Hexapuma*'s officers and enlisted personnel before she deployed, but she'd met all of them since. As the captain's wife, she was the head of the *Hexapuma* Support Group, the network of family members which the RMN officially recognized. She was the one in charge of interfacing between the support group and the Navy in general . . . and BuPers and BuMed in particular. The one who arranged periodic gatherings and dinners for the ship's dependents. The one who saw to doctors' appointments, birthdays, kids' school holidays, and all the thousand and one other details which inevitably cropped up as soon as a father or mother or a husband or a wife deployed. The fact that *Hexapuma* was such a new ship, with the reduced personnel made possible by the Navy's adoption of far more automation—and far less manpower redundancy—than in any prewar design, had helped. In fact, *Hexapuma*'s crew had actually been smaller than Terekhov's last ship, the light cruiser *Defiant*.

Which meant I had fewer condolence calls to make this time, she thought, her mood darkening again. *God, why do you do this to him?! Wasn't Hyacinth bad enough?*

But then she gave herself a mental shake, reminding

herself of how much she had to be grateful for. Unlike
HMS *Defiant*, *Hexapuma* had survived, and this time
the man she loved had come back to her without the
bleeding wounds the Battle of Hyacinth and the brutality of a Peep POW camp had left in mind, heart, and
soul. They were guaranteed a minimum of two weeks'
survivor's leave before he had to report back to duty,
too, and she intended to make him take every second
of that leave, no matter how much he itched to get
back to his ship to heal *her* wounds. And they were
going to be a wonderful two weeks, because despite
Monica, despite everything the universe had done to
him, he'd come home whole and complete, with the
demons of Hyacinth laid at last. And these were the
people who'd brought him back to her.

Nothing she ever did could repay the men and
women of his crew who'd survived with him and given
him back to her. She knew none of them would ever
think of it in those terms, any more than Aivars himself
did, but that didn't change what they'd done, where
they'd been with him, and her eyes burned for a
moment as she looked around the ballroom at the dress
uniforms and the comfortable conversational knots.

"The best crew God ever gave a captain, I think
you said?" she said now, reaching up to touch the side
of his face. "And how did they get that way, Aivars
Terekhov? I don't suppose *you* had anything to do
with it, did you?"

"Well, maybe it has been sort of a joint effort," he
acknowledged. "And I have to admit I'm nervous over
how many I'll be able to keep." He shook his head.
"I've been over the damages list with the yard dogs.
It's going to take a long time to complete our repairs,

and you know how BuPers is about raiding ships on the binnacle list! They've already as good as told me Ginger's going to be shipped off to *Weyland*, and God only knows what they're going to do with Abigail. For that matter, Ansten's due for his own command, and you *know* Cortez has to have a ship in mind for him. As soon as they actually let us dock her, they're going to start poaching my very best people. And on top of that—"

"Aivars, shut up," she said sweetly. He twitched and looked down at her sharply, and she shook her head. "You and I have been to this dance more than once, dear," she said then. "You'll deal with it, they'll go on to other duties, and they'll perform them just as splendidly as they did for you, because that's the kind of people they are. And one day we'll run into them again, when you and they are all disgustingly senior officers, and look back at this commission while you tell each other splendid lies about everything that's happened since. It's the way the Navy works. You know that as well as I do, and if you can't take a joke—"

"—then I shouldn't have joined," he finished for her, and she nodded.

"Exactly. And while you may be the commanding officer of HMS *Hexapuma*, she's not going anywhere at the moment and there isn't a solitary thing you can do to make those repairs go any faster than the Navy's going to push them anyway. So instead of dwelling on the inscrutable challenges of the future, why don't you and I invite our guests to be seated so Master Karl's henchpeople can serve?"

"You *do* have rather good ideas upon occasion, don't you?" He smiled. "And this is one of them."

He linked one arm through hers and led the way out to the center of the huge room. Heads turned and eyes tracked them, and the background murmur of conversation died as he raised his free hand.

"It's just been pointed out to me by higher command authority," he said easily into the silence, "that you were all invited here to eat. And those of you who know Chief Steward Agnelli will appreciate that there are certain forces of nature it's wiser not to resist. If we let Master Karl's dinner get cold, the consequences will be severe. So, if you'd all be kind enough to find your places, I think we'd better let his minions serve."

❖   ❖   ❖

Karl Koizumi, who'd ruled Sinead O'Daley's kitchen long before she'd become Sinead Terekhov, wasn't quite the tyrant her husband had implied. Not *quite*. He was, however, an absolute despot in his own realm, and given the quality of the meals he produced, there was no threat of any revolutions.

Terekhov had forgotten just how good a chef Koizumi was, and from the expressions of his officers and noncoms, this was a repast they'd spend years recounting over many another table. He remembered a few bull sessions like that of his own, especially when he'd been a junior officer, and it amused him that—

His thoughts broke off as Valentine Manning, Three Oaks' majordomo, slipped in through a side door and made his discreet way towards the head table.

Oh, shit, he thought, watching Manning's approach and taking in the majordomo's expression.

"Aivars," Sinead said. "Don't you dare—"

"Don't tell *me*," he replied. "You know Valentine

as well as I do. Do *you* think he'd be interrupting right now if he thought he had a choice?"

"Damn it, I haven't had you back for two *days* yet! They *can't*—"

She made herself break off, and he smiled crookedly at her.

"Of course they can," he told her, then turned his head as Manning slipped up behind his left shoulder. "Yes, Valentine?"

"I'm very sorry to interrupt, Sir, but I'm afraid there's an Admiralty courier here."

"A *courier?*"

Despite himself, one of Terekhov's eyebrows rose. He'd assumed he was about to be called away to an urgent com call, and an icicle went through him. The Admiralty didn't send couriers on "get back to us when you can" missions.

Damn you, Charlie, he thought, remembering the glance he'd shared with his brother-in-law. *Did you see this coming? And if you did, why didn't you—?*

He chopped the thought off, glanced at Sinead, and saw the same understanding in her suddenly taut expression. He squeezed her knee with one hand under the cover of the table, then looked back to Manning.

"Where is he?"

"She's in the Brown Salon, Sir."

"Very well." He inhaled deeply, folded his napkin and laid it beside his plate, and leaned across to kiss the lobe of Sinead's ear. "I'll be back as soon as I can," he promised.

"*This* time," she replied around an edge of bitterness not even centuries of a naval family could blunt, her green eyes suspiciously brilliant.

"This time," he agreed unflinchingly. Then he pushed back his chair and stood.

✧   ✧   ✧

"Sir Lucien will see you now, Captain Terekhov," the senior master chief petty officer behind the desk in the outer office said.

"Thank you, Senior Master Chief."

Terekhov took a final sip from the cup of coffee the uniformed steward had brought him on his arrival. He'd needed it, given the ungodly earliness of the hour. He set the cup on the coffee table, then stood, suppressing a bone-deep reflex to straighten his flawless uniform, and followed the noncom down a short, carpeted hall to a door of beautifully stained and polished ferran wood. His guide rapped once, sharply, on the door, then opened it and stood aside.

"Captain Terekhov, My Lords," he said, and Terekhov's nostrils flared as he heard the plural form of address.

That was all the warning he had before he found himself face-to-face not simply with Sir Lucien Cortez, the Fifth Space Lord and head of the Bureau of Personnel, but also with First Space Lord Sir Thomas Caparelli, the RMN's senior uniformed officer. *And* First Lord Hamish Alexander, Earl White Haven, who happened to be the Navy's civilian head.

Not to mention the current prime minister's older brother.

"Civilian," my ass, Terekhov thought as he continued into the spacious conference room without missing a stride. *He may not be in* uniform *at the moment, but if the Queen didn't need him in the Cabinet,* he'd *probably be commanding Home Fleet right now!*

The three monumentally senior officers stood as he approached, and White Haven extended his hand.

"I'm sorry we had to call you in so damned early, Captain Terekhov," he said. "And I hate the thought of dragging you away from your wife. But we've all been Queen's officers long enough to know that sometimes we just don't have a choice. And, before we go any further, I should point out that Lucien isn't the one putting the round pegs in the round holes this time. So if you're going to blame someone for what's about to happen, that particular buck stops with me."

"Not *just* with you, Hamish," Caparelli put in, and extended his own hand to Terekhov in turn. "There were several cooks involved in stirring this particular broth, Captain. Unfortunately, all of us came to the same conclusion."

"I hope you'll forgive me for saying you're making me a little . . . uneasy, Sir Thomas," Terekhov replied as Caparelli released his hand and Cortez extended his.

"That's because you have good instincts," White Haven said, and gestured for all of them to be seated.

He waited until they'd settled around the large table, then leaned back slightly in his chair, and despite his beautifully tailored civilian clothing, it was a senior admiral who looked out of his blue eyes at Terekhov, not a civilian.

"I'll come straight to the point. ONI, SIS, and the FO have all been through your reports—and more recent ones from Talbott—forward and backward. The consensus is that your analysis and conclusions were spot on, and we rather doubt whoever was pulling the strings behind your Mister 'Firebrand' and Roberto Tyler will just fold his tent and disappear. We think he may pause while he reloads, but he's not going to give up. Not after the amount of time, money, and risk he invested in his first attempt."

He paused, clearly inviting comment, and Terekhov cocked his head, gazing out the conference room's crystoplast windows at the Landing skyline etched against the morning sun, while he thought. Then his eyes returned to White Haven.

"If their intent was to prevent the annexation, My Lord, they've failed. They might decide not to throw good money after bad."

"If their intent was *solely* to prevent the annexation, yes," White Haven replied. "Unfortunately, we don't think that was the only thing they had in mind. And neither, if you'll forgive my saying so, do you, judging from your reports."

"I wouldn't say it was so much that I don't *think* that was the only thing they had in mind, My Lord." Terekhov shook his head. "It's more a matter of instinct—more a *feeling* than any kind of reasoned conclusion. But, no. I don't think we've seen the last of whoever it was, either."

"Well, whether we're all right about that or not," Caparelli said, "there's still that little eight-hundred-kilo hexapuma known as the Solarian League in the mix. Between the three of you, you, Admiral Khumalo, and Amanda Corvisart have handed OFS and the League their first real diplomatic black eye—the first one that really counts and can't just be swept under the carpet—in decades. All three of the admirals in this room fully supported Her Majesty's decision to approve your actions in Monica. That was incredibly well done in a very difficult position, and all of us know how easy it would've been for you to punt it back up the line and let some senior and better paid officer make the hard choices."

Terekhov felt his cheeks warm, but he looked back at the First Space Lord steadily, and Caparelli continued in the same level tone.

"You and your people did exactly the right thing, but Frontier Security isn't going to forgive and forget anytime soon, and it's a virtual certainty that the SLN's going to beef up its presence in Talbott's vicinity. I'd like to think even Sollies are smart enough not to push things at this point, but experience suggests otherwise. In fact, it's a lot more likely some Solly officer will decide to push back hard to restore Solarian prestige in the Verge."

Terekhov nodded slowly. Given the fact that Monica had been a long-standing Solarian ally—not to mention a fertile source of mercenaries to break other people's legs for Frontier Security—Caparelli was almost certainly correct. And if Manpower and whoever else had been involved in the attempt to kill the annexation decided to give the fire another kick or two...

"At the moment, it looks like the situation with the Peeps is in fairly good shape," White Haven took up the thread of conversation again. His deep voice was as calm as ever, yet Terekhov had an odd feeling that he was less happy about the Peeps than he wanted to sound. Which was odd, given Eighth Fleet's crushing victory at the Battle of Lovat...which had, after all, been won by his own wife.

"I'm sure we all would've preferred for President Pritchart's offer of negotiations to have been made in good faith," the First Lord continued. "It's unfortunate that that doesn't seem to be what happened, but I'm pretty sure Lovat has to've set them back on their heels. On the other hand—and this is classified, Captain—we don't yet have the new missile control systems as broadly deployed as we'd like. There's still a window of vulnerability, and we can't divert large numbers of wallers to Talbott as a show of force until it closes. We will be strengthening Tenth Fleet, and as soon as the situation vis-à-vis the Peeps permits, additional ships of the wall *will* be added to that list, but we simply can't do that yet.

"Because we can't, we'll be relying on lighter combatants, instead, and ONI's analysis—backed up in no small part by our examination of the hardware you captured intact at Monica—suggests those lighter combatants have an even bigger edge on any SLN units, especially with the new Mark Sixteen warheads, than we've ever been willing to assume. In other words, our more modern cruisers and destroyers should be able to hold their own against about anything the Sollies have below the wall. The problem is that the Sollies may not realize that."

"The problem," Caparelli amplified bluntly, "is that the Sollies damned well wouldn't *admit* that even if they did."

"Probably not," White Haven conceded. "And that, Captain, is the real reason we've sent Admiral Henke off to command Tenth Fleet for Admiral Khumalo. Well, that and the fact that she gave her parole when Pritchart sent her home. We can't deploy her against the Peeps until she's released from that parole, which happens to make her available someplace we need her even worse."

Terekhov nodded. He hadn't learned about Michelle Henke's survival until his return from Talbott, but from what he knew of her, she'd been an excellent choice for the senior fleet commander on Talbott Station. Much as he'd come to like and even admire Augustus Khumalo, he simply lacked the combat experience—and possibly what people still called the "fire in the belly"—Henke would bring to the job. She'd free Khumalo for the vital administrative duties of a station commander, which was where his true strengths lay, anyway.

The only thing that concerned him was her reputation for aggressiveness—the possibility that she might actually have *too much* fire in her belly. He supposed an unbiased soul might have made the same observation about him with a fair degree of accuracy, but Henke had made her name in cruisers and battlecruisers. From all accounts, she had a battlecruiser mentality, and from *other* accounts, she also had an ample share of the famed Winton temper. She was unlikely to tread lightly on any Solarian toes that got in her way, and the fact that she was the Queen's first cousin—and fifth in the succession, should anything happen to Elizabeth—could make any toe-stamping she did especially painful. Or especially . . . politically fraught, at least.

"What we have in mind is to send you back to Talbott." White Haven's expression was as unflinching as his tone. "It's not fair. If anybody deserves time at home, it's you. Unfortunately, sometimes Her Majesty's Navy can't afford to worry about 'fair,' and you're an especially valuable resource at this moment for several reasons. First, because you're a proven combat commander who's demonstrated he's willing to act on his own initiative. Second, because at this moment I very much doubt there's anyone in Manticoran uniform with a more formidable reputation in Solarian eyes. In that sense, we're sending you back out to be Admiral Henke's big stick, if it turns out she needs one. In addition to that, your Foreign Office background's going to be at least as valuable to her as it was to Admiral Khumalo. And, finally, it's clear from our correspondence with Prime Minister Alquezar and Baroness Medusa that no one has a better reputation—or better personal contacts—in the Quadrant than you do." He shook his head, his expression regretful. "The truth is, we can't afford to leave you on the beach, however much you might deserve it."

"I understand what you're saying, My Lord." Terekhov tried very hard not to sound like a man looking for an argument to convince his superiors not to send him. "But *Hexapuma* still hasn't been assigned a repair berth. And even after we get her docked and formally slotted into the queue, she's going to be in yard hands for months. Probably longer."

"Yes, she is, Captain." Terekhov's heart fell at the sympathy in Caparelli's voice. "That's why we're going to give her to Commander FitzGerald—along with his overdue promotion to captain."

Terekhov's felt his jaw tighten. It wasn't a surprise, not really. From the moment they'd told him they were sending him back out, he'd known they wouldn't be sending him in *Hexapuma*. And if he had to lose her, she couldn't possibly be in better hands than Ansten's. He knew that. And it didn't make it hurt one bit less.

"And I'm afraid that's not the worst of it, Captain," White Haven said quietly, and nodded to Admiral Cortez. Terekhov looked at him, and the Fifth Space Lord touched a key at his station. A holo appeared above the table—the holo of another *Saganami-C*-class heavy cruiser, sister to his own *Hexapuma*.

"HMS *Quentin Saint-James*," Cortez said. "She's the flagship of a new heavy cruiser squadron—the Ninety-Fourth—we've just stood up."

Terekhov nodded. Deep inside, a familiar sense of challenge warred with his grief at leaving *Hexapuma* behind. There was always that edge of excitement when it came time to assume a new command and turn it into a perfectly tempered weapon. It would take months, but the sheer satisfaction would—

But then his thoughts broke off as Cortez continued.

"The bad news, Captain, is that CruRon Ninety-Four leaves for Talbott tomorrow."

Terekhov stopped nodding and stared at him in shock. *Tomorrow?* He'd only gotten back from Talbott less than forty hours ago! How could he go home and tell Sinead he was leaving again *tomorrow?* Besides, he'd already taken command of *Hexapuma* on virtually no notice. Now they wanted him to take command of a brand-new heavy cruiser without even one full *day's* warning?!

"I know it seems insane," Cortez said, "but I'm afraid the decision to redeploy you—and the need to get CruRon Ninety-Four out to Tenth Fleet absolutely ASAP—doesn't leave us much choice."

"Sir, I understand what you're saying," Terekhov said again, after a long, ringing fifteen seconds of silence. "I think I do, anyway. But completely aside from the issue of leaving my wife again so quickly, I'm afraid I don't see any way I could assume command of an entirely new crew on such short notice! If nothing else, it would be totally unfair to *them*! We managed to get *Hexapuma* worked up to an acceptable standard on the voyage to Spindle, but we'd had at least a *little* time to shake down as a crew before we deployed. But less than *one day?*" He shook his head and looked at all three of the other men seated around the table. "With all due respect, My Lords, I don't see any way—"

"Excuse me, Captain Terekhov," Cortez interrupted. "I wasn't quite done."

Terekhov shut his mouth, and Cortez grimaced.

"First, you won't have to work up in *Quentin Saint-James*. Second, you won't be her CO; Captain Frederick Carlson's been with her for the last six months, supervising her completion and working her up. I think you'll be impressed with how well he's done that. In fact, every unit of the squadron's had at least two months' workup time, although they hadn't combined *as* a squadron at the time. In fact, *Marconi Williams* and *Slipstream* only joined a week ago."

Terekhov's expression was puzzled, and Cortez's grimace turned into a rueful half-amused and half-apologetic smile.

"We're not giving you *Quentin Saint-James*, Captain Terekhov. Or not as *your* command, anyway. We're giving you the entire squadron, *Commodore* Terekhov."

AUGUST 1921 POST DIASPORA

"If there happened to be a single word of truth in these 'assumptions' of yours—which there isn't, of course—you'd probably be a dead man sometime in the next, oh, thirty seconds."

—First Sergeant Vincent Frugoni, Solarian League Marine Corps (retired)

Chapter Fifteen

"MR. HARAHAP IS HERE, MA'AM."

The totally unnecessary—but highly decorative—receptionist stood aside, holding the archaic wooden door open as Damien Harahap stepped past him.

It was odd, Harahap reflected. Isabel Bardasano could have been a poster child for the Mesan "young lodges," the members of the Mesan corporate hierarchy who disdained the older tradition of blending into the "legitimate" Solarian business community. The ones who chose to flaunt their outlaw status, effectively giving the entire civilized galaxy the finger and daring it to do one damned thing about them. By and large, the members of the young lodges tended to be on the bleeding edge of every contemporary luxury, fashion, and fad, and judging from Bardasano's spectacular tattoos and body piercings, one would have guessed she shared that bent.

Instead, she chose to surround herself with deliberate archaisms. The office in which she'd initially interviewed him was part of her "public face" at Jessyk.

This was her actual office, the space from which she did her *real* work instead of simply maintaining her cover with the Jessyk Combine, and it was very different from that other office. The unpowered doors, the human receptionist, the old-fashioned hardcopy books lining the shelves in her office . . . It was almost as if they were a refuge, a place she could withdraw to, away from the reality of who she was and what she did on a daily basis.

The music playing in the background was another example of that. He didn't recognize the artist or the melody, but he suspected it might actually be a Pre-Diaspora recording which had survived all those centuries.

"Come in," she said crisply. "Sit."

He obeyed the command, taking a chair which, he noted, came equipped with the same sorts of sensors as the one he'd occupied for his first interview with her here on Mesa. Well, that was fine with him. As far as he knew, there wasn't anything he needed to hide this time around.

Of course, he could be wrong about that.

"Coffee?" she asked. "Something stronger?"

"Coffee would be fine," he replied, and she nodded to the receptionist.

"See to it, Samuel."

"Yes, Ma'am."

The receptionist disappeared and Bardasano tipped back in the huge chair behind her desk as she regarded the ex-gendarme thoughtfully.

"I could wish the rest of my people had your gift for concision," she said after a moment, stretching out one arm to tap the memo board lying on her blotter.

Like many executives of Harahap's acquaintance, especially those in the covert operations community, she preferred a handheld to a desk display.

"Your reports and analyses are well organized and quite thorough," she continued. "There's even some actual humor tucked away in them, but you still get the basis for your reasoning across quite clearly, and you even manage to get it done without a lot of excess word count. That's especially welcome around here, to be honest. Some of my other analysts obviously think we're paying them by the word! And you don't hesitate to offer firm conclusions, either, even when that might involve going out on a limb. Impressive."

She nodded slowly to herself, and Harahap allowed himself to nod back. She started to say something else, then paused as the receptionist reappeared with a silver tray holding an empty coffee cup, a large—*very* large; it had to hold at least two liters—self-heating carafe, and cream and old-fashioned sugar. He set it silently and efficiently at Harahap's elbow, then vanished once again, closing the door behind him.

"Samuel is sometimes a bit OCD," Bardasano observed, smiling as Harahap lifted the lid on the carafe and sniffed the aromatic steam, then poured into his cup. "On the other hand, he has a fairly good sense of how long my meetings are likely to run. Better than I do, sometimes. Judging by the size of that carafe, I'd say he expects you to be here a while."

"I don't have anything else scheduled for the day," Harahap replied, pouring cream and spooning sugar. He sat back in the sensor-equipped chair, legs crossed, and regarded her calmly across the cup.

"That's good, because there are a couple of those

potential out-on-a-limb conclusions of yours we probably need to consider pretty carefully. But before we get to that, I've come into possession of a tidbit you might find interesting."

Harahap raised his eyebrows in polite, silent interrogation, and she smiled. That smile held an edge he couldn't quite identify, but whatever it was twanged the instincts which had made him so effective in the field for so long.

"Our sources in the Talbott Quadrant have been . . . pruned back rather drastically," she told him. "On the other hand, as I'm sure you've concluded from the nature and content of the briefing materials we provided you with there, we have a *lot* of sources. I mention this because one of those sources is inside the Manties' Foreign Office, and his latest infodump makes interesting reading. Among other things, it gives us a better picture of who the hell Aivars Terekhov is than we had before. It's pretty impressive reading in that respect. But what you might find interesting is the fact that it was the activities of someone called 'Firebrand' that flipped Stephen Westman from *our* side of the equation into the support column for the annexation."

She paused, and silence filled the office, broken only by the background murmur of the music. She simply sat there, watching him out of those odd silver-irised eyes, her expression completely unreadable even by Harahap. It was obvious she was waiting for a response from him, and he sipped coffee for a moment, then lowered the cup.

"May I ask exactly how that came about?"

"That's hard to say for certain," she replied. "Off

the top of my head, it looks like you got too fancy and offended his principles."

Harahap frowned, running back through his conversations with Westman. The Montanan was as stubborn and bullheaded as a human being came, but he definitely had principles. He didn't bother to think his way through them and all of their implications, sometimes, but he had them—in spades. So it was entirely possible Harahap *had* offended them in some way, although he couldn't think of anything. Except...

"Would that have had anything to do with Agnes Nordbrandt?" he asked after a moment, and Bardasano's eyes narrowed with what might have been a trace of approval.

"I'd say that was a pretty good guess," she said. "Our source wasn't able to send us the actual report, only a summary of a general background briefing written from memory. But it does appear you got a bit too fancy by implying your approval for Nordbrandt's methods to someone like Westman. It seems Mr. Westman had no desire to find himself lumped in with her activities."

"I could see that," Harahap acknowledged in a dispassionate tone. "Westman saw himself as some kind of patriotic Robin Hood, and he's a lot smarter than Nordbrandt. He didn't have the mindset for terror tactics, but that was at least partly because he recognized how ultimately counterproductive they were, especially on a planet like Montana. Unfortunately, Nordbrandt saw things rather differently, and partly because of the communications lag, I didn't realize just how far into the terrorist camp she was prepared to go." He shrugged slightly. "If I wanted to convince him I was a serious player, a coordinator for a sector-wide 'resistance movement,' I had to at least drop names with him, and she'd made quite a reputation for her opposition—her *legal* opposition—to the annexation before she went underground. I have to say I wouldn't be surprised if he experienced some pretty serious qualms when she went off the rails into mass-casualty operations. If I'd realized she was going to do that, I would've tailored my approach to him differently."

"How?" she asked, and he twitched another shrug.

"I would've taken the position that sometimes a revolutionary has to work with unsavory allies. While I personally found her taste for bloodshed excessive and more than a little disgusting, actually, the committee I represented had decided to support her because however thuggish we found her, at least she was actually *doing* something. Obviously, Montana wasn't Split, and those sorts of tactics would be completely counterproductive there, which made me just as happy. I couldn't disagree with the committee's conclusion that she'd do a lot of damage to the annexation effort, but that didn't mean I had to like her strategy and tactics at all. Or that I wasn't afraid they might ultimately backfire on our entire movement if our connection to her became known."

"I see."

Bardasano frowned thoughtfully for a moment, then let her chair come upright and reached for her memo board.

"Interesting," she said as she brought it alive. "That's pretty much what I expected you to say."

She did *not*, he noticed, say she'd approved of his

response, and he sipped more coffee, his own expression tranquil while she scrolled through the files on her display. She found the one she wanted and looked back up at him.

"All right, let's look at the fruits of your recent labors. Why don't you start by summarizing the reasons you think Custis and Any Port would be bad investments for Janus?"

"Of course." He lowered his cup, holding it in his lap between both hands. "I'll take Any Port first, if you don't mind." He smiled briefly. "It's a much more clear-cut proposition than Custis, actually."

"Tell me about it."

"First, your basic intel package was badly off the mark." His voice was crisp but calm, almost dispassionate. "Whoever did the initial political analysis really needs to find another career. The idea that anyone in that star system was serious enough about reform to actually take to the streets was . . . well, let's just call it grossly overoptimistic. The current so-called opposition movement's basically a bunch of professional rowdies who never saw a riot they didn't like and naïve college students without a clue, all being used by a batch of 'reformist leaders' who really want to bargain their way up to the table—and the trough—in the existing system.

"According to your original brief, there were at least three potential targets for Janus. In fact, the only one that might conceivably have been useful was the Any Port Democratic Movement, but it only took one meeting with a representative of their central committee for me to realize—"

❖   ❖   ❖

"He's good," Isabel Bardasano said much later that evening, watching a spectacular sunset from the veranda of a mansion which officially didn't exist on an island that was supposedly a population-free nature preserve. "He's very good, actually. Even better than I expected."

"Really?" An old-fashioned rattan chair creaked as the man sitting on the other side of the small round table shifted position.

"I pushed him a little on the Westman-Nordbrandt business," she said. "Not very hard; just enough to let him know I had some potential . . . issues with the way he'd handled it. He didn't panic, he didn't bluster, and he didn't flounder. I have to assume he didn't have that information before I gave it to him, but he didn't even hesitate. He just told me why he'd done what he'd done and what he might have done differently if he'd been aware at the outset just how bloody-minded Nordbrandt was. I got the same sort of response three or four other times when I pushed on some of his conclusions from his recent field trip. He's smart, he's quick, and he's really in command of the material, Albrecht. It's obvious he actually did go through every damned bit of it, and his analysis was more comprehensive and tightly reasoned than ninety percent of the reports our own people generate. And he's got the mental agility to absorb new information and integrate it into his analyses—and strategies—on the fly. That's unusual in someone who provides that sort of painstaking evaluations. In fact, he's a very rare bird—a top drawer field agent who's just as good as an analyst."

"Somehow I doubt you'd be extolling his virtues this way unless you have something more . . . ambitious in mind for him," Albrecht Detweiler observed.

"He's a better analyst than ninety percent of the people I have all the way inside the onion," she replied bluntly, "but he's wasted doing prospector work. Besides, by now we've pretty much identified the star systems with the most potential for Janus. And much as I could use him in the home office, we couldn't get full utility out of him without bringing him fully inside, and frankly, at this point I wouldn't be willing to take that risk. But he doesn't have to know who's really calling the shots to be extraordinarily effective—he demonstrated that in Talbott."

"Where, as we've just discussed, he was directly instrumental in that bastard Terekhov's turning Westman and uncovering the Monica connection," Detweiler challenged.

"Once Terekhov uncovered that arms cache on Split and IDed our freighter somehow, Montana was falling into Manticore's pocket no matter what else did or didn't happen," she responded. "It was the *Marianne* and Binyan and his crew who blew that part of the operation. And apropos that topic, I argued rather strenuously against using the same ship to transport Technodyne's technicians and run arms deliveries. *That* was the link that pointed the Manties at Monica, not anything Harahap did."

"Point taken," Detweiler said after a moment. "So where do you think his talents would find their best and highest use?"

"In a lot of ways, I'd've liked to send him to New Tuscany to back up Aldona. He's already demonstrated he can work well with her, but we'd have had to bring him too far inside for that. Besides, she's already well launched on that, and throwing him into the mix at this late date would be a waste of resources. No, what I have in mind is to slide him back into what he was doing in Talbott. In particular, I'd like him to take some of the load off Partisan. Instead of sending him racing around eliminating bad prospects, I'd like to see him developing *good* ones for us. I think he's got the right mix of brains, audacity, and a dash of humor to handle somebody like the Allenbys in Swallow, for example."

"Um." Detweiler frowned, gazing into the sunset while he considered.

"We'd have to bring him far enough inside to make him potentially dangerous," he pointed out after a long moment, and she snorted.

"Albrecht, that was true from the instant Yucel ordered Eichbauer to work with us in Talbott! We've got serious operational exposure in Janus however we set it up and whoever we send out to handle the 'gardening.' And in a lot of ways, I'd rather risk losing him than our own deep cover people. For that matter, it wouldn't hurt our overall strategy if the Manties picked up a Solarian gendarme in the employ of a corrupt transstellar. That would probably help point them down the alley we want them to follow, and it would also pump more hydrogen into the fire when they parade him in the Solly 'faxes. The Sollies will claim he's not working for them, the Manties won't believe it, and the Solly public—or a big chunk of it, anyway—will buy Kolokoltsov's argument that it's all a Manty fabrication for nefarious purposes of their own."

She shrugged again, her smile turning briefly shark-like.

"He's too potentially useful for me to be *happy* about the thought of losing him, but if we *have* to lose somebody, I'd really prefer for it to be someone whose loss would actually push our ultimate objective forward, wouldn't you?"

"I'm inclined to trust your judgment, Isabel. But I think this is one we should probably take up with Collin, as well, since Janus was his brainchild from the beginning."

❖   ❖   ❖

"How's it going, Damien?"

"Can't complain, Rufino," Harahap replied as Rufino Chernyshev paused beside his restaurant table. "Would you care to have a seat, or would it be . . . inappropriate for the two of us to be seen together in public?"

"I don't have a guilty conscience," Chernyshev said with a smile. "Is there some reason you should?"

"Not here in Mesa." Harahap smiled back and pushed one of the other chairs out with his toe. "Sit down. The beer's pretty good here."

"They do have a fair selection," Chernyshev agreed. "What're you drinking?"

"Something called Old Tillman." Harahap held up the old-fashioned bottle. "Product of Manticore, if you can believe it."

"Oh, I can. Actually, it's pretty popular in these parts, despite the source."

Chernyshev sat and punched his order into the table terminal. A hover tray with a frosted stein and a bottle of Old Tillman arrived at his shoulder in less than thirty seconds. If it had taken more than forty-five, it would have been free.

"Is the security on this place"—Harahap twitched a raised index finger in a circular motion at the dimly lit restaurant's overhead—"as good as it claims?"

"Is any restaurant's security *ever* as good as it claims?" Chernyshev countered with a smile, watching the head on his beer as he poured carefully into the stein. Then he shrugged. "As far as anyone who might . . . how is it they put it in the bad novels? 'Wish us ill,' isn't it?" Harahap snorted in amusement, and Chernyshev went on. "As far as anyone like that's concerned, it's probably just as good as it claims. Now, where our esteemed *superiors* are concerned . . ."

He shrugged again. It was a very different shrug, and the whimsy had faded from his expression.

Harahap nodded. It was only to be expected that his new employers would keep an eye on anything their hired help got up to. It was interesting that Chernyshev was so willing to admit it, though. And his body language and tone were equally interesting.

Of course, he reminded himself, *someone as senior as Rufino seems to be might find it pretty damned useful to be considered "one of the guys" when it comes to bitching about the front office's . . . intrusiveness.*

"Well," he said out loud, "I don't have a guilty conscience where 'our esteemed superiors' are concerned, either. And I suppose it makes sense for them to keep an eye on their employees."

"Like I said when we met, it's nice to deal with a professional. To be honest, it took me a while to get as philosophical about it as you seem. And I'm willing to bet I started in this line of work at a considerably earlier age than you did, too."

Harahap nodded again, noncommittally. He suspected Chernyshev knew exactly when he'd first gone to work for the Gendarmerie.

"Should I assume you just happened along at this

particular moment—a coincidence, I might add, I would find difficult to believe—or are you here for a purpose?" he asked.

"No, I didn't just 'happen along,' and no, it's not a coincidence. Not that I'd turn down a nice bowl of the house *okroshka* and a skewer of the lamb *shashylk* to go with my beer. The beef and chicken *okroshka*'s especially good, if you haven't tried it. And the *pelmeni* aren't bad, either."

"Obviously, I should let you order," Harahap said with another smile. "So why not get the non-coincidence out of the way first so we can enjoy our meal?"

"Sounds like a good idea to me." Chernyshev set his stein on the table in front of him, drew a privacy unit from an inner pocket, and set it on the table beside the beer.

"Like I said, security's *probably* as good in here as *Starozhil* Aleksey claims it is, but let's not take any chances."

"Go ahead," Harahap invited, and Chernyshev switched it on and picked his beer back up.

"All right, Ms. Bardasano sent me to ask you to drop by her office again tomorrow morning. Around nine, let's say."

"Sent you to *ask* me?" Harahap said ironically, and Chernyshev chuckled.

"Those were her very words. Mind you, I think she'd be just a *little* irritated if it turned out you couldn't fit her into your busy schedule."

"By the strangest coincidence, I just happen to have an opening in my calendar tomorrow morning."

"I thought you might." Chernyshev sipped, then lowered the stein again.

"She also authorized me to give you a sort of preliminary brief on what she has in mind," he said in a rather more serious tone. "She'll want to handle the actual specifics herself, of course. She just wants me to give you a sort of...call it a general overview, since I had a hand in setting up a good bit of what you'll be dealing with. And, to be honest, one reason she wants me to is that she has a lot less actual field experience—especially in this kind of operation—than you or I do, and she's smart enough to realize it. One of the things I like best about working for her, to be honest. She understands there are aspects of Janus where someone who's been there and done that is a better choice as a briefer."

"Make sense to me," Harahap said with unfeigned approval. If he had a centicred for every desk-jockey who'd thought he knew everything there was to know about field ops and screwed the pooch...

"Well, in that case, let me start by saying your new assignment will be similar to what you've already been doing for us but that you're being moved up from prospector to handler. I imagine you'll be taking over existing relationships in at least some cases. In others, though—"

✦ Chapter Sixteen

THE CAPTAIN'S DINING CABIN aboard HMS *Tristram* was considerably smaller than that aboard the *Quentin Saint-James*. That said, however, it was far larger than any other destroyer's dining cabin Helen Zilwicki had ever imagined. Which, she supposed, shouldn't have been all that astonishing, given that *Tristram* was bigger than most navies' light cruisers and needed personnel space for fewer people than anyone else's destroyers.

Chief Steward Clorinda Brinkman watched like a broody eagle as her minions finished delivering food to the table and withdrew like wisps of fog on a breeze. She gave the entire cabin one more gimlet-eyed inspection, then nodded in satisfaction and followed the messmen out the cabin door.

"You were right, Naomi," Sir Aivars Terekhov observed with a smile. "She *is* a lot like Joanna, isn't she?"

"I think BuPers has a secret manufacturing facility somewhere that turns out stewards," Lieutenant Commander Alvin Tallman, *Tristram*'s XO, put in. "Of course, that could be simply my overactive imagination. There does seem to be a master template for *captain's* stewards, though."

"Only when it comes to bossing around their captains," Naomi Kaplan said from the head of the table. "Aside from that, they come in all sorts of flavors."

"I don't know about that, Ma'am," Abigail Hearns demurred. "I think Chief Steward Brinkman goes easier on you than most. She reminds me of my mother Sandra, actually. She doesn't so much boss you around as look at you with that reproachful gaze. Or, worse, she *trusts* you to do the right thing."

"And you think that kind of judo's better than just issuing orders?" Kaplan demanded, and Abigail shrugged.

"It's probably more effective in the long run. It at least leaves you the illusion you're the one making the decisions, too. And the Tester does teach us that it's by making decisions—and exercising our free will—that we grow and mature spiritually, so it's probably even good for you."

"Oh, thank you," Kaplan said dryly.

"You're welcome, Ma'am."

"I don't suppose I could give her back to you, Sir?" Kaplan asked, smiling at Terekhov, who chuckled.

"I'd love to have her, but . . . no, I'm afraid that particular transaction's not refundable."

"Pity." Kaplan sighed and shook her head wearily. "I suppose it's just one of the burdens of command."

"I'm sure you'll bear up under it just fine," the commodore consoled her.

"I'll try not to be too great a trial, Ma'am," Abigail assured her earnestly. "Of course, there is that bit about growing to meet your Test to think about."

"Well, I guess when a tactical officer's shown a

modicum of true talent, one just has to accept her occasional rough-around-the-edges spots," Kaplan said.

"I found that true aboard the *Kitty*, now that you mention it," Terekhov agreed. "Now what *was* that TO's name . . . don't tell me, it'll come to me . . . I remember it started with an 'N,' though."

"Ouch." Kaplan winced, then raised one hand in a surrendering gesture. "You win, Sir. Besides," she glared laughingly at Abigail, "it's always a good idea to let the senior officer win. You might want to write that down, Ms. Hearns."

"And so should you, Ensign," Terekhov informed Helen rather sternly as she cut another morsel of the delicious Montanan beef.

"Oh, I already have, Sir," his brand new, and extremely junior, flag lieutenant assured him. "I entered it under the chapter heading 'Sucking Up to Authority.'"

Terekhov chuckled and shook his head, then smiled at Kaplan's XO across the table.

"I sometimes think it's harder to figure out which is more stubborn, a Grayson or a Gryphon Highlander."

"Not much to choose between them, in my experience, Sir," Lieutenant Commander Tallman replied. "On the other hand, with a few exceptions, most of them do seem to do good work."

"That they do," Terekhov agreed. "Never a good idea to let their heads get too big for their berets, though."

Tallman nodded with an answering chuckle, yet he couldn't help thinking how few officers of Terekhov's seniority—and reputation—could manage to un-bend so thoroughly with his subordinates without in any way undercutting his own authority. Naomi Kaplan had the same gift, but it seemed even stronger in the commodore. No one could possibly doubt his deep affection for both Abigail Hearns and Helen Zilwicki, but only an idiot could have expected that affection to affect his judgment or the level of respect, discipline, and performance he would expect—and demand—of them.

"On a somewhat more serious note, Sir," Kaplan set down her wine and began buttering a second roll, "what do *you* think's going on with the New Tuscans?"

"Not anything we'd like." Terekhov shrugged and frowned in distaste. "Bernardus Van Dort and Admiral Khumalo asked me that, too, and like I told them, I haven't had enough time back in Talbott to form any considered opinion. That said, I wouldn't trust a single one of them in the same airlock with me.

"Their oligarchs—especially that idiot Yvernau—did everything they could during the constitutional convention to buy immunity from any domestic changes. And according to Baroness Medusa, they've been insisting ever since that their exclusion from the economic incentive package represents some kind of economic retaliation, not the inevitable consequence of their own decision not to join the Star Empire when they didn't get the special guarantees they demanded."

His frown deepened and he shook his head.

"They remind me an awful lot of the old Legislatural-ists, to be honest. I'm damned sure they're deliberately contriving these incidents in Pequod; I'm just not sure what they hope to achieve. But I don't like what I'm hearing about Cardot's take on all this one bit."

Helen felt herself nodding in agreement. Alesta Cardot was New Tuscany's minister of foreign affairs, and as Terekhov's flag lieutenant, Helen had seen the complete footage of Cardot's protest note about

"Manticoran provocations" in the Pequod System. The protest in question had clearly been aimed at someone besides Prime Minister Alquezar and Baroness Medusa, since the "provocations" were totally fictitious. Helen doubted Cardot would have discussed them in such detail—or shown so much visibly (and obviously) restrained outrage—over nonexistent affronts to New Tuscan's sovereignty if she hadn't intended that recording as future evidence of how dreadfully her innocent New Tuscan spacers had been treated by those horrid, arrogant Manties.

"I don't like it either," Kaplan said soberly, as if she'd just heard Helen's thoughts. "Especially since I can only think of one audience for her to impress."

"OFS," the commodore agreed with a nod. "To be honest, what worries me most is that we don't know if this was a brainstorm of Yvernau and Prime Minister Vézien, trying to pressure us into granting the economic concessions they still want, or if someone else's put them up to it for purposes of his own."

"Like the same someone who put President Tyler up to something, Sir?" Tallman asked quietly.

"I don't want to be looking under the bed for bogeymen just because of what's already happened, Commander. That's one reason I try to remind myself it's possible this was an internal brainstorm of the New Tuscan government. After all, this is only the second orchestrated effort to break our kneecaps out here."

"Once is an accident, twice is a coincidence, and three times is enemy action, you mean, Sir?" Kaplan said dryly, and Terekhov nodded.

"But the second time isn't *always* a coincidence," he pointed out grimly.

"You fill me with confidence, Sir."

"Well, I wouldn't panic just yet, Naomi. After what happened at Lovat, I expect the Admiralty should be able to reinforce us much more heavily sometime soon. Whoever pulled Tyler and Monica together with people like Nordbrandt has already demonstrated he's willing to do just about anything to get what he wants, but manipulating something like the League isn't a project that's going to proceed at lightning speed. No matter how corrupt the Sollies are—and trust me, I'm not about to underestimate *that*—" Terekhov's lips quirked, "any effort to organize some sort of repeat performance will have to burn a lot of time just sending conspirators back and forth. That should give us a window to build strength in the Quadrant before the puppetmasters' next move." He shrugged. "I'm sure we won't like whatever they have in mind, but, then again, New Tuscany may not like what *we* have in mind when it finally hits the fan."

"And Admiral Gold Peak's just the person to show them that," Kaplan agreed. "I pulled my snotty cruise aboard *Agni* when she was in command." She snorted softly. "I understand she hasn't exactly mellowed a lot with time, either!"

"I imagine that's one way to put it," Terekhov agreed. "And from everything I've ever heard about her, she's still a cruiser captain at heart. Like someone else I know." He smiled as Kaplan and Tallman chuckled, choosing not to mention any reservations about how desirable that might be in a fleet commander. "I'm sure she'll have quite a bit to say about New Tuscany when she gets back from Montana next month."

✦ Chapter Seventeen

My, you've been a BUSY *fellow, haven't you, First Sergeant Frugoni?* Damien Harahap thought, studying the imagery.

The man looking back at him from the holo display in his cabin aboard the yacht *Факел* had blond hair, blue eyes, and an improbably innocent expression. Or maybe it only seemed innocent because of what he knew about its owner.

He brought the dossier back up and paged through the screens with a pensive frown. First Sergeant Vincent "Vinnie" Frugoni, Solarian Marine Corps, with enough commendations and proficiency awards to fill a cargo shuttle. Wounded in action twice, mentioned in dispatches three times, and *twice* turned down recommendations for OCS. All that by only age forty-four—a virtual babe in arms in a society with third-generation prolong.

Obviously a lifer with no interest in a commission, Harahap reflected. *Until seven T-years ago, anyway*. He shook his head. *Somebody damned well should've been keeping a closer eye on* you, *First Sergeant*.

He pursed his lips, mourning the fact that not one of the League's myriad security services seemed to have even noticed First Sergeant Frugoni's abrupt choice in career changes. What the hell was wrong with those people? Anybody with half a brain should have realized that—

Be fair, Damien, he told himself. *You're actively looking for things like this, but there's no reason the Marines should've been. And there's no OFS or official Gendarmerie presence in Swallow, either. Anything that's going on there is on Tallulah's plate, not the League's, and I doubt* they're *going to advertise their more spectacular screw-ups to anyone outside the system. So I guess it's not* too *inexcusable that nobody seems to've noticed that Frugoni's decision not to re-up came barely five T-months after his sister was killed.*

Harahap's current employers, on the other hand, had come upon Frugoni working backward. The steadily gathering unrest in Swallow's Cripple Mountains had attracted the eye of one of Isabel Bardasano's analysts almost two T-years ago. The analyst in question had dived into its origins and discovered First Sergeant Frugoni when he realized how much of it stemmed directly from the death of Sandra Frugoni Allenby.

What a stupid waste that was, Harahap thought with genuine regret. *No wonder the Allenbys are mad as hell over it.*

Sandra Frugoni had arrived on Swallow as a Tallulah Corporation employee, but what she'd seen there had shifted her priorities radically. She'd given Tallulah notice within six months; within seven, she'd had her own medical practice, serving the men and women of the majestic, rugged Cripple Mountains, where isolation—and the fact that no one outside the Cripples gave much of a damn—made good medical care almost as rare as it had been on pre-space Old Terra. Her decision had resulted in an earnings drop of over seventy percent, not to mention the active harassment of her erstwhile employer, but she'd clearly never looked back. Harahap didn't know if she'd met Floyd Allenby before or after her decision to leave Tallulah's employ, and he had to wonder how that marriage would have worked out ultimately, given the fact that she'd been a third-generation prolong recipient and Floyd had never received even the first-generation therapies. That sort of thing often ended badly. But it might not have in this case... not that it mattered any longer, courtesy of an inexcusably stupid shoulder-fired surface-to-air missile.

And you'd already decided you were retiring to Swallow when the time came, hadn't you, Vinnie? It's not just your sister's death, is it? You're one of the ones with a conscience; I can tell. You didn't like some of the things the Marines have to do, and you'd had a bellyful, hadn't you? So you were looking for a place to settle down, maybe set up your own guide operation with your in-laws, watch your nephews and nieces grow up. But now there won't be any of those nephews and nieces, and that was a bad, bad mistake on Tallulah's part.

And then, of course, there was Frugoni's brother-in-law.

Harahap switched to another file—one that showed a weathered, tallish man with brown hair, brown eyes, sun-browned skin, a close cropped beard, and a nose that could have served as an ancient rowing galley's ram. Floyd Allenby was only thirty-two T-years years old, barely half his dead wife's age, and there were laugh lines among the weather-induced crow's feet at the corners of his eyes. But there was no laughter in that man's face these days.

A bit of the berserker there, Harahap decided. *Or maybe that's not fair. The man's a clansman, and his people are feudists. He's not* berserk; *he just has a highland clansman's notion of what constitutes justice and doesn't give a rat's ass what it takes to get it. If that means getting killed, he's okay with it, but that's not remotely the same as having a death wish. Better remember that, Damien.*

He closed the file and leaned back, listening to the music—it was one of the pieces Bardasano had been listening to during their interview, something called *Eroica* by some ancient composer named Bayhoven—while he thought.

Rufino Chernyshev had been spot on with his "guess" about the new responsibilities Bardasano had intended to offer Harahap. Which was about as surprising as the fact that sun tended to rise in the east. Chernyshev wouldn't have had that "chance conversation" with him if Bardasano hadn't approved it ahead of time. But Harahap had to admit that even his own suspicions had fallen short of his new employers' actual ambitions.

He wasn't foolish enough to believe she'd told him anything remotely like everything, and any information she'd given him about Operation Janus bore exactly as close a resemblance to the truth as her superiors wanted it to. That was something a field agent for the Gendarmerie learned to take in stride, but this time the stride had been just a bit *wider* than usual.

Whether or not he believed everything Bardasano had to say about this "Mesan Alignment," it definitely far greater resources than any transstellar—or *alliance* of transstellars—he'd ever heard of. And it was a very serious player; that much was obvious, because Bardasano had been forced to give him more background than he'd had if she'd wanted to make full use of his intelligence, as well as his skill set. He was positive she hadn't given him one thing more than she'd decided she had to, but even that restricted information was enough to underscore the sheer, audacious magnitude of the Alignment's operations. It seriously intended to *destroy* the Star Empire outright. And while Bardasano hadn't said so, it was obvious from what she *had* said—to someone like Damien Harahap, at least—that they'd been working on that for a hell of a lot longer than could be accounted for by Manticore's discovery of the Lynx Terminus.

I wonder how involved the "Alignment" was in Haven's decision to go back to war? Hell, given the scale these people seem to think on, I wonder how much it had to do with Haven's decision to go to war with Manticore in the first *place! Seems like an awful lot of work, though, and I wonder what their endgame is? It's got to be more than just punching out the Manties' lights!*

Yes, it did, but he reminded his curiosity bump that there were some things it was wiser not to know. Especially when one was a newly promoted operative in the employ of a hyper-paranoid interstellar conspiracy. But at least there were some surprising perks involved. Not least among them the vessel with which they'd provided him. *Факел* had been built on what was technically a dispatch boat's hull, but the dispatch boat in question had been larger than the bare-bones utility vessels used by most navies or data courier services. Officially, *Факел* was the *Christiane Hauptman*, a Manticoran-registered fast personnel transport for the Hauptman Cartel. That was concealed behind a false Solarian registry which listed her as the *Caroline Henegar*, for use when Harahap wasn't openly employing his cover as a Hauptman employee. Her actual builders and owners had never given her a name at all, only a hull number—DB-10024—so he'd felt free to bestow his own name for what he thought of as "internal use."

Captain Yong Seong Jin, DB-10024's commander, had been puzzled by his choice, initially. She'd never heard of a language called "Macedonian," but once he explained the name's origins to her, she'd been amused rather than affronted. That was good, since it had confirmed she really did have a sense of humor.

He suspected Yong was an ex-officer of the Mesan System Navy—or possibly not even "ex"—given the brisk efficiency with which she ran her small command. It was an interesting speculation, given what it would imply about the "Alignment's" relationship with the government of Mesa. What really mattered, though, was that she was about as professional as officers came. Not only did she obviously enjoy her command, she was smart, had an imagination she wasn't afraid to use, and was obviously aware of the . . . modalities covert operations required. He had no concern about her ability to support his mission without accidentally blowing their cover, which was more than he'd been able to say about some SLN officer with whom he'd been forced to work upon occasion.

In addition to the palatial comfort of *Факел*'s fittings, she was faster than any other ship aboard which he'd ever traveled. He was no hyper-physicist, and he had no idea how the "streak drive" accomplished its magic, but *Факел*'s interstellar speed was substantially higher than anyone else's. The fact that the "Alignment" had something like that tucked away in its pocket, reserving it solely for its operatives' use rather than making it available to the rest of the galaxy for a stupendous price, further underscored just how serious a player it was.

Nor was *Факел* the only goodie which had come his way.

He wasn't entirely happy about the new medical package his employers had provided. He'd seen too many ways in which suicide switches could be rigged even without access to someone's doctor, and he suspected that *his* new doctor would have been perfectly happy to do just that. That thought was enough to provoke the occasional bad dream, but they hadn't really needed any elaborate doctor's visits to set up something like that. There were much simpler ways to go about it, and he told himself firmly to look at the upside.

If Bardasano was to be believed, the booster to his prolong had just added close to another T-century to his expected lifetime. The ability to see in near-total darkness wasn't anything at which a field operative was likely to turn up his nose, either. And neither were the repair nanites swarming around his system. Bardasano had demonstrated their efficacy for him by slashing her own palm and then letting him watch as the deep cut closed and began healing before his very eyes. It was almost like carrying his very own regen clinic around with him, although he strongly suspected they violated the prohibitions on self-replicating, broad-spectrum biological nanotech. The times that sort of initially innocuous technology had gotten out of hand were enough to make anyone nervous, but if it was going to be wandering around the galaxy anyway, he might as well get in on it, himself. The oxygen reservoir implanted in his abdomen and the EM spectrum sensors implanted across his shoulder blades were well worth having, as well, and he'd been promised improved anti-disease nannies when he got back, as well. Unlike the repair nanites, they needed to be specifically coded to his own genotype so they could recognize any intruders, and there hadn't quite been time to get that done before he had to catch his shuttle for his new assignment.

And let's face it, he thought wryly, *nobody lives forever, anyway. Sure, Bardasano'll dispose of me in a heartbeat if I turn into a liability, but I already knew that. Probably be a lot harder for me to just . . . disappear now to avoid that, though. I wouldn't be at all surprised if my "regularly scheduled medical checkups" are going to include resetting some sort of dead man's switch from now on. That's how I'd've set it up, anyway. But the pay's good, the work's challenging, and as long as I don't trip myself up and blow an assignment, they'll keep me around and keep me in the field.*

In an odd sort of way, that was almost amusing, and he closed his eyes and smiled as he let the music sweep over him.

✧   ✧   ✧

"My God," Helga Boltitz said, shaking her head as she stared down into her drink. "I can't . . . I can't believe it."

"*You* can't believe it?" Helen Zilwicki shook her head, her expression grim, and Helga looked up quickly.

"I know it has to be worse for you," she said. "And I know I can't really imagine how *much* worse at this point, especially with no more information than we have. But it just seems so . . . impossible."

"That's certainly one way to put it." Helen inhaled sharply, then took a deep swallow from her stein of beer. She took her time before she lowered the stein again and looked at her table companion across it.

Helga Boltitz had to be one of the most beautiful women she'd ever met, and she'd met some really beautiful ones. For that matter, given her adoptive mother's life-long involvement with the Audubon Ballroom, she'd known quite a few women—and at least one man, she thought bitterly—who'd been genetically built from the ground up to be beautiful. People who bought pleasure slaves didn't want *ugly* property, after all. And that didn't even count the number of people who'd invested in the perfect profiles and skin texture biosculpt specialists provided all across the galaxy.

But Helga was from Dresden, where even prolong had only just become available. There were no biosculpt practices on Dresden, which meant she'd come by every bit of *her* attractiveness the old-fashioned way.

There were times when Helen—who was built on sufficiently compact and sturdy lines to have heard the dreaded adjective "healthy" applied to her person more than once—found it difficult not to resent people who drew the winning tickets in the "aren't-I-beautiful" genetic lottery.

Not always a good thing, though, is it? she asked herself. *You knew that even before you met Paulo. It's just—*

She chopped that thought off sharply. Better not to think about Paulo d'Arezzo just now. Not until they knew more.

"Sorry," she said, and managed a smile. "Didn't mean to take out any of my mad on you, Helga. It's just not *knowing*...."

"That much I really can sympathize with," Helga said. "When Minister Krietzmann got briefed on Commodore Terekhov's message and we found out you were all headed to Monica but we didn't have any idea what had happened after you got there ... That was pretty bad. And you're right, it was the fact that we couldn't know a thing about it for so long."

Helen nodded soberly. As Henri Krietzmann's personal assistant, Helga had been on the inside of that message loop right along the Quadrant's Defense Minister. So, yes. If anyone understood what Helen and every other Manticoran in Spindle were feeling at this moment, it was probably her.

"Well," she said out loud, looking around the noisy restaurant from their quiet, secluded little alcove, "I guess the good news is that we should be getting follow-on dispatches a lot more quickly than you guys could find out what had happened at Monica."

"I know."

Helga sipped her own beer. Since CruRon 94's arrival in the Quadrant, Commodore Terekhov's duties—and the Quadrant Cabinet's respect for his insights—had thrown her and Helen together on several occasions, and she'd decided she liked the young Manty. Of course,

Helen came from just a *slightly* different social strata than Lieutenant "Gwen" Archer, Admiral Henke's flag lieutenant and the only other Manticoran Helga had truly gotten to know. She certainly wasn't related to Empress Elizabeth, after all! But she *was* a Gryphon Highlander, with the sheer bloody-mindedness that implied, and that was something to which any Dresdener could relate.

"I wonder if they're going to release the news?" she asked quietly, and Helen glanced back at her quickly.

"They'll have to. It's not like the news services aren't going to be telling people about it pretty damned soon anyway," the ensign pointed out. "This is the biggest story to come out of the war in the last twenty T-years, Helga! The Solly services're going to be all over it, even if our own newsies weren't. Besides, Manticore figured out a long time ago that it's better to come clean when the shit hits the fan. You owe people that. And even if that weren't true, if you tell them what's really going on when the news is bad, not just when it's good, people tend to trust your word."

"I can see that," Helga agreed. "And I'm not saying any one should—or *could*—keep a lid on it forever. I'm just wondering if they're going to release the news *now*."

"You're probably in a better position to know about that than I am." Helen shrugged. "Off the top of my head, though, I'd say they probably will sit on it at least a while longer. Like I say, follow-up dispatches have to be en route. I'm guessing Prime Minister Alquezar and Baroness Medusa would just as soon have more information in hand before they start panicking everybody."

Helga nodded, listening to the restaurant diners'

cheerful, murmuring hubbub. Everyone seemed so upbeat, so cheerful. The possibility of a confrontation with the Solarian League might loom over them, but they were part of the Star Empire of Manticore now. The shield of the Royal Manticoran Navy extended over them, and, in the meantime, the annexation's impact on the Quadrant's economy meant a far better—and healthier—future for themselves and their children.

Except that that shield had just been dealt a shattering blow.

"Do you think it's as bad as the preliminary report suggests?"

"Probably not. Well, maybe." Helen grimaced. "After Lovat, I'd never've expected them to try something like this. A direct assault on the home system? That took what a friend of my dad's would call great big brass ones!"

"I don't think *anyone* would've expected it after so long," Helga said. "I mean, you've been fighting Haven for ages. If anyone was going to launch this kind of attack, why not do it a lot sooner? Wouldn't that've made more sense?"

"No." Helen shook her head. "Anybody who tried something like this was going to get royally reamed, even if they 'won.' That's the reason no responsible strategist would've signed off on it, even after we'd demonstrated the deep strike would work. In fact, I think the Commodore probably put his finger on what happened—or *why* it happened, at least."

Helga arched an eyebrow at her, and she tossed her left hand in a sort of throw away gesture.

"Sir Aivars," she said, using the title Terekhov had received at Baroness Medusa's hands, along with the

Parliamentary Medal of Valor, less than a week earlier, "thinks they did this—threw the dice and went all in—exactly because of what Duchess Harrington did at Lovat. They got reamed there, too, thanks to the new MDM control systems. Their birds have just as much range as ours, Helga; they just have less accuracy, and it gets crappier as the range extends."

Helga nodded. As Krietzmann's assistant, she'd been present when Terekhov briefed the Defense Minister and the rest of the Cabinet on the new Manticoran missiles. She didn't pretend to understand the technical details, but she understood the consequences of being able to utterly destroy an enemy at ranges from which she couldn't even hit your own ships.

"Well, the Commodore thinks they must've figured their only chance was to hammer us hard enough to force us to surrender before we got the new weapons broadly deployed. I don't think anyone in Nouveau Paris could've expected it to be a *good* chance, and they must have projected massive losses for their own side. But after the summit talks fell through and they saw what happened at Lovat, they probably decided it was throw the dice and take their own lumps in hopes of pulling it off or screen Mount Royal Palace with *their* surrender offer."

"And so all those people got killed," Helga said sadly, looking back down into her drink once more. Then she looked up quickly with something almost like a gasp. "Oh, Helen! I didn't mean to suggest that—"

"'S all right." Helen shook her head. "Oh, I'm worried about enough other people I know in the Fleet, but it doesn't sound like they got anywhere near *Hephaestus*. It must've driven Captain FitzGerald crazy to be sitting on his bridge doing nothing in the middle of something like that, but there's no way the *Kitty* could've done one damned thing until they get her repairs finished. So I'm not worried about *Hexapuma* or . . . or anyone aboard her."

Helga nodded with a relieved expression, but she found herself wondering which "anyone aboard her" Helen wasn't worried about. It sounded like a much more *personal* "anyone."

"Well," she said, "Admiral Gold Peak should be back in another three T-weeks or so. Maybe we'll have at least some good news for her when she gets here."

✦ Chapter Eighteen

VINCENT FRUGONI, LATE OF THE Solarian League Marine Corps, frowned down at his minicomp's display when someone settled into the seat beside him. He'd grabbed the redeye shuttle from the Capistrano spaceport deliberately, because it was usually the next best thing to empty. And as he glanced up from the display, he realized it was still the next best thing to empty. In fact, there were only seventeen other passengers on the entire eighty-seat shuttle. Like Frugoni, at least twelve of them had seized the opportunity to establish themselves in splendid isolation, unhampered by seatmates while they busied themselves catching up on either correspondence and com calls or sleep.

But not the yahoo in the seat next to *him*. Oh, no!

It wasn't that Frugoni begrudged the other fellow a seat, but he'd spent three T-decades in a military career that had seen him deployed aboard ship far more often than not. He'd had no choice but to put up with the close-packed proximity a warship's berthing spaces enforced. Now that he was out of the service, he treasured the breathing room civilians took for granted.

He gave the idiot beside him a moderately scathing look, but the newcomer only smiled, oblivious to the wattage with which First Sergeant Frugoni had incinerated decades of hapless recruits and privates. For just a moment, he found himself longing wistfully for the uniform and chevrons—and the authority that went with them—he'd left behind along with the rest of the Corps. Unfortunately, civilian life imposed somewhat different constraints. He hated giving up his current seat, for several reasons, but there were equally good reasons to change it, and so he sighed resignedly as he closed his minicomp, stood, and reached for his overhead bag.

"Why don't you sit back down, First Sergeant?" the intrusive civilian asked softly, and Frugoni froze. He darted another look at the other man, and the stranger smiled and patted the seat he'd just climbed out of.

"It's a fairly comfortable seat in a very good position," he pointed out. "And it'll be much easier for us to talk with you sitting in it. Probably less obtrusive than shouting back and forth across the aisle, too, now that I think about it."

"And why should I want to talk to you?" Frugoni asked just a bit sharply. "For that matter, who the hell *are* you?"

"Eldbrand, Harvey Eldbrand." The other man extended his hand; Frugoni looked at it with a marked lack of enthusiasm.

"I don't know any Eldbrands, I'm afraid."

"Oh, no. We've never met." The other fellow—Eldbrand—smiled, still holding out his hand until Frugoni finally shook it . . . briefly.

"However," Eldbrand went on then, "I do know some of the other people you know ... and I also know quite a bit *about* you."

"Here on Swallow, people take their privacy seriously." Frugoni's voice had taken on a much harder edge.

"I know," Eldbrand said calmly. "That's why you should sit back down so we can talk. I promise you'll find the conversation ... interesting. You may even find it useful."

"Useful how?"

Even as he asked the question, Frugoni knew he shouldn't have. He should have just shaken the guy's hand, told him he must have the wrong party, and gotten the hell away from him while the getting was good. But now he was half-trapped. One or two other passengers had glanced his way, seen him standing—and seen him talking to the stranger. That was likely to stick in their minds if anyone asked them any questions. And even if it didn't, the interior of every air shuttle in the Swallow System was covered by cameras. Given who he was and who his sister had been, the Fivers—the agents of General Tyrone Matsuhito's Inspectorate Five, the Swallow System's secret police—would be very interested in any imagery of him. If he made a point of walking away at this point, they'd want to know why. On the other hand, if he just sat back down ...

He hesitated a moment longer, then calmly took his bag from the overhead compartment, opened it, pulled out a book reader, then closed the bag and put it back. He settled back into his seat, smiled at his companion (although there was no smile in his blue eyes), and flipped the book viewer open.

"I don't like people who crowd me on shuttles," he said conversationally. "Especially people I don't know who say they know me."

"That's not what I said. I said I know a lot *about* you, which is true. And candor compels me to admit that I caught this flight because you did."

"Really?" Frugoni leaned back. "I think I'm liking you less and less."

"That's a pity," Eldbrand said cheerfully, "because once you get to know me, you'll find I'm a very useful sort of fellow."

"There's that word again—'useful.'" Frugoni shrugged. "You want to book a tour of the Cripples? That's the only interest I could see us sharing. I mean, no offense"—a bared-teeth smile gave the lie to the last two words—"but you don't exactly look like somebody who'd be 'useful' to me in a professional sort of way."

The stranger actually chuckled.

"Oh, not in the way you're thinking, anyway!" he said feelingly. "I doubt I'd last fifteen minutes in the Cripples, and I don't have any local business accounts or contacts that could help your charter service's bottom line. But that wasn't what I was talking about."

"Well, these days, that's all I'm *interested* in talking about," Frugoni told him. "I'm not in the Corps anymore, despite that 'First Sergeant' business. I run a charter service—a damned good one, if I do say so myself—but it's still in the startup phase. I'm not interested in focusing on anything else right now."

"Not *officially*, anyway," Eldbrand said, and Frugoni tensed.

"You really are looking for trouble, aren't you?" His expression was as calm as ever, but his eyes were hard.

"This isn't a good planet for people who go around playing—what's the term? Agent provocateur, I think. All I am these days is a businessman. Okay, I'm pissed off as hell at Tallulah, and Tallulah's pissed off at me for competing with them for scraps of the tourist trade. But I'm making it work—mostly because I've got so much better contacts up in the Cripples, which is their own damned fault—and that's what I'm interested in. I don't like Tallulah, but I've decided the only place I can really hurt them is in their cash flow, and that's exactly what I'm doing, in my own modest way. *All* I'm doing. If you're trying to imply anything else—or if somebody, and I'm naming no names, wants you to get me to implicate myself—you're wasting your time. I'll put on my dancing shoes and pop the champagne if something really, really nasty happens to Tallulah, but I'm not stupid enough to try to *make* it happen. So why don't you take your obscure comments and peddle them somewhere else?"

"First Sergeant—I'm sorry, *Mister* Frugoni—if I were a Fiver, or even working for the SFC, I wouldn't need you to implicate yourself."

Frugoni's eyes flared. He started to reply, then stopped, unwilling to give the other any additional openings. He hadn't expected a provocateur to accept his challenge that openly. Now that the extraordinarily ordinary-looking man had done just that, he had no idea what to say next. And in a case like that, the best thing to say was absolutely nothing.

"Relax," Eldbrand said, then snorted softly. "Sorry. That's the last thing you're going to do. Clichés seem to rise to the surface at a moment like this, though. What I meant was that I'm here as a friend, or at least a . . . benevolent neutral as far as the Cripple Mountain Movement is concerned."

Frugoni reached casually into his jacket pocket and the worn hilt of a Mark 63 combat vibro blade settled into his palm. He wouldn't be walking away if this went as badly as it was beginning to seem it might, he thought almost calmly. But if he wasn't, then neither was the other man.

"Three months ago," Eldbrand said calmly, "on one of your trips to Wonder, you left your hotel, went to a bar named O'Casey's—a fairly *disreputable* bar, actually—and had half a dozen beers with a lady of . . . dubious reputation named Gladys." He grimaced. "As assumed names go I suppose 'Gladys' is no worse than Harvey, but I believe that many years ago you knew her as Chief Petty Officer Gloria Stephanopoulos. That was during your deployment to support an OFS op—in the Dillard System, I think. Do I have that right?"

An icy chill settled in Frugoni's belly. He never moved a muscle, but those blue eyes had taken on an even colder tinge. One that anyone who'd ever seen combat with First Sergeant Frugoni would have recognized instantly. Eldbrand, however, appeared oblivious to it.

"For the sake of argument, let's assume I do have it right," he continued. "And let's also—just for the sake of argument—assume I know about your friend's various business enterprises, including the gunrunning. And let's further assume I know the reason you were drinking all that cheap beer in that really kind of horrible bar was that you hoped Gladys could connect you with one of her suppliers. Somebody who might be able to come up with a few hundred military-grade pulse rifles, and maybe a few SAMs and anti-vehicle weapons."

"If there happened to be a single word of truth in these 'assumptions' of yours—which there isn't, of course—you'd probably be a dead man sometime in the next, oh, thirty seconds," Frugoni said softly.

"Now that would be a great waste, First Sergeant. Oh, I know you're not a Marine anymore, but I'm pretty sure I'm talking to the First Sergeant right now, not the 'legitimate businessman' you really, really want Five to think you are. Think about this for a moment. If anyone with the Inspectorate—hell, anyone on Tallulah's payroll, for that matter!—knew what I've just demonstrated *I* know, why in the world would they try to entrap you? Trust me, if the local authorities had the information I have, you'd have been 'disappeared' the instant you set foot back in Capistrano. I don't know if they'd have gotten you alive—even if they had, I expect the Marines' anti-interrogation protocols would be causing their interrogators all kinds of grief right now—but they sure as hell wouldn't pussyfoot around 'entrapping' you!" He shook his head. "You know even better than I do that that's not the way Matsuhito or Karaxis operates."

Frugoni sat back in his seat, the not-yet-activated vibro blade still in his hand, while his brain raced. Every instinct still warned him this was some sort of setup, but Eldbrand had a point. Swallow wasn't a place where the authorities worried a lot about niggling little things like evidence or proof. Not anywhere outside the Highlands, anyway. If anyone in Rosa Shuman's government had suspected any of what this stranger had just laid out in such a devastating detail, they would have grabbed him first and worried about substantiating it later . . . right after they finished filling in the grave.

They damned straight wouldn't waste time stringing me along in hopes of getting to Floyd, either, he thought. _If there was any way they could get their hands on him or Jason or any of the others, they'd've done it years ago. Tyrone and Karaxis don't need any more "evidence" to go after the boys than they would to grab me, but they also know there's no way any of them're poking their noses out of the Cripples anytime soon. And they know damned well I wouldn't invite Floyd to do anything of the sort . . . and that he'd know it was bogus if I did! So what the hell_ does _this guy want?_

"This isn't the kind of conversation I should have with anyone, especially a total stranger, on a public shuttle," he said. "Assuming, of course, that the conversation was going to go anywhere, anyway."

"Actually, public air shuttles are very good places for this kind of conversation," Eldbrand demurred. "They've got video, sure, but I noticed your eyes before you chose the seat. That's why I said it was in a good position, and it is, isn't it? You know the pickups can't get a good look at your lips—that bulkhead by the drink dispenser cuts off the one on the left side of the cabin at row twelve, and the one furthest forward on the right side is behind us. Now, if we were to get up and turn around and face to our left about, oh, thirty degrees, the one hidden in the row twenty-three light fixture could probably get a pretty good angle."

Frugoni's nostrils flared. Swallow's security forces didn't waste a lot of time camouflaging their snooping systems. After all, all of them were completely legal under the current inventive interpretation of the Constitution. But Eldbrand had unerringly catalogued all the video pickups which might have provided grist for a lip reader, including the one that *had* been hidden in the light fixture he'd mentioned. Frugoni had done the same thing before he selected his seat, with an unobtrusive little device he'd acquired from Chief Stephanopoulos, and he wondered if Eldbrand had a matching unit in his pocket.

"As far as audio systems," Eldbrand continued, "I'm afraid the ones covering our current zone are suffering from unfortunate interference right this minute." Frugoni tensed, and Eldbrand shook his head. "Don't worry. I'm sure someone at Five will wonder if you had anything to do with it, but when they investigate, they'll find that the gentleman in 21-B is responsible. And if they examine his luggage, they'll find a small but expensive stash of controlled technology in it. It's mostly bootleg molycircs and some spyware nanotech, but there are a couple of jammers in there, as well, and one of them, unfortunately, is turned on at the moment. Faulty switch. I'm afraid he probably never even noticed.

"I suspect he'll have a hard time explaining that, especially when his employers find the fund transfer from Rappaport Industries. It's my understanding Rappaport and Tallulah are involved in a bidding war with OFS over Tallulah's continued control here in Swallow, and I'll bet the authorities are going to assume he's involved in gathering information that might be useful to Rappaport. It probably won't end well for him." Eldbrand's smile was cold. "But I wouldn't lose too much sleep over it, if I were you. He's a TSE investigator and he's been smuggling other tech—and mindbender—for years."

The growing unhappiness Frugoni had felt as Eldbrand talked disappeared abruptly. Under normal circumstances, he wouldn't have liked to think about what might happen to someone set up in the fashion the other man had described. But while Frugoni had nothing against anyone willing to smuggle outlawed technology past Tallulah and its Swallowan stooges, mindbender was something else entirely. There were, unfortunately, always people stupid enough to try "just a taste" of anything, even mindbender, but as far as Vincent Frugoni was concerned, people that stupid should be drowned at birth. Mindbender was one of the very few drugs which was outlawed on virtually every planet because of its hundred percent addiction rate and inevitable ultimately fatal side effects. The fact that it had a nasty habit of inducing hyper-violent psychoses in the ending phase of its users' addiction made the authorities no fonder of it.

If Eldbrand was telling the truth, then the sooner someone—*anyone*, even Matsuhito—took the supplier off the street as permanently as possible, the better.

And if he is *a bender-pusher, nobody's going to believe a single damned thing he says about how that jammer in his bag wasn't* really *his, either.*

It was always possible, he reminded himself, that Eldbrand really was a Fiver and that everything he'd just said was a fairytale. It was becoming more difficult to cling to that belief, however. And if the other man really knew as much about his own activities in Wonder as he claimed *and* he'd been able to identify and make use of the pusher, he was obviously a force to be reckoned with.

"How'd you know he'd be on this shuttle?" he asked after a moment.

"Because he's been on this shuttle every time he came back on-planet for the last sixteen or seventeen T-months," Eldbrand said. "I'm surprised you didn't notice him, First Sergeant. The first four times he used it, he was here because it's the one *you* always catch. He's not here to keep an eye on you any longer, of course. That's why the woman with the purple hair in 6-C is on board. But he knows security's lax on this flight—after all, he's seen it from the other side often enough—so he's been taking advantage of it for his own purposes."

Frugoni's eyes flicked to the purple-haired woman, then back to Eldbrand.

"Oh, yeah. They're still keeping at least one eye peeled where you're concerned." Eldbrand shrugged. "I expect they'd've invited you in for a little talk quite some time ago if not for your military record...and the Nixon Foundation. I don't know how long Luther and his people will go on poking around here in Swallow, but I doubt they'll leave before the contest between Tallulah and Rappaport gets resolved one way or the other. His entire team's basically paid for by a Nixon grant from Rappaport."

Frugoni looked at him thoughtfully, then nodded. That made sense, and it explained a few things. The Nixon Foundation was one of those Solarian organizations that did well by doing good. Something like ninety percent of its donations and other funding went into overhead, travel expenses, and bloated salaries, although it did seem a bit more serious than most of its ilk where investigating human rights offenses was concerned. Jerome Luther, the leader of its "fact-finding team" here in Swallow, had actually uncovered a genetic slave ring in the Cooper System, less than a hundred light-years from Sol. Unlike quite a few of the independent newsies Nixon deployed on its fact-finding missions, he had a League-wide reputation for serious digging, and Frugoni and the boys had wondered what brought someone with his media footprint to a backwater like Swallow.

"You know, Mr. Eldbrand, you seem to know an *awful* lot about what's going on here in Swallow for somebody whose accent makes it pretty damned clear that, as we say here, 'you're not from around here, are you?'"

"That's because my superiors have made a point of *learning* an awful lot about what's going on here in Swallow," Eldbrand replied calmly.

"And just why might that be? I doubt you're working for Rappaport, somehow. Don't tell me there's a third transstellar in the wood pile!"

"No, nothing that straightforward," Eldbrand said. "Let's just say—for the purposes of this initial conversation—that I represent a sovereign star nation which, for reasons of its own, is interested in supporting worthwhile causes like the Cripple Mountain Movement."

"Out of the bigness of its heart, I'm sure." Frugoni snorted. "Excuse me, Mr. Eldbrand, but I stopped believing in the Easter Bunny about the time I learned to head a football."

"I never said the star nation in question didn't have

ulterior motives." Eldbrand's tone was mild. "In fact, its motives are about as ulterior as they get. When you're likely to find yourself in a shooting war with the Solarian Navy, it's probably a good idea to find anything you can to ... distract the Sollies' attention from *you* and focus it somewhere else. So my superiors started looking for distractions, and what happened to your sister—and how your brother-in-law and his family reacted to it—was pretty damned visible a few years ago. It even made the mainstream Solly news services; that's why Nixon sent Luther out here in the first place—ostensibly, at least. The first data search we did on this neck of the woods turned up the coverage, and after that it wasn't hard to figure out roughly what was going on. Not when you're prepared to spend enough money and you have the kind of sources somebody like ... my superiors have, anyway. And, frankly, money's not a big issue for us. Not when we're looking at the alternative to spending it, anyway."

"I've seen this game played a time or two before," Frugoni replied, turning to look out the window beside him. "Usually by some fat-cat corporation trying to muscle in on somebody else's territory."

"Or by OFS," Eldbrand said quietly. Frugoni's eyes snapped back to his face, and he nodded. "Our people figured that was why you were already planning to leave the Marines even before your sister was killed, First Sergeant. You didn't like what happened in Al-Bakiya one bit, did you?"

"No," Frugoni said harshly. "And I especially didn't like the fact that OFS convinced Brisbane and her people that they'd support her and then threw all of them to the fucking wolves as soon as she'd given them the excuse to move us 'peacekeepers' into the system."

"And you're wondering if my superiors would do the same thing with you." Eldbrand nodded again. "Frankly, I thought that might be a problem for you. So one of the reasons I'm here is to do my best to convince you that won't happen here. I expect you to be a hard sell. I hope so, actually; I prefer working with people who have functional brains. But the truth is, we have every reason to want you to succeed ... and every reason not to get known as the sort of people who do the kind of thing OFS did to Andrianna Brisbane and the Al-Bakiyans. I'm afraid we won't get to that bit until we reach the 'I'll-show-you-my-cards-if-you'll-show-me-yours' stage, but I think once we do, you'll understand why I genuinely believe you'll decide we can be trusted."

"And if I don't decide anything of the sort?"

"Then I get back on my ship and head home, no harm, no foul." Eldbrand shrugged. "You're only one of several star systems we're looking at, to be honest. Given Tallulah's record, we'd be particularly happy to see it taken down, but we're in no position to be pursuing purely altruistic options. So if you and the Allenbys aren't interested, we'll wish you well and go looking for someone else to help."

"I see."

Frugoni leaned back in his seat, the book reader open in his lap, and contemplated his seatmate thoughtfully for the better part of two minutes.

"You've got my attention, anyway," he said finally. "I'd dearly love to know how you came by all your in-system information. Maybe I'll even find out. But you've impressed me, which I'm sure is what you had in mind, and your offer certainly sounds worth at least investigating. But I'm sure you understand I can't—and won't—try to speak for anyone else without checking with them first. So who—besides 'Harvey Eldbrand'—do I tell them we're talking to?"

"That's one of the things we find out when we get to the I'll-show-you-my-cards stage," the other man said. "For now, if you don't want to call me Eldbrand, how does . . . Firebrand strike you?"

SEPTEMBER 1921 POST DIASPORA

"I can understand why you might be a little...puzzled. And obviously it wouldn't be very smart of you to simply take my word for it that I'm one hell of a nice guy. On the other hand, we're not going to get anywhere if we both just stand here with the pulsers in our pockets aimed at the other fellow."

—Damien Harahap to
Tomek Nowak,
Lądowisko, Planet of
Włocławek

Chapter Nineteen

"GOOD AFTERNOON, ENSIGN ZILWICKI."

Helen turned towards the voice as the maître d' showed her into the restaurant's main dining room. Quillen's was one of the city of Thimble's better eating places, and its prices reflected that. But it was also close enough to both Governor Medusa's mansion and Augustus Khumalo's dirtside headquarters to be popular with the Navy.

"Lieutenant Archer," she said, nodding courteously to the red-haired, green eyed senior-grade lieutenant. He was seated at one of the restaurant's prized corner tables with one of the few people in Spindle Helen had gotten to know fairly well, and she smiled at his companion. "Ms. Boltitz."

"Would you care to join us?" Archer said. "We've only just placed our orders."

"Thank you, Sir," she said, although she had to wonder if she'd have been inviting any third wheels in his place. Admiral Gold Peak had been back in Spindle for less than two full days, after all, and she'd spent most of the first day coping with the results of the Battle of Manticore. Helen knew how much Commodore Terekhov had hated telling her about it, and Archer, as her flag lieutenant, had been just as frantically busy as his boss. He couldn't possibly have had the time to pick up the social threads here in Spindle, and if *she'd* been male and had a friend who looked like Helga...

Be nice, Helen, she cautioned herself. *After all, he is Admiral Gold Peak's flag lieutenant. There could be all kinds of legitimate business reasons for him and Helga to grab a quick lunch together.* She snorted mentally at the thought. *Oh, I'm sure it's "just business"!*

"What's this 'Ms. Boltitz' about, Helen?" Helga asked with a raised eyebrow as the maître d' pulled out Helen's chair. "Have I offended you somehow?"

"No, but this is sort of a formal venue," Helen replied, waving one hand at the crowded restaurant about them.

"And it would have been grossly disrespectful of the Ensign to allow herself to lapse into informality in the presence of an officer of such towering seniority as myself, Helga," Archer said sternly. "I'd've thought you knew that!"

"How *do* you fit that head of yours into a beret, Gwen?" Helga asked.

"It's difficult...difficult," he replied mournfully. "I have to have it sized up at least twice a week."

Helga chuckled, and he smiled at her, then turned back to Helen.

"I know we haven't had the opportunity to really introduce ourselves to each other, Ensign Zilwicki," he said. "On the other hand, we're probably going to spend a lot of time liaising with each other, so I thought that it might be a good idea for us to get to know one another. I didn't realize you and Helga had already met, although given another six months or so it *probably* would've occurred to me that the two of you must have, given what she does for Minister Krietzmann and what you do for Commodore Terekhov."

"It probably really would have, Helen," Helga told her earnestly. "He's *very* quick that way for someone with a Y-chromosome."

"And you're grossly disrespectful to someone of my advanced years, Helga," he said severely.

"Oh, forgive me!"

Helen smiled as she unfolded her napkin, draped it across her lap, and reached for the printed menu. She knew they were deliberately using their banter to put her at ease, but it was also clearly natural to them, and she was glad. Helga seemed like one of the nicest people she'd ever met, and the warmth in her eyes when they rested on Lieutenant Archer was obvious.

Helen allowed her own eyes to consider Archer thoughtfully while she considered what she'd been able to learn about him. Lieutenant Gervais Winton Erwin Neville Archer—no wonder he preferred the nickname "Gwen"—was probably six or seven T-years older than Helga. That made him ten T-years older than Helen herself, although he seemed as unconcerned by that as by the difference in their ranks. He had red hair, eyes as green as Helga's, and a snub nose. Given that he was a third-generation prolong recipient like Helen, he looked like Helga's kid brother, but there was nothing "brotherly" about his body language as he sat beside her at the table. He was also, as the second of his numerous given names indicated, a distant cousin of Countess Gold Peak and Empress Elizabeth, although he was obviously—and thankfully—immune to the towering sense of entitlement common to too many aristocrats of Helen's acquaintance. And, unlike many a Gryphon Highlander, she'd met quite a lot of those aristocrats.

And he doesn't have the drawl, either. Thank God.

A real live waiter appeared at her elbow to take her order and she considered the menu for a moment.

"Is the Montana sirloin shipped fresh, or has it been frozen?" she asked.

"At *Quillen's*?" The waiter looked deeply offended by the very thought.

"Then that's what I'll have, extra rare," she told him. "Just saw off the horns and show it the fire—briefly. Baked potato with sour cream and chives, and a side salad. Bleu cheese dressing. And do you have iced tea?"

"I'm afraid not, Ma'am." This time the waiter looked confused rather than offended, and she shook her head with a smile.

"Then just bring me a carafe of hot tea, lots of sugar, and a couple of tumblers of ice."

"Of course, Ma'am."

"Oh, and a couple of slices of lemon, too," she added.

"Certainly, Ma'am."

He disappeared and Helen looked back to see her table companions regarding her with quizzical expressions.

"Hey, they'd better get used to serving iced tea," she said. "I picked up a taste for it from the Graysons

I've met—like Lieutenant Hearns, Helga—and she's not the only Grayson serving with us right now."

"I can see that," Archer said. "It's your cooking instructions that seemed a bit...colorful."

"What?" She frowned, then snorted. "Oh, you mean the 'saw off the horns and show it the fire' bit?" He nodded, and she chuckled. "Sorry. I'm afraid I've been corrupted. That's the way Stephen Westman always orders it."

"Really?" Archer smiled. "Somehow I'm not surprised. Everything I've heard suggests Mr. Westman's a...larger than life character."

"That's definitely one way to describe him," Helen acknowledged.

"That's what I thought. Admiral Gold Peak wanted to meet him when we were in Montana, but there wasn't time. I hadn't realized *you*'d met him, though."

"Commodore Terekhov assigned me as Mr. Van Dort's personal aide while the *Nasty Kitty* played diplomatic tennis between Spindle, Split, and Montana. Mr. Westman and I got to know one another pretty well during his meetings with the Commodore and Mr. Van Dort."

Archer nodded, and she decided not to mention how much—and how painfully—she'd reminded Westman of Suzanne Bannister Van Dort, his best friend's sister...and Bernardus Van Dort's long-dead wife.

"Good. That gives me something else to pick your brain about." Archer shook his head. "Admiral Gold Peak's devoured every report she could get her hands on about events here in Talbott, and she's had me read 'em, too. She figures the more I know about them the better when it comes to handling her schedule. And

Helga's been a goldmine about Dresden and things here on Spindle, but you were right there while Van Dort and Sir Aivars talked Westman into laying down his guns, and he still seems to carry a lot of clout on Montana. Anything you can tell me about him would be more than welcome, Helen."

"Really?" Helen sat back, thinking, then shrugged. "Well, the first thing anyone needs to know about Stephen Westman is that he's a Montanan. They're all a little crazy, but he's crazier than most. In fact, he's almost as crazy as a Gryphon Highlander. I think he and my father would get along really well . . . assuming they didn't kill each other first. I remember the first time he met with us, and—"

✧　　✧　　✧

That Frugoni's a tough little bastard, Damien Harahap reflected with more than a trace of admiration as he closed the file. *I wish I'd been able to meet his brother-in-law, but that old saying about judging somebody by the company he keeps probably comes into play here. A man like Frugoni wouldn't play second fiddle to someone he didn't think deserved his support . . . and allegiance. That says one hell of a lot about Allenby right there.*

Which it did, of course.

He closed and security-locked the file. He'd let a couple of T-weeks pass before he went back for the final edit of his analysis of Swallow. It was always a good idea to let his thoughts settle and put a little distance between events and his considered judgment of them. But the *Факел* was approaching their next port of call, and it was time he turned his attention to the next system on his list.

This one was going to be tougher, he thought. Bardasano's people had created a credentialed cover that would make it absurdly easy to get into the system without being flagged as a potential subversive by the local security forces, but contacting the system's real subversives wasn't going to be easy, since first he had to figure out who the hell they were.

There had to be some, of course, however well hidden they might be. Even the most cursory examination of Włocławek made that clear. Although the material from Bardasano's analysts was a lot sketchier than anything he'd had going in on Swallow, they'd pulled together a comprehensive summary of the local power structure and political equation that could have served as a checklist for any regime intent on radicalizing its eventual executioners. It was just that those same analysts hadn't been able to point Harahap at any recognized contact point for the anti-regime movement which had to be bubbling away somewhere. And for all his cover's good points, it was likely to create a few initial trust issues where any such movement was concerned.

Part of the reason the analysts hadn't been able to pick out a contact point here was that they lacked the degree of access they'd had in Swallow because none of the League's transstellars had a finger in the Włocławek pie...yet. A couple were poking around the opportunities Włocławek offered, but so far the system's corruption—which was at least as bad as anything even a Solarian transstellar could have contrived—was entirely homegrown, and the failed reforms of the Ruch Odnowy Narodowej had only made it worse.

Much worse.

That sort of thing seemed to be inevitable when reformers were captured by the system. Harahap couldn't have counted the number of "National Renewal Movements" he'd seen end exactly the same way. In fact, it seemed to happen most often in the systems most desperately in need of reform. Probably because that was where one could always find someone most determined to protect the status quo by spreading around the corruption. Even the most fiery of firebrands—his lips quirked at his own choice of nouns—was a human being, and he'd yet to meet a human being completely immunized against avarice and the taste of power. Once reformers allowed themselves to be bought, they were almost always worse than the corruption they'd originally pledged to fight, and the current ugly unrest over the shoot-down of an air bus full of kids was one more indication that that was exactly what had happened in Włocławek.

Ziomkowski's real mistake was not purging the local kleptocracy, he thought now. *But that was because he was a* reformer, *not a revolutionary. He thought political power would be enough to "fix the system" without realizing the system itself* was *the problem. If he'd been ready to take a page from Rob Pierre and send a few thousand people to the wall, confiscate a few hundred fortunes, he might actually have achieved something. As it was . . .*

Harahap's problem was a lot simpler than Włodzimierz Ziomkowski's had been, because his employers didn't care whether the system was fixed or blown up, just as long as the effort to do the fixing—or blowing up—was sufficiently spectacular. They'd prefer for it to fail, and he understood why, but the locals were more than welcome to succeed, as far as he was concerned. In fact, in his opinion, Bardasano and her "Alignment" had gotten at least part of their strategy wrong. Discrediting the Star Empire in the Verge probably would go a long ways towards undermining its ability to engineer additional Talbott-style annexations, yet "proving" Manticore's guilt as a *successful* provocateur would do the Manties far more damage in the League.

When word of Operation Janus reached Old Chicago, Kolokoltsov, MacArtney, and the other Mandarins would seize the propaganda coup in both hands. They'd gleefully portray Manticore as a corrupt, expansionist, treacherous, imperialistic star nation, and the softheaded Core World idiots who bought OFS' self-billing as "a galactic force for good" would eat it up like candy. But the Mandarins would also recognize the danger a *successful* Operation Janus represented to what OFS *really* did in the Verge, and that would be intolerable to them. *That* was the ball upon which Bardasano and her superiors should be keeping their eye. Given the interstellar balance of power, the Solarian League was the only player with the potential to actually destroy Manticore. Anything that didn't motivate the League to do just that was dissipated strategic effort, however inherently worthwhile it might be on a purely tactical level.

Maybe it is, he told himself, reopening the Włocławek file and running his cursor down the index. *But that doesn't mean they aren't going to pull it off in the end. And Bardasano's insistence that Janus has to target at least a few star systems with no Solarian presence is smart, really smart. It puts the "Manties'" efforts even further out in the open, and it's going to make any of the other corrupt local system governments very wary of—and pretty damned hostile to—any extension of Manticoran influence into* their *backyards*.

He chuckled softly at the thought, and not just because he was a craftsman who respected good workmanship. No, Damien Harahap remembered his own childhood, and anything that made someone like the Włocławek *Oligarchowie* sweat was just fine with him.

Just remember you're not here to make sure they succeed, Damien, he reminded himself.

Tomek Nowak frowned thoughtfully as the utterly nondescript off-worlder walked down the old-fashioned sidewalk from the front door of Szymański i Synowie and turned right onto the pedestrian way.

The fellow might not look like much, but he did seem to get around...and to such interesting places. Szymański and Sons was far from the largest vendor of medical supplies in the city of Lądowisko. It *was* one of the capital's oldest firms, and it had somehow evaded the voracious appetite of the *Oligarchia*, but its market share had shrunk drastically over the last several decades. Nonetheless, it remained the primary supplier of the Siostry Ubogich, and the needs of Szpital Marii Urbańskiej and its satellite campuses outside Lądowisko were enough to keep its doors open.

Exactly what this fellow wanted with a Włocławekan medical supply firm was something of a puzzle, however, and Nowak didn't like puzzles. Especially not when the person at the heart of them seemed to be trolling for information.

All Nowak knew about him was that he represented the Oscar Williams Madison Foundation, a Solarian charitable organization well over three T-centuries old.

On the face of it, somebody working for a charitable organization might be expected to spend time talking to the Sisters and their suppliers, but that would only have been true if the organization in question was really what it claimed to be, and OWMF hadn't been that in a long time. Nowak himself knew very little about the foundation, but his friend Radosław Kot, who'd first noticed Mr. Mwenge, had used his journalistic contacts to do a little research.

Kot's well-honed suspicions had been roused when Mwenge arrived in a private Solarian-registry dispatch boat which appeared to be little more than a glorified—and luxurious—private yacht. He'd become even more suspicious when he discovered that the Biuro Bezpieczeństwa i Prawdy had given Mwenge only the most cursory of glances when he arrived. Indeed, the BBP had cleared him through customs with accelerated priority and he'd been met at the spaceport by a representative—admittedly, a fairly low-level one—of Hieronim Mazur's Stowarzyszenie Eksporterów Owoców Morza. That had been more than enough for Kot to dig deeper, and he'd discovered that the Oscar Williams Madison Foundation was quite well known in certain circles. The original organization had long ago been co-opted by the Office of Frontier Security, and while it continued to raise a great deal of money for its ostensible projects, ninety percent of those donations went into staff, overhead, and its directors salaries. In addition, it was liberally subsidized by OFS and various corrupt transstellars in need of good publicity in the League, where OWMF spoke fulsomely of its own good works in the poor, benighted star systems of the Verge . . . and of how generously OFS and whatever transstellar was currently paying it contributed to its efforts there.

Given the protests which had raged through the capital for three weeks after the air bus shoot-down—and the savage crackdown which had followed—that was exactly the sort of favorable PR the Party needed just now. Personally, Nowak thought Krzywicka and Pokriefke should be more focused on *local* opinion, but the *łowcy trufli* were always more worried about how opinion might affect business and tourism than about little things like blood in the streets.

That was probably enough to explain how Mwenge had breezed through security, and he was *certain* it explained the visits Mwenge had made to the Komisja Wolności i Sprawiedliwości Społecznej's offices here in Lądowisko. Bjørn Kudzinowski's "Freedom and Social Justice Commission" would be the logical agency to issue an off-world shill's marching orders. But that *didn't* explain the fact that he actually was contacting legitimate charitable entities here in Włocławek. Unless, of course, he hoped to use his contacts with them to dig for information on the local star system's subversive elements.

And given how half the Projects took to the streets after the air traffic hack went viral, Pokriefke has to be a hell of a lot more worried about any organized subversives than she was before. I may despise her, but unlike Mazur's, her brain actually works. Sometimes, at least.

Whatever else the stranger might be, however, Nowak had come to the conclusion he *probably* wasn't an agent of the BBP or the BDK. They seldom operated solo—which was wise, given how uniformly beloved they were—and there was no sign of any backup at all for Mwenge. That didn't rule out the possibility that he and his precious foundation were working for one of the *łowcy trufli* who'd gotten a sniff of the Krucjata Wolności Myśli's existence and launched a private venture to smoke it out, however.

No, it doesn't, Tomek, he told himself. *But if that's what he is, he's being awfully subtle, and that's not usually the hallmark of somebody working for Mazur or the other* oligarchowie. *"Subtle" isn't in enormous demand when you've already got the courts in your pocket.*

Mwenge moved on down the Mazowiecki Street pedestrian way, headed more or less towards Lądowisko Spaceport. If Nowak's information was correct, he had a shuttle on one of the private pads, so he was probably headed back to his ship. That might—or might not—indicate that his business (whatever it was) in Włocławek had been completed.

The smart *thing to do would be to just let him go his way while you go yours, Tomek, and you know it. The question is whether or not you're going to* do *it.*

He snorted at the thought, because it wasn't really a question at all.

He tugged his hat brim a bit lower, shoved his hands deeper into the warmth of his jacket pockets, bent his head against the winter wind, and matched the off-worlder's pace.

❖   ❖   ❖

Damien Harahap considered the imagery projected onto the contact lens in his left eye. The tiny optical pickup hidden in one of his rather ornate belt's ornamental silver conches gave him a hundred and sixty-degree view of the street behind him. It was a relatively simple bit of technology he'd found useful on many occasions.

The man ambling along behind him was a tallish, broad-shouldered fellow. He'd been there for the last four blocks, and he'd been waiting on one of the benches in the small park outside Szymański i Synowie when Harahap came back out. It was possible he'd simply had a hankering for fresh air. But given that the temperature was barely five degrees above freezing, it would have to be a greater than normal appetite for *cold* fresh air.

You, Damien Harahap, he told himself, *are a suspicious, distrustful, and generally paranoid fellow.*

He turned down a side street, moving away from the main thoroughfares and into a part of Lądowisko the Włocławek Bureau of Tourism really didn't want visitors to see. He passed a burned out storefront and wondered how long it had been boarded up. Had it been a casualty of the recent riots? Or did its charred, forlorn squalor simply represent the norm for this neighborhood? There was no way to tell, but the fellow behind him followed past it without missing a step, and Harahap nodded to himself.

Now for the interesting part, he thought. *This guy could be a BBP agent who'd like to ask you a few pointed questions, Madison Foundation credentials or no, given who you've been talking to for the last six days. If he's not that, odds are he's just an ordinary, garden-variety thug who's noticed how much cash you've been flashing around. Then again, it's always possible . . .*

Actually, he was reasonably sure his shadow wasn't

with the Biuro Bezpieczeństwa i Prawdy. If he had been, he'd almost certainly have already flashed a badge and started putting those pointed questions quite some time ago. And he probably would've shown at least a modicum of courtesy when he did, given who "Dupong Mwenge" worked for. But it was also possible he hadn't gotten the word on who "Mwenge" was, and the local regime's enforcers seldom objected to making their presence visible as a warning to their fellow citizens. Besides, agents of something like the BBP tended to come in two flavors: the subtle, unobtrusive sort (rather like one Damien Harahap), or else the truncheon-wielding, head-breaking sort. This fellow didn't fall neatly into either category.

Harahap's eyes narrowed as he approached a gate in the decorative but battered fence to his left. The wilderness beyond the fence had probably been a pleasant little park once upon a time—Lądowisko's original architects had tucked scores of small green spaces into the street grid of the capital's older sections—but now winter-gaunt trees loomed over mazes of underbrush which had devoured playground equipment and what had been shaded walks.

It was the sort of place muggers dreamed of, and Harahap began to whistle tunelessly as he stepped through the open gate.

❖　　❖　　❖

Now that's *an interesting development*, Nowak thought. *I think he must've spotted me. The question is why he's so obligingly wandering into such a handy dark corner. Somehow I doubt it's because he likes the color of my eyes.*

He followed his quarry—if that was what Mwenge

truly was—to the gate, then hesitated, conscientiously trying to think of some sort of BBP scenario that might make any sense. He couldn't. If the *czarne kurtki* suspected he was part of something like the Krucjata Wolności Myśli, they'd invite him downtown for a chat by breaking down his door in the middle of the night. They certainly wouldn't wave a mysterious off-worlder under his nose and expect him to fall into some kind of trap. Unless this was truly the first step in some convoluted attempt to infiltrate the KWM's membership.

You really ought to ask Tomasz before you go charging off half-cocked, he told himself. *You know you're too inclined to act first and think second... or third. And it's not like you're the only one you could be putting at risk.*

All of that was true, but he knew he wasn't going to ask anyone. Partly because there was no time—not if he meant to take advantage of the opportunity Mwenge had so courteously provided. But there was another reason. If Mwenge turned out to be one of the BBP's leg-breakers, Nowak would deal with him, one way or another. And if the *Biuro* ended up dealing with *him*, instead, at least he'd limit the damage to just himself.

Assuming the suicide protocols worked as promised, anyway.

He followed the other man into the park.

◇　　◇　　◇

Harahap turned sideways, edging through a gap in the overgrown bank of some unpleasantly thorny native shrub which squeezed tightly on the rutted path. On the far side, he found a small, muddy pond, heavily grown with some sort of reed. A thin skim of ice reached out across the shallows to where a single, forlorn waterfowl floated disconsolately. It was, he thought, a fitting metaphor for the gray, sullen despair-flavored discontent all about him ... except for the volcanic heat growing steadily hotter *under* that tide of dissatisfaction. Even making due allowance for the inherent stupidity of greed and a certain lack of imagination he found it extraordinary that none of the local security agencies seemed to grasp that the ice under their feet was as thin as the ice fringing the pond before him.

There was no ready exit from the pond's cul-de-sac, however, and he shrugged. He would have preferred to have a bolthole if he needed one, but sometimes an agent simply had to play the hand he'd drawn. He moved a few meters closer to the pond, then turned and faced back the way he'd come, still whistling and with one hand in his right coat pocket.

Nowak had never spent any time in this particular park, since he had an aversion to beating off muggers. Now, unfortunately, Mwenge had given him the slip. He had to be somewhere along one of the paths, but he'd managed to get around the initial bend and disappear before Nowak rounded it in pursuit, and the Włocławekan had no idea how those paths were arranged.

He stood very still, listening. The normal city sounds were faint and muted by the ratty, once elegant tenements that rose like some decaying ceramacrete canyon around the park. The cold, cutting wind was broken into little more than an unpleasant breeze by the same tenements, and as he cocked his head he heard—very faintly—the sound of someone whistling.

This is getting ridiculous. Why didn't he just leave a trail of breadcrumbs *like the kids in that old story?!*

Well, either it was an ambush after all or else this Mwenge really wanted to talk to him badly.

There was only one way to find out.

◇   ◇   ◇

As the man tailing him pushed through the same prickly gap, Harahap revised his size estimate upward. The fellow had very broad shoulders, too, and he carried himself like someone who spent at least an hour or so every day in the gym. He also seemed unsurprised to find Harahap waiting for him. His expression never flickered as he used his left hand to disengage a thorn-edged branch from the right sleeve of his coat; his *right* hand, however, stayed as firmly in his coat pocket as Harahap's own hand.

"I wondered when you'd be along," the ex-gendarme said calmly as his right thumb disengaged the safety on the compact pulser in that pocket. "Welcome to my office."

His left hand waved to take in their desolate surroundings, and the newcomer snorted in what seemed like genuine amusement.

"You wondered that, did you?" he said. "Well, I wondered why you were so obliging about showing me the way here."

"Sometimes you have to be 'obliging' to get the people you're interested in meeting to talk to you."

"Really?" The other man tilted his head. "And what makes you think I might be that kind of people? As far as I can tell, all you've done for the last week is talk to the kind of people someone working for a charitable foundation—especially one like yours—ought to be talking to. Which isn't at *all* the kind of people *I* am."

"No," Harahap conceded. "On the other hand, the people I do want to talk to would know what was going on with organizations like the Siostry Ubogich. And they'd probably get suspicious and come all over curious if someone from off-world started talking to those same organizations. Especially if that off-worlder let slip just how much he disapproved of the SEOM and the *łowcy trufli*." He smiled thinly. "And, while we're at it, I should probably point out that I'm none too fond of Minister Bezpieczeństwa i Prawdy Pokriefke, either."

He pronounced the Polish better than most off-worlders, Nowak noticed. At the same time, his accent was additional proof he *was* an off-worlder. But . . .

"You may not realize it, Mr. Mwenge, but that kind of talk can get someone in trouble here in the Włocławek. And for someone who's not fond of *Mała Justyna*, her *czarne kurtki* were awfully quick to get you passed through security when you arrived. For that matter, Hieronim Mazur's not in the habit of sending *Stowarzyszenie* representatives to greet his more trenchant off-world critics. Assuming they really are critics, of course." He smiled thinly. "I'm sure you can understand my confusion here."

Harahap smiled back as his earbug translated "*Mała Justyna*" into Standard English. "Little Justyna," was it? That was one his intel reports had missed, and he wondered how. Somehow the nickname didn't sound like a term of endearment.

"I can understand why you might be a little... puzzled," he said out loud. "And obviously it wouldn't be very smart of you to simply take my word for it that I'm one hell of a nice guy. On the other hand, we're not going to get anywhere if we both just stand here with the pulsers in our pockets aimed at the other fellow."

Harahap smiled more broadly as Nowak's eyes narrowed.

"Now," he continued in the reasonable tone of a man commenting on the weather, "I suppose it's possible you'd have no interest at all in talking to someone who, A, doesn't like what he sees in this system; B, managed to come up with a cover identity the local regime actually *welcomed* on-planet; and, C, might be in a position to provide someone here in Włocławek who didn't much care for his current government with assistance in *changing* that government."

He smiled again, more broadly, as the eyes which had narrowed went suddenly wide.

"By the way, I'll deny I ever said any of that if it should turn out you're actually a deep admirer of Pierwszy Sekretarz Krzywicka."

"And if I recorded it while you were saying it?" Nowak asked, sparring for time while he tried to deal with his astonishment.

"Well, in that case," Harahap reached into his left hip pocket and slowly and carefully extracted a small device and held it up, "I will be bitterly disappointed in the box of toys my superiors sent me out with."

"What's that?" Nowak's voice was suddenly deeper, sharper, and Harahap shrugged.

"Check your com," he suggested.

Nowak looked at him suspiciously for a moment, then raised his left arm, shooting his jacket cuff to look at the bracelet on his wrist. He gazed at it for a moment, then his eyes snapped back to Harahap.

"I'm afraid you need a new one," Harahap said pleasantly. "And this time you might want to invest in one that's hardened against directional EMP. On the other hand, I think I can be pretty sure any recorders hidden about your person are equally dead. And unless the pulser in your pocket's military grade—like the one in *my* pocket—I doubt you'll be able to shoot me very well. So if it's all the same to you, I'll take my hand out if you'll take your hand out and maybe we can talk like civilized men for a few minutes." He smiled again, and this time there was genuine warmth in the expression. "I promise not to ask you to make any commitments or even tell me who you are . . . this time. But judging from your actions, and unless you're a much better actor than I think you are, if you'll pardon my frankness, I think you'll find it worth your time."

Well, that went better than expected, Damien Harahap reflected an hour later as he watched his new acquaintance walk through the park gate and head back towards the heart of the city.

The Włocławekan hadn't fallen all over himself providing information about any secret organization he might or might not represent. And it was always possible he represented no such thing, although the fact that Harahap was still un-arrested strongly argued that he did. Barring that possibility—which would end badly for one Damien Harahap sometime very soon—he seemed to be exactly what Harahap had been looking for.

Tough, smart, and pretty damned ballsy, too, he thought. *And not just a low-level hanger on. Somebody else put him on to me, and he was either sent—or took it upon himself—to check me out.*

The Włocławekan had given him a name—Topór—which his earbug translated as "Axe" and probably bore about as much resemblance to his true name as Mwenge did to Harahap's. Aside from that, he'd spent almost the entire hour listening, with only an occasional question, while Harahap spun his spiel. Then he'd accepted the encrypted com combination and departed.

It would be interesting to see if he used it . . . and whether or not any second meeting he might arrange was a Biuro Bezpieczeństwa i Prawdy trap.

At least it'll keep life from being boring, Harahap told himself philosophically and resumed his interrupted walk to the spaceport, whistling once more and enjoying the brisk night while he thought about the PR strategy he was due to discuss with Bjørn Kudzinowski's senior assistant for off-world information.

It really *was* a marvelous cover.

Chapter Twenty

"SO, ADAM," KARL-HEINZ SABATINO leaned back with a tulip-shaped brandy snifter in one hand while he selected a cigar with the other, "I trust the funding arrangements are working out satisfactorily?"

Adam Šiml smiled—one might almost have said smirked—back at his host. His own snifter, with its seventeen centiliters of ninety-year-old Solarian brandy, sat on the inlaid end table of genuine Old Terran mahogany at his elbow as he leaned forward to select a cigar of his own from the humidor extended by Jiří Bradáč, Sabatino's personal aide.

"I certainly can't complain about the . . . promptitude with which the funds were transferred, Karl-Heinz," he acknowledged.

He unwrapped the cigar, snipped the end with the solid gold clippers Bradáč provided, and took his time lighting it with the attention to detail the task deserved. He rolled the fragrant, sweet-tasting smoke over his tongue, wallowing in the sensual pleasure with unfeigned delight and once again grateful to Lao

Than, the sixth-century Beowulfan physician who'd perfected the vaccine against cancer.

But then his mood darkened internally, although no sign of it touched his face, because he would have been even more grateful if that seventeen-T-century-old vaccine were currently available to every Chotěbořan. Before the *komár* plague, it had been; *since* the plague, it was available only to those prepared to pay for it in the clinics run by OFS and Frogmore-Wellington/Iwahara. As Frontier Security had pointed out, someone had to cover the expense of providing adequate medical care, and the fee wasn't exorbitant—only about thirty-six times what the vaccine cost. Of course "not exorbitant" was one of those relative terms, particularly for something that was a routinely available public health vaccination on other planets . . . and especially when Chotěboř's straitened economy meant the "not-exorbitant" fee was beyond the reach of all too many of the star system's citizens.

As were the standard therapies to prevent a dozen other diseases which no longer existed on properly administered planets which enjoyed a modicum of prosperity. Just as they hadn't existed on Chotěboř once upon a time.

But what the hell! A man couldn't expect to have *everything*, now could he?

The familiar resentment rolled through him, and he responded by making his smile a bit broader.

"Sokol can always use another sports complex," he said, "and quite a few of our stadiums and satellite fields need refurbishing." He shrugged. "Money's been tight for quite some time, Karl-Heinz, as I'm sure you understand. The ability to actually deal with some of those delayed repairs and renovations is going to make a lot of people very happy. Especially if we're in a position to base our future planning on an ongoing cash stream, as it were."

"I'm glad." Sabatino had his own cigar burning nicely and he blew a perfect smoke ring, watching with almost childlike delight as it drifted across the magnificently furnished library. Then he looked back at Šiml. "I can think of very few causes more worthy than your organization, Adam. I'm actually rather embarrassed that it's taken me this long to recognize just how beneficial Sokol's always been here in Kumang. And"—his hazel eyes narrowed ever so slightly—"if I can simultaneously earn Frogmore-Wellington and Iwahara a little goodwill by supporting them, I count that a beneficial secondary effect. A bit crass of me, I suppose, but I *do* represent businesses who exist to make a profit for their shareholders. If I can kill two birds with one stone, as it were, that's always a good thing, you understand. Especially when I have to justify expenditures to the accountants at the end of the day."

"Of course." Šiml nodded, drawing on his cigar. "And I understand how it might have taken a while for you to recognize just how worthy—and . . . beneficial— Sokol is. Or how beneficial it *can* be going forward, for that matter."

"That's exactly what I was thinking about when I approached you about the donation program." Sabatino beamed happily. "I trust the cash flow your Ms. Tonová and I have discussed will be adequate for your immediate needs?"

"For our *immediate* needs," Šiml stressed the adjective ever so slightly, "yes. It's more than adequate."

"Excellent. And"—Sabatino's eyes held his—"I'm sure we can address any future needs as they arise. Within reason, of course."

"Oh, of course," Šiml agreed.

Sabatino smiled again, remembering his conversation with Luis Verner and the system administrator's initial skepticism. To be honest, Sabatino had been a bit worried that Verner's concerns might have been better taken than he himself had cared to admit, once he started looking more closely at the proposition. Adam Šiml's reputation for civic-mindedness of the most revoltingly altruistic variety had appeared to be far better deserved than he'd assumed it could be. But Beowulf hadn't been settled in a day, and Karl-Heinz Sabatino hadn't achieved his current position by abandoning projects easily. He'd persevered, even though his initial personal contact with Šiml had seemed anything but promising. And it was working out very nicely, after all. According to young Bradáč's discreet taps into the Chotěbořian banking system, Šiml had skimmed just under forty percent off the top of Frogmore-Wellington and Iwahara's donations and grants to Sokol.

That was on the miserly side by the standards of Chotěboř's financial upper crust. Sixty or even seventy percent would have been closer to the norm, especially for an organization like Sokol, which could wrap itself—and its chief executive officer—in the mantle of all its manifold good works. But even forty percent was a welcome early sign. Once Šiml had settled fully into his new relationship, he'd undoubtedly increase his cut, and he was already responding—tentatively, to be sure, but responding—to subtle hints that his new patron might be willing to back a return to the political arena.

And what he's already taking is more than enough to put him under my thumb when he does, Sabatino thought, smiling benevolently at his guest. *He may not've taken as much as most of the other neobarbs on this benighted planet, but he's taken enough to shoot his reputation as a do-gooder immune to the attraction of filthy lucre right in the head. If his little arrangement with me ever becomes public it'll destroy him with his current support base—especially since it's such a contradiction of the front he shows everyone else.*

"It always does my heart good to be able to lend a helping hand to someone who devotes so much of his life and time to helping others," he said out loud. "And if I can make your own life a little easier in the process, why, that's even better from my perspective, Adam."

❖   ❖   ❖

"And how did dinner go?" Zdeněk Vilušínský asked pleasantly, and then chuckled as Šiml raised his right hand, middle finger extended.

"That well, did it?" the farmer said.

"The food was excellent and the brandy was even better," Šiml told him. "The problem was keeping it down, given the company."

"Is he really that much worse than, say, Cabrnoch or Kápička?"

"Depends on what you mean by 'worse.'"

Šiml crossed his library—much smaller and less grandly furnished than Sabatino's but filled with books and chips he'd actually read—and flopped into the chair behind his reading desk. Vilušínský followed him, settled into his favorite comfortable overstuffed armchair on the other side of the desk, and raised an eyebrow inquiringly.

"Cabrnoch's a pig in a trough." Šiml's calm, almost dispassionate tone turned the indictment of his star system's president into a flaying knife. "He's got every intention of hanging around and enjoying the hell out of his personal power for as long as he can, but he's also worried about what happens if he falls off the back of the *šavlozub*. You know as well as I do that he's grabbing cash with both hands and stashing it off-world to serve as his golden counter-grav if he has to make a run for it."

He paused, and Vilušínský nodded.

"That's bad enough, but Kápička's worse in some ways." He grimaced. "I wonder what Juránek thought he was doing when he recommended Kápička to Cabrnoch for Public Safety in the first place!"

"Probably that he had enough dirt on Kápička to guarantee he'd be the one who actually controlled the CPSF when push finally comes to shove between him and Cabrnoch—or anyone else, for that matter," his friend replied cynically.

"Then our esteemed vice president's even stupider than I thought he was." Šiml shook his head. "Kápička's got at least twice Juránek's IQ—which, admittedly, isn't that hard—and Juránek's a straight machine politician. Kápička isn't. And I doubt there's enough 'dirt' on Kápička for anyone to control him." Šimlr tipped his chair back. "There are occasions when I actually *like* the man. At least he likes football, and he's less addicted to living well at someone else's expense than Cabrnoch or Juránek. He's no saint, and he's sure as hell not passing up any 'legitimate' graft that comes his way, but I don't really think he's inherently vicious. The problem is that he genuinely believes that if all those 'subversive elements' get out from under Public Safety's heel, they'll launch some retaliatory reign of terror."

"And is he so wrong about what'll happen if our *jiskry* ever do find themselves in a position to retaliate?" Vilušínský asked softly.

"I hope he is, but I can't guarantee it," Šiml admitted with bleak frankness. "Some of our people—no, a *lot* of our people—are even madder than I am, and with good reason. People like Taťána Holečková, for example. Or Kateřina Lorenzová." He shook his head again, his expression even bleaker than his tone. "People who have dead or crippled or 'disappeared' family are going to want vengeance even more than they want justice, Zdeněk, and who are we to blame them? And that's where Kápička's logic breaks down. Every single name he adds to that list only creates more—and more bitter—opposition. Hell, for that matter, that's why some of his own agents've found their way into Jiskra, and you know it! In the end, his tactics are only going to make it one hell of a lot worse when the wheels finally come off."

"I notice you said 'when,' not 'if.'" Vilušínský smiled thinly. "That's one of the things I've always admired about you, Adam. Your optimism."

"I don't know if we'll manage to pull everything off the way we want to," Šiml replied, then snorted harshly. "I don't know if we'll manage to pull off *half* of what we want to! But you know as well as I do that the wheels *are* going to come off, one way or the other. It amazes me that people who sure as hell aren't stupid—like Kápička and Sabatino, or even Siminetti—can think they can go on forever without some kind of explosion."

"Adam, they know OFS and Frontier Fleet are standing behind them. Do you think for one second that someone like Verner would hesitate to break however many eggs it took to prop up his good friends at Frogmore-Wellington or Iwahara?" It was Vilušínský's turn to shake his head, his expression disgusted. "It wouldn't be the first time the all-benevolent OFS has been faced with a bunch of 'terrorist' neobarbs attacking their own 'openly elected government' and threatening the safety of the Solarian citizens whose investments are raising their system's standard of living to such heights! And"—his voice turned darker—"it wouldn't be the first time OFS courageously solved the problem by sending in the Solly Marines to kill however many of those 'terrorists' it takes, either."

"I didn't say the explosion would succeed," Šiml said grimly. "I said it's going to *happen*."

The two old friends looked at one another in the quiet library, and, after a handful of seconds, Vilušínský nodded. That, he thought, was the real reason Šiml had founded Jiskra in the first place. Adam Šiml was many things, but a natural revolutionary wasn't one of them. Vilušínský had never doubted his friend's loathing and hatred for someone like Jan Cabrnoch or Karl-Heinz Sabatino. Nor had he ever doubted Šiml's passionate desire to restore constitutional government and the rule of law to the Kumang System . . . or his personal courage and integrity. But what he was naturally was a teacher and a reformer, a humanist who abhorred the very thought of violence. Which, perversely, was what had finally carried him into active resistance. He was determined to impose some sort of control on that inevitable explosion he saw coming. To create a disciplined core that could both guide that explosion to success and restrain its excesses when it attained that success.

To save his homeworld from the blood guilt the demand of so many of its people for vengeance could so easily create.

For a man who's read so much history, he can be as blind as Sabatino, in his own way, Vilušínský thought now, sadly. *Or maybe he isn't blind. He's read a hell of a lot more of that history than I have, when it comes down to it. So he's got to know even better than I do how many revolutions have devoured leaders who were too moderate to suit the mob mentality. Maybe he's just willing to stand up and be devoured if that's what it takes to save Chotěboř's soul from itself. And if he is, what does that say about you, Zdeněk?*

He decided not to pursue that thought and gave himself a shake.

"I don't suppose Sabatino asked you for any receipts on your Sokol expense account, did he?" he asked, and Šiml chuckled.

"Hell no! He's just absolutely *delighted* at the proof that he's in the process of buying me off entirely."

Vilušínský didn't chuckle; he laughed out loud, instead.

Šiml was right when he said Karl-Heinz Sabatino was actually a very smart man. But he was a very smart man produced by a particular system and a particular mindset, and like many men—including, quite possibly, Zdeněk Vilušínský, he admitted—he seemed incapable of looking beyond that mindset. He saw the entire universe through the lens of his own experiences, his own expectations. And in his experience, everyone had a price.

Vilušínský had been as surprised as Šiml when the offer of a massive donation from Frogmore-Wellington Astronautics and Iwahara Interstellar landed on Šiml's desk at Sokol's central office. Květa Tonová, who was officially Šiml's secretary and actually his executive officer, had been stunned when she opened the message file and saw the amount Sabatino was offering to throw Sokol's way. It was the largest single contribution the sports association had received in well over a T-century, and the only string attached had been Sabatino's insistence on sitting down and personally discussing with Šiml what that money might be used to accomplish.

Šiml had been deeply suspicious, and neither he nor Vilušínský had doubted that the juicy offer contained any number of barbed hooks. In fact, he'd almost turned it down flat, because even though he'd been at a loss to imagine what Sabatino thought Sokol might accomplish for Kumang's absentee landlords, he hadn't expected it to be good for Chotěboř. But upon reflection, he'd decided to open the floodgate of cupidity as wide as Sabatino was willing to open it . . . if not for exactly the reasons the off-worlder might have expected.

As far as Vilušínský was concerned, anything that had happened more than, say, a thousand years ago was of limited interest, but Šiml was fond of truly ancient history, and he'd trotted out a quotation from some long-forgotten pre-diaspora revolutionary: "They will sell us the rope with which we will hang them," he'd said. If Sabatino wanted to pour money into the organization within which Šiml was building his movement, that was just fine with him.

Yet it had quickly become apparent Sabatino had rather more in mind than simply buying goodwill or inspiring Šiml to publicly endorse his policies or support the Cabrnoch government.

"You do realize Sabatino's little brainstorm has to be the most disastrous brilliant stratagem since Renato Alcofardo pissed away an entire star system by putting in the wrong puppet regime, don't you?"

"Only if it turns around and bites him in the ass the way Figuiera bit Alcofardo," Šiml countered. "And that means I have to be at least as smart as Figuiera was."

"I don't know about being as *smart* as he was, but I expect you're at least a much nicer person," Vilušínský said dryly. "I don't see any pogroms in your future."

"Assuming I have one of those, no." Šiml tipped his chair back farther. "Of course, that's what makes it so interesting, isn't it?"

Chapter Twenty-One

ERIN MACFADZEAN STOOD AND HELD OUT her hand as young Jamie Kirbishly escorted the tallish, very dark-skinned man into the office. Megan MacLean remained seated in the chair beside MacFadzean's, but her gray eyes were intent as Kirbishly's left hand made a tiny, almost imperceptible gesture. MacLean's gaze never flickered, although her body language might have relaxed a millimeter or two at the confirmation that their visitor was unarmed. Or, at least, that he wasn't armed with anything Kirbishly's sensor wand had been able to *identify* as a weapon, anyway.

"Mr. Bolívar," MacFadzean said.

"Ms. MacFadzean," the newcomer replied, shaking the proffered hand, and looked past her to MacLean. "Representative MacLean," he added with a respectful nod.

"Not any longer, I'm afraid, Mr. Bolívar," MacLean said, standing to extend her own hand. "Not for some time, now. I'm afraid I'm just a silver oak grower these days."

"Of course you are," Bolívar acknowledged with a slight smile. "That's what I'm here to talk to you about, after all. Mr. Hauptman was very pleased with Mr. Henry's initial analysis of the market possibilities here in Loomis. I won't pretend Mr. Hauptman's business analysts haven't identified quite a few other, potentially competing market openings, of course." He shrugged, his peculiar amber eyes, their irises heavily flecked with silver—evidence of some ancestor's fashion taste in genetic modification—bright as they met hers. "Personally, I'm very much hoping we find a way to do business in your star system."

"Well, yes, so am I." MacLean smiled back at him. "I hope you understand that my own silver oak plantations are still independently owned and managed, though. I'm afraid I won't be able to give you the sort of cut-rate prices SEIU is currently offering. On the other hand," her smile faded, "I *will* be able to offer you a long-term source, at least on a modest level, for a considerably longer period of time. I'm afraid I'm not a fan of Mr. Zagorski's harvesting practices. He's bringing a lot of timber to the market, but if you're interested in long-term purchases, he's not exactly doing our future supply any favors, Mr. Bolívar."

"Please, call me Toussaint," Bolívar said. "And I understand your point completely." He shrugged. "Mr. Hauptman's seen the results of that kind of . . . shortsightedness often enough. I suspect—in fact, I'm sure, given my instructions—that he's prepared to pay a reasonable premium to an independent supplier who can continue to meet his needs on a longer-term basis. The market for silver oak in the Star Empire's still relatively modest—it's not well-known there yet.

He expects it to grow once Manticoran craftsman and artists become more familiar with the wood's qualities, however, and he doesn't have any objection at all to keeping the supply limited in order to maintain the sort of price structure we envision. We'll also be looking at fairly substantial, regular shipments of seafood from Thurso, and the quantities of silver oak he's contemplating could easily be carried aboard the same freighters." The Manty smiled again. "Essentially, the profit on the seafood—which is a sustainable bulk commodity—will more than cover the transportation costs on the silver oak."

"I can see where that shipping model might make sense for him." MacLean nodded. "On the other hand, I think it would be wise for you, as his representative, to actually examine the plantations we'd be cutting for him. Should I assume you've been authorized to inspect them for him, Toussaint?"

Gray eyes held amber ones levelly for a moment, and it was Bolívar's turn to nod.

"Yes, I have." His tone seemed to say more than his words, but then he gave another of those warm, charming smiles. "I warn you, though," he added wryly, "that my expertise where silver oak's concerned is pretty superficial by Halkirk standards. I've boned up on the subject since Mr. Hauptman gave me this assignment, but I'd hardly consider myself any sort of silviculture expert."

"Fortunately, Ms. MacFadzean has all the expertise you could possibly ask for in that regard," MacLean told him. "In fact, she's my chief forester. Given that we're considering a long-term relationship with Mr. Hauptman's cartel—almost a partnership arrangement,

I suppose—I thought it would make sense to make her available to answer any of your questions. And, of course, to provide a personal tour of the stands."

"That would be most welcome," Bolívar said.

"I think that probably pretty much covers it from the air," Erin MacFadzean said the better part of two hours later.

She banked the air car slightly, cruising above the tops of the towering silver oaks at an altitude of two hundred meters. From that vantage, they could see for thirty kilometers, and the silver oak canopy stretched away, almost completely unbroken in every direction. At that, however, what they could currently see represented only about twenty percent of the MacLean family's holdings.

"I'm impressed," Bolívar replied, shaking his head. "I hadn't realized Ms. MacLean controlled this large a tract of timberland."

"Her family was one of the Loomis Expedition's first-shareholders." MacFadzean sounded faintly amused. "Nobody realized how lucrative the silver oak market was going to be at that time, and I suspect some of the other first-shareholders thought her ancestors were being foolish to take so much 'worthless woodland' here on Halkirk instead of holding out for a concession on Thurso." She shrugged. "Everyone already knew about the seafood potential from there, but only a handful—including Tammas MacLean—even suspected how much silver oak would be worth." She looked away from her passenger. "Or how much off-world interest it would spark," she added in a rather more somber tone.

"No, I can see how that might be." Bolívar's answering tone was carefully neutral, and MacFadzean inhaled deeply.

"I wonder if you'd care to walk through one of the stands we're currently harvesting?" she offered. "It's likely to be a bit noisy, but it would give you a 'ground-level' look at our harvesting techniques." She showed her teeth briefly. "I think you'll see why they're more sustainable than SEIU's current approach."

"I think that would be an excellent idea," Bolívar agreed, and she sent the air car scooting to the east.

Fifteen minutes later, the two of them stood watching logging crews carefully take down fifty-five-meter silver oaks. The long, straight trunks were close to five meters in diameter, and the harvesting crews were careful to leave every second mature tree—and *every* tree less than thirty meters tall—standing.

"Zagorski would take every one of them down," MacFadzean said, raising her voice to be heard over the sound of chainsaws and even old-fashioned axes. That voice was considerably more bitter than it had been. "There'd be nothing but stumps when that bastard was done, and he'd do a half-assed job of replanting."

"I take it he's not so very popular." Unlike Mac-Fadzean, Bolívar sounded almost whimsical, and she glared at him.

"You know damned well he isn't, or you wouldn't be talking to us," she said flatly. "I'm pretty sure there are bugs in most of our air cars, and I *know* all of our coms are tapped. It's a bit harder to plant bugs out here in the woods."

"Not impossible, I'm sure, though," Bolívar replied.

"Actually, pretty much, yes." MacFadzean shrugged. "We use a lot of autonomous drones to keep an eye on the state of the trees. Forest fires on Halkirk are a lot bigger economic disasters than they are other places in the galaxy, so not even MacCrimmon or MacQuarie complain too much about that. They're equipped with active as well as passive sensors, though, and I'm afraid we're not as well placed to do the kind of intensive maintenance SEIU does on its drones. That means about ten percent of them have . . . less than optimally efficient sensors which have a tendency to scramble electronics in their vicinity. It can be a real problem for our work crews' coms, actually."

"I see." Bolívar smiled. "Very neat. And for the same reason you use the drones out here you carefully *don't* sweep your air cars for bugs?"

"Oh, we sweep them occasionally . . . just not very well." MacFadzean bared her teeth. "The Uppies would be even more suspicious if we didn't, given Megan's role in the LRP. Besides, sometimes it's better to let the Uppies hear exactly what you're saying to each other, including an occasional conversation about how unhappy we are with the present management here in Loomis. The bastards wouldn't believe anything else we said, but it's amazing how careful we are to never suggest any extra-legal remedy for the situation."

"I see." Bolívar nodded, then looked at her very seriously. "Should I assume you *are* prepared to consider 'extra-legal' remedies?"

"We're headed that way," she replied, and shrugged as he raised his eyebrows. "Personally, I think it's inevitable we'll wind up doing exactly that. For that matter, Megan thinks the same thing. But she's been committed to...process-oriented reform, I suppose, for decades."

"In *Loomis?*" Bolívar inquired politely, and she snorted.

"She's an idealist, Mr. Bolívar. That's what makes people willing to follow her. Personally, I was a lot more skeptical than she was about the possibility of any meaningful sort of reform, but there didn't seem much else in the way of options. And when she organized the Loomis Reform Party, seven T-years ago, the LPP was actually promising 'free elections' under pressure from Zagorski's predecessor. I never liked the woman much, but she understood us one hell of a lot better than he's ever tried to. I doubt she ever intended the 'reforms' to go any further than window dressing, of course. What she wanted was something to let the locals vent and possibly even believe things would get better as a way to defuse the anger so many of us already felt." She shrugged again, and this time the shrug was sharp with suppressed violence. "I didn't really believe any 'reforms' were going very far then, and neither did Megan, but it was at least a chance. Until Zagorski came along and took the pressure off. At which point, we lost one of the two parliamentary seats we'd won in the very next election. It was about five months after that that Megan resigned the second one in protest over the way our voters had been intimidated and miscounted."

Bolívar nodded, and she turned away for a moment. Then she turned back to him.

"Sorry," she said, her voice a bit less harsh than it had been. "I know you already knew all that or you wouldn't have been talking to us. The thing is, though, that that's where Megan came from, and it's going to take her a little longer than it's taken me to decide we have to go beyond that. But at least we were able to convince her to begin setting up the Provisional Wing once we saw which way MacCrimmon was going to push MacMinn as soon as Zagorski gave him the nod. I think that's a pretty clear sign of where she's likely to end up."

Bolívar nodded again. He knew exactly when the Loomis Reform Party's underground, extra-legal branch had been organized, since MacLean's meeting with MacFadzean, Tammas MacPhee, and Tad Ogilvy was what had attracted Lieutenant Touchette's attention. MacPhee had held the other LRP seat in the local parliament, and he'd always been rougher around the edges than MacLean, while Tad Ogilvy was a very tough customer who'd organized the LRP in the city of Conerock. Both of them were rather less patient and more inclined toward direct action than Megan MacLean had ever been. Of course, he wasn't supposed to know who those people were—or even about the meeting.

"So how serious do you think she actually is?" he asked. "For a lot of reasons, I don't want to push any of you into doing anything you're not fully committed to. By the same token, though, as Mr. Henry said at his first meeting with you, we don't have unlimited resources. We need to invest them where we're likely to see the greatest return." He waved one hand in an almost apologetic gesture. "I don't want to be callous or cynical, but as much as we believe your situation here deserves support on its own merits, we can't afford to waste our effort if your people aren't ready to take our assistance and *act*."

"In all honesty," MacFadzean said frankly, "I can't give you an absolute answer. I will say Megan's going to have to be brought to that point gradually. At the moment, though, we're in the process of setting up what we've decided to call the Loomis Liberation League. We've been—*I've* been—having some very quiet conversations with people like Raghnall MacRory and his cousin Luíseach and...a few others. There are quite a lot of people who'd be inclined to support us and who we could probably count on to come out into the streets when the shooting started. I'm not talking to any of them yet, though." She shrugged yet again. "Some of them are noisy enough for me to be positive the Uppies have planted informants on them. At the very least, they're keeping them under surveillance, and the last thing we need is to be seen talking to them.

"My point, though, is that we're putting the ground-work in place and once it *is* in place, the pressure building here, especially with Zagorski's new logging policies, means it *will* be used."

"And have you had a discussion quite this frank with Ms. MacLean?" Bolívar asked shrewdly.

"No, not really," MacFadzean admitted. "Oh, she knows I think an open clash is coming, and she's stubborn enough she won't go down without a fight if it does. So after Nessa MacRuer arranged the meeting between me and your Mr. Henry, I told Megan I'd found a potential off-world source of financial backing and weapons. I didn't tell her exactly what it was, and I deliberately didn't mention your offer of naval support."

"Why not?" Bolívar cocked his head, and she sighed.

"Because she's not ready to hear about that yet. She's

a genuine patriot, and I think the thought of inviting *any* new interstellar interests into Loomis, given the mess SEIU's made here, isn't something she's ready to contemplate. I don't think she'd want me making any commitments in that regard just yet, and because she hasn't okayed anything like it, I'm not about to make any of them to you. Not yet. But I also think—no, I'm *sure*—that if you're able to provide us the kind of non-naval support Henry and I discussed it would be only a matter of time, and not a lot of that, before she decided to take the next step."

"I see."

Bolívar gazed up at the tree canopy for several seconds, his lips pursed in thought, then he looked back down at MacFadzean.

"I appreciate your honesty, but unless and until you're in a position to specifically tell us you *will* be planning on calling in naval support, we can't absolutely commit to provide it," he said. "We only have so many ships, and I'm afraid we're going to have to allocate them on what you might call a first-come-first-served basis. I'm sorry, but that's just the way it is. Having said that, I *think* we'd probably be able to peel off at least a couple of destroyers or a light cruiser or two on fairly short notice, which ought to be enough to discourage Frontier Fleet from anything too blatant in the way of support for MacCrimmon and Zagorski. And in the meantime, we could definitely provide small arms and even some crew-served weapons if you'd be interested in building up a stockpile."

"I'd be *very* interested in that." MacFadzean's eyes glowed, but then she frowned. "Getting them here, though—that might be a problem."

"We're talking about setting up a regular freight shuttle for seafood from Thurso," Bolívar pointed out. "From what I've seen of transstellars in general and SEIU in particular, nobody's going to turn up his nose or make any difficulties for somebody willing to buy the amount of fish we're talking about buying. And it's always been Hauptman policy to carry at least some small cargoes on spec for other destinations. When you couple that with the fact that we'll be buying silver oak from Ms. MacLean, I don't think there'll be much trouble about getting cargo shuttles down to the planet—particularly given how accustomed most of the local customs inspectors are to looking the other way for MacCrimmon's cronies and SEIU. I'm pretty sure we could get just about anything past them, as long as it's not full of fissionables or anything that . . . obvious, for the right baksheesh. And once we do get it down, I imagine all this lovely timberland"—he waved one hand at the surrounding silver oak—"would provide lots of places to hide any new toys you might acquire."

Chapter Twenty-Two

"SO WHAT DO WE *really* KNOW about this guy?" Mackenzie Graham asked a bit nervously. No, not really nervously, her brother thought. It was more a case of adrenaline lightly seasoned with apprehension.

"Only what I've already told you," he replied patiently.

"Which isn't one heck of a lot," she pointed out.

"Actually, it's less than that," he acknowledged. "But it's still time we—I—talk to him, Kenzie, and you know it."

"I just don't like the thought of your meeting with him in such a public place, Indy."

"What?" He cocked his head with a quizzical smile. "You think I should bring him here?" A small wave took in the crowded restaurant around them. The Soup Spoon always did well during lunch hour, given the quality of the food and the reasonable prices.

"No, of course not." Mackenzie shook her head quickly.

The Soup Spoon was their favorite restaurant, and had been for a long time. In fact, the Graham family had been eating in Tanawat Saowaluk's establishment since long before Bruce Graham had fallen afoul of the Seraphim System authorities. Long enough, in fact, that Tanawat was "Thai Grandpa" to Indy and Mackenzie. Because that relationship had been so long-standing, they could go on eating there regularly without arousing suspicion—and "just happen" to meet with any number of interesting people. They had to hold down the total numbers of such "chance encounters," but it was a public eatery, after all. And the fact that its proprietor, his wife, their surviving son, their older biological daughter, and their adopted daughter and her husband—plus two more of their servers—were all members of the Seraphim Independence Movement made it a perfect message drop. Almost anyone could come by for a bite to eat, which meant Indy and Mackenzie could get those messages to that same almost anyone without any personal contact at all.

And without saying a single word over any com when unfriendly ears might be listening.

"Bringing him here would be unusually dumb even for you," Indiana's loving sister continued. "But I'm not sure meeting him in a public library is a whole lot smarter."

"I have to meet him *somewhere*," Indy pointed out. "And sneaking off to meet in some dark corner somewhere is a whole lot more likely to point the scags in our direction. The odds might be pretty good they'd never notice, but if they *did* notice, they'd probably be inclined to wonder just why a Cherubim street hand's hiding in the shadows for a routine meet with an off-worlder." He shrugged. "Frankly, I think the library's the best combination of privacy and 'here I am in the open doing my day job' I could find."

Mackenzie nodded, more in acknowledgment than agreement, yet he had a point. From the beginning, he'd transacted a lot of his "graymarket" deals in the capital's library branches. They were a public space which still operated on a pretty close to round-the-clock schedule and they fitted well with the fact that he was a voracious reader. Indy spent hours parked in various library reading rooms, actually using the readers or hard copy books from the stacks, and neither of them doubted that the Seraphim System Security Police had a complete copy of his reading list, given what had happened to their father. That was why there were no "subversive" titles on it. But the library also offered a street hand like Indy a handy, cost-free place to meet clients, and it made a lot of sense to conceal the upcoming meeting as a regular business deal. It was just that every library was under twenty-three-hour-a-day surveillance by the SSSP.

Of course, every *public place is pretty much under scag surveillance,* she reminded herself. *And if this guy actually is what you're afraid he* might *be, it won't matter where Indy meets with him.*

"I think I should at least come with you," she said out loud, but Indiana's headshake was instant and firm.

"That's the *last* thing you should do, Kenzie," he said flatly. "You're a respectable cyber geek. We've been very careful about that, haven't we? You don't have anything to do with your disreputable brother's quasilegal transactions, except—maybe—to help with his bookkeeping. If the two of us turn up together anywhere for anything except a purely social moment—like, oh, lunch at the Soup Spoon—we're a lot more likely to start drawing the scags' attention, and you know it."

"But I don't like the thought of your—"

"I know what you don't like the thought of, Kenzie." His voice was much gentler, and he reached across the checkered tablecloth to squeeze her hand. "This is the way it needs to be, though. And if it should happen this guy really is a scag plant, you know what you have to do when they bust me, too."

She nodded unhappily, biting her lower lip. It might not do much good in the end, but they'd agreed long since that if Indy was arrested, Mackenzie must immediately denounce him to the authorities. It wouldn't make much difference to what happened to Indy; anyone O'Sullivan's scags arrested was automatically guilty unless he could come up with something sufficiently valuable to buy himself a get-out-of-jail card. But if she talked fast enough and loud enough it was at least remotely possible she could convince the authorities she hadn't been involved in any subversive activities on his part. It wasn't likely, but it *was* possible.

"Well, in that case, finish your *tam kha kai* and head on back to your office." He pushed back his chair and stood, bending over to kiss her cheek. "I'll screen you later this evening to discuss lunch plans for Wednesday."

"Sure." She reached up to touch the side of his face. "Just be careful, okay?"

"Always am," he assured her with a smile, and she watched him walk away, humming, with his hands in his pockets.

❖   ❖   ❖

Indiana Graham sauntered past the information desk at the Cherubim Public Library's Sinkler Street branch and nodded to the junior librarian stationed to keep an eye on things. The librarian nodded back without ever looking up from her own book reader. Indy spent enough time in her reading room to be a familiar face, although they'd never really spoken to each other.

He took the old-fashioned escalator up to the third floor and wandered down the hall to the main reading room. His eyes flicked to the left as he walked through the doorway and noticed the copy of a rather boring action novel on the reader at an unoccupied desk two cubicles over from the entrance.

He kept walking until he reached "his" cubicle— the one with four reader displays, from which he'd transacted so much street hand business. None of the other displays were in use, so he parked himself at the one farthest from the door and propped his feet inelegantly on one of the unoccupied chairs. From that position, he could watch the entrance without being especially obtrusive about it, and he punched the index key at the reader in front of him to call up the book he'd been reading during his last visit.

Seventeen minutes later, a tall fellow, with broad shoulders, fair hair, and gray eyes walked through the door and glanced around. He wore an off-worlder's clothing and he crossed straight to Indy's cubicle, smiled down at the chair whose seat was occupied by Indy's feet, then pulled out the chair across from him and sat with his back to the doorway.

"Come here often?" he asked.

"Fairly often," Indy acknowledged.

"You wouldn't happen to know where I might be able to find any reasonably priced *glühenden Nussbutter*, would you?"

"Depends on what you mean by 'reasonably,' I guess."

"Well," the newcomer regarded him levelly, "if it's too cheap, I'd probably esteem it too lightly."

"Actually," Indy lowered his feet from the chair and leaning forward as he spoke in a voice which wasn't especially loud but was also far from a whisper, "I could make you a pretty good deal on the *Nussbutter* if you really want it."

"Then I should probably buy some just to keep the scags happy, I suppose." The other man snorted. "I don't really expect to be using it here, you understand. I don't have any friends quite that close in Seraphim. Yet, at least."

Indy chuckled. The paste made from the *Liebender Nussbaum*—a native tree which bore at least a faint resemblance to Old Terra's walnut—possessed a natural bioluminescence which made it glow in the dark. It was also a powerful contact aphrodisiac, and it was often blended with a smorgasbord of euphorics. It was legal but regulated, and businesses had to be licensed to sell it. Given the amount of kickback it took to acquire one of those licenses, it carried a hefty price. By the same token, it was one of the items obtainable—for far less—on the graymarket and one which the authorities didn't try very hard to suppress.

"I'll give you my supplier's name," he said. "Try to buy enough to net me a decent commission."

"Of course," the other man said dryly. "On the other hand, that's not the real reason I'm here."

"No. So why don't you tell me why you *are* here? Oh, and while we're at it, why don't you tell me what I can call you?"

"For now, you can call me Clambake. And I'm pretty sure you already have a fair idea of why I'm here, given your people's choice of recognition phrases. And assuming I'm not wasting my time talking to you, of course."

"I don't know you . . . Clambake. For that matter, I don't know whoever you initially contacted. So I hope you'll forgive me if I don't fall all over myself to say anything which might be construed as . . . indiscreet."

It wasn't quite true that Indy didn't know who "Clambake's" first SIM contact had been. Which wasn't to say he knew that contact well . . . or wanted to. Richard Bledsoe was a low-level Mendoza of Cordoba freight supervisor at Tobolinski Field, Cherubim's primary spaceport, and he wasn't a savory sort of fellow. Like most of his ilk, he dabbled in smuggling, and in his case that sometimes included drugs and other prohibited substances which—in Indiana Graham's opinion—damned well *ought* to be prohibited. He was, however, in a position to be useful, and so he'd been recruited for a special SIM cell, a parking place for potentially useful contacts who were . . . less than fully vetted or trusted. That was one reason Mackenzie had been so uneasy over this meeting in the first place, because it had originated in a message passed up the chain from Bledsoe rather than resulting from a request sent down the chain *to* him.

"I can understand why you might hesitate to do anything 'indiscreet,'" Clambake conceded. "On the other hand, I'm sure you can understand why I'd be a little nervous about indiscretions myself. After all, I'm a stranger in town. I don't have any friends if the scags decide they don't like my face."

"There's a lot of that going around," Indy replied.

"All right," Clambake said after several long, dragging moments of silence. "I'm going to assume that since your people set up the meeting place we can talk here. Or do we need to go somewhere else?"

"As long as that display's up," Indy twitched his head in the direction of the reader to the left of the door, "the security system in this reading room's developed a glitch. It's still getting good imagery, but the audio pickup's on the fritz. It's a minor fault, but a real one. The kind of thing that happens when maintenance gets skimpy." He smiled thinly. "That happens a lot to the SSSP's equipment even without anyone's outside assistance, actually."

"What about lip readers?" Clambake's tone was more amused than challenging, and Indy snorted.

"Let's just say the image quality's not very good. In fact, it sucks." He shrugged. "Trying to run surveillance on an entire planet gets expensive, in both financial terms and manpower. One reason I like using libraries for my actual business meetings is that they don't get real high priority when the scags are handing out top-flight equipment or manpower allocations. Stupid of them, given how much fuel for subversion libraries hold."

"I see." There might have been a flicker of respect in Clambake's gray eyes, and he sat back in his own chair. "In that case, I suppose I should lay my cards on the table...to some extent, at least."

"That would probably be a good place to start," Indy agreed.

"All right, I will. I won't ask at this point whether or not you're sufficiently senior in whatever organization you people have to give me any commitments at this point. But I *am* going to assume they wouldn't have sent you if you weren't at least senior enough to hear me out and report back. So, for starters—"

❖ ❖ ❖

"Hi, Indy!" Mackenzie Graham said, smiling as her brother appeared on the com display.

"You free for lunch Wednesday?" he asked cheerfully, and her smile grew a bit broader—this time with relief—as the code phrase told her the library meeting had gone well. As far as he knew, at any rate.

"I guess I could fit you into my schedule," she replied. "I'm not positive, though." She frowned thoughtfully for a moment, then shrugged. "I know we just had lunch together, but if you haven't eaten dinner yet, I've still got some of that spaghetti Mom brought over the last time she was in town. Want to come by and I'll heat it up?"

"We could do that," Indy replied. "In fact, why don't we do this? You heat up the spaghetti, I'll grab a bottle of Chianti on my way, and there's still time for us to take in the sunset if we eat on the roof."

"Sounds like a deal to me. Thirty minutes?"

"Make it forty-five. The queues at the tram stops are running a little long."

❖ ❖ ❖

"You know, Uncle Thad *does* make good spaghetti," Indy said, sitting back from the table in the small dining area atop Mackenzie's apartment building.

Like much of Cherubim's architecture, Mackenzie's building had been erected long ago. It was barely ten stories tall, and while the neighborhood was considerably better than the one in which Indiana currently lived, it still wasn't exactly on the good side of town. Despite her "respectability," she remained the daughter of an enemy of the people, after all. Despite that, its occupants did their best to maintain at least some of the amenities, including the rooftop tables where they frequently dined.

This evening, as Indy had known would be the case, Mackenzie's neighbors most likely to eat up here were otherwise occupied. He wondered, sometimes, how those neighbors would feel if they knew how intensively he'd studied them, figuring out who they worked for, mapping their normal movement patterns. Digging that deeply into other people's lives made him a little queasy, as if he were becoming too much like Tillman O'Sullivan's scags. Unfortunately, he didn't have a lot of choice. Not if he meant to keep himself and his sister alive, anyway.

"Yeah, he does." Mackenzie used a bit of garlic bread to soak up the last of Thaddeus Lucchino's spaghetti sauce. "One thing we can be sure of is that at least she's eating pretty well," she added a bit more darkly.

"True," Indy acknowledged. Then he sat back with a glass of Chianti, gazing at the crimson and black coals of sunset's funeral pyre.

"So, are you going to tell me how it went?" Mackenzie asked in a somewhat lower voice as she drew her sweater closer against the undeniable chill of the breeze. "I'm assuming that's why we're eating up here, anyway."

"And here I thought you'd so cleverly set it up yourself!"

She stuck out her tongue at him, and he chuckled. Weather permitting, they ate on her apartment building's roof at least a couple of nights a week, and Indy had made a point of discovering exactly where the SSSP's bugs had been put. That task had been made easier by the fact that the bugs in question were fairly shoddy workmanship that hadn't been hidden particularly well. Obviously the scags didn't regard the apartments as a hotbed of subversive conspiracy. If they'd had the least suspicion of the discussions which had been held on this roof, they'd have devoted their best equipment—and their best maintenance techs—to making sure they heard every syllable. As it was, his and Mackenzie's favorite table happened to be located in what was very nearly a dead zone. Not quite—even scags were better than that—but close enough, especially on evenings like this when a brisk breeze blew across the microphones.

And the wind chimes I got Kenzie for her last birthday don't hurt, he thought cheerfully, listening to their musical but undeniably loud voice as the wind sent them clamoring into one another. He hadn't been stupid enough to hang it directly on top of a microphone, but he had hung it between their table and the nearest mic. As long as they kept their voices down, the chance of their being picked up was almost nonexistent.

"All right," he said. He drained his wineglass, then set it on the table and leaned forward, folding his hands and propping his elbows on the table top and dropping his own voice just a bit. "Either the scags have figured out what we're up to and set some kind of incredibly subtle and complex trap for us, or else this guy—'Clambake,' he said to call him—may be the real deal. In fact, he could be exactly what we need."

"I get very nervous when somebody we never heard of just turns up out of the blue to be 'exactly what we need.'" Mackenzie's expression was somber.

"You're not the only one." He smiled thinly. "And I didn't fall all over myself accepting his offer, either. I told him I was too junior to make any commitments—figured it couldn't hurt, assuming he *was* working with the scags, to keep them guessing about just who's in charge on our side—and I set up a contact procedure for when he comes back to Seraphim."

"Comes back?" she repeated, and he shrugged.

"He says he's got other people to talk to, and this will give *me* time to 'talk to my superiors' before we have to give him an answer. Frankly, I don't want to give him the impression we're rushing into anything even if he's completely legitimate. And if he's *not* . . ."

"Okay, I can see that. But what's this about 'other people'?"

"I wondered about that, too, Kenzie, so I asked. And that's where it got really *interesting*." Indy leaned a bit farther forward. "When he told me he'd hunted us up because the people he works for are in the business of supporting 'subversives' here in the Verge, I told him I didn't believe in the Tooth Fairy. He only laughed and admitted I had a point. But then he told me *why* they're willing to support people like us, and damned if it didn't actually make sense."

"Yeah. Sure!" She rolled her eyes skeptically, and he chuckled, but his expression and his voice were serious.

"I want you to think about this as critically as you can, Kenzie. I know I tend to jump as soon as I think the jumping's good, and we have to consider this one very, very carefully before I imitate any frogs. But if he's really who he says he is—and like I say, his story seems to me to make sense— we can't afford to *not* jump."

Mackenzie gazed at him for several seconds, her eyes shadowed in the deepening twilight. Then she nodded.

"Tell me," she said simply.

"Okay. Remember the stories we heard about what happened over in Talbott? Well, it seems they were accurate, and—"

❖   ❖   ❖

Rufino Chernyshev sat at his second-class table aboard the Krestor Interstellar liner *Mary Ellen*, savoring the *first*-class single malt in his glass and permitted himself a mild self-congratulatory glow.

He didn't know who the youngster he'd met in the library really was, although he suspected he was considerably more highly placed than he'd chosen to imply in whatever subversive organization was ticking away here in Seraphim. Chernyshev's preliminary briefing had been able to provide virtually no information on it—the Alignment was fortunate to have discovered its existence at all, much less learned anything about it—but unless he missed his guess, young "call-me-Talisman" was a member of its senior cadre.

Well, he had the pictures from his shirt-button cam, and one of their sources in Seraphim would have acquired a lot more information on him by the time he returned. In the meantime, "Talisman" and his colleagues would have plenty to think over. And—again, unless Chernyshev missed his guess—they'd jump at the chance for "Manticoran" support. Of course, he'd be better placed to shape his offer once he knew more about who he was dealing with, especially if that information offered an insight into exactly what had drawn Talisman (and, presumably, his associates) into attempting to build an effective resistance group.

Not that Jacqueline McCready and her administration didn't amply deserve to be kicked out on its collective ass, preferably with pulser darts delivered to at least a dozen ear canals in the process. God knew any number of people had perfectly legitimate reasons to do just that, and his impression of young Talisman was that he'd make a formidable foe. He might be inexperienced, but he clearly had good instincts.

Which is why I had to take care of that little house-keeping chore before I left. Not that it wouldn't have been worth doing on its own. I know we have to use whatever tool we can find in this business, but still . . .

When Isabel Bardasano started building the groundwork for Janus, she and her analysts had looked for any sources they already had in the star systems they'd identified as possessing potential for their purposes, and Bledsoe had been one of them. An organization like the Alignment never knew where it was likely to need a set of ears on the ground, and smugglers who were none too choosy about what they'd smuggle often drew the eye of Manpower, the Jessyk Combine, or any one of the Alignment's manifold black-market and criminal tentacles. Bledsoe had been recruited—by Jessyk—over ten T-years earlier, and his name had bobbed to the top for Janus, despite the fact that he was about as unreliable as a contact got, when he offered the information that he'd been approached by some kind of revolutionary group. Personally, Chernyshev wouldn't have trusted him as a dog-walker, much less a revolutionary, but the lead had been worth following up and he'd been instructed to accept recruitment. And it would appear they'd struck gold despite the unpromising geology.

Unhappily for Mr. Bledsoe, he'd turned out to be as stupid as he was corrupt and greedy. He'd actually suggested that, given his position inside the organization, he was worth more than the Alignment was already paying him. He'd suggested a modest little three hundred-percent raise, and—of course—Chernyshev had agreed.

Which was why in the next week or so—long enough to be sure Talisman wouldn't associate it with Chernyshev's visit—Richard Bledsoe would become the unfortunate victim of a fatal mugging. It wasn't that Chernyshev begrudged the extra money. It was that he'd had the chance to take Bledsoe's measure, and there was no doubt in his mind the smuggler would happily sell out everyone in sight. It would have been only a matter of time before someone like him dropped into SSSP headquarters and suggested he had some confidential information someone might be interested in. For that matter, someone stupid enough to try to turn the screws on his current employers might very well let something slip entirely inadvertently.

Which, Chernyshev thought, sipping the excellent whiskey appreciatively, wouldn't be happening now.

"They'll not do to my uncle what they've done to the rest of my family! But I'll pull the lads and lassies back onto MacRory land. We'll keep our heads down, mind our manners, and stay as far out of the public eye as we can. But know this, Megan MacLean—Hell won't hold what'll happen when the first Uppy sets foot on MacRory land after us!"

—Raghnall MacRory,
MacRory Militia,
Loomis system.

Chapter Twenty-Three

DAMIEN HARAHAP FROWNED AS the needle-nosed transatmospheric sting ship followed *Факел* into Mesa orbit and took up a position astern and outside the yacht's designated parking orbit. The good news was that the deadly little ship hadn't simply opened fire. The bad news was that neither Harahap nor any member of *Факел*'s crew had any idea why the star system's armed forces and security agencies had gone to such a state of hyper alert.

"Delta One-Niner-Seven-Three, power down your nodes," the sting ship's command pilot said over the com, his crisp tone just short of curt. "You'll be met by a Peaceforce shuttle that will transport your passenger. Confirm copy."

"Mike-Papa-Papa Seven-One-Two, Delta One-Niner-Three-Seven confirms copy your instructions," Yong Seong Jin replied. "We're powering down now."

"That's affirmative, Delta One-Niner-Seven-Three," the sting ship pilot said. "Have a nice day. Mike-Papa-Papa Seven-One-Two, clear."

"And what the *hell* was that about?" Harahap asked, and *Факел*'s skipper shook her head with an expression one of baffled anxiety.

"I don't know," she said. "In fact, I don't have the least damned idea...except that *whatever* it's about, it's not going to be good."

❖   ❖   ❖

Not good, Harahap decided several hours later, was a significant understatement.

No wonder the Peaceforce and the Internal Security Directorate have their panties in a wad, he thought grimly.

He could see the shattered ruins of Suvorov Tower from the windows of the apartment in which he'd been parked until Bardasano had time to talk to him. He didn't have a good angle—the view was constricted by residential towers which hadn't been involved—but what he *could* see suggested the official death toll reported by the 'faxes he'd so far seen was probably at least close to accurate.

Well, for certain values of "accurate," anyway, he corrected himself. *It must've been an interesting call. Do they understate the death toll, trying to convince everyone they're in complete control of the situation and there's no reason for their fellow citizens to worry about additional attacks? Or do they* overstate *the death toll to justify the security crackdown?*

At the moment, he was inclined to think it had been the latter. While he could see the wreckage of Suvorov, where the first "terrorist" bomb had gone off, he couldn't see Pine Valley Park...or, rather, where Pine Valley Park *used* to be. Nor could he see the ghetto towers where the "seccies"—the "second-class citizens" descended from the genetic slaves who'd earned manumission, back when the Mesan constitution had actually allowed for that—lived and labored for their betters. He could, however, make out armed air cars and sting ships of the Mesan Internal Security Directorate and the Planetary Peaceforce circling above the nearest of them. He was sure he could have seen the same thing above *any* of the seccy towers, since the planetary government had loosed the MISD upon them. Whether the hunt for the Audubon Ballroom terrorists being blamed for the attacks was genuine or simply a convenient pretext to hammer the seccies lest any of them get ideas about emulating the Green Pines Atrocity attacks was another interesting question.

I wonder... are they so insistent it was the Ballroom to keep the MOI out of it? I mean, sure, branding Manticore us the "Ballroom enabler" could have upsides for both the government and the Alignment, and having Zilwicki available as a public face for Manticore's support of Torch and all those other terrible Ballroom-associated things is tailor-made for that. But by treating it as terrorism directly linked to the seccies, they keep the MOI safely sidelined. And who does that suit better? The system authorities, or Bardasano's people?

The Mesan Office of Investigation was one of the best civilian police organizations in the entire galaxy. It was *also*, however, specifically prohibited from any involvement in seccy affairs, which only seemed odd until one examined the logic. The people who'd created the MOI wanted to make damned sure it remained a *police* organization with a genuine respect for the civil rights of Mesa's full citizens. The last thing they'd wanted was for the MOI to become a repressive, suppressive, callused institution accustomed to cutting corners in the investigation and prosecution of *citizens*. Under normal circumstances, one would have assumed the authorities would have pulled out all the stops and unleashed MOI's superb investigators and forensic specialists as part of the unyielding demand for answers. . . .

Unless, of course, someone doesn't want *those answers to ever see the light of day. But why would they want that? To cover the Alignment's tracks? Or to avoid anything which might undermine the justification for the seccy crackdown? Or maybe a combination of* both?

From all he'd been able to pick up so far, the current crackdown was the most savage any seccy had seen in at least fifty T-years. Harahap doubted the MSID was even trying to distinguish between anyone who might actually have been insane enough to launch a nuclear terrorist attack in *Mesa*, of all places, and those who'd had nothing at all to do with it. They were simply breaking heads—and necks—throughout the seccy districts to "send a message."

If Damien Harahap had had a credit for every government which had decided to "send a message" and, in the fullness of time, been handed its collective ass, he could have bought himself a nice little planet for his retirement.

Whoever this "Mesan Alignment" of Bardasano's is, it's not *the system government*, he decided, turning from the window and reaching for his bottle of Old Tillman once more. *Bardasano's way too smart to be part of something as ham-handed as the security forces here in Mesa. Hell, she's got me out prospecting for revolutionaries on planets where there's one hell of a lot less legitimate reason for rebellion than the seccies have right here in her backyard! Somehow I don't think she's stupid enough to miss the parallels.*

And then there was the minor fact that he was confident the Suvorov Tower bomb had never been set off by terrorists, whether from the Audubon Ballroom or strictly homegrown. And the reason he was confident was because he'd been to the facility *underneath* Suvorov Tower on his last visit.

From Rufino Chernyshev's body language as he'd escorted Harahap into the carefully unnamed facility, having him there hadn't been high on his list of Really Good Ideas. That, in turn, had suggested to Harahap that whatever the facility was, it was far more than simply the place Isabel Bardasano's private medical clinic called home. He'd scarcely been given a tour of the place—indeed, he'd seen only a lift shaft and lobbies on two floors, although the shaft panel had indicated there were at least a dozen levels below the ones he'd seen—but the security had been formidable. Formidable enough for him to find it extremely difficult to believe even the Audubon Ballroom, arguably the galaxy's most effective terrorist organization (or freedom fighters, depending upon one's perspective) had managed to smuggle a nuclear device into the tower.

Besides, nuclear acts of terror were far more apocryphal than actual. First and foremost, perhaps, because the use of nuclear fusion as a means of political protest was . . . frowned upon. Any group which resorted to *that* would unite every security agency in the galaxy—including the ones who were bitter enemies in every other way—to hunt them down. Even nuclear acts of *vengeance* were vanishingly rare, and Harahap found it difficult to believe even the Ballroom could suffer a sudden hankering for revenge sufficient to generate three separate nuclear attacks on a single bedroom suburb of the planetary capital. Besides, anyone who could get all three of those into place—especially through the security around Suvorov Tower—could certainly have taken out far more important and painful targets in Mendel itself.

The target selection itself was proof enough that whatever else might have happened, it hadn't been a coordinated terrorist operation. One deserted, near-derelict tower. One top-secret facility which obviously belonged to someone other than the system government. And one residential park where over three hundred children had been caught in the blast, not counting all the other civilians who'd died in the surrounding residential towers.

There'd been no reason to take out Buenaventura Tower. A little discreet investigation told Harahap it had been effectively uninhabited for over five local years while the city authorities dealt with more immediate projects. Demolishing a ceramacrete tower the better part of a kilometer in height was what one might call a nontrivial exercise. *Renovating* one of them was easier and much more cost-effective, but that didn't for a moment mean it was *cheap*. So until there was a pressing need for that space, Green Pines had elected to simply maintain its approach landscaping and façade while abandoning its interior to the local equivalent of rats, bats, snakes, and a double handful of squatters. All of which made it about as useless a target for a "terrorist strike" as Harahap could imagine.

The Pine Valley Park attack made sense only if one assumed the people behind it were unhinged... and unhinged people out for the maximum atrocity quotient didn't also waste nuclear devices attacking *empty* targets. Anyone who wanted to kill hundreds of kids would have hit a fully occupied residential tower, not one that had stood empty for years.

And then there was Suvorov.

Damien Harahap was no demolitions expert, but a man in his line of work picked up all sorts of odd bits of knowledge, and the planetary news feeds were still showing aerial shots of the blast sites virtually round-the-clock. He'd looked them over carefully, and he was convinced the device which had shattered Suvorov and inflicted significant damage on its neighboring towers had been detonated *under* the structure.

In fact, it had been detonated inside the facility to which Chernyshev had taken him. That was the only possible explanation for the pattern of destruction. And it hadn't been done by any "terrorist organization." Grievous as the damage was, it was also sharply contained. In fact, it was *so* sharply contained Harahap was certain he'd been looking at the aftermath of a suicide charge designed by the facility's owners to completely obliterate it while minimizing collateral damage.

Of course, "minimize" was a purely relative term for anyone willing to use a nuclear demolition charge inside a densely populated city.

But why? What could have possessed Bardasano's unnamed superiors to destroy their own facility? The only explanation that made even halfway sense was that their "Mesan Alignment" had fallen afoul of the system government. That the situation had been so dire they'd decided they had no choice but to destroy something as big, carefully hidden, and obviously expensive as the facility Harahap had visited lest its contents—and records, perhaps?—fall into...unfriendly official hands. But the major corporations—especially Manpower, Incorporated—*ran* the Mesan government, and Bardasano's Alignment was obviously in bed with at least several of those corporations, which made official displeasure unlikely. Besides, if Bardasano's people were in *that* much trouble with the local cops, *he'd* be having a lengthy discussion with someone in a uniform right now. Yet that only brought him back to the virtual impossibility of anyone else's getting a nuclear bomb through the security he'd observed.

No, something had gone wrong—something *internal* to the Alignment—in a major way. It might be being blamed on the Ballroom, and he could see all sorts of upsides to that from the viewpoint of the Mesan government, but whatever it had been, it hadn't been "terrorists."

All of which led to some very interesting speculation indeed.

❖   ❖   ❖

"I'm sorry it took us so long to bring you in for a proper debrief, Mr. Harahap," the man in the countergrav chair said.

He looked to be about Harahap's own age, although that was always tricky with prolong involved, and it would appear he hadn't gotten off unscathed during the recent excitement. Quick-heal had healed whatever soft tissue damage he'd taken in the T-month since the attacks (or whatever they'd been). There were still signs, though, if one knew where to look, which suggested some of that damage had been damned severe. More to the point, quick-heal was slower where bones were concerned, and the counter grav chair and the pair of folding canes hanging from one armrest—suggested the bone damage had been even worse.

"I've been watching the news feeds," Harahap replied to the semi-apology, and shrugged. "From what I've seen, you all have your hands pretty full. I can understand how schedules might have gotten . . . disarranged."

"Oh, they've certainly been that," the other man said dryly. "In fact, that's why I'm handling your debrief instead of Ms. Bardasano." His mouth twisted, his eyes bitter. "I'm afraid she was killed by the terrorists."

"I . . . see," Harahap said. That was one he'd never seen coming. Bardasano, dead? That was interesting, especially given his conclusions about where the Suvorov Tower bomb had actually been placed. In fact . . .

So if it wasn't terrorists, then maybe someone inside the Alignment managed to smuggle one in. Or maybe someone inside the Alignment just hacked the software and used a bomb the facility's builders had conveniently parked there for him? That would make a lot more sense than believing someone from the outside could smuggle one past their security. But if that's the case, what the hell is going on? Somehow I doubt it was just someone with a personal grudge against Bardasano!

"I'm sorry to hear that," he went on after a moment. "I can't say I'd really gotten to know her well, but I've always preferred working for professionals, and she was clearly that."

"Yes, she was," the other man agreed. "And, as you've probably already concluded, Isabel worked for me. That's why I'm handling your debrief. There's been some . . . significant confusion since the attacks. Frankly, there was more to them than just the damage everyone in general knows about. In addition to the nuclear devices that were used, we got hit with a highly sophisticated cyber attack." He sat back in his grav-chair, his expression one of profound disgust. "We're working on reconstituting the data that was destroyed or corrupted, but until we complete that we can't really bring any new people up to speed on ongoing operations. That's why debriefs like yours have to be handled by someone who already knows what's going on."

"I see," Harahap said again, filing away the additional evidence that whoever had hit the Alignment had done it from inside.

"For whatever it's worth," he went on, "I have the complete data set she gave me as part of my initial mission brief in the computers aboard ship."

"Really?" The other man straightened. "What sort of data set?"

"As far as I know, the complete raw data and a complete file of her people's analysis of it." The other's eyebrows rose, and Harahap shrugged. "I asked her for it because I wanted to make my own analysis. And from what I saw in the field, I think she really did give me all of it."

"That will be very welcome," the other man said. "I'm confident we can reconstitute all of it, ultimately, given how many places its bits and pieces were stored, but getting that big a chunk back intact will help a lot."

He sounded a bit less certain of his people's ability to do all that reconstituting than he probably wanted to, but that wasn't Harahap's problem.

"It was delivered to me originally hand-carried on chips, not transmitted," the ex-gendarme said. "I presume that was because of its sensitivity. I can go back up and bring it down myself, or I can give you the security codes to retrieve it without whoever you send wiping it . . . or blowing himself up."

"I think enough things have blown up already." The other man smiled thinly. "We'll probably send you back up in person. But first, tell me about your conclusions."

"Of course." Harahap settled back in his chair. "From this trip, the two that stand out to me as having potential for Janus are Włocławek and Swallow. Wonder's pretty much useless from Janus' perspective, but it has potential value as a place outside Swallow where our people can meet with one of the locals who's involved in the Cripple Mountain Movement up to his neck. He's got a legitimate business interest that takes him to Wonder on a semiregular basis.

"As I say, I don't see much point in looking for revolutionaries in Wonder. There is a lot of general unhappiness, but it's basically the same situation I found in Any Port. There's a lot of talk and any number of people who're willing to complain and *play* at rebellious attitudes—even turn out for protest marches—but that's as far as it's likely to go. I have a complete report on the system, including the analysis behind my conclusions. I brought that much down with me"—he opened his briefcase and extracted a data chip—"for someone else to crosscheck, but I really think any additional effort there would simply waste time and resources."

His debriefer took the chip with a nod, and Harahap sat back once more.

"Now, *Swallow*'s an entirely different situation," he said. "First, what's going on in that system's been brewing for years, and there's deep, personal involvement by a significant segment of the population. It's not the *biggest* segment, but it has a disproportionate amount of influence, and the people in it are about as bloody-minded as it comes. I spoke to one of them, and—"

◇   ◇   ◇

"He's good, Father," Collin Detweiler said several hours later. He and his father sat on the veranda of Albrecht Detweiler's island mansion, cold drinks in hand while they listened to the surf and enjoyed the sea breeze. "In fact, he's *very* good. Just as good as Isabel said he was."

"In that case, I have to wonder what conclusions he's drawn about Green Pines," his father said.

"I didn't ask him, and I don't intend to." Collin sipped whiskey, then set his glass down carefully. "For one thing, he knows damned well that the Gamma Center was under Suvorov."

"*He* knows about the Gamma Center?" Albrecht Detweiler's expression tightened ominously. "Just why the fuck does he know *anything* about the Gamma Center?!"

"He doesn't know how big it was, he doesn't know what we were doing down there, and he sure as hell doesn't have a clue about how important it was," Collin said soothingly. "Isabel was really rushed when she had him prepped, though. You know the suicide-protocol nannies have to be genetically coded *and* programmed before they can be injected. If she was going to get that done before she sent him out, the

Gamma Center clinic was the best place to do it. But I don't think you have to worry about anything he may have seen there. Among other things, she had Chernyshev personally escort him."

His father glared at him for another handful of seconds, then—slowly—relaxed back into his chair.

"All right . . . I suppose," he growled, then wagged an index finger. "I don't like it, though. We're getting way too close to be bringing any outsiders that deep into the onion."

"I suspect Harahap's figured out there *is* an onion, Father." Collin shrugged. "I don't think there's any way he could have a clue as to exactly *what* it is, though. And if we're going to make use of him—which I really think we should—we're just going to have to accept that when you use a man this smart, he's bound to figure out at least a few things you'd rather he didn't. The only way to avoid that would be to use people too stupid to do the figuring out . . . which would be a really, really good way to shoot ourselves in both feet."

"Granted. Granted!" Albrecht waved one hand. "And if you agree with Isabel that we need to use him, then I suppose I'm willing to sign off on it."

"I don't think we have a lot of choice, really." Collin shrugged again. "We're still trying to get ourselves reorganized after that cyber attack, and we lost both of Isabel's deputies—not to mention Jack McBryde—along with the Gamma Center. That means we're stretched thin for 'upper management' people all the way inside the onion, and *that* means we need to draft senior field operatives to fill the gaps. Frankly, I'm thinking we're going to have to pull Chernyshev in and give him Isabel's job."

"Are you sure about that?" Albrecht frowned. "He's been awfully effective in the field for a long time."

"Which is why we need Harahap to replace him—or at least *partially* replace him. Unfortunately, I can't think of anyone else we still have who (a) has the 'hands-on' field ops experience Isabel had, (b) is as fully briefed on her various ops as he is—you know she was using him virtually as a third deputy—and (c) is just as smart and capable as she was. And while it was never really a problem, he's also quite a bit more stable than she was. For that matter, his entire geno's more stable than the Bardasano line, and you know it."

Albrecht frowned some more, then nodded.

"Point taken," he said. "So how is Harahap going to replace him?"

"I'm going to give him primary responsibility for Włocławek and Swallow. I'll be sending him back to Mobius first, though. He made the initial contact there, so I want him to make the introductions for whoever replaces Chernyshev in that system. It's too far from the others for him to take it over permanently, though."

"I can see that." Albrecht nodded again. "The only thing that bothers me is that if he's as smart as you say, then the information we'll have to give him to steer things along properly is also going to give him a much better look inside than I'm really comfortable with."

"He may not get as deep a look as you're afraid he will, Father," Collin said, reaching for his whiskey glass once more. "And even if he does," he paused to sip from the glass, then smiled coldly, "he did make that trip to the Gamma Center clinic, didn't he?"

Chapter Twenty-Four

"WELL, IT'S CERTAINLY IMPRESSIVE, Luiz," Oravil Barregos, the Office of Frontier Security's governor for the Maya Sector, said.

"Please, Oravil." Admiral Luiz Rozsak winced. "We're traditionalists around here. A ship—even one that hasn't quite been completed yet—is *she*, not *it*."

"Really?" Barregos looked at the slightly shorter admiral, dark eyes innocent, and Rozsak snorted.

"All right, you got me." He shook his head and beckoned the governor through the open door into the very large, very comfortably furnished cabin—small suite, really—on the other side. "Am I really that predictable?"

"Only in some ways, Luiz. Only in some ways."

Barregos walked to the middle of the spacious flag officer's day cabin and turned to look at the smart wall which covered one entire bulkhead. The cabin itself was buried deep at the heart of the armored core hull of what would someday soon be the battlecruiser SLNS *Sharpshooter*. Its—no, *her*, he corrected himself

349

with a mental grin—originally assigned name had been *Defiance*, which he still thought would have been a perfectly splendid name, given the reason she'd been laid down. On the other hand, *Sharpshooter* was even better...and one hell of a lot more meaningful after the Battle of Torch.

The governor's mouth tightened, mental grins forgotten, as he thought once again of the losses, including *Sharpshooter*'s cruiser predecessor, Rozsak and his men and women had suffered defending the Kingdom of Torch and its ex-genetic slave citizens. He deeply regretted those deaths. He couldn't possibly regret what they'd died doing, but all those people, all those ships...

He shook his head sadly, eyes on the smart wall, gazing at the sun-burnished images of the other ships taking shape in the dispersed orbital yards of Erewhon. There were a lot of those ships, and construction on several of them was as advanced as it was in the case of Rozsak's flagship-to-be.

"I miss them too," Rozsak said quietly. He'd stepped up beside Barregos while the governor drifted in his own thoughts. Now Barregos glanced sideways at him, and the dark, trim admiral shrugged. "I know what you were thinking. I think the same thing a lot when I look at this." He jutted his chin at the smart wall. "I think about how Commander Carte and the rest of them never got a chance to see it. And about exactly how they'd look forward to those bastards in Old Chicago finding out about it."

"I know."

Barregos rested a hand on Rozsak's shoulder for a moment. Then he turned and seated himself in one of the day cabin's chairs and pointed at the identical chair facing it across a coffee table which looked like hammered copper.

"I realize this is actually your cabin, not mine," the governor said in a considerably lighter tone, "but seeing as how I'm the Governor and you're only the Admiral..."

"And so becomingly modest, too," Rozsak marveled, sinking into the indicated chair, and Barregos chuckled, wondering how certain members of his staff might have reacted to the admiral's flagrant lese majesty. No doubt many of them, especially in the outer circle, would have been outraged. Oravil Barregos wasn't. There might have been as many as three human beings in the entire galaxy he trusted as totally as he did Luiz Rozsak; there damned well weren't *four* of them, though.

"All of us would-be megalomaniac tinpot dictators are modest," he said in reply. "We only think we're half as godlike as we really are."

"One of the things I like most about you," Rozsak agreed affably.

"In addition to becomingly modest, however, I'm also a bit pressed for time," Barregos went on, his expression more serious, "and there are a few things we need to discuss under four eyes before we sit down with anyone else."

Rozsak nodded, his own expression attentive. "Under four eyes" was an Erewhonese idiom he and Barregos had adopted long since. It described a discussion between only two people—one secure from any eavesdropping and totally unrecorded. Which, given the nature of their discussions and the Solarian League's penalties for treason and mutiny, seemed like a very good idea to him.

"We're starting to get some questions—more of them than I anticipated, really—about just what the hell happened at Torch," Barregos said. "I know we managed to keep the real extent of your losses out of the news channels, thanks to how many of your units were 'off the books,' but it sounds like there's been some information leakage and the rumors about casualties are prompting a certain degree of interest. Or it could just be that for once Ukhtomskoy's actually done his job, instead."

"That's not really fair," Rozsak said mildly. "Ukhtomskoy's actually a competent fellow. He knows certain people don't want to hear any contrarian opinions, and he's damned careful not to give them any, once he's figured out who they are. But don't ever make the mistake of assuming he's too stupid to do his job. Jiri and I have both met him, you know, and he's a hell of a lot smarter than Karl-Heinz Thimár!"

Barregos nodded, albeit a bit unwillingly. The truth was that Adão Ukhtomskoy, the CO of OFS' Intelligence Branch *was* smarter—and considerably more imaginative—than Admiral Thimár, the head of the SLN's Office of Naval Intelligence. And it was also true that Rozsak and Commander Jiri Watanapongse, his staff intelligence officer, had met both men.

"All right, I suppose I should've said that it's possible that for once Ukhtomskoy's field people have done *their* job," he conceded. "At any rate, I've gotten a formal request for a 'more detailed and complete' report."

"But only from Intelligence Branch, *not* from ONI," Rozsak said thoughtfully. "Interesting. I wonder if that means Frontier Security and the Navy aren't talking to each other about it. Or about *us*, either."

"I certainly *hope* they aren't talking to each other about us!" Barregos shook his head. "That would be about the last thing we need at the moment."

"Ever the master of understatement." Rozsak's voice was desert dry. "Fortunately, I've had Jiri and Edie working on that."

"Ah?" Barregos arched an eyebrow. Commander Edie Habib (although she was now *Captain* Habib, even if no one outside the Maya Sector knew it) was Rozsak's chief of staff. She was also quite probably the smartest single member of the cadre of outstanding officers Rozsak had attached to himself over the years.

"I'll give you a copy of their craftsmanship before you head back to Smoking Frog," the admiral said. "It's really nice, if I do say so myself. Queen Berry and her people did a really good job of requesting our assistance for the sequences where I'm discussing our force availability with them. Gave me an excellent chance to substantially . . . understate our force numbers for the record, let's say. And once the two of them—and Ruth Winton—got done playing with the actual data, they'd built us a really exciting and totally bogus tactical log of the entire battle. I doubt it would stand up to any sort of intensive analysis, but I also don't think anyone in Ukhtomskoy's shop has the expertise to realize that on their own. They'd have to farm it out to someone at ONI, and you *know* how much they all hate sharing data with each other. Especially if one of them thinks there's a chance to catch the other one's service branch with its fingers in the cookie jar."

"That's probably true." Barregos nodded with an undeniable sense of relief. "Dare I assume your minions dealt with the diplomatic traffic and your formal reports to me equally creatively?"

"That they did. With all the proper date and time stamps, too. Can Jeremy and Julie get that inserted into the official files instead of the originals?"

"I'm pretty sure they can," Barregos said. Jeremy Frank, his senior aide, was twenty years younger than Rozsak, but he'd been with Barregos almost as long. And Julie Magilen, his personal secretary, office manager, and general keeper was Barregos' own age . . . and had been with him for better than half a T-century. They were at least as central to his and Rozsak's plans as Habib or Watanapongse, and just as loyal. In addition, Frank—his staff IT specialist as well as his aide—had built himself traceless backdoors in the strangest places.

"And what do these reports show?" the governor asked, and Rozsak shrugged.

"Everybody in Sol—from Bernard, over at Strategy and Planning, to Kingsford and Rajampet and even, God help us all, Thimár—knows we've been building ships out of the sector's own resources. God knows they've been just delighted at the notion that they wouldn't have to send any of their own hulls out here with the situation heating up with the Manties! So Edie sat down with Alex Chapman and Glenn Horton and actually designed the destroyers and cruisers we're supposedly buying from Erewhon."

Barregos nodded again. Admiral Alexander Chapman was the Erewhon Space Navy's senior uniformed officer, and Glenn Horton was his and Rozsak's local interface with the Erewhonese yards building the Maya Sector Defense Force. Of course, the MSDF didn't officially exist, but that was perfectly all right with Oravil Barregos, since the ships *in* it didn't officially exist yet, either.

And, he reminded himself, *it won't be so very long before the Maya* Sector Defense Force *becomes the Mayan* Navy. *And won't* that *frost some chops in Old Chicago?*

Assuming, of course, that he and Luiz Rozsak survived long enough for that to happen. Which wasn't precisely a given.

"The ships they came up with are going to raise a few eyebrows back home," Rozsak continued. "We kicked it around and decided even Thimár must be starting to get a clue that the Manties and the Havenites are building ships a lot more capable than anything the Navy has. We think it's unlikely anyone on Thimár or Kingsford's staff has even the remotest idea how *much* more capable, but the ships we designed for them are probably twenty or thirty percent more effective than anything in Frontier Fleet or Battle Fleet's inventory."

"Are you sure that's a good idea?" Barregos' tone made it clear he was simply asking a question, and Rozsak nodded.

"We have to show a qualitative edge to explain what we did to Manpower's mercenaries. Trust me, we knocked their order of battle down a lot in those new 'official' reports, but we still needed something to explain how the hell we beat them. Our options were either to have a lot more ships than we'd told them we're building, or else for the individual units to be more capable than anything in the rest of the Navy's inventory. And the whole reason we gave for using Erewhon to build them was to woo Erewhon back into the League's arms and away from its relationship with the Manties and Haven. It'll make sense to them that Erewhon had access to the Manties' warfighting technology and agreed to part with some of it in our favor. And if I know Thimár, he's going to immediately assume the new goodies we tucked into our ship designs are all the Manties have."

"And if they want us to send some of those new ships back to Sol for examination and evaluation?"

"Unfortunately, our losses at Torch were heavily concentrated in our new construction," Rozsak replied. "I'm afraid most of our surviving new-construction units were so badly damaged they'll either be in yard hands for months or else weren't worth repairing at all." He shrugged again. "Obviously, if they ask us to send some of them back, we will . . . as soon as they're available."

"How long do you think we can stall them that way?"

"Oravil, unless I miss my guess, we won't have to stall them a lot longer." Rozsak shook his head. "You've seen the same reports and news coverage I have. And Jiri passed along that movement order on Sandra Crandall's maneuvers. With Joseph Byng already in the Madras Sector and Sandra Crandall right next door with an entire damned fleet, what exactly do you expect to happen?"

"I expect them to lock horns with the Manties in a big way," Barregos said.

"Absolutely. And when they do, the Manties will hand them their heads."

"Really? From what Jiri had to say, Crandall's got an awful lot of firepower, Luiz."

"And she's almost as big a frigging idiot as Byng," Rozsak said caustically. "Not to mention the fact that I will absolutely guarantee you she hasn't got a *clue* about Manty missile capabilities. I could hand her the schematics on those big-ass multidrive missiles of theirs if we had them—hell, I could give her a working model!—and she *still* wouldn't believe it. She's got enough ships that even she should be able to get out with her force more or less intact, but only if she's smart enough to recognize the truth and pull back quickly enough. And there's no way in hell she's taking any of their star systems away from them."

"*If* that's what she's there to do, of course," Barregos pointed out.

"Of course it's what she's there to do. I'm not sure whether Manpower and Mesa are manipulating Rajampet and Kingsford or if Rajampet's using Manpower and Mesa to cover some devious end of his own. But there's no way in the galaxy that much of Battle Fleet got deployed way the hell and gone out to Madras unless someone intended it to accomplish something once it got there."

Barregos nodded slowly. Rozsak's analysis matched very closely with his own, and that might well mean . . .

"How soon will *Sharpshooter* actually be ready for service?" he asked. "I mean *really* ready, Luiz. Worked up and ready for combat."

"The entire first tranche should be out of the yards within the next two months," Rozsak replied. "For that matter, *Sharpshooter* should run her builder's trials within the next three or four T-weeks. Given the quality of the Erewhonese's workmanship, I expect we'll run official acceptance trials no more than a week or two after that. We can probably have all twelve in commission by, oh, late January. It'll be at least a couple of T-months after that before I'd feel comfortable taking them into combat, though. Actually, I'd want at least four T-months—call it the end of April—before I'd feel comfortable about committing them to action, and the wallers are a good ten T-months behind them."

"And what kind of missiles will they carry?"

"We've already taken delivery of full loadouts of Mk 17s from Chapman and Horton," Rozsak said. "On the other hand, it's also been suggested we might want to hold off on loading them into our magazines."

Their eyes met, and Barregos nodded ever so slightly. The political situation remained . . . convoluted, given the fact that Erewhon had deserted Manticore—with plentiful provocation, but still deserted—and delivered much of the Manties' war-fighting technology to the Republic of Haven just in time for the war between the Star Kingdom and the Republic to revive. As a result, Erewhon was in what might conservatively be called "bad odor" with Manticore at the moment, and the ESN had been frozen out of the new, improved, far more lethal current-generation Manty tech. But Rozsak's sacrificial defense of the Kingdom of Torch might be going to change that somewhat in Maya's case.

"Just how firm was that 'suggestion,' Luiz?" the governor asked now. "I've viewed your reports, but if you've heard something more substantial since you sent them in, I really need to know it now."

"It's not cast in ceramacrete yet," Rozsak admitted, "but it came directly to Jiri from Delvecchio."

Barregos sat back, his dark eyes thoughtful. Captain Rebecca Delvecchio, Royal Manticoran Navy, was the

Manticoran naval attaché in Erewhon. She was also, as everyone including—especially—the Erewhonese were perfectly well aware, the head of the Manticoran naval intelligence operation in the system. In the absence of the full ambassador who'd been recalled from Erewhon following Erewhon's departure from the Manticoran Alliance, Delvecchio was also carrying much of the diplomatic weight. After all, even when two star nations were royally pissed with one another, there still had to be some communication interface. As the Erewhonese put it, business was business.

"I don't think she's talking about all up, first-line MDMs even now," Rozsak cautioned. "For that matter, I'm not sure the *Defiants* could *handle* all up MDMs without some significant modification. But these *are* all pod-layer designs, and from what she's said, I think we may be looking at some of their older dual-drive missiles. It sounds like she's talking about—well, hinting about—older models of their Mark 16. Apparently they've still got a bunch in storage and the Manties don't consider them fully up to snuff against first-line Havenite opposition. Against *Sollies*, though..."

His expression was an odd mix of satisfaction, anticipation, and something almost like chagrin, Barregos thought. No Solarian flag officer, even one taking advantage of his own service's backwardness to become something else, was likely to do handsprings of delight over the conclusion that the mighty SLN had just become a third-power fleet. Things like that weren't supposed to happen.

"That's interesting," the governor said slowly. "That the Manties really may be willing to hand us something like that."

"Don't forget that we're basically talking outdated hardware—by Manty standards, at least," Rozsak cautioned him. "It's better than anything we could get anywhere else, and giving us actual examples will probably let us bootstrap the tech. But they're not giving us the keys to the Star Kingdom just yet."

"No, but it makes me wonder what else might be going on . . . and how it might factor into our own plans. For example, something funny's happening in Kondratii."

"Kondratii?" Rozsak's eyebrows arched.

The Kondratii System was less than a hundred and twenty light-years from the Maya System itself, and its inhabitants loathed Frontier Security and their transstellar overlords with a pure and burning passion. In fact, it was one of those places an OFS governor might expect to have to send someone like Admiral Luiz Rozsak and the Solarian League Marines to restore order.

Because of that, there was a page or so in Oravil Barregos' playbook where Kondratii was concerned. When the day came for the Maya Sector to declare its independence of the Solarian League, Kondratii would make an excellent addition to the new Mayan Federation. In fact, Barregos and Rozsak had drawn up a list of several star systems whose common interests would make them a natural fit as members of their new Federation, or at least its close allies and trading partners. And because that was true, Barregos had Renée Guérin, his senior civilian security advisor, and Brigadier Philip Allfrey, his senior Gendarmerie officer, keeping a close eye on the systems on that list.

Including Kondratii.

"According to Renée, something new's been added. There's always some lone wolf terrorist ready to squirt a little hydrogen into the fire in Kondratii, but it seems to her that some of the resistance movements are getting themselves better organized than they used to be."

"*Any* organization would be an improvement on how they 'used to be,' Oravil!"

"I realize that. But it looks to her like whatever's behind it is coming from *outside* the local system."

"Somebody's trying to destabilize it even further?" Rozsak frowned.

"Either that or they're trying to *stabilize* it . . . under new management."

"Are you suggesting it could be the Manties?"

"Right off the top of my head, it seems ridiculous," Barregos conceded. "That doesn't mean it might strike them the same way, though."

"For what conceivable motive?" Rozsak's expression was skeptical.

"To help make more trouble for the League." Barregos' expression was much more unhappy than skeptical. "Let's face it, Luiz. I'm sure they're genuinely grateful to us—to *you*—for defending Torch, and the Manties have a reputation for paying their debts. So I'm sure anything Delvecchio's telling you stems at least partly from that. But the Star Kingdom's also one of the best practitioners of *Realpolitik* around. It's had to be to survive. And while I'm sure they like us a lot," he smiled sardonically, "somehow I doubt they'd fall all over themselves to give us better weapons if they didn't figure it would help *them* as much as it's likely to help *us*."

"You're saying they not only have a pretty damned good idea of what we have in mind but that they'd like to see us move Sometime Real Soon Now?" Rozsak said slowly. "Sometime soon enough, for example, to help distract Old Chicago, OFS, and—just maybe—Battle Fleet from the Talbott Quadrant?"

"It's certainly possible. And if that's what they're thinking, then isn't it possible it would make sense to them to stir up places like Kondratii for the same reason? Especially if doing so encourages *us* to get off the centicredit?"

"That would be very devious of them," Rozsak said, with a certain admiration. "Almost as devious as *we* are."

"I didn't say I blamed them for it," Barregos agreed. "But if that *should* happen to be what they have in mind, I think it behooves us to find out everything we can about just how they might plan to pull it off." He shrugged. "And if all of this is pure paranoia on my part, it still won't hurt to have a better window into the internal dynamics of all the systems on our little list."

Chapter Twenty-Five

THE HOT DOG, DAMIEN Harahap decided, was one of the best he'd enjoyed in a long time. It was made of mutton, but "mutton" on Mobius was the product of the Mobian mountain sheep, a species unique to Mobius, which he privately thought had the potential to rival Montanan beef among the galaxy's gourmands. It had a deep, rich taste, and just a trace of onion and a somewhat larger trace of cheddar had been incorporated into this version of one of Mobius' hallmark specialties. His contact had suggested trying this iteration, and he was looking forward to trying several more before he left for Wonder and his scheduled—or at least *potentially* scheduled—next meeting with Vincent Frugoni.

He took another bite, then swooped a French fry through the ketchup and popped it into his mouth, then reminded himself to avoid eating too quickly. His contact had an hour-long window in which to meet him, and he'd really prefer not to have completely cleaned his plate and be sitting here, conspicuous among the diners at the other picnic tables, and look like he was waiting for someone.

Of course, I can always order another *of these, can't I?* he thought cheerfully, taking another bite of hot dog. *Besides, the view's nice enough for me play the tourist enjoying it without arousing too much suspicion.*

He looked out across his picnic table at the sizable lake at the heart of Central Park in the city of Landing—Mobius edition. The table sat on a small spit of land that extended into the lake, wide open to any watching eye, and he felt a modest stir of admiration for whoever had picked the site. Not only did the hot dog stand near the picnic tables do a brisk business, which could cover any number of people's "coincidental" meetings, but whoever had set the meet here—and for lunchtime—clearly understood that the best way to avoid bugs and directional microphones was to be so transparently open and aboveboard that no one pointed any of those objectionable devices one's way. In fact—

"Is this place taken?" a voice asked, and he turned back from the lake to find himself facing a man of slightly more than average height with dark hair and improbably bright blue eyes. The newcomer carried a tray loaded with not one, but two hot dogs, plus French fries *and* a largish serving of coleslaw. When Harahap looked up at him, he twitched his head, indicating the picnic bench on the other side of the ex-gendarme's table. "The other tables are packed," he pointed out, with a fair degree of accuracy, then smiled. "Besides, this is my favorite table. Especially on a day like this one."

"By all means, sit down!" Harahap invited. "And I can understand why you'd like the table. The view's really nice, isn't it?"

"And so is the breeze, when it gets as warm as it is today," the other man agreed. He set his tray on the table and seated himself, then cocked his head slightly. "Forgive me for mentioning it, but that doesn't sound like a Mobian accent."

"Because it's not." It was Harahap's turn to smile. "It's Manticoran." Which, he reflected, it really was. Maybe not Manticoran enough to fool a *real* Manty, but more than adequate to fool anyone else.

"A little far from home, aren't you?"

"When you work for the Hauptman Cartel, you get used to being 'a little far from home,'" Harahap replied wryly. "Still, it has its compensations. Like your system's hot dogs. A fellow I met on my last visit here suggested I try them. In fact, he specifically suggested I order Number Forty-Six from the menu." He met the other man's eyes levelly. "He said I'd really like it, and he was right."

"Really?" The other man smiled back at him. "Well, I've always liked Forty-Six, myself, but my real favorite is Number Thirty-One."

"I'll remember to try that," Harahap said as his table companion completed the recognition phrase. "On the other hand, I may not be the one making the trip next time." Something which could have been alarm flickered in the other's eyes, but Harahap continued unhurriedly. "Mr. Hauptman has a lot of interests, and I'm probably being transferred to another area—my specialty is prospecting for new contacts, you understand—and someone else, someone with a good track record for *developing* contacts, will probably be assigned to service any Mobian accounts if things actually work out here."

"I see."

The other man took a bite of one of his own hot dogs and chewed appreciatively. Then he swallowed.

"I suppose it would be convenient for me to have a name in any reports you may pass on to your . . . replacement."

"Oh, I think we'll just call you . . . Mr. Brown. *John* Brown. How does that suit you?"

"I think it should work just fine, Mr. . . . Dabilenaren, was it?"

"Yes, Ardagai. Ardagai Dabilenaren," Harahap extended his hand and "Mr. Brown" shook it firmly.

"Well, Mr. Dabilenaren," he said, "the same friend who recommended this hot dog stand to you spoke very favorably about his previous meeting with you. I hope you understood, though, that he wasn't in a position to enter into any binding agreements with your cartel?"

"Oh, of course! As I say, I'm a prospector. I'm used to situations like that. May I assume, however, that *you've* been authorized to make that sort of an agreement?"

"Let's say I have the authority to enter into a *tentative* agreement, assuming it does turn out we can . . . do business with one another." Brown took another bite of hot dog and chewed slowly while he let Harahap digest that, then swallowed. "Mind you, what your friend said to *my* friends sounded very promising. I think it could be a very profitable relationship for both of us, judging by what your friend said your own objectives were. But it isn't the sort of *final* decision I've been authorized to make."

"So exactly what sort of 'tentative' agreement do your friends have in mind?" Harahap asked, sitting back with his beer stein.

"Pretty much the one you discussed the last time

you were here," Brown said. "We're definitely interested in establishing the sort of communication channels you proposed. That sort of market support could make or break our own marketing efforts here in Mobius. And we're also interested in arranging to see some samples—hopefully a fair number of them—of the items you offered as a loss-leader to edge into the market. But I'm sure you'll understand that we have to be a little leery of binding commitments until we've actually taken delivery of them and established both that your cartel can supply them and that there won't be any...unpleasant surprises in the delivery chain. For either of us."

His eyes met Harahap across the table, and Harahap nodded.

"Oh, I can certainly see that. So, having said that, let's look at some nuts and bolts here. First, about those communication channels. The best way to—"

"—so I don't think you'll have any problems, assuming the weapons drop goes smoothly," Harahap said into the microphone, dictating the final paragraphs of his report as *Факел* departed Mobius orbit, headed for the system hyper limit and Wonder. That report would be dropped off in a public mailbox for the next Alignment contact to pick up when he arrived in-system. "Landrum's position with Somerton should make the actual drop fairly straightforward, unless these people's security is a lot more porous than I think it is. I've only promised them small arms and a few crew-served anti-armor weapons in the first drop, so bulk shouldn't be an enormous problem. I'd really like to get something heavier into their hands, but I think starting out fairly small will be more convincing—or reassuring, at least—to the locals."

He sipped whiskey for a moment, thinking about that, then nodded to himself and resumed.

"This visit's strengthened my impression that these people are a lot better organized than three-quarters of the would-be 'revolutionaries' out this way. I suspect 'Mister Brown' is considerably higher in their hierarchy than he wanted to admit, but he's also very smooth. I'd say he has strong nerves, and if he's as senior in their organization as I think he is, they strike me as very serious players.

"I've given him the 'contact codes' to request naval support from the 'Manties,' and we may need to be ready for things to pop here in Mobius sooner than we'd anticipated. Lombroso's decision to hold 'open elections' seems to've struck a much deeper nerve than he or his advisors thought it would. There's enough frustration that genuine political debate's beginning to creep into Mobians' day-to-day conversations, now that they're going to be allowed to actually vote, and that's never a good sign for a regime like his. I'd say the odds are at least seventy-thirty that he'll try to ratchet it back down once he realizes what he's started, and that's when the shit will really hit the fan. So our window to get these people primed may be narrower than we'd thought. Bearing that in mind, I recommend—"

◇   ◇   ◇

"Mr. Nyhus is here for his thirteen-hundred, Sir," Marianne Haavikko announced over Adão Ukhtomskoy's com.

"Oh, *wonderful*," Ukhtomskoy replied. Marianne had been with him for almost two and a half T-decades;

there wasn't much point in trying to hide his opinion of Rajmund Nyhus from her. She was also the complete mistress of her expression, and no one else—like Rajmund Nyhus—was going to hear him over her earbug.

"Well, I suppose there's no escape. Send him in."

"Of course, Sir," Haavikko said pleasantly, and Ukhtomskoy sat back in his chair.

The office door opened a moment later to admit a well-tailored man with very fair hair, a dark complexion, and blue eyes. He was rather shorter than Ukhtomskoy's hundred and eighty centimeters, but he had the look of someone who spent a lot of time working out.

"Rajmund!" Ukhtomskoy said, standing and holding out his hand with a very fair counterfeit of enthusiasm.

"Adão." Nyhus gripped the extended hand firmly. "Thanks for working me in on such short notice."

"You're the head of Section Two," Ukhtomskoy pointed out. "I'm in the habit of 'working in' my section heads when they say they need to see me." He smiled thinly, waving Nyhus into one of the chairs facing his desk before he sat back down himself. "Which isn't to say," he continued, "that I don't find myself wondering what's come up so suddenly."

"I know." Nyhus shrugged. "I hadn't seen the reports before our regular first-of-the-week meeting, though. Once I did, and once I had a chance to think about the analysis, I decided it probably shouldn't wait until Thursday, though."

"What sort of reports?" Ukhtomskoy frowned.

"There's something going on in the Verge—something *new*, I mean," Nyhus amplified. "There's a lot of unrest kicking up in our administered systems. And in some systems where we're only present in a support capacity, as well."

"Pardon me, but don't we always have a lot of 'unrest' in those systems?" Ukhtomskoy asked a bit tartly.

"I probably should've said *additional* unrest," Nyhus replied. "It's getting more organized, and we've got indications someone on the outside may be fanning the flames."

"Fanning them exactly how?"

"So far it's still largely straws in the wind," Nyhus admitted, "but there are rumors in some of our pipelines about promises of weapons—substantial *numbers* of weapons. And there are even some suggestions that someone's promising outside naval support."

Ukhtomskoy's eyes narrowed. This was the first he'd heard about anything like that from any OFS source, but there was that memo Noritoshi Väinölä had kicked over to him from the Gendarmerie a month or so ago. He'd written it off at the time as alarmism, some analyst with too much time on his hands seeing a pattern in what was actually chaos. But if Section Two was picking up some sort of confirming evidence, maybe this meeting with Nyhus wasn't going to be the usual complete waste of time.

"What kind of 'rumors' are we talking about here, Rajmund?" he asked a bit sharply, and Nyhus raised his right hand, palm up.

"You know how it is, Adão. We've got confidential informants scattered from here to hell and back, and every one of them wants to find something to convince us we ought to be paying him more. So I was a little . . . skeptical, let's say, when the first reports came in.

"Obviously, no one's going to be able to document anything like this, and I think some of my senior system agents are redacting the names of their informants." His mouth twisted briefly. "We've had too many of them burned because of sloppy information security along the chain to the home office, so it's not too hard to understand why they're reluctant to scatter names around. I've sent clarification requests back down the line, but it's going to take quite a while for them to get back to me."

Ukhtomskoy nodded impatiently. The lengthy delays in transmitting data over interstellar distances were any intelligence service's worst bottleneck.

"What concerns me is how broad a front these rumors and hints are coming in across," Nyhus continued. "It stretches—assuming there's anything to it—all the way from the Talbott Quadrant to the Maya Sector. In fact, it seems to extend even beyond Maya. And the other thing that concerns me is the name that seems to be associated with the promises of support."

He paused, and Ukhtomskoy scowled. One of the many things he disliked about Nyhus was his childish tendency to draw out revelations. Ukhtomskoy hadn't played "I'll-show-you-mine-if-you'll-show-me-yours" since high school.

Willingly, at any rate.

"And what name would that be?" he asked irritably.

"Manticore," Nyhus replied.

✧   ✧   ✧

"I think the hook's set," Rajmund Nyhus said later that evening.

He sat in a restaurant privacy booth, looking across the table at a very attractive platinum-haired woman who was dressed just a bit too cheaply and gaudily for her present surroundings. As part of his persona as a corruptible bureaucrat deeply in bed with every transstellar in the galaxy, he'd cultivated a public taste for cheap prostitutes willing to put up with fairly... stringent requirements. The fact that he actually enjoyed their services was an added cherry on top, but the real reason was to add texture to his corrupt, none-to-bright, rather seedy cover. Well, that and specifically to cover his meetings with his current "date."

Like him, Claire McGrath was a beta-line of the Mesan Alignment.

Technically, Claire was his "handler," but the truth was that Rajmund Nyhus was a *lot* smarter than most of his Frontier Security colleagues would have believed. He was also too valuable and too highly placed for anything but the most secure communication avenues, however, and Claire was exactly that. Among the other traits built into her line's genotype were photographic memory and the ability to almost perfectly mimic the exact tone and emphasis of anything one of "her" agents said to her. Nothing went out electronically or in hard copy; she carried every bit of it in her head, and the recipients of her reports could be confident she'd delivered them with every nuance of the agents who'd given them to her in the first place.

Best of all, from Nyhus' viewpoint, her line's designers had also included quite a bit of DNA from one of Manpower's more popular pleasure slave lines. In addition to a stunning figure, she had the hyper-driven libido that was genengineered into them, and without the all too often brutal "training" Manpower's slaves had to survive, she embraced that libido enthusiastically. She even enjoyed playing the roles Nyhus most enjoyed. He was looking forward to this evening's romp in his playroom, and both of them could claim with straight faces that all of the interesting noises she was going to make were a legitimate part of his cover. After all, it was a given that his apartment was thoroughly bugged by Frontier Security's own internal security agencies. It would never do to not live up to his cover, now would it?

In the meantime, though, the restaurant booth was clear of OFS' bugs. He knew it was, because it, too, belonged to an Alignment employee, although in this case, all he knew about the Alignment was that someone—he thought it was the local underworld—supplemented his official cash flow generously for operating his own restaurant. He made a comfortable profit out of the restaurant, as well, and all his clandestine benefactor required was that he make sure it was swept regularly and rigorously for spy devices expressly so that people like Nyhus could meet people like Claire in a very public but totally secure location.

And the fact that so many other people knew how secure it was covered the meetings of actual Alignment operatives. They simply disappeared into the background of everyone else using it for exactly the same purposes . . . which also helped explain why it showed such a comfortable profit.

"You think Ukhtomskoy's going to take it all the way up to MacArtney?" Claire asked now while the toes of one bare foot stroked his shin under the table.

"I doubt it. There's not enough urgency in anything I've fed him so far to push it that far up the queue this quickly. But I expect he will be bringing it up at his next conference with Väinöla and Mabley. Mind you, there are so many rumors flying around about Manticore this and Manticore that I doubt anybody—including Ukhtomskoy—will jump right out to endorse any of the stuff I gave him today. But he's definitely thinking about it, especially in light of that memo Väinöla handed him a few weeks ago. And, whatever else happens, I've got it into the official record that *my* local agents' 'confidential sources' are reporting Manty involvement, whether Väinöla's are or not. So when the time comes, that information will be there ready to point attention straight at Manticore."

"Good," Claire said. She sipped wine and smiled at him. "Let's go ahead and get the rest of your regular data dump out of the way, Rajmund. I'm feeling especially impatient this evening. I'm sure—" her smile broadened and she licked her lips slowly "—that your colleagues' bugs will get a *vigorous* workout tonight!"

Chapter Twenty-Six

"GOOD TO SEE YOU AGAIN, Rufino. I wish the circumstances were better."

Rufino Chernyshev nodded soberly as he shook Collin Detweiler's hand. Detweiler stood at the corner of his desk, still leaning on a cane, and his expression was less than happy.

"I wish the circumstances were better, too. And I hope what actually happened isn't as bad as the rumors I've heard."

"That would depend on the rumors." Detweiler smiled bleakly. "After all, the newsies' accounts only cover the visible parts of how badly we got hurt."

Chernyshev's face tightened.

"I was afraid that might be the case," he said. "Especially because I wasn't getting any official word from Isabel. I knew everyone must've been busy, but in the field we didn't know—"

"She didn't brief you because she's dead." Detweiler interrupted, his voice harsh, and despite himself, Chernyshev flinched. "We lost the entire Gamma Center,"

Detweiler continued. "And we got hit with a cyber attack that did one hell of a lot more damage—to data storage and com channels—than it should have, especially given how short a window it had to work."

"Shit," Chernyshev whispered, and Detweiler's face turned even bleaker.

"I'm not done yet. We also lost Luka...and Evigni."

Chernyshev's nostrils flared. Bardasano's death had half-prepared him for losing his clone brother Luka, because Luka had been her senior bodyguard. Anything that happened to her would have had to go through him, first. But Evigni—?

"How?" The question came out harsh and hard.

"We're still trying to put all of that together," Detweiler admitted. "We know the mechanics, and we've taken at least two seccies who were involved, though they seem to've been pretty peripheral. They were interrogated...thoroughly, and they told us everything they knew," his eyes were flint. "But what they had to say creates almost more questions than answers.

"One thing we're confident of is that Anton Zilwicki—and probably Cachat, too, though our interrogators are less sold on that one—were right here on Mesa. We don't know what they were after. I'm inclined to think *they* didn't know—that it was more a probe than an operation with a specific objective. But the evidence suggests they made contact with Jack McBryde."

"Jack?!" Chernyshev stared at him.

"That's what it looks like," Detweiler confirmed heavily. "Everything went to hell so quickly I doubt anyone'll ever put the narrative together—not completely. But Jack may've gotten a bad case of second thoughts. One of the Gamma Center scientists—an alpha-line named

Simões—suffered some kind of breakdown after his clone daughter was culled. It was a high-risk genome, so he should've been prepared, but he wasn't. Unfortunately, his superiors felt he was essential to the project he was working on, so Isabel assigned Jack to ride herd on him." Detweiler's lips twitched in bitter amusement. "Apparently, instead of Jack keeping him in line, Simões pulled Jack *out* of line."

"Jack always did have too much empathy," Chernyshev said. "That was what made him so effective managing assets when he was in the field."

"And it's exactly the reason I pulled him *from* the field," Detweiler agreed. "Anyway, somehow Jack and Zilwicki got together. We're guessing Jack spotted Zilwicki in a routine agent's report and that he's the one who initiated contact. It looks like he wanted to defect —and possibly take Simões with him—but that went south when the same agent whose report led him to Zilwicki contacted Isabel directly. At that point, she had no idea what was going on, so she headed for the Gamma Center to confront him, and she took both your brothers with her. From the surveillance images we've been able to pull together, it looks like Zilwicki and Cachat had an escape route through the old service tunnels—one that took them under Buenaventura Tower. When Jack realized they were running and leaving him to twist in the wind, he used an insurance policy—that's what brought down Buenaventura. But he obviously wasn't getting out himself, so he blew the suicide charge and took the entire Gamma Center—and Isabel, Evigni, Luka, the rest of her protective detail, and Zeke Timmons—with him."

"Zeke, too?" Chernyshev shook his head like a man

who'd taken one punch too many. Zeke Timmons had been his own immediate supervisor, and Bardasano's senior aide for field operations.

"Zeke, too." Detweiler nodded. "No one's sure what she was thinking, but if I had to guess, she took Zeke and Evigni because she hadn't realized what Jack was really up to and she wanted both of them along when she confronted him and demanded an explanation of the other agent's report."

"If she didn't know he'd turned, that made sense. And I really doubt it would've occurred to her that Jack McBryde, of all people, wanted to defect."

"That's what we think, too."

"So where are we now?" Chernyshev asked in the tone of a man deliberately changing the subject.

"Well, we've told the galaxy it was the Ballroom and that Zilwicki was in it up to his eyebrows." Detweiler chuckled grimly. "Since Jack blew him and Cachat—if Cachat really was with him—to hell before he blew the Gamma Center, *he's* sure as hell not going to dispute our version! And it's possible Jack didn't set off the nuke under Buenaventura, after all. According to the seccies we've interrogated, *Zilwicki* was the one who planted that charge."

"Excuse me? You're telling me Manticore really was supporting a Ballroom op here on Mesa? And they got *nukes* through our security fences?!"

"No. Oh, that's what we're telling the *rest* of the galaxy, but what really happened was that a bunch of seccy wannabe Ballroom types right here on Mesa stole the damned things from a construction outfit. We're not sure what happened to the built-in security programs, but Zilwicki had a hell of a rep as a hacker, so that probably explains it. Anyway, according to the seccies we took, the Buenaventura charge was supposed to go off after Zilwicki and his cronies had cleared the tunnels in their breakout. The service tunnel security pickups caught them still moving through the tunnels when the charge went up, though, so I'm inclined to think Jack figured out they had it and put his own trigger into it just in case they decided to depart without him. Either that or Zilwicki was a hell of a lot clumsier with the detonator than I think was very likely."

"And the bomb in the park?"

"According to the seccies we caught, that wasn't supposed to happen. The one who apparently knew where it *was* supposed to be set off died before we got that out of him, but he'd already confirmed that another member of their murderous little group went completely off the rails when Zilwicki's operation went to hell. He's the one who picked a more painful target and flew the bomb into the park, where he killed a couple of hundred kids *my* kids played with regularly. And damned nearly killed me, too, for that matter."

"And the cyber attack?"

"That had to be Jack." Detweiler's eyes were bleak and cold. "Zilwicki may have been a galactic-class hacker, but whoever set that in motion did it from deep inside. Our forensic people've managed to reconstruct a good bit of it, and it incorporated access codes and passwords Zilwicki couldn't possibly have had. I suppose Jack could've given them up to him, but even if he had, it's pretty clear the attack originated inside the Gamma Center just before the charge went off. So all the evidence says it was Jack."

"What did Zachariah have to say about it?"

"We've questioned him, of course, and he's cooperated fully. I don't think he had a clue what his brother was up to, and if you think about it, Jack wasn't the sort who would've involved Zach. I don't know what happened inside his head to cause him to turn, but he'd never've taken family with him."

"No. No, he wouldn't have." Chernyshev shook his head slowly.

"But that's basically where we are. At the moment, we're turning lemons into lemonade by selling the rest of the galaxy our version, and the Solly newsies are falling into line nicely. Of course the Manties are denying every bit of it, but even they can't *know* what happened, and Zilwicki's association with Montaigne and her Anti-Slavery League lunatics—not to mention Torch and the Ballroom—is working against them in a huge way right now.

"In the meantime, we've only started putting ourselves back together. That cyber attack hit Isabel's data storage hard—*really* hard. We've reconstituted about fifteen percent of it so far, but I'll be astonished if we ever get more than, say, a third of it back. The rest of it we'll have to pull back together the hard way. And with Zeke and Evigni both gone, we've got huge holes in our senior command structure. For now, we've had Yountz holding down the fort."

Chernyshev nodded; Raymond Yountz had been Bardasano's number two for domestic security. Given the aftermath of the "Green Pines Atrocity" it made sense to move him up into her chair, he thought. But Detweiler wasn't done yet.

"Unfortunately, I don't think we can leave him there.

There's too much popping loose—too much happening inside the onion, frankly, as well as the mess outside it. I need to pull Yountz back to deal with that, because nobody knows his shop as well as he does and we can't afford any—any *more*—dropped stitches, *especially* on the inside. We do *not* need another Jack at this late date! I've given him Steven Lathorous as an assistant, and that's helped, but he really needs to move back into his own chair as quickly as possible.

"Which brings me to you."

"Me?" Chernyshev frowned. "I don't know the domestic side at all, Sir!"

"No, but with Isabel and Evigni gone, you know more about *external* ops than anyone else I can think of. In particular, I know you were completely read in on both Janus and Oyster Bay. If we get Yountz back on the domestic side, he should be able to take care of that until you're fully up to speed, but we don't have anyone else—especially anyone with your field experience—to take over on Janus."

Chernyshev stared at him. He'd always avoided office duty like the plague, and he started to open his mouth to protest. Then he shut it again, and Detweiler nodded.

"So I suppose congratulations are in order," he said.

❖   ❖   ❖

The logging lorry with the MacLean Forestry Products logo moved sedately down the narrow, muddy lane through the towering silver oaks in a quiet whine of lift fans. The logging lorries of Halkirk were cheap, bare-bones versions of the more sophisticated transport available elsewhere, but they got the job done. This particular specimen was rather more battered than most, however...and if any suspicious soul had checked its transponder code, they would have discovered that it had been stolen three local months earlier from a dealership in Conerock.

Which probably won't do us a hell of a lot of good if the Uppies catch us, Erin MacFadzean thought. *It's worth trying, though, especially if MacQuarie has them keeping tabs on Megan's equipment. They're less likely to spot an off-the-books lorry in the first place.*

In theory, if the United Public Safety Force intercepted a load of military-grade pulse rifles in a lorry painted in the MacLean livery but stolen from a dealership a thousand kilometers from Megan's nearest stands of timber, they should assume someone else was trying to implicate her. That she wouldn't be stupid enough to point the finger at herself. The whole idea was rather more convoluted than MacFadzean liked, but Tad Ogilvy had convinced Megan it was worth trying.

The lorry reached a split in the trail and turned west, moving steadily away from MacLean land. In fact, they were moving into a dense belt of old-growth silver oak that belonged to one Nathalan Mundy, President MacMinn's treasury secretary. Once upon a time, it *had* belonged to the MacLeans, but Mundy's creative accountants had found a way to seize it from Megan's cousin Raibert for back taxes eight T-years ago. Somehow—as often happened in the Loomis System—when that seized property was sold at auction, Mundy's had been the winning bid. But he had no intention of cutting a single trunk until the scarcity Zagorski's harvesting policies were bound to produce had driven up the price.

In the meantime, that virgin woodland, untouched except for the forestry trails cut through it, was the perfect hiding place for the weapons which had begun to arrive as promised. Megan MacLean had grown up roaming her cousin's land as well as her own. She was intimately familiar with it, and she'd hired two thirds of Raibert's foresters when the IRS seized the land and took away their living. They knew lots of places to stash things, and the last place the Uppies would expect resistance groups to cache weapons was on a cabinet secretary's land!

This was the fifth—and final—trip to distribute Bolívar's initial shipment. The other four had gone without a snag, and once she had this load snugged away, she could pass word up the chain to arrange the *next* shipment. And if things went the way she hoped they would, Bolívar's *second* installment would deliver crewed anti-air and anti-armor weapons, as well.

And then the Loomis Liberation Front will start to grow some real *teeth*, she thought with a thin, cold smile.

❖   ❖   ❖

"I wish you'd be just a little less provocative, Raghnall," Megan MacLean said with a certain degree of asperity. "The last thing you need—*any* of us need—is to give MacCrimmon a pretext to bring the hammer down on us!"

"And what makes you think MacCrimmon needs a 'pretext' where anyone with the name MacRory's concerned?" Raghnall had the MacRory chin . . . and the MacRorys' gray eyes, which happened to be bright with anger at the moment. "You might be remembering what happened to my father and grandfather. You remember—the air-car accident?"

MacLean took a firm grip on her own temper.

What she really wanted to do was grab him and shake some sense into him. Unfortunately, he was twenty-one centimeters taller than she was, and stocky for his height. And, she conceded, he had a point. As the heirs of King Tavis III, the MacRory family had great big bull's-eyes pasted to their backs no matter what happened, and the amount of popular sentiment focused upon them only made it worse.

It wasn't that Tavis III had been a great king, because he hadn't. In fact, he'd been well-meaning but ineffectual and a bit weak, which was the main reason he'd abdicated following the bloody coup launched by Keith and Ailsa MacMinn's Loomis Prosperity Party. A stronger monarch might have attempted to rally support against the coup; Tavis had seen only the promise of still more bloodshed, and so he'd handed in his crown. Most people hadn't minded that much, and—after banning him and his entire family from politics—the MacMinns had allowed him to retire to private life, where he'd died of genuinely natural causes only a couple of years later. But the LPP had been less willing to take chances with his son, Angus, especially when people started talking about the good old days and "Good King Tavis" as SEIU started turning the screws on the Loomisian economy. As the unrest grew, more and more people started turning to the notion of bringing back the MacRory Dynasty.

Angus MacRory had known how that would end, so he'd stayed as far away from politics as he could. But Vice President MacCrimmon wasn't the sort to tolerate even potential threats, and whatever might have been the case for Tavis' death, there'd been nothing at all natural about his son's or his older grandson's. No one would ever be able to prove MacCrimmon had ordered their murder, but, then, there were a great many things no one would ever be able to "prove" in Loomis.

There was no doubt in the minds of Mánas MacRory, Angus' younger son, or in his nephew Raghnall. Like his father, Mánas had been as apolitical as possible, but after Angus and Seamus' deaths, that had become a frail protection, and Raghnall wasn't prepared to see his uncle murdered the same way. There wasn't much he could do to protect Mánas if MacCrimmon was prepared to come out into the open, but there was quite a lot he could do to preclude the sort of "accident" which had killed Seamus and Angus.

It was a sign of just how worried MacCrimmon was that Senga MacQuarie's Uppies *hadn't* moved openly when Raghnall organized the MacRory Militia out of his own family's foresters and likeminded volunteers. There were only two or three hundred of them, but they were armed—albeit with purely civilian weapons—and Raghnall had made it clear he and his people *would* protect his uncle and the rest of his family. They wouldn't stand a chance against Public Safety in a standup fight, but they also wouldn't go down *without* a fight, and no one in the LPP or SEIU really knew where that would end.

The result was a sort of tense truce—or, more accurately, a standoff—between the Militia and the system government. But it was a precarious balance, and as the current discontent and anger over SEIU's logging policies soared, it was becoming steadily more precarious.

"Raghnall, I understand how you feel," MacLean said now. "For that matter, I agree with what you just said.

But we need time—time to get ourselves organized. If something pushes MacQuarie into moving against you before the rest of us are ready to support you, it'll be a bloodbath that sees your uncle and you both dead. The rest of us won't be able to do a thing to stop that, and we both know MacCrimmon will seize the opportunity to do a thorough housecleaning of anyone he even suspects might oppose the regime. Which means the rest of us will go down right along with you."

"Time, is it?" Those gray eyes turned cold. "And what about all the 'time' you wasted on 'political reform,' Megan MacLean? The time you spent playing at politics while MacCrimmon murdered my grandfather and my father?"

MacLean bit down on a hot response. It wasn't easy, but she couldn't deny his point. In fact, a large part of her agreed with his accusation.

"I deserve that," she said after a moment, meeting those icy eyes levelly. "I thought I was making the right choice, but the truth is there *aren't* any 'right' choices anymore. It may've taken me a while to realize that, but I didn't start organizing the Liberation Front just to sit on my hands, Raghnall. I know why you're worried about your uncle, and you're right to be. But there are a lot of other people who've begun to see what you've been saying all along...and I'm one of them. We just need you to avoid letting MacCrimmon draw you into a false step until the rest of us can catch up with you and actually be ready to act. That's all I'm saying. Just give us time. *Buy* us time—please!"

Raghnall glared at her, but then the broad shoulders

sagged slightly and the icy fire in his eyes faded. It didn't disappear; it was simply banked.

"All right," he said. "I'll not go crawling on my knees to MacQuarie and surrender our weapons. That I won't do, not for you or God Himself! They'll not do to my uncle what they've done to the rest of my family! But I'll pull the lads and lassies back onto MacRory land. We'll keep our heads down, mind our manners, and stay as far out of the public eye as we can. But know this, Megan MacLean—Hell won't hold what'll happen when the first Uppy sets foot on MacRory land after us!"

DECEMBER 1921 POST DIASPORA

"She didn't really discuss whatever they talked about with me. I think she and Willie...had words over it, though. From what he very carefully hasn't said to me, it wasn't a very...productive conversation from his perspective. In fact, it's probably a little surprising both of them emerged intact. Of the two, my money would have been on Honor, understand. Willie would have been swinging above his weight."

—Hamish Alexander-Harrington,
Earl White Haven,
First Lord of Admiralty,
Star Empire of Manticore.

Chapter Twenty-Seven

A BRISK, COOL BREEZE swept up the avenue, snapping and popping among the brightly colored flags on the second-floor staffs of the buildings lining the street, as Abigail Hearns turned the corner and saw the ocean spread out before her. Dramatic clouds, piled high in billows and swoops of white but black and flat-bottomed with coming rain, swept in across that ocean. The rain was still several hours away, according to the met people, but it promised a tumultuous, lightning and thunder-streaked night, and she hoped she'd still be dirtside to enjoy it.

For the present she settled for filling her lungs with the freshness of un-canned air, feeling sunlight on her skin, and something inside purred in sensual pleasure. Any spacer who spent her life in artificial environments, hurtling between star systems, would have understood that pleasure, but it held a special savor for Abigail Hearns. She was a Grayson. Her homeworld's environment tried to kill its people every single day, and children weren't allowed outside without strict adult supervision until they were into their teens. Simple rain storms posed potential health risks as they scrubbed the heavy-metal planet's dust out of the atmosphere; breath masks to protect against that same dust on windy days like this were standard issue; and any natural body of water was far too contaminated for anyone to dream of swimming in. The majority of Graysons would have felt acutely uncomfortable in her place, but the years she'd spent off Grayson, first at Saganami Island and then serving on ships of the Royal Manticoran Navy, had changed Abigail Hearns in a lot of ways. One of those was her love—almost the addiction—of open spaces, fresh breeze, and sunlight untrammeled by anything remotely resembling an environmental suit.

She even liked walking in the rain . . . without an umbrella.

It was why she'd chosen to walk the six blocks to the restaurant, rather to the disgust of the tall, powerfully built Owens Steadholder's Guard lieutenant walking just behind her. Mateo Gutierrez *wasn't* a Grayson—by birth, at least—and while he had nothing against sunlight and fresh air—in moderation—he'd seen quite enough of both during his active-duty career as a Royal Manticoran Marine, thank you very much. And as the man charged with keeping Abigail Hearns alive at any cost, he was very much in two minds about his charge's taste for trundling around in a wide-open threat environment.

It was unlikely anyone here in the city of Thimble had any designs upon her life, but she was Steadholder Owens' oldest daughter. That made her an important political chip, whether for Grayson's internal politics or its relationship with the Star Kingdom, and there was always a chance someone would seek to cash that chip in. It was Gutierrez's job to be certain that didn't happen, and he was a man who took his duty seriously. Not to mention the very personal reasons he'd had to keep Abigail Hearns alive ever since a bloody, brutal day on a planet called Refuge in a star system called Tiberian. Mateo Gutierrez wasn't a man who found it easy to show emotions—or so he fondly believed—but he hadn't left the Marines and transferred to the Owens Guard on a whim.

Now something remarkably like an exasperated sigh of relief escaped him as the holo-sign of their destination flashed ahead of them.

"Oh, cheer up, Mateo!" Abigail scolded with a smile. "We're almost there, a little walk isn't going to kill you, and we both needed the fresh air. You can grumble all you want, but you were as tired of those bulkheads as I was!"

"There's a reason for all the taxis flitting around this city, My Lady."

"Yes, there is. And don't think I'm missing your evasion of my last point."

"Evasion, My Lady?" Profound innocence was an expression which did not suit Lieutenant Gutierrez's face.

"Evasion." She punched him lightly and affectionately on the shoulder, but then her own expression sobered. "And it's good to see all this, too." She waved one hand to take in the crowded slide walks, the curbside cafés, the delivery air vans, air cars—and, yes, taxis—buzzing by overhead. "Good to see people just being *people* instead of cat's-paws . . . or icons on a tactical display."

Her gray-blue eyes had darkened, and Gutierrez stopped a grimace before it ever reached his face. He knew exactly what that darkness was, but he couldn't exactly say that. So instead—

"Could see it just as well from a taxi's window, My Lady," he grumbled.

"You really *are* impossible, aren't you?" Abigail demanded, and laughed as she punched his shoulder again. But gratitude for the distraction accompanied the fresh humor in her eyes. "Well, there's the restaurant, so you can get me safely off the street in about, oh, another five minutes."

✧   ✧   ✧

Helen Zilwicki looked up as Lieutenant Hearns headed for their table, threading her way through the crowd behind the majordomo heels while Lieutenant Gutierrez followed at her heels, a ponderous cruiser keeping a watchful eye on the lively destroyer of his charge.

"Does he go *everywhere* with her?" Gwen Archer asked softly, and Helen chuckled.

"Pretty much, except the head," she replied. "Oh, he's got his own battle station aboard ship, but *off* the ship?" She shook her head. "At that, she's damned lucky she's a 'mere daughter'! That's the only way she got off with a *single* personal armsman. Someone like Duchess Harrington has a permanent *three*-man team everywhere she goes."

"Damn." It was Archer's turn to shake his head. "It's easy to forget she's a steadholder's daughter . . . until something like this comes along, anyway."

"Abigail has a tendency to stand stereotypes on their ears," Helen agreed, then stood and held out her hand in greeting.

"Abigail! I'm glad you could get shore leave."

"It *is* nice, isn't it?" Abigail shook her hand instead of giving her the hug she would have received in a less public venue. "It reminds me of Landing back on Manticore, in a lot of ways." Helen arched an incredulous eyebrow, and Abigail laughed. "Not the architecture and not the people, but the ocean. You Manties are spoiled by having oceans people can actually swim in! It probably takes a Grayson to appreciate them *properly*."

"You might want to discuss that with Duchess Harrington," Helen pointed out dryly. "Assuming you can get her off her sailboat long enough, of course."

"Point taken," Abigail acknowledged. "Of course, I could also point out that she *is* a Grayson . . . now," she added and turned to Archer as he stood. Under the strict letter of naval protocol, she really should have greeted him first, as Helen's superior officer, but it was a social occasion, after all.

"Lieutenant Archer," she said, shaking his hand.

"Lieutenant Hearns," he replied. "Or should that properly be 'Miss Owens'?"

"Only if you really like making enemies." She smiled. "On certain official occasions I have to put up with that. This isn't one of them."

Behind her, Lieutenant Gutierrez's eyes might have rolled ever so slightly, but Archer resolutely ignored that possibility.

"Good enough," he said, and waved for her to be seated.

She settled into the waiting chair, and Helen and Archer resumed their own seats. Gutierrez remained standing, somewhat to the chagrin of the waitstaff who seemed, for some odd reason, to find the next best thing to two massively-built meters of uniformed, *armed* watchdog plunked down in the middle of their restaurant moderately unsettling. Abigail would have invited him to join them, if she hadn't known how useless the invitation would be.

"So," she said, after their orders had been taken, "what's the latest buzz from high places, Helen? Or the latest buzz you can share, at least."

"Well, I'm afraid the Commodore hasn't shared any ultimate-cosmic-top-secret-shred-before-reading information with me. Has Lady Gold Peak shared any with you, Gwen?"

"Of course she has." Archer did his best to look down his snub nose at her. "And, equally of course, I am not in a position to share that privileged information with the plebeian junior officers clustered admiringly about me."

Abigail snorted in amusement. She'd only met Archer a couple of times, and then only in passing, but she'd suspected he had a sense of humor.

"Where *is* Helga when I need her?" Helen sighed, shaking her head. Then she reached into a pocket of her tunic. "Fortunately, she left me a pin to deflate you when you get too full of yourself. Let me see now. Where *did* I put it?"

She felt around in her pocket, and Archer laughed.

"I give!" he said.

"Good," Helen told him, then looked back at Abigail. "On a more serious front, I'm guessing the best news from your perspective is that we should see Admiral Oversteegen within the next ten days."

"Oh, good!" Abigail smiled broadly, and even Gutierrez allowed himself a much smaller smile. Michael

Oversteegen was as maddening a product of the Manticoran aristocracy as could be imagined, a perfect example of the drawling, lazy fop the Liberal Party loved to caricature. None of which mattered a bit to anyone who'd ever been privileged to serve under him, especially in places like Tiberian.

"I thought you'd like to know," Helen said. "But the fact that he's bringing another full squadron of *Nikes* and at least another squadron of *Saganami-Cs* with him is even better news from where I sit."

"Absolutely," Abigail agreed. "Especially after New Tuscany," she added, her expression darkening once more.

Helen nodded with a matching edge of bleakness. At least, unlike Abigail, she hadn't seen three-quarters of her destroyer division's ships blown out of space by six times as many battlecruisers while they orbited peacefully—and helplessly—around the planet of New Tuscany. The hit Helen had taken from that massacre had been nowhere near as savage as the one Abigail and the rest of HMS *Tristram*'s crew had sustained, although something still tightened dangerously inside her whenever she thought of Amandine Corvisart's death. She'd *liked* Corvisart, damn it!

At least the slaughter of Commodore Chatterjee's people had been avenged by the destruction of SLNS *Jean Bart* and the arrogant, stupid, supercilious, incompetent, egotistical, *stupid* admiral who'd opened fire on them. Abigail felt a deep, intense satisfaction at that thought, and if anyone had cared to point out that it was uncharitable of her, she wouldn't have given a single solitary damn. That didn't mean she was oblivious to the potential consequences for the Star Empire's steadily worsening relations with the Sollies, of course. Which was why the arrival of Michael Oversteegen's big, powerful and very, very dangerous battlecruisers would be so welcome. She couldn't think of anything in the Solly inventory—up to and including their best ship of the wall—that would really enjoying going toe-to-toe with a *Nike*.

Although, she added conscientiously, it would be far better all around if nothing of that sort ever happened, of course.

"Well, at least until the Sollies get around to restoring their computers, none of Byng's battlecruisers are going anywhere," Helen pointed out.

One of Michelle Henke's last steps before departing New Tuscany had been to trigger the security function in the surrendered battlecruisers' computer nets, using the access codes she'd demanded as the precondition to allowing Byng's survivors to surrender rather than following him straight to hell. The software had obediently lobotomized the ships, reconfiguring those nets from *computers* into pristine blocks of undifferentiated molecular circuitry. Every trace of data had been irrevocably erased, and while the molycircs themselves were just fine, it would require a properly equipped repair team to rebuild the matrices that turned them back into computers once again, and even then, they'd have to be completely programmed—from scratch—before those ships went *anywhere*. Until then, they were as effectively out of action as if Tenth Fleet had blown every one of them out of space along with *Jean Bart*.

"That ought to buy us some breathing space, anyway," Archer agreed with profound satisfaction. "Of course, after New Tuscany, any Solly with a functional brain would know better than to screw around with the RMN, anyway. Unfortunately, Sollies with functional brains seem to be just a little thin on the ground." His smile was tart enough to pucker every lip within fifty meters. "But with half their available ships stuck in New Tuscany orbit for the next four or five months, even *Sollies* may not do anything else stupid in the meantime."

"We can hope, at least," Helen said. "I'm not going to hold my breath, though."

❖   ❖   ❖

"So how are things back in Swallow, First Sergeant?"

Vincent Frugoni's blue eyes narrowed.

"I don't use that anymore, Mr. Eldbrand," he said. "Especially around here," he added a bit pointedly.

"Here" was The Busted Stein, a bar on the less-good side of Anatevka, the largest city—such as it was—on the planet Tevye and capital of the Wonder System, and Damien Harahap allowed himself to roll his eyes.

"I applaud your caution," he responded, after a moment, "and if it really bothers you, I won't use it either. But I didn't exactly pick this spot at random." He tipped back in his chair and twitched his head in the direction of the somewhat villainous looking bartender. "He does enough illegal business with enough unsavory characters out of this bar that no informant who likes his kneecaps is going to report anything that happens in it. And I personally swept it for electronic eavesdroppers when I arrived."

Frugoni considered that, then shrugged.

"Point taken." Frugoni pulled out a chair on the other side of the small, unsteady table and sat. "And it's probably paranoid of me to worry about it here."

"No," Harahap said after a moment. "No, it's not

paranoid at all, and I apologize." Somewhat to his own surprise, he meant it, too. "Tradecraft is tradecraft, wherever you are, and breaking it is never a good idea. Sometimes the smartass in me forgets that. Sorry."

Frugoni sat back, his expression faintly surprised, then chuckled.

"I'm glad to see I'm not the only smartass at the table."

"Well, I think that's probably an element in the character of most people who get involved in this sort of thing," Harahap observed. "And, trust me, there are times it helps. As long as you remember—the way I sometimes forget to—to keep it under control. In my defense, I'm actually pretty good at doing that under normal field conditions."

"As you say, we can probably dispense with at least some of our paranoia in a high class, upscale place like this," Frugoni said dryly, and it was Harahap's turn to chuckle. But then his expression sobered.

"Should I assume you found the opportunity to discuss my offer with your brother-in-law?" he asked quietly, leaning forward across the table.

"That's why I'm here. If I hadn't, and if he hadn't wanted me to follow it up, I wouldn't be," Frugoni pointed out.

"That was intended as what's known as a conversational gambit," Harahap told him with a smile. "I did say I could be a smartass, didn't I?"

"Yes. Yes, I believe you did. And—"

Frugoni paused and looked up in faint surprise as a waiter materialized at his elbow. Obviously he hadn't expected anything of the sort in an establishment like The Busted Stein.

"Drink?" the waiter inquired succinctly.

"It's sort of required if we're using the table," Harahap told the ex-Marine, indicating his own two-thirds full stein. "I'd stick with the beer, though. It's not great, but I'm not sure about all the ingredients in the harder stuff."

The waiter appeared unconcerned by Harahap's aspersions upon his place of employment's beverages. He only waited until Frugoni shrugged.

"Bring me one of those." He nodded at Harahap's stein, and the waiter grunted.

"Five credits," he said, proffering his memo board.

"*Five* credits?" Frugoni repeated, and the waiter shrugged. Frugoni glowered at him for a moment, then sighed. "All right. All right!"

He touched his uni-link to the waiter's board, authorizing the charge, and the Anatevkan turned and ambled away.

"This place gets better and better," Frugoni muttered, and Harahap laughed.

"Compared to some places I've done this kind of business, it's a palace, believe me!"

"What a fascinating life you must live," Frugoni said sourly. Then shrugged. "But, as I was saying, I've talked to the others. I'm not going to blow any smoke up your ass by pretending there aren't some serious reservations. Mostly because however good you make the offer sound, even the boys up in the high hollows are smart enough to realize that if it comes to a choice between us and *you*, you're going to pick you."

Harahap started to speak, but the other man held up one hand.

"I'm not saying any of us think you *ought* to pick anybody else if your people find themselves up against it, Eldbrand. You shouldn't. I'm just telling you everybody on our side recognizes that. Which means, among other things, that we're not going to let you any further inside. Not because we aren't grateful or anything, but there's that old saying about two people keeping a secret."

"'Any two people can keep a secret...as long as one of them is dead,'" Harahap quoted, and Frugoni nodded.

"Exactly. Bearing that in mind, are you ready to buy a possum in a sack?"

Harahap frowned thoughtfully. The "possum" of Swallow bore very little physical resemblance to the original Old Terran species, although it filled much the same ecological niche. It was also considered one of the delicacies of mountain cuisine, and he recognized the allusion to the mountaineer who'd sold a sack full of possums to a credulous flatlander...who'd gotten home to find the sack full of venom frogs, instead.

"Yes," he said simply, after a carefully metered pause, and Frugoni nodded.

"In that case, how do we do this?"

"Well, I can have five or six hundred pulse rifles and maybe three hundred man-portable SAMs delivered here in Wonder in about two T-months," Harahap said calmly, and watched Frugoni's eyes brighten. "I can throw in about twelve thousand rounds per rifle, too. It'll take something like another two T-months before I could get anything heavier—or more ammo, for that matter—in here. Of course, that's to Wonder. Getting them from here to *Swallow* may be a non-trivial challenge."

"How would they be coming in?" Frugoni asked, his eyes narrowing.

"Depends on how you want them manifested." Harahap shrugged. "I can get them through Wonder customs labeled as just about anything you want, but I think having your people try to pick them up here would constitute an additional element of risk. All in all, it'd probably be better to simply use Wonder as a staging point and ship them from here to Swallow. There's always the chance of their being intercepted by somebody at the Swallow end, but I think that would be less likely than the chance of something slipping if we try to juggle things here in Wonder."

"You're probably right about that." Frugoni pursed his lips thoughtfully. "I can think of a couple of approaches that might work, including straight up bribery. We might have to hit you up for some financial support to make that work, but at least three of Tallulah's Capistrano freight managers are greedy enough to overlook just about anything. In fact, one of them's been doing just that over medical supplies and some of the CMM's . . . nonlethal logistics." He smiled unpleasantly. "That gives us a certain amount of leverage, given how thoroughly he's screwed if his bosses find out what he's already been up to."

"Having a leash is always handy," Harahap said, "but *depending* on one can get risky."

"Agreed. That's why I'm not ready to just go ahead and tell you to ship them through him right now. And I don't suppose you'd like to get your own people picked up by Five if it turned out I was wrong."

"Not going to happen." Harahap chuckled. "However you want it shipped, we'll ship it. But we'll be using third-party carriers, and none of our people are getting any closer to Swallow than right here in Wonder. Trust me, it'll be better—and safer—for all of us." He shook his head. "You people do *not* need to have contact with a bunch of outworlders anywhere Matsuhito's people might notice it."

"True enough. But I hate to lose any time on the first delivery."

"No need to." Harahap shrugged. "It'll arrive here in Wonder in about two months, like I said. What needs to happen in the meantime is that you go back to Swallow and figure out exactly where you want the weapons delivered, how you need them packaged, and how you need them manifested. I've already set up a secure mail account here in Anatevka. If you can get back here within, say, five T-weeks—even six—and drop the information into that account, my . . . associates who get them this far can see to any repacking and relabeling you might need." He smiled cynically. "In that respect, a place like Wonder's just about perfect. Smuggling's one of the locals' major industries, and for some odd reason, they don't seem to have a whole lot of concern about Tallulah's tender sensibilities."

Chapter Twenty-Eight

TAMMAS MACCLACHER FROWNED AS his panel chirped. He laid his book reader in his lap and punched up his air car's HUD. At the moment, he was parked on the summit of a hill in the shade of a grove of mountain oak—silver oak's shorter (and less pricey) cousin—just off the main ground route from the capital and three kilometers inside Caisteal Òrach's eastern perimeter. It was a good spot from which to keep an eye on the ceramacrete ribbon of the ancient, old-fashioned roadway . . . and the hill gave enough elevation to substantially extend the range of his air car's somewhat illegally modified radar.

Now his HUD came up, and his mouth tightened, his frown turning into something harsher and colder, and he stabbed the com button.

"MacHutchin," a voice replied almost instantly.

"Elphin, it's Tammas," MacClacher said tersely. "I've got a dozen incoming, sixty-five kilometers out. No transponders, and they just came over Greentree Knob at less than a hundred meters."

"*Cac!*" A moment of silence, and then. "How fast?"

"About three hundred. They'll be there in maybe fifteen minutes."

"Got it."

The connection died, and MacClacher lifted his own air car off the ground and sent it scudding westward at well over five hundred kilometers per hour.

"Get your guns!"

Luíseach MacRory MacGill jerked up out of her chair as Elphin MacHutchin burst out onto the veranda.

"What are you talking about, Elphin?!" her father demanded, looking up from his after-lunch whiskey, but MacHutchin had his priorities straight.

"Keddy, fetch Peter and Georgina," he snapped, rather than answering that question. "I've called the air cars 'round. Tell them there's no time to pack!"

"Aye, Elphin!" Keddy MacRory jerked his head in sharp acknowledgment and went charging off the veranda towards the stables.

"Damn it, Elphin!" Mánas MacRory half-barked in exasperation. "What the hell are you on about?!"

"The friggin' Uppies're inbound!" MacHutchin half-snarled, turning back to him. "A dozen of MacQuarie's tac lorries! They'll be here in fifteen minutes!"

"*Shit!*" Luíseach's cousin Raghnall came out of his chair, gray eyes flashing.

"Are you sure about that, Elphin?" her father asked sharply.

"Young Tammas picked them up crossing Greentree Knob at treetop level." MacHutchin's voice was as bleak as his expression. "No transponders, twelve of 'em, and they're coming in at three hundred KPH flying nape-of-the-earth. What does that sound like to *you*, Mánas?"

Elphin MacHutchin had been Mánas MacRory's bodyguard for over twenty T-years, and his concern—his *fear*—turned that bleak voice hard as steel.

"It doesn't necessarily mean they plan on coming in guns blazing," Elspeth MacRory told her husband, laying her hand on his arm, her face tense, but Mánas shook his head as he laid his own hand over hers.

"Maybe not guns blazing, *gràidheag*," he said. "But nobody else would be sneaking in on us that way. And they wouldn't have that many vehicles unless they damned well meant business."

"We have to get you out of here, *Dadaidh*," Luíseach said urgently. "Now!"

"No." Mánas shook his head, his expression grim. "You and the children, yes, but I'll not run—not from our own land! It's a little enough the bastards've left us, and they'll not take this to go with it!"

Luíseach bit her lip. Caisteal Òrach, Golden Castle, was the last of the dozen or so royal estates which had once belonged to the MacRory Dynasty. Tavis MacRory had become King Tavis I largely because his family had been the single largest landowner on Halkirk, and he'd provided almost every hectare of the Crown's land by deeding it to the Crown at the time of his coronation. The deed, however, had clearly stipulated that it reverted to his family in the event that the monarchy was abolished. Tavis MacRory had been a hardheaded, pragmatic man who'd frankly doubted the monarchy *wouldn't be* abolished, eventually, and if his family was going to provide the Crown's lands, he intended to make sure it got them back if that happened.

Needless to say, the Loomis Prosperity Party had seen no reason it should be bound by a solemn contract. The MacMinns had simply taken over the vast majority of those lands as "government property"… and handed two thirds of it out to various cronies. The only real exception had been Caisteal Òrach, the smallest and least valuable of all the royal estates.

"If they get kicked out on their asses, we can always get it back," Raghnall pointed out. "And Luíseach's right. We've got to get *you* out of here, whatever happens, *Uncail*. If they get their hands on you two and the children, there's no one left."

"No one left to do *what*?" Mánas demanded. "D'you actually think there's a chance in hell of anyone 'kicking their asses out'?" Anger—not at his nephew—made his voice harsh, almost savage, and Raghnall shrugged.

"I don't know," he said simply. "But this I do know—if anyone ever *can* kick them out, they'll need a symbol to rally 'round. And, God help us all, right now, that's our family. It's *you*, and don't forget what happened to Dad and Granddad." His expression was carved out of granite. "If they want you gone, *arresting* you may be the last thing on their minds."

"He's right, Mánas," Elspeth said tightly.

"And where do we go?" Mánas' expression was bitter. "What hole will I crawl into?"

"Amulree," Raghnall replied. "They won't expect you there, given the way you and Huisdean tore into each other the last time you met."

"No, and I doubt Huisdean'll be all that damned happy to see us, either!"

Huisdean MacRory, who headed one of the cadet branches of the MacRory line, was a distant cousin, but he and Mánas had loathed one another since childhood.

"Which is exactly what I hope MacQuarie and Mac-Crimmon will think, too." Raghnall chuckled grimly. "I'm not saying Huisdean's one of your greater admirers, *Uncail* Mánas, but he's blood, when all's said, and a lot less fond of MacCrimmon than he's ever let on."

"You've talked to him about this?" Mánas demanded.

"Of course I have! And I didn't mention it to you because I knew what you'd say. But he'll put a roof over your head, and his lads will fight to keep it there. *If* you get yourself out of here before the Uppies land in the front yard!"

Mánas glared at his nephew like an irate bull, but then the fire in his eye faded and his shoulders slumped.

"You're right, *balach*," he said. "You're right. It just goes hard."

"I know, *Uncail*. But there's no choice. Now get *Antaidh* Elspeth—and yourself—out of here."

"And what about you?" Mánas demanded as he extended his hand to Elspeth, pulling her to her feet. "If they want me, they'll want you."

"Not so much as they're wanting *you* ... and Luíseach," Raghnall said grimly. "I'll not be heir unless something's happened to you, her, Peter and Georgina."

"He's right, *Dadaidh*," Luíseach said, and her voice was hard. She wasn't only Mánas' daughter; she was also second in command of the MacRory Militia. "Oh, they'll want him, too, but not so much as they want us and the kids."

"And you're right, *Uncail*," Raghnall said. "This *is* MacRory land, and there'll damned well be a MacRory on it when those bastards land!"

"We've no time to debate all this," MacHutchin pointed out sharply. He raised his uni-link to his ear, listening for a moment, then snorted.

"Keddy's got Peter and Georgina," he said. "He's loaded them into the stable air van instead of waiting for the air car. In fact—"

Everyone on the veranda looked up as the air van snarled into the air and headed west, directly away from the incoming UPS strike force.

"You can catch up later," Raghnall told Luíseach. "In the meantime, get your father and mother out of here. And keep your head down at Amulree."

Luíseach looked rebellious, but only for a moment. Then she nodded unhappily.

Two air cars sizzled in for landings, and Mánas, Elspeth, and Luíseach had just started for the veranda's steps when the door to the house flew open again.

"There's another lot coming in from the west!" Steaphan MacHutchin, Elphin's son barked. There was a military-grade pulse rifle over his shoulder, and he threw its duplicate to his father as he came. "Another dozen of the bastards!"

"Damn it to hell!" Raghnall snarled. "Go, *Uncail*! Get out of here *now!*"

"Steaphan, you're with Luíseach in the second car!" Elphin snapped, checking the pulse rifle's magazine.

"Aye!" his son acknowledged, and took Luíseach's elbow, half-pulling her down the steps while Elphin followed Mánas and Elspeth towards the nearer air car. Fifteen or twenty more militiamen came boiling out of Caisteal Òrach's outbuildings, all of them armed, and three-man crews atop the main house were stripping the camouflage panels from the pair of roof-mounted anti-air tribarrels Raghnall had acquired from Erin MacFadzean.

Raghnall claimed a pulse rifle of his own while he watched the air cars lift off and streak away—to the north, this time, not due west—and wondered if his uncle understood the real reason he'd stayed. Oh, he'd meant it, when he said there'd be a MacRory on MacRory land when the Uppies landed. MacMinn and MacCrimmon had spilled too much MacRory blood for it to be any other way. But if MacQuarie's strike commander realized Mánas, Elspeth, and Luíseach had already left, their chance of eluding capture would go from slim to nonexistent. The longer he and his militiamen stalled the Uppies, made them think their quarry was in the house behind him, the better the escapees' odds became.

It's not like I ever thought we could stop the bastards. I just never told Uncle Mánas that. Best case, MacCrimmon and MacQuarie would've backed down rather than risk an open fight when people are already so pissed over Zagorski's policies. But if they insisted on taking him in, there was never any real chance we could stop them. But if I'd told him that, he'd've pitched three kinds of fits about "running out" and leaving me to stall.

Unlike Mánas, Luíseach had always known exactly what Raghnall had in mind. She hadn't liked it one bit, but she had children to think of. Raghnall didn't. That gave him a greater degree of freedom, and he switched his uni-link into Caisteal Òrach's general net.

"All right, *gaisgeach*," he said. "Get to your places, but nobody fires a shot unless *I* say so. We're buying time, not starting a bloody war!"

One or two of the militiamen—and women—looked

rebellious, but heads nodded, and he wasn't concerned with his lads and lasses' discipline. In fact, he was a lot more worried by the Uppies' *lack* of discipline. Hopefully, they'd see the rooftop tribarrels and decide talking beat shooting. And when they did—

"Oh my God!" someone shouted, and Raghnall wheeled around as the stable air van came hurtling back out of the west... pursued not by a UPS tactical van but by a military-grade sting ship in the livery of Star Enterprise Initiatives Unlimited's in-house security arm. The van slewed sharply in midair—Keddy was clearly trying to put it back on the ground—but Raghnall's eyes were still widening in horror when the sting ship's bow mounted pulse cannon fired.

The burst of ultradense thirty-millimeter ceramic darts shredded the air van like an old-fashioned chainsaw. The vehicle tipped crazily and then simply disintegrated in a massive ball of exploding fuel.

"Bastards!" Raghnall heard someone else screaming with his vocal cords, and the pulse rifle snapped to his shoulder. Military-grade or not, it would have been useless against the heavily armored sting ship.

The rooftop tribarrels weren't... and the gun crews were no longer waiting for anyone's permission.

The sting ship pulled up sharply, banking away from the murdered air van, and ran straight into a torrent of fire from both tribarrels. One sleek wing disintegrated, and the sting ship cartwheeled out of the air. It plowed into the surrounding forest at better than six hundred kilometers per hour and exploded.

"Under fire!" Raghnall heard Elphin MacHutchin's voice over the uni-link com channel an instant later. *"We're under fire!* We're—"

The voice stopped abruptly, and Raghnall MacRory's face was stone as understanding roared through him.

They never meant to "arrest" anybody. His thoughts were colder than ice and more implacable than any glacier. *It was Dad and Granddad all over again. But they're not going to be able to sell it as an "accident" this time.*

And they damned well aren't going to have it all their way, either.

He looked at the tattered, flaming wreckage where fourteen-year-old Peter and nine-year-old Georgina MacRory had just died and inhaled sharply.

"Find your positions," he said coldly, and wheeled to face the armed men and women who stood staring at the same wreckage. "If they want us bad enough, they'll have us . . . but not until we've killed a shit pot of *them* first!"

✧   ✧   ✧

"—don't care *what* MacCrimmon or MacQuarie say!" Burgess Stirling snarled. "That was goddamned well a fucking *assassination*, and every one of us knows it!"

Wordless, savage agreement rolled around the table under the light of the hissing pressure lantern, and Megan MacLean's heart sank as she heard it. Not because she disagreed with a single thing Stirling had said, and not because the same fury didn't throb in time with her own pulse beat. But because—

"We're still not ready!" Nessa MacRuer looked at the others pleadingly. "I know how all of you feel—*I* feel the same way! But we aren't *ready* yet!"

"That doesn't matter," Tammas MacPhee grated. "I agree with you, Nessa, but it doesn't *matter.* They've started something none of us can stop, any more than

MacCrimmon could stop it—not at this point. And let's face it—if we're not able or willing to move now, after something like *this*, we never *will!*"

"Damned right," Stirling growled.

His organization, the Red Fern Association, had consistently pushed for a more confrontational stance. They'd wanted street demonstrations, provocations, even riots. They hadn't worried about burned out shops and businesses, or even broken heads and bodies in the street. In fact, they'd *wanted* broken heads, wanted the Uppies to overreact and squirt hydrogen straight into the furnace of Halkirk's growing unrest. Megan MacLean understood that perfectly, and she'd never much cared for Stirling or his methods.

But that didn't mean he was wrong now.

She looked around their meeting place, at the bare stone walls and dirt floor. Any physical meeting between the leaders of the Loomis Liberation League was incredibly dangerous, but so were electronic conferences, and some meeting places were less dangerous than others. Like this one. The long-abandoned cellar was a relic of the very first wave of colonization, and the house above it had burned to the ground over two T-centuries ago. It wasn't on MacLean's land—this parcel actually belonged to one of Nessa MacRuer's clients, but it was being managed with no intention of selling it. And it was close enough to Elgin for any of the LLL's leaders who lived in the capital to reach without too much difficulty, yet far enough away to be outside the intense scrutiny the UPS maintained in Elgin and Halkirk's other cities and towns. Better still, the land had gone back to forest after the house burned. By now, some of the trees growing around and over it were more than a T-century old, and that dense canopy could conceal a lot of private air cars and foot traffic.

So she wasn't worried about their present physical security. It was where she saw this meeting *leading* that frightened her.

"Burgess and Tammas are right, Nessa." Tad Ogilvy was looking at MacRuer, but MacLean knew he was actually speaking at least as much to *her*. "Some things can't be allowed to stand. If we let them, we surrender the very thing that brought us together in the first place! And on a more practical note, we don't have *time* to get 'ready.' MacQuarie's turning the damned planet inside out looking for Luíseach and Gavin. If she finds them—if they go the same way her father went—they cut the heart right out of popular resistance."

"Don't get too carried away, Tad," Fenella MacKail said a little sharply. Ogilvy and MacPhee both glared at her; Stirling's expression went considerably beyond that, and MacKail waved one hand in a frustrated gesture. "I agree public opinion's hugely in the Mac-Rorys' favor now, but do we really think *that's* the foundation we want to build an armed revolution on?"

MacKail was a high school teacher, and it was her fury at the way in which the schools had been turned into an arm of indoctrination by the LPP which had driven her to rebellion. She was, however, much more urban than most of the Liberation League's other leadership, and her opinion of her rural fellows wasn't incredibly high. And the one Prosperity Party policy with which she'd actually agreed was the abolition of Loomis' constitutional monarchy. In her opinion, monarchy was an incredibly stupid form of government, and Tavis III's performance during and after the LPP coup was her primary example of that. In a lot of ways, MacLean agreed with her, but . . .

"*Successful* revolutions depend even more on emotion and commitment than on firepower," she said now. "There has to be something—some*one*—who can carry that commitment, be the focus of it. And at this moment, Burgess and Tad are right. All that passion and anger's focused on the MacRorys and, especially, Luíseach. And given the strength of that anger, whether or not *we* want to move may be completely beside the point."

Agreement rumbled around the cellar, and she wondered if she was glad, because MacRuer was absolutely correct. They needed more weapons—and heavier ones—before they mounted any move against the UPS and SEIU's armed security force. A couple of more months, another shipment or two, and they'd be in a far stronger position.

But they didn't have a couple of more months.

No one knew exactly how Luíseach MacRory's air car had evaded the strike on Caisteal Òrach. Personally, MacLean suspected it was the incredible fury with which Raghnall MacRory and his militia had fought back. No one was going to confirm the Uppies' losses—for that matter, official spokesmen continued to insist their casualties had been extraordinarily light—but the firefight had raged for better than fifteen hours, and Senga MacQuarie had been forced to call in UPS units from as far away as Conerock. In the end, they'd killed Raghnall and almost every single one of his supporters, but they hadn't died easily, and the way MacQuarie's tactical commanders had focused on them *had* to be the primary reason Luíseach had successfully squirmed through their grasp and disappeared.

She and her husband Gavin were in hiding. No one knew where, and they had no intention of telling anyone, but they'd managed to get out half a dozen communiqués, including proof both of them were alive. And at the moment, with the murder of her parents and her children, Luíseach MacRory was not simply the only living heir of Tavis III, but the living, breathing personification of all of Halkirk's blazing fury.

And there could not conceivably be a single person in the entire Loomis System more bitterly determined to crush the current regime than the woman who'd begun styling herself Queen Luíseach II.

I don't blame her, I sympathize with her entirely, but God has she ever upped the ante for all of us! MacLean thought.

Well, maybe it was time someone did just that.

"Whatever we think of the timing," she said, making eye contact with each of the other men and women around that table, "this is a moment and an opportunity when we *have* to act. All of you know how much I would've preferred to settle this at the ballot box, or at least with peaceful demonstrations. But if I'd ever really believed we could do that, the MacRory Massacre would have changed my mind. So as I see it, the question isn't whether or not we begin our revolution now; it's *how* we begin it. We've looked at a dozen models for that, including at least three where our hand is forced by events beyond our control. I think we're all agreed that that's what just happened . . . which means it's time we dusted those off and decided exactly where to begin."

✦ Chapter Twenty-Nine

"HEY, JESS! DID YOU HEAR who caught your sensor ghost?"

Lieutenant Commander Jessica Epstein glanced over her shoulder but never stopped running. Commander Francis Drescher was her immediate superior in Perimeter Security Command, the command charged with maintaining and operating the exquisitely sensitive long-range sensor platforms which watched over the Component A of the Manticore Binary System. He was also, like her, one of the RMN officers who liked to actually run—not simply run *in place* on a treadmill—for exercise, and one of the perks of serving aboard HMSS *Hephaestus*, the Star Kingdom's primary industrial platform, was that there was actually room in which to do that. In fact, this entire three-kilometer long tube had been converted for that very purpose.

The one thing that Lieutenant Commander Epstein truly resented about Commander Drescher (aside from the fact that romantic involvement between officers in the chain of command was strictly forbidden by the

Articles of War...damn it) was that he was the next best thing to five centimeters taller than she was, with much longer legs. At the moment, those longer legs were bringing him up rapidly from behind, and she knew that she'd soon have a clear view of his remarkably attractive posterior as he passed her and left her—figuratively—in his dust. But he could damned well catch up with her first, if he wanted to talk!

Which he proceeded to do with irritating promptness.

"No," she said as he drew even with her shoulder and slowed down—damn him!—to keep pace with her. "I was off-watch by the time they sent anybody."

"Well, I think you're *gonna* hear about it," Drescher said with a grin. "It was the Cepheids. And the really good part? Looks like it really was a ghost. And a little birdie told me Bridget has one of her SCA meetings coming up Sometime Real Soon Now."

"Oh, *crap.*" Epstein shook her head, her expression chagrined.

Lieutenant Commander Bridget Landry was the CO of HMS *Dagger*, and *Dagger* was a unit of DesDiv 265.2, commanded by Commander Michael Carus and known as the Silver Cepheids because of its scouting expertise. Landry also happened to be one of Epstein's close friends—they'd been at Saganami Island together—and a member of the Society for Creative Anachronism. A member who reveled in the painstakingly accurate recreation of costumes from societies the rest of the galaxy had forgotten about seven or eight hundred T-years ago.

At the moment, courtesy of the very faint hyper signature picked up by one Lieutenant Commander Epstein's section and kicked up the chain by that same

Lieutenant Commander Epstein, DesDiv 265.2 was approximately one light-month from *Hephaestus*. And from Drescher's broad grin—it would never have done to call it a *smirk*, of course—they damned well hadn't found anything when they reached the signature's locus. Which meant it truly had been a sensor ghost...and that SOP required Cepheids to maintain and overwatch on the location for the next two T-weeks.

"She going to miss her meeting?" Epstein asked with a certain resignation.

"Dunno," Drescher said cheerfully. "I only know she has one coming up because she's supposed to partner with Hammond over in Maintenance. I don't know about Bridget, but *Hammond's* royally pissed over the possibility that she'll miss it. Sounds like the two of them had something special planned."

"Wonderful." Epstein rolled her eyes. "She is *so* going to give me hell if she does miss it!"

"Nah." Drescher shook his head. "She won't *give* you hell; she'll just make your life a *living* hell. But don't worry. She'll forget all about it in a year or two."

"Oh, thank you *so* much, Frank!"

Epstein threw an elbow, but he danced nimbly aside without even breaking stride and grinned at her. Then his expression sobered...a bit, at least.

"Kidding aside, Jess, it's probably not a bad thing. We're all still kinda on edge after what the Peeps pulled. Having something to do besides brood on who got killed can't be a bad thing. Besides, if the Admiralty's gonna let Bridget play with a destroyer all her own, every so often they're likely to insist she do what *they* want her to with it. I'm sure she'll understand that. Of course, whether or not she'll *admit* she does..."

"Remind me to leave an old pair of gym socks in your skinsuit to reward you for making me feel so much better, Frank."

"What I'm here for." He gave her another grin, then turned on the hydrogen and sped up the passageway ahead of her.

And his posterior looked just as fine as ever.

"They never got a sniff of the spider, Sir," Commander Theresa Coleman said, studying the tactical imagery in the depths of the main tactical display on MANS *Mako*. "That's a standard picket formation. If they had a clue where we really are, they'd be headed our way."

"It looks that way to me too, Theresa." Admiral Frederick Topolev nodded. "But let's not get too confident," he went on, waving an admonishing forefinger in his chief of staff's direction. "For one thing, they may have seen us just fine and decided not to tell us about it by coming after us. Don't you think their Home Fleet might like the opportunity to micro-jump a couple of squadrons of their damned podnoughts right on top of us before we could hyper out again?"

"Well, of course, Sir." Coleman seemed a little taken aback, but she rallied gamely. "They *might* think that way, but that'd be more like something a batch of Sollies might try. If they really wanted to keep us from hypering out, they'd have to wait until we were inside the hyper limit, and there's no way *Manties* would be stupid enough to risk losing track of us in the month or so it's going to take us to get that far inside."

"Of course they wouldn't," Topolev agreed. "And you're right, unlike the Sollies the Manties know their ass from their elbow. I'm just suggesting we shouldn't get too tightly wedded to how dazzlingly clever we are until we've gotten back up to speed, deployed the pods, and pulled out again." He shrugged ever so slightly. "To be honest, I agree with you pretty much down the line. But we're getting this"—he gestured at the display's tactical icons—"on tight laser links from the platforms we left behind. Everything we've seen suggests the Manties' platforms are at least as good as ours, and pretty damned stealthy. I don't *think* they could have deployed a sensor shell tight enough to pick up the spider without our catching them at it, but there's not any proof of that just yet, either."

Coleman nodded soberly, because the admiral had a point. The Mesan Alignment Navy was one of the youngest fleets in the galaxy. In fact, it was in the process of carrying out its first combat operation . . . and using what had been supposed to be training ships, prototype test-beds for the actual battle fleet still under construction, to do it. The Royal Manticoran Navy, on the other hand, was hundreds of T-years old, with a peerless tradition of victory, and more than two decades of brutal warfare against the People's Republic of Haven under its belt.

Probably pretty damned hard to overestimate the bastards, she thought. *But if you've got to make a mistake, it's better to do that than to underestimate them. On the other hand, they're not really ten meters tall and covered with hair. And they can't have a clue about the spider. We have a hard time tracking it, and we know exactly what we're looking for. Be a bit hard for them to pick up something they don't even know exists!*

In many ways, the spider drive was the crown jewel of the Alignment's war-fighting technology, the product of many decades and billions of credits of research, and the deciding factor in making Operation Oyster Bay possible. The primary sensor used by every navy to detect and track hostile vessels under power was the Warshawski, a highly refined version of Adrienne Warshawski's original gravitic detector. The enormous gravitic footprint of a starship's impeller wedge, even at relatively low power, was glaringly obvious at enormous ranges, whereas *active* sensors had strictly limited reach against targets as small (relatively speaking) as a warship. Even with the best stealth fields in existence, the passive detection range against a starship wedge was at least six or seven times the range any active system was going to manage against that starship's hull. So it made far more sense to use those passive systems to look for impeller signatures and search for electronic emissions.

But Task Force One's stealth was just as good as the Manties'—probably a little better, actually—so there were no electronic emissions to spot. And the gravitic signature of the spider drive was tiny, compared to any impeller wedge. *Mako*'s gravitic cross-section was about on a par with an extremely stealthy recon drone, and the Manty destroyers scrambled to investigate the "sensor ghost" of their very cautious, very gradual alpha translation into n-space were a couple of light-hours astern of her. With all due respect to Admiral Topolev, no way in hell were those destroyers going to see the flagship.

And neither is anyone else, she thought grimly. *I don't know that Oyster Bay's going to work as well as everyone hopes. One thing I do know is that no plan ever works as perfectly as it sounds like it should.*

But those people behind us don't have a clue, and the first thing anybody ahead of us should know about it is going to be a cloud of graser torpedoes coming in out of absolutely frigging nowhere.

Which, when she came right down to it, would work just fine for her.

✧   ✧   ✧

"Excuse me, My Lord, but Foreign Secretary Langtry's on the com. He'd like a moment of your time, if that's convenient."

Hamish Alexander-Harrington, the Earl of White Haven, looked up from his conversation with Captain Fargo, his Admiralty chief of staff.

"Did he say what he wanted to speak about, Eddie?" he asked.

"No, My Lord." Senior Chief Edward Neukirch shook his head. "He said it would 'just take a minute,' though."

"I see."

White Haven's smile might have been the tiniest bit sour. Sir Anthony Langtry was an old and close friend, but in many ways, and despite a lengthy diplomatic career, he was still a colonel of Marines at heart. He was inclined to do things as informally as possible, which, as a general rule, White Haven—who'd dealt with entirely too many bureaucrats—found a breath of fresh air. Sometimes, though, Langtry's tendency to go straight to his fellow cabinet members rather than through channels could be . . . counterproductive. Quite often, someone else, lower down the feeding chain, could have answered his current question without pulling someone like, oh, the First Lord of Admiralty, out of a conference with his chief of staff.

"Put him through, Eddie," White Haven continued

after a moment, pushing his counter-grav float chair across his spacious office from the conference table to his desk. Neukirch, who'd had ample opportunity to learn his boss' ways, timed things almost perfectly. The earl had a wait of no more than ten seconds before the desktop display lit with Langtry's face.

"Hello, Tony," he said. "What can I do for you this afternoon?"

"Is there time to catch Honor before she hypers out for Nouveau Paris?" Langtry asked, and White Haven's eyebrows rose at the lack of any greeting.

"No," he replied after a moment. "Eighth Fleet made its alpha translation over an hour ago. Why?"

"Damn." Langtry grimaced, but the word came out almost mildly. "I wanted to get her the information before she talks to Pritchart."

"And what information would that be?" White Haven inquired affably enough that Langtry snorted in amusement.

"Sorry. Sorry!" He held up a placating hand. "Don't mean to be mysterious. It's just that those bastards in Mesa have tossed us another hot potato. According to Lyman Carmichael's dispatch from Old Chicago, they've just handed the League a formal note accusing us of orchestrating a nuclear attack on their citizens."

"What?!" White Haven twitched upright. His eyes widened in disbelief, but narrowed again almost immediately. "That business in Mendel?"

"Right in one." Langtry nodded, his expression sour, and White Haven swore mentally.

The stories about what certainly sounded like a terrorist incident coming out of the Mesa System had been wildly confused . . . and confusing. It took time for information to come so far, despite the huge volume of traffic through the Manticoran Junction, and what information they'd received so far had been incomplete, internally inconsistent, and unclear as hell. The one thing they *did* know was that Mesa had—predictably— immediately insisted the Audubon Ballroom was behind it. Which, given the Ballroom's savage, extra-legal campaign against Manpower in particular and genetic slavery in general, wasn't really as unreasonable of them as White Haven would like to think. But this...

"They're saying *we* did it?"

"They're saying we enabled and *sponsored* it, not that we actually did it ourselves." Langtry snorted. "They're also making it pretty damned clear that the only reason they aren't accusing us of doing it ourselves is because they're such sophisticated diplomats. If they weren't, they'd probably be as crass, crude, and direct as, oh, *we* were after that business with Monica, and come right out and say we did it."

"On what conceivable evidence?" White Haven demanded, and Langtry's expression turned more sour than ever.

"Well, that's the main reason I wanted to talk to Honor before she left. Not just because I don't want her blindsided in Nouveau Paris if Haven's ambassador gets a dispatch home to Pritchart before Eighth Fleet gets there. I mean, I *don't* want her blindsided, but the real question I wanted to ask her is what she knows about anything Anton Zilwicki may've been up to lately."

"Zilwicki?" White Haven cocked his head.

His wife had a long-standing relationship with the Antislavery League and (some would have said) with the Audubon Ballroom. There were times—many of them—when that relationship became just a tiny bit of a problem where a duchess, steadholder, fleet admiral, and personal confidante of not only Elizabeth III but Protector Benjamin Mayhew was concerned. There was, however, no way in hell Honor Alexander-Harrington was ever going to change her spots in that regard. She'd imbibed her hatred of genetic slavery and Manpower with her mother's milk—literally—and that hatred burned with a cold and terrible fire. So it wasn't at all surprising Catherine Montaigne and Anton Zilwicki had become personal friends. Nor was it surprising that Montaigne and Zilwicki's...involvement with people like Jeremy X, the theoretically retired head of the Audubon Ballroom, should splash over onto her.

"I know Zilwicki visited her aboard her flagship before Lovat," he said now, slowly. "She didn't really discuss whatever they talked about with me. I think she and Willie...had words over it, though." He grimaced. "From what he very carefully hasn't said to me, it wasn't a very...productive conversation from his perspective. In fact, it's probably a little surprising both of them emerged intact. Of the two, my money would have been on Honor, understand." His grimace turned into a smile. "Willie would have been swinging above his weight."

Langtry chuckled. White Haven's younger brother William—Baron Grantville and Prime Minister of Manticore—had inherited his full share of the famous Alexander temper. The foreign secretary found himself wishing he could have been a fly on the wall when that temper ran into Honor Alexander-Harrington's calm, cool, absolute refusal to do one iota less than *she* thought duty demanded of her, and damn what anyone else thought.

"Why are you worried about Zilwicki?" White Haven went on. "Given what you've already said, I can't think of any *good* reason for you to ask about him."

"According to Mesa's note, their conclusion—based, as I'm sure we'd all expect, on a careful and dispassionate examination of all the evidence—confirms that notorious Ballroom sympathizer Anton Zilwicki was directly responsible for the Green Pines attack. They say they have conclusive evidence he was on Mesa, that he was involved with the 'Ballroom terrorists' who actually planted and detonated the bombs, and that *circumstantial* evidence which—for some reason—they haven't been able to absolutely confirm 'at this time' strongly suggests he was there with the direct sanction of the Manticoran government. They seem to be implying that we provided him and the Ballroom with support as a reprisal for their involvement in what happened in Talbott. Which, of course, they hasten to point out, never happened outside our own paranoid imagination or, conversely, outside our evil, imperialist Machiavellian attempts to turn Solarian public opinion against the blameless citizens of Mesa."

"What a load of horse shit," White Haven said sourly.

"Of course it is. On the other hand, there's no denying he's been closely affiliated with the ASL and people who are at least ex-Ballroom 'terrorists.' I mean, the man's *daughter* is Queen of Torch and Jeremy X is her minister of war!"

"Yes, and Elizabeth's niece is her best friend and basically runs Torch intelligence for her," White Haven pointed out.

"I never said Zilwicki was the only Manticoran with connections to Torch," Langtry riposted. "And did I say something to make you think *Mesa* wasn't pointing that out right along with Zilwicki's nationality? Or the fact that he used to work for ONI? Or that he's become something of a personal friend of the royal family ever since he helped save Ruth Winton's life in Erewhon?"

"No, you didn't," White Haven's sourness had turned positively corrosive. "And of course the bastards would trot that out, too."

"Exactly." Langtry shrugged. "But that's why I'm looking for anyone who knows what he may actually have been up to. I was hoping Honor could tell me, because from what you've said it doesn't sound like Willie can. That means the only person here in the Old Star Kingdom who *might* know is Cathy Montaigne. And I'll let you guess how the newsies—and the frigging Mesans—will react if they find out the Foreign Secretary is 'hobnobbing' with the notorious Anton Zilwicki's even more notorious paramour, supporter of interstellar terrorism, mouthpiece of mayhem, and general all-round longtime anti-Mesa fanatic Catherine Montaigne!"

"Then I'd recommend making sure no one finds out," White Haven said, "because I don't think there's anyone else who could possibly tell you, now that Honor's on her way to Nouveau Paris."

He smiled slightly at Langtry's expression, which he understood perfectly.

"Good luck," he said sweetly. "I think you're going to need it."

❖   ❖   ❖

"Well, which do you want first, Hago? The good news, or the bad news?" Captain Merriman asked.

Commander Hago Shavarshyan pushed back from his console and looked at her, not without a certain trepidation. Sadako Merriman was a petite, fine-boned woman, with a pronounced epicanthic fold and long chestnut hair, and under normal circumstances, Shavarshyan didn't mind resting his eyes upon her one bit. Of course, she was off the market, given her relationship with Commodore Thurgood. No one was supposed to know about that, but the truth was that everyone did. Besides, Shavarshyan would be a piss-poor excuse for an intelligence officer if he didn't even know who his own boss was sleeping with.

Something about her current expression's combination of chagrin, resignation, and sympathy made Hago Shavarshyan profoundly nervous, however.

"Gee, thanks for the choice, Ma'am," he replied. She said nothing, and, after a moment, he shrugged. "I guess we might as well start with the good."

"All right. The *good* news is that Admiral Crandall and her task force will be leaving us shortly. Thank God."

Shavarshyan could only nod at that. He and Merriman were both Frontier Fleet, which was less than dust on the boot heels of any Battle Fleet flag officer like Sandra Crandall. Shavarshyan had been unfortunate enough to meet quite a few Battle Fleet officers, but the only one he could think of who'd rivaled her towering combination of arrogance, overconfidence, choler, and stupidity had been Admiral Josef Byng. Now that the Star Empire of Manticore removed him from the gene pool, Crandall found herself in sole possession of that very special niche in his cherished memories, and the sooner God was good enough to get her the hell out of the Meyers System—and, for that matter, the entire Madras Sector—the better Shavarshyan would like it.

From Merriman's expression, however, the other shoe hadn't dropped yet.

"All right," he said cautiously. "I'll grant that that's good news, Ma'am. Why do I think it's not *unalloyed* good news?"

"Because you're a first-rate intelligence officer with a clear-thinking, incisive mind," Merriman suggested. "And because I already gave you a pretty damned big hint."

"That must be it," he agreed sourly. "So why don't you go ahead and give me the *bad* news now, Ma'am?"

"All right." The captain's tone turned much more serious—Shavarshyan might almost have said *ominous*. "The bad news comes in two parts. The first part is that the reason she's leaving us is to move directly to Spindle and demand the Manties turn over Admiral Gold Peak and her senior officers for trial on charges of murder and surrender every single ship that was present at New Tuscany."

"She's *what*?" Shavarshyan was surprised, all things taken together, that his question came out so calmly.

"She's going to Spindle with her entire task force to collect heads, and she doesn't give much of a damn how much breakage there is," Merriman said grimly. "In fact, I think she's hoping for one hell of a *lot* of breakage. What she really wants to do is rip off Gold Peak's head and piss down her neck, and she informed Commissioner Verrocchio that she intended to move out within forty-eight hours. That was the day before yesterday, and I'll be absolutely astounded if she gets those Battle Fleet scows underway this week. But once she gets there, she intends to commit what the dictionary programs call 'an act of war.'"

"Don't you mean *another* act of war, Ma'am?"

"You're not going to win any popularity prizes pointing that out, Hago. Besides, she *is* an admiral, even if it's only in Battle Fleet, where competing skill levels leave a little to be desired. I think you'd be well advised to remember that."

"Excuse me, Ma'am?"

Shavarshyan felt more than a little taken aback. He knew exactly how Merriman thought of Crandall. For that matter, her comment about Battle Fleet flag officers' skill levels only underscored the contempt most Frontier Fleet officers felt for their Battle Fleet counterparts. Which made the implied reprimand of her last sentence even more surprising.

"I said you'd be well advised to remember she's an admiral," Merriman told him. "Because it's occurred even to her that if she's planning on rushing off into the Talbott Sector and committing the Solarian League to a potential war with the Star Empire, it would behoove her to have someone with at least a modicum of background knowledge about Talbott along. In fact, she's formally requested that we temporarily assign someone with that sort of knowledge to her staff."

Shavarshyan stared at her in horror, and she nodded slowly.

"I'm afraid you just drew the short straw, Hago. You've got twenty-four hours to tidy up your desk and pack. Then you're reporting aboard *Buckley* for a little voyage."

"It's not that we're not 'fond' of Mr. O'Shaughnessy. We're *very* fond of him, actually. Sort of the way you're fond of a cousin you know is really, really smart...and still want to strangle from time to time."

—Admiral Augustus Khumalo,
Royal Manticoran Navy,
CO, Talbott Station

✧ Chapter Thirty

IT WAS A BEAUTIFUL NIGHT, decided Colonel Kirsten MacChrystal as she followed Bhaltair, her four-year-old Hypatian Mountain Hound, down the park jogging path. The stars were just coming out in a sky cloudless enough to be visible even here, in the heart of the capital where sky glow so often killed visibility, and Thurso was a gorgeous, brilliant sapphire almost directly overhead, pouring its light down. The park's artfully landscaped lighting managed to provide more than enough illumination without violating the . . . intimacy of the night, the air was cool enough to be fresh without nipping, and a gentle breeze danced and murmured in the trees. It felt good to be out of the office, especially on a night like this, and she chuckled to herself as Bhaltair disappeared into the banks of flowering hibernia that fringed the path.

He was a big, cheerful, always curious dog who asked nothing more than an hour or so in the evening out with his person, and MacChrystal was perfectly happy to give it to him. The Hypatian was an ancient breed, produced in the Hypatia System over a thousand years ago out of a crossing of the even more ancient Rottweiler and Greater Swiss Mountain Dog. They were big—Bhaltair tipped the scale at just under eighty kilos—playful, and generally gentle, but they were also ferociously protective.

That was one of the reasons Bhaltair had come into her life, because the United Public Safety Force was not the most universally beloved organization in the Loomis System, and Colonel MacChrystal was the commanding officer of its Elgin Division. The woman in charge of the system capital's police force could reasonably expect to be unpopular with a great many Loomisians.

That was also the reason MacChrystal was always accompanied by a ten-man security team when she took Bhaltair for his evening walk in Hendry Park. And why Hendry Park's jogging paths were closed to the public for thirty minutes before and after Bhaltair's walk. The team maintained a moving perimeter, far enough out that she could at least pretend she was out alone with Bhaltair but in visual and electronic contact with one another at all times. She really wished she could just leave them the hell home at moments like this, yet she wasn't remotely stupid enough to venture out into a public park without precautions. She supposed she could always have someone else take Bhaltair out—a point which had been made rather strongly by Alastair MacKeggie, the commander of her personal detachment—but she refused to give the bastards the satisfaction. Captain MacKeggie was of the opinion that she was probably even more unpopular than usual in the wake of the Mánas MacRory "arrest attempt," and he was undoubtedly right, but MacChrystal had learned long ago that the one thing she absolutely couldn't do was to let anyone even think she'd been intimidated.

Besides, she loved nights like this and she wasn't about to give them up in fear of the sort of crackpot scum who were so upset over the MacRorys.

Bastards had it coming anyway, she thought, inhaling deeply as she filled her lungs with the hibernia's scent. *If they didn't want their heads broken, they should never've organized their frigging "militia." Did they* really *think we could let that kind of challenge pass? Especially now, of all times?!*

She snorted, irritated at herself for letting thoughts of Luíseach MacRory MacGill disturb her at a moment like this. The bitch couldn't hide forever, and when they found her, she'd follow the end the rest of her troublesome family had. It was only a pity Kiley had missed her when he made a clean sweep of the rest.

Whatever the public might have been told, Senga MacQuarie's instructions had been singularly clear on that point. None of the MacRorys were to survive their "arrest," and the existence of the "MacRory Militia" had offered the perfect pretext. Whether or not the "militia" actually intended to fight was beside the point; the UPS' after-action reports would make it perfectly clear that it was the militia who'd provoked whatever happened by opening fire even before the arrest force had announced its identity.

Never expected the sons of bitches to put up that *sort of fight, though,* she acknowledged sourly.

The militiamen's final casualties had been total—the UPS squads who'd shot the wounded and handful of prisoners in the back of the head had made sure of that—but casualties had been heavy for the assault force, too. Over ninety of MacChrystal's troopers had died, with another thirty-five wounded. There was also the minor matter of sixteen armored tac vans, one command vehicle, and a pair of SEIU sting ships. They'd managed to keep a lid on their actual losses—or she thought they had, anyway—but they'd made one hell of a hole in her own command, and they hadn't done much for the UPS in general.

And in the confusion, MacGill and her husband got away. Damn *I hate it that that happened! And,* she acknowledged, *Senga wasn't any happier about it.*

Well, MacQuarie would just have to deal with it, she told herself. And so far her people had things under control. They'd met the "demonstrations"—it was against official policy to call them "riots"—with a maximum of force and a minimum of tact. A couple of hundred arrests and several hundred broken heads had whipped the "demonstrators" back to their kennels, and they hadn't heard a peep out of them in the last week and a half.

I don't care what Touchette says. If anything more "organized" was going to happen, it'd have started by now. You'd think a Gendarme would've figured that out if anyone could! These bastards don't have the guts to—

Her head snapped up as she heard a sudden, ferocious growl from Bhaltair. She whipped around towards the shrubbery where he'd disappeared . . . just as the pulser dart struck one centimeter below her right eye and her head disintegrated in a cloud of crimson and gray mist.

✧   ✧   ✧

"Don't spare the hydrogen, Ira," Johannes Grazioli said as his air limo sped through the cloudless Halkirk night. His chauffeur glanced at him in the small com screen by his knee, and Grazioli chuckled. "I'm in a hurry tonight," he said.

"Yes, Sir," Ira Valverde acknowledged solemnly, and returned his attention to the HUD. He didn't doubt his employer was "in a hurry tonight." Technically, he wasn't supposed to know—although, to be honest, Grazioli didn't seem to give a damn who *did* know—about the pair of underage sisters waiting in the SEIU executive's luxurious Rotherwal apartment. For that matter, the mere existence of the Rotherwal apartment was supposed to be a deep, dark secret. Which it was, officially at least, since a senior SEIU executive (and they didn't come a whole lot more senior then Johannes Grazioli, Senior Executive for Logistics, Loomis System) wasn't supposed to have a "secret" pied-à-terre.

Someone with Grazioli's tastes *needed* a private hideaway, however. There were rumors, which Valverde believed, that he'd been caught with his fingers in the Manpower cookie jar in his previous post in the Bessie System. The SEIU Board of Directors had an unusual puritanical streak where genetic slavery was concerned, so if the rumors *were* true, it spoke well for Grazioli's connections that he was still employed. By the same token, it probably explained how he'd ended up in a system like Loomis and as the *number two* member of the hierarchy, rather than as System Manager. Given the ... esoteric nature of Grazioli's chosen entertainments, there wasn't much question in Valverde's mind just how he'd found himself in bed—literally—with Manpower.

Assuming, of course, there'd been any truth to such libelous rumors.

Fortunately, that was none of Ira Valverde's business, and he concentrated on his flying.

Sakue Yampolski, the head of Grazioli's protective detail, didn't have that luxury. Unlike Valverde, she had to know everything there was to know about the man she was responsible for protecting. She wished she didn't. For that matter, she wished Grazioli had the common decency to at least *try* to conceal his appetites from her. Unfortunately, he seemed to have no·clue why he ought to. Indeed, she sometimes suspected that in his own mind, her own diminutive stature and slender build put her into the category of his preferred sex toys, despite the fact that she was very nearly eighty T-years old. It was a good thing that, whatever his other failings, he was smart enough not to try to play games with his own security chief.

Especially since I would gleefully cut off his balls and tie them around his neck for a bowtie, she thought, and smiled at him from the facing seat as she allowed her imagination to dwell lovingly upon the possibility.

As a general rule, it was a bad idea for the head of someone's protective detail to think he'd look so much better dead. But it was better to be honest with herself. And however Yampolski might feel about him, it was her job to keep the sick bastard alive, so she'd do it and take a certain professional pride in the doing. Besides, it wasn't as if he was the first waste of good DNA she'd been assigned to protect over the sixty T-years of her career.

At the moment, however, she wished he was at least·a little bit brighter than he was. Sakue Yampolski had seen a lot of neobarb unrest in her time, and she didn't like what she was seeing on Halkirk.

She remembered a line from a really, really bad holo-drama. Things were "quiet, too quiet," especially after the MacRory fiasco and the violent demonstrations it had provoked, and she didn't buy into the theory that the UPS had crushed that unrest once and for all. In fact, she thought Ottomar Touchette's analysis was on the money, which made this no time for someone like Johannes Grazioli to prance around out in the open.

And I don't really care whether or not he *thinks anyone knows about the frigging apartment*, she thought behind that concealing smile. *I know for damned sure a whole* lot *of anyones do, and a bunch of them would be just* delighted *to kill his sorry ass*.

That was why she'd had the entire apartment build-ing swept for surprises. Fortunately, it was a small building, not one of the residential towers seldom seen outside Elgin, so sweeping it wasn't all that hard. And she had six members of her team on the floor directly beneath Grazioli's penthouse. Nobody was getting to him that way, and she'd arranged for a rapid bugout if that seemed indicated.

❖   ❖   ❖

"Are you sure you don't want to come down and at least have some supper, Sakue?" Grazioli asked, and smiled. "I'm likely to be several hours, you know."

"I'm aware of that, Mr. Grazioli," she said, wonder-ing if he realized just how...scummy that smile of his looked. "But I've got plenty of paperwork I can catch up on while you're occupied." She smiled back and gestured at the limo's data terminal.

"If you're sure," he said, and headed for the lift from the rooftop landing pad to his penthouse.

Yampolski watched him go, then keyed her com.

"He's headed down, Rick."

"Copy," Rick Fernandez, the senior member of the detail keeping an eye on the apartment building, replied. "Did he invite you down for a drink?"

"If that was the only thing he'd had in mind, I might've accepted," she said caustically, and grimaced when he chuckled. "Listen, you'd better just be grateful he's as hetero as he is. Otherwise, he'd be looking at *your* ass, boy-oh!"

"He may be, anyway," Fernandez replied. "His girlfriends are late."

"Oh?" An eyebrow arched. "Do we know why?"

"Their 'uncle' screened about thirty minutes ago." Yampolski could hear the shrug in Fernandez's voice. "Said they'd be delayed. Something about their air taxi's routing getting screwed up."

Yampolski's other eyebrow joined the first, and she frowned. The pimps who provided Grazioli's playthings knew he didn't like to wait. In fact, they'd move heaven and earth to *avoid* keeping him waiting. And that...

"I don't like this, Rick," she said as every instinct in her body started to jangle. "Turn him around as soon as he gets there."

"He won't like that, Sakue," Fernandez said with pronounced trepidation.

"What you mean is he'll kick, scream, holler, and bitch the whole way," Yampolski corrected. "And, frankly, I don't give a good goddamn if he does. He can take it up with Frazier. And if Frazier wants, he can damned well pull me from Grazioli's detail. Hell, I wish he would! But in the meantime, we're getting his ass out of here and back under cover until I find out why the girls are late."

She'd opened the sliding panel to the pilot's compartment while she spoke, and her raised right forefinger made an urgent "wind it up" motion at Valverde as the chauffeur looked up from his book reader. He gawked at her for a moment, then tossed the reader aside, and she heard the whine as the turbines spooled up.

"I don't like unexplained schedule changes, especially now," she continued to Fernandez, "and I'm damned—"

The shoulder-fired Hydra III was old, outmoded, and obsolete, but its warheads still packed one hell of a punch. The blast-incendiary warhead's performance against any armored target was fairly anemic, but the penthouse wasn't armored. And neither was the air limo.

The four warheads didn't impact exactly simultaneously, and Sakue Yampolski had one fleeting moment to realize that at least Johannes Grazioli had died before she did.

❖   ❖   ❖

It was raining in Conerock as Lieutenant Ranald Ross' personal vehicle screeched to a halt. He was out of the air car and halfway to the station house entry before the hatch cycled closed behind him.

He hit the front door like an earthquake, barely pausing for the security computer to recognize his biometrically linked personal transponder and open it, and Kenneth Bevan, the duty sergeant, looked up from his solitaire deck with a startled expression, then leapt to his feet.

"Lieutenant! What're you doing here?! Sir," he added belatedly.

"Get your ass in gear, Sergeant!" Ross snapped so sharply Bevan blanched. Ross was normally an easy-going boss. He didn't tolerate any slackness, but neither was he the type to collect scalps for minor infractions like a little solitaire game at three o'clock in the morning.

"Yes, Sir!" Bevan barked, coming to attention. "I'm sorry, Sir, I didn't—"

"What the hell are you talking about, Bevan?" Ross demanded.

"I—that is . . ." Bevan looked at him helplessly, and the lieutenant glanced at the cards scattered across the duty desk in front of the noncom.

"Oh Christ, Bevan!" Ross rolled his eyes. "I could care less about the damned *cards*! Haven't you been listening to *Freiceadan* at all?!"

"*Freiceadan*, Sir?"

Bevan's confusion was complete, Ross saw. The sergeant was a good man, solid and reliable, but he wasn't exactly the most mentally agile person Ross had ever known. And clearly he *hadn't* been listening to the United Public Safety Force's internal news channel.

"According to *Freiceadan*, somebody just shot Colonel MacChrystal in Hendry Park." Bevan gawked at him. "Sounds like they took out her entire detail at the same time. In fact, it *sounds* like her damned dog was the only survivor—the bastards just stun-gunned *it!* And they took out Major Kiley, his air car, and *his* entire detail at what sounds like *exactly* the same time."

Bevan went even paler. It didn't take a mental giant to see the connection between MacChrystal and Jordan Kiley, the man who'd officiated over the MacRorys' murders. But Ross wasn't done yet.

"On top of that, Zack MacLennan just screened from Rotherwal. Somebody blew hell out of that sick bastard

Grazioli's little playpen about nine minutes ago. And on top of *that*, I can't get Major Farquhar to answer her com. So, if it's all the same to you, Sergeant, I think we'd better get ourselves organized, don't you?"

"Uh, Yessir! Right away, Sir!"

Bevan stabbed a button on his panel and the general alarm wailed from every speaker in the station house... and, at only slightly lower volume, from the personal com of every UPS trooper assigned to it, wherever they might be. Startled voices answered from the squad room where the ready response force had probably been playing poker, rather than solitaire, and Ross headed for his own office at a half-run. He'd been unable to reach Amanda Farquhar, the commander of UPS' Conerock Division, over his personal com, but his office com should be able to nail down her current location from her personal transponder. He hoped so, anyway, because he sure as hell wanted to talk to her!

Sergeant Bevan looked up as the front door opened again, and his tense, worried expression eased as Alexina Morrison and Lachlan MacLaurin burst through it. They weren't supposed to be on duty tonight, but unlike the sergeant, they obviously *had* been listening to *Freiceadan*. Both of them were only privates, but Bevan knew Ross had earmarked them for promotion after the next proficiency exam, and both of them were geared up in full tactical rig.

"Good to see you," he said as they jogged across the lobby towards him. "The Lieutenant's in his office, and—"

The burst from Morrison's flechette gun hit him at the base of the throat and decapitated him.

The body flipped backward, and MacLaurin went by the brand new corpse at a run. He disappeared down the short hallway to the squadron, and the hard, sharp discharges of *his* flechette gun vanished into a terrible scream of agony.

Lieutenant Ross' reflexes betrayed him. He charged straight out of his office, pulser in his hand...which was exactly what Private Morrison had expected. She was waiting, half-concealed behind the duty desk, and the shrieking flechette darts hit Ross squarely in the face before he ever saw her.

She reached across the desk and hit the button that overrode the security computer. The station house's doors all opened at the same instant, and forty more armed members of the Loomis Liberation League charged through them.

✧   ✧   ✧

"Stop squealing about it and *fix* the damned problem!" Nyatui Zagorski snapped from the com display. "We've goddamned well paid you people enough, so get your thumbs out of your asses and get a *handle* on this!"

Tyler MacCrimmon gripped his hands tightly together behind him and managed not to snarl back at the SEIU exec. It wasn't easy.

"We're *trying* to get a handle on it, Nyatui." His voice was less even than he could have wished. "At the moment, we're having just a little bit of difficulty down here, though."

"'*Difficulty*'?" Zagorski repeated. "What you've *got* down there, Mister Vice President, is a frigging disaster! Do you have any idea how much SEIU equipment those bastards have already torched?!"

"Yes, I do," MacCrimmon replied. "I'm a bit more concerned about all the *people* they've *killed*, though. Including Johannes Grazioli and Jock MacRathin."

Zagorski had opened his mouth. Now he closed it again and sat back in the chair behind his enormous desk.

"I knew about Grazioli." His volume had dropped by at least fifty percent. "This is the first I've heard about MacRathin, though. Is that confirmed?"

"Yes," MacCrimmon said tightly. "And while Johannes' murder could have had something to do with his . . . tastes in entertainment, Jock's sure as hell didn't. I've got confirmation of the assassination of at least twenty-five senior government and UPS officials *so far*." He emphasized the last two words harshly, his eyes locked to Zagorski's. "But that's not the only people these lunatics are killing, and they hit the Cooperative's Elgin office about twenty minutes ago. MacRathin was in his office with three other board members when someone tossed in a hand grenade to keep them company. And another bunch of the bastards got into Admin and set off some kind of bomb right in the middle of the Cooperative's main data storage. The Uppies have retaken the two lower floors, but they're in one hell of a firefight with the sons of bitches upstairs!"

"Shit," Zagorski muttered. The Silver Oak Cooperative played an important role in SEIU's "management" of Halkirk. The front organization, completely staffed and administered by native Loomisians, functioned as the primary conduit for silver oak without getting SEIU directly involved in hammering any effort by the producers to raise prices. Jock MacRathin, its CEO, had managed the majority of Grazioli's contacts and contracts with the local growers and loggers...and had been, if possible, even more despised than Grazioli.

"Look," MacCrimmon pushed into the temporary break in Zagorski's tantrum, "everyone down here's doing his best to 'get a handle on it,' but this is no local disturbance. It's going on in Elgin, Conerock, Rotherwal, and at least ten other cities and major towns. That means it's planned and *orchestrated*. MacQuarie's in her HQ, coordinating operations, and I really need to be over there helping her do that. So that's where I'm going. My staff will keep you updated, but right now I need to be concentrating on that. So if you'll excuse me."

He reached out, cut the connection, and headed for his office door.

⟡　　⟡　　⟡

"—don't care where the frigging guns *came* from," Nathalan Mundy snarled. "What I *care* about is what the bastards are doing with them right now!"

The treasury secretary glared around the conference table in the basement of the United Public Safety Force's main building in Elgin.

"And the *reason* I care about that is that they seem to be kicking our asses!" Mundy added.

Senga MacQuarie flushed angrily. She opened her mouth, but someone else spoke before she could flay Mundy.

"I agree the situation is...messy," the voice said. It belonged to Frinkelo Osborne, the Solarian "trade attaché" who was actually the Office of Frontier Security's senior man on the planet. "And I know you've suffered heavy casualties and a lot of property damage. Believe me, Mr. Zagorski's called that to my attention in no uncertain terms! But I think it's important that no one panic here."

"*Panic?*" Vice President MacCrimmon looked at him as if he had two heads. "This isn't 'panic,' Mr. Osborne. Nathalan might not be the most tactful person in the universe, but he *does* have a point. In the last two T-weeks, we've lost control of Conerock, Harlach, MacQuinnville, and Ohlarhn. That's four of our regional administrative centers, and I'd like to point out to you that there were only *twelve* of them to begin with. As nearly as we can tell, they've acquired every Safety Force armory in all of those cities, too, and at this moment, Secretary MacQuarie's probably lost close to half of her people."

"I understand that, Mister Vice President," Osborne said. "But however serious the situation may be, it's still a long way from *hopeless*."

He gave the Prosperity Party's leadership the most confident expression he could summon up. The truth was, however, that he wasn't *quite* as confident as he sounded—by a margin of no more than, oh, three or four hundred percent. And the truth was *also* that for a centicredit and a cup of cold coffee he'd let every damned person in this room go straight to hell. If anyone had ever deserved to have his planet burned down around his ears, it was MacCrimmon and his cronies, and he didn't even want to think about what might be necessary to save their skins. One thing he did know, given how far things had already gone: it was going to be ugly. In fact, he was sinkingly certain that it would be even uglier than he could imagine.

Unfortunately, Nyatui Zagorski had already dispatched his own report to the home office in Lucastra.

Osborne doubted his version of events was going to even mention the not so minor role SEIU's policies, arrogance, and security force's brutality had played in creating them, but that report was the one SEIU's patrons would be sure got read in Old Chicago. That meant it would be the one upon which the Office of Security ultimately acted, whatever Osborne did.

It's not going to matter, Frinkelo, he told himself bitterly. *Whatever you want, HQ's made it clear enough you're here to support Zagorski's operations. The last thing any of your esteemed superiors need is a glitch in their personal cash flow from SEIU. So however much you'd love to watch him and all his local stooges hang—however much you may hate what it'll take to save their worthless asses, instead—that's not on the program this month.*

"I'd be inclined to agree that it isn't hopeless *yet*," MacCrimmon said after a moment. "I hope you'll pardon my pointing out that it seems to be *headed* that way, though."

"Of course I understand your concerns, Sir," Osborne said. And he did.

In the wake of the precisely coordinated, carefully targeted strikes in half a dozen cities, popular support had rallied to the "Loomis Liberation League" like a hurricane. The simmering unrest over SEIU's logging policies had never been far from the surface. The fury spawned by the murder of ninety percent of Mánas MacRory's family had brought it to a roaring boil, and the LLL's initial successes had reached deep into that unrest with the proof that UPS and SEIU's own security forces could be hurt. Not simply hurt—defeated. *Destroyed.*

Ottomar Touchette had warned Osborne it was coming, and Osborne had dutifully passed the Gendarmerie lieutenant's analysis on to his own superiors. Not even Touchette had expected things to boil over this quickly, however. And the UPS' increasingly vicious tactics, the product of its own fear and desperation, were only pumping more hydrogen into the furnace. On the other hand...

"Mister Vice President, I've already sent my dispatch boat to McIntosh. There's a permanent Frontier Fleet detachment there. I sent the boat off five days ago, so it ought to reach McIntosh in another five or six days. When it does, I'm sure naval support at the very least—possibly even a company of Marines or an OFS intervention battalion—will be on its way here absolutely ASAP."

Every Loomisian in the underground room was looking at him now, eyes bright with the light of drowning men and women who'd suddenly seen a rope thrown in their direction.

"All you have to do is hold on," Osborne told them. "Just hold on for another couple of T-weeks, three at the outside, and then I guarantee it'll be the people on the *other* side's turn to worry!"

Chapter Thirty-One

"I'D REALLY LIKE A LITTLE more time to think about things before Admiral Gold Peak sends Lieutenant Commander Denton on to Manticore," said Gregor O'Shaughnessy from Baroness Medusa's com display.

"Forgive me, Gregor," she said dryly, "but unless I'm very much mistaken, you've just *had* better than a T-month to 'think about things,' haven't you?"

"Well, yes. I suppose what I should've said is I'd like a little more time for you to consider my report and the two of us—and Prime Minister Alquezar's Cabinet, of course—to kick it around before *Reprise* heads for Landing."

"Somebody back on the Old Terra said 'Ask me for anything except time,'" Medusa replied. "And it's not as if *Reprise* is the only courier available to us. I understand exactly why Lady Gold Peak wants her on her way yesterday. We're lucky as hell Denton spotted all those superdreadnoughts—and that the two of you were smart enough to pull out as soon as he did rather than trying to deliver my note to Commissioner

Verrocchio anyway—and she's not about to waste any of that luck. The Admiralty needs that information absolutely as soon as possible, and I'm pretty sure they'd really, really like to have Commander Denton and his people there for the most exhaustive debriefing they can arrange. Let's just worry about getting that into the pipeline first. We'll take our time to make sure we've considered all the political implications and *then* get our own messenger off."

"Yes, Ma'am," O'Shaughnessy said. "I'd just like our thoughts about those political aspects to get there at the same time as the military data. It's not that—"

"It's an imperfect galaxy, Gregor," Medusa interrupted. "We'll just have to do the best we can. And I suppose I should probably point out that it's up to Admiral Gold Peak to determine when a warship under her command departs for Manticore. She might get just a little cranky if I tried to order her to hold *Reprise* while I got my own thinking in order. Especially since she's quite well aware that I have four perfectly serviceable dispatch boats in orbit around Spindle. For that matter, I suspect I could probably hire another one if I really needed to."

"Yes, Ma'am. Understood."

"Good. But having said all of that, I want you here in my office fifteen minutes after *Reprise* reaches Spindle, understood?"

"Yes, Ma'am."

"Then I'll see you then. Clear."

Medusa cut the connection, then tipped back in her chair and looked across her desk.

"There are times," she said mildly, "when I understand why you military types aren't unreservedly fond of Gregor, Augustus."

Augustus Khumalo smiled and shook his head. He'd taken a pinnace down from HMS *Hercules*, his superdreadnought flagship, for the regular mid-week conference with Baroness Morncreek and Joachim Alquezar later that afternoon. Because he'd already been at Medusa's official residence when Michelle Henke's first message to the imperial governor arrived, he'd actually beaten O'Shaughnessy's com transmission to her.

"It's not that we're not 'fond' of Mr. O'Shaughnessy," he said now. "We're *very* fond of him, actually. Sort of the way you're fond of a cousin you know is really, really smart...and still want to strangle from time to time."

"You can't imagine how that relieves my mind." Medusa's tone was desert dry, but then she gave herself a shake and let her chair come back upright.

"Still, he does have a point. The political implications are going to be about as hairy as anything I could imagine. I know he doesn't trust you Neanderthal military types' judgment in all things, and I think it's silly of him to worry that an 'unbridled' military report may prejudice thinking in the Foreign Office and the Cabinet. But deciding exactly what us political authorities should be advising will be a handful. And I really would like our analysis and recommendations to reach Manticore before the Admiralty starts issuing movement orders."

"Understood."

Khumalo nodded. Despite the uniform he wore, his responsibilities and decisions carried an unavoidably political aspect. In effect, he was not simply the military commander on Talbott Station, but also the First Lord of Admiralty in Alquezar's local Cabinet.

"I can't argue with that," he continued, "and one thing we can be pretty sure of is that Earl White

Haven and Admiral Caparelli aren't going to let any grass grow under their feet when they start considering new deployment orders. Like you just told Gregor, we're incredibly lucky Denton—and Gregor—made the smart choice and headed straight back here. The question is how close behind them Crandall might be. Assuming, of course," he added, his tone even drier than Medusa's had been a moment earlier, "that this *is* Admiral Crandall and that she *is* headed our way."

"Assuming that," Medusa agreed, and rolled her eyes.

Michelle Henke had brought a treasure trove of information home from New Tuscany, including the entire classified database of every battlecruiser in the late, unlamented Admiral Byng's task force. A complete copy of that data had already been forwarded to Manticore, where ONI would indulge in a gleeful orgy of analysis, so *Reprise*'s report that she'd detected seventy-odd ships of the wall in the Myers System wasn't going to come at the Admiralty quite as cold as it might have. But while Byng's files had contained the information that Battle Fleet was conducting some sort of training exercise clear out here in the Verge, those ships were supposed to be in the McIntosh System, not Meyers. There might be all sorts of innocent reasons for them to have changed their station, but according to the testimony of members of the New Tuscan cabinet (who'd fallen all over themselves cooperating with Admiral Gold Peak), the mysterious Aldona Anisimovna had informed them of Crandall's presence as part of seducing them into serving as Manpower's cat's-paw. That implied all sorts of ugly possibilities, given Manpower's earlier effort to prevent Talbott's entry into the Star Empire.

And it also implies that this Admiral Crandall's just as likely to do something spectacularly stupid as Byng was, the governor reflected grimly. *It'd be a mistake— as I'm sure Gregor would point out—to* automatically *assume she's stupid enough to attack us, but that's where the smart money would go. And we'll get hurt a hell of a lot less if we assume that's what she'll do and she* doesn't *than if we assume she won't... and she does.*

"I'm sure Admiral Gold Peak and her people are discussing that very point as we sit here," she said. "In the meantime, I think we'd better ask Joachim to get hold of Henri Krietzmann. Under the circumstances, it couldn't hurt to have the Quadrant's minister of war present for our regular weekly get-together, now could it?"

❖   ❖   ❖

"Colonel Weng is here, Brigadier."

Brigadier Noritoshi Väinölä, CO of Solarian Gendarmerie Intelligence Command, grimaced and checked the time display in the corner of the report he'd been reading. One thing about Weng Zhing-hwan, he thought; she was punctual as hell.

Well, that and she was actually willing to *think*, which was unfortunately rare in the upper reaches of the Solarian League's intelligence services.

"Send her in," he told his secretary, closing the report on his memo board.

His office door opened a moment later and Lieutenant Colonel Weng stepped through it.

"Zhing-hwan," he said, nodding in greeting, and she nodded back.

"Good afternoon, Sir," she replied, and one of Väinölä's eyebrows rose at her unusually formal tone.

Her memo requesting this meeting had sounded routine, but there was nothing "routine" about her expression. Or her body language, for that matter.

"You said you had something we needed to discuss." He rose and headed across to the comfortable armchairs arranged around the coffee table in the corner of his office nearest the window that looked out across Lake Michigan. A carafe of coffee and another one of hot tea for the lieutenant colonel were waiting on the table. He poured himself a cup, settled into one of those armchairs, and pointed at another one. "Should I assume whatever it is might be just a tiny bit more important than your memo seemed to imply?"

"Yes, Sir," Weng said. "I'm afraid it is. Or that it *may* be, anyway."

She sat, but she didn't pour herself tea, even though it was her favorite blend. Väinölä's platinum hair was even fairer than Weng's, but he was twenty centimeters taller than she, and his dark brown eyes had a pronounced epicanthic fold. Now those eyes narrowed at her unusual abstention. It was the only really overt sign of anxiety she showed, and he took a slow, deliberate sip of coffee while he reflected upon how unlike her it was to show any at all.

"And why might that be, Colonel?" he asked, lowering his cup.

"Because I think Rajmund Nyhus is deliberately feeding Frontier Security bad information," she replied bluntly.

"Now that," Väinölä said softly after a ten-second pause, "is an interesting...assessment. And it brings to mind two questions. First, why do you think that? And, second, why are you telling *me* about it?" He paused again, cocking his head. "Now that I think about it, there's a third one, isn't there? *Why* is he doing it? Assuming he is, of course." He smiled thinly. "You can answer them in order."

"Yes, Sir."

Weng drew a deep breath. She opened her own memo board, but she didn't look down at it, and her blue eyes met his levelly.

"I try to stay at least broadly informed about what's going on in the other intel shops," she began.

"That would be a reference to your semiregular tête-à-têtes with Lupe Blanton?" Väinölä asked pleasantly. "The ones in which you share privileged internal information from the Gendarmerie with a minion of Frontier Security?"

"Well, yes, Sir." Lieutenant Colonel Weng shrugged ever so slightly. "You and I have discussed the way intelligence data bottlenecks often enough, and I've known Lupe for a long time. She's always respected the confidentiality of anything I gave her . . . just as I've done with her."

"And she's also one of the few people in Ukhtomskoy's shop with a working brain." Väinölä sipped more coffee. "I can't say I'm wildly enthusiastic at the notion that anyone on that side of the aisle's getting a look inside our intel gathering process. At the same time, I'm familiar with the need for workarounds to fill in holes in our own information, and Blanton's one of the good ones, even if she did end up in OFS. So what can you tell me—without violating the confidentiality of anything *she* told *you*, of course—about Nyhus cooking his reports to Ukhtomskoy?"

"Actually, Lupe knows I'm bringing this to your

attention, although her suspicions about what Nyhus is doing depend on information I shared with her, rather than the other way around. Do you remember a memo from Braxton Reizinger I copied to you back in June?"

Väinölä frowned, searching his mental files, then shook his head.

"Sorry, no."

"It's not like you don't have enough other reports to read, Sir, and we didn't really have anything concrete, anyway. But one of his analysts—Master Sergeant Roskilly—bird-dogged some interesting reports to him, and he forwarded them to me. Reports about levels of unrest out in the Verge."

"Roskilly!" Väinölä snapped his fingers. "I *do* remember her, although she was only *Staff* Sergeant Roskilly when I had the Verge Desk. And I think I remember your memo, too, now. Something about deliberate provocations and outside support?"

"Yes, Sir." Weng nodded. "I asked Reizinger to keep Roskilly on it and to keep me informed, and I've been coming steadily to the conclusion that she's absolutely right. Somebody definitely *is* stirring the pot in at least a dozen star systems, and Roskilly's right when she points out that, given the distances involved, it has to be the result of an *interstellar* effort. The problem is that Nyhus seems to've picked up on the same thing—which, to be perfectly honest, struck me as unusually competent for him—but he's drawing radically different conclusions. Or that's what he's telling Ukhtomskoy, anyway."

"What kind of radically different?"

"If you remember Roskilly, you know how good she

is," Weng said just a bit obliquely, "and she's been working this hard. Despite which, she hasn't been able to nail down who might be responsible for it. None of our sources have been able to shed any light on that, which hasn't kept some of them from speculating, of course." Her lips twitched. "And a lot of the speculation, not too surprisingly, perhaps, given what happened in Monica, has focused on the Manties."

"I'm not surprised." Väinölä snorted. "By this point, certain people are seeing Manties under every bed in the galaxy!"

Weng nodded. She knew her boss shared her own conclusions about just who'd done what to whom in the Talbott Sector.

"Roskilly's problem is that no matter how far down she drills, there's no reliable information on who's poking up the fire, whatever certain people may be suggesting. None."

"And this is significant because—?" Väinölä raised both eyebrows.

"Because according to what Lupe tells me, Nyhus is telling Ukhtomskoy he has 'solid evidence' from 'confidential sources' that the Manties *are* behind it. Now, I suppose it's always possible Frontier Security has better 'confidential sources' in the Verge than we do, but if that's the case, it'll be the first time it's ever been true!"

Väinölä chuckled harshly. There wasn't a lot of amusement in the sound.

"You're suggesting he's fabricating that evidence and hanging it on 'confidential sources' to keep anyone from catching him at it," he said.

"That's exactly what I'm suggesting, Sir. And what

worries me quite a bit is that I can't answer that third question you posed. I know he's in bed with dozens of transstellars, including Manpower, so on the surface, there're plenty of people he might be shilling for. Given Frontier Security's—well, *Verrocchio's*, anyway—involvement in that business in Talbott, I'm inclined to focus on Manpower and Kalokainos as his most probable ... patrons. I might've added Technodyne to that, if Technodyne didn't already have enough trouble coming down on it. But if this is happening on the scale it *looks* like it is, it's way too widely spread to be any transstellar, or even any consortium of transstellars, I can think of."

"But if it's not somebody like Manpower or Kalokainos, then doesn't Manticore become the logical prime suspect?"

"In some ways, yes," Weng conceded. "But there's no evidence of that. That's what I keep coming back to. Nyhus isn't just suggesting the possibility, or even the probability, that it could be the Manties. He's telling Ukhtomskoy his sources say it *is* the Manties."

"And if he's telling Ukhtomskoy that, then Adão doesn't have much choice but to kick it up to MacArtney," Väinöla said slowly.

"Exactly. Sir, can I ask if you've heard anything about this coming back down the chain?"

"You can ask, and the answer is that I haven't. Which, I presume, answers my *second* question. The one about the reason you're bringing it to my attention."

"Yes, Sir. I don't know what's happening here, but Lupe and I both think there's a hell of a lot more going on under the surface than we know about. I don't want you—us—getting blindsided by it. And if you'll pardon my saying so, if Ukhtomskoy really has passed this up to Permanent Undersecretary MacArtney, you *should* have heard something coming back down-chain."

"Yes, I should have." Väinölä's tone was grim. "If nothing else, they should be asking for a crosscheck from us, shouldn't they?"

"Yes, Sir, they should."

Weng's eyes were somber, and Väinölä grimaced. He could think of several reasons that might not have happened, but none of them were good. And he knew exactly what the lieutenant colonel carefully wasn't saying.

In his considered opinion, his immediate superior, General Toinette Mabley, the Gendarmerie's commanding officer, hadn't been the best choice for her job . . . and not just because one Noritoshi Väinölä could have been promoted into it, instead. Mabley wasn't the smartest person he'd ever met, and he knew she'd been a compromise choice resulting from intense negotiations between Nathan MacArtney, Omosupe Quartermain, and Taketomo Kunimichi. Interior, Commerce, and Defense all had legitimate interests in the Office of Frontier Security, but those interests often conflicted, and none of them had been willing to sign off on someone who would favor one of the other department's interests over their own. For that matter, none of them had been willing to accept a nominee who'd make waves for his or her department. And so, rather than competence which might prove . . . unruly, they'd chosen mediocrity. Mabley liked things just the way they were, and she would dutifully follow any order—or even any pointed suggestion—one of her political masters threw her way.

So the question, he thought bleakly, *is whether MacArtney's just quietly kept any reports from Ukhtomskoy to himself, or whether he's told Mabley to sit on anything that might challenge those reports? Or, for that matter, if Mabley's decided all on her own not to share Nyhus' suspicions with those of us who might have been expected to confirm—or deny—them?*

And what do I do now that Zhing-hwan's brought this sack of snakes to my attention? I can't go to Mabley and tell her an OFS intelligence section CO's deliberately falsifying information for his superiors. First, because there's no proof he is; second, because that could spark exactly the kind of turf war somebody like Mabley really, really hates; and third, because for all I know, MacArtney—or any of the other Mandarins, for that matter—could just as easily be in the pocket of whoever's doing this.

He glowered down into his coffee cup, grappling with possibilities and consequences, and wondered just how the hell he was supposed to handle *this* one.

Chapter Thirty-Two

BRILLIANT SUNLIGHT POURED DOWN from a polished sky dotted with isolated, almost painfully white clouds. The temperature was a sweltering thirty-four degrees, but a brisk breeze helped, stretching the brightly colored pennants on the staffs which ringed Jankulovski Stadium into briskly popping, starched stiffness. The stadium's high, stepped seating completely enclosed the football pitch, protecting it from the breeze's worst effects (and cutting it off from most of the *cooling* effect, unfortunately), but it was still affecting play, especially the goalies' punts. Given the heat, it wasn't too surprising drink vendors were doing excellent business, and Chotěbořian beer had always been good. And strong. It was evident that at least a few spectators had already overindulged in it, as a matter of fact, but Sokol's security people—many of them off-duty city police—had the situation in hand and people were actually behaving themselves quite well, under the circumstances.

That wasn't always the case at a heavily attended football game on Chotěbor, and despite the heat, the stadium was packed. It was standing room only—and scalpers had made respectable fortunes selling tickets, including quite a few to seats that didn't actually exist—as the Benešov Dragons squared off against the Modřany Sabres in one of the most anticipated games of the year. Nor had the game disappointed the fans to this point. There were 38,000 seats in Jankulovski...and not one of them was unoccupied as the Dragons' right winger faked outside, then reversed to cut inside the Sabres' left center back. The entire audience came to its feet as he crossed the ball with a perfect pass to Petr Bednář, the highest scoring active player in the Kumang System. Bednář took the ball with his left foot, drove past the Sabres' *right* center back, and then crossed his dominant right foot behind his left in a perfectly timed rabona kick that caught the Sabres' keeper charging to his right. It was beautifully executed, and the ball sliced into the upper right corner of the net for Bednář's five hundred and fifth career goal.

"*Yes!*" Daniel Kápička surged to his feet in the president's box, both clenched fists raised over his head. "*Yes!* God, that was *beautiful!*"

"Yes, it was," Adam Šiml agreed a bit more calmly. He'd risen from his own seat, if only to get a better view over the sea of heads between him and the pitch, and now he shook his own head as he settled back down again. "I remember when Petr first started playing with one of the local Sokol teams. He was only a boy—what? about twelve, I think—and he liked gutsy, flashy plays even then. Fortunately, he had the athleticism to pull them off! Did you see that bicycle kick goal he scored against the Ravens last week?"

"I certainly did! And speaking of fortunate things, it's

fortunate Sokol gave him the opportunity to develop that athleticism. You've done that for an awful lot of players over the years, Adam. I don't know where football would be without you people," Kápička said warmly, settling back down in the comfortably upholstered seat.

The sliding crystoplast panels at the front of the box could have been closed to produce a bubble of air-conditioned coolness, but Šiml hadn't even contemplated suggesting it. Minister for Public Safety Kápička had been a punishing soccer player in his youth, a box-to-box midfielder who'd thrived on the position's demand for stamina and relentless hard work. He'd played at both lower school and college levels, although he'd never quite made the cut for one of the professional teams. Not as a starter with one of the teams that was regularly in contention, anyway, and he wasn't the sort to settle for "second-best" at anything. But he was still an avid fan. He wanted to be able to feel the crowd's excitement physically in the waves of sound as the packed stadium cheered, whistled, and applauded, and he wore a huge smile as he listened to it now.

The truth was, Šiml reflected as he sipped from his own beer stein, that there were quite a lot of things about Daniel Kápička he actually respected. He was ambitious, he worked hard, and he demanded the same from his subordinates. He was also scrupulous about rewarding those who met his expectations, loyal to those he considered friends, and generous on a personal level, sometimes even at the expense of the ambition which was his driving force. Unfortunately, he was also perfectly happy to cooperate with the transstellars exploiting the Kumang System. Worse, he'd made Jan Cabrnoch's security forces even more powerful, driven by both that personal ambition and his conviction that only Public Safety stood between order and anarchy.

And he was one of Sokol's enthusiastic boosters, as well. Šiml had no doubt he'd been absolutely sincere in the praise he'd just offered, and he was maintaining his own support for the organization—so far, at least—despite a certain awkwardness where Cabrnoch was concerned.

Or, rather, where Cabrnoch's feelings for Sokol's *executive director* were concerned.

I wonder how much longer Daniel can keep that up? I'm sure this is a political calculation he'd like to ignore, but I doubt he'll be able to pull that off much longer. I'm sure Žďárská's giving him an earful about me, anyway!

Or possibly not, now that he thought about it. Zuzana Žďárská wasn't actually stupid. In fact, she had a pretty good mind, on those occasions when she chose to exercise it. But her natural default was "blunt object" mode, and because that normally worked for the System President's chief of staff, she'd gotten out of the habit of practice where more subtle approaches might have been indicated.

In this case, though, she might actually have decided a modicum of caution was in order. She had to realize—and Šiml was positive *Kápička* had realized quite some time ago—that Karl-Heinz Sabatino had become Adam Šiml's newest Best Friend Forever. Neither of them—nor Cabrnoch, for that matter—could possibly believe that was because Sabatino had suddenly developed a late-blooming passion for Chotěbořian athletic organizations. And it was damn sure that Kápička and Minister of the Treasury Ludmila Kovářová had a pretty good idea of how much of Sabatino's generous support *wasn't* going into new stadiums, equipment, or personnel costs.

That must be particularly galling for Žďárská, he thought cheerfully, since Treasury had become her go-to agency for dealing with Cabrnoch's real or perceived political rivals or enemies.

Kovářová was a very good economic technician. Unfortunately, like everyone else in the Cabrnoch Administration, she considered graft one of the perks of her office and was perfectly prepared to screw over the citizens of Chotěboř in order to open the taps of her personal wealth. She was also prepared to adopt a "purer than the driven snow" public attitude when her often creative accountants discovered one of her political *opponents* had been abusing the public's trust with shady economic deals or by evading his or her legitimate tax burden. That normally made her a perfect tool for Žďárská, but no Chotěbořan was stupid enough to go after anyone Sabatino had decided to support.

That's got to really frost all three of them, he reflected with profound satisfaction. *And as long as they're stymied, Daniel can go right on enjoying my invitations to share the presidential box at games like this one. If they're crass enough to point out that I'm not exactly Cabrnoch's favorite person, he can always point out that he's staying close enough to keep an eye on me until they figure out what Sabatino has in mind. And as soon as he drops Sabatino's name, they're going to pull in their horns.*

He leaned back, nursing his beer, and smiled.

✧   ✧   ✧

"Hell of a game," Šiml said, several hours later.

He and Zdeněk Vilušínský sat on the veranda of

Vilušínský's sprawling "farmhouse"—someone from one of the poorer parts of town might have called it a mansion, despite its antiquity—nursing chilled tumblers of vodka. The temperature had dropped nearly seven degrees out here in the country, and the night air was actually close to chill. The starscape glittered overhead, and the sound of wind in the trees, insects, and the lonely, haunting whistle of a *výr šedý*, the most proficient of Chotěboř's nocturnal avian predators, provided a welcoming stillness after an exceedingly busy day.

"Hell of a game," he repeated, shaking his head. Despite Bednář's spectacular goal, the Sabres had won 3–2 on a penalty kick with less than fifteen seconds on the clock. "Went right down to the wire." He sipped vodka. "And Daniel was so happy about my generosity in sharing my box that he insisted on treating me to a five-course banquet at Koš Chleba to pay me back." He raised his free hand to his lips and kissed the back of his thumb. "Magnificent! I wonder what the little people had for dinner?"

Vilušínský chuckled, but he also shook his own head rather more seriously.

"I'm glad you had a good time. And you can damned well take *me* to Koš Chleba, next time I'm in the capital! But don't get too carried away. He's a long way from stupid, and if he figures out what you really have in mind, he probably won't bother taking it to Cabrnoch or Žďárská. He'll go straight to Sabatino."

"I know." Šiml tipped back his chair, stretching out his legs and resting his heels on the veranda's railing while the fitful breeze stirred his hair. "And I also know Jan and Zuzana have to be getting nervous by now. It doesn't matter to them that I've been careful to avoid any overtly political moves, either. Sabatino's doing that *for* me, whether I want him to or not."

"Do you think he really sees you as an alternative to Cabrnoch?" Vilušínský seemed torn between hope and cynicism.

"Frankly, I'm not sure *he* knows whether or not he does." Šiml sipped more vodka. "I suspect he started the entire thing as more of an insurance policy than anything else. He could've been thinking about simply setting me up as a sort of façade opposition—a popular face for a 'legitimate political process' that might divert some of the growing unhappiness. If he figures he's turned me into a suitably pliable sock puppet, though, he really may decide to go ahead and pull the plug on Jan. Honestly, that would be the best possible outcome from our perspective, wouldn't it?"

"It could be. It could also get you killed, Adam." Vilušínský's tone was very serious now. "It could get you killed by Cabrnoch—or your good friend Kápička, or even Siminetti—if they thought there was a way to fob off Sabatino with some sort of plausible deniability. For that matter, they might go ahead even without deniability, on the theory that Sabatino couldn't afford to replace them if he no longer had someone—like you—waiting in the wings."

Šiml nodded soberly, but Vilušínský wasn't finished.

"And even assuming that didn't happen, assuming Sabatino went ahead and supported a regime change that put you into the presidency, what happens if—or when—he figures out what you *really* have in mind? Or Verner does?"

"Probably something unpleasantly permanent," Šiml conceded. "And Karl-Heinz and OFS have their hooks deep enough into Public Safety they could certainly engineer a tragic assassination or even a 'spontaneous coup.' Unless, of course, there was another armed, organized group that could *spark*—you should pardon the verb—a counter-coup in favor of the legitimately elected president."

"That's a pretty significant 'unless,'" Vilušínský pointed out. "And that assumes Kápička doesn't figure out what we're doing or Cabrnoch doesn't decide to swat you first. Or, for that matter, that Sabatino doesn't realize how you're really spending all those funds you're transferring out-system! Somehow, I don't think pulse rifles are the sort of 'retirement account' he wants you investing in."

"Probably not, but it's not very damned likely he'll find out about that part, especially with Pastera handling my investment portfolio and Martin keeping an eye on things from the shipping end. It was very generous of him to suggest I avail myself of Michal's services, don't you think?"

This time, Vilušínský laughed out loud. Too many Chotěbořans found themselves working for their trans-stellar landlords or those landlords' cronies, since that was really the only game in town. In Michal Pastera's case, he'd sought employment in Kovářová's Treasury Department right out of college, and—like any good, ambitious servant of the people—jumped ship to the private sector at the earliest possible moment. Over the past several T-years, he'd worked his way up to a senior position in Frogmore-Wellington's caretaking operation in Kumang. Frogmore-Wellington and Iwahara's investment in Kumang might be tiny by transstellar standards; in absolute terms, an enormous amount of money went in and out, and someone had to handle the equivalent of the giant corporations' interstellar petty cash purchases.

That was what Michal Pastera did for Karl-Heinz Sabatino . . . who had no idea he'd gone to work for Kovářová in the first place on the orders of his Jiskra cell leader.

Martin Holeček, on the other hand, was a coreworlder who'd come to Kumang as a freight supervisor for Iwahara Interstellar. But he'd lived in Kumang for over ten T-years, and he'd married a local girl.

Taťána Holečková had suffered a certain degree of harassment over her decision to marry him. In fact, some of her longtime friends had turned their backs on her for of it. She'd found that painful, but it had also helped her with Public Safety and Iwahara's local security staff. She was one of the collaborators who'd cast their lots with the Cabrnoch Administration and the transstellars, and her occasional clash with estranged friends bolstered that impression.

In fact, however, appearances could be deceiving. Táňa loved her husband deeply, despite his employer, but the *komáři* had claimed over half of her family. She was fiercely protective of its surviving members, and two of her younger cousins had been in the wrong place at the wrong time when anti-government/anti-transstellar leaflets were being handed out. Neither of the boys had been involved; they'd simply been there when the Chotěboř Public Safety Force decided a message needed to be sent. Both of them had survived, but one of them had suffered traumatic brain injury . . . which, of course, the CPSF blamed on those vicious, antisocial, anarchist leaflet-printers, who'd provoked the violence by wantonly attacking the champions of justice and public order.

Martin—who'd known both boys and never believed a word of the official story—had been so furious he'd decided to resign from Iwahara, but Táňa had convinced him to stay. He hadn't really understood why, at the time; but he'd understood perfectly a year later when she recruited him into her Jiskra cell.

And his position with Iwahara put him in a perfect position to pass certain cargoes of farm equipment whose contents didn't *quite* match their official manifests to destinations on the planetary surface.

"I'm sure my good friend Karl-Heinz feels nothing but reassured by the thought of having Michal ride herd on me," Šiml continued. "And in the meantime, I *know* he's aware Jan is feeling progressively less fond of me. In fact, he's told me not to trouble my head over it, since he has the situation under control. He wasn't *quite* so crass as to say things will stay that way exactly as long as I go on playing ball with him, but the implication was pretty clear. In fact, it was clear enough I'm inclined to think he *is* seriously considering supporting regime change if the general level of unhappiness keeps climbing."

"Really?"

"Really. There's not much point setting up a way to cover your bets if you're not willing to use it when it looks like everything's falling into the crapper. Or when it looks like the ungrateful recipients of your corporation's largess might actually be thinking about seeking membership in something like the Star Empire of Manticore, anyway. On the other hand, it probably wouldn't hurt to . . . improve my position with him, and I think there may be a way to do just that."

Chapter Thirty-Three

"WELL, AT LEAST IT'S a more pleasant venue than the last one," Damien Harahap observed dryly as the tall, fair-haired man who went by the name of Topór dropped into the chair on the far side of the table.

"It seemed like a good idea to avoid any deserted parks," Topór replied. "Nasty things can happen in parks. Never know who you'll meet there. And besides being more comfortable, I doubt you're going to be frying any of my electronics this time around." He showed his teeth in a thin smile. "Not unless that directional pulse of yours is a hell of a lot more directional—and short-ranged—than I figure it is."

He had a point, Harahap reflected.

An ice cream parlor might not strike someone as an enterprise likely to thrive in winter, especially on a planet whose climate hovered on the cool side of the ones humans preferred, but while it would never do to call the place packed, it was doing remarkably brisk business. That probably had something to do with the indoor ice-skating rink which it faced. At the moment, he and Topór sat under a gaily striped

canopy just outside the waist-high boundary wall around
the rink. The music blaring from overpowered speakers as the crowd of skaters whirled around the ice
provided a nice security touch, too. He had trouble
hearing Topór even when the other man raised his
voice; the possibility of someone else happening to
overhear them was slight, to say the least.

And Topór had taken the seat that put him between
Harahap and the open-air control room for the fellow
managing the ice rink's sound system and lights. Clearly
he calculated that any EMP pulse powerful enough
to take out yet another recorder would probably fry
the control room's electronics, as well.

Which, Harahap conceded, *might be just a* tad
*difficult for even a fearless interstellar secret agent
such as myself to explain away when the authorities
express mild curiosity about how that peculiar event
might have come about.*

Topór might not be a professional, but he appeared
to have good instincts. That was nice.

"Since I don't really visualize any need to disable
any recording devices—or weapons—during this conversation, your precautions, although well taken, aren't
really necessary. This time, anyway."

"Glad to hear it." Topór unsealed his coat and
withdrew a small pouch and a pipe. Harahap wasn't a
huge fan of tobacco, but quite a few of the ice cream
parlor's patrons were smoking. Indeed, a canopy of
smoke drifted overhead—not heavy, but clearly visible.
So he supposed there was no point protesting as Topór
opened the pouch, leaned back in the rustic wooden
chair, which creaked a bit ominously under his solid,
well-muscled weight, and began stuffing the pipe.

"The recorder wasn't that big a problem," he continued as he worked, "but replacing pulsers here on Włocławek is a copper-plated bitch."

"Would it help to say I'm sorry about that?" Harahap asked innocently, and Topór chuckled. Then he looked up as the adolescent waitress appeared.

"*Poproszę gorącą czekoladę,*" he said.

"*Oczywiście,*" the young woman replied, and headed for the counter.

"Hot chocolate does make more sense than my ice cream cone, I suppose," Harahap observed. "I have to wonder how it tastes with tobacco, though."

"So you speak Polish, *Panie* Mwenge?"

"No. I just loaded a translation program. It's pretty simpleminded and damned literal," he tapped his unilink's earbug, "so it doesn't help a whole lot turning Standard English into Polish anyone here in Lądowisko would recognize, but it does have its moments."

"I can see where that might be the case," Topór agreed. "And as for your question," he flipped a permatch alight and lit his pipe carefully, "that depends on the tobacco and the chocolate, I suppose."

Harahap nodded a bit dubiously, and the Włocławekan chuckled. He started to say something else, then paused as the waitress returned with a steaming mug of hot chocolate and a tall carafe from which to replenish it.

"*Dziękuję, kochanie,*" he said, and spun a coin through the air to her. Her right hand snapped out like a striking serpent, and he grinned as she caught it. "Don't worry about change," he told her.

"*Dziękuję!*" The waitress gave him a huge smile, since that coin was worth at least three times the cost of his chocolate. It was also non-electronic. The local tax authorities didn't like hard currency—cash transactions were far harder to track—which meant there'd be no record of her unexpected income.

She scampered off, still smiling, and Harahap raised an eyebrow at Topór.

"Not that I'm criticizing," he said mildly, "but was that really a good idea? A tip that size will stick in her mind if any unpleasant people ask about you or me."

"People around here tend to develop a sudden case of amnesia when the *czarne kurtki* ask questions," Topór replied. "Especially about big tippers." He smiled even more broadly. "Besides, that's not very likely to happen. I'm afraid quite a lot of the local riffraff like the ice cream and hot chocolate here. I don't suppose more than, oh, fifteen percent of the black-market deals in Lądowisko get negotiated around these tables. And two-thirds of them involve the black jackets. If they aren't actually providing—or buying—whatever's being dealt, then they're collecting a piece of the action for protection."

"I'd just as soon not be hobnobbing with any of Ms. Pokriefke's officers," Harahap said a bit sharply. "If they're running a protection racket and you and I aren't paying them, they might get just a little huffy."

"Who said I wasn't paying them?" Topór asked calmly. "I do pretty well in my day job, but nobody in Lądowisko's going to turn up his nose at a chance to pick up a little extra income on the side, and I happen to like Sarduchan pipe tobacco." He drew on his pipe, then lowered it and blew a perfect smoke ring. "The import duties on that are pretty damned high, so I keep myself in smokes by selling it myself on the side. I show a nice profit, actually."

"I see." Harahap considered that, watching the smoke ring drift up to join the overhead haze, then shrugged. "Well, I'm happy for you that you've found a way to make your vice pay for itself. That's not exactly what *I'm* offering to provide, though. Should I assume that the fact you used the contact code to set up this meet indicates you're interested in what I *can* provide?"

"I think you can safely assume that, yes," Topór replied. "There are a hell of a lot of details that'll have to be worked out first, of course."

"At the moment, I imagine I probably have a lot better feel for that than you do." Harahap chuckled briefly. "This is what I *do*, after all. From what you just said, though, should I also assume I'm going to have to work out those details with someone besides you? Or in *addition to* you?"

"Yes, you should," Topór agreed. "So why don't you finish up your ice cream cone while I finish up my chocolate, and then the two of us should go for a little tram ride."

Progress, Damien my boy. Progress! Damien Harahap told himself that evening as he settled into the comfortable spaceport hotel room suitable for a lower mid-level bureaucrat with the Oscar Williams Madison Foundation. He would have preferred something more palatial, but it was certainly adequate. And it was convenient for his meeting tomorrow morning with yet another clutch of KWSS bureaucrats eager to find out how the Oscar Williams Madison Foundation would burnish Włocławek's halo for the League. He loathed those meetings, but he had no intention of blowing them off or being anything other than intent, focused, and highly efficient during them. Harahap's superiors had the connections to make sure the Foundation did exactly what Hieronim Mazur was paying it to do. For that matter, Harahap—or, rather, Dupong Mwenge—truly was an OWMF employee, and the Foundation connection was going to come in handy if Harahap started shipping in "medical supplies" for the Siostry Ubogie. Covers didn't come any better than that, and he'd do whatever it took to maintain it.

Even endure another meeting with that pompous ass Mazur, he told himself, and shuddered.

But then his thoughts returned to his afternoon with Topór.

I'm still not at the top of their organizational tree, he thought. *Not quite. But I suspect "Grot" is pretty damned* close *to the top.*

The tram had deposited him and Topór on a slushy, old-fashioned sidewalk outside an only moderately rundown apartment building. It had reminded him in some ways of the "one-sun" in which he'd met Agnes Nordbrandt in the city of Karlovac. Of course, narrow, squeezed-in tenements were much the same all across the Verge; form followed function, after all.

One difference, though, he reflected. *"Grot" is a lot closer to* sane *than Nordbrandt ever was.*

He reminded himself that it wouldn't do to rush to any premature judgments in that regard, but Grot could scarcely be *less* sane! Besides, Harahap had decided he liked the man. And he wondered about that code name. It translated as "spearhead," which could just be a coincidence, but Harahap had found himself wondering if the choice of that particular alias had been a bit of a Freudian slip on someone's part. Certainly Grot struck him as exactly the sort of fellow who might be "spearheading" an underground organization. Especially one with a name like "the Free Thought Crusade." There was a definitely professorial air about Grot, with an extraordinarily sharp brain lurking close behind it, and it had been obvious he had something very like a mentor's relationship with Topór.

He'd also spoken with remarkable—and rather proprietary—assurance about the Krucjata Wolności Myśli's objectives.

But he's still not the fellow in charge, Harahap decided, leaning back and watching the local soccer channel on his suite's smart wall. *He's near the fellow in charge, but they aren't going to bring me into a face-to-face with the guy who's really calling the shots. Not this quickly . . . if they're ever willing to do it at all, and in their place, I damned well wouldn't be. But by the same token, they had to introduce me to someone high enough up to pass judgment on my reliability and utility. And it has to be someone whose judgment they respect. Judging by Topór's attitude, that's exactly who Grot is. And, to be fair, he's obviously a very, very smart fellow. I don't think he's the type to take anything for granted. Unfortunately for him, he's a little too honest to realize what a cunningly deceitful fellow I am.*

He was a bit surprised to discover he actually regretted that. He'd *liked* Grot, and he found himself hoping even more strongly that the KWM might succeed here in Włocławek.

But whether they do or not isn't really my concern.

What matters is that I have my foot well and truly in the door. We'll just have to see what Grot has to say when he gets back to me tomorrow. And in the meantime, he decided, watching a particularly spectacular save, *the local teams aren't half bad.*

❖   ❖   ❖

"So both of you think we should take Mr. Mwenge up on his offer?" Tomasz Szponder asked, pouring vodka into Jarosław Kotarski's glass.

Tomek Nowak sat at the other end of the desk in Szponder's Wydawnictwo Zielone Wzgórza office with a glass of honey mead, and the pleasant scent of his pipe tobacco clung to his sweater, tickling Szponder's nostrils. Now he raised his glass slightly in Kotarski's direction, obviously inviting the older man to respond first.

"We both know Tomek can get a little... overenthusiastic sometimes," Kotarski said now, with a smile. "In this case, though, I think he's right. Whatever else 'Mr. Mwenge' may be, he's not working for the *czarne kurtki*. Mind you, that doesn't necessarily mean he *is* working for *us*, but that old saying about my enemy's enemy comes into play, I think."

"I don't like how cozy he is with KWSS," Szponder said. "Having him zipping in and out of their offices adds an entirely unnecessary level of risk to anything *we* have to do with him."

"Actually, that could work for us," Nowak put in. Szponder cocked an eyebrow at him, and Nowak shrugged. "He *is* going to be 'in and out of their offices' whenever he's in-system, and they're all going to know why he's here. That means he's probably the only outworlder in the entire system they *won't* be watching for contact with dangerous revolutionaries. If we. screw up, we're likely to lead *Mała* Justyna to *him*, but I don't think he's very likely to lead her to *us*."

"Tomek has a point," Kotarski agreed. "And I've done some research on Manticore. Besides what falls into the 'everybody knows' category, I mean." He. snorted. "And I've discovered that in Manticore's case, what 'everybody knows' in the Solarian League is even farther off the mark than usual. I'm not prepared to propose them for sainthood, but this is one of the only two star nations to equate the genetic slave trade with piracy and actually execute slavers taken with slaves on board. *And* they apply the 'equipment clause' to determine whether or not a ship *is* a slaver. They were one of the prime drafters of the Cherwell Convention, for that matter. They have a reputation for being the sort of traders who could skin one of our own *oligarchowie* and then sell his hide back to him, and nobody gets that reputation without being pretty damned ruthless from time to time, but they also have a reputation for genuinely respecting the rule of law."

Szponder made a moderately incredulous sound, and Kotarski laughed. ·

"Remember what I used to teach, young man," he said. "I don't use terms like 'respect the rule of law' lightly. But I can tell you that—reading between the lines—the thing that really, really pisses the Sollies off is the number of times the Manticorans have told the League in general and Solly *transstellars* in particular to pound sand. Well, that and the number of times they've helped other star systems stand up to their neighbors, including the League. I found several verified instances of that, including a system called

Marsh, another one called Idaho, and a third—the most important by a huge margin—called Grayson."

"Out of the bigness of their hearts, I suppose?"

"Surprisingly, I think that actually may have played a part in several of their decisions."

Both of Szponder's eyebrows arched in surprise at Kotarski's tone, and the ex-professor laughed again. It was a considerably harsher sound this time.

"I know our own beloved political leadership makes it hard to believe that sort of thing, but do try to remember that not even Włocławekan politics were *always* corrupt. For that matter, if you really believe all politicians are automatically and irrevocably corrupt, just what exactly do you think is going to happen to *you* if we actually pull this off, Tomasz?"

"Don't think I don't spend the occasional night worrying about exactly that." Szponder looked down into his vodka, then raised his eyes to Kotarski's. "I think about Włodzimierz a lot, sometimes. If it weren't for Grażyna, I'd probably worry about it even more than I do."

"As long as you *do* worry about it, it won't happen," Kotarski said almost gently. "But my point is that there really are political leaders who *prefer* doing the right thing whenever that's feasible. Most of them realize—or at least I hope to God they do—that it won't always be feasible, but that doesn't mean the right thing isn't their default setting. And what's impressed me most from the research I've done since Tomek's first conversation with Mr. Mwenge is that Manticore seems to recognize the *pragmatic advantage* of doing 'the right thing.'"

"Advantage?" Szponder cocked his head.

"People trust Manticore to keep its word because they have historical evidence Manticore *does* keep its word," Kotarski said simply. "I'd say Manticore thinks carefully about the pros and cons before it *gives* its word, however. In the cases of both Marsh and Grayson, they needed military bases in the region, and in each case both sides recognized it was a matter of mutual self-interest and advantage for all parties involved. But *also* in both cases, Manticore went far beyond the minimum it had to do. It was building *allies*, not just bases from which to operate. They poured enormous amounts of their own resources into those systems, and over the course of their relationship, both Marsh and Grayson—especially Grayson—have made huge economic and industrial progress . . . and paid Manticore back two or three times over." He shook his head. "Don't think for a minute that the Manticorans didn't have their eye on that potential return on their investment from the outset, either. I think the Manticorans seek that sort of relationship not simply because of that 'default setting' of theirs, but because those relationships have paid off so powerfully for them over the T-centuries. Whatever their bottom-line motive, though, any star system they approach only has to look at Grayson to see how the Star Kingdom of Manticore interacts with its friends and allies. That's the reason all those systems in the Talbott Sector voted to join this new 'Star *Empire* of Manticore,' Tomasz.

"And what I see when I look at Mr. Mwenge's offer is the pragmatic military advantage to Manticore in helping us if at the same time that distracts the Solarian League from concentrating on the Star Kingdom. That's on the one hand. What I see on the *other* hand is the damage Manticore could do to literally T-centuries of reputation if it turned around and threw us to the wolves. If it comes down to a life-or-death decision, one in which their own survival or a truly vital core interest would be threatened if they didn't let us drown, then they probably would. Anything short of that, Manticore won't do that."

"I think Jarosław's right," Nowak said quietly. Szponder looked at him, and he shrugged. "We're all agreed the lid is blowing off here in Włocławek, one way or the other, sometime soon, but I think Mazur genuinely believes Pokriefke and the *czarne kurtki* can keep it clamped down forever.

"He's wrong, and we all know what'll happen if he finds that out and there's no one to take effective control when people finally go into the streets and just don't care how many of them get killed this time around." Nowak's expression was somber, his voice grim. "It'll be bloody, it'll be messy, it'll be destructive as hell, and what Mazur and the other bastards in the *Oligarchia* will do when they realize they can't stop it is call in Frontier Security to hammer the lid back down, no matter who they have to kill or how much of Włocławek's future the Sollies demand as their thirty pieces of silver.

"That's what all of this is about, Tomasz. I know how important it is to you that we get back to what *Włodzimierz* Ziomkowski stood for, and I agree with you a hundred percent. But I'll be honest. What matters more to me immediately, what keeps me awake at night worrying about my wife and my kids, is what happens if the explosion comes and there's no one to take the controls and steer. No one with the organization and the firepower to *impose* control and kick hell out of the *Oligarchia*, Krzywicka, Pokriefke and the goddamned BPP *before* they have time to whistle up Frontier Security and Frontier Fleet. And right now, we *can't do that*. We just can't, and all of us know it. That's why we had to use the Krucjata to tamp *down* the riots after SEOM shot down that airbus."

"And you think Mwenge—the Manticorans—will give us the firepower we need?" Szponder said, and it wasn't really a question.

"What I think is that no one *else* will," Nowak said unflinchingly.

"Tomek has a point," Kotarski said. "And while we're making points, don't forget they're offering us *naval* support, too. That implies interstellar recognition of us as the legitimate Włocławekan government by one of the most militarily and economically powerful star nations in the galaxy. And on the purely military side, it also suggests that the *łowcy trufli* will have a hell of a problem convincing OFS and Frontier Fleet that crushing us would be another low-cost operation."

"So both of you advise accepting the offer?"

Szponder looked back and forth between his two senior lieutenants—his theoretician and his tactician— and it was obvious he was asking for *advice*. That he intended to make the decision himself in the end.

Kotarski and Nowak glanced at one another, then turned back to him and nodded firmly.

"It's a risk," Kotarski said, his tone as unflinching as Nowak's had been moments earlier. "And if we're wrong about trusting the Manticorans, it could be disastrous. But if we're not wrong, it's the best opportunity God's ever going to offer for stopping everything we're all dedicated to stopping."

Silence hovered, and then Kotarski chuckled. It was so sudden both of the others looked at him in astonishment, and he waved one hand at them.

"Sorry! It's just that I actually *liked* Mr. Mwenge. Quite a lot, really. I've been working on preventing that from affecting my thinking, but I can't help it. And at least he has a sense of humor!"

"I don't recall him cracking any jokes while we talked," Nowak pointed out, and Kotarski snorted.

"Oh, but he did! In fact, it's been a running joke since the moment he...introduced himself to you in that park, Tomek."

"What kind of joke?" Nowak demanded. He seemed a little affronted, Szponder noted, which probably had something to do with his own jealously guarded reputation as a practical joker. "I didn't hear any jokes!"

"Yes you did, you just didn't know it. I didn't limit my research only to Manticore and its foreign policy. I took a look at Mr. 'Mwenge' as well. The name struck me as a little odd, so I went into the University's library banks."

He paused, and Nowak nodded. When the Uniwersytet Mikołaja Kopernika Department of History was ordered to terminate Kotarski's teaching position, the department had somehow forgotten to terminate his access to its computers. His colleagues' "oversight" had warmed Kotarski's heart, but it had also proven extremely useful to the Krucjata Wolności Myśli. And as an ex-professor turned hobbyist, he made a point of puttering around in the library banks on a regular basis, doing research on the most disparate topics he could think of, as a cover for his occasional, deadly serious forays for information the KWM truly needed.

"Well, it turns out that 'Mwenge' is a word in a very ancient language, one called Swahili," Kotarski said now. "And what it translates as is 'Firebrand.' I haven't run down 'Dupong' yet, and I don't intend to, since I'd just as soon not draw any attention to him if someone's monitoring my data searches, but I'm willing to bet it means the same thing—or something very like it—in yet another ancient language."

"You mean—?" Szponder said, his own eyes lighting with amusement.

"Exactly. He's literally *told* Pokriefke and Mazur and all those *aparatczycy* over at KWSS that he's here to burn their house of cards down around their ears, and they're too damn stupid to realize it!" He shook his head with another chuckle. "How can I *not* like someone with that sense of humor?"

FEBRUARY 1922 POST DIASPORA

"Excuse me, Mr. Frinkelo, but this is exactly what the Eridani Edict is intended to prevent, and the Constitution obligates the League to *enforce* the Eridani Edict, not violate it!"

—Commander Bryson Neng,
Solarian League Navy,
XO, SLNS *Hoplite*

✦ Chapter Thirty-Four

"ALL RIGHT, PAUL."

Innis MacLay rested one powerful hand on his son's shoulder. What he really wanted to do was to ruffle the boy's hair the way he had when Paul had been much younger. But fourteen-year-old adolescent pride got in the way of that sort of open display of affection these days. And if that was true under normal circumstances, it was even truer today, Innis thought.

"I'm counting on you," he continued instead, looking into Paul's eyes. They were the same hazel as his mother's, and they met his father's gaze steadily. "I've no doubt there are still a few Uppies about the countryside, and I'll expect you to keep your mother and the girls safe. You'll do that for me, aye?"

"I will, Da."

Paul's voice was deeper than it had been, Innis realized. It hadn't truly broken yet, but it was closer than it had been. Had it truly changed that much in the two months since the Rising had begun?

His eyes burned for just a moment at the thought,

and his grip tightened on his son's shoulder. Then he turned and knelt to sweep the eleven-year-old twins into a huge hug.

"And *you'll* be minding your mother, too, the pair of you!" he told Jennifer and Keeley sternly, his voice a bit gruffer than it had been with Paul. They looked back at him—Keeley with a demure, obedient expression that went poorly with the devilish gleam in her eye and Jennifer with darker, softer eyes, shadowed with anxiety. "I said *mind* her," Innis told Keeley giving her a little shake, and squeezed Jennifer tighter with his other arm.

"Like always, *Dadaidh*," Keeley promised.

"Lord save your *màthair*, then!" he sighed, and stood, holding out his arms to his wife.

She burrowed into them, more worried than either of her daughters but determined not to show it, and he hugged her close.

"And when will you be home again?" she asked, hugging him back.

"Well, that's not a thing I can tell you, *Rùnag*," he told her. "From the looks of things, it'll not be long, but MacCrimmon and MacQuarie've fooled us a time or two. Still and all, I'll be surprised if it lasts another month." He squeezed her again, then stood back so that he could smile down into her face. "We've friends at the spaceport still, and MacCrimmon's shuttle's on thirty-minute notice to lift." He winked. "I'd say that sounds like a man as might be thinking it's time to be getting off-planet and maybe even out-system."

"Pray God it is," she said much more softly, eyes suspiciously bright as she gazed up at him. "And just you be remembering that a great, towering *fùidir* such as yourself's a bigger target than most!"

"Oh, aye, I'll remember, *Rùnag!*" he reassured her, laughing as she called him a clown.

But then his smile softened. He gave her one last squeeze and felt his throat trying to close. Perhaps Paul was even more like him than he'd thought, he reflected, because he was damned if he'd say another word and let them hear the crack in his voice.

He picked up his pulse rifle, slung it over his shoulder, smiled at the four most important people in the entire universe, and headed out the door into the bright, breezy morning.

Chattan MacElfrish, not so many years older than young Paul and full of fire, was waiting with the air car. He looked up from his book reader, shoved it into a pocket, and hit the ignition button to fire up the turbine as Innis opened the door and climbed in beside him.

"The family's good, then?" he asked.

"Aye, they are," Innis replied.

"Then that's the way it should be," the unmarried Chattan told him as he lifted the air car off the ground. "It's good they'll be waiting for you when it's finished, Innis. I envy you that." He smiled, then checked the time and nodded in satisfaction. "And in the meantime, we've some Uppy arses to kick! I'm thinking we should make Elgin by lunchtime."

"I don't suppose there's any *good* news?" Tyler MacCrimmon growled as he settled into his chair at the head of the conference table.

The big, tastefully—and expensively—furnished briefing room was well lit, with the presidential seal inlaid in silver and gold into the enormous, hand-polished silver oak slab of the table. That seal belonged to him now, since he'd exercised the constitutional provision which let him "temporarily" relieve Alisa MacMinn of her office on the grounds of exhaustion. That was a much kinder word than "senility," and the press releases all assured the Party faithful the Beloved Leader would return to office as soon as she recovered.

Even her most fervent supporters seemed to feel that giving her a little . . . vacation might be a good idea under the present circumstances.

Crystal decanters of expensive off-world brandy and whiskeys gleamed behind the wet bar at the far end of the room, and burnished silver carafes of coffee or tea sat before each of the people seated around the table. Soft music played, the whisper of the air conditioning sent tiny, almost imperceptible shivers up the hideously expensive spidersilk drapes which concealed the smart wall when it wasn't in use, and feet were silent in the thick, deep pile of the midnight-blue carpet.

The entire scene reeked of wealth, of power and privilege, and the people in it were as expensively attired and perfectly groomed as the briefing room. Not a hair was out of place. And yet, Frinkelo Osborne thought from his lowly seat, half a dozen places down from MacCrimmon's, the air seemed heavy and stale. Not in any physical sense, perhaps, but laden with the stink of fear and weighted down by the invisible heaviness of desperation.

MacCrimmon's question hung in that heavy air, unanswered. None of his cabinet ministers seemed eager to meet his eye, and he glowered at them for several seconds, then swiveled his eyes to Keith Boyle, the Loomis System's secretary of war.

"Well?" he said flatly.

"There hasn't been much change since yesterday," Boyle replied. He twitched his head at the uniformed officer sitting beside him. "General Renwick's just returned from an inspection of our front-line units. I won't say his report is hugely optimistic, but we don't seem to have lost any more ground overnight."

"Well, *that's* a relief," MacCrimmon growled. "What about taking any ground *back?*"

"That's . . . not going to be easy." Anger flashed in Boyle's eyes, although he was careful to keep it out of his voice. "If we had more manpower, we might be able to accomplish something along those lines. As it is, I've instructed General Renwick to impress upon his people that we can't afford to *lose* anything else before we're relieved."

MacCrimmon's jowls flushed. For an instant, Osborne thought the Acting President was going to lash out at Boyle, but then his nostrils flared and he sat back in his chair, visibly leashing his anger, and gave a single, jerky nod.

That was better than Osborne had really expected. MacCrimmon had always had a tendency to find scapegoats for his own failures and make examples when others failed *him*, and that tendency had become more pronounced as the LLL closed in on Elgin. Fortunately, even he seemed to realize this disaster was very little of Keith Boyle's making.

Osborne's own sources indicated that Boyle probably would have loved to launch a coup that put himself in control, but there'd never been much chance of that. Mostly because the Army had been reduced to a mere eighty thousand men and women over the course of the

last several decades as first Lachlan MacHendrie and
then his protégée Senga MacQuarie built up the United
Public Safety Force at the Army's expense. After all, as
they'd pointed out time and again, there was no one
for an army to *fight*, but MacCrimmon could always
use more policemen! And besides, they'd added much
more quietly in MacCrimmon's ear, did he really want to
trust someone like *Boyle* with any *real* combat power?

Which was why the UPS actually had actually been
provided with more light armored units than the Army,
and why there'd been so many heavy weapons tucked
away in various UPS armories scattered around Halkirk.

Heavy weapons which had found their way into
the rebels' hands, in all too many cases.

Osborne glanced at the spidersilk drapes, and he was
just as glad they were drawn. If they'd been open, the
smart wall's display would have made dismal viewing.
After fifty-six days of fighting, the Prosperity Party's
loyalists held exactly two of Halkirk's twelve regional
administrative centers. They still controlled Elgin—
or most of it, anyway—and there'd been no serious
fighting on Thurso or in Red Bluffs, Glenquoich, or
Gilliansbridge, the next three largest cities on Halkirk.
But seventy-five percent of the smaller towns and
cities had gone over to the Liberation League, and
probably as much as fifty percent of the population
outside those major cities actively supported Megan
MacLean and her fellows. Personally, Osborne suspected that Ottomar Touchette's estimate of *seventy*
percent was closer to the mark. In fact, among the
loggers and foresters who were the backbone of the
system's economy, the percentage was even higher,
thanks to Nyatui Zagorski's policies.

That was also a huge part of the reason the Party loyalists had been driven back into the larger towns and cities. The UPS had learned that going into the woods after well-armed, motivated men and women who spent their entire lives there was a good way to lose troopers and their equipment.

It doesn't help any that MacLean and her people came so close to completely decapitating the UPS in the opening hours, either, he thought. *I may not've thought much of Colonel MacChrystal as a human being, but she had a lot better idea about how to organize field operations than MacQuarie or any of the other HQ chair warmers. Not to mention the fact that losing her and two of her three deputies created enough confusion the Liberation League damned near managed a* coup de main *right here in Elgin that could have ended the entire rebellion in the first forty-eight hours!*

He shook his head mentally, careful to keep the ever-increasing contempt he felt for the men and women in the briefing room out of his expression. If a single one of them had possessed enough sense to pour piss out of a boot—and the spine to argue with Zagorski—before this bitched up disaster began . . .

"Any more on MacGill's location?" MacCrimmon continued.

"Not really," MacQuarie admitted. "There are reports she's in Conerock, but we're just chasing rumors at this point, I'm afraid." She shrugged unhappily. "We're tapping a lot of their com traffic, but not enough, and they're surprisingly good at communications discipline. They almost always use code words rather than giving names or places in the clear, and they're obviously using a lot of dead-drop mailboxes. We've found and shut down over a thousand of them, and I'm pretty sure we've only scratched the surface. And on top of that, it looks like they use couriers to physically deliver messages whenever time permits."

"Well, that's useful," MacCrimmon said acidly. His support for Senga MacQuarie was running thin, and although her dark eyes glittered she had sense enough to keep her mouth shut.

"All right, bottom line time. Our projections indicate the bastards will take Elgin away from us within the next four days," MacCrimmon said to Osborne, his voice flat. "Right now, we've got them confined on the western perimeter, but they're constantly burrowing deeper. More to the point, our orbital sensors show them concentrating for a push through Swantown, and we don't have anybody left to stop them. Once they break through the Army's cordon, they'll come in behind the Public Safety troopers holding the western side of town."

Osborne nodded soberly. Swantown—a wealthy "bedroom community" suburb of Elgin—lay along the Swan River, on the southwestern edge of the capital. If the Liberation League secured Swantown, the hard-pressed Uppies being slowly driven west would be flanked . . . at which point, panic would turn their stubborn retreat into a rout. Especially since they knew what was going to happen to them if they fell into the Liberation League's hands after the increasingly vicious "reprisals" and atrocities of the last four or five T-weeks.

And what MacCrimmon *hadn't* said was that the fall of Swantown would also mean the loss of Elgin

Spaceport...the off-world escape route for the Prosperity Party's upper echelon and their family members.

"I understand, Mister President," the "trade attaché" replied.

"I believe you told us we could expect relief from McIntosh within three T-weeks 'at the outside,'" MacCrimmon continued. "While I wouldn't want to sound like I doubt you, that was almost *six* T-weeks ago."

"I know, Mister President." Osborne nodded again. "I know. And all I can tell you is that the relief force *must* be underway to us right now."

✧ ✧ ✧

"An' keep your bloody *heads* down!" Alexina Morrison, who'd been a private in the United Public Safety Force less than two months earlier, shouted the furious reminder as the first hypersonic pulser darts began to hiss and crack overhead. "We need to take the fuckin' *tower*, not to get your worthless arses killed!"

A couple of the foresters under her command actually grinned at her, but most of the other forty-five men and women of her assault team only nodded grimly. They'd seen too many killed because of a moment's carelessness. Besides, they'd come to regard Alexina Morrison with near idolatry. Not only had she and her partner been instrumental in taking Conerock in the first place, but she'd been in the forefront of the vicious streetfighting in Elgin from the very beginning...and she was still alive. That was a not insignificant accomplishment for someone who persistently led from the front.

"All right," she continued in a slightly less penetrating tone, "when we hit the freight entrance, Tammas'll go right and head for the lift shafts. Regina, you'll go left and take out the maintenance and engineering control room. The rest of you will follow *me* straight for the lobby. All of you got that?"

Heads nodded, and she gazed at all of them for a moment, then jerked her head at the waiting objective.

"All right then, let's get to it," she said grimly.

Captain Dugald Dempster cringed as a new crescendo of explosions tore through the smoke billowing up to his left. Theoretically, he commanded an entire UPS company; what he *actually* commanded were thirteen troopers supported by a single light tribarrel, and the tribarrel was running low on ammo.

"*Anything* from HQ, Morag?" he asked, trying hard to keep the desperation out of his voice.

"No," Sergeant Morag MacCuffie, his single remaining noncom said flatly.

MacCuffie was a lifer, hard as nails and with about as much compassion or mercy as a claw hammer, and her squad had been one of the first to be assigned to reprisals. Most of that squad was dead now, which was how Dempster had inherited her. He'd never liked her much, but at least he could count on her not to fold on him. If for no other reason than the number of people on the other side who'd see to it that she took a long time dying.

"Time to go," she continued in that same, flat voice, her eyes tracking steadily from left to right and back again as she peered through her helmet's vision-enhancing face shield. Even with it, she couldn't see a damn thing through all the smoke and dust. "Left flank's going to cave in the next five minutes, and we haven't heard squat from MacWilliams in over half an hour."

"If we pull out, we leave Brecon wide open," Dempster objected, jerking one thumb at the avenue they'd been ordered to hold "at all costs." There'd been a *lot* of those sorts of orders over the last couple of weeks.

"And if we don't, we're all dead, and the frigging street's open *anyway*," MacCuffie pointed out acidly.

She had a point, Dempster conceded. On the other hand, Brecon Avenue was one of Elgin's central corridors. The rebels had learned the hard way not to advance in the air, since not even their captured UPS tac vans could stand up to the Army's shoulder fired SAMs. Of course, what the rebels probably *didn't* know was that the Army had exhausted virtually its entire supply of them.

Should've had more SAMs of our own, Dempster thought bitterly. Unfortunately, no one in Public Safety's upper echelons had ever visualized a situation like this. He wondered if that same upper echelon leadership had spent the last month or so regretting the Army's systematic emasculation as bitterly as one Dugald Dempster did. Personally, he'd have loved to leave this streetfighting shit to someone—*anyone*—else!

There wasn't anyone else, however, and the UPS had lost too much of its light armor in the first week or so to parcel out any of its remaining Solarian-built Scorpion light tanks or Panther armored personnel carriers. The survivors were being held as a central reserve—that's what he'd been told, anyway—and even the locally built Soighnean GEV command vehicles were in short supply. Which meant the only way to keep the bastards from infiltrating their merry way all the way to SEIU Tower was to hold the critical intersections with infantry.

And if they *didn't* hold the critical intersections...

"Raise somebody at Dunwoody's CP," he said, hoping he sounded calmer and more confident than he felt. "Tell the Major that if we don't get some support up here in the next five—"

The Liberation League had very few Hydra IIIs left. They did have a few, though. It had taken three hours for the missile crews to work their way to a suitable firing spot, but they'd found one on the tenth floor of a building that overlooked Brecon Avenue. Now two of the missiles impacted directly on Captain Dempster's position.

Unlike Sakue Yampolski, Dugald Dempster and Morag MacCuffie had no time to recognize the agents of their destruction.

❖   ❖   ❖

"Excuse me, Ma'am, but I have a burst transmission for you from a Mr. Osborne," Lieutenant Hughes said respectfully, and Captain Francine Venelli, commanding officer, SLNS *Hoplite*, looked up from her hamburger with a resigned expression. Her ship had crossed the Alpha wall little more than half an hour ago. In fact, she was still thirty-three light-minutes from the Loomis System's twin habitable planets, which meant the message must have been banged off pretty much the instant Loomis Astro Control picked up her command's translation. God, she *hated* officious, self-important bureaucrats who seemed totally unaware of the limitations of light-speed transmissions.

"Of course you do, Aaron," she sighed. "He couldn't possibly wait for us to get close enough to have an actual *conversation*, now could he?" Hughes looked a little uncomfortable, and she waved one hand at him. "That was what's known as a rhetorical question," she explained.

"Yes, Ma'am."

Venelli suppressed a strong desire to roll her eyes. For a communications specialist, Aaron Hughes had an unfortunately literal turn of mind and a . . . less than lively intellect. There were times when Venelli thought—uncharitably, she knew—that he might have made a perfectly acceptable Battle Fleet officer.

Now, Frannie, she told herself. *Be nice. You wouldn't wish* that *on anyone, even Aaron.*

The reflection had more point than usual, given Venelli's most recent experience with Battle Fleet. *Hoplite* had been homeported in the McIntosh System for the last four and a half T-years, and for the most part, it had been a relatively pleasant—or at least painless—tour. Until Sandra Crandall and her damned task force arrived and made itself even more insufferable than Battle Fleet usually did. Had the fact that Crandall knew substantially less than squat about Frontier Fleet's job of keeping a lid on the pot out here in the Verge kept her from assuming command of every damned ship in the sector, whether they were part of her task force or not? It had not. And had she had a single frigging clue what to *do* with that command once she had it? She had not.

Which simply reconfirmed Francine Venelli's opinion that Battle Fleet was about as useful for the Navy's *real* job as a screen door on an airlock. It wasn't that she begrudged them their useless, shiny superdreadnoughts and all the other toys the Navy kept buying them instead of the battlecruisers and light cruisers Frontier Fleet really *needed*. She did, but that was the way it had always been and the way it would always be—Frontier Fleet would suck hind teat and then be expected to do the Navy's real work with half the hulls it needed.

Like most of Frontier Fleet, Venelli actually took a backhanded pride in her people's ability to get the job done with entirely old, worn-out equipment. It was Battle Fleet's *attitude* that pissed her off, and she'd wanted to dance a jig when Crandall decided to pull out so abruptly for the Madras Sector. The one thing she'd been afraid of was that Crandall might have ordered the McIntosh detachment to join her flag, but her worry had been needless. After all, what would a Battle Fleet admiral need with mere Frontier Fleet units, even if the commanders of the Frontier Fleet units in question had some actual first-hand familiarity with the region in which she was about to operate?

But Venelli had barely had time to crack a good bottle of wine to celebrate her restored freedom before the message from Frinkelo Osborne arrived and Governor Annetje Slidell—who was not, in Captain Venelli's carefully considered opinion, the sharpest stylus in the OFS box—had dispatched *Hoplite*, along with the light cruiser *Yenta MacIlvenna* and the destroyers *Abatis* and *Lunette*, to see what the hell was going on in the Loomis System.

Whatever it was, it hadn't sounded good, but Venelli hadn't seen Osborne's actual message. Of course she hadn't! What possible reason could have induced Governor Slidell to share a dispatch from the senior OFS officer with the Frontier Fleet officer ordered to assist him? Obviously, *Francine Venelli* didn't need that sort of information, anyway, and her orders had been short and succinct: "Go to Loomis. Report to Frinkelo Osborne. Do whatever he needs you to do."

At least they had the advantage of brevity and simplicity, she thought. But she didn't expect "whatever he needs you to do" to be one of her more enjoyable experiences. Those sorts of orders seldom were. Which brought her back to her lunch and Osborne's damned burst transmission.

"Well," she said, looking back down as her cabin steward set the bowl of potato salad at her elbow, "we're still seven hours out from Halkirk orbit, and I'm still hungry. Copy the message to my com queue. I'll take a look at it after lunch." She allowed herself a modest grimace. "The galaxy will still be here in twenty minutes, and I'll be damned if I'm going to let this Osborne kill my appetite *before* I eat!"

Chapter Thirty-Five

"HI, DAMIEN!" RUFINO CHERNYSHEV met Damien Harahap at the door and extended his hand. "Good trip?"

"Fast, anyway," Harahap said, shaking his hand and smiling. "I've decided I like the streak drive."

"You're not the only one." Chernyshev chuckled and pointed Harahap at the small conference table in the corner of his spacious office. "It's working for us in a lot of places right now, even if we do have to be careful about not arriving somewhere 'impossibly' early."

"Yeah, but Captain Yong could pull out the stops on the way back to Mesa. All the way from Włocławek in less than a month." Harahap shook his head. "If you guys ever decide to go public with it, you'll make a fortune from the passenger and high-speed freight operators!"

"Afraid that won't be happening any time soon," Chernyshev said as they settled into the comfortable chairs at the conference table. He lifted the coffee pot on the table and quirked an eyebrow at Harahap.

"Thanks," Harahap agreed, and held out one of the cups while Chernyshev poured. Then he sat back, sipping the excellent coffee.

"You seem to have settled in nicely," he said after a moment, waving the cup in a gentle circle that indicated Chernyshev's office.

"I suppose so." Chernyshev's smile was a bit sour. "Can't complain about the pay, and I'm seeing a lot of interesting stuff I wouldn't have seen before, but I do miss being in the field."

"I was going to say that at least bureaucratic chair warmers don't have to worry about getting themselves shot like field agents do, but given how you came by this promotion, I suppose that's not as humorous as it might have been."

"No, I guess it's not," Chernyshev agreed. He sipped coffee himself, then shrugged. "Still, the Manty Navy has a saying that probably applies." Harahap tilted his head inquiringly, and Chernyshev snorted. "If I can't take a joke, I shouldn't have joined," he said, and Harahap snorted in amusement.

"I've scanned your report," Chernyshev continued in a down-to-business tone, "but I haven't had time to actually *read* it. I did go through your conclusions section, though. I was particularly struck by your assessment of Włocławek."

"I'm pretty confident I still haven't met the fellow who's really in charge," Harahap replied, "but 'Grot' impressed me. And whoever *is* in charge doesn't dillydally. Grot got back to me in less than twenty-four hours to accept our offer. And he came up with some ingenious suggestions for how to get our shipments through Włocławekan Customs, too."

"Are you really as confident as you suggested that Grot and his buddies might actually pull this off?"

"That's always the question, isn't it?" Harahap shrugged. "My gut feeling is that they'd have a damned good chance, especially if we can get two or three loads of weapons through to them. May I ask why you're curious about their chances? I mean, are you asking because we want them to *fail* to make sure the Manties get splattered with sufficient opprobrium?"

"Frankly, we probably don't care too much either way," Chernyshev said. "Not yet, at least. We *do* need at least some of these people to crash and burn fairly spectacularly, if we're going to discredit the Manties in the Verge. But I think your suggestion that having some of them *succeed* will contribute more to accomplishing Janus' objectives in the *League*. If we did want to put the blocks to Grot and his friends in Włocławek, though, how would you go about it?"

"Burn one of the weapon shipments," Harahap replied promptly. "We'd have to make sure that whoever runs them in genuinely believes he's working for the Manties, but that would be the quickest way to blow the wheels off and make sure Manticore gets the blame. The downside would be that the Manties wouldn't get blamed for throwing Grot's people to the wolves. It would just be one of those operational fubars that happen once in a while, not a deliberate abandonment."

"I know." Chernyshev nodded. "That's one of the considerations the original Janus planners sort of overlooked. We can't pull the carpet out from under any of them before they actually pull the trigger without undoing a lot of the anti-Manty aspects."

"I'm sure there'll be plenty of opportunities for things to go totally off the rails without any involvement on our part," Harahap said.

"Truer words were never spoken," Chernyshev told him, and snorted harshly when Harahap looked a question at him.

"MacLean's people are currently kicking the shit out of the Prosperity Party in Loomis," he said.

"So soon?" Harahap sounded surprised, and Chernyshev waved his coffee cup.

"Apparently MacCrimmon was stupid enough to try to kill off the MacRorys. Personally, I suspect that was another Zagorski brainstorm. Anyway, the Uppies botched it but still managed to kill enough of them to push the Liberation League over the edge."

"Damn." Harahap shook his head. "I didn't expect *that* to happen!"

"Neither did anybody else. The good news for MacLean and MacFadzean is that at least we got the first couple of weapon shipments through to them first. But we were still in the seduction stage, in a lot of ways. Henrique Chagas—you don't know him, but he's a good man—took over when you were reassigned, and we knew tensions were still climbing, but MacLean obviously didn't want to take to the streets any sooner than she could help. Obviously, that changed."

"Have they used their hotline to 'Manticore' to ask for naval support?"

"Not that we know of. For that matter, MacFadzean and MacPhee were still working on bringing MacLean along when Henrique was last on-planet. We don't know for sure that MacFadzean even told her about the offer of naval support. Of course, our latest info's almost four T-weeks old, so there's no telling how the situation may've changed. Based on what we've heard so far, though, it looks an awful lot like they're going to take the planet away from MacCrimmon—and maybe even SEIU—pretty handily all by themselves."

His eyes met Harahap's, and they both smiled. Neither of them would lose any sleep over what happened to someone like Tyler MacCrimmon or Nyatui Zagorski.

"In the meantime, however," Chernyshev went on a more briskly, "we're going to assign you responsibility for Seraphim, too. I did the initial spadework there myself, but with me stuck in this damned office, I have to hand it off to someone. Given the personalities, I think your touch would be well suited to bringing them along. They're not what I'd call close enough to Włocławek and Loomis to be exactly *convenient* but that would be true of just about anyone else I could assign them to, and with the streak drive, it shouldn't be *too* bad."

"Whatever you say. I hope you remember that bit about it's not being 'convenient' if I end up dropping a ball because of transit times, though."

"If it happens, it happens," Chernyshev said philosophically. Harahap looked mildly skeptical, and Chernyshev chuckled. "I can put that in writing for you, if you'd like."

Harahap's lip twitched, but he shook his head.

"Thanks awfully, Rufino, but somehow I doubt that would save my ass if it goes south and someone farther up the food chain wants someone to hang for it."

"Of course it wouldn't, but think how much better you'd feel knowing I'd at least tried to save your neck!"

They traded the smiles of field agents who understood how bureaucrats played the game. Then Chernyshev set his coffee cup down and leaned forward, folding his hands on the conference table in front of him.

"One of the reasons I wanted to see you this morning was to personally brief you on Seraphim, Damien. The background's a little tricky, but it's certainly one we can work with. The first thing I think you need to bear in mind is—"

❖   ❖   ❖

"What do you mean there are no Marines?!"

Acting President Tyler MacCrimmon stared at Frinkelo Osborne in disbelief. Or perhaps a better term would have been "shock," Osborne thought.

"Mister President, when I sent Governor Slidell my request, no one had any way of knowing the situation with the Manties was going to go as completely off the rails as it has," he replied. "From the Governor's covering dispatch, Admiral Crandall pulled in every Marine detachment she could find before she headed off for Spindle. The Governor tried to pry loose at least some ground troops, but she's got fires of her own to stay on top of in McIntosh. She spent several days looking for troops—that's most of the reason for the delay in responding, in fact—then decided she needed to get the requested *naval* support off to us as soon as she could. She says she should have at least a battalion or so of Gendarmes she can loan you in another couple of weeks."

"*Another* couple of weeks?!" MacCrimmon stared at him. "In 'another couple of weeks' MacLean and those lunatics will own the frigging planet! At which point, a *division* of Gendarmes wouldn't do us any good!"

"Mister President, once they know we have orbital support, I'm sure MacLean and the others will realize they have no choice but to pull back. At that point—"

"What have you seen out of them so far to suggest they're that close to rational?" MacCrimmon demanded. "And even if MacLean and MacGill were willing to do anything of the sort, all our intelligence suggests the rest of the bastards would refuse to lay down their weapons! That's why we *need* ground troops—*Solarian* ground troops, that'll prove the League is backing us! The ground troops you *promised* us."

Osborne clamped down on an angry temptation to point out that he hadn't *promised* MacCrimmon anything. It wouldn't have done any good. Besides, he admitted a moment later, he'd certainly used the possibility of sending in the Marines to damp down the acting president's panic. And now that those Marines had failed to arrive, that tamped down panic was flaming up once more, all the worse because of how hard MacCrimmon had clung to the promised lifeline. Osborne could see literally see the fear driving anything remotely like reason out of the acting president's eyes.

"Governor Slidell *will* be sending a ground force," he said as reassuringly as he could. "I regret that she didn't have it available when my dispatch arrived. It never occurred to me that a Battle Fleet admiral would requisition the entire Marine force assigned to McIntosh." *Which*, he carefully didn't point out, *was never more than a single understrength battalion to begin with.* "I'm sure the Gendarmes, at the very least, are in the pipeline right now."

"And I'm telling *you* this has to be stopped *now*," MacCrimmon grated.

"Mister President—"

"If we don't have ground troops, we'll have to do it another way," MacCrimmon interrupted. "From orbit."

Osborne looked at him in shock. Surely he couldn't mean . . .

"As the President of the Loomis System, I can request military assistance from the League on my own authority," MacCrimmon went on in a flat, terrible voice. "Please inform Captain Venelli that I'm invoking the assistance clause of our agreement with the Office of Frontier Security. Secretary Boyle and Secretary MacQuarie will provide the targeting coordinates."

"He can't be serious." Francine Venelli stared at the face on her com display. "That would . . . that would—"

"That would kill a hell of a lot of people," Frinkelo Osborne filled in for her. "Unfortunately, it's not our call."

"Not our *call*?" Venelli glanced across her desk at Commander Bryson Neng, *Hoplite*'s executive officer. Then she looked back at Osborne. "Forgive me for pointing this out," she said more than a little caustically, "but whether or not it's our call, it'll damned well be our *KEWs!*"

"I realize that, Captain." Osborne closed his eyes for a moment, then shrugged, his expression unhappy. "Unfortunately, Frontier Security signed a standard assistance agreement with the MacMinns over thirty T-years ago. And under its terms, the President is entitled to ask for—and the League is obligated to *provide*—'all required military assistance' when the local government determines that it's necessary."

"Excuse me, Mr. Frinkelo," Neng put in, "but this is

exactly what the Eridani Edict is intended to prevent, and the Constitution obligates the League to *enforce* the Eridani Edict, not violate it!"

"I'd love to tell the locals that," Osborne said bitterly. "But Attorney General MacGwyer's already pointed out to me that the Eridani Edict specifically exempts planetary governments dealing with insurrection and civil war. And Secretary of War Boyle's assured me that he's prepared to sign off on the target list as constituting actual military objectives, not simply terror strikes." He raised one palm-up hand into his com's field of view in a gesture of helplessness. "So the bottom line is that they really can 'request' this."

"They've got orbital infrastructure of their own," Neng pointed out. "If they want kinetic strikes, let them carry them out themselves!"

"No, Byron," Venelli said, her voice heavy. He looked at her, but she continued before he could protest. "They've got orbital infrastructure, but none of it's weaponized. Do you really want a bunch of civilians de-orbiting cobbled up KEWs? God only knows what kind of effective yields they'd wind up with! For that matter, they'd be lucky to hit the right town! And at least three of the targets on this list are coastal. If they dump an outsized hunk of orbital debris into an ocean, Lord only knows how much of a tsunami they could churn up!" She shook her head, her expression grim. "No, if this is going to be done, it needs to be done by somebody who can at least hit the right target and not kill anybody else."

"But, Ma'am—"

Venelli's raised palm stopped him, and she looked back at Osborne.

"If I'm supposed to do this," her voice sounded like crumbling granite, "I want official authorization—*written* authorization—from President MacMinn herself. And I want it clearly specified *in* that authorization that the demand for this came from the local system government after I'd voiced strenuous protests. And I want those protests *communicated* to them, too, Mr. Frinkelo! There's not going to be any laying this off on an 'out-of-control' battlecruiser CO."

"President MacMinn is...incapacitated," Osborne replied. "MacCrimmon's the Acting President under the Seventh Amendment to the Loomis Constitution. I assure you, the constitution's quite clear on his current legal authority."

"Then I by God want the relevant constitutional language included in that written authorization! Maybe *that* will—"

She cut herself off, but Osborne heard her anyway and shook his head sadly.

"He's running—they're *all* running—too damn scared, Captain. I understand why you want the documentation, and you'll have it within the hour, I'm sure. But just making them sign off on it by name in the official record isn't going to make them stop and think. Not now."

"Maybe not. But I can frigging well give it my best shot first."

"Yes, you can. And between you and me, I hope you have a lot more luck in that respect than I did. I'll get that documentation to you ASAP. Osborne, clear."

✧   ✧   ✧

"What did you say?" Megan MacLean's face went white and she stared at Tammas MacPhee. "*Starships?*"

"I just found out," MacPhee said harshly. "The

bastards are sitting on the information, but our people on the inside say there's a lot of com traffic going on between Boyle's office and whoever's in command."

"Dear God." MacLean turned from her friend to stare sightlessly out across the smoke-hazy vista of the city of Elgin. The LLF controlled half of that city now, and they'd overrun the spaceport. They had the MacMinn Administration—although everyone knew it was really Tyler MacCrimmon calling the shots now—on the ropes. Just another few days, and MacCrimmon would be either surrendered, dead, or fled!

And now this.

"We're not equipped fight Marines in battle armor, Megan," Tad Ogilvy told her bluntly. "We could probably cost them a few people, but not enough to stop them. Uppies in armor would be bad enough; Solarian *Marines* who know what the hell they're doing are a whole 'nother proposition, though."

"What about intervention battalions?" Erin Mac-Fadzean asked. "We could handle *those*, couldn't we?"

"If that's what they were stupid enough to send... maybe," MacPhee said. "Even there, it'd be a hell of a lot uglier than anything we've seen yet."

"'Ugly' I can handle." MacLean rubbed her temples with both hands. "But this could be a lot worse than that, Tammas, and you know it."

"Even if we order the lads and lassies to lay down their weapons, you know a third of them won't," MacPhee said. "Stirling, for example. The only way you'll get his people's guns would be to pry them out of their cold, dead hands!"

"If that's what it takes, I'd be willing to do that

myself rather than risk a kinetic bombardment of the entire damned planet!" MacLean snapped.

"It's not likely to come to that," MacPhee argued. "Outside the towns and cities, we're too well dispersed and camouflaged for them to pick our people out for bombardment. And it'd be even harder to find individual targets in any of the urban areas. Besides, not even MacCrimmon could be crazy enough to take out our own towns and cities!"

"Do you want to bet your people's lives on that?" MacLean demanded.

"I'm just saying that until they at least *threaten* us we don't have any evidence of *what* they'll do. We can probably convince the majority of our people—even Stirling's—to accept at least a temporary cease-fire, and that'll buy us a little breathing space. Then, when MacCrimmon issues his demands, we already have a firebreak in place while we try and talk sense into the hard cases."

"And what kind of 'sense' would that be?" Mac-Fadzean demanded bitterly. MacPhee looked at her, and she pointed out the window at the smoke-laden air. "What do you think will happen to the leaders of this 'treacherous' rebellion if we surrender? Do you think somebody like MacQuarie or MacCrimmon would take her boot off the backs of our necks? After we've come this close, scared them this badly? Hell, no, they won't! They'll keep that boot right where it is until they get the pulser darts into the backs of our heads!"

"And if the alternative's a kinetic bombardment?" MacLean shot back angrily. She shook her head. "No, Erin. Tammas has probably come up with the best of the bad options available to us." She looked her second-in-command straight in the eye. "Pass the word. We're standing down and holding in place until we know exactly what they're going to demand."

"Targeting queue uploaded and locked, Ma'am," Lieutenant Commander Sharon Tanner told Captain Venelli. Her tone and expression made it clear what she thought of that targeting queue, Venelli thought. "Atmospheric penetrators deployed and ready. Prepared to execute on your command."

"Thank you, Commander," Venelli said, speaking to her tactical officer much more formally than usual.

She glanced at the com displays showing Captain Alec Sárközy of the *Yenta MacIlvenna* and Commanders Gwang and Myrvold of the *Abatis* and *Lunette*. None of them had been assigned any of the targets on Boyle's list. *Hoplite* had more than enough launch capability to handle all of them, and Venelli refused to spread the guilt around if she could help it.

Their expressions told her all she needed to know about how *they* felt about their orders, and their eyes looked back at her grimly. She forced herself not to wilt under the anger in those eyes—anger she knew wasn't directed at *her*—and drew a deep breath.

"Very well, Commander Tanner," she said. "Execute."

"Executing, aye," Tanner replied harshly and punched a button.

Eighty-seven seconds later, nine regional administrative centers which had gone over to the LLP ceased to exist. As did eight smaller towns, seven staging areas, and four major ex-UPS district bases . . . along with just over 3.3 million citizens of the Republic of Loomis.

Chapter Thirty-Six

"SO I'LL EXPECT TO SEE you and Mother for dinner Wednesday," Sinead Patricia O'Daley Terekhov said into her minicomp. "If you're late, I'll feed your supper to Alvin and Theodora," she continued in a stern voice. "You know how much German Shepherds like roast beef, and Theodora's due to drop her litter sometime in the next week. She's eating for eleven at the moment, and she's getting 'notional' about her diet, too. Last night, she ate two of my shoes—from different pairs, of course! So don't think I won't fend off her crazed appetite with your beef Wellington if you don't make it, Charley!"

She grinned, imagining her brother's reaction to the voicemail when it arrived. At the moment, he was on Gryphon, which would have made any kind of real-time conversation impossible even if there'd been an FTL link between Manticore-A and Manticore-B. Still, she had plenty of time to transmit it to the regular morning Admiralty courier. Light-speed transmission time between the Manticore Binary System's two components was almost eleven hours, whereas messages aboard the Admiralty couriers who jumped back and forth every four hours on a regular schedule—or more frequently, if an emergency message came up—made the transit in about half an hour. Use of the couriers was partly a security measure, since highly classified messages were routinely hand-carried, anyway. For routine traffic where time—or security—wasn't a significant issue, laser transmission was cheaper, although the difference wasn't as great as one might have thought, given the necessary infrastructure.

Another advantage the Admiralty couriers afforded Navy personnel and their families, however, was that space aboard them was available on a first-come first-served basis for physical packages, as well as electronic messages. Sinead had already taken advantage of that this morning.

Tomorrow was Captain (JG) Ginger Lewis' birthday, and Aivars had told his wife about Ginger's hobbies. For someone who'd spent her entire naval career in engineering, it probably made sense that Ginger was an inveterate model builder, but she also hand-fabricated and painted miniatures. Why she didn't simply go ahead and print them out instead of individually sculpting them in wax, then preparing the molds, then casting them in old-fashioned resin obviously perplexed Aivars, but Sinead understood it perfectly. She loved her husband, she knew how much he loved her art, and he was one of her greatest boosters, but he simply didn't understand how the artist's creative process worked. Didn't grasp the sheer, sensual satisfaction of being "hands-on" at every stage in the conception and production of a thing of beauty...or of sculpting the wax by hand instead of simply programming the printer. Sinead did, just as she understood the passion for creating hand-built art of any sort, and she'd spent the better part of a week—and pulled more than one string with an old family friend in BuShips—to come up with the old-fashioned model of HMS *Wayfarer*.

Officially, the *Caravan*-class Q-ships were still on the Official Secrets List, for reasons Sinead found difficult to understand. The armament and capabilities of the converted freighters had been leaked to the press shortly after Duchess Harrington's return from Silesia, and detailed schematics of the pre-conversion *Caravans* had been available from open-source publications like *Jayne's* for at least three T-decades. But, no! The Navy had, by God, classified the Q-ship design fourteen T-years ago, and it was *staying* classified!

Fortunately, there were ways, and Captain Fenris had agreed to release the necessary information for one of his own senior master chief petty officers to fabricate the pieces of a detailed model just over a meter and a half long. In white resin, so she could spend weeks getting the paint exactly right.

Even packed flat, the pieces—individually printed from the master builder's draft—filled a carton two meters long, fifty centimeters wide, and seventy-five centimeters deep . . . and weighed almost thirty kilos. Putting it together—and painting it—would keep even Ginger Lewis occupied for weeks, and Sinead looked forward to her reaction to the gift.

The completed model would be too large to keep aboard ship, given normal space allotments, but Ginger's newly assigned quarters aboard HMSS *Weyland*, the major space station orbiting Gryphon, were considerably larger than those aboard most warships. She'd be close enough to home to have it stored dirtside if she needed to, for that matter. In fact, Sinead had already hit on the ideal way to "store" it when she was next deployed out-system. After Captain Fenris agreed to release the information Senior Master Chief Glendie needed, Sinead had approached Commodore Leschinsky, current History Department Chairman at Saganami Island, and suggested to him that it was past time the *Caravans*—and especially *Wayfarer*, the most famous of them all—were suitably represented in the Academy's museum. And the fact that *this* model would have been built by one of *Wayfarer*'s surviving engineers (there'd been only twenty-one, and this was one who'd received the Osterman Cross for her performance in *Wayfarer*'s final engagement) would lend it even more historical significance.

There were advantages, she thought complacently, to growing up in a Navy family. And it was particularly satisfying to use some of those advantages for Ginger Lewis.

Sinead could see why Aivars had been so taken by Ginger. Some wives, she knew, would have been nervous about the relationship between their husbands and such an attractive young woman, but Sinead wasn't. She saw why Ginger might remind Aivars so strongly of her—they had the same coloring, they were the same height, and both had the same slender but solid build. In fact, Ginger looked like exactly what Aivars had come to regard her as: Sinead Terekhov's younger sister . . . or daughter.

Sinead's mouth tightened for just a moment, eyes dark with memory, but then she inhaled deeply and shook her head, once. No, she understood what drew her husband not simply to Ginger Lewis but to other young women, as well, like Abigail Hearns, or Helen Zilwicki...or Ragnhild Pavletic, and there wasn't anything remotely romantic or sexual about it.

I really should tell Ginger about Nast'ka the next time I see her, she thought now. *And I should see her sometime soon. She's too sturdy a personality to feel like she's being slotted into someone else's place, but there* is *some subtext here she should probably be aware of. Besides*, she grinned suddenly, *it'll give me an excuse to pop over to* Weyland!

Vice Admiral Claudio Faraday, who'd recently assumed command of the RMN's primary R&D installation, was another O'Daley cousin she hadn't seen in too long. If she hopped over to Manticore B for a daytrip, she could probably inveigle an invitation to *Weyland* for lunch, and it would be only reasonable for her to see Ginger and young Paulo d'Arezzo while she was there. In fact, Claudio would almost certainly invite them to lunch, as well, since he undoubtedly knew they'd been with Aivars at Monica. And career-wise, it wouldn't hurt Ginger or Paulo to be brought to their CO's attention on a more personal basis.

Yes, that was an excellent notion, she thought with another, broader smile. And from what Aivars had let drop, she should be able to amuse herself gently teasing Paulo about Helen. Now, would Ginger *help* her do the teasing? Or, as a considerate superior officer, would she provide covering fire for Paulo?

Sinead snorted in amusement, then glanced at the time display on the shuttle's forward bulkhead. They were well behind schedule, thanks to a twenty-minute ground delay, but the shuttle should be docking with *Hephaestus* in another twenty-five minutes or so. Technically, with Aivars' promotion and redeployment to Talbott, there was no longer a direct connection between Sinead and the *Hexapuma* families. Ansten FitzGerald, however, was unmarried. Amal Nagchaudhuri, who'd become *Hexapuma's* executive officer, *was* married, but Rebecca Nagchaudhuri was a professor of hyper physics who'd accepted a one-T-year guest lectureship at Clemson University on Old Terra shortly before *Hexapuma* deployed to Talbott. No one had expected the ship to return as soon as she had, and the opportunity to teach at what was widely regarded as the first or second best multi-spatial research school in the Solarian League wasn't lightly come by. Her teaching commitment would end in another few months, at which time she and their two sons would come home to Manticore. But until she did, neither of *Hexapuma's* senior officers had a spouse handy to step into Sinead's role. Lieutenant Commander Brenda Howell, who'd been assigned to Ginger's old position as chief engineer, did, but Lewis Howell was only twenty-five. That was a tad young for the job, so Sinead had agreed to stay on until Rebecca got home.

Oh, sure, Sinead! What a sacrifice you're making! You know damned well that you're going to miss them all when Rebecca does turn up and evicts you from your matriarch status!

Well, maybe she would, but she didn't have to admit that to a living soul. And in the meantime, she'd be having lunch with Ansten, his officers, and at least thirty of *Hexapuma's* dependents at Dempsey's in another couple of hours. Where, she was reasonably certain, she'd discover just how disappointed those officers were that the *Nasty Kitty* had been denied the chance to serve under Aivars for the Battle of Spindle.

The catastrophic defeat Countess Gold Peak's command had handed Sandra Crandall in Spindle—some of the newsies had taken to using the term "battle of annihilation," which was probably fair enough, although more of her ships had been captured than destroyed outright—was still reverberating through the Navy. God only knew what would happen on the Solly side of the fence once word got back to Old Terra. No wonder all the Nasty Kitties wished they'd been along!

She sat back in the comfortable seat, listening to the classical music offering, and gazed at the forward bulkhead display, which was centered on the slowly, steadily growing HMSS *Hephaestus*. Sinead Terekhov literally couldn't have counted the number of times she'd been to that huge, sprawling hive of activity, but it never lost its fascination for her. When she'd been a girl, visiting her naval-officer father's workplace, it had been far smaller than it had become as a result of King Roger's buildup, but even then, daytrips to *Hephaestus* had been one of her favorite treats. The later, massive military construction requirements of the war against the People's Republic of Haven had driven that growth even farther and harder, yet that only made it still more fascinating to an older and wiser Sinead who truly understood what it meant and represented.

Today, the station was no longer simply huge... it was *stupendous*. Its central spine was over a hundred and ten kilometers long, and branches and lobes reached out in every direction. The longest of the secondary arms was sixty kilometers in length, and it wouldn't be the longest for long. The entire, enormous, perpetually expanding agglomeration of industrial modules, habitats, shipyards, hospitals, communications and banking offices, and freight terminals stretched out with the total lack of grace possible only in microgravity, yet *Hephaestus* had its own beauty. Flanks gleaming in Manticore-A's reflected light were separated by chasms of total blackness where that sunlight couldn't reach, and constellations of warning lights, navigation beacons, and docking stations blazed like their own galaxies along the space station's skirts. It was hard to believe, looking at that child's model on the bulkhead display, that there were two million human beings bustling about inside the station, and Sinead found herself wondering—again—how many of those two million ever stopped, stepped outside the lack of wonder of their familiar daily routines, to consider just how marvelous *Hephaestus* was.

Well, maybe they *don't*, she thought. *But gawking, awestruck visitors like me can always make up for them!*

❖   ❖   ❖

"What the *fuck?*"

Jansen Mandrapilias, third officer of the liquid gas tanker *Bernike*, looked up sharply from the shipping manifest he'd been updating for their arrival at the Draco Seven orbital refinery. At the moment, *Bernike* was accelerating steadily away from *Hephaestus*, fourteen minutes and 691,000,000 kilometers out from the station on her regular bi-monthly round-trip to Draco, the central of the Manticore-A's system's three gas giants. Trundling back and forth between the refinery and *Hephaestus'* enormous tank farm wasn't the most exciting occupation in the world, but there was a certain solid satisfaction to the job.

Besides, Jansen had earned his watch-standing ticket just last December, barely two T-months ago, so it was all still brand, shiny new for him. Especially when the Skipper had seen fit to hand over to "Mister Mandrapilias" after clearing the *Hephaestus* departure perimeter. Zinaida Merkulov, who had the sensor watch, on the other hand, was at least two and a half times Mandrapilias' age and made it a point of pride never to be surprised by anything. In fact, Jansen rather suspected the Skipper had left her unofficial instructions to keep an eye on the newbie, given that she was something of a legend in the Hauptman Cartel's service who probably should have retired at least a T-decade or so ago. Unfortunately for those who felt she'd earned a vine-covered cottage somewhere, she routinely maxed the cartel-wide proficiency tests every year. In fact, she'd been seriously pissed this year when she came in third, instead of first.

She'd also been known to refer to one Jansen Mandrapilias as "Sonny" on certain off-duty occasions.

Under some circumstances, that could have led to a discipline problem, but not aboard *Bernike*, and not with Zinaida Merkulov, who was always professional *on* duty. Which made the totally unexpected outburst even more shocking than it might have been out of someone else.

"What?" Jansen demanded now, but she ignored him. She was punching numbers into her console at lightning speed, and then she whipped around to Cathal Viñas, the helmsman of the watch.

"Hard skew one-two-five, niner-seven-zero!" she barked. *"Now!"*

Jansen's mouth dropped open, but Cathal had known Zinaida longer than Jansen Mandrapilias had been alive, and he recognized the hammered-battle steel urgency of her tone.

He snapped his joystick hard over, sending six million tons of tanker into a steeply climbing starboard turn. Warning hooters sounded as she departed radically from her filed course profile, and Jansen could already hear the reaming Management would give *all* of them when ATC levied the fines. If they docked his pay to cover it, he'd still be working it off when he was twice Zinaida's age!

"Zinaida, what the *hell* do you think—?!"

Then another alarm sounded, and Jansen's eyes jerked back to his own panel. He'd never heard that strident, two-toned, ear-piercing wail outside a training simulation, and he couldn't really believe he was hearing it now.

But he was.

Something slammed into the interposed belly of *Bernike*'s impeller wedge and vanished with the instantaneous ferocity of a several hundred thousand-kilometers per second gravity gradient. But something else *missed* the wedge. It came sizzling through the tanker's wide-open throat on a reciprocal course with a closing velocity of over 60,000 KPS, crossed the wedge's interior at a sharp angle in approximately five-thousandths of a second, missed her enormous hull by no more than sixty or seventy kilometers, and went racing out the wedge's kilt.

Then it was gone. The collision alert continued to sound, and Mandrapilias felt echoes of terror that hadn't had nearly long enough to register at the time whiplash up and down his nervous system. His head jerked around to Zinaida.

"What the fuck was *that*?" he demanded.

He didn't know—then—that he would never, *ever* forgive himself for not reporting the incident instantly to ATC. Not that three and a half minutes of warning would have done any good.

Even the inner reaches of a star system represent a vast volume, against which even the largest spacecraft is very, very tiny. On the face of things, collisions and near collisions between spacefaring vessels were low-probability events, even for those moving along well-traveled shipping lanes. They weren't made any more likely by the fact that an active impeller wedge was among the galaxy's most . . . energetic energy signatures, which made it very hard for even the least attentive sensor tech to not see one coming. And, of course, Astro Traffic Control kept a very close eye on the multi-billion tons of military and civilian shipping passing through the Manticore Binary System at any given moment.

But the interlopers slicing into the heart of the Manticore System at twenty percent of light-speed, cutting straight through the heart of the primary shipping lane from the Draco Seven gas facility, didn't care about ATC, and their lead wave wasn't using an impeller wedge to accelerate. It was using something the Royal Manticoran Navy had never heard of, and it was unlikely any other sensor tech—especially any *civilian* tech, with commercial-grade sensors—would ever have noticed the tiny gravitic anomaly which had drawn Zinaida Merkulov's attention. She hadn't felt any sense of alarm, really; only the inveterate curiosity which had led her to her career in the first place. It was an itch she lived to scratch, and she'd redirected the sensors Klaus Hauptman had been kind enough to provide for her personal use towards it.

She never actually "saw" the incoming graser torpedoes at all, but she'd tracked those gravitic anomalies coming straight at her ship and extrapolated their trajectory in the nick of time.

The rest of the Manticore Binary System was less fortunate.

◇   ◇   ◇

Sinead was watching the display when it happened.

The shuttle was the next best thing to a hundred thousand kilometers from *Hephaestus*, but its optical heads had zoomed in until the space station's crazy quilt geometry completely filled the display. Even if they hadn't been designed to be the stealthiest attack platforms yet built by human hands the graser torpedoes which had slashed past *Bernike* were far too distant and far too tiny to appear in any optical display. The missile pods following on their heels were somewhat less stealthy, but they were also coming in on a purely ballistic trajectory, far astern of Oyster Bay's vanguard and falling steadily farther astern as the torpedoes' spider drive accelerated them towards their targets.

Sinead wasn't alone in not seeing them. *No one* saw them . . . until several million lifetimes too late.

Admiral Topolev's task group had continued in-system for just over a month after its stealthy arrival, until it reached its deployment point, one light-week from Manticore, with a velocity of twenty percent of light-speed relative to Manticore-A. That was when it deployed its missiles and its torpedoes and then disappeared tracelessly back into hyper. The weapons it had left behind had continued coasting through space at their initial launch velocity, their sensor heads protected against particle erosion by special nose caps, until they reached their pre-programmed attack locus. Then they blew the protective caps, receipted the tactical updates from the incredibly stealthy scout ships which had been sent ahead to gather that data for them, and updated their targeting queues.

At five hundred thousand kilometers, the graser torpedoes fired, and Sinead Terekhov cried out in horror as HMSS *Hephaestus* disintegrated.

It was nowhere near as sanitary as "disintegrated" might imply, of course. It couldn't be, when scores of grasers, each more powerful than most heavy cruisers' main battery weapons, ripped into a totally unarmored civilian target the size of *Hephaestus*. The torpedoes were deliberately yawing on their axis as they fired, sweeping their beams across the greatest possible volume of the station, and their projectors lasted three full seconds before they burned out.

Three seconds while they closed at 60,000 KPS.

Those grasers smashed into *Hephaestus* like a chainsaw into warm butter. And, like the butter, *Hephaestus* simply splattered across space. Chunks of wreckage—some big as battlecruisers—arced outward from the center of destruction like obscene meteors. Secondary explosions vaporized entire sections of the station as fusion plants—not just those of *Hephaestus*' internal power net, but of the dozens of merchant vessels and warships docked to load or unload cargo or for repairs—lost containment in sun-bright boils of plasma.

The explosions spread from the graser impact points, racing outward, like flame along a dry tree branch. They grew, reached out to one another, embraced, *merged*, until they became a single terrible vortex of destruction that rivaled the power of Manticore-A itself.

Sinead's shuttle spun madly, swinging to interpose its own impeller wedge between itself and the wreckage belching out of that hellish maw of devastation, but the optical heads, obedient to their uncaring computer's programmed imperatives, swiveled to keep the station—or what had *been* the station—centered on the screen. It glared there, like some prevision of the lava fields of hell, and Sinead O'Daley Terekhov pressed both hands to her mouth, her vision streaked by blinding tears, sobbing uncontrollably as she watched the nightmare which had come for HMSS *Hephaestus* consume the Star Kingdom of Manticore's primary industrial platform and more than two million human beings... including the entire crew of HMS *Hexapuma*.

Chapter Thirty-Seven

"SO, IS THAT EVERYTHING?" Adam Šiml asked, tipped back in his comfortable chair.

There was a certain overly patient edge to the question, and Marián Sulák snorted. He'd known Šiml for well over forty T-years, and he recognized testiness when he heard it.

"Adam, you could easily have gotten out of here on schedule if you'd really wanted to. It's not like this couldn't have been settled over the com! Not that a confirmed autocrat like yourself would have considered that for a moment, of course. How *did* you survive all those years in academia?"

Šiml glowered at him, but his eyes twinkled as he shook his head.

"You know, Marián, I haven't spent all this time sitting here in Zelený Kopec because of how much I admire your handsome face. I'm a very busy man these days, and I was supposed to be in the air to Velehrad thirty minutes ago!"

"Yes, you were. Now look at Hana and tell her,

with a straight face, that the little boy in you who likes playing with models isn't absolutely content to be sitting here right now!"

Šiml looked across the conference table at Hana Káňová, the solidly muscled director for construction on Sokol's regional Zelený Kopec board. Káňová, a past planetary champion fencer, had known him for a much shorter time than Sulák—a mere twenty T-years, in her case—but from her expression, she didn't expect him to be able to take up Marián's challenge. He had the impression—no, he was certain—she was less than delighted with the origin of the funds flowing into Sokol's infrastructure accounts, but she *was* delighted by the way they let her catch up with long-deferred construction and, especially, repairs. Although, in this case, as it happened, she was doing both.

"Actually," Šiml pointed an accusatory index finger at the youngish man sitting at her elbow, "it's Ondřej's fault. He should never have brought those plans to the conference."

"I believe it was your suggestion that I bring them ... Sir," Káňová's executive assistant replied. In fact, in addition to being her assistant, he was also her nephew, and he'd known Šiml since the day he'd turned fifteen. As a rule, Sokol tried to restrict nepotism in its paid staff, but that was hard on a planet like Chotěboř, where nepotism and cronyism had become the order of the day. In Ondřej Bilej's case, however, Šiml had no problem with the system, since Bilej also happened to be one of the best three or four architects Šiml knew, with a special gift for sports complexes.

Even if he was a wiseass.

"That has nothing to do with the case, you young

klouček," Šiml shot back now "You know my weaknesses! As such, as a dutiful employee of Sokol, you should've taken steps to *protect* my schedule rather than supinely acquiescing in something you damned well knew would seduce me into breaking it!"

He pointed the same finger at the holographic model of the new multi-sport complex glowing between them. It was spectacular, with no fewer than four football pitches, each with its own bleacher seating, plus a pair of gymnasiums, six tennis courts, and a pair of what were still called Olympic-sized indoor swimming pools. It was going to replace no less than three existing facilities here in Zelený Kopec, all of which dated from well before the *komár* plague and had begun falling apart T-years ago. It was also going to cost several million credits, which would actually be considerably cheaper than trying to properly refurbish the present facilities. Under the old scheme of things, they'd have had no choice but to refurbish anyway, in the tiny dribs and drabs they could squeeze out of the budget, which would probably have taken at least ten or fifteen T-years. Under the *new* scheme of things, his new best friend Sabatino had agreed to cough up complete funding for the project.

"To be perfectly honest," Bilej admitted with a smile, "it did cross my mind that you were likely to have a lot of questions, Mr. Šiml. And I should probably admit I always enjoy taking you inside the nuts and bolts. Still, I think it's just a little unfair to put *all* the blame on my plate."

"Surely you don't expect him to *admit* that?" Marián chuckled. "Adam's life is totally untrammeled by anything as limiting as the schedule constraints we mere mortals put up with. If it weren't for Květa, he'd never get anywhere on time!"

"Now that is *not* true!" Šiml protested. "Why, I was actually *early* once—about three years ago, it was, for a faculty meeting, I think—and Květa didn't have anything to do with—"

The ear-shattering explosion shook the office, rattled the windows violently, and completely demolished the executive parking area outside Sokol's Zelený Kopec offices.

✧   ✧   ✧

"Adam!" Karl-Heinz Sabatino held out his hand with a concerned expression as Adam Šiml walked down the shallow steps into the outsized sunken living room. "My God! You could've been killed!"

"I know." Šiml gripped his hand and shook it firmly. "And I have to admit, I never saw it coming. Nobody did."

He grimaced as Sabatino released his hand and pointed him into one of the huge armchairs by the picture window overlooking the capital's skyline from atop Zlatobýl Tower. Zlatobýl, at the very heart of Velehrad, was the tallest tower in the capital, and the yearly rent on Sabatino's penthouse—which occupied its entire top floor—would have built two sports complexes the size of the one in Zelený Kopec.

The spectacular view was a bit limited today, unfortunately. The skies over Velehrad were dark, heavy with black-bellied clouds despite the early afternoon hour, and raindrops battered the crystoplast window. Lightning flickered behind the towers on the far side of Náměstí Žlutých Růží, pulsing in the belly of those clouds, and the rumble of thunder was loud enough to be heard despite the penthouse's soundproofing. Sabatino glanced out into the thunderstorm's violence and shook his head.

"Maybe we should have—seen it coming, I mean," he said. He turned back to Šiml, and his eyes had turned hard. "Politics can be a much more dangerous game than anything Sokol sponsors, Adam. I'll admit it never occurred to me that something like this might happen, but maybe I should've remembered some of the players don't worry a lot about the rules."

"You know," Šiml said, "it's at least remotely possible this was purely personal, Karl-Heinz." Sabatino looked skeptical, and the Chotěbořan shrugged. "I'm not saying I'm incredibly unpopular these days, but there has to be at least someone I've royally pissed off over the years. For that matter, don't forget how many people *did* absolutely hate me back in the bad old days when we still didn't have a cure for the *komár*." He shook his head, allowing more than a trace of bitterness into his expression. "It's hard to blame people who lost someone they loved for feeling that way...especially after Jan worked so hard to make me the scapegoat. I'd thought most of that had faded. In fact, I'm positive *most* of it has, looking at the 'faxes and the political columns, but this really could've been someone whose opinion of me *hasn't* changed, you know."

"Funny you should mention that." Sabatino's voice was grim, and he barked a laugh when Šiml lifted an eyebrow. "That's exactly what Cabrnoch told me *he* thought had happened."

"Well, he *has* to say something," Šiml pointed out. "And to be fair—although being fair to Jan isn't all that high on my priority list—there hasn't been time for any kind of determination. They're just starting the investigation, you know. It's entirely possible he genuinely doesn't have any better idea of who may've been behind this than you and I do."

Sabatino snorted and looked back out into the storm. He obviously suspected that Jan Cabrnoch had a very good idea of who'd planted the bomb in the brand-new air limousine he'd provided for Adam Šiml.

"Well, we'll see what his 'investigation' turns up," he said in that same grim voice. "And I've already requested that Gunnar be kept apprised of its progress. *Personally* apprised."

Šiml's eyebrow rose again. Gunnar Castelbranco, the head of security in Kumang for Frogmore-Wellington and Iwahara, was a hard, ruthless, not particularly nice, but highly intelligent fellow. He was also far more concerned with getting results for his boss than about any toes he might step on in the process, and he probably knew where all the political bodies of the Cabrnoch Administration were buried. No one in that administration was likely to miss the significance of Sabatino's insistence that Castelbranco be kept "personally apprised" of the investigation's findings.

"I appreciate your concern, Karl-Heinz," he said, after a moment, "but having Gunnar looking over Cabrnoch's and Kápička's shoulders isn't going to make my relationship with either of them any better."

"I realize it might have that effect," Sabatino acknowledged. "in fact, I thought about that before I spoke to them. Some things are more important than others, though. I don't want anything happening to you, Adam, and something damned well nearly did." He turned back from the window and smiled thinly at his guest. "And, while I've come to value our personal friendship, we both know my concern here goes well beyond that."

Šiml looked back at him, then shrugged in acknowledgment.

"Of course I understand that," he said. "I just don't want you getting too firmly wedded to the notion that this *had* to be political. It may have been. In fact, I'll be honest and admit I find it a bit difficult to believe any of those people who might be pissed off at me would be *sufficiently* pissed off to try to blow me up in midair. That doesn't mean it *can't* be what happened, though. And while I appreciate that your involving Gunnar's intended to protect me, I hope it's not going to . . . further polarize my relations with Jan. I don't think it's going to help either of us if this dumps more poison into that relationship."

"Be honest, Adam!" Sabatino actually chuckled as fresh thunder crashed and re-echoed over Velehrad. "'That relationship' was pretty damned 'poisoned' when he froze you out of the government in the first place. When I started pouring funds into Sokol, it got about as bad as it ever could!" He shook his head. "No, whether any of his people were actually involved in this or not, he'd have danced a jig if it succeeded, and you know it. Under the circumstances, the benefit of making him aware that I'm . . . casting a protective wing over you, let's say, far outweighs any possible negatives."

"I just don't want this to complicate our plans, Karl-Heinz."

"I hope it doesn't, either, but it may actually have simplified our *priorities*," Sabatino pointed out. "And," he looked up as a uniformed maid stepped into the open living room door and knocked lightly on the doorframe, "I see supper's about ready. Let's let this rest until we've eaten. But I've asked Gunnar to drop in after supper to discuss getting you some full-time security of your own." Šiml opened his mouth to protest, but Sabatino shook his head. "I'm not talking about any of *our* people. If nothing else, I wouldn't want to 'taint' you with that off-world patina. And I'm sure you don't want a bodyguard following you around wherever you go. But whoever tried to kill you once may try twice, or even three times, and he only has to get lucky once. Besides, after what was clearly an attempt to murder you, I doubt any of your friends in Sokol—or anywhere else, for that matter—will think it's out of line for you to acquire at least a little protection. So be prepared to humor me on this one."

He pushed himself up out of his chair before Šiml could respond, and laid one hand on the Chotěbořan's shoulder.

"Now come eat before it gets cold," he said.

❖   ❖   ❖

"I thought I'd better screen you directly, Adam," Minister for Public Safety Kápička said from Adam Šiml's com. Five days had passed since the explosion had demolished Šiml's limousine, the Zelený Kopec executive parking area, and the thankfully unoccupied cars belonging to Marián Sulák and Hana Káňová which had shared it with the limo.

"Why *shouldn't* you screen me, Daniel?" Šiml cocked his head. "It's not as if you don't have my com combination," he pointed out mildly.

"Well, no, it's not," Kápička agreed. "But this isn't personal, Adam. It's not even about football."

"Actually, I sort of suspected that," Šiml said gently. "I was trying to put you at ease."

"I appreciate the effort, but I think I'd best get on with it." Kápička seemed to brace himself. "Our forensics people have finished their analysis of the explosive residue. In fact, they finished it day before yesterday, but I asked Jaromír Lepič to have them run the entire test protocol again. I got the results from him about twenty minutes ago, and he's probably passing them on to Gunnar Castelbranco right now. In fact, I've asked him to make sure Captain Price gets them for System Administrator Verner's information, as well."

"This is all sounding very ominous, Daniel."

"What it *is* is embarrassing, and maybe worse than that," Kápička said. "According to the taggants, the bomb that took out your limo came from us."

"*Us*'? Which 'us,' Daniel?"

"CPSF," Kápička sighed.

"What?" Šiml sat up straighter. "That was a *Public Safety* bomb?!"

"No!" Kápička said quickly. "I *swear* to you, Adam, that nobody in Public Safety had a damned thing to do with it! Or, at least," he added with the air of someone trying to be scrupulously honest, "if there was any involvement by someone in my shop, it was purely personal and I haven't been able to find a single person with a motive to harm you in any way. And the instant we got that first taggant analysis, I pulled out all the stops looking for someone like that, I guarantee you!" He shook his head. "No. The explosives were manufactured for our SWAT teams, but it looks to us like someone stole them."

"Stole them," Šiml repeated carefully, and Kápička waved one hand.

"I know how that sounds. It's the only answer I can think of, though," he said, then paused and shook his head unhappily. "Actually, as much as I hate to admit it, we have the occasional problem with CPSF equipment—including weapons, sometimes, I'm afraid . . . finding its way onto the black market. We do our best to keep it quiet, for obvious reasons, but it *does* happen. From what Lepič's already turned up, I'm afraid this is another instance of that."

"I see." Šiml looked at him levelly for several seconds, then shrugged. "I can't pretend I'm happy to hear about that, Daniel. For a lot of reasons."

"I know. Don't blame you, either. And—" Kápička chuckled sourly "—I don't think Castelbranco's going to be happy to hear it either. But I'm being as honest as I can when I tell you I've looked hard—in fact, I'm *still* looking hard—but I've found absolutely no evidence that . . . anyone in government service, let's say, had anything to do with that explosion."

That, Šiml reflected, was as close as Kápička could come to naming names like Cabrnoch or Žďárská, and from his expression, he was either totally sincere or one of the better actors Šiml had ever seen.

Or, more likely, a combination of both.

"Well," he said finally, "I appreciate your informing me. And I see why you thought you should do it in person. I know you have a lot of people already looking over your shoulder on this one, Daniel, but I hope you understand that if you discover any more about these mysteriously missing explosives, I'd really like to hear about it. Especially if there might be any more of them floating around out there in the possession of whoever already tried to kill me once."

"Of course I understand!" Kápička nodded sharply. "And I promise you that anything I find out will be forwarded to you immediately."

"Thank you, Daniel. I appreciate that, too. And now, I'm sure you have things you need to be doing, so I'll let you go."

"Thanks, Adam. I'll be in touch. Clear."

Šiml's display went blank, and he sat back with a cheerful smile which might have startled Daniel Kápička.

You're not going to find out who sold these *explosives on the black market*, he thought with intense satisfaction, *because that's not what happened. No, you're going to find out that* these *explosives were in that air lorryload that crashed over in Bílá Voda last year. Of course, they never actually got* into *the lorry, but I suppose the explosion was energetic enough it's not surprising your crash investigators didn't realize that.*

His smile turned into something suspiciously like a grin. At the time, he'd been more than a little irritated with the *jiskry* who'd arranged that accident. They'd been careful, and while the CPSF could readily track the explosives back to a specific delivery lot, the paperwork tracing where every *part* of that delivery lot had gone was much more problematical. No one would be able to prove the part of it used to blow up his limo *hadn't* been aboard that lorry. And the trio who'd actually engineered the theft had no official connection to the lorry, the explosives, or even the shipping order, so he'd been forced to accept their cell leader's judgment that it had actually constituted a very low risk. Despite which, he and Vilušínský had sent back very firm instructions to never—ever—do something like that again. The quantities of weapons and explosives which could be diverted to Jiskra that way might have been very useful, but not useful enough to risk alerting Siminetti or Kápička to the fact that members of the CPSF might belong to a secret subversive organization.

Of course, we never thought about them being useful this *way,* he reflected. *Actually makes me feel a little guilty for the nastygram we sent them when they did it.*

❖ ❖ ❖

"Let me put this as clearly as I can, Zuzana," Karl-Heinz Sabatino told the red-haired woman on his com. "I'm not happy. I'm not happy at all."

"I understand that, Mr. Sabatino," Zuzana Žďárská said. "and, I assure you, President Cabrnoch isn't any happier than you are. But, frankly, this is something you should be taking up with Minister Kápi—"

"I've already spoken with Daniel," Sabatino interrupted. "And Gunnar Castelbranco's discussed it—in some detail—with both him and General Siminetti. However, under the circumstances, and in order to avoid . . . misunderstandings, I feel it would probably be a good idea for me to make my feelings clear to *you,* as well."

Žďárská closed her mouth. She maintained a politely attentive expression with the practiced ease of a lifetime in politics, but anger glittered in her eyes. Sabatino saw it, and it didn't bother him a bit. Especially not since there was more than a little apprehension to keep it company.

"Thank you," he said. "You see, Zuzana, I've been trying to figure out why someone might have wanted to kill Adam Šiml, of all people. I mean, the man's uniformly beloved among sports-minded Chotěbořans, isn't he? And Sokol is one of the relatively few institutions here on Chotěboř that's universally popular. Oh, I know there was some ill feeling when he originally left government service, but that's all in the past." His eyes bored into her. "And, just between you and me—and possibly President Cabrnoch—the past is where that ill feeling had better *stay*. I'm aware Daniel and General Siminetti have been singularly unsuccessful in their effort to determine just how explosives delivered to CPSF's SWAT teams could have ended up in the back seat of Adam's air limo. I'm sure they're doing their very best to unravel that mystery even as we speak." He smiled with very little humor. "In the meantime, however, speaking both as one of Adam's many personal admirers and, yes, friends, but also as the representative of Frogmore-Wellington and Iwahara Interstellar, I'd like to point out that on behalf of my employers, I may find myself required to . . . rethink my relationship with the current administration if it should happen the local authorities are unable to prevent the murder of a philanthropist of Adam Šiml's stature. The loss of someone who's become our most visible connection to Chotěbořian social causes and corporate charitable contributions would make me really, really angry, I'm afraid."

He smiled again, the expression thin and cold.

"I do trust you'll convey my deep concern in this matter to the President."

Chapter Thirty-Eight

"I'M NOT SURE THAT'S a good idea, Sinead." Lisa Katherine O'Daley's blue eyes were dark, her expression troubled, and she shook her head as she gazed at her daughter. "I know you'd like to get away, but if Aivars isn't expecting you—"

"No, he's not expecting me," Sinead O'Daley Terekhov interrupted, her tone rather more clipped than she normally used with her mother. "He's not expecting the news he's going to get in another week or so, either. I'd just as soon he saw *me* as soon after that as I can arrange."

"Sinead—" Lisa began, then stopped, looking at the pain in her daughter's green eyes. She knew that same pain echoed in her own, but it went even deeper for Sinead.

Thirteen days had passed since the murderous attack the newsies had already dubbed "the Yawata Strike" after debris strikes on Sphinx destroyed the entire city of Yawata Crossing. There'd been 1.25 million people in Yawata alone. The best current estimate was that over *seven* million civilians had been killed, combining losses on the planetary surfaces with what had happened to the Star Kingdom's major space stations. No one had released numbers on *military* casualties yet, but everyone knew they'd been hideously high, as well, and Lisa doubted there was a single family in the Manticore Binary System who hadn't lost someone they loved. God knew *Lisa* had! In fact, she'd lost over thirty coworkers—some of whom she'd known for upwards of forty T-years—in the First Interstellar Bank of Manticore's *Hephaestus* office. And at least ten of her late husband's friends and colleagues had died in the destruction of the *Hephaestus* headquarters of Brookwell, O'Daley, Hannover, and Sakubara, the partnership he'd helped build into one of the Star Kingdom's half-dozen most successful investment management firms.

They came from old money on both sides of the family, the O'Daleys did, and a precious lot of good that did in the face of so much pain and loss.

But at least I was in Landing when it all happened, Lisa thought. *Sinead wasn't. Sinead saw it happen. Maybe that's the difference. But . . .*

"Have you discussed this with Charley?" she asked.

"No." Sinead sat back on the small settee on the other side of the coffee table and looked out the four hundredth-floor office's floor-to-ceiling window across the city of Landing. It looked so . . . normal, she thought. How could it look that way after what had happened?

"No," she repeated, looking back at her mother. "He's still on Gryphon, I think. Besides, I'm pretty sure he's too busy to talk to me right now."

Her mother snorted. Like Sinead, Lisa knew what

Charles O'Daley really did at the Foreign Office. If there was one person who was turning over every rock for any clue as to who'd attacked them, her son was that person. And he probably blamed himself for every one of the millions of dead. After all, it was his job to have known about whoever had committed that atrocity. The fact that no one else in the entire Star Empire had seen it coming would never blunt his bitter sense of self-blame.

There was a lot of that going around, she reflected.

She climbed out of her chair and crossed to the window. She looked out it, her thoughts paralleling her daughter's, although she didn't know it, while she thought about guilt, responsibility, and pain. Then she turned back to Sinead.

"You and Aivars discussed your going with him when he first deployed to Talbott," she pointed out. "You decided against it then because he was going to spend so little time in any single star system. So when you come down to it, will you *really* be any closer to him—effectively, I mean—than you are right here at home?"

And if you're not, you'll be alone with all this pain, where I can't reach you, either, she carefully didn't say.

"I don't know." Sinead replied. "But I know I won't be any *farther* from him. And for at least the immediate future, he may be spending more time in Spindle, given what just happened there. And I *need* to be there with him, Mother...because of what just happened *here*."

"And how would you get there?" Lisa asked gently. "You can't just book a suite on one of the Hauptman Cartel liners, you know."

The devastation of Manticore's orbital infrastructure had locked down all regularly scheduled civilian shipping routes. Eight passenger liners had been caught at *Hephaestus* or *Vulcan*, Sphinx's equivalent. All of them—and everyone aboard them—had been destroyed. Even Lisa, with all her contacts as First Interstellar's CEO, didn't begin to have a complete count on how many freighters and cargo and personnel shuttles had been swept into oblivion along with them. It was going to take time to sort out so much death and destruction.

"The Navy still has ships in the pipeline," Sinead replied. "I talked to Terry Patterson day before yesterday." Her nostrils flared. "Claudia was on *Vulcan* with her ship. And Peter had gone out to have dinner with her."

"Oh, God," Lisa breathed as the fresh pain hit.

Commodore Terrence Patterson, Admiral Patricia Givens' deputy at the Office of Naval Intelligence, had been one of Charles' personal friends for many years. He and his family had been O'Daley houseguests on dozens of occasions, and her eyes burned as she remembered his daughter, his son-in-law, and their two children . . . who would never see their mother or father again.

"I didn't know," she said softly, looking at her daughter, and Sinead smiled. It was a sad smile, one that quivered just a bit.

"I expect it'll be months before we know everyone we've lost." Her voice was husky, and she cleared her throat almost viciously. "I didn't know when I screened Terry, either. His yeoman told me before she put me through." She looked away from her mother. "I almost hung up before he came on the com. I mean, what was I going to *say* to him after that? But Chief Powell had already told him I was waiting, and I couldn't just cut and run." She looked back at Lisa. "And do you know what the very first thing he said to me was?" Her voice turned husky again, wavering around the edges, and her eyes brimmed with tears. "He told me how sorry he was to hear about *Hexapuma*."

"Oh, Sinead."

Lisa crossed quickly to the settee and sat beside her. She put her arm around her daughter, and Sinead let her head rest on her mother's shoulder while her eyes burned. They sat that way for almost a full minute before Sinead drew a deep breath and straightened.

"Anyway," she patted her mother's knee and made her voice sound almost normal, "I knew he wouldn't have time for idle conversation, given what must be going on at the Admiralty right now. So I went straight to the point and asked him if he thought the attack would affect dependent passages to Spindle."

"'*Dependent*,' sweetheart?" Lisa cocked one eyebrow, and Sinead smiled at the welcome edge of humor in her mother's tone.

"For certain values of the word, yes, Mother. Especially if it helps get me where I want to be aboard a Navy transport at a time like this."

"Oh, I see!" Lisa nodded. "And what did he have to say?"

"He said he didn't know."

"And this was a surprise to you?"

"Not really. But he suggested I might ask Captain Mathis over in BuPers, so I did. And he says the Navy's pulling in every transport it can find. They're obviously going to have a lot of personnel transfers—God knows they'll probably have to pull shipyard techs from every station we've got just to sort through the wreckage—and until they know where they're going to be transferring people to and from, all nonessential personnel movement's on hold."

"That sounds less than promising."

"At least some transports will still be moving back and forth, Mother. They have to be, however disrupted normal shipping may be," Sinead said. "And he told me he could put me on the standby list on an as-available basis aboard one of them. I told him to go ahead and do that, but there's no telling how long I'd have to wait. I thought about taking *Kaisers Witz*, but Captain Marco told me about her forward alpha nodes." She smiled crookedly. "I guess it's lucky he couldn't get her moved up in the repair queue."

Lisa nodded, silently grateful in more than one way that the small but well-appointed yacht her own father had commissioned sixty T-years ago had still been waiting for a repair slip on *Hephaestus* when the attack came in.

"So it looks like I'm stuck, for now at least," Sinead conceded. "But I'm not giving up, and Captain Mathis promised to let me know if anything opens up." She smiled again, less crookedly. "Being married to the man who won at both Monica and Spindle seems to carry a few perks I hadn't counted on."

❖   ❖   ❖

"Captain Lewis?"

Ginger Lewis looked up from her book reader's article on gravitics sensor maintenance techniques. There was nothing new in it, but reading old manuals was a lot less depressing than following the news channels.

"Yes, Senior Chief?"

"Captain Mathis can see you now, Ma'am."

"Thank you, Senior Chief."

She switched off the reader, slid it into her pocket, and followed the petty officer down a remarkably long hall, even for Admiralty House. He turned a corner, then rapped on an old-fashioned, unpowered door, opened it, and stuck his head into the office beyond.

"Captain Lewis is here, Sir."

"Thank you, Clement," a voice said, and the senior chief stood aside, holding the door for Ginger.

She stepped through into a moderate-sized office. It was buried too deeply in Admiralty House for windows, but a smart wall was configured to show a busy ski slope, complete with cloudless blue sky, brilliant sunlight, and flying cascades of powder snow as somebody slalomed past the camera. It was probably from someplace on Gryphon, Ginger thought, and felt her mouth stiffen as she thought about what she'd left behind to answer BuPers' summons. It was only by the grace of God and Vice Admiral Faraday's surprise evacuation drill that she was still alive. Too many of the people she'd met aboard HMSS *Weyland* in Gryphon orbit, people who'd begun the process of becoming colleagues and friends, had been less fortunate.

"Captain Lewis, reporting as ordered, Sir," she said.

"Captain." The extraordinarily tall, heavily tanned, brown-haired officer behind the desk had a pronounced Gryphon accent, which suggested her guess about the ski slope's location had been on the money, and he stabbed an index finger at a chair. "Sit," he invited.

"Thank you, Sir."

Ginger sat obediently while he looked back down at a memo on his display. He had to be almost two meters tall, she thought, and dauntingly fit. From the looks of him—and bearing that smart wall in mind—he probably spent a lot of time on skis. Then he looked back up at her with blue eyes which seemed even brighter in that tanned face.

"I'm sure you're wondering why you're here," he said with the air of someone getting right to the point, but then he paused as if inviting a response.

"I am a little curious, Sir," she admitted. "Obviously, BuPers needs to find somewhere to put me after what happened to *Weyland*. Given how...chaotic things are, I didn't expect to be ordered to report personally at Admiralty House, though." She smiled faintly. "It seemed like an awful lot of trouble for BuPers to go to where one squeaky new junior-grade captain's concerned. Especially"—the smile disappeared—"with everything else you have to worry about just now."

"Actually, that 'everything else' is why you're here, Captain Lewis," Mathis told her, and tipped back in his chair, stroking his walrus mustache with an index finger while he considered her.

"I have a slot to fill," he said then, "and when I plugged the requirements into the personnel database, your name came out."

"May I ask what kind of slot, Sir?"

"It happens, Captain, that there was a conference on *Hephaestus* on the twenty-sixth. One of several, I'm sure." His mouth tightened. "This particular conference, however, was a meeting of ship's captains and their execs chaired by Vice Admiral Toscarelli."

Ginger winced. Anton Toscarelli had been the Royal Manticoran Navy's Third Space Lord, the CO of the Bureau of Ships. His death aboard *Hephaestus* had already been announced, but somehow Mathis' words gave that death an immediacy it hadn't had before.

"The reason I mention this," the other captain continued, "is that among the officers attending that conference were the CO and XO of *Charles Ward*, one of the new *David Taylor* FSVs. Her electronics officer was also on the station for a briefing on the newest Lorelei platforms." He grimaced. "Effectively, that pretty much decapitated the ship's entire command structure, particularly since the EO had taken along her assistant and the Tacco had hitched a ride to have lunch with his fiancée at Dempsey's. At that, though, she was luckier than four other ships with senior officers at the Vice Admiral's conference, because she wasn't actually docked at the station."

Ginger winced again, harder, trying to picture what the loss of every department head except Astrogation and Medical must have done to *Charles Ward*'s ship's company. But even as that thought went through her, she felt her interest quickening. If the ship needed a new chief engineer, too...

"What do you know about the *Taylors*, Captain?" Mathis asked.

"Only what I've read in the *Proceedings*," Ginger admitted. "I know the operational concept behind them, but I've never actually seen one, I'm afraid."

The *Taylors* were a new departure in support ships whose pedigree owed at least a little—conceptually, at least—to the *Trojan*-class AMCs. Far smaller than mammoth repair vessels like HMS *Ericsson*, whose technicians had helped rebuild *Hexapuma* after the Battle of Monica, the *Taylors* ran to around three million tons, only about twenty percent bigger than the new *Nike*-class battlecruisers.

The challenge handed to BuShips' designers had been to produce a "fast combat support vessel" which combined substantial repair capability and a modest capacity as an ammunition/stores ship in a package which was fast enough to stay with a detached force of battlecruisers. The result was the FSV, a ship which could be configured—and *re*configured—at need to fulfill a spectrum of missions, and the result looked . . . odd the first time someone saw it.

Oh, the forward twenty percent of a *Taylor*'s outboard profile looked pretty much like a standard bulk carrier's hull, with a few other features thrown in. But stretching aft from that was a long, relatively narrow tube—a central core which contained the basic ship systems and life support—that terminated in what looked for all the world like a warship's after hammerhead. Four full-length ribs projected outward from the core, designed to serve as attachment points to mate the core hull with four quarter-hull section modules. Those modules included straight cargo carrying variants, but also those fitted with machine shops, as ammunition carriers, or even as personnel transport quarters and life support.

Their smaller dimensions limited the size of the modules they could mount, and the maintenance module had only about twenty percent of an *Ericsson*'s machine shops and fabricator capacity. It also meant they could carry fewer spares than an *Ericsson*, even with a cargo module dedicated to that specific purpose, but the dorsal ribs extended beyond the outer profile of the modules—and the permanent hull section—and were fitted as full-length mooring points for the RMN's standard CUMV(L)s. That created four "cargo racks" that provided a substantial external cargo-carrying capacity, since the various marks of Cargo Unmanned Vehicles (Large) could be used for spares—or for ammunition or general stores. They'd even been provided with a module suitable for turning them into long-term LAC tenders...and they required less than a quarter of an *Ericsson*'s crew.

They also had military-grade sidewalls, and they were armed.

It had always been RMN policy that repair and ammunition ships had no business involving themselves in combat, to begin with, and that hull volume aboard a service ship was too valuable to waste on weapons they wouldn't need. The Janacek Admiralty, however, had decided differently, and the *Taylors* were the result. The forward hull section contained a heavier armament than most light cruisers, taking full advantage of the RMN's off-bore missile capability, and—as part of their *Trojan* DNA—eight launch bays for LACs.

The truth was that the *Taylors* had represented a solution in search of a problem, in Ginger's opinion, when she'd first heard the scuttlebutt about them. She'd been able to imagine instances in which they'd be valuable, but those instances would be relatively rare, so she'd questioned the diversion of resources into their construction. Unfortunately—or fortunately, she supposed, depending upon one's viewpoint—the class's initial units had been well advanced when the

People's Republic of Haven reinitiated hostilities. They'd been pushed to completion to clear the slips for new war construction and, somewhat to the Navy's (and Ginger Lewis') surprise, they'd proved extremely useful. There were never enough Navy-owned service ships—especially with the Navy's expanded role in Silesia, the acquisition of Talbott, and the enormous deployment of relatively light units as part of Operation Lacoön—and none of the "taken up from trade" merchant ships being pressed into service could possibly have matched a *Taylor*'s sheer versatility. And even though a *Taylor* cost a good bit more than a "regular" repair ship on a per-ton basis, it cost a lot less in absolute terms, even allowing for its armament and integral LAC squadron. That meant the Navy could build more of them, and despite their Janacek pedigree, BuShips was doing exactly that.

"Well, you're about to see one from the inside," Mathis told her.

"Yes, Sir," she said. "I'm not really familiar with how the *Taylors*' command structure's arranged," she continued. "How does the ship's engineering department interface with the repair and support component?"

"It's all one department," Mathis replied. "The EO runs both sides of the shop."

Ginger suppressed an automatic blink of surprise. It definitely hadn't worked that way aboard *Ericsson*.

"Sir, I've never run a dedicated construction or repair department," Ginger pointed out. "That's one reason I was assigned to *Weyland*. I've spent almost my entire career in shipboard assignments. The way it was explained to me, BuPers detailed me to *Weyland* to pick up more 'yard dog' expertise, and I'd think that kind of background would be in demand running the engineers aboard something like a *Taylor*."

"That's all right, Captain. That's not what you're going to be doing."

"It's not?" Surprise startled the question out of her, and he snorted.

"No." He shook his head. "What we have in mind for *you*, Captain Lewis, is something a little more challenging. Welcome to your new command."

She stared at him in disbelief, and he lifted a chip folio from his blotter. He tossed it across to her, and she caught it automatically, still staring at him.

"I suggest you get started reading up on your new ship, Captain Lewis," he told her dryly. "They're holding a shuttle for you. If we're lucky, there'll be time for your personal gear to catch up, but I wouldn't count on it. Hopefully, you'll have at least a few days—maybe even a couple of weeks—to settle in. It's definitely going to take me at least a day or two to round up the rest of your senior officers. But as soon as we can get her squared away, *Charles Ward* is going to be headed for Talbott."

⋄　　⋄　　⋄

"Well, damn," Henrique Chagas growled as the news feed scrolled up his display aboard the "Hauptman Cartel" freighter decelerating towards Thurso.

So much for this part of Operation Janus, he thought sourly. *Crap.*

It must have been an interesting call for the local news channels, he reflected. On the one hand, advertising to the galaxy at large that you'd just killed two or three million of your own citizens with kinetic strikes that took out entire cities wasn't exactly good for your star system's public image. On the other hand, driving that point home for anyone foolish enough to think about emulating Megan MacLean's revolutionaries had to be pretty high on Tyler MacCrimmon's to-do list. And since the "free and independent" news media of the Loomis System did exactly what the Loomis System's government told it to do, that was exactly the message the newsies had delivered.

He froze the feed, looking at the imagery of the crater the KEWs had left where the city of Conerock used to be. There'd been no survivors at all from that one, according to the newsies, and it hadn't been a lot better than that for any of the other targeted cities. That would have been more than enough, he was sure, to have ended the rebellion, but if official reports were to be believed, every single member of the LLF had been killed or captured following the government's successful assault to retake control of Elgin. Megan MacLean, Erin MacFadzean, Tammas MacPhee, and Tad Ogilvy were all confirmed dead according to Senga MacQuarie's official communiqués. There was no specific mention of Luíseach MacGill or her husband, which was an interesting omission, but it was depressingly clear the Loomis Liberation Front had been totally crushed.

And not one frigging mention of the Manties in any of this crap, he thought disgustedly. *All that work right down the toilet!* He glowered at the ugly hole where Conerock's neat homes and families had once been and shook his head. *You'd think they could've taken at least* one *of the bastards alive and gotten them to talk about their "Manticoran sponsors," but, no! MacCrimmon and MacQuarie couldn't even get that* right!

He growled an obscenity, killed the feed, and punched in a com combination. The ship's captain appeared on his display almost instantly, and Chagas smiled sourly at the worry in the other man's eyes.

"Don't sweat it, Captain," he said. "Under the circumstances, there's more than enough 'local unrest' hereabouts for a reasonable merchant skipper to give the system a miss until things settle down. Go ahead and jettison the arms shipment just in case, but I think the 'Hauptman Cartel' is going to pass on picking up this particular load of seafood."

"Yes, Sir." The captain made no effort to disguise his relief. "Back to Mesa, then, Sir?"

"Might as well," Chagas said morosely. "*This* system's a total bust."

❖   ❖   ❖

"Oh, damn," Ginger Lewis muttered as the com signal pinged at her.

She thought about ignoring it—Captain Mathis had been right; she had a lot of reading to catch up on, she was due to go aboard *Charles Ward* in less than an hour, and her baggage *hadn't* caught up with her—but for all she knew sanity had broken out at the Admiralty and one of Mathis' superiors was screening her to tell her it had all been a mistake.

Part of her hoped that was *exactly* what it was.

The signal pinged again and she hit the acceptance key, opening a window in the corner of her display. Then she twitched upright in her shuttle seat.

"Ms. Terekhov!"

"I've told you before, Ginger. Ms. Terekhov is Aivars'. mother. *My* name is Sinead."

"Well—" Ginger began, then stopped, closed her

mouth, and smiled. "Sorry. I'll try to remember, but it's hard. I still think of you as 'the Skipper's wife,' I'm afraid."

"I understand, but I hope you'll find it a little easier to think of me by my first name now that you're a CO yourself."

"You heard about that?" Ginger shook her head. "I think somebody's made a serious mistake, to be honest."

"Nonsense!" Sinead Terekhov said sternly. "That's not a thought you're allowed to entertain, young lady! When they pull out the captain's chair for you, you *sit*, and whatever else you may do, you never let anyone think your posterior isn't completely comfortable in it. I trust that's clear?"

"Aye, aye, Ma'am," Ginger acknowledged wryly, and Sinead snorted.

"Better. Honestly, Ginger, you'll do just fine. I know you didn't see it coming, but there are a lot of things we haven't seen coming lately."

"That's for damned sure," Ginger agreed. They gazed at each other for a handful of seconds, each of them thinking of all the people she'd never see again. Then Ginger cleared her throat.

"May I ask why you've screened me . . . Sinead?"

"Well, partly to congratulate you on your new command. My spies reported it to me about ten minutes ago."

"Thank you." Ginger's smile was a bit lopsided. "They told *me* about it about twenty minutes before they told *you* about it!"

"The Navy can be like that even under normal circumstances. Under these, you're lucky you got *that* much warning!"

"I know. But you said that was part of the reason you'd screened," Ginger pressed and cocked one eyebrow. Sinead Terekhov had become one of her favorite people, but she did have all that reading to do.

"Well, the other reason was to ask you for a small favor," Sinead said. "You see..."

⋄   ⋄   ⋄

The shuttle braked, then shivered as the boat bay tractors reached out and locked. Ginger put away her reader and gazed out the port, watching the bulkhead markings slide by as the shuttle moved vertically up the cavernous, brilliantly lit well of the bay. That bay was larger than most warships, even superdreadnoughts, boasted because of the outsized parasite work boats it was designed to host at need. Then the shuttle shivered again, harder, as the docking arms locked, the umbilicals engaged, and the boarding tube ran out.

Less than three hours had passed since the moment she walked into Captain Mathis' office in Landing.

"Good seal, Ma'am," the flight engineer announced.

"Thank you, Chief." Ginger made herself sound calm, as if things like this happened to her every day, even as a little voice screamed that BuPers had made a dreadful mistake. But then she remembered her conversation with Sinead Terekhov, and smiled ever so slightly.

She waited until the petty officer unsealed the hatch, then reached for the grab bar and swung herself from the shuttle's artificial gravity into freefall for the brief passage down the boarding tube to the boat bay gallery. She floated to the matching grab bar at the gallery end of the tube, caught it, and twisted, moving feet-first from the tube's zero-grav into the gallery's standard one gee. She landed with the grace-ful, spinal-reflex proficiency of thirteen T-years spent almost continuously on shipboard and saluted the absurdly young-looking midshipwoman wearing the brassard of the boat bay officer of the deck.

"Permission to come aboard, Ma'am?" she requested formally.

"Permission granted, Ma'am." The youngster return-ing Ginger's salute looked more than a little nervous, even uncertain, and Ginger suppressed an urge to pat her on the head and tell her everything would be all right.

Instead, she glanced at the midshipwoman's name-plate and nodded as her brain pulled the information out of storage. Paula Rafferty, twenty-one T-years old, assigned to *Charles Ward* for her snotty cruise. She'd only come aboard the ship five days before the Yawata Strike, poor kid. And the only reason she was still alive was that, as the most recently arrived of the ship's four midshipmen, she'd still been aboard when the others all drew leave aboard *Hephaestus*.

Snotty Row must feel like a mausoleum, Ginger thought compassionately. *I wonder if the others' effects have been cleared out yet? I guess that's one of the things the new captain's going to have to find out about.*

"Thank you, Ms. Rafferty," she said out loud and looked around the spotless gallery. The "new air car" smell of a ship fresh from the builders enveloped her, but aside from Rafferty and one maintenance tech, it was empty, with no sign of a proper side party or anyone senior to the midshipwoman.

"I'm sorry, Ma'am," Rafferty said quickly. "We didn't have notification you were aboard the shuttle

until it was already docking. Commander Nakhimov
is on his way, but—"

She broke off with visible relief as the nearest lift
slid open. A lieutenant commander jogged out of
it, and Ginger's memory offered up another name.
Dimitri Nakhimov—Dimitri *Aleksandrovitch* Nakhimov,
actually—*Charles Ward*'s astrogator. He was about ten
T-years younger than Ginger, with fair hair and gray
eyes. He was also fifteen centimeters taller than she
was, but very slightly built. He didn't look *fragile*,
precisely, but no one was ever going to mistake him
for a native of Sphinx, she thought.

"Captain Lewis," he said as he came to a halt.
"I apologize for not meeting you, Ma'am! We didn't
know—"

"That's all right, Mr. Nakhimov," Ginger interrupted.
"Ms. Rafferty already explained about that." She smiled
crookedly. "I imagine it's going to be a while yet before
we get all the confusion cleared away."

"Yes, Ma'am," Nakhimov acknowledged.

"I take it you're the senior officer aboard?"

"Yes, Ma'am." Nakhimov's nostrils flared. "Actually,
I'm the most senior officer *period*, I'm afraid."

"I know." Ginger nodded sympathetically, but her
voice was cool and professional. "I only asked because
I understand from BuPers that Commander Hairston is
en route to us now. No one seemed to have an official
ETA for him, though, and I wondered if he'd beaten
me here. Obviously," she smiled thinly, "he hasn't.
But I realize the ship's casualties have been heavy,
and I know that's dropped a lot of responsibility on
you—and on you, Ms. Rafferty," she added, glancing
at the midshipwoman. "According to BuPers, they've

found most of the replacements we're going to need."
Something flickered in Nakhimov's eyes, and she faced
him squarely. "I know it's going to hurt to see so many
strangers' faces. Trust me, I've been there a time or
two myself. But what matters right now is that the
ship *needs* us . . . and she's going to need *them*, too."

"Yes, Ma'am! I didn't mean to imply—"

"And you didn't, Commander," she interrupted again,
and shook her head. "You'd be more than human if
you weren't reeling a little, and I'm sure seeing me in
Captain Whitby's command chair's going to be hard,
too. But what we have is what we have. We're all just
going to have to dig in and make it work."

"Yes, Ma'am."

"All right." She inhaled sharply. "In that case, Commander, I think you and I should probably move to
the bridge."

"Yes, Ma'am. This way, please."

Ginger followed him to the lift car, then preceded
him into it as he stepped respectfully to one side.
She allowed him to punch their destination into the
panel—after all, at the moment she was still a guest
aboard *his* ship—and stood with her hands clasped
behind her, watching the location display flicker and
change.

The trip took longer than she'd expected. There'd
been no time to absorb much about her new command's *physical* layout—she'd been too busy soaking
up all she could about the state of its crew—and
Charles Ward was the biggest ship she'd actually
served in since *Wayfarer*'s cruise to Silesia. Her
bridge was a long way from the boat bay, and no
doubt Ginger's own trepidation made the trip seem

even lengthier than it was. But, eventually, the lift car eased to a stop, the doors slid open, and she stepped out onto the support ship's command deck.

That bridge was bigger than she'd really expected, too, and it didn't look like any repair ship's bridge she'd ever seen. Mostly that was because none of those other repair ships had boasted stations for a tactical officer, her assistants, and an electronic warfare officer. At the moment, however, that huge, brightly lit bridge seemed oddly underpopulated thanks to the holes the Yawata Strike had torn in the ship's senior ranks.

Only two other officers were waiting for them: an extremely youthful junior-grade lieutenant with engineering insignia and, beside her, one of the most striking women Ginger Lewis had ever seen, with vividly green hair, amber eyes, and the caduceus of a surgeon lieutenant. Both of them came to attention as she stepped onto the bridge, and the enlisted personnel manning the bridge stations rose and came to attention, as well.

"Stand easy," she said, and crossed to the command chair which was about to become hers. She stopped beside it, touched a key on the chair arm, and listened to the musical tone sounding throughout the ship. She waited a moment, knowing that everywhere throughout the mammoth hull men and women were stopping, turning to face bulkhead displays in response to the all-hands signal. Then she reached into her tunic, and the archaic paper crackled as she broke the seals, unfolded her orders, and looked into the command chair's com pickup.

"From Admiral Sir Lucien Cortez, Fifth Space Lord, Royal Manticoran Navy," she read, as five T-centuries of commanding officers had read before her, "to Captain (Junior Grade) Ginger Lewis, Royal Manticoran Navy, Fifth Day, Tenth Month, Year Two Hundred and Ninety-Four After Landing. Madame: You are hereby directed and required to proceed aboard Her Majesty's Starship, *Charles Ward*, FSV-Three-Niner, there to take upon yourself the duties and responsibilities of commanding officer in the service of the Crown. Fail not in this charge at your peril. By order of Admiral Hamish Alexander-Harrington, Earl White Haven and First Lord of Admiralty, Royal Manticoran Navy, for Her Majesty the Empress."

She fell silent and refolded her orders, then turned to Nakhimov.

"Mr. Nakhimov," she said formally, "I assume command."

"Captain," he replied, equally formally, and there was more than a hint of relief in his eyes, "you have command."

"Thank you." She looked up. It took her a moment to find the duty quartermaster, and she made a mental note to familiarize herself—thoroughly—with the bridge layout at the earliest possible moment. Then she located him.

"Make a note in the log, please, Chief Houseman," she said, reading his nameplate.

"Aye, aye, Ma'am," the chief replied, and a shiver went through Ginger's nerves as, in that moment, she truly became HMS *Charles Ward*'s mistress after God. She inhaled deeply and turned back to the command chair's pickup and all the waiting men and women who had just become *her* crew.

"I know none of you expected to see me in this

chair," she said quietly, resting one hand on the chair back. "I didn't expect to be here, either. But the Service is bigger than you and bigger than me. When someone falls, someone else steps into her place and finishes the job. That's the way it's always been; that's the way it is today, when a lot of people are stepping into other people's places.

"What happened here in Manticore, in our own home star system, represents the worst defeat in the Royal Manticoran Navy's entire history. Proportionately, we lost fewer *ships* in the Yawata Strike than we did in Axelrod's attack four hundred years ago, but our personnel losses were enormous, our industrial capacity's been savaged, and the loss of civilian life—the lives we're supposed to *protect*, people—was intolerable. Here, in this ship, you've experienced your own part of that catastrophe. You've lost officers, shipmates, *friends*, and at this moment, you have to be still reeling from that. Believe me, I *know*. I was at Monica. I served with Duchess Harrington aboard *Wayfarer* on my very first deployment. I know what it is to turn around and see the holes where men and women you knew, worked with, respected, even loved are just . . . gone, and it may be even worse when the ship's undamaged. When everything seems just like it was yesterday . . . except that so many people are dead, blotted away when we weren't even looking. There's no easy way to deal with that, and the people we've lost in the Yawata Strike will be with us all for a long, long time.

"But so is our duty. There's an ancient ballad— one that goes far back beyond the first day a human being ever left the Sol System. Despite that antiquity, though, I think three lines of it are relevant to us, here, today, twenty-five hundred T-years later.

> "I am hurt, but I am not slain;
>   I'll lay me down and bleed a while,
>   And then I'll rise and fight again."

She looked directly into the pickup.

"We're hurt, people. We're bleeding. But whoever did this to us made a *bad* mistake, because we aren't *slain*. And as God is our witness, we *will* rise and fight again."

She stood there, looking out of the displays all over the ship—all over *her* ship—for another ten seconds. Then she squared her shoulders.

"Carry on," she said quietly, and cut the connection.

Chapter Thirty-Nine

THE COM SIGNAL PINGED.

Helen Zilwicki frowned as the sound pulled her out of the memo on her display. She'd discovered, rather to her surprise, that she actually liked some of the paperwork coming across her terminal as Sir Aivars Terekhov's flag lieutenant. Some of it, frankly, was boring as hell, yet there was something...satisfying about managing the Commodore's agenda and calendar.

And given the most recent news from home, anything she could find to keep her mind occupied was a welcome diversion from simply sitting around and worrying.

The com pinged again and she sighed, then called her expression to order, and opened a window.

"Ensign Zilwicki," she announced formally, then allowed herself a small smile as Gervais Archer's face appeared. "How can I be of assistance, Sir?" she inquired formally, since the com request had come in over *Quentin Saint-James'* official net, not on her personal combination.

"Good afternoon, Helen," he replied. "I'm afraid I'm not screening because of anything I need from you." He seemed to inhale. "The Admiral just received a follow-up on the flash dispatches from home."

Something icy seemed to congeal in the pit of Helen's stomach. Something about Archer's normally cheerful eyes . . .

"It's worse—a lot worse—than the original dispatch estimated," he continued. "We already knew *Hephaestus* and *Vulcan* were both gone. Now we have confirmation the bastards took out *Weyland*, as well."

Helen winced. She knew Terekhov, Gold Peak, and Khumalo had all assumed *Weyland* must have been targeted as well—that anyone who could get through Manticore-A's defenses to take out *Hephaestus* and *Vulcan* would have done their damnedest to kill *all* of the Star Empire's major industrial nodes. That made the confirmation no less devastating, and she locked down hard on her purely personal reaction to the news.

"Best estimate is over seven million civilian dead and probably close to one-point-six million military personnel," Archer continued grimly. Then his eyes met hers directly over the com. "And the real reason I'm screening you is to inform you that *Hexapuma* was still docked at *Hephaestus*." Helen felt her face freeze, and Archer shook his head with sad sympathy. "I'm sure not all of her people were aboard, but nobody who was made it out," he continued softly. "I'm sorry, Helen, but the Admiral wanted to you and Sir Aivars to hear about it before the official briefing."

"I . . . understand," she said after a seeming eternity spent fighting for control of her voice. "And I'll inform him immediately, of course." She paused and cleared her throat. "I . . . don't suppose you have any sort of breakdown on *Weyland*'s casualties?"

"No, I'm afraid I don't." He seemed a bit surprised by the question. "We've got confirmation of the station's destruction, though, and if she got hit the same way *Hephaestus* and *Vulcan* did, there can't have been very many survivors."

He didn't ask why she'd asked, and she bit her lip—hard—in gratitude for a moment. Then her nostrils flared as she inhaled deeply.

"Thank you, Gwen," she said. "I know you didn't enjoy telling me that. And please thank Lady Gold Peak for me, too. I'm sure the Commodore will feel the same."

❖   ❖   ❖

"Enter!" Sir Aivars Terekhov called as the admittance chime on the flag bridge briefing room's door sounded. He looked up from his conference with Commander Pope and Lieutenant Commander Lewis and smiled as the door opened. "Helen!" he greeted the newcomer. "Already finished beating the schedule into submission?"

"I'm afraid not, Sir," she replied, and his smile vanished instantly as her tone registered. The adjective which came most readily to mind where Helen Zilwicki was concerned was "sturdy," and in far more than merely physical terms. Yet today she seemed . . . brittle, and her eyes were suspiciously bright.

"What is it, Helen?" he asked in a much gentler tone, feeling Pope and Lewis look at each other and then at him and his flag lieutenant.

"Lieutenant Archer just screened me with a message from Admiral Gold Peak, Sir," she said in an unnaturally level voice. "We've received amplification on the flash dispatches from Manticore. Apparently, the original casualty estimate was low."

She paused, and something about her manifest unwillingness to continue sent an icy chill through Sir Aivars Terekhov. He'd had two T-days to come to grips—intellectually, at least—with the devastating attack, but all of them had been dreading the more detailed dispatches they knew would follow once the Admiralty and the Grantville Government had time to begin sorting out the true extent of the damage.

"How low?" he asked.

"According to Lieutenant Archer, we lost between eight and a half and nine million people, Sir, and *Weyland*'s destruction's been confirmed. And"—her voice wavered ever so slightly—"so has the *Kitty*'s."

"What?"

Terekhov heard his own voice ask the question, but he didn't remember telling it to. All he could do was stare at his flag lieutenant, understanding—now—the bright sheen of unshed tears, while his mind tried to cope with the totally unanticipated shock.

Why are you so surprised? a corner of that mind asked itself. *You knew she'd be in yard hands for months. Where the hell* else *did you think they'd send her for that? Of course she was at* Hephaestus! *You just didn't want to think about that, did you?*

No, he hadn't. But now he had no choice, and he drew a deep, steadying breath that seemed to help remarkably little.

"Personnel losses?" His question sounded preposterously calm in his own ears.

"Total, Sir." The first word came out in bits and

pieces and she blinked hard, fighting to control her voice. "Some of her people were probably out of the ship," she continued huskily. "I don't know how many . . . or who. And even if they were," despite her hard-held control a single tear trickled down her cheek, "they were probably just somewhere else in *Hephaestus* and . . ."

Her voice trailed off completely, and she stood there, gazing at him through a silvery shimmer of tears.

Terekhov's jaw tightened. He seemed about to reply, but then he stood instead and crossed the briefing room deck in two strides. Her eyes began to widen in question, but his arms went around her before she could speak.

She stiffened. Embracing one's flag lieutenant wasn't exactly forbidden by Regs, but the service's *traditions* came pretty damned close to that, for a lot of reasons, most of them very good ones. But Terekhov didn't seem to care, and all Helen felt in that moment were the arms of the father who couldn't be there for her—the father who was all too probably as dead as the men and women of HMS *Hexapuma*. She tried to draw the Navy's formalities about her, reached for the armor of an officer on duty, and they crumbled in her hands.

"I know, Helen." His voice rumbled in her ear, and the tears burst free as one hand rose to gently cup the back of her head. "I know."

❖   ❖   ❖

Alcohol was only one of several substances prohibited in a naval officer's private quarters. That prohibition did not apply to flag officers and captains, of course, but then again, flag officers and captains presumably found it more difficult to drink themselves into a drunken stupor without anyone's noticing. It wasn't that the Royal Manticoran Navy prohibited off-duty drinking; it was simply that the RMN prohibited *drunkenness*, whether on duty or off. It was that distinction which prevented the private possession of alcohol—among other substances—from becoming a court-martial offense unless it was abused. At which point, as Abigail Hearns' father was fond of saying, "Hell wouldn't hold" the consequences for the officer in question.

At the moment, she didn't much care about Regs, and she lifted the bottle of Silver Falls Select and refilled Helen Zilwicki's glass.

"I don't really drink, you know," Helen told her.

"I know. That's why this is the last glass you're getting." Abigail smiled faintly. "Under the circumstances, though, I don't see how it could hurt."

"I'm not *drunk*," the ensign replied, although her very careful enunciation suggested that might not be entirely accurate.

"I know that, too," Abigail reassured her, capping the bottle she'd borrowed from Mateo Gutierrez and sliding it back into a drawer. She was glad Mateo's taste in liquor was so good, although her own glass still contained a centimeter or so of the warm, golden glory she'd poured into it at the beginning of Helen's visit.

She settled back into the chair in front of her small desk and picked up that glass to take another tiny sip while Helen sat on her neatly made up bunk. Then she smiled again, sadly, at her guest.

"Might not be the worst thing in the world to *get* you a little tipsy, though, Helen," she suggested.

Helen looked at her, and she shrugged. "I'm just saying you've been carrying a lot around with you ever since we heard about Green Pines. Piling this on top of everything else..."

She let her voice trail off, holding Helen's gaze.

"I'm not the only one who's lost people," the younger woman said almost angrily after a moment. "Everybody's lost *someone!* For that matter, you and the Commodore lost just as many people aboard the *Kitty* as I did. Why can't I just...you know." She waved her whiskey glass vaguely. "Why can I just...deal with it like he does? Like *you* do?"

"I'm not going to bring up anything about faith, or the Test, or any of those other Grayson notions about how to deal with loss," Abigail said calmly. "Mind you, I've found they really *do* help me at times like this. But don't think I'm 'dealing with it' as handily as you seem to assume. And neither is Sir Aivars. I do think, though, that it's hitting you—and him—even harder than it's hitting me or Captain Kaplan. We've lost the *Kitty* and all of our friends who were with her; you and he have lost a lot more than that. Your father, his entire squadron at Hyacinth. You've got more to deal with than we do. Including what happened to *Weyland*."

Helen had been looking down into her glass. Now her eyes snapped back up to her friend's face, and Abigail shook her head.

"Of course you do," she said softly. "And I wish I could tell you he's fine. But I can't, and you know no one else can, and somehow, Helen, you're going to have to deal with that until you do know, one way or the other."

"But I never had time," Helen half-whispered. "I never really had time to tell him." Tears welled, sliding down her face, and her lips trembled. "All of them, Abigail. *All* of them! And I never had the time to *tell* him. I think...I think he knew, but I should've *told* him. I knew how much he distrusted...personal relationships. I knew *why*, and...and I didn't want to...to scare him off by going too fast. But I should've *told* him, and I didn't. And now I'll never be able to, and...and..."

Her voice broke, and Abigail put her glass back on the desk. She crossed to sit on the bunk beside her friend and drew her into a fierce embrace.

"You don't *know* you'll never be able to, not yet," she said softly, fiercely. "Maybe you won't, and maybe the Tester *will* let you. But, trust me, Helen. I know exactly why he's always 'run scared' where anything like the way the two of you feel is concerned. I'd probably feel the same way if I knew I'd been genetically designed as a 'pleasure slave' by those Mesan monsters. Of course it's hard for someone like him to trust his *own* emotions, much less anyone else's! But don't forget, I was your training officer in the *Kitty*. I got to know all of 'my' snotties pretty darned well before we got back to Manticore, and whatever else Paulo d'Arezzo may have been or not been, one thing he *wasn't* was stupid!" She smiled a bit mistily through her own tears, hugging her weeping friend with one arm, stroking her hair with her free hand, and shook her head. "You may not have *told* him, honey, not in so many words, but trust me, he knew. I promise you, he *knew*."

Chapter Forty

"SO," BRIGADIER SIMEON GADDIS said sourly, cupping his hands in front of his mouth and blowing on them as he stepped out onto the observation platform and the cold wind off Lake Michigan whistled around his ears. He glanced back and forth between Lupe Blanton and Weng Zhing-hwan with an edge of suspicion... or perhaps the proper noun was *apprehension*. "What brings us all together on this fine, brisk March morning?"

"It *is* brisk, isn't it?" Lieutenant Colonel Weng acknowledged cheerfully, watching that same wind shred the steam rising from her hot cup of tea.

"Actually, it's cold enough to freeze off certain important portions of my anatomy," he replied tartly. "Couldn't we have found someplace out of the wind for this clandestine discussion?"

Gaddis was from the southern hemisphere of Shakin in the Bootstrap System, and Shakin's *average* temperature was well above Old Earth's. Old Chicago in March, especially anywhere near the lakefront, was like a foretaste of hell as far as he was concerned.

"It's not a 'clandestine discussion,' Sir," Weng admonished him. "It's just three professional colleagues out to enjoy the morning sunshine."

"And if you think anyone is going to believe that, you need to find another line of work, Colonel," the very tall, muscular brigadier—he was forty centimeters taller than Blanton and almost thirty centimeters taller even than Weng—replied. "Although," he continued grudgingly, "I will concede that it's nice to see at least *some* sunshine after the last couple of weeks."

The brigadier had a point, Weng conceded. The temperature in Old Chicago in March seldom dropped below about minus seven degrees, and the *average* low was somewhere around freezing. For the last week or so, however, it had plunged well below that average, and the bright morning sunlight reflected dazzlingly off the white snow bordering the Solarian capital's heated walkways and roadways.

And he also had a point that no one who noticed the three of them chatting was likely to think they'd just happened to run into one another. On the other hand, the three-hundred-and-twelfth-floor observation deck was on the west side of Smith Tower, and Smith Tower happened to house JISDCC, otherwise known as the Joint Intelligence Sharing and Distribution Command Center. As such, all three of them had every right to be there, although they seldom were. In theory, JISDCC was supposed to keep all the Solarian League's myriad intelligence agencies on the same page. In fact, the "sharing" and "distribution" bits of the Center's charter got very short shrift. Still, there were appearances to maintain, especially given the currently worsening situation vis-à-vis the Star Empire of Manticore, so it wasn't exactly *preposterous* for them to have dropped by. In fact, they'd each casually mentioned to various colleagues that they were off for a visit to show how seriously they took that situation, even though everyone knew the visit wouldn't actually accomplish anything...except to rack up bureaucratic brownie points against future need. And each of them had carefully—and "coincidentally"—engineered the time of his or her visit to ensure that they would, in fact, wander through Smith Tower on their flag-showing expeditions at roughly the same time.

And with all three of us in the same place at the same time, it would look suspicious if we didn't get together for a brief huddle, she reflected. *Not that anyone would actually expect us to tell each other anything substantive. It's all just part of the coup-counting part of the job.*

"This shouldn't take all that long, Sir," she said out loud. "Lupe and I just need a little advice."

"And you couldn't just screen me about it?" Gaddis demanded even more sourly. "I have a perfectly nice, warm office, you know."

"And there are probably quite a few people keeping track of the conversations you have from it," Blanton put in. Gaddis looked at her with arched eyebrows and she shrugged. "I'm sure you take the same kind of precautions Zhing-hwan and I take, Sir. But I also know all your official calls are logged, and I'd just as soon not have anything point people at this particular conversation."

"I hope you know how paranoid that sounds," Gaddis observed, and both women smiled with very little humor.

"And are you going to tell us paranoia isn't a survival tool in our business?" Weng asked him.

"No." He shook his head. "No, probably not. To be honest, though, I have to wonder why 'spooks' want to talk to a straight cop like me. Or, for that matter, why you couldn't have simply sent me an interoffice memo about it, Colonel," he said, looking at Weng rather pointedly. "Unlike Lupe here, we're in the same chain of command, after all."

Weng nodded, although it wasn't quite as simple as the brigadier had just implied. Gaddis was the equivalent of her own immediate superior, Brigadier Väinölä, but in the Gendarmerie's Criminal Investigation Division rather than Intelligence. That meant he was an actual working cop, with very little involvement in the Gendarmes' support for OFS out in the Verge. He was also remarkably apolitical for someone who'd risen to his position, and he'd gotten there largely because he knew where too many bodies were buried. A *lot* of people would have preferred to see someone a bit more ... amenable to the political realities of the Solarian League's upper echelons in his job, but they'd had to be very careful about trying to break the bureaucratic kneecaps of someone with that much ammunition. And everyone knew he was a cop's cop, determined to do his job and prepared to exhume any of those bodies he needed to if someone got in his way. As such, he tended to be regarded as some sort of rogue elephant and given a wide, wide berth by the majority of the intelligence and law enforcement community's senior members, many of whom had good reason to worry about any exhumations he might undertake.

And that, of course, was the reason she wasn't about to send him any direct memos. As he'd just implied, he had very little interest in the sorts of intelligence Weng Zhing-hwan and Lupe Blanton were *supposed* to develop. That meant there was little official pretext for them to route reports to him, and everyone in the intelligence community knew it. In turn, *that* meant any official contact would be likely to draw attention... and if there was any truth to the suspicions they'd begun to nurture, the *last* thing they needed was to be caught sharing information with what was probably the one man in the Solarian League's senior law enforcement who'd earned a reputation for going wherever the evidence led him and damn the political consequences.

"We're both Gendarmes, Sir," she said now. "We aren't really in the same chain of command, though, are we?"

"No. But is there a reason *you're* talking to me instead of Noritoshi Väinölä?" Gaddis' tone had turned stern, and his eyes were hard. "He and I *do* exchange information from time to time, you know. And we have those meetings—you know, the ones where we get together with General Mabley once every couple of weeks?—where we talk about all sorts of things. More to the point, I've known him for a long time. If you're about to tell me he's involved in something I need to be taking official cognizance of, you and I may have a problem, Colonel."

"Sir, Brigadier Väinölä knows about most of what we wanted to talk to you about. I haven't told him quite *everything* we've picked up because, frankly, if I did, he'd be legally obligated to report my conclusions to General Mabley. And I don't want to put him in that position any more than Lupe wants to put Adão Ukhtomskoy into the same position over at Frontier Security."

"Why not?" Gaddis sounded rather more wary, and Weng smiled crookedly.

"We're not violating any laws, Brigadier. For that matter, we're not even violating any regulations. What we *are* doing would probably come under the heading of...deliberately withholding raw data from our superiors to protect our sources."

"Why does that word 'probably' make me nervous, Colonel?"

"Because you've been around Old Chicago a long time, Sir," Blanton put in. She turned her back to the lake, her hands shoved deep into her pockets, and looked up at the towering brigadier. "The problem is that Zhing-hwan and I—and I'm pretty sure Brigadier Väinöla—are coming to the conclusion that there's some truth to the Manticorans' claims that the League's being manipulated. Which leads us to the conclusion that anyone doing the manipulating must be plugged in at what I think we could agree would be called a very high level."

"The sort of level where they might hear about it if the two of you started sounding any alarms through official channels?"

"Exactly," Weng said. She sipped tea from her insulated cup, treasuring the hot tea's warmth in the cold, windy morning...and wishing her stomach didn't feel quite so cold for an entirely different reason. "At the moment, neither Lupe nor I are concerned about our physical safety," she continued after a moment, not completely truthfully. "But if the Manties are right, these people don't give much of a damn how many other people get killed. I'd imagine that what you've seen from the Technodyne investigation could be considered evidence pointing in that direction."

Gaddis looked at her for a moment, then nodded slowly.

"We haven't been able to prove Technodyne was *directly* involved in supplying those terrorists in Talbott," he said. "Partly, Ms. Blanton, I'm afraid that's because quite a few of your Frontier Security people out in the Verge have been ... less than forthcoming, let's say. But there's no doubt in *my* people's minds that even if Technodyne wasn't directly shipping the weapons, they knew all about that part of the operation. We don't have the same kind of access into—or leverage against, for that matter—Manpower or any of the other Mesan players, but the mere fact that they're involved, assuming the Manties aren't completely out to lunch, would certainly indicate no one's worrying very much about body counts."

"And judging by what happened to Admiral Crandall, they're *getting* body counts," Weng said flatly.

"Are you seriously suggesting this 'manipulation' goes deep enough to move seventy or eighty ships of the wall around like tiddlywinks?" Gaddis demanded.

"Yes, Sir." Her voice was so quiet he could barely hear it over the wind, but she met his eyes very levelly. "That's exactly what we're afraid of."

The brigadier looked back and forth between both women, and they looked back at him, no longer trying to conceal the anxiety in their eyes. Only the wind spoke for several seconds. Then he inhaled deeply, turned away, and rested both hands on the observation deck's railing as he gazed out into the cutting wind.

"That's a very scary proposition," he told that wind. "It's also pretty far out. I hesitate to use any adjectives like 'hysterical' or that 'paranoid' one again, but I'm sure you understand how our esteemed superiors would regard the notion."

"That's why we need you, Sir," Blanton said. "Unlike either of us, you're a department head, and you're right—we're both 'spooks,' but you're a cop. We understand intelligence gathering and analysis, but neither one of us has a clue about how to launch an *investigation*. For that matter, neither Brigadier Väinölä nor Adão have the . . . facilities or expertise—or the jurisdiction!—to launch any investigations. But one thing we're pretty sure of is that if there's any basis for our suspicions and they kick those suspicions upstairs through our own chains of command, whoever the manipulators are, they're going to pull out all the stops to *quash* any investigation you might otherwise be requested to undertake."

She did not, Gaddis noted, mention the distinct possibility that they would also take steps to "quash" the troublesome analysts who'd disturbed their comfortable bottom-feeding muck.

"And what exactly do you want me to investigate?" he asked.

"We've written up everything we've turned up so far, Sir," Weng said.

She set her teacup on the railing next to his right hand and reached into her coat pockets for a pair of gloves. She pulled them on and reclaimed her cup. When she did, there was a data chip on the railing.

He glanced down at it out of the corner of one eye but made no immediate move to pick it up.

"You wouldn't have discussed this with anyone over in Admiral Thimár's shop, I suppose?"

"Sir, I don't know anyone in ONI well enough to approach them with something this ... tenuous, especially when it has so many sharp edges," the colonel told him.

"I know a couple of people in Section Four," Blanton said. Section Four was the Office of Naval Intelligence's counterintelligence command. "Frankly, I'd be really worried about the security of anything over there, though. And, well, there's always Admiral Yau."

"Tell me about it," Gaddis muttered.

Yau Kwang-tung, Section Four's CO, had towering family connections ... which happened to be his sole qualification for his position. The fact that he had it anyway probably said a great deal about how anyone could hope to manipulate something as gargantuan as the Solarian League, the brigadier reflected now. Obviously, no one could *possibly* pose a genuine threat to the League or to the Solarian League Navy! That being the case, there was no need to put someone competent in charge of their counterintelligence duties.

"There's a reason I asked," he said, turning to face them and leaning back against the rail. In the process, his right hand just happened to sweep up Colonel Weng's chip. "Do either of you know Captain al-Fanudahi?"

"Daud al-Fanudahi?" Weng asked. Blanton only looked blank, and Gaddis nodded to the colonel. "I know the name, Sir, and I know he's on just about every senior Navy officer's shit list. That's about it."

"Captain al-Fanudahi is a very interesting fellow," the brigadier said slowly. "It happens that the main reason he's on the Navy's 'shit list' is that he's been telling people for years that the Manties have pulled way ahead of us in terms of weapons development. I'll let you imagine how someone like Fleet Admiral Rajampet or Admiral Polydorou over at Systems Development reacted to that."

"Not well," Blanton said with a wince, and Gaddis nodded.

"That sums it up pretty well, actually," he said. "These days, after what happened to Crandall at Spindle, they're at least calling him in for the occasional briefing, but he's still very much a voice in the wilderness."

"I'm sorry, Sir, but I don't see where you're going with this," Weng said. He cocked an eyebrow at her, and she shrugged. "If Captain al-Fanudahi's already marginalized, how much ability to help push something like this along would he have? For that matter, if I remember correctly, he's in Operational Analysis. That would be Admiral Cheng's department, and with all due respect, Cheng's not a lot sharper stylus than Admiral Yau. And, again with all due respect, I'd be almost as worried about OpAn's ability—assuming it had the willingness in the first place—to maintain security about this."

"Al-Fanudahi's *assigned* to OpAn," Gaddis replied. "From what I can see though, he figures he *works for* the entire Navy. That's how he made himself so unpopular, and I suspect a man like that's probably been looking at aspects of our current situation that go way beyond Operational Analysis' formal responsibilities."

"Are you suggesting we should approach him, Sir?" Blanton asked. Her opinion of the idea was painfully evident from her tone, and Gaddis snorted.

"No, I'm not suggesting anything of the sort...yet, Ms. Blanton. What I am suggesting is that we need to start counting noses, thinking about who we *could* approach assuming we discover there's any validity to these suspicions of yours. I think Captain al-Fanudahi belongs on that list, and Brigadier Osterhaut over at Marine Intelligence might be another. I know she's technically part of Admiral Thimár's command, too, but the Marines pretty much run their own shop. Something about getting burned once or twice—or a dozen times—too often by faulty intel from their naval associates."

"If you think we need to bring them in on this, Sir, I'm willing to defer to your judgment," Weng said, meeting his eyes steadily. "I'm not going to pretend I'm *eager* to do that, you understand."

"And I don't think we should do anything of the sort, either. Or, as I say, not *yet*, anyway." He raised his hands to his mouth and blew into them again. "Let me take a look at what you've got so far. For right now, I don't plan on sharing it with *anyone*. Not until I'm convinced there's something more here than two very smart analysts who may—or may not—be imagining things. I'll get back to you, either way. If I come to the conclusion that you're onto something, though, I'll have to start asking *someone* at least a few questions." He lowered his hands and his smile was bleak.

"Just between the three of us, I'm not really looking forward to that if you are."

APRIL 1922 POST DIASPORA

"It's a bit drastic, but to paraphrase an ancient pre-diaspora politician a friend of mine turned up a while ago, 'The Solarian League is like a hog. You have to kick it in the snout to get its attention.'"

—Admiral Michelle Henke,
Countess Gold Peak,
CO, Tenth Fleet,
Royal Manticoran Navy.

Chapter Forty-One

"COMING UP ON FINAL BEARING in twenty seconds, Ma'am," Lieutenant Commander Nakhimov announced.

"Very good," Ginger Lewis acknowledged as HMS *Charles Ward* picked up her orbital station-keeping marks after three hard days of exercises in Manticore-B's Unicorn Belt. She watched the maneuvering display while CPO Dreyfus gentled away her last few meters per second of velocity, then nodded as the numbers trickled across the digital readout and, exactly on the mark, fell to zero.

"On station," Nakhimov said. "Impellers going to stand by."

"Very well done, Astro. And you, Chief," Ginger said.

"Thank you, Ma'am," Nakhimov responded, and Dreyfus smiled briefly, then returned her attention to shutting down her board.

Ginger looked at the back of the chief petty officer's head for a moment. Angelina Dreyfus was one of the best helmswomen she'd ever seen. At only thirty-six, she was on the young side for a CPO, but she had the gift.

She was also the member of *Charles Ward*'s bridge crew who most worried Ginger.

It was ironic, in some ways, she supposed. She was only ten years older than Dreyfus—which was at least as young for a starship captain as Dreyfus was for a CPO—and they were within a couple of centimeters of each other in height. Not only that, they both had red hair. In fact, they favored one another a great deal, aside from the fact that Dreyfus had blue eyes, instead of green. Ginger suspected they had similar senses of humor, as well...normally. But Dreyfus' older brother had been the night shift manager in Dempsey's *Hephaestus* restaurant. He'd been her only sibling...and her parents had been dining in his restaurant when the Yawata Strike hit. She'd taken their deaths hard, and it was obvious she remained a long way from coping with her loss.

She was scarcely alone in that. Most of Ginger's new crew had lost someone—family, close friend, crewmate. In her own case, the entire crew of *Hexapuma*; in *Charles Ward*'s case, virtually all of the ship's senior officers. Not that it stopped there; almost a quarter of her crew had been aboard *Hephaestus*, enjoying what was supposed to be their last leave before they deployed to Talbott while their ship lay sixty thousand kilometers off the station, unable to find docking space. Thank God Captain Mathis' "couple of weeks" had expanded rather significantly! And not just because Ginger had needed the time to settle in. Her new crew needed that time even more desperately than she did.

The duty bridge crew had watched the space station blow up before their eyes, which certainly explained

the state of shock which had gripped the entire ship
when Ginger read herself aboard. Of course, the same
thing could have been said of just about every ship
in the Manticore System, but the *Charles Ward*—her
crew was still trying to decide between *Charley W*
and simply *CW* as a nickname—had taken a more
grievous internal hit than almost any other ship to
survive Many of the other surviving units had lost
some key personnel, given the numbers of both officers and enlisted who'd had errands to run aboard
Hephaestus, Vulcan, or *Weyland*; none of them had
lost her entire senior command echelon.

Or eighty percent of their snotties, she reminded
herself grimly, glancing to where Paula Rafferty sat at
Nakhimov's shoulder, closing down Astrogation under
his supervision. She couldn't quite make up her mind
how well Rafferty was dealing with her isolation in
Snotty Row, but at least Ginger had made sure she
had someone riding herd on the midshipwoman.

She smiled, inner grimness easing slightly, as she
moved her gaze to Tactical and the fair-haired, gray-
eyed, improbably handsome ensign holding down the
junior tactical officer's slot.

Charles Ward's losses had left BuPers scrambling
for replacement personnel. Well, Admiral Cortez was
scrambling for replacements *everywhere*, to be fair,
and that meant an awful lot of officers were being
hastily slotted into positions which would normally be
held by people far senior to them. The captain's chair
of *Charles Ward* was a rather pointed case in point,
as a matter of fact. The ancient tradition of stepping
into "dead men's shoes" hadn't really changed that
much, she supposed.

But there had been a couple of upsides from Ginger Lewis' viewpoint. One of the severest losses to *Charles Ward*'s enlisted structure had been Master Chief Petty Officer Elijah Tebo, her boatswain. As the senior noncommissioned officer aboard, the bosun was a key member of any ship's company, and Tebo's death aboard *Hephaestus* had left a gaping hole. But the destruction of HMSS *Weyland* had left Ginger with a replacement she might not have been allowed to choose without the severity of the Navy's overall losses. If Angelina Dreyfus was young to be a chief petty officer, then Aubrey Wanderman, at thirty-four, was even younger to be a *master* chief petty officer, but there'd never been a doubt in Ginger's mind who she wanted as *her* boatswain. She suspected Aubrey must have been as terrified by the prospect as she'd been by the thought of assuming Captain Whitby's chair, but he'd come a long, long way—light-years!— from the hesitant, nervous young grav tech, fresh out of advanced training, who'd reported aboard HMS *Wayfarer* the better part of fourteen T-years ago.

Well, so have I, I suppose, she conceded. *And Paulo's come quite a ways in the last year and a half, too*, she added, watching Ensign d'Arezzo lean closer to Lieutenant Commander Raymundo Atkins, *Charles Ward*'s new tactical officer, as the two of them discussed something on Atkins' display. He was barely three T-years older than Paula Rafferty, but his calm, confident demeanor was clearly reassuring to the midshipwoman.

Which is good, since I don't think we'll be seeing any replacements for the other snotties, she thought more glumly. *Paula's going to rattle around in there like a dry pea in a two-liter bottle. Thank God she's got somebody on the commissioned side remotely close to her own age! And it probably doesn't hurt that Paulo's such a nice piece of eye candy.*

That thought, she discovered, came perilously close to sparking an inappropriate giggle from *Charles Ward's* CO, but it was certainly true. The only downside she could see was the possibility that Paulo's looks, added to the quiet strength of his personality, might tempt young Paula into inappropriate thoughts about her superior. Knowing how Paulo felt about the origin of his perfect profile, strong chin, and chiseled lips Ginger had no fear anything inappropriate would *happen*, but that might not keep Paula from . . . yearning in that direction.

It sure as hell wouldn't've kept me from "yearning in that direction" when I was her age, Ginger admitted. *He* is *a tasty-looking fellow, isn't he? In fact, I'm still a little surprised by how long it took* Helen *to realize that aboard the* Kitty.

She shook herself out of her reverie and rotated her command chair to face the dark-haired, hazel-eyed commander standing at her shoulder.

"I think they all did well, Mister Exec," she told him, making sure her voice was loud enough for everyone on the bridge to hear. "In fact, they're doing well enough I'm no longer nervous about deploying to Talbott next month. Please make the entire ship's company aware of that for me."

"Of course, Ma'am," Commander Fred Hairston replied.

He was a burly, broad-shouldered man, twenty-five centimeters taller than Ginger, whose Sphinxian accent reminded her of Duchess Harrington. He was also fifteen years older than she was, and she'd been afraid that age differential—and the fact that, unlike her, he was a Saganami Island graduate—would create a certain tension between them. So far, all he'd been was a tower of strength, however, and she smiled at him.

"Thank you," she said, then checked the date/time display. Another thirty-one minutes till lunch, she noted, and climbed out of the command chair.

"You've got the ship, Fred. I'm pretty sure Jared's starting to wonder where I am—after all, it's not like I had anything *important* to do this morning—and Gareth and I have more paperwork to beat into submission after lunch."

Hairston's eyes twinkled at her resigned tone, but he only nodded.

"I have the ship, aye, Ma'am," he acknowledged with grave formality, and she nodded back.

"Then I'll leave her in your hands," she said, and headed for the lift shaft.

The lift car deposited her outside her quarters, and the Marine sentry reached behind himself to hit the admittance key and open the door for her.

"Thank you, Simpkins," she said as she stepped past him.

"You're welcome, Ma'am."

The captain's quarters aboard HMS *Charles Ward* were vast beyond belief for someone who'd been a commander less than seven T-months ago. Ginger supposed a three-million-ton ship could afford the space, but it still struck her as scandalously wasteful, and her new steward—something else she'd never expected to have—poked his head out of his pantry.

"Table's already set, Ma'am," he said, twitching his head in the direction of her dining cabin. "I'll be ready to serve in five minutes."

His tone rather clearly implied that she'd better be ready to *eat* in five minutes, too, and she nodded meekly.

"That will be fine, Jared," she said, and went to take her place at the head of the ridiculously large table in the ridiculously vast dining cabin.

Actually, she reflected as she looked around the compartment, this was probably the one aspect of her quarters that wasn't on too grand a scale for her taste. It was far larger than anything she'd ever need for her convenience, but she'd already discovered that it was scarcely large enough for her *needs*. She'd been only a noncom herself when she served under Honor Harrington aboard *Wayfarer*, but even so she'd realized the value of Lady Harrington's practice of dining regularly with her officers, and she'd had plenty of opportunities since to compare captains who *didn't* follow that tradition with those—like Sir Aivars Terekhov—who did. She'd known which category *she* wanted to fit into, and those shared meals had done more to bind *Charles Ward*'s command team together than even she had been prepared to believe they might.

Stewards Mate 1/c Pallavicini arrived with her salad in considerably less than the specified five minutes. He placed it in front of her, along with a cruet of her preferred balsamic dressing, poured iced tea—a taste she'd picked up from the Graysons with whom she'd served—into her glass, and then disappeared back into his pantry.

Ginger looked rather bemusedly at the salad. It

was fairly spectacular, garnished with cheese, bacon bits, boiled egg, and what she was fairly sure were Sphinxian anchovies. It was also at least fifty percent bigger than she needed, and she could smell the spaghetti sauce—the *delicious* spaghetti sauce, damn it!—of the entrée coming on behind like Juggernaut.

I have *to do something about him,* she reflected, reaching for the salad dressing. *I know he means well, but if he keeps this up, he'll have me weighing two hundred kilos inside of six months!*

In her calmer moments, she knew it was unlikely even Pallavicini could quadruple her body weight, but it didn't *feel* that way as she contemplated his notion of a "light luncheon." This was his first assignment as a captain's steward, and he seemed grimly determined to see to his new captain's care and feeding, however *she* might feel about his ministrations. She strongly suspected that at least half of that was compensation on his part, because he'd been on a planet-side liberty on Manticore when the light cruiser *Calliope* was destroyed in the Yawata Strike. He couldn't do much about his dead shipmates, but the loss had imbued him with a fierce . . . protectiveness probably wasn't the right word, but it came close, where his new captain was concerned. His reaction to her original suggestion, when she'd first come aboard, that a *small* salad and possibly a tuna fish sandwich and a glass of milk were more in line with her normal preference for lunch had warned her this was going to be an uphill fight. Of course, where the captains of RMN starships were concerned, convincing their stewards they actually were capable of sealing their own shoes—unassisted—when they absolutely had to was *always* an uphill fight. Given his obvious response to *Calliope*'s loss (and her awareness of it) this hill was being a bit steeper than usual, though.

And it didn't help one damned bit that he was such a good cook, either.

Maybe if I get Doc Massarelli involved? Yeah, that's an idea! Get her to discuss things like caloric intake, high blood pressure, obesity, and things like that with him. It'll sure be a hell of a lot easier than developing the willpower to just not eat *the stuff when he puts it in front of me!*

She chuckled at the thought, poured the dressing, and reached for her fork. She'd just taken the first bite when Pallavicini turned back up ... with the inevitable plate of delicious, butter-saturated garlic bread. He set it on the table and turned to go, but her waving hand caught him before he could. She finished chewing her mouthful—which, of course, was just as delicious as it had looked, damn him—and swallowed, then cleared her throat.

"Do me a favor, Jared. Pass the word to Gareth that I need to talk to him."

"Of course, Ma'am. The first thing after lunch."

There might, Ginger reflected, have been a certain repressive emphasis on the word "after," but she elected to let it pass in dignified silence.

"That should be fine," she said instead.

❖   ❖   ❖

"So, is that about everything, Ma'am?" Senior Chief Petty Officer Gareth Yamaguchi asked ninety-odd minutes later, running his eye back over the notes he'd jotted on his memo board.

SCPO Yamaguchi was Ginger's yeoman ... inherited,

like her ship, from Captain Whitby. Unlike most of *Charles Ward*'s crew, Yamaguchi had been with Joanna Whitby for over five T-years. He'd been more than "just" her yeoman, as any good yeoman always was, and it still showed in his eyes, sometimes, when he and Ginger worked together. He was also ten years older than she was, and there were times she thought a part of him resented seeing someone so young take Whitby's place. If that was true, though, he never let it affect his calm, professional attitude where his *new* captain was concerned.

"I think so," she said, leaning back in the chair behind the desk in her day cabin. "The most immediate bit is tidying up and signing off on those supply list requests for Lieutenant Primikynos before we pull out for Spindle." She smiled wryly. "I think he's too efficient for my own good. I never quite seem to catch up with him. Or maybe what I really mean is *he* never has to catch up with *me!*"

"No, Ma'am," Yamaguchi agreed. "The Lieutenant *is* good. Probably because of all those years he spent as a merchant spacer." The yeoman smiled suddenly. It wasn't often that Ginger saw one of his smiles, but when they came, they illuminated his entire face. "If you'd like me too, Ma'am," he suggested, "I imagine I could come up with some . . . creative requests that would make the Lieutenant work for it for a change. Especially if I got Jared involved." The smile turned positively wicked. "We haven't requested anything at all esoteric for your cabin stores, you know. There's got to be an opportunity there!"

"You, Gareth Yamaguchi, are a wicked man," she told him with a chuckle. "However, I will admit that a certain ignoble part of me is highly in favor of the idea. Why don't you and Jared put your heads together and come up with a potential 'challenge list' for me to look over?"

"Of course, Ma'am." Yamaguchi's smile faded, but the gleam stayed in his eye, and Ginger treasured it.

"In that case, I think we're about done, and—"

"Excuse me, Captain," Pallavicini interrupted respectfully, poking his head in through the day cabin door.

"Yes, Jared?"

"You have a com request, Ma'am. It's Ms. Terekhov."

"Ask her to hold five seconds while Gareth and I finish up, then put her through," Ginger said with a smile.

"Yes, Ma'am."

The steward's head disappeared, and Ginger looked back at Yamaguchi.

"As I was saying, I think we're about done. Please do make sure to get those notes typed up for me before the department head meeting, though."

"Of course, Captain."

Yamaguchi closed his memo board, gathered up his minicomp, and headed for his own cubbyhole of an office. Ginger watched him go, then punched the key which had begun flashing on her desk com.

"Good afternoon, Ginger," Sinead Terekhov said from the display.

"Good afternoon, Sinead."

It no longer felt quite so strange to address Aivars Terekhov's wife by her first name. In fact, it was easy. Like her husband, Sinead had an innate ability to put people at ease, and in her case, the constraints of rank—and of the relationship between a junior officer and her superior—didn't come into play. Although, when Ginger thought about it, the difference between their family backgrounds would probably have been a problem for some of Sinead's social peers. The O'Daleys and the Longs had been around a long, long time, and Ginger really had very little idea how wealthy Sinead was... except that the proper adverb had to be "very." Her own family, on the other hand, was solidly middle-class, and Ginger had begun her naval career as enlisted. She imagined there were quite a few people from Sinead's background who would have been just a *bit* less genuinely warm to someone from hers.

In fact, I damned well know *there are! I've* met *some of the bastards.*

"What can I do for you?" she asked, and Sinead wrinkled her nose at her.

"Actually, I wanted to see if you'd be free to join me for dinner this evening, or possibly tomorrow night?"

"I'm afraid I couldn't make it today. I'm having a working dinner with my senior officers. Tomorrow night would probably work." Ginger thought, rubbing the tip of her nose with her left index finger. "Commander Lawson, Lieutenant Primikynos, and I have a meeting tomorrow with a rep from Logistics Command, but I *should* be clear of that no later than fifteen hundred. Call it sixteen hundred, to be on the safe side. That could put me in Landing by seventeen-thirty."

"That would be more than early enough. Can I go ahead and pencil you in? It's not anything formal. And in light of what you've said about Steward Pallavicini, I'll *promise* to serve something light!"

"God!" Ginger laughed. "*Thank* you for that! I

know he absolutely means well, but I'm going to get Dr. Massarelli to beat him about the head and ears."

"You see? You *are* developing good tactical instincts!" Sinead smiled. "Screen when you leave the ship, and I'll have the limo pick you up at the port."

❖   ❖   ❖

"So, overall, I'm completely satisfied with our people's performance," Ginger said from the head of the table.

Pallavicini and the stewards mates he'd enlisted for the evening had cleared away dinner. Now her senior officers sat back in their chairs, coffee cups and dessert dishes in front of them, and looked back up its length at her.

Fred Hairston sat at the table's foot, flanked by Kumanosuke Lawson, *Charles Ward*'s engineering officer, and Lieutenant Commander Nakhimov. Raymundo Atkins sat to Lawson's left, and Lieutenant Yolande Cornelisz, the ship's electronic warfare officer, faced Nakhimov across the table. Lieutenant Traxton Sughavanam, Ginger's communications officer, sat to Cornelisz's right, facing Lieutenant Oliver Primikynos, and Lieutenant Benjamin Marsden, CO of HMLAC *Nożownik* and the senior member of *Charles Ward*'s LAC squadron, sat to Primikynos' right, while Surgeon Lieutenant Sying-ni Massarelli sat directly to Ginger's left.

"I know it's been hard on all of them," she continued now, cradling her own cup in both hands. "All of us—aside from Sying-ni and Dimitri—are new to them, and to be honest, I can't really imagine, even now, what it must be like for a ship's company to lose that many of its senior officers in a heartbeat."

She shook her head sadly. "In that respect, we're all really looking in from the outside."

"That's true in one sense, Ma'am," Massarelli said.

The surgeon lieutenant was, by any measure, the most visually striking person Ginger Lewis had ever seen. Her hair's natural color was a vivid emerald green. Her eyes were a shade of amber Ginger had only seen once, in a German Shepherd, and their pupils were vertical slits, not round. Her fingernails were much stronger and narrower than those of any other human Ginger had ever met, and her ears were elongated and almost triangular in section, their tips pricking through that improbably green hair. When she moved, it was with an extraordinarily graceful, curiously sinuous carriage which only underscored her feline appearance.

Thanks to her personnel file, Ginger knew the source of the obviously massive engineering in Massarelli's genetic heritage. Like Paulo d'Arezzo, it had been provided courtesy of Manpower, Incorporated, although at least in Paulo's case no non-human DNA had gone into the mix. Sying-ni Massarelli was the granddaughter of yet another liberated genetic slave who'd chosen to settle in the Star Kingdom of Manticore and take the surname of the captain whose cruiser had liberated him from a Mesan slave ship.

Ginger wondered if there'd been any temptation on her grandfather's part to attempt to have his own genegineered appearance muted or even completely smoothed away in his children. She was quite certain Dr. Massarelli would have felt no inclination in that direction, however. She wore that green hair, those cat eyes, those pointed ears, as a conscious badge of pride, a proclamation of her refusal to hide her slave heritage . . . and her own personal declaration of war.

Interesting contrast there, between her and Paulo. Or at least between her and the old *Paulo,* Ginger thought. *I wonder if they've discussed it?*

"True in what sense, Sying-ni?" she asked out loud.

"In the sense that you're all relative newcomers, and that our people took a really heavy psychological hit. But *every* man and woman in the Navy—for that matter, in the entire *star system*—has taken a hard hit. You and the XO and everyone else sitting around this table are no different in that respect." Those amber, catlike eyes circled the other faces. "I know we're all concentrating on pulling the rest of the crew up out of the depression, the posttraumatic shock of what happened, and to be honest, I think most of us are doing a pretty fair job of that. But it would be a mistake—a *serious* mistake—for us to underestimate or, even worse, deny the extent to which this has affected *us*."

"Do you really think we're doing that, Doctor?" Commander Lawson asked, and his voice was a little tight, a little hard around the edges.

Massarelli looked at him calmly for a moment, then nodded.

"Yes, Sir. I do."

Lawson's naturally dark complexion got a shade darker and his jaw tensed. For a moment, he seemed to hover on the brink of saying something sharp, but then his nostrils flared and he shoved himself back in his chair without speaking.

Ginger watched him with understanding and an edge of concern. As *Charles Ward*'s engineering officer,

Lawson would be absolutely critical to the ship's success, and she was worried about him. Like Nakhimov and Hairston, Lawson was a Sphinxian. But while Hairston had lost a cousin and her three children in Yawata Crossing, virtually Lawson's entire family had lived in or around the small city of Tanners Port...which had been obliterated by the debris-spawned tsunamis.

It was abundantly clear that Hairston had taken the attack *very* personally, but the XO had focused that anger outwardly. He was looking for necks to break, and he spent a lot of time with Raymundo Atkins and his tactical section. Lawson seemed to be focusing his rage, his fury, *internally*, however, and that could be a very bad thing. Especially since he was four years older than Ginger and clearly felt his own engineering experience—he'd been a *Hephaestus* yard dog for three years and commanded a major shipbuilding module for his last year there—made him more qualified than her for the captain's chair aboard a ship like *Charles Ward*.

Ginger was prepared to deal with that...resentment on his part if she had to, and as long as he kept it under control, she didn't blame him for feeling it. She didn't *agree* with him, but she didn't blame him, either, and she understood it wasn't necessarily something he'd *chosen* to feel. But if that internal anger of his locked up with a feeling of grievance, of having been passed over for something that was his just due...

Don't borrow trouble, she told herself. *So far, he's done his job, and there hasn't been a hint of his letting anything get in the way of that. I know why Sying-ni's worried about him, though. I could see him eating a pulser dart one night. But until it looks like it may actually be reaching that point, I don't have any basis—or any valid reason, for that matter—to think about requesting his relief. And if I did try to have him replaced, and if BuPers could actually come up with someone as a replacement, it'd probably finish him off once and for all. The man's hanging onto his duty because right this minute, it's all he has left.*

"I think that's a very valid point for all of us to bear in mind, Sying-ni," she said after a moment, meeting the surgeon lieutenant's eyes but watching Lawson from the corner of her vision. "I know *I* haven't really dealt with my 'survivor's guilt' yet." She smiled with very little humor. "I imagine it'll be a while before I can draw a deep enough breath for that, and I won't pretend I'm not grateful it will. But you're right. We do need to bear it in mind."

She glanced away from Massarelli, letting her eyes circle the table. Lawson's face might have clenched a little tighter, but he looked back levelly enough when it was his turn to meet her gaze, and she nodded in satisfaction. Then she took a sip of coffee, set the cup down, and squared her shoulders.

"However," she said more briskly, "that's probably enough reflecting on gloom and doom for the evening. In fact, I think we've covered everything that needed covering as a group...and I understand from my spies that we have several fair to middling spades players in our senior command crew."

Several people chuckled, and Commander Hairston's hazel eyes gleamed. Calling the XO a *hard-core* spades player was rather like calling the Tannerman Ocean damp, and Oliver Primikynos wasn't far behind.

"I have a few other points I'd like to discuss with some of you," she continued, "but I don't see any reason to do it in a stuffy, formal setting. So if Jared"—she looked over Hairston's head to where Pallavicini had poked his head back out of his pantry—"would be good enough to find the cards, I think we've earned a little bit of relaxation."

Chapter Forty-Two

"I HAVE TO SAY, Mister President, that I was a little surprised by the menu," Michelle Henke said.

"Really?" President Warren Suttles looked back at her with a smile. The President was on the short side of medium height—for a Montanan, anyway—with dark hair going white at the temples. He was a small-framed man, with well-manicured hands, and Henke couldn't shake the feeling that he looked more like a professor at a small college somewhere than the president of an entire star system. "I hope it was a *pleasant* surprise?" he continued.

"Oh, it was delicious!" she assured him. "It was just that given the way the beef you produce here is Montana's hallmark, I'd rather assumed it was also a staple of any state dinner."

"Figured that might be the case." Suttles' smile turned into something much closer to a grin. "It's a good idea to cut against the grain, every so often, though. And sage hen's something else we do pretty well on Montana. 'Course I understand it's not quite the same as the *original* sage hen."

"Not hardly." The new speaker was a considerably taller, fair-haired man standing with them in the Musselshell Ballroom, the biggest one in the Beaverhead Hotel, the tallest luxury hotel in Estelle, the capital of the Montana System. "Spent three of the worst years of my life on Old Terra," Chester Lopez, the Montanan Attorney General continued. "Didn't want to go, but Dad insisted DeVry was the only place to get a *real* law degree." He snorted harshly and waved the whiskey tumbler in his hand in a disgusted arc. "Never really understood that, since they don't pay any damned attention to their own laws. Anyway, I tried the 'original' sage hen while I was there, and I don't believe I've ever been quite as disappointed in something in my life."

He shook his head gravely, but amusement gleamed in his dark eyes.

"That bad, was it, Chester?" Suttles asked with the air of a man obediently offering an opening.

"Wasn't rightly *bad*," Lopez replied in the tone of a man trying to be fair. "Sure was on the scrawny side, though. I told the cook I'd expected a grownup bird, and he told me that was what it was. Seems like the 'original' variety never gets to more 'n about three kilos."

"*Three?*"

"That's right, Mister President," Lopez assured him, and returned his gaze to Henke. "Now, the *Montana* sage hen's not considered even moderately well grown till it hits nine, maybe ten kilos, Countess Gold Peak. And the one we had to table tonight was probably closer to twelve."

"Well, it was certainly delicious," Henke said with a chuckle. She'd discovered on her first, brief visit to

Montana that *nothing* on Montana wasn't bigger—and, of course, better—than anything any other planet might boast. And, to be fair, looking at something like the Sapphire Mountains' New Missouri Gorge tended to substantiate a lot of that. "I'm not at all disappointed in missing the beef—especially since I'm sure I'll see plenty of it while we're here."

"Can't say we're sorry to see you here, either, Admiral," another voice said.

Henke turned to find herself facing Commodore Francine Cody of the Montana Customs Patrol. The MCP, which was in the process of being folded into the *Talbott Quadrant* Customs Patrol, was the closest thing to a navy Montana had possessed before the system's annexation into the Star Empire. It had never amounted to more than a handful of light, sublight patrol craft, but within those limits it had been a professional and well-trained force, and Cody was its senior officer. She was also a very tall, rangy woman, almost as tall as Henke's best friend, Honor Harrington. She had a much deeper voice than Honor's, however, and her brown eyes were dark.

"Especially not after what happened at Spindle... and Manticore," Cody continued, and those dark eyes held Henke's levelly. Suttles looked a little uncomfortable and seemed about to say something. But then he stopped with a small headshake. Lopez, on the other hand, only smiled.

"Don't want to sound alarmist or try to push you into a corner," the commodore went on, "but I'm just a mite nervous over what's likely to happen if you were to pull out. Being as we're sort of... exposed here in Montana."

"I fully realize that, Commodore," Henke replied. "Actually, of course, *Tillerman* is a bit more exposed to anything coming out of the Madras Sector than Montana," she pointed out, "but we're fully aware of the threat to Montana. In fact, that's why I'm here instead of with the Tillerman detachment." She sipped champagne, then shrugged slightly. "I think we can take it as a given that what happened to Crandall's pretty much defanged anything from Madras, so I don't really anticipate a serious threat out of Meyers any time soon. And you're right; from the perspective of an attack direct from the League—or from any... independent star systems, let's say—Montana's the more exposed. As for how long we'll be here, that's not really a question I can answer, because so much depends on future events. I *can* say we have no intention of pulling out of Montana unless there's a direct, credible, and more serious threat to another system in the Quadrant... *or* unless the strategic situation changes in a way which requires offensive action."

"Offensive action against the League, My Lady?" Suttles was clearly nervous about that thought, Henke noted.

"Well, Mister President," she said dryly, "no one in the Star Empire's contemplating a counteroffensive against the Kingdom of Oz."

The storybook reference went right past him—not surprisingly; Henke only knew about it because of her friend Honor's interesting reading tastes—but he obviously understood her context just fine. And he didn't seem particularly pleased by it, she noted, and castigated herself for excessive levity.

Again.

"What I mean, Mister President," she said in a more serious tone, "is that we've already been attacked by the Solarian League, and at this time we can't know what they're going to do next. If there's an ounce of sanity in Old Chicago, they'll denounce Crandall's actions and apologize for them. Unfortunately, there's been very little evidence of sanity anywhere in the Sol System for quite some time. So it's entirely possible that we are, indeed, going to find ourselves in a shooting war with the Solarian League."

Suttles' eyes had grown wider at her frankness, but she continued levelly.

"The Empress has already instructed us to activate a long-standing contingency plan. We call it Operation Lacoön, and under that ops plan, the Navy is currently in the process of securing control of every wormhole we can reach and closing them to all Solarian-registry shipping." She saw Cody wince in understanding of what that meant, but went on for Suttles' benefit. "Once those wormholes are closed, the Solarian interstellar economy's going to effectively come to a standstill. Some shipping will still get through, but it'll all have to be re-routed and our best estimate is that even after they re-route, which will take them T-months, if not years—they'll be operating at *maybe* fourteen or fifteen percent of their pre-Lacoön levels. To get back up to, say, fifty percent, they'll have to at least quadruple their merchant tonnage, and *that's* not going to happen tomorrow, either. And if those wormholes stay closed to them, they'll *never* get much above sixty percent of where they were before we shut them down."

She paused and gave the system president a cold, hard smile.

"I don't care how big their economy is, that's going to hurt them, Mister President—hurt a *lot*. The idea is to cause sufficient pain to encourage Undersecretary Kolokoltsov to . . . rethink the sort of belligerence Josef Byng and Sandra Crandall have displayed. It's a bit drastic, but to paraphrase an ancient pre-diaspora politician a friend of mine turned up a while ago, 'The Solarian League is like a hog. You have to kick it in the snout to get its attention.'"

Lopez snorted and even Cody's lips twitched, but Suttles shook his head.

"Kicking something the size of the Solarian League in the snout strikes me as a . . . risky undertaking, Lady Gold Peak," he said.

"Of course it is. Unfortunately, given what's already happened at Spindle, there's nothing we can do that *isn't* risky, one way or another. It's the Empress' opinion"— she emphasized the title ever so slightly and saw the awareness that she was speaking of her own first cousin flicker in his eyes—"that audacity and firmness are our best recourse. I'm sure Baroness Medusa's dispatches will lay out the Crown's intentions in much greater detail for you, but essentially, our position's very simple. We won't seek additional military confrontations with the League, but we *will* be firm in the face of additional Solly provocations. And if *they* seek additional military confrontations, we'll give them to them." She showed her teeth briefly. "I believe New Tuscany and Spindle have demonstrated that, for the foreseeable future, our war-fighting technology's hugely superior to anything the League has. If it comes to more open combat, the Solarian Navy won't enjoy the experience one bit. And if it *does* come to additional open combat, if the idiots in Old Chicago who're allowing themselves to be manipulated *escalate* the conflict between the League and the Star Empire, then, yes, we'll adopt the most offensive operational stance we can. Any war we fight against the League has to be as short and decisive as we can make it, because there's nothing magical about our current tech advantage. It's the result of the better part of eighty T-years of R and D and combat experience. That's not something the League's going to be able to duplicate in a heartbeat, but it's not something it *can't* duplicate if we give it long enough.

"So, in answer to your question, Commodore, we'll be here for as long as the League is prepared to *not* escalate. In the event the SLN should head in Montana's direction, we'll be prepared to 'kick it in the snout' hard enough to convince it that it should damned well go somewhere else. But we'll also be thinking in terms of taking *offensive* action should that happen, and that will obviously require the redeployment of my main combat power elsewhere. Of course, by that time, I tend to suspect the Sollies will be a little too busy wrestling with the hexapuma to be sending anything nasty *your* way."

❖   ❖   ❖

"Midshipwoman Zilwicki, I believe?" a deep voice asked.

Helen turned quickly and found herself facing a tall, blond-haired man in a spotless white Stetson whose crown band of hammered silver and amethyst gleamed under the ballroom's lights.

"Mr. Westman!" She smiled broadly and extended her hand. "It's good to see you again."

"And me 'thout even a pulser," Westman said with a slow smile of his own, shaking her hand firmly. Then he looked across her shoulder and extended his hand to the officer who'd just walked up behind her.

"Commodore Terekhov."

The two men were very nearly the same height, with very much the same coloring, although Westman—the younger of the two—looked older. Partly that was because he was so weathered and tanned, but mostly it was because he was a first-generation prolong recipient while Sir Aivars Terekhov was third-generation.

"I'd like to think," Terekhov replied, shaking the proffered hand, "now that we're all citizens of the Star Empire, that we could be a little less formal, Mr. Westman. My name's Aivars."

"Pleased t' meet you, Aivars." The skin around Westman's blue eyes crinkled. "Remind me a lot of another fella I met. Right pushy, he was. Navy captain, I think. Sure do favor."

"Well, that's interesting. *You* remind *me* of a cowboy I met once. Stubborn fellow. Got himself into what I think you Montanans call 'a heap of trouble.'" Terekhov chuckled. "Of course, in the end, it all worked out. He might've been stubborn, and he might've been a bit *hasty*, but nobody ever called him stupid."

"Might want t' spend a mite more time talking t' some of my friends and neighbors 'fore you go making rash statements like that," Westman told him. "And speaking of stupid," he looked back down at Helen, "I'd heard 'bout the Captain's promotion, but seems t' me you didn't have *this*"—his index finger brushed the single white stripe on her dress uniform's shoulder board—"last time you were here."

"No, Sir." She elevated her nose. "I, Mr. Westman, am now an *ensign*."

"Which," Terekhov explained dryly, "you can think of as the larval stage of an officer."

"I bet you didn't think that when *you* were one, Sir," Helen replied demurely. "Of course, that was long enough ago I can see where you might have trouble remembering."

Westman chuckled, and Terekhov smiled, pleased by the reemergence of the Helen Zilwicki who'd first come aboard *Hexapuma*. For the first few days after news of *Hexapuma*'s destruction—followed by the arrival in Spindle of Solly newsies who'd pursued her for stories about her "terrorist father" like raucous hyenas—she'd been quiet, subdued, with the sturdy independence and humor which were so much a part of her quenched. But she'd recovered since. Sir Aivars Terekhov wasn't foolish enough to think there weren't still plenty of dark spaces in her emotions, but the link the voyage from Spindle had given her time to heal. But then—

"And how're the rest of your 'Nasty Kitties'?" Westman asked.

There was a moment of intense silence, a tiny bubble of stillness in the crowded ballroom, and Westman's lips tightened as it registered. He looked Terekhov in the eye, and the commodore shook his head ever so slightly.

"I am deeply and sincerely sorry to hear that," the Montanan said after a moment, his normal drawl hardly noticeable. "I'd heard it was wicked. Never occurred to me *Hexapuma* was caught in it." He inhaled deeply. "How bad was it?" he asked quietly.

"As far as we know at this time, none of them got out," Terekhov said even more quietly, and Westman winced.

"*Shit*," he said with soft, terrible intensity, and rested

one hand on Helen's shoulder. She looked up at him again, and the echoes of her pain looked out of her eyes at him, but there were no tears. She truly had healed—some, at least—and she held his gaze levelly.

"Can't tell you how sorry I am t' hear that," he said, and he was speaking to her, not to Terekhov. "I know what you and your ship did for all of us—and especially for me, right here in Montana. No way I could ever pay you back for that, but"—his hand tightened on her shoulder—"that doesn't mean I'm not ready to try. You need anything, anything at all—either of you," he looked back up at Terekhov, "you let me know. Might be I won't be able t' get it for you, but that sure's hell doesn't mean I won't *try*."

"Are you going to need anything else for the next hour or so, Sir?" Helen asked as she followed Terekhov towards the boat bay lift shafts.

The four days since the state dinner had been a whirlwind of activity for most of Tenth Fleet's senior officers. The normal peacetime schedule of shore visits would have been arduous enough, given Montana's recent inclusion in the Star Empire and the Navy's awareness of the importance of establishing a positive relationship with the star system's political leaders and people. That was more important than ever, under the current circumstances, however, and so the Navy's officers had found themselves submerged in a tsunami of purely social events—although nothing could truly be "purely social" at the moment—plus a grueling marathon of planning conferences with the local authorities.

Helen and Terekhov had just returned from the commodore's most recent speaking engagement. She knew he loathed them, but unfortunately for him, he was *good* at them...not to mention the most popular single Manticoran in the entire Talbott Quadrant. Which meant he was spending far more time than he preferred in morale-boosting public appearances...and that Helen was spending that time, as well.

Now he cocked his head and gave her a quizzical look.

"Only the next hour or so?" he asked.

"Well, Sir, I'm way behind on my exercise schedule. What I'd really like to do is spend thirty minutes or so working out with Chief O'Reilly—assuming he's free— and then catch a shower before lunch."

Terekhov nodded. Tamerlane O'Reilly, one of Lieutenant Commander Olga Sanchez's chief petty officers in *Quentin Saint-James'* engineering department, happened to be about the only person in the ship's company who could match Helen in *Neue-Stil*, her preferred weaponless combat technique. And she had a point, he thought. As his flag lieutenant. Her duties had expanded over the last few days as badly as his own had. No wonder she was behind on her workouts.

"I think I can spare you. It will be a great hardship, of course. Why, I'll probably have to punch up my own files on the computer or something equally arduous. However, always bearing in mind how important it is for a Queen's officer to keep himself—or herself—physically fit, I will make the sacrifice."

"Oh, thank you, Sir!" she replied in suitably awe-struck tones.

"Go." He raised his right hand flipping the fingertips towards the lift shaft. "Go! Enjoy yourself without so much as a thought for my own grueling labors in your absence."

"Aye, aye, Sir," she said with a grin, and he smiled after her as she sped off.

◇   ◇   ◇

HMS *Quentin Saint-James* was a *Saganami-C*-class heavy cruiser, with the small ship's company her high degree of automation made possible. As such, even a mere ensign—especially a mere ensign assigned to the commodore whose flagship *Jimmy Boy* happened to be—had a cabin to herself. It wasn't an incredibly *huge* cabin, and if there'd been another extraordinarily junior female officer assigned to Commodore Terekhov's staff they would have shared it, but that wasn't the case, and Helen was just as happy as she stepped out of the shower, toweling her short hair vigorously.

She tossed the towel on to the unused bunk and stepped in front of the mirror, turning to see the back of her right shoulder, and shook her head with a grin. The Chief had gotten through to her with a combination she hadn't even seen coming, and she'd thought for a moment she'd dislocated her shoulder when she hit the mat. She hadn't, but the bruising promised to be spectacular and she imagined the shoulder was going to be stiff and tender for a while.

Probably be a good idea to drop by sickbay and see what Doc Zhin can do about that. I doubt she's going to be willing to waste any quick-heal on me—more likely to point out to me that "pain is a teacher we do well to heed." She shook her head. She's as bad as Master Tye that way! But I bet she'll at least come up with some old-fashioned aspirin. Funny how something can be around that long and still be the first thing a doctor reaches for when—

Her thoughts paused as a reflection of the blinking

green light on the base of her desk terminal caught her attention. It hadn't been there when she discarded her sweats and headed for the shower, and she wondered who the message was from.

I hope the Commodore didn't wind up needing me anyway! I really needed that workout, but I'd hate to not be there if he did need me.

She reclaimed her towel and wrapped it around herself like a sarong, then perched in the desk chair and keyed the display. The header of a recorded message came up, and she frowned. It was an inter-ship message, which meant it wasn't from the Commodore, but she didn't recognize the originating address. *Charles Ward?* What kind of name was that for a ship?

Well, I guess it's no sillier than Quentin Saint-James *or* Marconi Williams, *even if I never heard of him—whoever he was*, she thought as she punched the play key. *I wonder what he d—*

Her thought chopped off in mid-word as the display image dissolved into the face of the message's sender. She stared at it, unable—or maybe unwilling—to believe what she was seeing as the playback began.

"Hi, Helen," Paulo d'Arezzo said. "Sorry I haven't been able to get a message to you sooner. It's been crazy! But they *promise* me a dispatch boat's pulling out for Spindle this afternoon. I don't know if you've heard about the *Kitty*." His face twisted, but he continued unflinchingly. "She never had a chance when they took out *Hephaesteus*, but I'm fine—*fine*, you hear me? And Captain Lewis and Senior Chief Wanderman are fine, too. In fact, we're all in the same ship now. There was a drill on *Weyland* that had all the R and D staff dirtside when the attack came in. And Aikawa made it too. He wasn't in the ship when they hit us. He was in transit between Manticore and the station."

He paused, his recorded lips seeming to tremble just a bit, as he came to the end of that first, rapid-fire spurt of words. Then he drew a deep breath, and his gray eyes were dark and shadowed when he spoke again.

"It's . . . sort of hard to believe *anyone's* still alive," he said softly, "and the one person I most need to talk to about it's off in some ship named *Quentin Saint-James*. I wish to hell you were right here right this minute, but, *God*—! When I heard about what happened to *Hephaestus*—and to the *Kitty*—I went down on my knees because Captain Terekhov'd taken you with him. I've run scared where people are concerned for too long, Helen. But the Yawata Strike clarified a lot of things for a lot of people, and one of the things it clarified for *me* is how I feel about *you*. I think you feel the same—or I sure hope you do, because I'm going to be a real pain in the ass if you don't!"

His lips quivered again, this time with a smile—or Helen thought it was a smile, anyway. She wasn't really sure, because she was crying, she realized—crying so hard she could hardly even see the imagery, even as she laughed—and her hands rose to cover her mouth.

"Look," he went on, "the *CW*'s deploying to Spindle as soon as we get the new personnel worked up. And when we get there, I'm taking you to the best restaurant in Thimble. And after that, we're finding a hotel, and—"

He went on talking, and Helen Zilwicki took one hand away from her lips and touched his face on the display—the face she'd known she would never see again—with trembling fingers while it wavered and swam through her tears.

Chapter Forty-Three

"MARIKA!" IBTESAM VAN DER LEUR exclaimed. "I'm so glad you were able to come!"

"Thank you, Ibtesam," Marika Zygmunt replied with somewhat less enthusiasm as she shook van der Leur's hand. "Your memo made it sound urgent enough that the Board thought it would be a good idea to send a representative. I hope you understand, though, that since I'm not an officer of the corporation, I'm not in a position to make any sort of binding agreements tonight. Assuming, of course, that that's the purpose of our meeting."

"Oh, I understand entirely." Light glinted off of van der Leur's cybernetic eyes and her smile turned just a little condescending, for several reasons. Not that her employers were in any position to be condescending to their rivals at the moment, in Zygmunt's opinion. "But you are a member of the Board, with all that lovely stock," the other woman continued brightly, "and I'm sure the Board will value your practical experience in this matter just as much as I will."

"I suppose we'll just have to see," Zygmunt responded equally brightly, then tried not to wince as Immacolata Yemendijian, Manpower, Incorporated's CEO, crossed the room to put an arm around her and kiss her on the cheek.

"It's good to see you, Marika," she said.

"Immacolata," Zygmunt replied.

She not only didn't wince, she managed not to draw back visibly, which constituted a major triumph of the will. It was impossible for her to imagine a first name less suited to Yemendijian's actual personality, and that kiss was more than a pro forma peck, although much less...intense than the one Zygmunt knew van der Leur would have preferred to give her. The thought made her skin crawl. In fact, it made her think longingly of her days as one of Jessyk's senior starship captains when she could have put several hundred light-years between the two of them. Unfortunately, that had been T-years ago, before she'd inherited her parents' stock and traded her command deck for the loathsome swamp of corporate politics as practiced in Mendel.

She nodded to Yemendijian and stepped past her to shake hands with Menendo Wirschim, Technodyne of Yildun's senior VP for Operations on Mesa. He looked a little nervous, but that was understandable. He'd done the corporate equivalent of stepping into a dead man's shoes when his predecessor was recalled to the Solarian League as one of the numerous casualties of the Battle of Monica.

"Good evening, Menendo," she said, and his smile was a bit more thankful than that of a senior transstellar's bureaucrat was supposed to be.

"Good evening, Marika," he replied, and nodded

to the considerably shorter, black-haired, and badly overweight man standing beside him. "I don't believe you've met Ivan Tuero. He's our Director of R and D here in Mesa."

"Mr. Tuero," Zygmunt said, shaking his hand in turn, and Tuero smiled, his olive-dark eyes twinkling.

"Please, call me Vancheka," he told her. "I'm a working stiff, not really someone accustomed to these sorts of high-level meetings. I understand you actually used to work for a living the same way I do, Captain Zygmunt."

"That was a long time ago," she said, but she also bestowed an even broader smile upon him.

The temptation to smile faded as she looked across the room and saw Maximilien Beaudry, van der Leur's deputy. Beaudry was Director of Logistics in Kalokainos Shipping's Columbo Region, and he stood by the wet bar, martini in hand with Vitorino Stangeland, Manpower's VP for Sales and Marketing. There was no love lost between Kalokainos and the Jessyk Combine, but it wasn't Beaudry's presence which had banished the smile she'd shared with Tuero. Stangeland was a mousy little bureaucrat of a man, yet he was just as morally corrupt as Yemendijian—albeit without her . . . exotic tastes and sadism. Being in the same room with either of them was enough to make Zygmunt's skin crawl.

"Marika!"

Zygmunt brightened a bit again when Gerhaus Yang swept down upon her. She and Yang were very much of a height, but where Zygmunt had dark hair, dark eyes, and a trim figure kept that way through vigorous exercise, Yang was, frankly, spectacular. There was obviously some good, solid genegineering in her family, and biosculpt hadn't hurt one bit. Coupled with that long red

hair, those arctic blue eyes, and a richly curved figure
Zygmunt deeply envied, she could hold her own physically in any company. She was also one of the smartest
women Zygmunt had ever met, and she'd personally
built Sapphire Technologies of Mesa into the primary
builder for the Mesa System Navy. More to the point,
she clearly felt much the same way Marika did where
Manpower was concerned, and the two of them had
known one another since Zygmunt's spacefaring days.

She was accompanied by Óttar Nagatsuka, Sapphire's
VP for Weapons Research. Nagatsuka was the youngest person present—aside from Lucindé Myllyniemi,
Stangeland's Assistant VP for Sales and Marketing—and
there were persistent rumors that he and Yang were
lovers, which obviously explained how he came to head
Sapphire's second most important division at such an
absurdly tender age. Given that Yang's preferred form of
exercise occurred in bedrooms, and that her cheerfully
equal-opportunity appetites were well known, that was
probably inevitable. In fact, however, Nagatsuka had
been happily married to Francisco Smirnov for almost
as long as Zygmunt had been married to Bradley Mykos,
and he was just as relentlessly monogamous as she was.

She shook hands with Nagatsuka and exchanged a
hug with Yang which was as welcome—and genuine—as
Yemendijian's had been distasteful.

"Well, now that we're all here," van der Leur said,
looking just a bit pointedly in Zygmunt's direction,
"why don't we find something to drink and get down
to the dreary business at hand. I'm sure we can all
find something much more enjoyable to do with our
time after we get that out of the way."

Zygmunt punched her order into the wet bar,

accepted her tall, iced—and, in her case, nonalcoholic—drink, and followed the others as they settled around the large conference table. It was interesting, she thought, how the natural pecking order established itself with van der Leur at one end of the table and Yemendijian at the other, flanked by Stangeland and Myllyniemi. As the sole member of the group with no satellite in attendance, Zygmunt settled between Myllyniemi and Yang, which put a lot of X chromosomes on that side of the table, she reflected.

Van der Leur waited until everyone else was seated before she took her own chair, which wasn't totally inappropriate, since she *was* the one who'd sent out the invitations, but was typical of her arrogance. Although Yang was the most beautiful person in the room, Zygmunt had to admit that van der Leur was the most . . . visually striking. She was barely a hundred and fifty centimeters tall, with crimson hair—not *red*, crimson—even more tattoos than most members of Mesa's "new lodges," and the polished, featureless silver of her eye implants. Unlike most people with cybernetic vision, van der Leur had traded in a perfectly serviceable pair of organic eyes, and Zygmunt wondered sometimes exactly what that said about her.

"I'm sure all of us have been following what's happening out in the Verge," she said now, with unusual brusqueness, for even her hyper-aggressive personality. "What many of you may not have realized, however—although I'm sure Marika's aware of it—are the probable ultimate consequences of this unprecedented seizure of wormholes the Manties have embarked upon."

More than one of her audience's expressions flickered at her assumption of ignorance on their part,

Zygmunt noticed. Not that van der Leur cared; she had more of the typical transstellar's arrogance than most, difficult though that was.

"If this is allowed to stand," she informed them, "the consequences for the Solarian League's economy will be somewhere between dire and catastrophic. I'm well aware—" she showed her teeth for a moment "—that as Kalokainos Shipping's local CEO for Operations, I'm automatically . . . disinclined, let's say, to look favorably upon anything coming out of Manticore. But I invite any of you who haven't already done it to have your operations people run their own analyses of what this will do to the interstellar movement of goods and services and the people who do that moving. Frankly, quite a few of the smaller lines will go belly-up very, very quickly, and some of the major players are likely to follow suit, if this goes on for very many T-months."

Well, you've got a point about that, Ibtesam, Zygmunt reflected. *Not that you give a single good goddamn what happens to the* crews *of your ships.*

"That's bad enough," van der Leur continued, "but what's even worse, in a lot of ways, are rumors I'm beginning to hear out of the Verge."

She paused, those featureless eyes swiveling around the table. Silence hovered for several seconds before Immacolata Yemendijian cleared her throat.

"And which rumors might those be?" she asked. "Frankly, *I* haven't heard anything good coming out of the Verge—especially, given what you've just said, where the frigging Manties are concerned—for a long time."

"By an interesting coincidence," van der Leur told her with a thin smile, "the ones I have in mind *do* concern the Manties. And the reason I invited this particular group to discuss those rumors this evening is that it seems to me that there's a certain . . . reluctance in Old Chicago to tackle those rumors effectively."

Zygmunt managed not to blink. She couldn't disagree about the *effectiveness* of Sollies' efforts to deal with the Manticorans, but that was scarcely due to anything remotely like "reluctance." Or *sanity*, for that matter. Thanks to the Visigoth wormhole, news of the disaster at Spindle had reached Mesa well over a month ago. Zygmunt's own career had never included naval service, but no one who'd ever skippered a starship could fail to understand how catastrophically Sandra Crandall's fleet had been crushed . . . despite the fact that the Manties hadn't had a single ship heavier than a battlecruiser. The jury might still be out on precisely how the RMN had managed that, but the consequences were abundantly clear. And van der Leur wanted the SLN, having just lost one hand to the buzz saw, to stick in *another* one?

"Precisely what kind of 'rumors' are we talking about, Ms. van der Leur?" Menendo Wirschim asked after a moment. "And could you explain to us exactly how you expect the League to deal with them 'effectively'?"

"Why, yes, I can!" She smiled brilliantly at the Technodyne executive. "And when I do, I think you'll understand exactly why I invited you and Mr. Tuero over for drinks, Menendo."

Rufino Chernyshev tipped back his chair and waved expansively in a "come in" gesture as Lucinde Myllyniemi appeared in his office doorway. The tall, blond haired young woman—for a prolong society, fifty-one was barely out of babyhood—shook her head and smiled as she accepted the invitation.

"So, was it as bad as you anticipated?" he inquired as she settled herself on the corner of his desk.

"Being in the same room for almost four hours with Ibtesam van der Leur and Immacolata Yemendijian?" She shook her head, kicked off one shoe, and put her foot in his lap. "Rufino, nobody could possibly 'anticipate' something as thoroughly 'bad' as *that*."

Chernyshev chuckled and began massaging her foot. He and Myllyniemi had known one another since he'd been a thirty-three-year-old junior instructor at the Mesan Alignment's agent training facility on Mesa and she'd been an especially precocious fifteen-year-old student. He could still see a lot of that fifteen-year-old's reckless humor in the confident, seasoned agent, and her hobby—she was a marathoner who routinely worked out under an extra twenty percent of gravity—kept her as slender and graceful as she'd ever been.

And the two of them had been on-again, off-again lovers ever since she'd turned eighteen.

Of course, he reflected affectionately, watching her almost visibly purr as his fingers worked skillfully along her foot, *quite a few people could say that about their relationships with Lucinde*.

"So, aside from the company, how was it?" he asked.

"Well, your little birdies were *mostly* correct. I'm not sure how this is going to impact our plans, though. You know, it would really help at a moment like this if we had someone a little more highly placed in Manpower's official hierarchy."

And if we did, you wouldn't have to carry water for us with Manpower, would you? Chernyshev thought with a certain degree of compassion . . . and a lot more sympathy. *But somebody has to do it, and your reward for doing it so well is to be stuck with it for the foreseeable future.*

Manpower, Incorporated, was extraordinarily useful to the Mesan Alignment, but it was also the single most hated, most reviled transstellar in the entire explored galaxy. Right off the top of his head, Chernyshev couldn't think of a single one of the Alignment's military, political, or philosophical opponents who wouldn't cheerfully shoot every Manpower executive. None of those opponents had ever heard of the Alignment, however. Not yet. And the Alignment intended to keep it that way for as long as possible. Towards that end, having Manpower regarded *solely* as a corrupt, morally bankrupt, and incredibly depraved business entity was absolutely essential, and it was equally important to keep anyone with a direct connection to the Alignment as much in the shadows as possible.

For the Alignment's purposes, Immacolata Yemendijian and Vitorino Stangeland were perfect. They actually were everything the galaxy thought Manpower was, and neither of them had any inkling of the Alignment's existence. Two or three members of the Manpower Board were also members of the Alignment, but all of them were fairly low-profile, and no Alignment operative had ever risen above the middle management level. People at that level could accomplish a great deal to . . . shape Manpower's activities, but none of them were in positions to formulate official policy. True, half a dozen of the largest shareholders were Alignment fronts, but none of them knew exactly who actually gave them their instructions. There still had to be someone—someone who understood the Alignment's ultimate objectives—in that "official hierarchy" of Lucinde's, and that was where she came in.

Privately, Chernyshev knew, she considered Manpower a perversion of the Detweiler Philosophy and believed the Alignment should have cut its ties with the corporation long ago. She might understand the advantages Manpower created; that didn't mean she *liked* them. Fortunately, it also didn't prevent her from steering Vitorino Stangeland with consummate skill. In fact, Stangeland was convinced he was the one doing the driving, and the fact that he would very much have liked to become one of her lovers was a lever she used very effectively. In fact, Chernyshev never doubted that if it ever became necessary for her to actually allow Stangeland into her bed, she'd do it with a smile.

And then go stand in a shower for the next three days.

"You know I've passed that observation of yours along," he told her now. "And I sympathize. But I have to admit, I was a stronger supporter of the notion before I inherited Isabel's chair and realized how really effective you are over there." She made a face, and he patted her ankle. "No, I mean it! You *are* effective. And, while I probably shouldn't be telling you this, I doubt you're going to have to put up with it a lot longer." Her eyes narrowed, and he nodded. "We're definitely moving into the end game."

"Thank God," she said. Then her nostrils flared, and she leaned back, bracing herself with her hands on the desk behind her. "I'm not sure how that endgame's going to work out, though. Especially if van der Leur's suggestions wind up bearing fruit in Old Chicago."

"And those suggestions were—?"

"Well, the general anti-Manty groundswell's building nicely. Of course, we could pretty much count on van der Leur to want Manticore burned to the ground, but she and some of the others—including my own dear Immacolata!—are picking up rumors of growing unrest in the Verge. *And* they're leaping to the conclusion that Manticore must be the one squirting the hydrogen. But they also seem to feel the SLN isn't taking things seriously enough. From what van der Leur said, Volkhart Kalokainos and his father plan on turning up the pressure on Kolokoltsov and the other Mandarins to increase Frontier Fleet's presence in the Verge in general and in the trouble spots in particular."

"Really?" Chernyshev chuckled "And how do they plan to convince Frontier Fleet captains—those who have working brains, of which there are more in Frontier Fleet than Battle Fleet—to rush in where Crandall chose to tread?"

"By offering the Sollies Technodyne's second-generation improved shipkillers," she told him, and he stopped smiling.

"The *second*-generation birds?" he said with the air of a man making certain he'd heard correctly.

"That's what she said, and Wirschim and Tuero both seemed to know exactly what she was talking about."

"I see."

Chernyshev frowned as he contemplated the idea. Lucinde didn't know about Massimo Filareta's orders to attack the Manticore Binary System. Nor did she know about the *first*-generation Technodyne shipkillers with which his ships had been supplied. Shipboard ordnance wasn't Rufino Chernyshev's strong point, either, and from everything he'd learned, even the best of Technodyne's new hardware remained markedly inferior to the Manties'. But the second-generation weapons were essentially identical in performance to the Mesan Alignment Navy's current shipkillers. The idea of handing them to the Sollies, giving the Manties a good look at them before they had to deal with any MAN units, might not strike the people in charge of the Alignment's naval posture as a good idea.

Unfortunately, he couldn't see a way to stop van der Leur and the others. As Lucinde had just said, they didn't know anything about Operation Janus. If they *had* known, they'd have been as opposed to it—for their own perfectly logical reasons—as the SLN or the Manties, and if they did offer the League a substantially upgraded missile capability, the Mandarins might well jump at it.

And if they do *start beefing up the Frontier Fleet presence in the Verge, they get a lot more likely to catch one of our people wandering around between resistance movements. That could be . . . unfortunate.*

"Well," he said finally, giving her foot one last caress and removing it from his lap, "that's interesting. Might even work, although I doubt the Sollies will like what the Manties do to them even if they do get their hands on Technodyne's new goodies. You did good, Lucinde—again. But then, you always do."

"Damn straight," she told him, slipping her shoe back on with a smile. "And my reward for that is your taking me to dinner at Chez Umberto's. After which," her smile grew positively sultry, "I may have a little reward for *you*, as well."

Chapter Forty-Four

"...so, as soon as we had *Carolyn* and *Argonaut*'s people off Shona Station, we withdrew our own people," Captain Jacob Zavala said, sitting across the table in HMS *Artemis*' flag briefing room from Michelle Henke. "Lieutenant Hearns executed that whole part of the business *extremely* well, Milady. Her Lieutenant Gutierrez ran the nuts and bolts, but she was the one who put it together and made it work. I've written a letter of commendation I'd like to go into her permanent personnel file."

"Append it to your formal report and I'll see to it that it does," she told him.

"Thank you, Milady. The truth is, *all* my people did well. The one thing I truly regret is the destruction of Vice Admiral Dubroskaya's battlecruisers." The small captain's face turned grim, his eyes dark. "I should have launched a demonstration salvo, like Captain Ivanov in Zunker."

"From what you've already told me, Jacob, that's clearly a case of being wise—and unjust to yourself—after the fact." He looked at her, and she met his eyes levelly. "Five *Rolands* didn't have the magazine capacity to fool around wasting rounds on 'demonstrations,' and you know it. When Governor Dueñas 'quarantined' our ships, he deliberately set up a confrontation just like this one, and Dubroskaya knew exactly what he was doing. Hell, she and her ships were the most important *part* of it, the thing that gave him the firepower to think he could pull it off! I'm not saying that should have earned her and so many of her people a death sentence, but I *am* saying it was other people's decisions that set up everything that happened. I'll go over the final report, of course, and Commander Adenauer and I will analyze your targeting decisions just as carefully as you could possibly want. But I'm already pretty sure what we're going to find that without a better baseline for how well the new Mark 16s would perform against battlecruisers, your targeting decisions were entirely appropriate."

She continued to hold his gaze until he nodded ever so slightly, although she suspected he didn't fully agree with her. Not yet, at least. It was going to take some time for him to get past the feeling that all those deaths had been avoidable.

Well, of course they were avoidable, Mike! she told herself tartly. *It's just that none of the people who could've done the avoiding happened to be wearing* Manticoran *uniforms!*

"Between the battlecruisers and the Gendarmerie troops on Shona Station, total Solarian casualties were about six thousand," Zavala said. "No native Saltashan was even injured, as far as I know. Because the Governor refused all communication after we put our people aboard the station, I had to complete the negotiations to arrange our people's extraction without any more violence with Lieutenant Governor Tiilikainen. I've included complete recordings of all our conversations in the final report. My impression is that if she'd been in charge from the start, none of this would've happened. She didn't say so in so many words, of course—it *was* an official communication—but it's pretty clear this was all Dueñas' brainstorm."

"Pretty much what I assumed going in." Michelle sat back in her chair. "I just wish he hadn't been stupid enough to get so many people killed. And, Jacob, while you're kicking yourself about Dubroskaya, remember you gave *her* every chance to be not-stupid, too."

"Yes, Milady. At any rate, once we'd recovered the ships, Captain Chou decided to take *Carolyn* on to Montana. She should be arriving in another couple of weeks; she's not one of the fast freighters serving the beef trade. With Lacoön shutting down the League, Captain Lyriazis decided to divert from Merge and Even Star, so he took *Argonaut* to Lynx, heading back to Manticore."

"Good, Jacob. Very good. Unless I find something totally bizarre in your final report, I'll be endorsing your actions with my strongest approval when I forward my own report to Admiral Khumalo and Baroness Medusa. From everything I've seen so far, you and all your people performed brilliantly."

"We tried, anyway, Milady," he acknowledged.

"Which was exactly what I expected out of you when I sent you," she said, rising from her chair. He followed suit, and she walked him to the briefing room door. "I think your people are entitled to a little leave," she continued, "and there are some really good restaurants here in Montana. Why don't you see about letting them sample some of them?"

"I think that would be a wonderful idea, Milady," he replied with a smile.

"Good! And try one or two of them yourself."

"Of course, Milady."

He came briefly to attention, then stepped through the briefing room door to the midshipwoman waiting to escort him back to the boat bay. Michelle smiled after him for a moment, then returned to her chair and frowned thoughtfully.

As she'd told Zavala, she couldn't blame anyone besides Damián Dueñas, Vice Admiral Oxana Dubroskaya, and Major John Pole for the death toll in Saltash. Not that she expected the *Sollies* to see it that way. On the other hand, she was all done worrying about how Sollies reacted to anything. If an OFS system governor impounded Manticoran merchant vessels—and their crews—and refused to release them, then the Solarian League was just going to have to live with the consequences. And given the RMN's record on commerce protection, Dueñas damned well should've known what would happen.

Still, she reflected, *you could've sent something a little more impressive than five destroyers, Mike. You know how arrogant Sollies are. Maybe if you'd sent Michael's battlecruisers—or even Terekhov's cruisers— Dubroskaya would've been smart enough to back down before she got herself and so many other people killed.*

She thought about that for another moment, then shrugged. There were always the "could'ves" and "should'ves" after *anybody* got killed, and like she'd told Zavala, the ultimate responsibility for those deaths lay with the people who'd been stupid enough to manufacture the incident in the first place.

She nodded, and then smiled slightly. She'd come to know Sir Aivars Terekhov much better since his return to the Talbott Quadrant. She understood exactly why so many people thought so highly of him—not just out here, but back home—and he and her other squadron commanders were due to dine with her this evening aboard her flagship.

He'll be proud enough of young Abigail to bust his buttons, she thought, using one of her mother's favorite archaisms. *Now, what's the best way to tease him about how well another of "his girls" has done?* She snorted. *Maybe I should have Gwen screen Zavala and tell him to join us and bring his officers?*

She grinned impishly and reached out to punch Lieutenant Archer's combination into her com.

✧   ✧   ✧

"It's time," Tomasz Szponder said, sitting back from the table, coffee cup in hand.

"Are you certain of that?" Jarosław Kotarski leaned forward, left elbow propped on the arm of his chair, and an index finger stroked his mustache. "We've barely begun the real prep work, Tomasz."

"That's not what I meant." Szponder shook his head. "What I meant is that it's time for us to start thinking about actual strategies. *Active* strategies."

"What sort of 'active strategies'?" Grażyna Kotarska, Jarosław's wife, asked.

She was a small but sturdy woman, with short brown hair, and just as much a revolutionary as her husband. Unlike him, though, she was still employed by the Włocławek Department of Education...as a kindergarten teacher, where her superiors probably figured she couldn't do much damage. At the moment, she and Tomek Nowak had been stacking dessert plates to clear the table, and she cocked her head and fixed Szponder with a bright, demanding eye.

"Oh, I'm not planning on blood in the streets tomorrow, Szytylet." Szponder used her KWM code-name with a crooked smile. "But friend Firebrand's demonstrated his bona fides pretty conclusively. So now that we know we really do have that sort of support, we need to start thinking about how to use it."

"But not tomorrow," Kotarski said, sitting straight again and nodding in approval.

"No, not tomorrow, Jarosław," Szponder reassured him. "Tomek and I have been kicking around numbers for a while now. Based on the two shipments Firebrand's gotten through to us, and assuming he makes his projected future delivery schedule, we'd have enough weapons—military-grade weapons—to begin a guerrilla campaign in two or three T-months. But we're all agreed that isn't the way we want to go."

He looked around the Kotarski table again. His own wife, Grażyna, was at the opera tonight. Aside from her, the people around that table were effectively the entire central cell of the Krucjata Wolności Myśli, and he saw agreement in every face.

He knew all of them would support exactly that sort of a campaign...if it was the only alternative to admitting defeat and letting people like Hieronim Mazur and Agnieszka Krzywicka continue crushing the Włocławekan people. Yet despite the enormous dissatisfaction with the Ruch Odnowy Narodowej and—especially—the Stowarzyszenie Eksporterów Owoców

Morza, the preponderance of firepower would have been overwhelmingly on the side of Justyna Pokriefke's BBP and General Sosabowska's SZW. Not even Firebrand's weapons deliveries could hope to change that, simply because of the size of the security forces.

That was why the KWM's original strategy had focused on education, on attempting to "grow" that sense of dissatisfaction into something which might produce enough pressure to force at least limited reforms without "blood in the streets." Unfortunately, events since the Lądowisko airbus shoot-down had amply demonstrated that that wasn't going to happen.

There'd been a dozen demonstrations—two of which had degenerated into outright riots—once the hacked version of the air-traffic control records had become general knowledge. At first, Pokriefke's Biuro Bezpieczeństwa i Prawdy seemed to have tried to contain things without bloodshed, but perhaps the KWM had done its work too well. Or perhaps it was simply the RON's chance to discover how extraordinarily difficult it was for any repressive regime to allow "just a little" protest.

Whatever the cause, the demonstrations' size had grown swiftly and the demonstrators' demands had begun to reach beyond accountability for the murder of children. They'd begun to reach into the system which could *allow* the murder of children . . . and then cover it up. That was the point at which the BBP had called out the riot battalions and the *czarne kurtki had* started making examples. And *that* was the point at which the demonstrators had responded with riots in Lądowisko which had lasted for over two days, in the wake of which martial law had been declared not just in the capital, but in *every* major city, and those who spoke their minds too rashly had started...disappearing.

Tomasz Szponder was coldly and bitterly certain none of those vanished citizens would ever be seen again. And if the RON and *Oligarchia* were prepared to go that far, the possibility of *peaceful* reform no longer existed...if it ever truly had. That was precisely why he'd finally started stockpiling weapons.

But *non*-peaceful reform carried its own grim imperatives, and despite the KWM's preliminary work, it would take T-months—probably *T-years*—to build a guerrilla movement with a genuine chance of success. While they were doing that building, they'd almost certainly come to the KWM's attention. In fact, the weapons caches they'd already established significantly increased the odds of that happening, even in the relatively short term. And even if they somehow produced that kind of movement, they'd still get a lot of people killed... and offer Mazur and Krzywicka the perfect pretext to call in OFS. Neither of them would really want to do that, because they knew how the Solly transstellars would move in as soon as they let OFS in the door, but they'd a hell of a lot rather see everybody else in the star system become Solarian helots than lose *everything* in the wake of a successful revolution.

Especially as long as they got to be the slaves' overseers.

Nor would it take long for OFS and Frontier Fleet to respond if they did send for help. Thanks to the Włocławek-Sarduchi warp bridge, Włocławek was little more than a week away from the Frontier Fleet naval base in the Warner System, which also happened to be the location of an OFS sector HQ.

"The thing is," he continued, "now that the Manties have agreed to provide naval support, we've actually got a chance even if Mazur and Krzywicka whistle up the Sollies. We'd have to coordinate carefully, but we have the com channel 'Firebrand' set up for us."

"'Coordinate' what, Tomasz?" Kotarski asked with a frown. "It sounds like you have something specific in mind."

"I do." Szponder sipped coffee, then lowered the cup and set it very precisely on the table in front of him.

"Tomek and I have been looking at this from the moment Firebrand turned up, even before Manticore delivered the first arms shipment. We haven't said anything about it, both for security reasons and because until we had proof we can rely on Manticore, what we've been thinking about would've been insane. Now, though, we might actually be able to pull it off."

"Pull what off?" Grażyna asked softly. She sank back into her chair, leaning forward and folding her arms on the table while she looked intently into Szponder's face, and there was a strange little smile on her face. "What have the two of you been hatching?" She shook her head. "I've thought for weeks now you were up to something!"

"Guilty," Tomek acknowledged with a smile of his own—one that bordered on a grin—then twitched his head in Szponder's direction. "Although, to be fair, it was mostly his idea. I only got behind and pushed because I liked it so much!"

"If it's something that appeals to *Tomek*," Kotarski said dryly, "it fills me with dread."

"Oh, it's not *that* bad," Szponder said. "But if we don't want a guerrilla war, and if we don't want to degenerate into nothing more than terrorists, our only option is a coup. And if Tomek and I are right, and assuming I get confirmation from the Manticorans that we can have naval support here in Włocławek when we need it, I think we just may have come up with a way to make a coup work."

✧   ✧   ✧

"Christ!" Michael Breitbach muttered, staring at the HD.

The System Information and News Service's camera-drones circled over the boulevard between the O'Sullivan Tower and Freedom Park as the Scorpion light tanks in Presidential Guard colors moved in, and the live feed wasn't cutting away to the sort of canned fluff it normally used to sweep unpleasant events under the rug. SINS reported exactly what President Lombroso wanted reported, and what Lombroso and General Olivia Yardley obviously *wanted* at this moment was for the citizens of Mobius to understand that anyone who got too uppity was asking not simply for a truncheon to the head but a pulser dart to the brain.

"I can't believe this," Yolanda Somerset said in the tone of someone who wished she truly couldn't. "What's Yardley *thinking?!*"

She shook her head and leaned against Breitbach's shoulder as they sat in bed, watching the atrocity which had been a peaceful demonstration unfold. She was also a member of the Mobius Liberation Front's executive cell and one of the very few people who knew Breitbach was the MLF's leader.

"She's thinking she can do whatever the hell she wants. After all, she's got the fucking tanks, doesn't she?!" Breitbach snarled. "But this . . ."

The two of them watched the tanks grind inexorably

forward, watched the swirls of panic reaching out as the crowd of demonstrators tried to get out of the way. If those bastards didn't stop pretty damned quick, Breitbach thought, they were going to start running over people. Some of the demonstrators were already being knocked down and trampled as the crowd realized what was coming at it, but that was probably what the bastards had in mind from the beginning, and—

"*Oh, Jesus!*" Somerset cried.

Her fingernails dug bleeding furrows in Breitbach's forearm, but he scarcely noticed as he jerked upright when the oncoming tanks suddenly opened fire on the unarmed crowd. The heavy, hyper-velocity tribarrel darts tore through the demonstrators, ripping bodies apart, spraying blood and tissue. The tanks went right on advancing, still firing...and then an antitank launcher opened fire from the O'Sullivan Tower's thirtieth floor. One of them exploded, and a second tank erupted in a blue-white blaze of burning hydrogen an instant later. They switched their suddenly frantic fire from the fleeing, bleeding crowd to the source of that deadly fire. Ceramacrete vaporized, windows blew inward, flames gushed from shattered interiors, fire alarms wailed, and a *third* Scorpion exploded.

"Is that *us?!*" Somerset demanded through her tears as the entire boulevard erupted in exploding vehicles, bodies, *pieces* of bodies, and spiraling clouds of flame.

"I don't know," Breitbach said hoarsely. "Probably." He shook his head sharply. "We didn't tell our people not to participate in the demonstration—we never saw this coming! Damn it, the son of a bitch invited demonstrations with his frigging talk about *elections!* Who'd have thought even he—?!"

He made himself stop and draw a deep breath, then turned to look into Somerset's tear-filled brown eyes.

"I don't know," he said more quietly as yet another Scorpion blew up. "But who the hell else on Mobius has access to antitank launchers? Only us, courtesy of Dabilenaren and his friends!"

"But you never authorized anything like that!" Somerset jerked her head at the chaos on the HD.

"No, I didn't, but some of our cell leaders—Kazuyoshi Brewster comes to mind—might've decided to deploy them anyway." He bared his teeth. "In fact, I wouldn't be a bit surprised if that's *exactly* what happened. I know Glenda helped plan the march, and Kaz has access to the weapons cache in Allerton. It would be like him to cover his wife's bets this way."

"And he's always been a loose warhead," Somerset said harshly.

"One way to describe him," Breitbach acknowledged. "But he's also a good man, and if Lombroso and Yardley hadn't pulled *this* shit"—he jabbed an index finger at the HD—"no one would ever've known they were there. I'm not saying I'm not pissed off at him for running that risk, Yolanda. But God knows how many more of those people would already be dead if those launchers *weren't* there."

"You're probably right," she conceded, "but what's this going to mean down the road?"

"If I had the answer to that question, I'd be God and we wouldn't need the Liberation Front to deal with Lombroso," he replied grimly. "I'm willing to bet he's going to scream for outside help, though."

He climbed out of bed and reached for his clothing.

"I've got to talk to Kayleigh," he said. "Send her the code for the Bendan Terrace apartment."

❖   ❖   ❖

"Well, *this* sucks." Commodore Francis Thurgood tossed the hardcopy report onto his desk. "I really, really don't want to hear this kind of shit, Sadako!"

"I'm aware of that," Captain Merriman replied rather more serenely than most of Thurgood's subordinates would have, given his tone. On the other hand, Captain Merriman had certain advantages those other subordinates didn't have. "I'm your senior intelligence officer, though, remember? I'm afraid that makes it my job to bring you this sort of news."

"I know," Thurgood growled, leaning back in his chair and running his fingers through his hair. "I know! And however little I may like it, the truth is, I'd a hell of a lot rather have you giving me good intel than the kind of crap Yucel and that bitch Crandall prefer! Or *preferred*, I guess I should say in Crandall's case." He shook his head. "You know, I'm not a big fan of the Manties, but if I could figure out how, I'd send Gold Peak a case of champagne for taking Crandall off the board!"

"I agree. On the other hand—speaking as someone with a proprietary interest in your continued well-being, as well as as a dutiful intelligence officer—I should probably point out that going around saying that to anyone else might not be the very best idea you ever had."

"Point taken." He managed a genuine smile.

"Better," she said, and crossed to perch on the corner of his desk. She was little more than two thirds his height, and she looked absurdly young to be wearing a captain's uniform. Of course, she was third-generation prolong, and Thurgood was only second-generation.

"Now," she continued, "do you want to hear my analysis of what this is likely to mean for us?"

"I would," he replied, and meant it. Sadako Merriman wasn't just the woman he'd fallen in love with; she was also the best intelligence officer he'd ever had.

"All right. If the Admiralty's serious about being 'more proactive' out in the Verge with these new wonder missiles from Technodyne, we're probably going to see at least some of them coming our way, given our proximity to the Manties' Talbott Quadrant. How *soon* we see them's another question, of course. And, frankly, if what we've been hearing about the Manties' missiles is anywhere near accurate, I'm inclined to doubt Technodyne just happens to have a real equalizer in its back pocket."

"So you think this is all moonshine and hot air?"

"No." She shook her head. "No, I'm inclined to believe Technodyne really did have something better than they handed Tyler at Monica. I just find it hard to believe they've got something—got *anything*—as good as the Manties' current-generation hardware. You and I both know there's nothing *magic* about the Manties' missiles, but they damned well spent a long time developing them. There's no way Technodyne's come up with matching weapons this quickly.

"The problem, of course, is that our esteemed Battle Fleet colleagues and civilian superiors are likely to be clutching at straws. Or, rather, the *civilians* are going to be clutching at straws and Battle Fleet's head is so far up its collective ass that it's in acute denial over

Manty weapons capabilities. So both sets of idiots are going to push this 'proactive' stance, if not for exactly the same reasons."

"Which brings us to our *immediate* civilian superiors," Thurgood growled.

"Exactly." Merriman's expression turned grim. "I'm not sure what's going on with Hongbo, and I know Verrocchio's scared as hell that the Manties are going to come our way if the situation keeps going farther and farther into the crapper. I don't know if he's scared *enough* yet, though, and Yucel sure as hell isn't. I know the Gendarmerie imposes strict IQ limits on its brigadiers, especially the ones it sends out to the Verge, but she's exceptionally stupid even for one of them. She's going to eat this 'proactive' stuff up with a spoon, and she's going to push Verrocchio to think exactly the same way."

"And if she succeeds, Verrocchio really *is* likely to see the Manties come calling," the commodore said glumly. "At which point, he'll expect *us* to do something about it."

"Exactly," his intelligence officer said again.

❖   ❖   ❖

"Vincent!"

Vincent Frugoni paused and turned around as someone called his name. A tallish, fair-haired man farther down the slidewalk waved to draw his attention, and Frugoni stifled a frown. What he wanted to do was to keep right on walking; what he actually did was to step off the belt and wave back.

"Jerome," he said in greeting as the other man caught up and stepped off beside him. "What can I do for you?"

"Just wanted to touch base," Jerome Luther replied, shaking the proffered hand. "I've got a lead on the real reason Parkman was screaming for all that extra security the day your sister was killed. And if my source is right, and if I can confirm it, then it was just as frigging stupid as you and your brother-in-law have said it was all along. There wasn't any credible 'threat.' He wanted the paperwork to justify an increase in TSE's budget here in Swallow, and he figured the memos going back and forth between his people and Karaxis would provide it."

"And you really think you're going to get that confirmed?" Frugoni asked skeptically. There were times he believed Luther truly was determined to unravel the whitewash of Sandra's death. Most of the time, though, he remembered the newsy worked for the Nixon Foundation. Besides, even if he got his information confirmed, it wouldn't change anything. Nobody back in the League cared what happened someplace like Swallow, and the Shuman Administration sure as hell wasn't opening any investigations!

"Probably not," Luther conceded. "Not going to keep me from trying, though." He grinned suddenly. "By now, Shuman, Karaxis, and Parkman have me so frigging pissed I'll keep right on digging if only to piss them off back!"

"Well, that's refreshingly honest!" Frugoni said with a genuine chuckle. Luther's charm was one of his stocks in trade, and despite himself, the ex-Marine couldn't help liking him.

"Yeah, I guess it is. Well, see you around."

"Sure." Frugoni shook hands again and turned back towards the slidewalk to the air-car park, but Luther snapped his fingers loudly.

"Oh, almost forgot!" he said. "Picked up an interesting tidbit. Something that might interest your in-laws...assuming, of course, that there was any truth at all to the base canards being leveled against them by the Administration."

"What sort of tidbit?" Frugoni's eyes narrowed slightly.

"It appears Frontier Fleet's planning some sort of change in its deployment stance. Something to do with Manticore—or that's what I hear. And as part of whatever the hell they're doing, they just pulled out Deston's destroyers."

The Solarian newsy had stopped smiling. His brown eyes met Frugoni's blue gaze very levelly, and Frugoni reminded himself not to frown. Nobody in Tyrone Matsuhito's Inspectorate Five would find a chance encounter between him and Luther surprising or particularly alarming, given the newsy's entire ostensible reason for being in Swallow to begin with. But they might just wonder why Luther was telling him that Commander Francine Deston and her destroyer division—the only Solarian naval units in the entire star system—had been pulled out.

Of course, I'm *not to sure why he's telling me,* the retired noncom thought. *Or whether or not he's telling me the* truth. *I guess it's always possible he approves of the CMM. On the other hand, he's being funded by Rappaport, and Rappaport would love to see Tallulah taken down a peg. The only problem with that is the fact that Rappaport wants to* take over *from Tallulah, not see us kick* all *the transstellars out of Swallow.*

"That's interesting...assuming it's accurate, of course," he said, after a moment. "If I happen to run into Floyd, I might mention it to him."

"And tell him I still want that interview!" Luther said with another grin. "I'll even wear a blindfold while you escort me up into the mountains!"

◇   ◇   ◇

"Well now, that's right interesting," Floyd Allenby said. He whipped the tip of his fishing rod expertly, and the fly landed exactly in the eddy from the mountain waterfall. "'Pears to me might be an opportunity here."

"Makes me nervous, Floyd," his cousin Jason Mac-Gruder replied, looking up from where he was cleaning the four sunburst trout Floyd had already reeled in. "Seems just a mite too...convenient, if you know what I mean."

"That's because you're a pessimist by nature, Jase," Vincent Frugoni told him. The ex-Marine sat leaning back against a sunbaked boulder, open beer in hand while he watched the cousins work. "Mind you," he continued, "pessimists are disappointed a lot less often than optimists."

"Why, thank you, Vinnie," MacGruder said. "Soon's I figure out whether that's a compliment or an insult, I'll know whether or not you get to eat tonight."

Frugoni chuckled, but his eyes were serious as he turned back to Allenby.

"All I can tell you for certain, Floyd, is that all our contacts inside the Army, SFC, and Tallulah agree that Frontier Fleet's pulled Deston out of the system." He shrugged. "Obviously we can't take that as gospel— our contacts could be wrong, or they could've been turned. And we don't have as many of them as I'd like, anyway. But when all the ones I've been able to check with agree, then I think we have to go with the assumption that it's *probably* true."

"And if it is?" Allenby asked, his eyes on his fishing fly. "You're thinking it's time for that—what did you call it? 'Trojan horse,' wasn't it?—of yours?"

"Maybe it is," Frugoni said seriously. "We've got more people than we ever had before. Thanks to Eldbrand, we've got guns for them. Thanks to Lazlo and Rachel, we've got the pilots. And if the Manties come through with the naval support, we're golden."

"Mighty big 'if' in there, if you don't mind my sayin'," MacGruder observed.

"Gonna be a pretty fair-sized 'if' in anything we do, Jase," Allenby replied thoughtfully. "And Vinnie's got a point. Haven't had our skies clear of Frontier Fleet bastards in a long time, and this time we've got the guns and the bodies to take advantage of it. Assuming Vinnie's brainstorm works, of course."

"And also assumin' we can take out Karaxis' HQ on schedule. Hope you didn't forget that minor detail." MacGruder seemed extraordinarily placid about the possibility.

"No. No, haven't forgotten," Allenby said. "Haven't forgotten a thing."

JUNE 1922 POST DIASPORA

"Damn. Wish he'd been smarter."

— Master Sergeant
Alexandra Mikhailov
Solarian League Marines
(retired)

Chapter Forty-Five

"CLEARANCE READINESS FROM Junction Central, Ma'am," Lieutenant Sughavanam announced. "We're number ten for transit."

"Thank you, Traxton," Ginger Lewis responded as the scarlet "10" appeared beside *Charles Ward*'s icon in her maneuvering display. Technically, the next few minutes were Dimitri Nakhimov's responsibility, but no captain ever let someone else make her first wormhole transit. So instead of Nakhimov, she raised her eyes from the display to look at Angelina Dreyfus.

"Put us in the outbound lane, Chief."

"Aye, aye, Ma'am," Dreyfus replied. Skilled fingers played the control buttons set into her joystick with a maestro's skill, and the three-million-ton starship responded with thistledown-grace. Ginger watched the icon on the maneuvering display settle exactly into its proper position, and then Dreyfus looked up from her own display.

"In the lane, Ma'am."

"Nicely done," Ginger acknowledged and switched her attention to the visual display.

There was a strangeness to the traffic through the Manticoran Wormhole Junction's termini. She was far from surprised to see it, but the strangeness still seemed profoundly... unnatural.

It wasn't so much that there was less traffic— although there *was* less of it—than that the inbound lanes were so sparsely populated, without the conveyor belt-like progression of incoming freighters, passenger liners, dispatch boats, and couriers. That was Operation Lacoön, she thought. Manticore's far-flung merchant fleet had returned home, the traffic serving the Solarian League had ceased entirely, and while the traffic to non-Solarian destinations was actually picking up, there was still far less of it. According to her intelligence briefings, that non-Solarian traffic would be increasing, possibly dramatically, in the very near future, though. The abrupt cessation of the decades of cold and hot war with the Republic of Haven was in the process of opening enormous new economic possibilities for both nations, and a lot of the idled carrying trade was already picking up charters to Havenite destinations. Perhaps as much to the point, there were a lot of independent and nominally independent star systems in the Verge, and many of them would be delighted to trade with Manticore rather than the Solarian League... assuming the Star Empire was still around to be traded with.

That was a qualifier she didn't much like, and she told herself once again that she and her crew weren't deserting their posts. It wasn't like the *CW*—at least the crew had settled on that much, she thought, lips twitching in an almost-smile—could have contributed much to the system's defense when the Solarian battle fleet everyone knew was en route actually arrived. Nor would the sizable detachment of cruisers and destroyers accompanying the *CW* to the Talbott Quadrant have made much difference to such a clash of titans. Somehow she doubted that made any of them any happier to be leaving at this particular moment than her own people were.

Besides, she told herself, *it's not like Home Fleet hasn't found a perfectly suitable replacement for our own mighty armament.*

She snorted mentally at that, her eyes on the endless chain of ships headed *out* of the Manticore Binary System. Most were freighters and transports headed for Talbott, or for the repair yards at Trevor's Star which were being upgraded as rapidly as possible to provide some fragment of the fleet support which had been lost in the home system. Others, however, were headed for the Beowulf Terminus, although there were fewer "freighters" in that transit queue than the casual observer might suspect. Or she hoped to hell any "casual observers" *did* suspect, anyway.

Charles Ward moved steadily forward with the other Talbott-bound vessels. The far smaller—and more lethal—cruisers and destroyers ahead and astern of her were minnows beside her bulk, although *she* was dwarfed by the even larger vessels headed for Beowulf.

CPO Dreyfus held their place in the outbound queue without further orders, and Ginger punched up Engineering as they neared the departure beacon. Kumanosuke Lawson's face appeared on the small display by her right knee.

"Engineering," he acknowledged.

"Commander," she said, rather more formally than

she might have spoken to another of her officers. "Stand by to reconfigure to Warshawski sail."

"Aye, Captain," he said. "Standing by to reconfigure."

Ginger nodded and watched the cruiser ahead of the *CW* drift farther forward. The other ship hesitated for just an instant, and then blinked out of existence, and the number on Ginger's maneuvering display changed to "1."

"Cleared to transit, Ma'am," Sughavanam said.

"Good. Tell Junction Central thanks," she replied, and looked back at Dreyfus. "Take us in, Chief."

"Aye, aye, Ma'am."

Charles Ward drifted ahead at only twenty gravities, aligning herself perfectly on the invisible rails of the Junction, and Ginger watched her display intently. It was a good thing the RMN believed all its engineering officers should be bridge-certified "just in case." There'd been plenty of times when she'd seriously resented the requirement that an engineer spend time in maneuvering simulators and on actual starships' bridges. Then again, she'd never expected to find herself *commanding* a starship, either. Or, at least, not without a stint as a major hyper-capable ship's XO first!

Of course, I did have that time as the Kitty's *acting XO in Monica until Ansten got back on his feet, didn't I?* she thought around a familiar flicker of pain for *Hexapuma* and all the friends who'd died with her. *That has to count for something.*

No doubt it did, but she cherished no illusions about her ability to emulate a ship handler like Aivars Terekhov or Duchess Harrington. Which made it no less important to demonstrate—to herself, as well as her ship's company—that she was at least competent in that respect.

Charles Ward's light code flashed bright green as the big support ship settled into exact position, and Ginger looked back at her com display.

"Rig foresail for transit."

"Aye, aye, Ma'am," Lawson replied. "Rigging foresail . . . now."

The *CW*'s impeller wedge dropped abruptly to half strength as her forward nodes reconfigured to produce a circular disk of focused gravitation over three hundred kilometers in diameter.

"Stand by to rig aftersail on my mark," Ginger murmured as *Charles Ward* continued to creep forward under the power of her after impellers.

A new readout appeared as that steady motion slid the rigged Warshawski sail steadily deeper into the focused funnel of hyper-space that was the gateway to Talbott. The readout danced rapidly higher as the sail began drawing power from the tortured gravity waves twisting eternally through the Junction, and Ginger watched them carefully. She knew she had a window of almost thirty seconds, but that didn't mean she wanted to be sloppy, or—

The dancing numbers crossed the threshold. The foresail was now drawing sufficient power to provide movement, and she nodded sharply at Lawson.

"Rig aftersail now!"

"Rigging aftersail, aye, Captain."

Whatever demons might be following Kumanosuke Lawson around, he ran his department like a precision chronometer, and *Charles Ward* twitched ever so slightly as her impeller wedge disappeared entirely and a second Warshawski sail sprung to life at the far end of her hull.

The transition from impeller to sail was one of the trickier maneuvers with which a helmswoman had to deal, but Angelina Dreyfus' skilled hands gentled the big support ship through the conversion with barely a quiver. She held the ship rock-steady, and Ginger's fingers tightened on her chair arm as a familiar queasiness assailed her. Few people ever really adjusted to the sensation of crossing the wall between n-space and hyperspace, and her stomach seemed to have more trouble with it than most. The fact that the gradient was so much steeper in a junction transit only made that worse, but at least it would be over soon, she reminded herself as she concentrated on maintaining her serene expression.

The maneuvering display blinked, and for an instant no human sense or chronometer had ever been able to measure, HMS *Charles Ward* ceased to exist. In theory, it wasn't *truly* instantaneous, although no one had ever been able to confirm that theory experimentally. Ginger wasn't hugely interested in "theory," however, and she concentrated on controlling her nausea as her ship snapped—whether "instantaneously" or not—across better than six light-centuries in that fragment of time no one could measure.

That nausea spiked abruptly, but then it eased once more, vanishing with the transit energy radiating from *Charles Ward*'s sails, almost as quickly, and she sighed in relief.

"Transit complete," Chief Dreyfus reported.

"Thank you. That was well executed," Ginger replied, watching the numbers spiral downward once more. "Engineering, reconfigure to impeller."

"Aye, aye, Captain. Reconfiguring to impeller now."

Charles Ward folded her wings back into her impeller wedge and moved forward more rapidly, accelerating steadily away from the terminus in the wake of the cruiser which had preceded her.

✧   ✧   ✧

"Can I get you anything else, Ma'am?" Jared Pallavicini inquired. "More coffee?"

"No, Jared, I think we're fine," Ginger replied. "Just leave us the Glenlivet and the glasses, and we'll take it from there." She smiled. "I promise I'll buzz you if something else occurs to me."

"Of course, Ma'am." Pallavicini produced the required glasses, gave each a ceremonial swipe with a spotless napkin, and placed them precisely on the table, flanking the whiskey bottle. Then he withdrew, closing the pantry door behind him, and Ginger heard a chuckle from the far side of the table.

"What?" she asked, looking at her guest.

"You're making progress with him," Sinead Terekhov replied. "I don't think he offered you more Alfredo sauce more than twice!"

"Don't you go picking on Jared," Ginger told her with a twinkle. "And for God's sake don't say anything about more food where he might hear you! Sying-ni's done wonders with him, and I don't want you undoing her good work!"

"Not for anything in the world," Sinead reassured her, and they smiled at each other as Ginger uncapped the bottle and poured. Then they sat back, glasses in hand, at the table in the dining cabin which seemed much larger with only the two of them.

"That's good," Sinead said, sipping from her glass.

"I can't really claim a very discerning palate where whiskey and wines are concerned," Ginger admitted. "I know I really liked Glenlivet when Captain Terekhov introduced me to it, though." She shook her head with a bittersweet smile of memory. "I wasn't the only one in the *Kitty*'s wardroom who decided to stock up when I got the chance. Didn't realize how much it *cost*, though!"

"I wouldn't necessarily call Aivars' palate 'discerning,'" Sinead said, after a moment. "But he does have good instincts—in most things, not just wines or liqueurs. And when he makes up his mind about something—or someone—he doesn't look back or second-guess himself."

"I know what you mean. The Captain—well, Commodore, I suppose—isn't exactly what anyone might call wishy-washy." Ginger smiled, but the smile faded and her gaze turned a little troubled.

"What?" Sinead asked as the brief silence drew out, and Ginger shook herself.

"Oh, I'm just wondering—maybe worrying a little—over how he's going to react to the entire notion of our being *allied* to Haven." She looked her guest in the eye. "He never actually talked about it, Sinead, but I looked up the official record on Hyacinth. I know what happened to so many of his people, and how badly he was hurt himself. And he tried to hide it in Nuncio, but I knew . . . When he found out the 'pirates' were renegade StateSec ships, I knew how it hit him. I don't know if he ever realized I did, but Ansten FitzGerald and I both knew."

"I'm not surprised," Sinead said quietly. "And I wish I could tell you how he's likely to react. Oh, I know how he'll react *intellectually!* He's a very smart man, my husband, and only an idiot would think this was anything other than the best news we've had since the Battle of Spindle. But emotionally...that's likely to be harder. And it may be even harder when he finds out how many of our friends—not just all the people on *Hexapuma*, but people like Peter Patterson and his wife—we've lost." She inhaled deeply and shook her head. "I think he'd actually laid the ghosts of Hyacinth after Monica, but now..."

"Well, if anything's likely to help him deal with all that, it would probably be seeing you." Ginger smiled again, more broadly. "That portrait he keeps in his cabin is nice, but I suspect it's not *quite* as nice as having the original in hugging range."

"Oh, not simply *hugging* range, dear girl!" Sinead said with a wicked chuckle, and Ginger laughed.

"The truth is," she said after a moment, "that I'm really pleased to have you aboard, and I'm looking forward to the Commodore's reaction when you just turn up. He needs something to shake up his routine, you know. But I can't help thinking you'd have been more comfortable on one of the personnel transports."

"Nonsense!" Sinead sipped more whiskey. "They pack you into one of those things like canned peas! And that's especially true now. If I was aboard one of those transports, I'd probably be sharing a single state room with at least one other anxious wife." She shuddered delicately. "No, thank you! I've done that in the past. Besides, you and your officers are far better company than I'd find over there. I especially like Dr. Massarelli, and young Paula is a sweetheart!"

"Well, I wish you'd at least let me move you into

better quarters," Ginger protested. "We've got more space aboard the *CW* than any other ship I've ever served in, Sinead! For that matter, I have an entire additional sleeping cabin right here. It's *got* to be more comfortable than the bunks down there in Snotty Row!"

"I am not yet feeble," Sinead replied with a grin, "and I'm not going to bounce you—or one of your other officers—out of your quarters. It was kind enough of you to offer me a lift in the first place. Besides," her grin faded, "Paula needs the company."

And that, Ginger reflected, was entirely true.

She'd never imagined, when Sinead Terekhov told her she'd been granted priority for naval transport and that she'd like to accompany *Charles Ward* to Talbott, that she'd choose to make the voyage in the quarters normally assigned to the ship's midshipmen. For that matter, she was reasonably certain *Sinead* hadn't considered that possibility...until she arrived onboard and discovered that Paula Rafferty was all alone down there.

"I won't pretend I'm not grateful for the way you're... looking after her, Sinead," she said, after a moment. "I'm not too sure how happy the Commodore's going to be with me when he finds out I let you travel in steerage, though!"

"You just leave Aivars to me." Sinead's smile returned. "Besides, he'll understand."

"You're probably right about that." Ginger shook her head, gazing down into her whiskey glass. "I think he tries to hide it sometimes, but he always seems to be able to spot anyone under his command who's in trouble. Don't get me wrong, Ansten FitzGerald stayed on top of everything that happened to any of the *Kitty*'s people. But it just always seemed that whenever I looked up, the Commodore was always... I don't know. He was just always *there*, whenever anyone needed him."

"That's Aivars' way," Sinead said. "And...there's probably another reason it seemed that way to *you*, dear."

Ginger's eyes snapped up from her glass, meeting Sinead's across the table, and her mouth opened. But Sinead held up her hand before she could speak.

"Ginger," she said gently, "I don't for one instant believe anything *remotely* improper ever happened between you and Aivars. One of the very few immutable certainties of this universe is my husband's fidelity. But ever since his return to active service, he's had an even greater tendency to...mentor, let's say, promising young officers. Especially promising young *female* officers."

Ginger had closed her mouth again, but her eyes were still distressed, and Sinead shook her head.

"I've known Aivars Terekhov for the next best thing to fifty T-years, and because of that, I know he'd never allow favoritism to color his actions or his decisions. But I come from a Navy family myself," she said with, Ginger reflected, massive understatement, "and I also know he understands a senior officer's responsibility to groom, train, and *support* promising junior officers. He'd do that for anyone he thought was as good at her—or his—job as you are. But there's a reason he's especially supportive of his female junior officers. A reason which applies rather strongly in your own case, I suspect."

"A reason?" Ginger repeated when the older woman paused.

"Yes." Sinead's eyes softened. "You look a great deal like me, Ginger. But you look even more like Anastasia."

"Anastasia?"

"Our daughter," Sinead said quietly, and Ginger stiffened.

"Nastyen'ka was never interested in the Navy, unnatural child that she was," Sinead continued with a wistful smile. "She was interested in planets, and she begged, pleaded, and pestered until she got her way. She was a little too much like both her parents in that respect, I think. But about the time Aivars returned to active service after the Battle of Hancock, she was accepted into the Sphinx Forestry Service's intern program. I never saw her happier in her life! And then, about a year later, she fell from a crown oak during a treecat rescue mission and her counter-grav failed to activate."

Ginger inhaled sharply, and Sinead nodded.

"She suffered catastrophic brain trauma," she said in a steady voice. "The SFS airlifted her out immediately, but she was gone by the time they reached the trauma unit. If she'd lived, she'd be about a year younger than you are now."

"I never..." Ginger shook her head, and Sinead reached across the table to lay one hand on her forearm.

"Ginger, Aivars would have recognized the qualities which make you the officer you are even if you'd been male, two meters tall, and covered with hair! And I am *not* telling you he values you because you remind him of Nastyen'ka. I'm simply saying he sees an echo of her in *every* promising young woman he meets, and that because you look so much like her, he probably sees that echo even more strongly in your case. And one of the reasons I'm telling you this is that *I* do, too. Neither of us thinks you're a replacement for our daughter, and both of us value you for who you *are*, but I think it's right for you to know about her. And perhaps it'll help you understand why I'm perfectly content down in 'Snotty Row' with young Paula. She's a Queen's officer, not a child, but she's also young woman who's lost her entire family. If she needs a *non*-Navy shoulder to cry on, just a bit, I have one that's perfectly serviceable."

❖   ❖   ❖

Well, well, well, Rufino Chernyshev thought. *Isn't that interesting?*

He pursed his lips, whistling softly for several seconds as he considered the message which had just reached him through the covert channel to "Manticore" Damien Harahap had set up for Tomasz Szponder and the Free Thought Crusade.

A part of him felt almost guilty, he realized. That was probably inevitable—to really succeed at this sort of thing, an operator had to be able to genuinely empathize with the people he was manipulating—but what he mostly felt was intense satisfaction.

He gazed at his display for another few seconds, then nodded and opened a window to post a memo and keyed his microphone live.

"Confirm receipt," he said, watching the words appear. "Assure them support will be there within twenty-four hours either side of their proposed execution date."

Chapter Forty-Six

"SHUMAN CENTRAL CONTROL, this is Victor-Lima-One-Seven-Seven. Request final docking clearance."

"Hold one, Victor-Lima," the thoroughly bored traffic controller aboard the *Donald Ulysses and Rosa Aileen Shuman Space Station* (more commonly—and not especially affectionately—known as *Dumber Ass*, from its initials), the Swallow System's primary space station, replied. "Checking the boards."

"Roger, Shuman Central. Victor-Lima-One-Seven-Seven copies. Holding at the approach beacon."

The controller brought up her schedule, and flight VL177 blinked a bright, authorized green. Well, of course it did. VL177 was a Tallulah mining shuttle, and Tallulah's shuttles and courier boats and freighters—and the armed sting ships of Tallulah Security Enterprises, based right here on *Dumber Ass*—went wherever the hell they liked and did whatever the hell they wanted, although why a mining shuttle was coming *up* from Swallow was an interesting question.

Probably down for some major overhaul, she thought.

Damned things may not be configured *for atmosphere, but that doesn't mean they can't handle it if they have to. And if they go slow enough!*

"Victor-Lima-One-Seven-Seven, Shuman Central. I have you on the schedule. You are cleared to dock at the Alpha-Tango-Seven beacon. Confirm copy."

"Shuman Central, Victor-Lima-One-Seven-Seven copies cleared to approach on docking beacon Alpha-Tango-Seven. Initiating thrust."

"Confirmed, Victor-Lima. Have a nice visit," the controller said and watched her radar as the bulky shuttle's reaction thrusters—impeller wedges were banned this close to the station—sent it towards its assigned docking bay.

❖　　❖　　❖

"Well, so far so—" the shuttle pilot began.

"Don't say it!" the purple-haired woman in the copilot's seat cut him off sharply. He looked at her, one eyebrow quirked, and Staff Sergeant Rachel Lamprecht, Solarian League Marines (retired) shook her head. "You don't go around jinxing perfectly good operations that way," she told him severely. "I thought we'd taught you people that, Truman?"

"Guess I forgot," Truman Rodriguez replied with a casual air that fooled neither of them. "And, by the way. If I forgot to mention it before we lifted, thanks for coming along."

"De nada," Lamprecht said, waving one hand.

Rodriguez nodded and turned back to his controls. She might have waved it off, but he hoped she knew how much he'd meant it. Unlike him, the only dog Lamprecht—or, for that matter, Laszlo Hiratasuka and Alexandra Mikhailov—had in this fight was their decades-long friendship for Vincent Frugoni. That was something a Swallowan could understand—even an adopted Swallowan like Rodriguez—but it still wasn't her fight.

It *was* Truman Rodriguez's fight, though. He was as much an immigrant to Swallow as Vincent Frugoni and Sandra Allenby, and his job as a Tallulah Resource Extraction Enterprises pilot paid remarkably well, for the Swallow System. But he'd been assigned to this star system for over thirty T-years. He had a wife, four kids, and an extended family which included Floyd Allenby.

And I've seen what something like Tallulah means for my kids and my grandkids, however good it may look for me, he thought grimly. *No freaking way is that happening to my girls!*

"Docking collar in fifteen minutes, Vinnie," he said into his mike. Then glanced over his shoulder at his flight engineer.

"Send it, Joyce," he said, and Eileanóra Allenby's niece nodded.

"Sending," she said, and tapped a transmit key.

❖   ❖   ❖

"Fifteen minutes, Jase! Signal just came in!"

"Then I reckon it's 'bout time we got this here excursion underway," Jason MacGruder replied.

At the moment, his air lorry was cruising idly through the MacIntyre Gap, coming up on Fort Golden Eagle, the central command post of the Swallow System Army. Since the Swallow System had a unified military, that meant Fort Golden Eagle was the central command nexus for all of Swallow's armed forces. More to the point of MacGruder's present perspective, however, was that it was also the SSA's central equipment depot. At any given time, somewhere around eighty percent of Felicia Karaxis' ground combat vehicles and more like eighty-five percent of her aircraft were neatly lined up at Fort Golden Eagle. The numbers were a bit lower than that at the moment, given the presence Karaxis had built up around the Cripple Mountains in response to the Cripple Mountain Movement, but that was fine with MacGruder. The CMM knew exactly where all those armed air cars, APCs, and light tanks were . . . and thanks to Eldbrand's generosity, there was something they could do about it.

Just as MacGruder was about to do a little something about Fort Golden Eagle.

He touched the transmit key on his dashboard com.

"Gemma, you got those power cells for me?" he asked casually.

"Told you I did," a voice came back. "Why? You running low?"

"Nah," he said, feeding more power to the turbines and settling to a slightly lower altitude as he accelerated down the Gap towards Fort Golden Eagle. "Just checkin'. Know you can be a bit forgetful sometimes."

"Ha!" The reply came back with fine disdain. "That's rich, coming from *you!* But don't worry. I'll get 'em to you right on time," Floyd Allenby's sister told him.

"That's a real comfort," MacGruder replied, and smiled as the Fort Golden Eagle perimeter beacon came up on his HUD.

❖   ❖   ❖

"What does that idiot think he's doing?" Major Brinton Avery demanded as the civilian icon swept towards the outer perimeter. "Don't tell me he doesn't know this is restricted airspace!"

"Dunno about that, Sir," the duty sergeant replied. "Got a lot of people taking the shortcut through the Gap. Some of 'em aren't all that careful about their navigation, either."

"Well, this *one*'s about to get his ass in a heap of trouble!" Avery said, and hit the guard frequency.

"Unidentified civilian traffic at three hundred meters, eighty-five kilometers, west-southwest, this is Golden Eagle Flight Ops. You are entering restricted airspace. Turn away immediately."

Nothing happened for a moment, then—

"Golden Eagle Flight Ops, this is Tallulah-Sierra-Niner-Two," a voice came back. "I know it's restricted airspace. Check your clearance list."

Avery frowned and snapped his fingers at the duty sergeant, then pointed at her terminal. *He* hadn't seen anything about a Tallulah special flight when he came on duty!

"Nothing showing here, Sir," the sergeant said after a moment while the air lorry swept steadily closer.

"Tallulah-Sierra-Niner-Two, Golden Eagle Flight Ops. I do not—repeat, do *not*—show you on the clearance list. Turn away now."

"Look, laddie," the voice came back, "if you want to explain to General Karaxis why the stuffed snow bear Ms. Hampton told me to deliver to her for Mr. Parkman isn't in her office by sundown, that's fine with me. But if you don't want to explain that, then you'd better find me on your list!"

Oh, crap, Avery thought. *The one thing that'll get my ass canned in a heartbeat is to piss off the General. But, damn it, they* aren't *on the list!*

He punched in a command, swiveling the main

camera head, and his frown deepened as the oncoming lorry sprang into sharp focus on his visual display. The vehicle was definitely painted in Tallulah's livery, and its shiny, freshly polished look suited someone delivering a personal gift to Felicia Karaxis from Alton Parkman. It was a full-sized Torro-class heavy-lift lorry, not a merc van—way too big to be transporting a single snow bear. But, of course, that wasn't necessarily the only thing it had aboard.

None of which solved his problem.

He frowned for another long moment's thought, then drew a deep breath as the lorry crossed the *inner* perimeter.

"Tallulah-Sierra-Niner-Two, Golden Eagle Ops," he said. "You are not—repeat, *not*—cleared to the primary field. Divert to Bravo Three. You'll be met by a security team and—"

❖   ❖   ❖

"...a security team and—"

"Reckon it's about time." Jason MacGruder's tone was relaxed, almost casual, but sweat beaded his forehead as the glanced at the young man seated beside him. "Jessop?"

"Go for it," Jessop Allenby replied tautly.

MacGruder slammed the throttle through the gate and the turbines, borrowed from one of Cripple Mountain Search and Rescue Command's high-speed, heavy-lift rescue ships, howled.

❖   ❖   ❖

"Good seal," the docking bay controller announced as Truman Rodriguez's shuttle settled into the buffers and the personnel tube mated with its hatch.

"Thank you," Rodriguez acknowledged pleasantly,

then smiled as Vincent Frugoni and ninety heavily armed men and women stormed through that tube and into *Donald Ulysses and Rosa Aileen Shuman Space Station.*

Fortunately for the bay controller, he was a very fast-thinking man. He got his hands up in less than 2.5 seconds.

❖   ❖   ❖

"What the—?!" the duty sergeant began, and Brinton Avery's stomach turned to ice as he realized he'd waited too long to divert the Tallulah air lorry.

It sprang forward at at least twice its listed maximum velocity, and a corner of his brain wondered exactly what had been done to its engines. It was only a very *tiny* corner, though. All the rest of it was focused on the deadly stream of cluster munitions spilling from its belly hatch. The programmable weapons' stubby wings popped out, they banked sharply away from the lorry, and Avery watched in something that longed desperately to be disbelief as they blanketed Fort Golden Eagle's primary ground armor park in a red-and-white surf of chemical explosives.

His hand darted out without any conscious decision on his part and his thumb jammed down on the emergency alert button. Alarms began to warble all over the base, duty sections raced to man their weapons, but no one had expected anything like this! As he watched, the improvised bomber changed course. It swept across the parked air cav mounts and atmospheric sting ships with that seemingly inexhaustible store of cluster bombs still tumbling from its belly hatch, and the bright blue flare of exploding hydrogen reservoirs ripped through them in its wake. It didn't get all of them, of course, but it got *most* of them. And as it dropped down on the deck, screaming across the military reservation at just under Mach 1, false panels on its exterior blew free and a quartet of Rattlesnake Ground Attack Missiles blasted from their concealment.

One of the pre-programmed, precision guided weapons took out the three ready-duty sting ships on the parking apron. The second impacted directly on the base's central air-defense station; and the third and fourth blew the transmitting masts atop Felicia Karaxis' HQ building into blazing wreckage.

✧   ✧   ✧

The man in the Tallulah Security Enterprises uniform looked up in astonishment as the door to TSE's on-station com center opened abruptly and half a dozen heavily armed men and women swept into the compartment.

"*Don't!*" the tall, brown-haired woman at their head said sharply, but instinct had already betrayed him. His hand scrabbled at the pulser holstered at his side, and a single shot from the ugly flechette gun in her hands cut him almost in half.

"Damn," Master Sergeant Alexandra Mikhailov (retired) said almost mildly. "Wish he'd been smarter."

✧   ✧   ✧

Major Avery stared sickly at the flame, smoke, and debris rising in the air lorry's wake, trying to understand how a single vehicle could have wreaked such havoc. Flames vomited from the HQ block, the Rattlesnake hit on Air Defense Central sent an evil, anvil-headed cloud heavenward, and he saw men and women bursting out into the open, staring up in shock and confusion. The lorry squatted low to the ground, screaming directly west across the thousand-square kilometer area set aside for training maneuvers at barely fifty meters. No one on the ground was remotely capable of effective action as it swung further north, streaking back up MacIntyre Gap at that same, preposterous speed.

And as it sped north, drawing every eye to its passage, over a dozen more heavily modified civilian vehicles—lorries, vans, and at least one search-and-rescue skimmer—came slicing up from the *south*.

Air Defense Central's destruction fatally compromised Fort Golden Eagle's aerial defenses, and those vehicles spread out across the base. Heavy tribarrels, delivered courtesy of Harvey Eldbrand and fitted to most of those "civilian vehicles," spat rivers of explosive darts. They went through the surviving air cavalry mounts and the armored ground vehicles like chainsaws of fire, leaving broken, blazing wreckage in their trail, and two of them swooped down on the already blazing HQ block and put a dozen smaller missiles—mixed high explosive and incendiary—into the SSA's central command nexus.

❖   ❖   ❖

Leroy Yelland looked up from his cards as the ready room door slammed open.

"What the f—?!" he began, then froze and sat very, very still as Master Sergeant Mikhailov showed him the muzzle of her flechette gun.

Abiola Wilhelmsen, the other ready-duty sting ship pilot, and Ramiro Maxwell, one of the squadron's maintenance techs, sat just as still. Wilhelmsen laid his cards face down on the table and carefully raised both hands. Maxwell simply sat paralyzed, his eyes huge.

"Nice to see some sanity this time," Mikhailov said with a thin, cold smile. "Now if the lot of you will come this way, please?"

Her twitched flechette gun summoned all three TSE employees out of their chairs like a magic wand. Two of the armed civilians with her took charge of them, ushering them roughly, though not brutally, out of the ready room and into the lounge area next door.

As they entered the lounge, Yelland saw another forty or fifty TSE and Tallulah Corporation personnel seated at the food court's tables. One of his own keepers used her military-grade pulse rifle to point at an unoccupied table.

"Why don't you fellas have a sit-down?" Her genial tone fooled none of them. "You just keep your hands on the table top or the top of your heads, whichever you prefer, and you'll do just fine. Let those hands go wanderin', though, and—"

She shrugged, but one glance at the pair of flechette gun-armed men positioned to cover the entire room without intruding into one another's lines of fire completed the sentence quite adequately in Leroy Yelland's opinion.

He sat with his back to the rest of the lounge and his mind raced in at least a dozen directions at once, like an entire cage of crazed hamsters, while it tried to figure out what the *hell* was happening. Then his eyes widened as a quartet of men and women in flight suits jogged past the lounge's open door.

❖   ❖   ❖

"Good morning, people," Vincent Frugoni said as the lift car's doors opened and he and the fifteen CMM fighters with him stepped out onto *Dumber Ass'* central control room. Another thirty of his people had peeled off on the way here—moving with the smooth precision of the Solarian Marines, thanks to Alexandra Mikhailov's training—and secured the route from the shuttle bay to the space station's electronic brain.

The control room personnel whirled at the sound of his voice, and he heard someone swear in surprise as the CMM's numbers—and armament—registered.

"This space station is now under the control of the Cripple Mountain Movement," he continued, mostly accurately. "As of this moment, all communications are down unless *I* tell you differently. That includes *you*, Ms. MacDerry!" he said sharply as one com tech's hand twitched towards her panel.

She snatched her hand back into her lap and stared at him goggle-eyed, more surprised by the fact that he knew her name than that he'd seen her hand move. He smiled and twitched the muzzle of the pulser in his hand.

"In fact, just to keep any of your colleagues from doing anything foolish, why don't all of you move over here by Commander Hewitt." He nodded almost companionably to the station's administrator, standing rigid and still frozen in shock. "That way we can keep an eye on all of you without getting cricks in our necks," he told MacDerry. None of them moved for an instant, and his face hardened. "*Now*, people," he said in a quiet tone more terrifying than any bellow, and feet scrambled suddenly to obey him.

"Better," he said.

"Yo." Floyd Allenby answered his com laconically and listened for a moment, then nodded. "Thanks,"

he said, equally briefly. He cut the connection and punched in another combination, looking down through the icy, crystal Cripple Mountains' morning at the Swallow System Army's Camp Justice, well over two thousand meters below him.

He could think of very few less appropriate names for the sprawl of temporary barracks, the vehicle park, and the air cav mounts parked on its small airfield. Although, he reflected, there was a certain amount of "justice" in what was about to happen to it.

The com chimed at him, announcing the establishment of the programmed conference call.

"Sandra's coming," he said quietly.

Colonel Brenda Johnson sipped orange juice, then set the glass back down and reached for her fork once more. Johnson was a member of the System Security Force, and the SSF was the component of the system's military which corresponded most closely to an actual police force. As such, she sometimes wondered how she'd wound up in command of Camp Justice. She was a Lowland girl, and these mountains were cold enough to freeze the ass off a statue. The people who lived in them were no great prize, either. But at least the food was good, and—

The first shoulder-fired missile came shrieking down the morning sky from the high ridge to the east. It slammed directly into the tank farm for Camp Justice's ground vehicles and air cav, and a huge fireball of exploding hydrogen soared into the heavens. The next half dozen missiles—with blast-fragmentation and incendiary warheads—landed a heartbeat later, ripping into the camp's crowded barracks and mess halls.

Men and women screamed in agony as they were blown apart, scourged by blast and shrapnel, or set afire. Some of the wounded rolled on the ground, beating at their flaming clothing. Others simply ran in panic, and the wind of their passage fanned the flames higher.

The launchers along the ridgeline reloaded, and a second wave of explosions ripped through the camp's vehicle park. Armored units exploded and air cav mounts tumbled end for end as the shockwaves clawed at them.

Then the mortars to the north opened fire, adding their heavier, even more destructive hate to the holocaust, and the three heavy tribarrels concealed on the slope eight hundred meters below Allenby's position opened up, pouring their devastating fire into the sea of smoke and flame.

Colonel Johnson, her XO, and *his* immediate subordinate were all dead before the first tribarrel dart arrived on its target. And at exactly the same moment, at six other locations covering the approach to the Cripples, six other base commanders' breakfasts suffered the same fiery interruption.

"Now you two just remember the plan," Rachel Lamprecht said in a calm, matter-of-fact tone as she and Staff Sergeant Laszlo Hiratasuka (also retired) led the way into the launch bay. "The important thing is for both of you to take your time getting the feel of the controls, right?"

Joyce Allenby nodded, hoping she didn't look as nervous as she probably did, and glanced at Orrin MacGruder. She and Orrin were highly skilled pilots. In fact, both of them carried Unlimited Licenses, and Orrin had taken the Swallow Trans-Atmospheric Racing Association's Donald Ulysses Shuman Memorial Cup in the last season before Sandra Allenby's death. Neither of them, however, had ever piloted a sting ship in their lives.

Fortunately, that was exactly what Lamprecht and Hiratasuka had spent the last twenty or thirty T-years doing. And they'd rigged simulators aboard a pair of *Sky Shark*-class racing ships when they arrived as "tourists" on one of Vincent Frugoni's charters from Wonder six T-months ago. It wasn't the same as actual sting ship cockpit time, but it was a hell of a lot better than nothing!

"Remember," Lamprecht continued as they crossed the bay to the two ready-duty ships, "TSE uses Lanza Corporation's *Relámpago*-class ships, and the *Relámpagos* actually aren't quite as hot as the *Sky Shark*. They're more maneuverable out of atmosphere because they've got heavier grav plates that let you pull higher gees, but their top acceleration rate's a good ten gees lower."

The shaven-headed Hiratasuka was punching commands into the bay's central console, and green standby lights flickered to amber above the docking hatches of a second pair of sting ships while the automated systems began loading missiles onto the external racks.

"They've got a lot more endurance, too, of course," Lamprecht went on. "What matters most at the moment, though, is that with those Frontier Fleet bastards gone, we've just taken control of the only exo-atmo armed ships in the entire frigging star system." Her smile was fiercely predatory, and her brown eyes glittered. "I don't think Shuman and Parkman are going to like that one little bit!"

Chapter Forty-Seven

"MS. TEREKHOV IS HERE, SIR," the midshipman escort said, and Admiral Augustus Khumalo walked around his desk with his hand held out as the elegantly dressed red-haired woman stepped into his day cabin.

"Ms. Terekhov!" he said as her slender hand disappeared into his far more massive one. "I can't tell you how pleased I am to meet you."

His tone, Sinead noted, was sincere. But it carried an edge which suggested his pleasure at seeing her might not be completely un-flawed.

"Admiral," she responded, and smiled at him, then turned to her escort from the boat bay and shook her hand, as well. "Thank you for taking such good care of me, Ms. Pittman," she said, and the young woman smiled, then faced the admiral and braced to attention. He nodded dismissal, and she disappeared back out the door as Sinead turned back to Khumalo.

"Aivars didn't have very long at home before they deployed him back out here, but he told me how much he respected—and appreciated—your response to his discoveries about Monica," she said. "And I've viewed all the reports on the news channels. So, before we say anything else, let me tell you how very grateful I am for your decision to support him." She shook her head. "I come from Navy families on both sides, you know. So I understand exactly what sort of risks you took when you did that."

"Oh, well," the tall, powerfully built admiral seemed a bit nonplussed, and he patted her hand once before he released it, took her elbow, and guided her to the old-fashioned, unpowered but sinfully comfortable couch in the corner of the large compartment.

"There really wasn't any option," he said as he seated her, then sank into the facing armchair. "I mean, his logic was compelling, he'd shown an enormous amount of moral courage in acting upon his conclusions, and if he was right—and I believed he was—then it was essential to take swift, decisive action." He smiled crookedly. "The truth is, he'd already taken the *decisive* action, and it was undoubtedly easier to support him after the fact than it would have been to make the same decision in his place."

"Even if that's true, it doesn't detract one bit from the moral courage it took to back him so completely once you got there." Sinead shook her head again. "And it wasn't exactly 'after the fact,' either, since you had no idea what had happened, how the Solarians might react, or when—or *if*—you'd be reinforced from home. I admit I'm rather proud of Aivars, but don't sell yourself short, Admiral. I promise you, *Aivars* never will."

Khumalo smiled and dipped his head in brief gratitude, but his brown eyes were intent as he leaned back in his chair.

"I appreciate that," he said, "but while I'm very pleased to see you here aboard *Hercules*, I'm also surprised. No one warned any of us you were coming."

"That's because I only decided to come after the Yawata Strike," she replied, green eyes darkening, and he nodded.

"I assumed that was the case," he said quietly, "and I can't tell you how devastated I was personally by what happened to *Hexapuma*. I know we lost a lot of other ships, a lot of other *people*, but she was... special. To a *lot* of people out here, not just to me." He shook his head sadly. "But I'm afraid Aivars is forward-deployed to Montana, not here in Spindle."

"Captain Lewis already shared that information with me." Sinead shrugged. "We noticed as we came in that there seem to be very few warships here in Spindle at the moment."

"No, there aren't. Frankly, we're thin enough on the ground that I'd like to shortstop some of Captain Grierson's units right here. I think, though, that Admiral Caparelli's right. Admiral Gold Peak needs them worse than I do."

"I'm sure that's true," she said. "And while I hope we'll be here in Spindle long enough for me to renew my acquaintance with Baroness Medusa, I'm also eager to catch up with Aivars."

"I see," he said, and that slight edge was back in his tone. He looked at her steadily for a moment, then inhaled and squared his shoulders.

"I'm afraid I don't think that's a very good idea, Ms. Terekhov," he said. She arched an eyebrow at him, and he leaned forward in his chair. "I'm sure you want to see your husband. And I'm confident he'd love to see you, too. But we've adopted a strict policy where Tenth Fleet's dependents here in Talbott are concerned. The situation's highly fluid. We don't know which way the Sollies are likely to jump next, and that means we don't know where Lady Gold Peak's units are going to be. For that matter, we're not certain where they actually *are* right now, given the delays in message transmission. Because of that, we're quartering all Navy dependents here in Spindle rather than forward-deploying them. To the best of my knowledge, your husband's squadron's in Montana, but they may not be there next week, and we're not in a situation that allows any of our units to be officially homeported anywhere here in the Quadrant. So, while I understand your reasons for coming all the way out here, I think it would be best all round for you to remain in Spindle, as well. I'll be delighted to include any personal messages from you to him aboard our next dispatch vessel, and I'm sure *Quentin Saint-James* will cycle back through Spindle...eventually."

"I'm afraid I have no intention of remaining in Spindle," Sinead replied.

"And I'm afraid, Ms. Terekhov, that I'm going to have to insist. And not just because we can't be positive where your husband is at the moment. Oh, that's a significant part of my thinking—somehow I don't think he'd be happy about the notion of your chasing around trying to catch up with him. But—and this is the real reason Tenth Fleet's in-Quadrant dependents are here in Spindle—this is also the safest place for you just now. We have enough missile pods in orbit to prevent anything the Sollies are likely to scare up from breaking our defenses."

"I'm sure I'd be equally safe on any planet protected by Admiral Gold Peak's ships," Sinead said.

"Perhaps you might be. In fact, once you got to Montana and safely down on-planet, you'd probably be just fine," he acknowledged. "But before you got *to* Montana, you'd be aboard a Queen's ship in a war zone. And, forgive me for saying this, Ms. Terekhov, but I have the strangest suspicion that if you discovered upon your arrival that your husband's squadron has been deployed elsewhere, you'd immediately set out for wherever 'elsewhere' might be. And that, I'm afraid, would take you directly into an area of active operations."

"I have Admiralty authorization to travel aboard the *Charles Ward*, Admiral," she told him just a bit frostily.

"Forgive me for pointing this out, but that authorization was for travel to *Spindle*, not to Montana," he said in a tone of genuine regret.

"As the station commander, you could extend that authorization," she observed rather pointedly.

"I could...but I won't." He shook his head again. "I deeply admire and respect your husband, Ms. Terekhov. And I believe I truly do understand why you want to join him. But I'm afraid I can't permit it."

"I can't *believe* that man!" Sinead fumed.

"Oh, *I* can," Ginger said from the other side of the table. The expensive Thimble restaurant surrounded them like some rich, quiet cocoon, and she snorted as she reached for her wine glass. "And, to be completely honest," she continued, "I think there's some point to his argument, Sinead."

"Traitor!" Sinead shook a finger at her across the table-cloth. "Don't you dare get all 'reasonable' about this!"

Ginger chuckled and sipped her wine, then her expression sobered a bit.

"Seriously, Sinead. I might not worry as much as Admiral Khumalo does, and I doubt I'd feel too concerned if you continued forward on a personnel transport. Not even Sollies are going to be deliberately shooting at unarmed people-haulers, except by mistake. But the *CW*'s a legitimate target, and as crazy as things have been out this way—hell, *everywhere!*—there really is the chance someone could get into range to do that shooting. I don't plan to face the Commodore and tell him I let you get killed aboard my ship."

"Don't be silly. First, nothing's going to happen to 'your ship.' Second, if it did, Aivars would never blame *you* for *my* stubbornness. And, third, the personnel transports aren't continuing forward, either." Sinead glowered down into her own wineglass. "The Admiral's unloading everybody he can right here in Spindle because he plans on packing them to the bulkheads with reinforcements for Admiral Gold Peak."

"Well, there you are." Ginger shrugged. "I'm sorry, and I know it's disappointing, but there's really not anything I can do about it. And I won't pretend I'm entirely brokenhearted that I can't, for all the reasons the Admiral's already given you. I like you, Sinead. I like you a lot."

"Thank you." Both Sinead's voice and eyes softened. "I appreciate that. But neither you nor Augustus Khumalo are going to prevent me from doing exactly what I came out here to do. I trust you understand that?"

"Sinead, somehow I doubt *anyone's* stopped you from doing exactly what you wanted for a long, long time," Ginger told her. "But that doesn't mean the Navy's going to help you do it this time."

"Then I'll just have to do it without the Navy," Sinead said composedly. "In the meantime, rather than continue to argue or berate you for your indescribably treacherous support of Admiral Khumalo, why don't we order? I understand the Beef Wellington is marvelous here."

❖　　　❖　　　❖

"This," Adam Šiml said quietly to Filip Malý, his recently acquired personal bodyguard, "is not looking good."

Malý, who'd risen to the rank of lieutenant in the Chotěboř Public Safety Force before Šiml had selected him from among the dozen or so officers Daniel Kápička had personally recommended to him, nodded. In fact, he thought, his new boss had a pronounced gift for understatement.

It was raining hard, and it was winter in the planetary capital of Velehrad. The temperature hovered only a few degrees above freezing, the football pitch was a frigid sea of mud and water—every time the Mělník Warriors' keeper came out of the net curtains of spray flew everywhere—and the players were cold, wet, miserable...and more than a little pissed. In fact, the game should probably have been postponed (or moved to one of the covered stadiums) but the playoff schedule was already complicated and the weather front had moved much faster than the forecasters and weather satellites had predicted. In fact, the sun had been shining brightly through the gathering clouds less than forty-five minutes before the start of play.

And the first rain had begun to fall three minutes into the first half.

Of course, the weather wasn't the *only* thing on Šiml's mind just now. The rivalry between the Warriors and Velehrad Lions was of ancient lineage, dating back—quite literally, in this case—to the years the Kumang system was first colonized, when the Lions had been the *Lvi* and the Warriors had been the *Válečníci*. It was also bone-deep and bitter at the best of times, which today wasn't. The winner of tonight's game went on to the planetary finals; the loser went home, and neither club had any interest in doing that. Nor did their fans, and the home crowd had been expressing its disapproval of the officials for most of the second half. The fact that the Lions had advanced to this point only because they'd eliminated the Benešov Dragons on the basis of the away goals rule after tying their semi-final match with them made the home team's partisans no happier, because the Lions' regular-season record against the Warriors was one-and-three . . . and the Warriors' fans had made their opinion of the way the Lions had "squeaked into" the playoffs abundantly clear.

The players on the field were pulling no punches. It was a wet, brutal, aggressive game, and each team had already been yellow-carded at least once. In the Lions' case, there were no fewer than three of them, including one on Štěpán Jura, their star striker. From where Šiml sat in his warm, dry box, the officials were doing an excellent job under extraordinarily trying circumstances, but he was hardly surprised diehard fans sitting in the cold, drenched open didn't share his opinion.

And the fact that they were in the last two minutes of the second overtime period with the score still tied 2–2 wasn't making them one bit cheerier. If the Lions couldn't score in the next hundred and twenty seconds, they'd be eliminated in exactly the way *they'd* eliminated the Dragons, because the Warriors had scored seven regular season goals in Velehrad during the regular season and the Lions had scored only three in Mělník.

Šiml punched a combination into his com.

"Yes, Adam," a voice responded instantly.

"I'm not sure if it's going to be worse if the Lions score or if they don't, Eduard," Šiml told Eduard Klíma, Sokol's Director of Safety and Security. "Either way, this could get ugly."

"No! You *think*?!" Klíma had known Šiml since they were boys, and his own profound worry burned through his sarcastic tone. Then Šiml heard him draw a deep breath at the other end of the com link.

"I've screened the Velehrad PD for extra officers," he said. "And they're watching the game live downtown, so they already had a pretty good idea how things're looking. The Commissioner's calling in every off-duty cop he can, and they're handing out the riot gear."

"And our own people in the stadium?"

"I've passed the word—to the cops working the crowd, as well as our people—and they're ready to cover the touchline if anybody tries to storm the field. We're trying to get more of the PD's people in here to cover the exits and at least try for crowd control if it turns ugly, but frankly..."

His voice trailed off in the verbal equivalent of a shrug, and Šiml sighed. Chotěbořian football crowds in general weren't noted for reserve and calm during the playoffs. And, unfortunately, the Velehrad fans were even less noted than most for off-field restraint. All of which suggested that unless—

A massive roar went up from the crowd as the Lions' right wing cut inside the Warriors' left wing back and headed the ball sharply to Jura. The entire stadium came to its feet as the striker feinted to the inside, then cut toward the outside. The center back turned to intercept in a blinding blur of motion, mud, and spray, and—

The ball bounced away, spinning out of bounds, and Štěpán Jura lay on his back both hands clutching an obviously broken leg.

Trainers and medical personnel rushed onto the field. It took them several minutes—minutes during which the crowd noise rumbled with mingled anger and shock—to get Jura's leg splinted, lift him onto the counter-grav stretcher, and get him off the field. Finally, though, it was time to resume play . . . and the referee handed the ball to the Warriors.

For just an instant, shocked silence enveloped the stadium. Then the cheers and whistles began from the Mělník side of the field one bare instant before the Velehrad crowd realized that not only had no penalty been called, but the throw-in had been awarded to the *Warriors*.

"Oh, shit," Eduard Klíma said almost conversationally over Šiml's com, and then all hell broke loose.

✧　　✧　　✧

"Christ, Zdeněk!"

Adam Šiml strode back and forth across his office like a caged, unkempt tiger, badly in need of a shave, a shower, a change of clothes, and at least ten uninterrupted hours of sleep. He ran his fingers angrily through his hair, his expression ugly, and his voice was harsh with much more than his obvious exhaustion.

"What a frigging nightmare!" he jerked out. "Bad enough for a *football match*, but this—!"

"It would've been a lot worse without you, Adam," Zdeněk Vilušínský said. "A *lot* worse. I don't think anyone else could've done as much to get them out of the streets again."

"And that's going to be one hell of a lot of comfort to their families, isn't it?" Šiml grated, and Vilušínský was forced to nod unhappily.

The riot in Velehrad Stadium had spread rapidly. At least some of the fans had smuggled truncheons past security—Klíma and the Velehrad Police were asking some very tough questions about just how *that* had happened—but there'd been plenty of beer bottles and temporary overflow seating to use as improvised weapons. And then the riot inside the stadium spilled out into the capital's streets. The replay video of the incident—which clearly showed Jura sliding on the treacherous footing and going down with no contact between any defender and him *or* the ball—hadn't done one thing to quell it . . . especially when some Lions supporter announced it was obviously computer-generated to justify a terrible call! The insanity to which rabid sports fans could fall prey never failed to amaze Adam Šiml, even after all these years.

But once the riot hit the streets, it had only grown in fury, and hastily assembled riot police had moved in. Unfortunately, no one had seen the madness coming. The cops had been assembled on too little notice, and there'd been too few on duty at the outset to deploy in the department's standing riot control plans. They'd done their absolute best, Šiml knew . . . and, in too many cases, they'd simply been plowed under. Ground cars and trams had been overturned, windows smashed, shops and businesses looted. Then the arson had started.

And that was when Jan Cabrnoch ordered Daniel Kápička to deploy the Safety Force to support the city police and "restore calm and public order."

To his credit, Kápička had argued, but Cabrnoch had simply repeated the order. And, as Kápička had feared—and Šiml could have predicted—the instant CPSF uniforms appeared in the capital's streets, what had been a riot of infuriated sports fans became something else entirely. All the resentment which had festered since the Náměstí Žlutých Růží demonstrations had exploded and, for the first time in anyone's memory, rioters—regular citizens, many of whom had been nowhere near the Stadium—actually attacked the CPSF with their bare hands.

Šiml and Sokol's leadership had done everything humanly possible to quell the rioting. They'd been *everywhere*, with Šiml at their head, helping fight fires, helping medical teams, appealing over bullhorns and on the public boards for calm, *pleading* with the rioters to just *go home* to their families. They'd snatched what sleep they could *when* they could, and there'd been damned little of it. For that matter, Šiml's face and torso had been badly bruised when he'd personally intervened at one point and been trampled for his effort.

"Three days, Zdeněk! *Three days!*" He was literally shaking with anger. "If that *idiot*—no, if that frigging *murderer*—hadn't sent the Safeties into that mess, we could've . . . we could've—!"

Words failed him, and he kicked a chair clear across the office. It crashed into the wall and bounced back, and he swore viciously. Then he whirled to face his oldest friend.

"Three hundred and eighty-seven dead," he snarled. "That's the *official* count, but you and I know damned well it's low. And even Cabrnoch admits to four *times* that many badly injured! God only knows how many *more* people who got hurt didn't report to hospital in the middle of all that! And that *bastard* in the Presidential Palace is still passing it off as only sports enthusiasts and thugs who got out of control." His lips worked for a moment and he actually spat on the floor. "Oh, there were 'out-of-control thugs' out there, and *most* of the bastards were wearing uniforms! I will fucking *kill* the miserable piece of shit with my own hands!"

Vilušínský glanced at Filip Malý, who stood attentively against the wall beside the office door. The younger man's expression was as ugly as Šiml's, which was hardly surprising, since there was a very good reason Šiml had selected him from Kápička's nominees. CPSF lieutenant or no, Malý had been a member of Jiskra for over five years.

"Adam, please. Take a deep breath."

"*Take a deep breath?!*" Šiml glared at him incredulously, and Vilušínský shoved up out of his chair and glared right back at him.

"Yes," he said harshly. "I know how furious you are, and I'm just as angry—don't think for an instant I'm not! But I also know how *exhausted* you are. You're not thinking clearly, and God knows you've got every excuse for it! But you have to control yourself. If you don't, if you lose it and openly attack Cabrnoch *now*, what happens to Jiskra and everyone in it?"

Šiml stared at him, and Vilušínský pressed on quickly.

"I know you never wanted what's just happened, but you need to recognize the opportunity in it."

"Opportunity? *What* opportunity?" Šiml demanded, and Vilušínský drew a deep breath. It was a sign of Šiml's fatigue and fury that he hadn't already seen the opening for himself, he thought.

"There are five things you need to consider," he said. "First, this nightmare's brought the opposition to Cabrnoch to a boil. It may cool a bit in the next few weeks, but it'll be there for a hell of a long time. Second, Sabatino and Castelbranco are going to realize that just as clearly as you and I—or Cabrnoch—do. Third, you did more—you and Sokol—to get people back out of the streets and pull the injured out of that goddamned mess than anyone else on the frigging planet. And, fourth, *because* of that, at this moment you're the most popular man in the star system. I know this isn't the way you'd have chosen to bring any of that about, but it's already *happened*, Adam. And that's my *fifth* point, because now that it has, you *have* to control yourself. You've got to go on being the voice of calm reason. Because I can't think of anything that could've done a better job of convincing Sabatino that Cabrnoch's in trouble . . . and that you're *definitely* the best candidate to replace him."

Chapter Forty-Eight

GOVERNOR ORAVIL BARREGOS TURNED from his contemplation of the brilliantly illuminated towers of the Shuttlesport skyline as Jeremy Frank, his senior aide, opened his office door.

Frank stood aside, waving another man courteously through it, then followed the visitor. At a hundred and eighty centimeters, Barregos and his aide were of much the same height, but the newcomer was ten centimeters taller than either of them. He was also very broad-shouldered, deep-chested, and dark complexioned, and something about his chin reminded Barregos of Prince Michael Winton, the Duke of Winton-Serisburg.

Which probably shouldn't have been surprising, under the circumstances.

"Governor," Frank said, "allow me to introduce Mr. Håkon Ellingsen."

"Mr. Ellingsen." Barregos extended his hand and forbore mentioning how unlikely he found that name in connection with that chin and complexion.

"Governor." Ellingsen's grip was strong, without being overpowering, and a white smile flashed. "Thank you for agreeing to see me...after hours, as it were."

"I have to admit I'm a little perplexed by your request for anonymity," Barregos replied as he and his visitor settled into facing chairs at the small conference table in the corner of his large office while Frank produced cups and a tall carafe of coffee. "Aside from the obvious fact that you're up to something you'd just as soon nobody in the League found out about, I mean."

"Actually, it's not just the Sollies we're worried about this time around," Ellingsen said. Frank held the carafe over his cup, and the Manticoran looked up and nodded. "That's our *primary* concern, of course," he went on as the aide poured, "but I'm sure you're aware of this 'Mesan Alignment' Captain Zilwicki and Agent Cachat uncovered."

"Queen Berry's relayed at least some of your...suspicions to us." Barregos nodded. "Frankly, I'm inclined to think there's something to them." He shrugged. "It could explain several 'coincidences' that've bothered me for decades now."

"Odd. We've had much the same experience." Ellingsen's teeth flashed again. This time no one could have mistaken it for a smile. "But that's one reason I'm maintaining such a low profile. We're still trying to figure out where the 'Alignment' might have its own sources, and I think we can all take it for granted that anything it heard about and thought would hurt our position vis-à-vis the League would be whispered into someone's ear in Old Chicago just as quickly as their little dispatch boats could get it there."

"That would appear to be a reasonable assumption," Barregos acknowledged with a wintry smile.

"In addition, of course," Ellingsen continued, "given the current state of affairs, it probably wouldn't be to *your* advantage if Kolokoltsov and the other Mandarins found out you were even talking to us."

This time, it was the Manticoran's turn to shrug, and Barregos nodded.

"That's undoubtedly true. And to be honest, that's why I'm a little puzzled to be speaking to you instead of having this passed through Torch. We're in regular contact with them, and Permanent Senior Undersecretary Kolokoltsov's well aware of our treaty relationship."

"And that would make it much more reasonable—and less suspicious—for you to talk to an envoy from Queen Berry," Ellingsen agreed. "Unfortunately, this is very closely held, and the decision was taken—at a considerably higher level than my own—not to read Princess Ruth or Queen Berry in on it."

"I see." Barregos' eyes narrowed. "That's . . . very interesting."

"I thought you might find it that way."

Ellingsen sat back in his chair, nursing his coffee cup, and regarded the governor levelly for several seconds. Then he squared his shoulders and sat upright once again, with the air of a man coming to the critical point of his visit.

"I hope you'll forgive me for saying this, Governor, but we've been watching developments here in the Maya Sector and a certain very quiet . . . evolution in your relationship with Erewhon. We're also aware your local defense force is . . . a bit more powerful than anyone in Old Chicago realizes, let's say. Based on what we know, our analysts have reached certain conclusions in regard to Maya, and that's what brings me here. You see—"

"Well, damn," Luiz Rozsak said mildly as he stirred minced garlic, rosemary, salt, and coarse-ground black pepper into the olive oil.

Barregos sat patiently, well accustomed to his admiral's habits, while Rozsak finished stirring and then rubbed the mixture into the large beef tenderloin on his counter. He worked carefully, painstakingly coating every square centimeter of surface, then opened the hood of the gas grill. He adjusted the gas jets on its right side and used a pair of tongs to lubricate the hot end of the grate with an oil-soaked rag. Then he lifted the tenderloin and settled it onto the grate with a sizzle, closed the hood, wiped his hands on his apron, and turned back to the governor.

"Given how much the Manties seem to've figured out, I have to wonder if they have sources in Erewhon we don't know about."

"No one ever said their ONI was incompetent, Luiz," Barregos pointed out. "I tend to doubt Captain Zilwicki's likely to keep any deductions he may've reached about our intentions a deep dark secret where Admiral Givens is concerned, either. On the other hand, given the amount of . . . insight Ellingsen demonstrated, I actually suspect a lot of his information came from Erewhon via Nouveau Paris now that Pritchart's signed on for this Grand Alliance of theirs."

"That would make sense," Rozsak conceded, checking his chrono and then beginning to chop romaine lettuce on a sideboard. "And I suppose it's reasonable they'd keep this very closely held. I'm still a little surprised they've decided to leave the Torches in the dark about it, though."

"I thought about that, but actually, I'm not sure I wouldn't have reached the same decision, given the fact that Jeremy X and Web Du Havel both have such long-standing connections with the Ballroom," Barregos said, and snorted as Rozsak raised both eyebrows at him. "I'm not saying the Ballroom doesn't know how to maintain operational security, Luiz! No, what might have kept me from bringing Torch in is that the Ballroom already has its fingers in so many pies, a lot of which involve planets that would just *love* to kick OFS into the nearest supernova. It would have to be awful tempting from Torch's perspective to make this sort of offer to their friends in that kind of situation."

"And every time they did, it would increase the chance of its leaking." Rozsak nodded. "I suppose that does make sense. But what about Delvecchio? She's right here in Maya, and she's effectively promised Jiri delivery of those Mark 16s we talked about in November. If she's carrying that kind of information back and forth, why not use *her* as the conduit?"

He finished chopping the romaine, deposited it in a large salad bowl, then reopened the grill's hood and turned the sizzling tenderloin to sear the other side.

"I raised that point with Ellingsen, actually," the governor replied.

"And he said?"

"Two things. First, Elizabeth, Pritchart, and Mayhew have apparently decided it makes more sense for the Manties' Foreign Office to take the lead in this. And because it's so tightly held, they're not bringing anyone in on the Navy side unless and until they absolutely have to. And, secondly, they sent Ellingsen straight out from Landing both because it's a shorter communications loop and because eliminating as many relay points as possible cuts down on the number of chances for something to be misconstrued or misunderstood."

"Which would be a very bad thing under the circumstances," Rozsak observed as he began cutting onions and tomato for the salad.

"Oh, I think that's at least a *mild* understatement," Barregos said dryly, and the admiral chuckled.

He went on slicing for at least another full minute, never looking up from his cutting board, then raised his eyes to the governor once more.

"At this point," he said, "all twelve *Sharpshooters* are fully commissioned and worked up. We haven't taken delivery of any Mark 16s yet, but Delvecchio's provided us with operational profiles on them, so we've been able to work up our tactical crews with them in simulations, as well as the Mark 17s. We still don't have any of the superdreadnoughts, though, and we won't before February. So even given the kind of firepower we can produce, we're not ready to stand off Battle Fleet by ourselves."

He checked his chrono again, then reopened the grill, turned off the burners under the tenderloin, slid it to the cool end of the grate, and turned the single burner at that end to medium. He inserted the temperature probe, closed it again, and turned back to Barregos.

"So I suppose the question is how much fleet support the Alliance is prepared to give us. From what you've said, they've got a lot of irons in the fire right now with this 'Operation Bastille' of theirs."

"Ellingsen was playing that close to his vest," Barregos said. "How many irons they've got at the moment, I mean. But when I mentioned what Renée's been picking up from Kondratii he more or less admitted that was the Manties. So they've obviously been working on this for quite a while, which I'm willing to bet means that saying they have 'a lot of irons in the fire' understates the situation by, oh, no more than a light-year or so."

"Which lends more point to my question."

"Indeed it does. I made that point to him, too, since the Mandarins would have to make squashing *us* a much bigger priority than dealing with someplace like Kondratii."

"And he said?"

"And he said they fully understand that. By the same token, that would make us far more useful to them as a distraction, and from a cold-blooded, pragmatic standpoint, that also makes us worth a considerably larger investment in tonnage. According to Ellingsen, they're prepared to meet any 'reasonable requirement' we might suggest."

"That *we* might suggest?" Rozsak repeated, and the governor nodded.

"They don't expect us to buy a pig in a poke, Luiz. He says that if we're interested, he can be back here by late next month with a representative from Alexander-Harrington and Caparelli to discuss force levels directly with you."

"Well, in that case," the admiral said with a smile, beginning to toss the salad, "I'm all in favor of listening to whatever the Admiralty's representative has to say."

❖   ❖   ❖

The com chimed and she punched the key to open a window in the middle of the calendar she was annotating for Commodore Terekhov. All she saw was *Quentin Saint-James'* wallpaper and the icon of a voice-only connection. Then a voice spoke.

"Howdy, Helen," Stephen Westman said. "Tell me, would it happen the Commodore—and you, of course—would be able to join me at The Rare Sirloin for dinner in a couple of hours, say?"

"I just happen to be working on his schedule right this minute," she replied with a smile. "I think he's planning on a working dinner here on the flagship, but that hasn't been set in ceramacrete yet. If that's *not* what he has in mind, he could probably be on the ground in Estelle by, say, nineteen hundred your time. Can I tell him whether this is a social invitation or if it's a case of your going back to your wicked ways?"

"No, I *haven't* 'gone back to my wicked ways,' young lady!" he said, and she heard the smile in his voice. Then his tone sobered. "But it 'pears somebody else may have something along those lines he wants to talk about."

"Along the lines of what the Mesans tried to pull here in the Quadrant, you mean?" she asked more sharply. "I imagine he'd be *very* interested in anything like that. I'll have to ask him, though. Have you got a moment?"

"I don't mind holding," he said.

"Then I'll be back with you in a sec," she said, and punched Sir Aivars Terekhov's com combination.

"Yes, Helen?" Terekhov said a moment later.

"Sir, I've got Stephen Westman on the line. I know you were thinking about having supper with Captain

Pope, Commander Stillwell, and Captain Carlson, but he'd like to invite you—and me—to dinner at The Rare Sirloin at nineteen hundred this evening."

"Would he?" Terekhov cocked his head. "Should I assume you think I ought to accept his invitation instead?"

"Actually, Sir, I think that might be a good idea," she said seriously. "From what he's saying, he thinks he's stumbled across something related to what the Mesans were trying to pull here in the Quadrant. If I had to guess, Sir, I think he's probably bringing it to you because he knows you better than any of Admiral Gold Peak's other senior officers."

"I see." Terekhov's eyes had narrowed. They stayed that way for a moment, then he nodded. "Well, if that's what my flag lieutenant thinks, then it's probably worth following up. Nineteen hundred, you said?"

"Yes, Sir. I think that would give you time to make it dirtside after your captains' conference this afternoon."

"In that case, tell Mr. Westman we'll be there."

"Yes, Sir." She cut the circuit and brought the connection to Westman back up. "Mr. Westman?"

"Yes?"

"Sir Aivars says he'll be happy to join you for dinner. We'll see you at nineteen hundred, if you want to go ahead and make reservations."

"Fine!" Westman said in a satisfied tone. "Tell the Commodore I appreciate it, and I'll see both of you then. Clear."

◇   ◇   ◇

Helen followed her commodore into the dimly lit, incredibly expensive restaurant. As always, the combination of dim lighting, soft music, delicious aromas, and peanut shell-littered floor struck her as distinctly incongruous. But it was very Montanan, she admitted, just like the exposed overhead beams and the snarling Montana cougar's heads mounted on the walls.

The maître d' personally escorted the two of them— *well, actually*, she thought, *he's escorting the* Commodore. *I'm more of an afterthought*—to their table. Westman and a stranger were already seated, waiting for them.

The Montanan stood, offering his hand to Terekhov. The two men shook firmly, and then Westman turned to Helen. In *her* case, though, she got a hug. Which, she thought, was a far cry from the hostility with which he'd initially met her and the Commodore.

"Aivars, Helen," he said then, waving at the very ordinary-looking man, "allow me t' introduce Mr. Ankenbrandt—Michael Ankenbrandt. He's a purchasing agent for the Trifecta Corporation out of Mobius. Came to talk to me about beef this morning."

"Mr. Ankenbrandt," Terekhov acknowledged as he and Helen took their seats and Westman sat back down. "I'm sure you and Mr. Westman had a very interesting conversation about beef. I'm not entirely sure why he thought *I* should meet with you, though."

"Actually, Commodore," Ankenbrandt replied, "I didn't ask to speak to you specifically. I told him I needed to speak to the senior Manticoran naval officer here in Montana."

"And I figured the chance of me gettin' him in t' talk t' Admiral Gold Peak in any kind of a hurry ranged somewhere from short of slim t' none," Westman put in. "'Sides, I figure someone as suspicious and ornery as you'd make a pretty fair first-stage filter."

"Suspicious I'll give you," Terekhov said with a smile. "But I don't think a Montanan ought to be throwing around words like 'ornery' where anyone else is concerned. Come to think of it, that's probably truer for some Montanans than for others!"

"Point," Westman acknowledged with a smile. "On th' other hand, I still don't have any damned idea what it is Mr. Ankenbrandt wants t' talk to a senior officer about!"

Terekhov considered him for a moment, then turned a cool blue gaze upon Ankenbrandt.

"I'm certainly not *the* senior officer in Montana at the moment," he said. "On the other hand, if you want to talk to her, I'm afraid you'll have to convince me first. So what's this all about?"

"That's a . . . complicated question, Commodore," Ankenbrandt replied, and glanced sharply in Helen's direction.

"Ensign Zilwicki is my flag lieutenant." There was an edge of frost in Terekhov's voice. "I don't propose to send her to sit at the kiddies' table while the adults discuss serious matters."

"Sorry." Ankenbrandt colored slightly, and his tone sounded genuinely apologetic. "It's just that—Well, the truth is I guess I'm nervous—scared as hell, really—about this whole thing. And I never expected to encounter so much of your Navy here in Montana."

"Then why did you come here?" Terekhov asked.

"Actually, what I was *supposed* to do when I got here was to send a prearranged, coded message on to Spindle," Ankenbrandt said. "No one in Mobius expected Admiral Gold Peak to actually be here, in Montana, when I arrived. This information needs to get to her absolutely ASAP, and when I realized she was *here*, I also realized this was the best opportunity to get it delivered. And my . . . superiors were paying pretty close attention to the rumors coming out of the Quadrant after the Battle of Monica. They briefed me on everything they knew about it, and that suggested to me that Mr. Westman here might be able to . . . facilitate contact with her."

"Why not go directly to the Navy? Or to someone in the Montana system government?"

"Because my initial contact with Mr. Westman could be covered by my employer's instructions to find a source of beef here in Montana," Ankenbrandt replied reasonably. "To be honest, I'm not fully comfortable about talking to two uniformed RMN officers in a public place, but Mr. Westman insisted I had to . . . pass muster with you before I'd have any chance of reaching Admiral Gold Peak. Things are moving so fast in Mobius that I decided I had no choice but to take the chance."

"Why?" Terekhov asked. "No offense, Mr. Ankenbrandt, but what could events in Mobius possibly have to do with Admiral Gold Peak?"

Ankenbrandt looked acutely unhappy. He sat for several seconds, playing with a steak knife and staring down at the light reflected from the flat of the blade. Then, finally, he drew a deep breath and looked back up at Terekhov.

"I know you won't have been briefed on a single thing I'm about to say," he said. "Admiral Gold Peak will have been, though."

"And?" Terekhov prompted when the other man paused again.

"I represent...a group in Mobius which has been discussing certain things—very quietly—with a... representative of your Star Empire," he said slowly. "In the course of that discussion, we were promised support—*naval* support—under certain circumstances."

The soft background music made the silence around the table even more profound, Helen thought. That silence lingered for a dozen heartbeats before Terekhov leaned back in his chair.

"Naval support," he repeated carefully, and a tense-faced Ankenbrandt nodded. Terekhov pursed his lips, then tilted his head. "You're right, this isn't anything *I've* been briefed on. So, before we go any farther, let me be sure I understand what's being said. You're telling me the people you represent—other than the Trifecta Corporation, that is—are planning some sort of action in Mobius that will require outside naval support and that the Star Empire of Manticore's *promised* you that support?"

Ankenbrandt nodded again.

"I can only assume, then," Terekhov said softly, "that you're talking about some form of...active uprising against your own system's government? And you're saying *Manticore's* offered you actual direct, *open* support for that?"

"Yes," Ankenbrandt said tersely. Then he grimaced. "Nobody in Mobius expected to need to contact you this soon. It wasn't supposed to happen for months yet. But last month what was supposed to be a peaceful political demonstration—President Lombroso announced new elections several T-months ago; it was only supposed to be window dressing, but some people actually took him seriously—turned ugly. In fact, it turned *damned* ugly."

The unremarkable-looking man looked far less unremarkable, as hatred twisted his expression. "Lombroso turned Scorpion tanks loose on them," he continued harshly. "Casualties were . . . heavy. And some of our people had smuggled some of the antitank weapons your people've shipped in to us into positions covering the demonstration. So now we've got hundreds of civilian dead and wounded and the Presidential Guard knows *someone's* managed to get modern weapons past Customs." He shook his head. "Under the circumstances, we think Lombroso's going to call in OFS and Frontier Fleet, and when that happens, we're going to need that naval support."

He met Terekhov's eyes levelly.

"We're going to need it *badly*," he said, very, very quietly.

Chapter Forty-Nine

"SO," LUCINDE MYLLYNIEMI SNUGGLED up against Rufino Chernyshev, her head on his shoulder, and her breath was warm on his ear. "Now that I've had my wicked way with you, are you ready to tell me what's been on your mind all night?"

"You realize that if I tell you, I'll have to kill you," he said, stroking one hand down her flank, and she purred.

"Nonsense," she told him. "I'm far too valuable an asset."

"Oh, in *so* many ways," he agreed with a smile. Then his expression turned more serious. "Actually, there *is* something I need to brief you in on, although I hadn't really planned on doing it under these circumstances."

"Well, *I* don't have any problem mixing pleasure with business." She nipped the lobe of his ear.

"So I see." He smiled again, then rolled up on an elbow to look down at her. "The thing is that Alpha-One's authorized Operation Houdini."

Myllyniemi went very still, eyes even darker than

usual, and he let her absorb the implication. Despite her senior—and completely trusted—position as one of the Alignment's more senior agents, she had no idea Albrecht Detweiler even existed, far less who he might be. She *did* know where "Alpha-One" stood in the Mesan Alignment's hierarchy, however, and that was all she needed to know to understand what she'd just been told.

Operation Houdini was the codename for the systematic removal from Mesa of everyone inside the Alignments' "inner onion." Altogether, that probably came—although it was only an estimate on her part—to fewer than a hundred thousand people . . . at the outside. Vastly more people belonged to the Alignment, but none of those other people knew the Alignment's true purpose and objective.

Unfortunately, it wasn't going to be as simple as just loading all of them aboard passenger liners and sailing off into the sunset. She knew that, too. Among other things, there was plenty of physical evidence which had to be erased if the secret was to hold. At the same time, the inner onion had been planning for precisely this moment for the better part of a hundred and fifty T-years. She'd had to know at least that much because of her position in the Manpower hierarchy. But from Chernyshev's tone . . .

"I take it there's a certain . . . time pressure?" she said slowly after a long, thoughtful pause, and he nodded.

"Yes, there is." His voice was considerably more serious. "Without going into a lot of details that you don't have the need to know, the Manties and this 'Grand Alliance' with Haven are likely to kick the ever loving crap out of the Sollies a lot more quickly than we'd originally anticipated. Mind you, it's a long way from a given that Manticore can actually *beat* them. The League's so damned big that it's awful hard for me to visualize a situation in which the Manties both militarily defeat it *and* manage to impose any sort of lasting peace terms. Even assuming our long-term plans succeed almost perfectly, there's still going to be a Solarian League, and it's still going to be bigger than the Star Empire of Manticore. If the Manties hammer it hard enough to make the Mandarins in Old Chicago actually knuckle under, there's going to be a hell of a lot of revanchism rolling around inside it, too. So whether or not Manticore wins an immediate *military* victory, sooner or later the Sollies are going to be back—this time with matching weapons—for another round."

Myllyniemi nodded. She'd known the broad terms of the Alignment's ultimate strategy. Again, it was something she'd needed to know to make intelligent decisions when she couldn't seek direction from above. She knew precious little about the *details*, for excellent reasons, but she was aware that the Alignment intended ultimately to place itself in the position of powerbroker between the remnants of a greatly diminished Solarian League and its primary interstellar competitor in order to play the two of them against each other. The assumption—up until the last twenty T-years or so—had been that the League's probable competitor would be the People's Republic of Haven.

That had undergone just a *bit* of revision lately, of course.

"The problem," Chernyshev continued, "is that, given what happened in Spindle, it's obvious the Manties" military advantage is even greater than we'd projected. And when Haven decided to throw in with them instead of finishing them off while they were vulnerable, our attack on their home system—and, yes, that *was* us, in the unlikely event that you'd failed to figure that out already—isn't going to buy all the advantages we'd hoped for. Oh, it was still worth doing, but we'd really have preferred for Pritchart and Theisman to use the opening to take the Star Empire off the board once and for all. Instead, they're *supporting* Elizabeth, and it's likely that's going to embolden the Manties to push their military advantage even harder rather than to pull in their horns. In particular, our analysts suggest Admiral Gold Peak's just as bloody-minded as her cousin . . . and perfectly ready to use however sharp a sword she needs on any Gordian Knots that come her way."

"Like Mesa," Myllyniemi said.

"Exactly. And that's particularly bothersome now that we know Zilwicki and Cachat got home alive and took one of the scientists who was actually *inside* the onion with them. That's not only what inspired Pritchart's brainstorm; it raises the question of what she—and Manticore—are likely to do now that the Alignment's intruded into the light."

"I see the logic," she said, reaching up to lay one hand along his cheek. "If we have to rush Houdini, though, it's going to be . . . messy."

"Yes, it is," he agreed grimly. He let himself slide back down, laying his other cheek against her breast, and his eyes were shadowed. "The Green Pines attack offers an opening I don't think anyone's happy about, but we're going to use it anyway." His lips tightened. "I know the Manties're telling the galaxy Zilwicki and

Cachat had nothing to do with the park explosion, and I'm willing to concede they didn't actually plant the bomb themselves. But those seccies goddamned well wouldn't've *had* the damned bomb in the first place if not for them. I'm looking forward to paying them back for that. In the meantime, though, there are going to be more strikes by 'Ballroom terrorists' here on Mesa. We can use the explosions to 'disappear' a lot of the people we'd otherwise be pulling out more gradually and simultaneously erase a lot of physical evidence."

"That sounds like a lot of collateral damage," she said unhappily.

"Because that's exactly what's going to happen," he said even more grimly. "I don't like how high the body count's going do be. I'm pretty damn sure *Alpha-One* doesn't like it, for that matter. But that doesn't mean it won't be effective, and the Manties aren't likely to give us enough time to do it any other way."

"I understand," she said quietly.

"Under the original Houdini plan, you're scheduled for the third extraction flight," he said more briskly. "Obviously, that's subject to change, depending on how the original plan is modified. In any case, though, you're going to have to coordinate with pulling out our people on the Manpower board as well. That's one reason I'm telling you about it now."

She nodded silently, and he smiled suddenly, lifting himself on his elbow again and cradling her face between his hands before he kissed her slowly and lingeringly. Then he pulled back, still smiling, and she smiled back, despite the ghosts in her eyes.

"And in the meantime," he said softly, "why don't

you and I find something to distract ourselves from business?"

❖ ❖ ❖

Commander Tremont Watson, Frontier Fleet, tried very hard to keep his unhappiness from showing as SLNS *Oceanus* decelerated toward orbit around the planet Mobius. As a general rule, he was rather proud of belonging to Frontier Fleet—an organization which actually did useful things—rather than Battle Fleet, but at this moment he wished he was almost anywhere else in the galaxy than in *Oceanus'* command chair.

"Coming up on the mark, Sir," Lieutenant Gillespie, his astrogator announced, and he nodded.

"Thank you, Sandra," he said briskly.

"And what we do now, Sir?" Lieutenant Commander Fred O'Carroll, his executive officer asked very quietly in his ear.

"And now, Fred, we find out exactly what Brigadier Yucel has in mind." He smiled thinly. "I can hardly wait."

❖ ❖ ❖

"Carlton! What the hell are *you* doing here?!" Kayleigh Blanchard demanded as one of the Mobius Liberation Front's riflemen escorted the tall, rather narrow-shouldered man in Landing City Police Department uniform into her command post. "For that matter," she added, her eyes narrowing, "how the hell did you get here without being *shot*?"

"And good afternoon to you, too, Kayleigh," Captain Carlton Carmichael replied sourly. "Nice to see you."

"Well, of course it is . . . I guess," Blanchard said, reaching out to shake her old boss' hand. In fact, he'd once been her partner, before his promotion and her resignation. "But my questions stand. How *did* you get here? And why?"

"I walked across Cloverdale Boulevard waving a white flag," he said. "I think Lieutenant Collins was under the impression I intended to negotiate a prisoner swap and then come home again." He smiled thinly. "She's going to be disappointed."

"And once he got to our side of the street," the suspicious looking rifleman said, "he asked us to deliver him to you. By name." He shrugged. "If he's got a tracer on him, he swallowed it—or stuck it up his ass—and none of our scanners found it."

"That's okay, Kai. I know him. I've known a long time, in fact. Although," she added a bit pointedly, "I'm still waiting to find out why he's here."

"I'm here because Ochoa told me Petulengro's just informed him there's a Gendarmerie intervention battalion on its way into orbit," Carmichael said grimly, and Blanchard's jaw tightened. Colonel Grigori Petulengro headed the LCPD's Security and Intelligence Branch; Major Ashton Ochoa commanded the Criminal Investigation Branch, which made him Carmichael's direct superior. "Petulengro's a weasel," the police captain continued flatly, "but Ochoa's always been square with the troops—you know that. So I figure he's telling the truth. And I also figured that *you* had to be on the other side somewhere. So you need to tell whoever's in charge that this Brigadier Yucel's brought along a batch of Solly Frontier Fleet ships. I don't think she brought them just to look pretty, and after the way you've been kicking Lombroso's ass for the last couple of weeks, I doubt he's likely to be a big fan of moderation, either. Under the circumstances, I think you'd better get on the com and let your people know what the hell is likely to come down on their heads sometime real soon now, Kayleigh."

❖   ❖   ❖

"Thank God you're here, Brigadier!" the fair-haired, beefy-faced man on Francisca Yucel's com screen said. "My God! It's been a *nightmare* for the last two weeks! Where have you *been?!*"

"I appreciate your concern, Mr. Frolov," she told Trifecta Corporation's Mobius planetary manager. "And I assure you Commissioner Verrocchio dispatched us the moment Ms. Xydis'—and President Lombroso's, of course—dispatches reached him."

"Couldn't you have gotten here any *sooner?!*" Frolov demanded. The man had small, brown eyes that rather reminded Yucel of an Old Terran pig. "Do you have any idea how much *damage* these lunatics have done to Trifecta's assets? Not to mention all of our employees who've been killed or injured!"

That last sentence had the feel of an afterthought, the brigadier thought. Not that she had any problem with that. She understood her job, but vast though her contempt for the Verge's neobarbs might be, it was entirely possible that her contempt for transstellar flunkies like Frolov ran even deeper.

It would've been a very close run thing, at any rate.

"Obviously, I've just arrived, Sir," she told him. "I'm still in the process of gathering information. Once I have it, I assure you, we *will* take action."

"What sort of 'information'?"

"Mr. Frolov, I need to know what the situation on the ground is before I can do anything about it," Yucel explained as calmly as possible. "And, with all due respect, I really need to speak with President Lombroso's government, as well. As you know, the request for OFS support came from *his* office."

She emphasized the pronoun, holding Frolov's gaze, and those piggy eyes blinked as she reminded him of the *official* reason—and Trifecta's fig leaf—for her presence.

"Oh! I mean, of course! I only—"

"Ma'am, I have President Lombroso for you," her com officer interrupted politely.

"I'm afraid I have to go now, Mr. Frolov. I'll keep you informed." Yucel killed the connection before Frolov could respond and turned to the com officer. "Put him through."

"Yes, Ma'am."

An instant later, President Svein Lombroso appeared on her display. He looked far less spruce and well-groomed than his official file imagery, she noted, and the same was true of the crowd of men and women in the conference room with him. She recognized Angeliki Xydis, Frontier Security's representative in Mobius; General Olivia Yardley, the Presidential Guard's commander; and Friedmann Mátáys, the CO of the Mobius Security Police. She didn't have a clue who any of the others were, and they didn't matter anyway.

"President Lombroso, I'm Brigadier Francisca Yucel," she introduced herself crisply. "I'm here on behalf of the Office of Frontier Security in response to your request for support with a full intervention battalion. In addition, I'm accompanied by four Navy destroyers and the light cruiser *Oceanus*. How may the Solarian League assist you, Sir?"

✧   ✧   ✧

"Yes, Augustus?"

Estelle Matsuko, Baroness Medusa and Her Imperial Majesty's Governor for the Talbott Quadrant, set down her teacup with a smile as Augustus Khumalo appeared on her com display. Early morning sunlight spilled into her spacious office, and the remnant of a small omelette and accompanying croissant sat on the blotter in front of her. Her staff had given up attempting to break her of her habit, acquired during her days on the planet Medusa, of eating breakfast at her desk. She was far too set in her ways to change... especially when she could gaze out of her office window across such a gorgeous stretch of ocean.

"You're up early," she observed, and he smiled back in acknowledgment. He was not what some deplorably perky people persisted in calling "a morning person."

"Yes, Milady, I am," he said. "I've spent quite some time over the last couple of days thinking about Lady Gold Peak's report and our interview with Mr. Ankenbrandt. And about her request for additional ground forces from the Quadrant Guard."

"I'm sure we all have," Medusa's smile faded. "In fact, when I haven't been 'thinking about it,' I've been having *nightmares* about it. Should I assume some new aspect of it's occurred to you?"

"Not precisely, no. I suppose what I actually should've said was that I've been thinking about your authorization for her to respond to any more messages she receives by providing the promised support just as if it had really been us talking to them in the first place."

"You're not having second thoughts about the policy, though," Medusa said, studying his expression thoughtfully. "So that means you've had some additional thoughts about how best to *implement* it?"

"That's exactly what I've been thinking about." He nodded. "And Captain Grierson's stop on his way forward to Lady Gold Peak with the reinforcements from home is responsible for the notion I've had."

"And what notion would that be?"

"Well, before we forward-deployed Tenth Fleet, when Admiral Gold Peak and I proposed organizing the Quadrant Guard to support our Marine strength by combining the planetary combat forces here in Talbott, we didn't really have hard numbers on the size and availability of those forces."

He paused, one eyebrow raised, and she nodded.

"Since then," he resumed, "Mr. Krietzmann's office has been compiling those figures. I have his preliminary numbers—and I stress they're *only* preliminary at this point—and if they're accurate, I think it might be possible to dispatch a much larger reinforcement than she probably thought we could when she sent us her request. None of the pre-annexation planetary armed forces were all that huge for entire star systems, but they weren't exactly tiny, either, and there were a lot of them. That gives us some pretty impressive absolute numbers from which to slice off manpower for her. Integrating them into a single force with a single operational doctrine's going to take time, so at the moment we're retaining 'national units' as individual formations when we start putting the building blocks together. Eventually we'll get beyond the 'allied units' state of affairs to a truly integrated force; we just aren't there yet. There's more commonality of equipment than we'd expected, though—most of the local star systems bought Solarian hardware before the annexation—and we're converting the units that *didn't* buy from the Sollies to Manticoran equipment first. We'll switch the others over later.

"But my point is that it looks very much to me as if we've got a lot more combat power we could deploy forward a lot more quickly than we thought we could. The biggest problem's likely to be transport because, at the moment, Tenth Fleet—the entire Quadrant—is shorter on troop lift than warships. When Captain Grierson reaches Montana, Lady Gold Peak will have a lot more light units that can respond to assistance requests. But she's still going to be very short on both planetary combat elements *and* on the lift to move the ones she does have around, and that could get ugly if more Mobiuses turn up. I doubt the home system's going to be able to send us much in the way of additional troop strength, but I've sent the Admiralty an urgent request for additional troop *transports*. She's going to need at least some of those, whatever happens, and I don't know how many of them I'll be able to get, but I'd like your permission to begin organizing for the biggest troop lift to Montana the Guard can support."

There was silence for a moment, and then Baroness Medusa nodded.

"For a bluff, unimaginative naval officer, you *do* have some knacky notions from time to time, don't you Augustus?" she said with a smile.

✦ Chapter Fifty

RUFINO CHERNYSHEV'S COM CHIMED softly. He glanced at the time display and grimaced. In fact, his expression was rather stronger than a mere grimace—"scowl" would probably have been too strong a noun, although it came close—and only partly because so many things in the galaxy seemed determined to go wrong at the same moment. He'd discovered that he hated office work just as much as he'd expected to, but at least there was a sense of satisfaction in getting it right... usually. Sometimes, though, there *was* no "right." And some of the people involved in those not-right outcomes—one of whom was undoubtedly here for her scheduled appointment—were not his favorite people in the universe.

There was no point in putting this off, though, so he keyed the com.

"Yes?"

"Ms. Marinescu is here, Sir," Samuel Hairston, the secretary he'd inherited from Isabel Bardasano along with this office, confirmed. His voice was as pleasant and professional as ever, but Chernyshev had discovered that Hairston was even smarter than he was good-looking. And when they'd discussed his calendar for the day, it had been evident to him that Hairston liked Janice Marinescu as little as his new boss did.

Well, that's fair enough, Chernyshev thought now. *Only very strange people* do *like scorpions, after all.*

"Send her in, Samuel," he said out loud, making no effort to hide the resignation in his tone, since only Hairston could hear him over his earbug.

"Of course, Sir."

The office door opened almost instantly and a tall, square-faced woman with striking features and dark hair and eyes came through it. Chernyshev remained seated rather than rising to greet her, and something flickered briefly in those dark eyes. It might have been irritation, or it might have been anger, and Chernyshev could live with either of those. Janice Marinescu was ten or fifteen T-years older than he was, and she was good at her job, but she was also the sort who pushed the limits of anyone *else's* authority, and until Isabel Bardasano's death, she'd technically been senior to Chernyshev. They'd been in different chains of command, fortunately, but he suspected she was one of several people who thought *they* would have been a far better fit than one Rufino Chernyshev for Bardasano's suddenly vacated position, and he had a pretty shrewd notion of what would happen if she sensed anything remotely like an opening to test the limits of *his* authority.

"Janice," he said with a brief nod towards the chair in front of his desk.

"Rufino," she acknowledged as she sat. There might

have been just an edge of challenge—or possibly of simple testing—in her use of his first name. On the other hand, there might not have been, and he reminded himself not to let how much he disliked her color his perceptions.

Not exactly falling all over herself to congratulate me on my "promotion," though, is she?

"I had a conversation with Albrecht and Collin yesterday," he told her.

"Let me guess," she responded sardonically. "About recent events in Manticore, by any chance?"

He nodded. He wasn't surprised by the accuracy of her prediction; he'd never thought she was stupid.

"I'm sure you've been thinking just as hard as the rest of us about ways this can ... impede our plans once it becomes general knowledge," he said. "The fact that Zilwicki's alive to dispute our version of Green Pines is bad enough. Thank God we never actually claimed our security people had killed him on-planet!" He shook his head. "There were actually a few people over in Propaganda who thought that would've been a good idea. They even wanted to exhibit 'his' body to prove we'd gotten him and that he'd *definitely* been behind the attacks. I understand Collin changed their minds by pointing out what happened to Haven when they claimed to have executed Harrington!"

"It's nice to avoid shooting yourself in the foot," Marinescu agreed with a thin smile.

"Or at least limiting yourself to the loss of a single toe when you do." Chernyshev's smile was even thinner than hers had been. "It's bad enough that Manticore's going to be able to produce him as a counter witness, but we could live with that. Of course the man they sent to execute nuclear terrorism on an independent planet is going to swear up and down that he never did it! The fact that *Pritchart* obviously believes him, though—believes him enough to proclaim the existence of the Alignment and actually travel to Manticore personally to negotiate peace—is just a little harder to wave away. And the fact that *anything* about the Alignment's creeping into the limelight, coupled with Gold Peak's ... proactive stance in Talbott, has the potential to go from really, really bad to disastrous a lot more quickly than anyone wants to think about. Which brings me to the reason for this meeting."

He let his chair come fully upright, and his expression was somber.

"Albrecht has decided to execute Houdini," he said flatly. "He's decided to execute it now, and on an expedited basis."

"That could be ... complicated," Marinescu replied after a moment.

"Complicated doesn't begin to describe it." Chernyshev snorted harshly. "It's Albrecht's thought that we can kill two birds with one stone, though."

"Let me guess," she said again. "He figures we can use more 'Ballroom terror attacks' to cover the accelerated withdrawals. And if we do that spectacularly enough, anything Zilwicki—or Pritchart, for that matter—says about the Manties' lack of involvement will sound rather less convincing to Solarian public opinion."

"And to Mesan public opinion, for that matter." Chernyshev kept his voice level despite his vast personal repugnance for the entire idea. Marinescu, on the other hand, actually smiled in approval ... which illustrated the main reason he despised her so. Of course, it was also the main reason she'd been appointed to her current position five T-years ago.

The Bardasano genome carried some unfortunate instabilities, and Chernyshev knew there'd been serious consideration of simply culling it. The proposal had been rejected because it also produced so many highly capable, downright brilliant individuals. Isabel Bardasano had been an outstanding case of the genome's good points outweighing its bad, in point of fact. So far as Chernyshev was aware, on the other hand, there was no known history of instability in *Marinescu's* genome...which hadn't prevented Janice from being—in his considered opinion—a stone-cold psychopath.

She'd been one of the Mesan Alignment's most effective "wet work" specialists for decades, because she was smart, she was tough, she was quick-thinking... and she really, really liked killing people. If she hadn't been so far inside the onion, she'd have fitted in perfectly with Manpower, although her tendency to kill people probably would have cut into even Manpower's profit margin. He hadn't doubted for a moment that she'd actually *like* the notion of setting off nuclear devices in urban settings.

Having his expectation confirmed wasn't exactly a good thing in this instance, he reflected.

"I know you haven't had much warning," he told her, "but I'll need to see an action plan as soon as possible. Albrecht wants it yesterday. Me, though—I'm willing to let you have until the day after tomorrow to get it right."

"Gee, thanks."

"He's serious about moving this quickly, Janice." Chernyshev grimaced. "He realizes rushed planning is the best way to screw up, so he's willing to be reasonable, but we can't let any grass grow under our feet on this one. And your initial action plan doesn't have to be perfect. I'm sure Collin will want to review it and tweak it a bit, so think of this mainly as a starting point."

"What kind of time window do I have?"

"Until the end of October," he said flatly.

"October?" she repeated, and her expression was much less cheerful than it had been a moment earlier. "To *complete* the operation?"

"October," he confirmed. He understood her less than delighted reaction. They were already well past the middle of June, which gave her barely four months to complete an operation which had originally been scheduled to take over two T-years. "I did say we couldn't let any grass grow, didn't I?"

"I don't know if we can do it in four months—physically, I mean." It wasn't—quite—a protest, but it came close, and he shrugged.

"We're not the ones setting the available time, Janice. Zilwicki and Pritchart are doing that. Put yourself inside Elizabeth Winton's mind for just a moment and think about what they're telling her. You've just gotten confirmation from one of your most trusted operatives that there's a clandestine organization which helped manipulate you back into a shooting war with the Republic of Haven and which—just incidentally—was almost certainly responsible for the attack on your home star system that killed several million of your citizens. According to the President of the Republic of

Haven—with which you've been at war, cold or hot, for the better part of a T-century, by the way—she not only believes your agent's information, but she's willing to negotiate a peace treaty with you so the two of you can go after the bad guys together. *And* as coincidence would have it, your first cousin just happens to be in command of a fleet that could easily destroy at least a third of the entire Solarian League Navy in a standup fight and, equally coincidentally, just happens to be less than two hundred light-years from Mesa. Now, from what you know of Elizabeth Winton, how do *you* think she's likely to react?"

"Shit," Marinescu said.

"Exactly. The only things that may work in our favor are Solarian gullibility, the consequences of Oyster Bay, and message time.

"First, the entire idea of this 'Mesan Alignment' they've come up with is too fantastic for any serious thinker to accept for a minute. I guarantee you that no one in the League, especially in Old Chicago, is likely to believe—or admit they believe—Zilwicki's version of what happened here on Mesa. I'm pretty sure we can spin this as a desperate Manticoran attempt to evade responsibility for its unprovoked terrorist assault on Mesa, and Malachai Abruzzi's Ministry of Information's talking heads will get behind that and push hard.

"Second, despite what I just said about Gold Peak's combat power, what happened to Manticore's industrial infrastructure has to leave them a little more cautious about direct confrontations with the League. Any assault on Mesa would clearly escalate their problems with the Sollies, even if Mesa's never been a member of the League. It would play too perfectly into the narrative Kolokoltsov and his friends are constructing. They have to know Abruzzi would jump on it as proof of who's *really* pushing the confrontation, and there are plenty of Sollies who would eat that up with a spoon.

"And, finally, the communications loop will play into things, too. According to our latest information, Gold Peak's currently in Montana, and it'll take quite a while for any message from Manticore to get to her there. But don't get too comfortable about how *much* it'll affect things. Sure, it'll take time for any orders to attack Mesa to get to her, but once they arrive, she'll be just *delighted* to come kick Mesa's ass right up between its ears. Manticore's hated Mesa for T-centuries just because of the slave trade, Janice; the discovery of the Alignment's existence is only going to vindicate that hatred in their eyes. Gold Peak would want Mesa's scalp under *any* circumstances; after Oyster Bay, she'll come a-running just as fast as her little starships—well, her great big, *nasty* starships, actually—will go. In fact, the only real question's whether or not she'll be interested in letting any of the system navy's ships surrender after she gets here."

"All right. All right, I can see that." Marinescu waved one hand, her brow furrowed as she considered all the myriad ways in which her carefully orchestrated plans for Operation Houdini, the systematic, traceless removal of the key personnel of the Alignment's "onion" from Mesa, had just gone belly up. "And I can see why Albrecht wants to use 'terrorist incidents' as cover. In fact, that's the only thing that could even make it possible! That doesn't guarantee it'll work in the end, though. There are going to be ... loose ends that have to be tied up, no matter how smoothly everything goes, and there won't be time to make them disappear quietly. You do realize that?"

"Of course I do, and so does Albrecht. If you see a better option, I'm sure he'd be delighted to hear it."

"It's going to be even messier from the get-go than our existing Houdini plans ever envisioned," she continued, ignoring his last sentence. "I mean a *lot* messier, Rufino. Right off the top of my head, I'd be astonished if the collateral damage doesn't at least double even before we start tying off those loose ends."

"I know," he sighed. The difference between them, he thought, was that for Marinescu that was simply a tactical problem, not a moral one. "And because the 'collateral damage' is going to be so much higher, I think we're likely to have some problems with some of our . . . moderates."

"Screw 'em," she retorted. "I don't say I'd do it this way as my first choice, but the truth is, it could be a useful filter, Rufino."

"Filter?"

"If they're so frigging softhearted, so gutless, they can't recognize pragmatic necessity when it's staring them in the face, then they're probably not up for the long haul, anyway, whatever they may've thought going in. And if that's the case, we should cull them right now. If we're going to be setting off nukes anyway, it shouldn't be too hard to make them disappear before any cold feet get a chance to produce more Simões or Jack McBrydes!"

"There may be some point to that," Chernyshev said after three or four seconds. "Unfortunately, we need some of the people you're talking about, and once they've had a chance to put things into perspective after the fact, most of them will probably settle down. Even if they don't, they'll all be in Darius, which means none of them would find himself or herself in Simões' position. So, if it's all the same to you, Albrecht would really prefer for us to get them there alive."

"He's in charge." Marinescu shrugged. Obviously, a few hundred lives one way or the other didn't much matter to her. "But if you're not going to let me cull them, how do you keep them in line when the bombs start going off?"

"We start by getting the most essential—and most . . . problematic—ones off-planet right now." Chernyshev extracted a chip from his desk drawer and flipped it across to her. "I had Psych do a quick run of the alpha and beta lists, looking for the individuals most likely to have . . . issues with Albrecht's Ballroom option. They're all on the chip, and they're sorted both in order of how likely they are to respond poorly and their value to the Alignment. You're authorized to start collecting the most critically important this afternoon. We'll need cover stories for some of them—especially the ones with family who aren't on the Houdini lists—but I want at least the top third of them out of Mesa by the end of the week."

"We won't be able to send them direct to Darius on that kind of timetable," Marinescu pointed out.

"I know. We'll have to go with the backup routes." It was Chernyshev's turn to shrug. "It wasn't why we've built them in the first place, but the arrangements are in place. It'll just take them longer to get there."

"And give them more opportunity to run, if they're inclined to do that."

"I doubt very many of them would be, but that's a

point worth considering," Chernyshev conceded. "So I guess that means we'll have to give them babysitters."

"I won't have very many people to spare," she objected. "Putting this together and making it work in this kind of time frame is going to be what I think the navy calls an 'all-hands evolution.' I'm going to need everybody. For that matter, I may have to draft people from some other departments, and right off the top of my head, I think somewhere around eight or ten percent of the key staff earmarked for the extraction teams under the existing Houdini plans aren't even on-planet right now! Finding 'babysitters' without making dangerous holes in my operational people won't be as easy as you seem to think it is."

"I didn't think it would," Chernyshev said coolly. "On the other hand, this may be something up the Gauls' alley."

"Ah?"

Marinescu sat back in her chair, her expression thoughtful. GAUL—the Genetic Advancement and Uplift League—had been a part of the Mesan Alignment from the beginning, and its members had proven useful on more than one occasion. It had also tended over the T-centuries to become a sort of collecting basket for the most fanatical supporters of the Detweiler Plan, however, and like fanatics in general, they were perfectly comfortable with . . . extreme solutions. The Gauls served as the security force of last resort for the inner onion of the Alignment. There weren't actually all that many of them, but they had a fearsome reputation within the Alignment, which made them useful out of proportion to their actual numbers when the velvet glove seemed unlikely to suffice.

Most Gauls would have been quite willing to strap a nuclear device to their backs and walk into a crowded restaurant to execute one of the "Ballroom" attacks the revised Houdini would require, and Marinescu had already started thinking about ways she could use them. But Chernyshev had a point. It would be difficult to imagine a more ... diligent babysitter—and gaoler—than a Gaul. And it would be impossible to imagine one who could be more intimidating to someone who might consider desertion in transit.

"All right," she said after pondering it for a moment. "That could work."

"In that case, I think we're probably done—for now, anyway," Chernyshev said. "I'd like to see a preliminary draft of your action plan before we talk to Albrecht and Collin about it, but that's your side of the shop, not mine. For the most part, I'm perfectly content leaving it in your hands."

"I appreciate that."

She climbed out of her chair, and those dark eyes flickered again—this time with something which could have been contempt. But that was fine with Chernyshev, up to a point, at least. She was one of those people who confused eagerness to kill with *willingness* to kill, and it couldn't hurt to have her dismiss him as someone disinclined to dirty his own hands with what had to be done if he could avoid it. She was unlikely to go so far as to buck his authority, whatever she thought—not while she knew he had Albrecht Detweiler's full-blooded support—but if the time ever came ...

"Samuel will see to it that anything you send him reaches me as quickly as possible," he said.

"Got it." She nodded. "Until later, then."

Chernyshev watched her walk out of his office and frowned thoughtfully as the door closed behind her.

❖   ❖   ❖

Division Chief Jules Charteris hit the play button on his uni-link when he saw the blinking light. He routinely silenced the com function during meetings of his staff—or with his superiors—in the Ministry of Economics, so it wasn't uncommon for him to find messages waiting.

"Hi, Jules!" his wife Lisa's voice said in his earbug. "Sorry I missed you, but something's come up. I just found out I won't be home for supper tonight. Or for quite a few nights, I'm afraid. There's some kind of hush-hush conference out on McClintock Island. I just had time to run home, pack a bag, and catch the shuttle. I don't have all the details—and I couldn't share them with you if I did, Honey; you know the drill—but I wouldn't be surprised if this keeps me tied up for quite some time. Maybe even a couple of months. According to my boss, there are a lot of details that need tidying up after what happened at Green Pines. I'm sorry we didn't have any more warning than this, but somehow the galaxy has a habit of going its own way, doesn't it? Love you!"

The message ended, and Charteris frowned unhappily. As a member of the Mesan Alignment, he understood the need for what Lisa liked to call "operational security." He had to practice quite a lot of that himself, given his position in the system government. But he sometimes thought his wife should've gone into police or intelligence work rather than pure science. She seemed to actually *enjoy* playing these sorts of games, which was more than Jules could say for himself. And precisely why was anyone "tidying up" anything about Green Pines at this point, almost a full T-year after the attacks? That was the kind of silliness of which the "spooks" were so inordinately fond!

He didn't like the thought of "maybe even a couple of months" parted from her, either, but it wouldn't be the first time. She'd been sent out-system on a couple of occasions—once for the better part of a T-year—and at least this time she'd be on the same planet with him. That was something. Her superiors—at least half of whom seemed as childishly paranoid as Lisa sometimes got—might even let her give him the occasional com call!

He sighed and headed for the lift shaft to his office. If Lisa wasn't coming home tonight anyway, he might as well use the time to deal with some of the unending backlog on his computer.

✧　　✧　　✧

"Have you heard anything from Zach, Mom?" Arianne McBryde asked from Christina McBryde's com display.

"You mean as in in the last few hours?"

"I mean since this morning." Arianne sounded more than a little anxious, Christina noticed.

Arianne was the youngest of her four—three, now, she reminded herself with a familiar spasm of pain—children, with the ferociously sharp intellect the entire family seemed to share. She was an outstanding chemist and a scientific advisor to Brandon Ward, the Mesa System's CEO, with a career of which any woman could have been proud. But she was still Christina's baby girl, and hearing that anxiety in her voice was like a dull knife in Christina's heart.

"I had a voicemail from him in my message queue this morning," she said. "He sounded just fine, Honey."

"I think I probably got the same one," Arianne said. "Was it about that conference he's been called away to?"

"The one on McClintock Island, yes." Christina nodded. "Why?"

"Oh, I don't know . . ." Arianne shook her head. "He just sounded . . . worried, I guess."

"Oh, Sweetheart! He didn't sound 'worried' to *me*! Preoccupied, I thought—I'll give you that—and God knows we've all had plenty to feel preoccupied about lately." She cocked her head, smiling sadly at her daughter. "Are you sure it's not the date that's making you worry about him, Ari?" she asked very gently.

Arianne's face stiffened. She said nothing at all for at least ten seconds, then her nostrils flared as she inhaled deeply.

"Maybe it is," she admitted. "It's just that . . . just that . . ."

"Just that you miss Jack, Sweetheart. We *all* do. But it's been a year now, and just because *he* was in the wrong place at the wrong time when those horrible people set off those bombs doesn't mean anything terrible is going to happen to Zach, too. You know that, don't you? I mean, up here." Christina tapped her temple with an index finger. "Not here." She pressed the palm of the same hand to her chest, over her heart. "It's going to take all of us a while yet to really accept what happened, I think. I know I still wake up missing him, and so does your Dad. And JoAnne, too."

Arianna's blue eyes gleamed with unshed tears and she nodded mutely. She'd always been close to her big brother, and the fact that he was one of the hundreds of people whose bodies hadn't even been found after the Green Pines terrorist attacks was hard for her. Christina knew that, because it was hard for *her*, too. But she still had three children, she reminded herself, and it didn't matter that Arianne was fifty T-years old, either. It was still a mother's job to be strong for her children.

And if being strong for your kids helps carry you through the darkest bits, so much the better, she thought.

"Tell you what," she said more briskly. "Why don't you and George come over to supper tonight? Your dad's got the evening off, and I'm pretty sure I can pry JoAnne loose for the evening, too. It's about time the two of you got off the decicredit and actually set a date for the wedding. In fact, if you don't think it would sound too morbid, I think you might consider setting it for the anniversary of the day we lost Jack."

"Oh, Mom! I *couldn't*."

"Oh, yes you could." Christina felt her own eyes burn, but she smiled at her daughter. "I know you wanted Jack to be there, and I know he planned on being there. Well, it's not his fault that he won't be. But picking that date would be a way to celebrate his *life*, Ari, and you know as well as I do that what he'd want most in all the universe would be for you to get on with *your* life. I'm not saying it's a great idea. I'm saying that I think you should consider it. And that you should definitely plan on supper at home tonight. I've still got time to throw together a carrot cake, and you know how much Jack loved those!"

❖   ❖   ❖

Zachariah McBryde stood beside Lisa Charteris watching the display as the blue and green jewel of Mesa dwindled into the immensity of space. He didn't know the name of the ship they were on, although he supposed it was at least possible someone would let that obviously cosmically important information slip before they reached the first transfer point. He was damned if he could see any reason to keep it secret, anyway. Although the fact that *he* couldn't see a reason didn't mean their keepers couldn't.

He carefully avoided looking over his shoulder at S. Arpino, the keeper under whose eye they currently were. He wasn't sure where Zhilov, the second Gaul assigned to their small party, was at the moment. Probably someplace where he could keep *his* eye on the other . . . evacuees. For the life of him, Zach couldn't see the need for such continual—and overt—surveillance. Sure, some of the evacuees slated for removal under Operation Houdini might have second thoughts when the time came. Like Lisa, for example, whose husband wasn't on the list. Jules didn't have a clue about the inner ring of the onion any more than Zach's family did, and that—unfortunately—made it especially important to leave him behind.

So, sure, Lisa might have wanted to change her mind. For that matter, *Zach* might have felt the same way, especially after the cloud of suspicion which had gathered over Jack in the wake of the Green Pines Atrocity. He still didn't know what it was that they'd thought Jack might have done, but he was honest enough to admit—to himself, at least, and very quietly—that the way they'd pressed him during their investigation had really, really pissed him off. Pissed him off to the point of having a few second thoughts himself about the Alignment's true objectives and the entire Detweiler Plan. But he'd never seriously considered not reporting in when the Houdini activation code was passed. Not really.

Of course you didn't, he thought sardonically. *And the fact that Marinescu personally came to collect you and handed you straight over to Frick and Frack to go directly to the spaceport didn't have a* thing *to do with how cheerfully you accepted your movement orders!*

He smiled mirthlessly at the thought, because the one thing Jack had truly gotten through his skull over their years inside the onion was the need for operational security. And, as Jack had pointed out, there was no way to really know how someone would respond to conflicting imperatives before the moment actually came. Somebody, somewhere was going to try to avoid being extracted because of a wife, a lover, a child. It was *going* to happen, and the lack of warning, the hastiness with which Houdini had actually been mounted, could only make that worse. That was why Marinescu had turned up with the Gauls in tow to... discourage any second thoughts.

Yeah, I don't like it, but I understand it. But that still doesn't mean they have to keep watch over us every instant. We're aboard a frigging starship, for God's sake! We can't run, we can't hide, and we can't even talk to anybody else. So why the hell can't they at least back off just a little? They'll have plenty of warning to turn the wick back up before we reach the first transfer station.

"Did *you* get a chance to actually talk to your family?" Lisa asked him quietly.

Her head twitched ever so slightly, as if she'd

started to turn and look over her shoulder before she stopped it, and Zach turned his own head to look at her. Apparently she'd decided Mr. S. Arpino could go to hell if he didn't approve of her chosen topic.

"Not directly, no," he replied after a moment. "I got to record messages for all of them, but what's his name—Haas, Marinescu's XO—vetted them before they got dropped into their message queues. You talk to Jules?"

"Not directly." She sighed. "I left him and the kids voicemails, and I understand why I couldn't tell them where I'm really going, but I do wish I'd at least been able to talk to them face-to-face one last time."

"I know. But, you know, thinking about it, it may actually be easier this way. I'm not saying I wouldn't have preferred actually talking to my mom and dad one last time, but it would've been hard to keep from tearing up while I did. And if I did that, they want to know why. So maybe the Powers That Be know what they're doing, after all."

"It just feels so... dishonest," Lisa said. "I don't mean the disappearance itself or anything like that. That's necessary, and I understand that. But I hadn't realized I'd feel so guilty over just disappearing out of their lives—especially Jules', if I'm going to be honest. The girls are all grown, they have their own lives and families, and I'll miss all three of them like crazy. I hadn't really thought about how much I'd miss the grandkids, either. Maybe I just... didn't *want* to think about it, you know? But Jules and I have been married for over forty years, Zach. I *hate* the thought of his thinking I cared so little about him that I just... vanished."

Zach nodded sympathetically, and his sympathy was genuine. On the other hand, this was exactly why neither he nor Jack had ever married, ever started families of their own. They'd known—as Lisa had surely known—that the Alignment was entering the endgame stage of its long, shadowy existence. Oh, no one had expected Houdini to come this abruptly, no one had anticipated the way the Star Kingdom of Manticore—and now the Republic of Haven—would so completely overturn all the careful timetables, but they'd known it couldn't possibly have been more than another half-century or so. For people with prolong, and especially for alpha and beta-liners with prolong, a half-century was actually a fairly brief interval. Lisa had to have known she was likely to run into exactly this sort of situation when she married Jules in the first place, so it wasn't as if she hadn't realized she was offering up hostages to fortune.

But I suppose the brain and the heart don't always work smoothly together, and she really did love him. That's always been obvious. And maybe, down the road, she'll be able to remember all the good parts, all the joy, without feeling like she just abandoned them all. And it's not like they all died, or anything. She may be dead as far as they know, but she'll always know they're still there, still living and loving and remembering her. That's not so shabby, when you think about it.

"Well, nobody's told me so, you understand," he said out loud, resolutely ignoring the Gaul behind them, "but my brother Jack used to be up to his armpits in this kind of operation. Based on conversations I had with him, Marinescu and her people are going to have to come up with explanations for our disappearance. We can't just inexplicably drop out of sight without raising the very questions Houdini's supposed to prevent. It won't be the *real* explanation, and in that sense I suppose we are being dishonest with the people we've left behind. But it'll be the sort of explanation that makes it clear we didn't deliberately disappear. And that means Jules and your daughters—and my family—won't think we just abandoned them. I imagine the simplest way to do that will be to convince everyone we're dead. Probably in an air-car accident, or stepping in front of a ground car, or something like that. It may not make Jules any happier about losing you, but he's not going to blame you for running away from him if he thinks you're dead. And the truth is that you really didn't have much more choice than you would've had about a real air-car accident, Lisa. We're both too deep inside the onion for any other outcome. So, in a way, we're not being dishonest with the people we love at all. We didn't leave them because we *chose* to; we left them because we're part of something that didn't *give* us any choice."

"I suppose you're right." Lisa smiled up at him, briefly, then patted him on the arm. "And at least if I had to drop my entire life without any warning at all, I've still got at least one friend I can talk to about it. That's something."

"And once we get to Darius, we'll probably find out we have quite a few friends who were on the list," Zach told her, covering the hand on his forearm with his own. "Once we get past the upheaval, it'll sort itself out, Lisa. It always does."

❖   ❖   ❖

Rufino Chernyshev reached the final screen, closed the report, and sat back in his chair with a frown. Not because Marinescu's proposals weren't workable. In fact, he suspected, the fact that they *were* workable was what bothered him the most.

Not your call, he reminded himself. *And not really your responsibility, either. Which doesn't change the fact that you wish like hell you were still out in the field getting shot at somewhere, instead.*

His frown turned into a scalpel-thin smile, and he shoved up out of his comfortable chair to take a quick turn around his spacious office. Exercise, physical exertion—that was something else he missed about the field. Gym time just wasn't the same, somehow. Maybe because there was no adrenaline rush to go with it? But at least his workspace was big enough he could actually work up a sweat if he tried hard.

Marinescu's revised Houdini plan should accomplish everything Albrecht Detweiler wanted. Probably. The one imponderable was how long the Manties would give them, because it would take time to set the stage for Marinescu's "incidents." And even if that hadn't been true, they'd have to lift more personnel out in much bigger chunks than the original Houdini plan had envisioned. Rather than moving people in dribs and drabs, they'd have to put as many as several hundred warm bodies each aboard a much smaller number of ships. That promised to be ticklish. The existing plan had called for them to evacuate no more than eleven or twelve hundred critical personnel per month, and that would have been no problem at all. The normal mortality rate from all causes in the Mesa System ran to about four percent. In a star system with the next best thing to thirteen billion citizens, "disappearing" an additional 0.0000001% of the total population each month wouldn't be even a blip. But they couldn't do it that way under the accelerated timetable, and pulling out thirty or forty times that number in a single month, the way the new plan envisioned, would be something very different. Hence the "terrorist" scenario.

But even with "terrorist attacks" to explain people's disappearance, physically *moving* that many bodies would be another serious challenge—one which precluded the original intention of sending them out in small groups aboard ships which were part of the normal traffic flow. That meant juggling shipping movements to get the needed transport where it was required at the *time* it was required, and that equated to additional risk. And to the use of . . . suboptimal vessels in too many cases.

Marinescu's right about that, too . . . damn it. An awful lot of our people are going to have to travel aboard Manpower's slave transports. In fact, they'll have to travel in the slave quarters—*and won't they just love* that!

He was entirely happy that he wouldn't be the one listening to alpha and beta-liners from the upper strata of Mesa's scientific, political, and financial sectors who'd just found out they were traveling in the same quarters as *genetic slaves*. He didn't care who *did* end up listening to them, as long as it wasn't him!

And it beats hell out of what's going to happen to an awful lot of people right here on Mesa, he reflected grimly.

One of the aspects of Marinescu's revised plan that

he least liked was the way she'd cut down on the evacuation lists. A lot of people who'd thought they'd be leaving on that far distant day when Operation Houdini was put into effect wouldn't be. Marinescu had concluded that there simply wouldn't be time and personnel lift capacity enough to pull all of them out on the accelerated schedule, and she'd cold-bloodedly narrowed the list by removing "nonessential" names from it.

But the people to whom those names belonged couldn't be left behind, either, because they knew too much about the inner onion. None of them were deep enough inside to know the details—that was why she'd classified them as "nonessential" in the first place—but all of them were aware of the existence of the Detweiler Plan, and the galaxy at large could not become aware of its existence yet. The fact that Herlander Simões was available to spill what *he* knew about it to the Manties and the Havenites was bad enough; if a few thousand more Herlanders turned up right here on Mesa to confirm his "lunatic ravings" things could get very bad. And so, quite a few loyal members of the Alignment would gather at their evacuation points . . . only to become additional victims of those vicious "Ballroom terrorists."

He didn't like it. In fact, he *hated* it. But there truly wasn't another option, and Marinescu was reptilian enough to embrace that without flinching. Which confirmed a decision Chernevsky had made some time ago . . . without bothering Albrecht or Collin Detweiler about it.

But if all those people were going to die anyway, then surely he could at least make their deaths mean something. Contribute to the movement to which they'd dedicated their lives, even if at the very end that movement was forced to sacrifice them. The mere fact that they were "terrorist victims" would strengthen the narrative Albrecht and Marinescu were constructing, but there were going to be so many angry voices—Mesan and Manticoran, on both sides—shouting so stridently that the narrative was likely to get lost in the weeds. Unless...

He paused in his pacing, his eyes widening, and then he smiled. In fact, he chuckled at the first truly amusing thought to come out of the entire Houdini bloodfest. He crossed to his desk and punched the key on his com.

"Yes, Sir?" Samuel Hairston's voice replied almost instantly.

"Samuel, I need a message sent to Old Terra."

"Of course, Sir. To whom should I address it?"

"To Audrey O'Hanrahan," Chernevsky said with a broad smile. "I think it's time our wandering girl paid us a visit and did a nice human relations story right here on Mesa."

JULY 1922 POST DIASPORA

"Tell me, Elizabeth. Do you really think *Mike Henke* wouldn't've gone right ahead and responded exactly the same way even if the Governor had told her not to?"

—Lady Dame Honor
Alexander-Harrington,
Duchess and Steadholder
Harrington,
CO Grand Fleet.

Chapter Fifty-One

THE SKY OVER LAKE MICHIGAN was gorgeous, a flawless vault of midnight spangled with the glittering lights of mankind's original starscape and so clear of clouds not even the sky glow from the Solarian League's capital could hide it. The light-spangled flanks of Old Chicago's towers, rising sheer and tall out of the lake, reflected from its mirror-smooth surface like brighter, far more numerous stars, and the breeze rising from the water was a welcome kiss of coolness through the evening's residual heat.

Brigadier Simeon Gaddis sat on the balcony of his five-hundredth-floor apartment, gazing out across that panorama, and sipped thoughtfully at the tall, cold drink in his hand.

It seemed so calm, so peaceful, he thought. As if everything was just the way it had been before word of the Battle of Manticore reached Old Terra. Before the Navy discovered that Massimo Filareta's entire fleet had been captured or—in the case of what sounded like at least half his superdreadnoughts—destroyed by the "Grand Alliance" of Manticore and the Republic of Haven.

Never saw that one coming, he reflected. *Which probably says something about my own underestimate of what Manty weapons can do. But Manticore and Haven allied with each other? Maybe some of the spooks saw it on the horizon, but me?* He shook his head. *And whatever anyone like that idiot Nyhus has to say about it, that strikes me as pretty conclusive evidence the Manties—and the Havenites—are damned serious about this "Mesan Alignment" they claim is out there. Unless he wants to come up with something else that could make them not just stop shooting at each other but both shoot at us after the last eighty or ninety T-years of hating each others' guts!*

All of which gave added point to the information Lupe Blanton and Weng Zhing-hwan had shared with him.

He'd been through their documentation at least a dozen times in the months since they'd handed him their data chip. He'd been damned careful to keep that chip out of anything except his own personal, standalone reader, too. And he'd done a little very quiet, very cautious poking around of his own.

So far, as much as he'd have liked to conclude they were suffering paranoid delusions, he'd found no evidence of anything of the sort. Worse, he'd come to the conclusion that Rajmund Nyhus was actively manufacturing evidence that Manticore was orchestrating the unrest sweeping through the Verge. Gaddis was willing to concede that assuming Manticoran involvement was a natural leap, given the state of war—now a formal, *declared* state of war, thanks to the

Manties—between the League and the Star Empire. But Nyhus' reports (which Gaddis wasn't supposed to be seeing) were far too definite in their conclusions in that respect. The brigadier couldn't even have begun to guess how many other falsified documents he'd seen in the course of his career had carried that taint of fitting together too deeply, too perfectly. No, he was convinced they were a put-up job—or at least filled with data, much of it sketchy, to say the very least, which had been skillfully shaped into a deliberately misleading mosaic. So either Nyhus was a hell of a lot smarter than Gaddis had ever believed he was, or else he was fronting for someone.

Most likely, he's just being someone else's mouthpiece. Of course, that leaves the question of who "someone else" is. It really could be just your typical rotten-to-the-core transstellar trying to break the Manties' kneecaps, but I don't think so. I think Lupe and Weng are onto something, and that scares the shit out of me.

He took another small up from his glass, feeling the alcohol glow its way down his throat, and sighed.

And now Natsuko's getting involved, he thought glumly. *I wonder if she even begins to guess just how risky that could be?*

Given the choice of which of his subordinates he most trusted, he would have picked Lieutenant Colonel Natsuko Okiku without hesitation. And not just on a personal level. He'd seen her work—worked *with* her—for over ten T-years, and he'd learned to trust her instincts. She was quite young for her rank, not yet forty-three, but she was as determined to catch the bad guys—whoever they were and whatever friends they might have—as Gaddis himself. And she was also as sharp as they came and a brilliant, tenacious investigator who simply would not give up once she had her teeth into a problem. That was what made her so incredibly valuable.

And it was also likely to get her killed.

Gaddis was reasonably certain—but *only* reasonably certain—no one else had noticed her covert meetings with Captain Daud al-Fanudahi. He couldn't be positive, but he was pretty sure Major Bryce Tarkovsky, from Meindert Osterhaut's shop in Marine Intelligence, had also been privy to several of those meetings, and he knew Irene Teague had been present. That said quite a lot right there, since Captain Teague was Frontier Fleet and al-Fanudahi was Battle Fleet. But the question in Gaddis' mind was exactly what *Okiku* was doing as part of that thoroughly ominous little gathering.

No, he told himself. *It's not a "question" at all. What scares you is that you're pretty damned sure al-Fanudahi reached out to her through Tarkovsky for exactly the same reasons Lupe and Weng came to talk to you, Simeon. And, knowing Natsuko the way you do, you're equally sure what she told them.*

He drank again, then sighed once more, set the glass down, and reached for his personal com. He punched in a combination.

"Yes, Sir?" a voice replied, no more than ten seconds later.

"I know it's after hours, Natsuko, but there's something I'd like to discuss. Could you drop by my office about oh-nine-hundred tomorrow morning?"

"Of course, Sir. Should I ask what it's about?"

"Nothing that won't keep until then," he said calmly. "See you tomorrow."

"Yes, Sir. Good night."

"Night, Natsuko."

He cut the connection and gazed out over the placid, brilliant starscape of the water and the more distant, far vaster starscape of the heavens, and wished with all his heart the galaxy truly was that peaceful.

But it's not, Simeon. And if Natsuko's going to put her butt on the line, you damned well need to be out there at least covering her back. Besides, his lips quirked briefly as he reached for the glass once more, *you'll be a much more difficult target than one more lieutenant colonel who's only trying to do her job.*

"So, what do you make of all this?" President Eloise Pritchart waved one hand at the display where they'd just finished viewing the latest dispatches from the Talbott Quadrant.

"Well," Empress Elizabeth Winton replied, "I'm sure I'm naturally inclined to go along with Mike—Countess Gold Peak—simply because she's my cousin, but I think she's made a pretty compelling case, actually."

"I've known Mike almost as long as you have, Elizabeth," Honor Alexander-Harrington observed, "and I've never known her to go off after wild hares...in her professional capacity, at least." Her lips twitched. "Now, in her *personal* life, from time to time..."

"Just be glad you never knew Aunt Caitrin when she was Mike's age." Elizabeth shook her head and rolled her eyes. "That aside, however, should I assume you endorse her conclusions?"

"Of course I do." Honor shrugged. "I suppose I ought to admit I'm genetically predisposed—you should pardon the expression—to be suspicious as hell wherever

Mesa and Manpower are concerned. Having said that, it makes perfect sense from their perspective, given what we know about the 'Alignment' thanks to Captain Zilwicki and Agent Cachat. It's probably not costing much more than their efforts in Monica did, and look at the potential payoff from their side! I doubt they'd anticipated what we did to Filareta last month, but they have to know how this would be the equivalent of a red flag for OFS and the Mandarins. Given what Lacoön's doing to the League's cash flow, they literally can't afford to lose Verge systems. So this is guaranteed to draw the strongest response the Sollies are capable of. In the meantime, it'll play wonderfully to the Solly public when Abruzzi's shills at Education and Information present it as yet more evidence of our 'imperialist' ambitions. As for what happens when 'our' promised naval support doesn't turn up on schedule . . ."

She shook her head, her expression grim, and Benjamin Mayhew nodded.

"As someone whose star nation's been the beneficiary of Manticoran trustworthiness, I can tell you exactly how valuable the Star Kingdom's reputation for keeping its word really is."

"And as someone who was royally shafted by that bastard High Ridge, you've also had first-hand experience of what happened when the Star Kingdom didn't *keep* its word, too," the Earl of White Haven said grimly.

"I wouldn't go that far, Hamish," Benjamin disagreed gently. "I never thought the *Star Kingdom* wasn't keeping its word. I do have to wonder, though, how his and Descroix's foreign policy played into the thinking behind this."

"I'm sure it did," Pritchart said. "On the other hand, Arnold Giancola's . . . creative editing must've been at least as much a part of it. The way you and I were proclaiming diametrically opposed versions of our diplomatic correspondence did Manticore's reputation a lot of damage, I'm afraid, Elizabeth."

"Couldn't have done it if High Ridge hadn't set the stage for it," Elizabeth replied. "Which is taking us a little afield. Your question was whether or not I think Mike's uncovered an actual Alignment operation, and my response is that I definitely think she has. And I also completely approve of Baroness Medusa and Admiral Khumalo's reaction to it."

"I do too," Honor said, with something that looked suspiciously like a grin. Elizabeth quirked an eyebrow at her, and Honor chuckled. "Tell me, Elizabeth. Do you really think *Mike Henke* wouldn't've gone right ahead and responded exactly the same way even if the Governor had told her not to?"

"No," the Empress acknowledged. "Although I think it's remotely possible that if they'd sent her orders not to respond to any requests for assistance she'd at least exercise a little restraint about the *way* she responded."

"Sure you do." Honor shook her head.

"The reason I raised the question in the first place," Pritchart said, "is that I agree entirely that Baroness Medusa and the Admiral acted correctly . . . and that there are a couple of other points I think should be considered."

"What sort of points?" Elizabeth asked.

"First, it's important that as another member of the Grand Alliance the Republic be seen standing firmly with Manticore on this issue," Pritchart replied. "We can't afford to let the Mandarins think they see any daylight between us when you begin answering aid requests and we announce what's actually going on. I've discussed this with Tom Theisman and the other members of my Cabinet who're still here in Manticore, and they all agree. So I kicked it around a little more with Tom, and I'd like to offer some reinforcement to your Tenth Fleet."

"What sort of reinforcement did you have in mind?" White Haven asked.

"We were thinking about sending Lester to lend a hand," Pritchart said, and smiled at the Manticorans' expression. "Oh, not our entire component of the Grand Fleet." Her smile faded. "If the Sollies stay as stupid as they've been so far, you'll probably need that firepower a lot closer to home. But it occurred to us that if we peeled off one of his task forces—possibly minus a squadron or two of wallers and reinforced with additional light units—they'd substantially increase Admiral Gold Peak's firepower. His superdreadnoughts would be available if the League sends yet another fleet into Talbott in Crandall's wake, and the light units would increase Admiral Gold Peak's flexibility when those assistance requests start coming in. I'd also like to make some additional Marines available to her, but I'm afraid we'd have to collect them from home, first."

"That's a very generous offer, Eloise." Elizabeth Winton's eyes were as warm as her tone. "And I'll accept it gratefully. You're right about the firepower helping, but I think your point about showing solidarity's even better taken."

"You said you had a *couple* of points," Honor said.

"Yes, I did. And my second point is that I believe we need to spread the word on this. I don't see any way we could possibly get to all the planets who think they've been talking to you—not in time to keep an awful lot of them from walking straight into this. Especially not since first we'd have to figure out where those planets *are*. But one thing that's become clear is that this Alignment doesn't think small. That being the case, why should it limit its operations to systems in proximity to Talbott?"

"That's an ugly and entirely plausible possibility," Mayhew said slowly.

"Well, after that occurred to me, I asked myself where the next most likely spot might be, and it occurred to me that they've already tried to destroy Torch once. In light of that, I can't think of any reason they wouldn't spread this particular rat poison in Torch's vicinity. If they can sell the notion that what's happening in Mobius is part of a Manticoran effort to expand its frontiers, then building a defensive zone around Torch would make at least as much sense to their customers. And if the Alignment could simultaneously drive a wedge between the Republic and Erewhon by suggesting to the Erewhonese that our new ally is deliberately destabilizing their vicinity—no doubt at least partly because you're still angry over their signing an alliance with us—that would have to be a good thing from its perspective."

"I don't like that thought at all," White Haven said after a moment. "And I especially don't like it if what we think is happening in the Maya Sector really *is* happening. The last thing we need is to alienate Barregos.

And the *next*-to-last thing we need—assuming we're right about his plans—is for something to pull his superiors' attention in his direction before he's ready."

"That's exactly what I was thinking," Pritchart agreed.

"So you want us to pass this information along to Erewhon and Barregos," Elizabeth said.

"I think it would be wise." Pritchart nodded. "I know Erewhon still isn't your favorite star nation, Elizabeth. On the other hand, I suspect at least a handful of people might've said the same thing where the Republic of Haven was concerned up until recently."

"I suspect they might have," Elizabeth agreed with a slight smile. "Besides, I never really blamed *Erewhon* for what happened. Oh, I was more than moderately irked when they handed all that technology over to you people, but it wasn't as if High Ridge hadn't done everything humanly possible to drive them into your arms! Besides, our economic sanctions have slapped them pretty firmly on the wrist for that. And given the interstellar equation that seems to be working out in their neck of the woods, I think getting back onto good terms with them—and staying there—would be in the best interests of everyone involved."

"Daud, meet Lieutenant Colonel Weng," Natsuko Okiku said.

Captain Daud al-Fanudahi looked at the woman beside Okiku. She was a good fifteen centimeters taller than Okiku, and despite her surname, she was as fair-haired and blue-eyed as Okiku was black-haired and brown-eyed. And while they were the same rank and both of them wore Gendarmerie uniform, Weng's bore the hour-glass shoulder flash of the intelligence branch and not the scale balance of the Criminal Investigation Division.

"Colonel Weng," he said, extending his hand.

"Sir," she replied. Her grip was firm and she met his eyes steadily, both of which he decided—hoped— were good signs.

The three of them stood in Records Room 7-191-002-A, the same "active records repository" in which Okiku had first met with him, Irene Teague, and Bryce Tarkovsky barely two weeks earlier.

"I hope you won't take this wrongly, Colonel," he continued after a moment, "but I'm afraid I know very little about you."

"Which means you wonder what the hell use I could be and that you're a little nervous about meeting me at all," Weng said with a smile, and he nodded.

"Rather more bluntly phrased than someone of my own exquisite tact would have put it, but, yes."

"Well, I sure as hell hope that's what you're wondering," she said. "If it isn't—and if you're not worrying just a little over my *real* motives—there's something wrong with your brain."

"Like I told you, Daud, Brigadier Gaddis vouches for her personally," Okiku said.

Al-Fanudahi nodded. He was still a little bemused by the way Gaddis had swooped into "his" effort to determine who and what was manipulating the Solarian League . . . and to what end. He was deeply grateful, of course, but it made him more than a little nervous, too. If Gaddis had picked up on his core group's activities, who *else* might have noticed them? And the sense that everything was accelerating, speeding ever more rapidly into the unknown—and the dangerous—only made that nervousness worse.

"Yes, I know," he told Okiku, then turned back to Weng. "And if the Brigadier's prepared to vouch for you, that's good enough for me from a security perspective. I'm just not clear on exactly where you fit into our little conspiracy."

"Well," Weng said, "while you've been coming at this from one end, some interesting intelligence has fallen into my lap over in the Operations Division. I think Brigadier Gaddis is of the opinion that we need to combine my information with yours. Because if there's anything to your suspicions, Captain—and I'm afraid I think there is—there's an entirely new component you don't know anything about yet. You see—"

Chapter Fifty-Two

"FRANKLY, SINEAD," BERNARDUS VAN DORT said, "I'm not absolutely convinced Khumalo isn't right about this." He smiled slightly. "And I *am* convinced he's not going to be at all happy when he hears about your—our—plans."

He and Sinead Terekhov shared a table, gazing out over the ocean from the terrace of Mathonwy's, one of Thimble's most exclusive restaurants. Seabirds, mostly native species, but with a sprinkling of imported Old Earth gulls, rode the wind, seeming to hover motionless overhead before darting down to snatch some unwary tidbit from the water's surface. Storm clouds were rolling in from the east, but it would be hours yet before they reached the beachfront, and the sands were littered with sunbathers above the scalloped white line of gentle surf while heads bobbed against the waves offshore.

"At the moment, the thought that the good Admiral will be...irked only increases my enthusiasm," she told him. "And, frankly, I stopped asking anyone's permission about my movements about sixty T-years ago."

"Believe me, I understand." He shook his head. "Aivars described you to me, you know. I believe one of the things he said was 'stubborn as the day is long.' Which, coming from him, filled me with dread, you understand."

"I am *not* stubborn. In fact, I've never understood why the entire galaxy seems determined to apply that adjective to me."

"Of course you haven't."

He sipped wine, then his expression turned serious.

"The truth is, I wouldn't let you book passage if *Gertuida* wasn't armed . . . and *Iconoclast* wouldn't be keeping her company. I might not have been able to keep you from booking it aboard someone else's ship, but I wouldn't have helped you do it." He looked at her very levelly, and she nodded.

The Rembrandt Trade Union had had transitioned into Rembrandt United Shipping when the Talbott Sector's incorporation into the Star Empire of Manticore obliterated all internal customs duties. RUS remained the Talbott *Quadrant*'s biggest single shipping consortium by a sizable margin, however, although competition was beginning to appear, and the Van Dort family's dominant position in the Trade Union had been maintained in it.

RMS *Gertuida* was a six-million-ton freighter, not a passenger ship, but like most of the RTU ships she'd been equipped with a small number of extremely comfortable passenger suites for the Union's—and now RUS'—executives. Rather fewer of the Trade Union's ships had been armed, but not only was *Gertuida* one of them, she'd recently emerged from a refit in which her armament had been upgraded to Manticoran standards. Her missile defenses had been strengthened significantly, her own missiles had been upgraded to be at least as good as anything anyone outside the Grand Alliance was likely to possess, and she'd been equipped with a military-grade inertial compensator and particle screening to match. In fact, she would have made a formidable privateer, Sinead reflected. With the light cruiser *Iconoclast* in company, she should be more than equal to any threat she might encounter en route to Montana with her cargo of military spares, ammunition, and general stores.

And I can tell from his eyes he's remembering what happened to his wife and daughters, she thought. *I wonder if he knows Aivars told me about that?*

She felt a sudden surge of tenderness for the man who'd become her husband's friend and reached across the table to lay a hand on his forearm.

"I truly appreciate what good care you're taking of me. Aivars is lucky to have you for a friend."

"From where I sit, the luck's on the other side," he told her. Then he smiled. "You just be sure to tell him I put up a valiant struggle before you browbeat me into circumventing his station commander!"

"Oh, I promise!" she laughed.

❖   ❖   ❖

The luxurious vessel plowed across another ocean, three hundred light-years from the Spindle System, in a white smother of spray under a dome of sky polished to dark cerulean by scudding white clouds. The wind was out of the west at around forty kilometers per hour—what was still called a Force Six on the Beaufort Scale on every planet settled by humanity—piling up four-meter waves, but the *Grażyna* was just over two hundred meters long. She'd been built to take anything up to and including a Force Eleven in stride. The Wiepolski Ocean's current conditions weren't even enough to impart much in the way of motion, and Tomasz Szponder and his guest sat on the afterdeck, watching the fishing lines that trailed aft from the heavy-duty rods in the brackets at the corners of the deck.

Or that was what they were doing as far as any overhead imagery might have reported, anyway.

"So you and Tomek are satisfied?" Jarosław Kotarski said.

"As satisfied as we can be," Szponder replied. "It's the neatest solution we can think of, now that the Manties've promised their warships will arrive in the right time window. I'd really love to pull this entire thing off with nobody at all getting killed, but that's unlikely." He shook his head sadly. "The best we can say is that this way the smallest number of people are likely to be killed."

"I'm in favor of that," Kotarski said, yet his expression was worried.

"You know we're not going to find a better opportunity, Jarosław."

"Yes, I do. That doesn't mean I'm not...nervous at the prospect."

"And you should be. But I don't really see Krzywicka or any of the others turning down my invitation, do you?"

"From Party Number Seventeen on this *Dzień Przewodniczącego*?" Kotarski laughed. "And on Szafirowa Wyspa? Oh, I think you can count on most of the *aparatczycy's* attendance!"

"Exactly." Szponder nodded. "It means coming out into the open, and that's enough to make me at least as nervous as *you* are." He shrugged. "But it's absolutely our best chance to get all of them—probably even Pokriefke, this time—in one place, at one time, and in a situation under our control."

"And what about Mazur?" Kotarski asked, and Szponder grimaced.

"I've discussed that with Radosław and Kinga," he said. "Their opinion is that this year, he'll *have* to attend."

Kotarski still looked skeptical, but he also nodded. Radosław Kot wasn't simply a journalist, and Kinga Kowalewska wasn't just an artist. As it happened, Kinga—who was active on the literary café scene, as well as a well-known painter—was a confidential informant for the BBP. In fact, she'd been recruited by the black jackets specifically because of her relationship with Kot. His youthful record as a "hooligan," which was political-speak for "troublemaking dissident," would have made him an object of official interest even without his decision to become a newsy, so Justyna Pokriefke's secret police had "suggested" to Kinga that if she wanted to stay out of the BBP's black book herself, she should keep an eye on her longtime lover.

Of course, the BBP hadn't realized both of them were already members of the Krucjata Wolności Myśli.

More to the point at the moment, Radosław and Kinga were the best analysts the Krucjata had where the day-to-day realities of the *Oligarchia* were concerned. Szponder was a member of the *Oligarchia*, but they were *students* of it. They'd focused their attention upon it with all the tenacity which had made Radosław a successful reporter even in Włocławek, and their grasp of its internal dynamic was actually better than his. And that meant their estimate of Hieronim Mazur's response to an invitation to spend *Dzień Przewodniczącego* as Szponder's guest was probably the best anyone could have given.

And, Kotarski conceded to himself, *even he's likely to feel compelled to . . . modify his routine a bit this year.*

Mazur had made a point of never joining the Ruch Odnowy Narodowej. That hadn't prevented him from contributing generously to the Party's coffers; influence buying was an old, well-understood game among the Włocławekan elites. But he'd deliberately chosen to maintain official separation between himself and the Party's *aparatczyków* as part of the pretense that the RON remained the vigilant guardian of the people, dedicated to their well-being and the sworn foe of any who would oppress or exploit them. As such, he normally avoided Party functions, including *Dzień Przewodniczącego*—Chairman's Day—the planet-wide holiday on which the Ruch Odnowy Narodowej celebrated its rise to power.

But this Chairman's Day would be different. Not only would it be the thirty-fifth anniversary of the successful culmination of the *Agitacja,* but this year was also the one hundredth anniversary of Włodzimierz Ziomkowski's birth. The reform party he'd founded had become something very different from anything he'd ever intended, but that only increased the fervor with which it embraced his life as the emblem of its virtue.

"I'd really prefer more preparation time," Szponder continued, "but we've got a month. That should be more than long enough for the critical strike teams, and from the viewpoint of operational security, the shorter the timeframe, the less likely something is to leak to Pokriefke or any of her *czarne kurtki*."

"That's true enough," Kotarski agreed. "And the fact that you've already stashed so many of Mwenge's weapons on Szafirowa Wyspa won't hurt, either!"

"No, it won't." Szponder smiled. "Remind me to thank Hieronim—later, of course—for mobilizing the fisheries for us. And just think how appropriate it is to take back Włodzimierz's revolution on Szafirowa Wyspa! Somehow, wherever he is, I expect him to be more than a little amused by the irony, don't you?"

Kotarski didn't smile; he *laughed*.

The furiously angry planetary unrest spawned by the Lądowisko airbus shoot-down had spread to the men and women who manned the Stowarzyszenie Eksporterów Owoców Morza's enormous fishing fleet. Over a dozen of the murdered children aboard that airbus had come from fishery families, and many of their grieving parents' coworkers had joined their demand for justice. They'd actually had the temerity to march in protest demonstrations in downtown Lądowisko. Mazur and the SEOM management hadn't liked that at all, so they'd made examples by terminating the dead kids' parents for taking unauthorized time off. And they'd made it clear they'd fire anyone else guilty of the same offense.

Over a hundred other workers, some of them key low-level management employees, had defied their edict, and they'd followed through with the promised firings. It had hurt productivity, but there were always enough people on Włocławek desperate for work that the downtick had been manageable, and that had made it an acceptable price for choking off visible political unrest.

Yet that hadn't ended the unrest in question; it had simply driven it underground. The KWM had enlisted dozens of members from the fishing boat crews and processing plant staffs even before the airbus was shot down. After Mazur's declaration of war on political dissidence, recruiting had surged. And that meant the SEOM's own fishing boats had transported the weapons Dupong Mwenge had supplied to the KWM across the Wiepolski to Szafirowa Wyspa, Sapphire Island, the private island the Szponder family had owned for the better part of three T-centuries.

It wasn't an especially huge island, but at forty-one kilometers long and almost twenty-four kilometers broad at its widest point, it wasn't exactly tiny, either. In fact, it had a total area of just under five hundred square kilometers, most of which remained in a virgin state, aside from a handful of isolated beach houses and Prezent do Praksedá, the enormous, landscaped estate Szponder's great-great-great grandfather had built for his great-great-great-grandmother.

That much space had provided plenty of room to conceal the KWM's small arms and crew-served weapons. And the Ruch Odnowy Narodowej's original charter had been signed in the grand dining room of Prezent do Praksedá.

Under the circumstances, Kotarski reflected, *Tomasz has a point. I've never been all that sure about afterlives, but if there is one, Włodzimierz's going to laugh his ass off if we actually make this work.*

❖   ❖   ❖

"It's good to see you, *Ma'am*." There was a twinkle in Commander Naomi Kaplan's eye as she emphasized the rank title, and Ginger Lewis waved one hand in an airy gesture.

"Always good to maintain one's seniority over the little people," she said complacently, and Kaplan chuckled and looked at her own tactical officer.

"You should make a note of that, Abigail," she advised.

"Before I can think about maintaining anything, first I have to get senior to someone," Abigail Hearns pointed out. "Not that such an unworthy thought would ever cross my mind. Unlike you heathen Manticorans, Graysons understand how important it is to maintain an appropriate humility in our dealings with those less fortunate than ourselves."

"*Sure* you do," Ginger said. "I've noticed how shy and retiring you are."

The three of them sat in comfortable chairs in her day cabin, and she smiled at the younger woman. Abigail smiled back, although there'd been some suspiciously damp eyes when they arrived aboard *Charles Ward* as her guests. Abigail was fairly certain it hadn't been a coincidence Aubrey Wanderman happened to be in the boat bay, personally supervising the side party when they came aboard, either. Paulo d'Arezzo would be joining them for supper when he came off-watch in about ninety minutes, and despite his noncommissioned rank, Wanderman would be there as well.

At which point, she reflected, forty-five percent of HMS *Hexapuma*'s total surviving personnel would sit down around a single dinner table.

With plenty of room to spare.

"I'm only sorry you missed the Commodore and Helen," she said as that bittersweet thought went through her.

"It happens...a lot," Ginger observed. "And maybe it's just as well Admiral Khumalo bumped Sinead—Ms. Terekhov, I mean—off the *CW* in Spindle." She shook her head. "Somehow I don't think finding out she'd missed him by less than forty-eight hours would have been a happy thought for her. In fact, I'm pretty sure she would have broken something. Probably a *lot* of somethings." She chuckled. "That's a lady who knows what she wants, and she's about through waiting for the Navy to let him come home again."

"Hard to blame her," Kaplan said. "It's not like they *left* him home very long."

"And they do have a tendency to send him off on...challenging missions," Abigail agreed.

"That's something I wanted to ask you two about," Ginger said. "What's all this business about Mobius? All I know about it is that Mitya Nakhimov, my astrogator, tells me it's about two hundred light-years from here. I'm assuming there's a *reason* Admiral Gold Peak's sending an entire division of *Saganami-Cs* off to it?"

⬥ Chapter Fifty-Three

"BE SEATED, LADIES AND GENTLEMEN," Rear Admiral Craig Culbertson said as he walked briskly into the flag briefing room, accompanied by Captain Roscoe Weisenthal, his flag captain, and Captain Helena Sammonds, his chief of staff. "I apologize for my tardiness," he continued, crossing to his chair "Captain Weisenthal's XO had a point that needed clarification."

He sat, and the assembled squadron and division commanders who'd politely ignored his command to seat themselves, followed suit. He smiled and shook his head, then tipped back his chair. He was a tallish, sandy-haired man with a full, neatly trimmed beard, and he normally smiled a lot. Today, though, his smile faded quickly and his brown eyes were intense as they swept the men and women around the briefing room table.

"I assume you're all waiting with bated breath to discover the reason for this summons," he said, "and I won't keep you in suspense. The primary purpose of this meeting is to discuss with you the possibilities Captain Grierson's arrival from Manticore present. I realize his cruisers and destroyers scarcely represent a vast increase in our combat power, but they do significantly increase the total number of platforms available to us. So it's occurred to me that Admiral Gold Peak might expect us to do something with that availability."

He paused and, here and there, a head nodded. Mike Henke had left Culbertson's CLAC squadron—already understrength by one carrier, even before HMS *Cloud* had been detached to accompany Sir Aivars Terekhov to Mobius in response to Michael Breitbart's second, desperate request for assistance—to cover Montana. She'd left him two divisions of *Saganami-C*-class heavy cruisers—Prescott Tremaine's CruDiv 96.1 and Captain Otmar Kenichi's CruDiv 94.2—and a pair of destroyer squadrons. The first division of Terekhov's CruRon 94 would return to Culbertson's command as soon as he'd completed his mission to Mobius, but no one knew exactly how long that mission was likely to take, since no one knew the situation he'd find when he arrived there.

In terms of defending Montana, Culbertson's remaining five CLACs, supported by eight *Saganami-Cs* plus the large number of Mark 23 missile pods aboard his munitions ships, should be adequate to deal with any likely Solarian threat. In the meantime, the rest of Tenth Fleet was in the process of uniting in the Tillerman System for a direct attack on Meyers, the administrative capital of the Office of Frontier Security's Madras Sector. Culbertson had no qualms about Gold Peak's decision to take the war to the Sollies—not after she'd received confirmation Massimo Filareta was about to attack the Manticore Binary System—but it had left him with too little butter for his bread where additional Mobius-like situations might be concerned.

Of course, she hadn't known—then—how the Second Battle of Manticore had worked out. Culbertson did, and that was part of the reason for this meeting.

"My current thinking," he continued out loud, his expression grimmer, "is that we really don't know how many other places these Alignment bastards may have promised desperate people Manticoran support. Admiral Gold Peak's instructions to answer any support request have been confirmed by Governor Medusa and Admiral Khumalo. But she didn't know at that point how decisively Filareta would be defeated or what sort of reinforcements that might free up for us here, and until Captain Grierson arrived, we were far too shorthanded for her to have contemplated our doing anything more . . . proactive than waiting for someone to come calling. And, frankly, Mobius was damned lucky to find the Admiral here when Ankenbrandt arrived. He wasn't looking for the Navy in Montana; he only expected to send a message on to Spindle. So I don't think we should assume anyone else is going to be sending messages *here*, however badly they need help. They're more likely to send them direct to Spindle, exactly the way Ankenbrandt intended to do before he found us here. Or, as Commander Fremont"—he nodded to Commander Louis Fremont, his staff operations officer—"suggested to me the other evening, they're likely to not send them to *us* at all."

One or two people frowned, and Culbertson snorted.

"The point the Commander made to me over supper the other night—ruined my digestion, too, I might add—is that if *he'd* been in charge of setting up this operation, he'd also have set up 'communications chains' that went either to the Alignment . . . or nowhere at all." He smiled bleakly. "Unfortunately, that theory fits entirely too well with the sole case we know about. The only reason Mr. Breitbart's messengers came to Montana was that after the attack on Trifecta Tower, the situation on Mobius disintegrated so quickly he had to improvise, using his *own* communications assets rather than the ones the 'Manties' set up for him. After Commander Fremont made his suggestion, I went back over everything both Ankenbrandt and Ms. Summers said before they were sent on to Spindle. Neither of them ever mentioned what sort of communication channels their 'Manticoran' contact had established, but it was clear they were operating *outside* those channels because of how suddenly the situation had worsened. And that leads me to believe Commander Fremont's almost certainly correct about what was *supposed* to happen when they asked for help.

"Which further suggests that if anyone *else* needs our help, they're going to be telling the wrong people about it."

He paused, and the silence was deafening as his officers digested the implications.

"If that happens," he resumed after a moment, his eyes cold, "thousands of people—maybe hundreds of thousands, or even *millions*—are going to die thinking the Star Empire of Manticore—*our* Star Empire, Ladies and Gentlemen—betrayed them. And I've decided that's not going to happen anywhere we can do anything about it."

"I think we're all onboard with that, Sir." Scotty Tremaine's voice was harsh. "May I ask how you plan to go about it, though?"

"Indeed you may, Captain." Culbertson let his

chair come upright, planting his forearms solidly on the table top. "Captain Grierson's arrival gives us far more light platforms than Admiral Gold Peak ever contemplated when she drafted our instructions. Captain Zavala's Saltash operation also gives us a far better meterstick for how effective those light platforms can be, even against heavy Frontier Fleet units. My primary responsibility at this time is the defense of Manticoran citizens here in Montana, but that doesn't mean I can't take advantage of that effectiveness and those platforms. What I intend to do is to organize at least three, hopefully four, task groups of light cruisers and destroyers. I'd like for each of them to have a core of at least one division of *Rolands*, to give them some long-range firepower. I may break up your division, Captain Tremaine, to assign a *Saganami-C* to each of them, as well. And I also intend to attach a single freighter—I'm looking at our smaller support ships first, but I'm willing to commandeer civilian ships from the supply chain Admiral Khumalo's set up for us here in Montana, if I have to—with a load of Mark 23 pods and a pair of dispatch boats, so they can send for more help if they need it.

"While Captain Sammonds organizes that, Commander Fremont and I will go through every scrap of intelligence we can turn up, trying to identify star systems in our vicinity—within a couple of hundred light-years, let's say—the Alignment may have targeted. Frankly, I doubt we'll find enough information to make meaningful determinations, but it may at least help us prioritize a bit. Either way, though, I intend for those squadrons to depart Spindle within forty-eight hours—seventy-two, at the outside."

He paused, and Commodore Madison, the CO of his second CLAC division, raised an eyebrow.

"And do what when they get there, Sir?" he asked in the voice of someone who suspected he already knew the answer to his question.

"The gloves are off now," Culbertson said flatly. "You've all seen the reports on Second Manticore. As Duchess Harrington told Filareta, if war's what the Sollies want, then war is what they're damned well going to *get*. By this time, Kolokoltsov and the other Mandarins have received the Grand Alliance's formal declaration of war, and Admiral Gold Peak is already moving on the Madras Sector. That being the case, I see no reason we shouldn't take a few offensive steps of our own. I intend to take or destroy any Frontier Fleet units in those systems. In addition, we will seize any Solarian civilian shipping as legitimate prizes of war . . . and if our people should just happen to walk into another Mobius situation"—those bleak, brown eyes circled the table again—"then they can damned well do something about it."

❖   ❖   ❖

"So you're Stephen Westman," Sinead Terekhov observed.

"Indeed I am, Ma'am." Westman doffed his Stetson and swept a remarkably graceful bow as she finished stepping from the boarding tube to the shuttle pad. Then he straightened, blue eyes glinting under the bright Montana sun. "An' from the portrait Aivars keeps in his cabin, you must be Sinead."

"And you figured that out all on your own," she marveled with a smile.

"Ma'am, I know Montanans have a reputation for

not havin' the very quickest brains around," he said earnestly. "Howsomesoever, that's not really fair. Why, *most* Montanans're just as smart as anyone else you might meet. Then there's the ones like me. The ones who need a mite of help t' know when t' come in out of the rain. But we *do* try, really . . . and I s'pose I might's well add that Captain Lewis warned me you'd most likely be along." He shook his head with a smile of his own. "I should've realized old Bernardus'd come up with a ship for you."

"Aivars does seem to have made friends in the oddest places out here," she agreed, extending her hand.

"He's the kind of man does that," Westman agreed, and raised her hand to his lips rather than shaking it. Then he tucked it into the crook of his left arm and waved his right arm at the pad lift.

"I understand you have that effect on people, too," he said with a smile. "An' Captain Lewis warned me you were . . . 'a force of nature,' I b'lieve she said."

"No? Did she really?!" Sinead laughed. "I'm not nearly that fearsome, Mr. Westman!"

"Don't think I said anything 'bout 'fearsome,'" he replied. "However, soon's she told me that, I reserved the Presidential Suite at the Comstock—that's the best hotel here in Estelle—for you. Been holdin' it for the last week, waitin' for you and Bernardus t' get around Admiral Khumalo." His smile broadened, but then his expression softened and he patted the hand in the crook of his arm "Reckon that's the least Montana—and I—can do for Aivars till he gets back here."

❖   ❖   ❖

"Well, there they go, Sir," observed Helena Sammonds, standing on HMS *Elf*'s flag bridge as she and

Craig Culbertson watched the icons accelerating steadily towards Montana's hyper limit. "At least we made your deadline. But you're dumping a lot of responsibility on some fairly junior captains," she added.

"Of course I am." Culbertson turned from the display. "I think they're up to it, though. And whether they are or not, I agree with Admiral Gold Peak. I'm not letting thousands of people who trusted us die thinking we betrayed them."

"And that bit about destroying any Frontier Fleet units they meet?"

Sammonds, Culbertson knew, wasn't second guessing him. What she *was* doing was giving him one last opportunity to consider his instructions to the commanders of those improvised task groups, check his orders one last time for potential improvements, while they were still in com range.

"Admiral Gold Peak was right about that, too," he said. "She couldn't know we'd formally declare war after Filareta attacked the home system, but it wouldn't really matter either way."

He shrugged and twitched his head sideways at the display.

"All they're going to run into out here in the Verge is Frontier Fleet. I know Frontier Fleet's one hell of a lot more competent than Battle Fleet, but I'll be astonished if there's more than three or four warships in any of the systems on our list. I could be wrong about that. And if the Alignment's plans to ginger up resistance movements have borne fruit, I suppose the locals may have requested additional support. Even so, the most they're going to see is a handful of battlecruisers, and Zavala demonstrated what the

Mark 16 G can do to Solly battlecruisers. Every one of those ships has additional pods limpeted to their hulls, and we've assigned one of Tremaine's *Saganami-Cs* to each task group. I know he hated breaking up his division, but if just five *Rolands* can dismantle four Solarian battlecruisers with a single salvo, then three or four of them backed by a *Saganami-C* can handle anything they're likely to run into out here. And whatever the Sollies may think, we're at war with the bastards now, Helena. So if there's anyone out here stupid enough to pull the trigger rather than cut his wedge and surrender when he sees Manticoran warships entering his system, he'll deserve whatever the hell he gets."

✦ Chapter Fifty-Four

"GOVERNOR," HÅKON ELLINGSEN SAID as Jeremy Frank escorted him once again into Oravil Barregos' office.

"Mr. Ellingsen." Barregos held out his hand. "And this is—?" He raised his eyebrows at the much smaller man at Ellingsen's side.

"Abernathy, Governor," the newcomer said. "Captain Vitorino Abernathy."

"I see." Barregos shook his hand in turn, and then nodded to the man who'd risen from the chair beside his desk. "And this is Admiral Rozsak."

"A pleasure to meet you Admiral," Abernathy said, shaking his hand in turn. "We've heard a lot about you. The stand you made to defend Torch..." He shook his head in obvious admiration, and Rozsak shrugged.

"We had a commitment. A moral one, as well as a treaty."

"I'm aware of that, but your people paid almost as heavy a price—heavier, in absolute terms—than Duchess Harrington paid in Grayson. That's something any Manticoran can admire."

Rozsak shrugged again, this time a little uncomfortably, and Abernathy let it drop.

"I suggest we all sit down and get to it," Barregos said after a moment, directing his guests to the small conference table. "Would either of you gentlemen like anything to drink? I anticipate being here a while, and snacks are available. On the other hand, Luiz here is something of a cook, and he's offered to feed us all if we take a break in two or three hours."

"According to the Admiral's dossier, 'something of a cook' is something of an understatement." Ellingsen smiled. "I'll gladly sit down to any meal he'd care to offer."

"I hope you still feel that way *after* you've eaten," Rozsak said with an answering smile.

"I'm not too worried about that, Admiral," Ellingsen replied, and set his small briefcase on the table. He opened the sophisticated security locks and extracted a chip folio and a compact holo unit.

"It occurred to me that we could save some time by letting Secretary Langtry explain things to you personally, Governor," he said, and popped one of the chips into the player. A moment later, the distinguished image of Sir Anthony Langtry, Foreign Secretary of the Star Empire of Manticore appeared above the reader. He was seated behind a desk in an obviously formal setting, with the skyline of the city of Landing visible through the window behind his left shoulder. Ellingsen cocked an interrogative eyebrow at Barregos, and, when the governor nodded, pressed the play button.

"Governor Barregos," Langtry said, "I appreciate your willingness to continue these conversations with

Mr. Ellingsen. Obviously, we—the Star Empire and the Maya Sector—have a great deal to discuss, and we're not going to get all of it worked through in a single session. I feel it's important for you to know precisely what we're thinking here in Landing, however, so I've recorded this message. Mr. Ellingsen is fully in my confidence, and he can expand on any point where you feel additional clarification is necessary or desirable."

He paused for a moment, as if to allow that to settle, then continued.

"Essentially, we find ourselves needing all the allies we can get. The Republic of Haven's willingness to stand with us against Solarian aggression's been a godsend. Frankly, especially after the Yawata Strike, I doubt our position would be survivable without President Pritchart's full-blooded support. But 'survivable' isn't necessarily the same as *good*, I'm afraid, and that doesn't even consider this 'Mesan Alignment' we've only recently learned exists. As you and Admiral Rozsak are probably better aware than most, we possess a significant advantage in war-fighting capability at the tactical level. *Strategically*, our ultimate prospects are far less hopeful. The population base and industrial power of the Solarian League are many times that of the Star Empire and Republic of Haven, combined. Eventually, even Sollies—no offense"—he smiled tightly—"have to recognize our advantages . . . and seek to acquire the same capabilities for themselves.

"Given enough time, they *will* succeed in doing exactly that."

Langtry paused again. This time his expression was bleak, and he sipped from the coffee cup on his desk before he resumed.

"Our best—perhaps our only—hope is to defeat the League quickly, in the shortest possible war. In large part, to conclude hostilities before the League can fully mobilize its R and D against us, but also to end the fighting with as little additional loss of life and destruction of property as possible. The less damage we do, the fewer Solarians we kill, the better our chance of concluding a peace settlement that avoids the sort of revanchism which would send the League back to war with us as soon as its weapon-makers duplicate our advantages.

"And that's what brings us to Maya."

The foreign secretary looked directly into the camera.

"It's become clear the Mandarins will never conclude a negotiated peace. It's stupid, and ultimately self-destructive, but they appear to be convinced they've crawled too far out on the limb to back down. They're prepared to kill as many people as necessary to buy the survival of their personal power and the system that gives it to them, and the fact that they aren't answerable to any effective political oversight is what's allowed them to do that. So for any negotiated settlement to become possible, the Mandarins have to go. And because there's no political mechanism to remove them, we must create a situation in which the League Assembly—or at least sufficient of the League's member star system—*create* that mechanism out of a sense of self preservation.

"We hope to convince them they *must* take action if the League is to survive. You no doubt know even better than I just how much outright hatred for Frontier Security and the League in general exists in the Verge, and how thoroughly justified it is. We propose to give that hatred, that legitimate yearning for independence from the political and economic system which has raped the Verge for so long, a voice in order to multiply the threats the Core Systems can recognize. We believe a flare of widespread unrest—and calls in Old Chicago from the threatened economic interests for its suppression—will generate a Core World perception, even among those who don't realize how critical to the League government's budget the revenues squeezed from the Verge truly are, that the League is sliding towards dissolution. Towards that end we've been promoting discussions with . . . action-oriented reform elements in many of the Protectorates and quite a few nominally independent star systems. It's been our policy to avoid encouraging anyone we feel has a less than even chance of success, since it would do neither them nor our cause any service to promote rebellions which fail. Where we believe the chance of success exists, however, we stand ready to provide both weapons and naval support.

"Obviously, I'm speaking to you because we're aware, in at least a general sense, of your apparent plans in the Maya Sector. We believe an independent Maya under your governance would be a vast improvement over the present arrangement, and it would clearly be in our self-interest to engender friendly relations with such an independent star nation. It would also be in our interest to repair our relationship with Erewhon and generally shore up the strategic flank of both the Star Empire and the Republic of Haven in your vicinity.

"Because of that, I now formally offer you an alliance with the Star Empire and the Republic. For obvious reasons, this isn't something any of us would be announcing publically anytime soon. However, Mr. Ellingsen and Captain Abernathy are authorized to discuss with you what sort of military—and economic—support you might require in order to succeed in your...endeavor."

He paused again, then smiled slightly.

"There's an old, old piece of pre-diaspora political wisdom I think applies to all of the League's adversaries. 'If we don't hang together, we will all hang separately.' It would seem to me, and to my Empress and President Pritchart, that it would be far wiser of the Grand Alliance and the Maya Sector to hang together at this moment.

"Langtry, clear."

"Well, that's a sight I never expected to see. Or that I never *wanted* to see rolling towards me, back in the day, anyway," Captain Loretta Shoupe said.

She, Commander Ambrose Chandler, and Captain Victoria Saunders stood with Augustus Khumalo in his ancient flagship's CIC watching the displays. And, Khumalo had to admit he shared her sentiments; it wasn't a sight *he'd* ever expected to see, either.

"Just as glad no one expects me to repel the invasion," Captain Saunders said dryly. "*Hercules* is a game old bitch, but she'd be just a bit outclassed by *that*."

She twitched her head at the display, and Khumalo snorted.

"Vicki," he told his flag captain, "no disrespect to *Hercules*, but if you even suggested going up against that kind of firepower, I'd not only relieve you of command, I'd have you committed!"

Eloise Pritchart and Thomas Theisman had done Lester Tourville proud when they detached him from the alliance's Grand Fleet. Although he'd given up

Vice Admiral Sampson Hermier's entire task force and lost one superdreadnought squadron from each of his two remaining task forces, those task forces had each received two additional squadrons of battlecruisers and an additional flotilla of light cruisers in exchange. Altogether, the new, revised Second Fleet boasted two hundred and thirty-one warships. With its fleet train of attached ammunition and service ships, over two hundred and fifty Havenite starships were decelerating steadily towards Spindle . . . and thirty-two of them were modern SD(P)s, although—like Tenth Fleet's existing superdreadnought strength—none were equipped with Keyhole-Two.

"How much do we know about Tourville, Sir?" Saunders asked. "I know he was in command of the lead Peep—Sorry; I guess I'd better watch that. I mean, I know he was in command of the lead *Havenite* element when they hit Manticore. And I understand he commanded the ambush force that dropped out of hyper to box Filareta when the *Sollies* hit Manticore."

She shook her head, clearly still bemused by the speed with which the implacable hostility of the last five or six decades had disappeared.

"I figure all of that—and the fact that they picked him to command these people"—she twitched a gesture at the display—"indicate he's pretty good, but I don't really have a feel for *how* good."

"I think that's a question for my always well-informed staff," Khumalo said and cocked his head at Chandler. "Ambrose?"

"According to reports, Ma'am," his staff intelligence officer told Saunders, "he's more or less the Havenite version of Duchess Harrington. Or maybe

Lady Gold Peak, actually, since he's got a reputation as a cowboy, the sort of fellow who'd be comfortable on Montana." Saunders chuckled, and Chandler shrugged. "I'm inclined to think that reputation's... somewhat exaggerated, though. After all, there are those who'd describe Admiral Gold Peak the same way—that's why I said he might be more a Havenite Countess Gold Peak than a Duchess Harrington—and we all know they'd be wrong about *her*. I think they'd be equally wrong about him, because I doubt a real 'cowboy' would've compiled the combat record he has. Duchess Harrington's the only commander who's ever beaten him, and he's the only commander who's ever beaten *her*, although, to be fair, the odds were sort of stacked in his favor that time."

"While you're being 'fair,' Ambrose," Loretta Shoupe said dryly, "you might want to remember that the last time Duchess Harrington beat *him*, she had Apollo... and he didn't."

"That's a valid point," Khumalo agreed. "But the important thing here, Vicki, is that Admiral Theisman and President Pritchart have sent us the man who's almost certainly the best fleet commander they have." It was his turn to shake his head. "I would really, *really* hate to be the Solly admiral sent out to attack Talbott now that we've got both those cowboys—or cowgirls, as the case may be—to kick his ass," he added in tones of profound satisfaction.

✧   ✧   ✧

"Governor Medusa," Lester Tourville said, stopping exactly three meters from Estelle Matsuko's desk. He braced to attention and bowed ever so slightly—a nice balance, she decided, between the Republic of Haven's aggressive egalitarianism and the sort of formality most people associated with monarchies. The treecat on his shoulder watched the two-leg ritual with bright, interested eyes . . . and what she suspected was amused tolerance.

"Admiral Tourville," she replied, rising and walking around the desk to extend her hand. "You are a *most* welcome visitor."

"Thank you, Milady," he replied, shaking the offered hand, and his bushy mustache quivered slightly as he smiled. Then his expression sobered. "I'm afraid Manticorans haven't always been happy to see me in the past. I hope that's not going to be a problem for anyone out here."

"If it is, I assure you Admiral Khumalo, Admiral Gold Peak, and I will all stamp on it with both feet the instant it rears its head." She met his gaze levelly, despite their substantial difference in height. "You fought for your star nation just as they've fought for theirs, and we all know a lot more now about *why* we were fighting each other. More to the point, your Navy stood up to confront the Solarian League with us *despite* how long we've been fighting one another. If we have any anti-Haven bigots out here, I *want* them to show themselves, because as soon as they do, I *promise* you they'll be on their way home. And not with any glowing letters of commendation in their personnel files!"

Tourville glanced from the corner of one eye at the treecat on his shoulder. The 'cat nodded ever so slightly, and Medusa carefully took no note of the interchange. She'd been informed that the treecats had begun providing what amounted to bodyguards for key members of the Grand Alliance's leadership, although she hadn't realized one had been attached to Tourville. Obviously, though, he'd already gotten into the habit of letting his six-limbed companion evaluate the sincerity of those with whom he came into contact.

"I'm deeply relieved to hear that," he told her soberly. "There are still people in my Navy, some of them on my own staff, who have ... reservations about our cooperation with the Star Empire. Not on any sort of political or professional level, but more on a ... personal one, I suppose. I imagine that's inevitable, given how many of our friends and fellow officers—in both navies—have been killed fighting each other. But I assure you that you won't find any 'bigots' in Second Fleet, either. Or, if you do, at least, they'll be headed home on the same ship as *your* bigots."

"That sounds more than fair to me, Admiral," Medusa said warmly. "And on behalf of myself, Prime Minister Alquezar and his Cabinet, and Admiral Khumalo and the Royal Manticoran Navy, I hereby invite you, your staff, and as many of your senior officers as you'd like to bring along for a banquet this evening. Regular service dress uniform will be fine. This isn't going to be a tedious formal affair. Instead, Treasury Minister Lababibi has arranged the Spindle version of a clambake." She smiled. "Be sure to warn your officers they're likely to be wandering barefoot in the surf before the evening's done!"

❖　　❖　　❖

"Well, damn," Craig Culbertson said mildly. "*This* is unexpected!"

"That's one way to put it, Sir," Helena Sammonds replied. The chief of staff stood at the seated admiral's shoulder, gazing at the dispatch on his display. "Sort

of wish we'd known it was coming before we sent off
your 'prospectors,'" she added.

"A valid point," Culbertson acknowledged. "I wonder if we should send some of our new cornucopia
after them?"

"Probably not a good idea, unless we can scare up
enough escorts to look after them, Sir," Commander
Fremont said from the other side of Culbertson's desk.
The admiral looked at him, and the ops officer shrugged.
"Given the way our 'visits' are going to be stomping on
Solly toes left and right, having an unarmed, unescorted
transport full of troops turn up on their doorsteps after
our task groups have moved on might get messy."

"Something to that, Sir," Sammonds said. "Quite a
lot, actually."

Culbertson nodded, and he knew they were right,
but the temptation was still hard to resist.

He punched a key and shifted his screen to the direct
feed from the main display in the big carrier's combat
information center. It was currently configured to show
the entire Montana System to five light-minutes beyond
the hyper limit. The green beads of three fleet transports
accelerated steadily across it towards Montana orbit,
and he shook his head. None of them were exceptionally large—the biggest probably massed no more than
a couple of million tons—but according to the dispatch
they'd transmitted ahead of themselves, they carried
upwards of fifty thousand trained combat personnel and
their equipment, including light ground armor, elderly
but still effective sting ships and atmospheric aircraft,
and copious amounts of ammunition.

"I sure wish Lady Gold Peak had known this was
coming before she headed off for Madras," he said.

"And all God's children said 'Amen!'" Lieutenant Commander Gert Spinrad, Culbertson's astrogator put in fervently. At thirty-six, Spinrad was the youngest member of his staff, only about five years older than his flag lieutenant, and he'd spent two years with the Grayson Space Navy.

There were times Culbertson suspected it had affected his brain.

Nonetheless, he had a point. Those fifty thousand troops would have been worth their weight in any commodity anyone cared to nominate when Admiral Gold Peak crossed the Meyers alpha wall. But the *rest* of the dispatch—!

"Do you think they can really come up with that many more men?" he asked, looking up at Sammonds and Fremont. "A *million* of them?"

"Well, Admiral Khumalo *did* say they'd turned up more manpower than they expected," Sammonds pointed out with a crooked smile. "And he won't be providing them to anyone until and unless he can scare up the transport for them. On the other hand, I have to say this does offer a certain . . . greater flexibility going forward, shall we say?"

Helena, Culbertson reflected, had quite a way with words.

❖   ❖   ❖

"That's an impressive list of 'supporting elements.'" Captain Edie Habib, Luiz Rozsak's chief of staff, sat back in her chair, left elbow on the chair arm while she rested her chin on that palm and her right hand toyed with a lock of dark brown, reddish hair. "First time I ever heard of three complete squadrons of wallers 'supporting' a dozen battlecruisers!" she said wryly.

"Agreed." Rozsak sat in his own chair, tipped back while the two of them studied the force analysis on the briefing room's main wall screen. "Ellingsen and Abernathy actually offered us a fourth squadron, but I didn't want to impress our new allies as being overly greedy, so I declined with becoming modesty."

Habib chuckled, then sat straighter and looked at her admiral.

"This is going to make our job a lot easier, Luiz," she said much more seriously. "When do we get to sit down with them and start serious planning?"

"That's the one fly buzzing around in my ointment," Rozsak said. There was just a hint of sourness in his tone, and Habib's brown eyes narrowed.

"Abernathy says that in the wake of Filareta's attack on the Manties' home system, they're concerned by potential SLN action against Beowulf or the possibility Kingsford and the Mandarins will be stupid enough to mount another, even bigger attack on Manticore. He also told us their intelligence is picking up rumors that someone—probably Technodyne and this 'Alignment'—is promising to provide the Navy with—and I quote—'second-generation improved shipkillers superior to anything you saw at Torch.'" He shrugged. "Given those circumstances, he says, at the moment their planning focus is on nailing down as many loose ends as they can in their own defenses—including the Haven System's, just in case anyone in Old Chicago's feeling that crazy. It'll probably be at least a couple of months before they could shake loose enough staff to do any sort of serious joint planning. So what they'd really prefer is to make a virtue out of necessity and give us a free hand in formulating our joint ops plans on the basis of this force structure."

He twitched his head in the direction of the wall display.

"They're giving us carte blanche?" The brown eyes which had narrowed widened in surprise, and Rozsak nodded.

"Abernathy was authorized to tell us they're prepared to conform to our planning unless they see some serious problem in it. Apparently, since we're going to be the 'public face' of our little secret alliance, they're willing to let us call the shots. Ellingsen also pointed out that since we'll be the ones most exposed to risk in this instance—and since they assume we have to be more familiar with the local strategic situation than they are—it's only reasonable to let us put our imprint on the planning from the earliest stage. And, as I say, they figure we'll probably be less distracted by other pressing operational concerns. Like whether or not someone's planning on invading our home star system."

"I suppose that makes sense," Habib said. "Mighty generous of them even so, though." Then she snorted. "Well, I guess anyone who's ready to send us three *squadrons* of SD(P)s has already demonstrated her 'generosity'!"

"I know. It's just . . ." Rozsak shook his head. "It's just that Abernathy seemed . . . less nuts-and-bolts oriented than I would have expected from someone in his position."

"What do you mean?"

"I had the feeling he was more of a spook than a shooter, I guess," the admiral replied. "I really wish I'd had Jiri there to take a read on that. He's got good instincts for that kind of thing."

Habib nodded in understanding. Commander Jiri

Watanapongse, Rozsak's staff intelligence officer, was one of the sharpest "spooks" the chief of staff had ever met. Meticulous and logical to a fault, he also knew when to trust his instincts.

"You could be right about that," she said after a moment's consideration. "About his being a spook, I mean. You did say their Foreign Office's taking lead on this. It'd make sense, if it's as tightly held on their side as they've indicated, to grab somebody seconded to diplomatic service, or maybe from ONI, for this."

"I know. In fact, that's what I told the Governor, because it does make sense. In a way, at least. Personally, though, I'd've found a shooter with the right security clearance and sent him, instead. I'd've wanted to be sure *my* shooters' perspective was represented from the get-go. And I would've done my damnedest to keep compartmentalization on my side from throwing any grit into the gears."

"Grit?" Habib cocked her head. "That sounds like you're thinking about more than just the fact that they sent an intelligence guy on what was primarily a diplomatic mission anyway, Boss."

"I suppose it does, and it may just be pre-opening-night nerves on my part." Rozsak smiled suddenly. "After all, we've been working towards this for a *long* time, Edie. We've known exactly what we wanted to do, and we planned accordingly. So when Santa Claus suddenly sweeps down the chimney and offers to open his pack when we're finally on the verge of pulling the trigger, my first reaction is to worry about any place it might cause potholes in all that planning."

Chapter Fifty-Five

"IT'S NOT GETTING ANY BETTER, Karl-Heinz," Adam Šiml said somberly.

He and Karl-Heinz Sabatino sat in the Zlatobýl Tower penthouse, once again looking out over the Velehrad skyline and the canyons of its streets. There were no thunderstorms this time, but a cold, dreary, gray rain sifted down, enough to chill the soul even from the penthouse's warm luxury.

And all too accurate a reflection of the planetary capital's mood.

"At least no one's getting killed in the streets," Sabatino said, equally somberly, and Šiml nodded.

He still despised everything Sabatino stood for, and the man's calculating manipulation of the Chotěbořian economy appalled him. He wasn't going to make the mistake of thinking Sabatino would let anything stand in the way of his Solarian masters' plans, either. Yet the anger in Sabatino's eyes seemed genuine. Perhaps, Šiml thought, because his normal calculations didn't think about Chotěbořans as *people*. He thought of them as game pieces, market forces, and political tokens to be maneuvered for Frogmore-Wellington and Iwahara Interstellar's benefit. The riots—and the death toll—had reminded him of the flesh and blood human beings behind those game pieces and tokens.

Or maybe he's just pissed off because he can see it'll be bad for business in the long run, the Chotěbořan reminded himself.

Either way, his displeasure with the Cabrnoch administration was obvious.

"No, no one's dying in the streets…right now," Šiml let some of his own bitterness show. "There will be soon enough, though. Daniel's managed to clamp down the lid, but there's a lot of pressure underneath it, and *keeping* it clamped down is another matter entirely."

"I know." Sabatino shook his head. "Gunnar's people are telling me the same thing you are. For that matter, it's what that pain in the ass Holowach's telling Luis Verner. In fact, *he's* insisting there's some kind of *organized* resistance to Cabrnoch bubbling away under the surface."

"Really?" Šiml frowned, if not for exactly the reasons Sabatino might have expected.

He'd always suspected Major Holowach was a lot smarter—or at least more effective—than Gunnar Castelbranco. It was unlikely Holowach had as many sources and paid informants as the corporate security chief did, but all indications were that the Gendarmerie major and Captain Price, his senior analyst, were less likely to accept a thesis because it happened to agree with what their superiors wanted to hear.

"Has System Administrator Verner said what kind of 'resistance' Major Holowach's worried about?"

"No, not specifically." Sabatino shrugged irritably.

"Besides, if there was any *organized* movement out there, it would've taken advantage of the football riots!"

"Yes, I suppose it would have," Šiml agreed. "Assuming it was ready to move when the riots erupted, of course."

"Well, if it wasn't ready to move *then*, then it's never going to be ready!" Sabatino said dismissively. "Which doesn't alter the accuracy of your observation." He shook his head. "I've been worried about Cabrnoch's judgment for some time, but even so, I never expected him to order the CPSF into the streets that way. What the hell was he *thinking*?"

"Probably the same thing he was thinking fifteen months ago in Náměstí Žlutých Růží," Šiml replied tartly. "I know I have a lot of personal reasons to detest the man, Karl-Heinz, but all personal animosity aside, it's beginning to look to me like the only response he knows is to bring the hammer down on anything that *might* threaten his power base. And in the long run, that's only going to make it worse. If you compress a spring too far, when the pressure releases there's no telling how far it's going to recoil!"

Sabatino nodded glumly, looking down into his wineglass. Then he looked up and squared his shoulders.

"The truth is, Adam," he said, "that when he ordered the clampdown on those demonstrators, I thought it was the right move, too. Given what was happening in Talbott, it seemed like a really bad time to actively encourage political unrest. God only knew where it might've ended! But since then—and particularly, to be honest, since I became acquainted with you—I've realized you're right. I may not like Holowach, but he had a point when he said the political system here on Chotěboř's lost its 'elasticity.' I asked him what the hell that meant, and he said that when a government's unable to allow *any* public expression of discontent, it means two things. First, it means that government's lost the ability to respond effectively to the *causes* of that discontent. A response doesn't necessarily have to consist of making concessions, he pointed out, but the causes themselves have to be addressed and the pressure has to be relieved somehow, and when a government can't do that, it's in trouble. But, second—and I think this may be what you're getting at where Cabrnoch's concerned—it means the government in question is operating in what he calls a 'fortress' mentality. It's drawn its lines, and anything at all that threatens its position *has* to be hammered. And that, as he pointed out, only creates martyrs."

Šiml nodded, honestly impressed by both the caliber of Holowach's analysis and by Sabatino's willingness to admit it might be valid.

"So what do we do about it?" he asked quietly.

Sabatino gazed out the windows for a long moment, then stood. He walked to the windows and turned his back to them to face Šiml.

"Cabrnoch has to go," he said flatly. "Verner doesn't begin to have the Gendarmes—or the fleet support— to forcibly suppress any sort of general insurrection. And, frankly, given the way the galactic situation's developing, it'd be a frigging disaster even if he could. The probable damage to the system's infrastructure would represent a significant economic hit for Frogmore-Wellington and Iwahara, which wouldn't make the home office happy. The number of people who'd probably get killed would be even worse, from my perspective. And with the Manties only sixty-four light-years away, the chance of keeping that kind of public unrest nailed down without *someone's* inviting them in a la Talbott would be pretty low."

Šiml nodded again, hoping his surprise didn't show. That was about the clearest—and most accurate—estimate of the situation in Kumang he'd ever heard out of Sabatino.

"I know you figured out from the very beginning that I wasn't throwing money at Sokol only because I like football and swimming pools," the system CEO said wryly. "I also know you've done well financially out of our...relationship. And I strongly suspect you also realized from the beginning that I visualized you as a...political counterweight, call it, for Cabrnoch. It's been apparent for several years that public support for his administration's been eroding. So, yes, I invested in Sokol—and in *you*—to have that counterweight ready if I needed it. And I won't pretend I did it because I'm a great humanitarian and philanthropist. I did it because it made cold, hard sense from a pragmatic business viewpoint.

"Having said that, though, and bearing in mind what happened out there in the streets last month, I think you may represent the best chance Chotěboř has."

Silence fell. It hovered for the better part of a minute, then Šiml climbed out of his own chair and crossed to the windows, looking out across the city from Sabatino's side.

"Let me be clear on this, Karl-Heinz," he said quietly. "Are you seriously suggesting removing Jan from office and putting me in his place?"

"Yes," Sabatino said simply.

"And how do you expect to do that? Even if elections meant anything, he doesn't have to face one for another two T-years. And if System Administrator Verner doesn't have the . . . coercive power to suppress a popular insurrection, where does he get the coercive power to forcibly disarm the Public Safety Force?"

"It won't come to that." Sabatino's tone was flat, confident. "I can make Cabrnoch what they used to call 'an offer he can't refuse.' And I can do the same for Vice President Juránek." He shrugged. "First, I've got a *lot* of money, Adam. I can probably buy Juránek for less than one year of what we've been paying Cabrnoch. Cabrnoch may be a little more expensive—or want to be, anyway—but I expect he'll change his mind when I explain the alternatives to him. Alternative One is that he accepts my offer, resigns gracefully, receives a luxury villa on the Cragmore Ocean beachfront in the Boyle System, and a lifetime income at about fifty percent of what he's getting now. Alternative Two is that he *rejects* my offer, at which point I withdraw all financial support, begin supporting public demands for a recall election, and drop evidence of several T-decades of political corruption, malfeasance, human rights abuses, and other illegal activities into the news channels before *you*, as the spokesman for the recall referendum movement, request System Administrator Verner to petition the Office of Frontier Security to oversee the referendum's vote in order to assure that it's fair, open, and represents the actual desires of the people of Chotěboř."

He smiled thinly.

"Which do *you* think he'll choose?"

❖　❖　❖

"Do you think he's serious?" Zdeněk Vilušínský asked.

"Yes, I think he is," Šiml replied. "He wants my answer within twenty-six hours."

"Damn," Vilušínský said almost prayerfully.

"Don't get carried away," Šiml said more sharply. Vilušínský looked at him, and he shrugged. "I'll admit I actually find myself liking Sabatino—a little, at least—and that what he's talking about here probably does represent the best way to engineer some sort of soft landing for the anger out there." He twitched his head at the window and the nighttime city streets beyond it. "But he's still the local representative for Frogmore-Wellington and Iwahara, and he has absolutely no intention of taking his—their—hand off the economic throat of this star system. I think he's genuinely unhappy about the number of people who were killed and injured last month. In fact, I don't think he ever remotely imagined something *that* bad was likely to happen. After all, the casualties from the riots were thirty or forty *times* as bad as those from the Náměstí Žlutých Růží demonstrations. I think that shook him—maybe even badly—but ultimately, he's loyal to the people who pay him."

"Are you saying he expects you to simply take over from Cabrnoch and be a new face doing the same things?"

"No. I think he expects me to come in and make at least some genuine reforms. But he doesn't want anything more than a façade democracy, Zdeněk. I think I might even be able to get him to open the spigots a little bit where the system's economic health is concerned, but that's about as far as it's going to go."

"I have to say, even that would be a vast improvement over where we are now," Vilušínský said. "And if it let you get your foot in the door, gave you a base to work from, then—"

"No," Šiml said again, more forcefully. He shook his head. "Gradualism *might* work, but historically, that fails more often than it succeeds in a situation like this. If we don't want our 'reforms' captured by the system, just turned into something that legitimizes Frogmore-Wellington and Iwahara's positions, we have to rip the present power structure out by the roots. Even if Sabatino was willing to let me do that, the people running the current establishment wouldn't, and if they have enough time, they know all about ways to short-circuit any effort to reform it. If he gives us 'a foot in the door,' we have to put our shoulder into it and drive that door all the way open. Not sometime in the future—immediately."

"How?"

"Between Michal Pastera's acquisitions and Martin Holeček's . . . creative manifesting, we've got enough modern small arms here on-planet to equip two thirds of our *jiskry*. After what happened last month, I don't think we'd have much trouble motivating our people if we saw an opportunity."

"What kind of 'opportunity' do you have in mind?" Vilušínský asked warily.

"Cabrnoch resigns, Juránek does the same, there's a special election to replace them, and I win, courtesy of Sokol and Sabatino's backing." Šiml paused and Vilušínský nodded, watching his face closely. "I take office and spend a week or so, maybe a month, settling in. Then I invite Daniel Kápička and, possibly, Sabatino to a meeting—not in the Presidential Palace, but a quiet meeting at my house. They attend the meeting,

a couple of hundred of our armed *jiskry* take them
into custody—hopefully without killing anybody—and
I go on the air, announce Daniel's resignation, and
order the dissolution of the CPSF. At which point,
a few hundred more *jiskry* immediately move in and
take over the CPSF armories and the main barracks
in Velehrad."

"You really think Kápička's people would lie down
for that?"

"I think there's a *chance* they would," Šiml said.
"I don't know how *good* a chance, but definitely a
chance. And if the Velehrad riots showed anything last
month, it's that there really are people—a lot more
of them than I thought there were, frankly—willing
to take to the streets even without any organized
leadership. If we offer them that leadership, if we tell
them they're defending the new, reform government,
and if our *jiskry*—and, for that matter, the people
we already have inside the CPSF—are there to provide leadership and an armed cadre, I think they'll
respond. It may not be the bloodless coup you and
I would prefer, but I think we could probably hold
bloodshed to a minimum, and I believe—genuinely
believe, Zdeněk—that it would *work*."

"And do you have a page in this plan for Verner,
Frontier Security, and Frontier Fleet? You *know*
Frogmore-Wellington and Iwahara are going to scream
that Sabatino's being unlawfully detained and that your
'seizure of personal power' is flagrantly illegal under
our own Constitution!"

"Yes, I do," Šiml acknowledged. "And I do have a
page in my plan for it." He smiled coldly. "As Karl-Heinz
pointed out to me just this evening, Montana—and the

Star Empire of Manticore—are only sixty-odd light-years away."

❖   ❖   ❖

"Excuse me, Governor," Julie Magilen said, "but there's someone I think you'd better see."

Oravil Barregos looked up from the never ending flood of paperwork with raised eyebrows. Magilen had been with him for almost thirty T-years, and she was his personal secretary and office manager, definitely *not* his receptionist. He couldn't remember the last time *she'd* told him someone wanted to see him, especially someone without an appointment, and something about her tone...

"By all means, Julie," he said, bookmarking his place and closing the file he'd been perusing. "Who is it?"

"I think I'll let her introduce herself, if that's all right with you, Sir."

"Of course it is," he replied, his expression slightly puzzled, and glanced at the tall, red-haired man seated in the corner of his office as she stepped back through the door to collect his visitor. Vegar Spangen had headed his personal security detail for almost as long as Magilen had run his office staff. Now he stood and moved casually to one side, unsealing his tunic and placing himself where the governor wouldn't be in his line of fire if that became necessary.

Which it won't, of course, Barregos told himself. *On the other hand, a little constructive paranoia never hurt anyone.*

Magilen returned, and Oravil Barregos frowned as a tallish woman followed her into the office. It took a moment, since she was in expensive, well-tailored civilian clothing, but he'd done his homework well, and he felt his eyebrows trying to disappear into his hairline as he recognized her. If she'd been in uniform, that uniform would have been the black and gold of the Star Empire of Manticore, not the white of the SLN. It would also have borne the shoulder flash of the Office of Naval Intelligence and the four broad gold cuff bands of a admiral.

"Admiral Givens." It took every year of his political experience to keep the utter astonishment out of his voice. "This is an...unexpected honor."

"I certainly hope it's 'unexpected,' Governor Barregos," the Second Space Lord of the Royal Manticoran Navy said dryly. "If it's not, I'm afraid I'm about to get you into a lot of trouble with Old Chicago."

"Actually," he replied with a smile, "I think we're already in a fair way to getting me into trouble with the Mandarins. Of course, hopefully they won't know about that for another few months."

"Oh." Givens cocked her head. "You're that far along?"

"Excuse me?"

This time he couldn't keep the surprise out of his tone, and she frowned. For some reason, her expression sent a chill through him, and he waved at the same conference table where he'd met with Ellingsen and Abernathy.

"Why don't you have a seat, Admiral," he invited, "and tell me why Empress Elizabeth has sent her senior uniformed intelligence officer all the way to Maya?"

❖   ❖   ❖

"She said *what?!*"

Luiz Rozsak stared at Oravil Barregos' com image, and the governor tried to remember if he'd ever before seen Rozsak display an expression of sheer, stunned disbelief. He didn't think he had. In fact, he doubted *anyone* had. In this case, though, God knew the admiral had every excuse.

"She said she'd come to Smoking Frog personally instead of simply sending a message—or a messenger—because Elizabeth and President Pritchart felt it was important to impress upon us the seriousness with which they view a false-flag operation the Alignment appears to be running. One in which they pretend to be Manticoran agents provocateur and make all sorts of promises about weapons and naval support in order to provoke insurrections that will divert Solarian resources from the Grand Alliance." He smiled thinly. "Does that remind you of any conversations you and I may have had recently? Like, oh, three days ago?"

"Son of a *bitch*," Rozsak said. Then he shook himself, and his eyes hardened. "I *told* Edie Abernathy was a spook, not a shooter. But, God, Oravil! It took great big brass ones to waltz into your office and sell us that bill of goods. Damned if they didn't do it, too!" Those brown eyes got even harder. "I don't like being played for a fool, but they managed it nicely, didn't they?"

"I think there was a politician back on Old Terra who said something about being able to fool some of the people some of the time, but nobody being able to fool *all* of the people *all* of the time," Barregos replied. "And I have to say Admiral Givens' reaction when I told her about our recent visitors and showed her the security cameras' imagery was . . . energetic. She was *not* amused."

"Well, they took a hell of a chance, but they did

their prep work, didn't they?" Rozsak tipped back in his chair. "That holo of 'Langtry' was a nice touch, too. If Givens hadn't come out here in person, I might've been inclined to wonder which batch of Manties we should be listening to!"

"I know. And I'm wondering about 'Mr. Ellingsen's' resemblance to the Winton Dynasty, too. Biosculpt, you think?"

"Almost certainly," Rozsak agreed. "Bastards thought of everything, didn't they?"

"Just about. Although, if I hadn't mentioned those missiles Delvecchio's promised us to 'Ellingsen' on his first visit, you might've tripped Abernathy up when you started talking force levels. I find that more than mildly irritating."

"You're probably right, but the bastard was quick on his feet. He might've brushed through it anyway. And there's no point kicking yourself over it at this point. For that matter, I'd've done the same thing in your place. Why not? You were talking to one Manty about another Manty, and both of them were supposedly on our side." Rozsak shrugged. "The important thing is that now we know. I wonder..."

His voice trailed off and Barregos tilted his head. "Wonder what?"

"Oh," Rozsak smiled almost beatifically, "I'm just hoping Captain Abernathy plans on dropping in on us again. I'd *really* like to discuss our joint operational plan with him."

"I'd pay money to see *that* conversation," Barregos said feelingly. "In the meantime, though, you, Richard Wise, Commander Watanapongse and I have to sit down and go back through all those rumors about 'unrest' we've been hearing out of places like Kondratii. If there's anything to them—if these 'Alignment' bastards really are trying to touch off a wave of rebellions in *our* neighborhood—I think we should make it clear that we take . . . a dim view of that sort of shenanigans."

"Just how 'dim' a view did you have in mind?" Rozsak asked.

"Interesting you should ask. I've just been discussing that very point with Admiral Givens, and she's going to join both of us for dinner. I think you should fix something special, because afterward, the three of us are going to give some thought to how we might make the punishment fit the crime."

Chapter Fifty-Six

"CAN YOU *believe* THIS?" Jan Cabrnoch demanded. "Who the hell does Sabatino think he is?"

The Kumang System President looked considerably less photogenic than usual as he glared at his chief of staff. His dark hair—dramatically silver at the temples—seemed to bristle with anger, and his normally piercing blue eyes blazed with fury.

At the moment, the last thing in the universe Zuzana Žďárská wanted was to answer his question. Unfortunately, not answering it wasn't an option.

"I don't know who he thinks he is, Mister President," she said, with rather less than total truthfulness and addressing him far more formally than usual. *In*formality seemed contraindicated at the moment. "But I think this is a panic reaction to last month," she continued "If we just ride it out, then—"

"*Ride* it out? Christ, Zuzana! He's 'requested' an answer by this afternoon! How the *hell* am I supposed to 'ride out' a five-hour deadline?"

Žďárská bit her lip, trying frantically to think of a response.

Cabrnoch exploded out of his chair and began stalking back and forth across his office's deep carpet with angry, jerky strides. He frequently paced while wrestling with problems, but never like today. He'd been president for thirty-five T-years, and in all that time Žďárská had never seen him so elementally furious.

Of course, he'd never before been told he'd just been fired, either.

"This is *your* fault!" Cabrnoch snapped, whirling to stab an index finger at her. "You were the one who advised me to send in the Safeties when those lunatics started burning down Velehrad!"

Žďárská started to open her mouth, then closed it firmly. That accusation, she thought, was totally unfair. She hadn't *advised* him to send them in; she simply hadn't argued when *he* decided to do it! But if she *said* that . . .

"Mister President," she said instead, "it's obvious Mr. Sabatino's reacting to the riots. It doesn't really matter to him *why* anyone rioted. What matters is that the level of violence—violence provoked by the *rioters*, not the Velehrad PD or the CPSF—has him scared that there's still more unrest on the horizon. But there's no provision in the Constitution for the simultaneous resignation of both the President and the Vice President! Whatever Mr. Sabatino may want, there's no legal way to *give* it to him! I think we should make that point. At the very least the legal obstacles have to give him pause, and once he's been forced to stop and think about the difficulties involved, there's an excellent chance his initial panic will ease."

"Hah!" Cabrnoch snorted. "He's had damned near a month for his panic to 'ease,' Zuzana. What the hell makes you think he'll change his mind just because I tell him 'Oh, I'd love to resign, but I can't do it legally?' He'll only demand we change the frigging Constitution, too!"

"Even if demands that, it'll take time, Mister President. And our people control the news channels and the electoral process."

"For *now*," Cabrnoch grated. "If he starts waving money around, how long will 'our people' still be '*our* people'?" He shook his head angrily. "He'll yank them out from under us and throw their support behind that bastard Šiml. You *know* that's who he's planning on bringing in to replace me!"

He had a point, Žďárská admitted bleakly, and anger of her own churned through her at the thought. She'd taken so much *pleasure* in kicking Šiml's sorry ass out of Jan Cabrnoch's path to power. And the bleeding-heart had been so holier-than-thou in his 'principled opposition' to Cabrnoch's—and Zuzana Žďárská's—rise to the top. She'd helped turn him into a pauper, banished to his pathetic position at Sokol, and now *this*. Cabrnoch was right about what Sabatino had in mind . . . and if he fell from power, what happened to *her*? Especially if *Šiml* took his place? She rather doubted anyone was going to offer *her* a golden grav harness or any off-planet retirement villas!

Cabrnoch stopped his furious pacing and dropped back into his enormous desk chair. His shoulders sagged, and when he shook his head again, it was no longer an angry gesture. This time, it was one of resignation, and an icy chill ran through Žďárská as she watched the energy flow out of him.

"Mister President," she began, "I don't—"

"It's over," he cut her off flatly. She stiffened, and

he leaned back, his expression grim. "He's got all the cards. If I don't accept his 'generous offer' he'll call in his OFS lapdogs. If he drops all that evidence on the news channels and starts buying support for his recall petition, Verner will jump to give it official OFS backing. And if that happens, you and I'll be lucky if we don't go to prison as part of the window dressing for a Frontier Security takeover of the entire system."

"But—"

"There aren't any 'buts,'" Cabrnoch said. "If he didn't have Šiml sitting in the wings as a replacement, it might be different, but he does. So I suppose I should start giving some thought to how to compose my letter of resignation, don't you think?"

❖   ❖   ❖

"Is he really going to resign, *Teta* Zuzana?" Edward Klíma sounded as if he couldn't believe it. "Just roll over and *give up*?"

"He doesn't think he has any choice," Zuzana Žďárská told the man she'd personally picked to head Jan Cabrnoch's security team. Klíma wasn't the brightest LED on the display, but he was a long way from stupid, and he was also her cousin. There were over thirty T-years between them, which was why he called her *Teta*—Aunt—rather than cousin, and he'd always been very loyal to her. And despite the nepotism which had earned him his position, he was also good at his job . . . and proud of his position as the president's chief bodyguard.

"But he's the *President!*" Klíma protested. "Nobody can *make* him do anything he doesn't want to!"

"Unfortunately, in this case someone can," she said bitterly. "As long as that *zkurvysyn* Šiml's whispering in Sabatino's ear, the deck's just too heavily stacked against him, Edward."

Klíma glowered at her for a moment, then turned and walked angrily out of her office. She thought about calling him back, but what was the point? She wasn't going to be able to make him any happier, and nothing would change. Besides, she had more pressing concerns, if Cabrnoch really was going to resign. One thing she damned well wouldn't have in a Šiml administration was a job, so it was time to start reminding certain important people about all the bodies she'd helped bury over the last three T-decades. She was sure she could convince them to contribute to her retirement fund if that was the only way to keep those bodies safely interred.

She punched up her contacts list and placed the first call.

❖   ❖   ❖

"I sure hope this works the way you think it will, Adam," Zdeněk Vilušínský said as the armored air limo Karl-Heinz Sabatino had financed settled towards a parking slot outside the restaurant.

"I do too. But while I try to remind myself that nothing's certain—or foolproof—it's hard to see how it won't. At least as far as the election's concerned. Hell, Zdeněk! You and I'd win an *honest* election! Assuming anyone on Chotěboř would recognize one of those after thirty-five years of Cabrnoch."

Vilušínský nodded, although he was less certain about his own ability to win the vice presidency in an honest election. Šiml's stature, especially since the Velehrad Riots, would have made his election to the presidency a shoo-in, but both of them represented

Chotěbor's agrarian interests. Admittedly, agriculture was a critical component of the planetary economy, but it wasn't the *only* component, and in any sort of open, honest election, a running mate from one of the major cities would probably have been a better choice.

Fortunately, this wasn't going to be an open, honest election, however much both of them might have preferred that. And it probably would have been at least moderately . . . injudicious for a system president planning to engineer what amounted to a coup against the Constitution to select a running mate who wasn't part of the plot.

"You're probably right," he said out loud. "I guess I just find it hard to believe everything's coming together this way. Or maybe I'm afraid that if I *let* myself believe it's all going to work I'll jinx it! Either way, I'll feel a lot happier after Cabrnoch announces his resignation this evening."

"Me, too," Šiml admitted as the limo touched down neatly.

The turbines whined as they spooled down and Filip Malý climbed out of the passenger side front seat and opened the rear door. Šiml smiled at Malý and climbed out of his own seat.

"Thank you, Filip," he said.

"You're welcome, Sir." Filip smiled back, although his eyes continued to scan the local slidewalk and sidewalks. "Just polishing the apple with you. I always did want to work Presidential Security, and now—"

The pulser dart crackled past Šiml's right ear with the pistol-crack of its hypersonic velocity. It struck the limo and punched a pin-sized dimple into the vehicle's thick armor, and Malý reacted instantly by dropping a shoulder into Šiml's chest and driving him back into his seat, behind that protective armor.

Šiml tumbled awkwardly backward, sprawling across the seat he'd just climbed out of, while his brain tried to catch up with what was happening. He landed heavily and bounced, then shoved himself back into a semi-sitting position as Malý wheeled away from the limo, his right hand darting inside his tunic to produce his own pulser.

Another dart shrieked past Šiml, passing through the still-open door, and he heard Vilušínský swear viciously as the dart creased his cheek, opening a bloody slash like a razor blade, before burying itself somewhere in the limo's luxuriously upholstered interior.

Malý moved sideways, screening that open door with his own body, and the pulser in his hand rose. It fired... and in the same instant, a third pulser dart slammed into—and through—the light armor he wore under his tunic.

Blood exploded from between his shoulder blades and he dropped without a sound.

✧   ✧   ✧

"I want that bitch arrested, charged, and damned well *convicted!*" Karl-Heinz Sabatino snarled.

"Mr. Sabatino, I understand you're angry. For God's sake, I'm angry! Adam Šiml's a personal friend of mine! But there's no evidence Ms. Žďárská had anything to do with this," Daniel Kápička replied.

"The hell she didn't!" Sabatino snapped from Kápička's com display. "The son of a bitch was her own cousin—and Cabrnoch's security chief, for that matter! You think the two of them didn't know *exactly* what he was doing?!"

"Frankly, no, I *don't* think they did," Kápička said. "And, for what it's worth, neither does Adam."

"Adam's entirely too trusting a person," Sabatino fired back. "And who else had a motive to see him dead?"

"Mr. Sabatino, I don't doubt Klíma was motivated by President Cabrnoch's decision to resign. And like anyone else who can count to twenty, he must've realized Adam's the most likely person to succeed the President. But everything I've seen so far indicates he acted on his own. I don't doubt his relationship to Ms. Žďárská played a part in his motivation, but I think she was genuinely shocked by his actions. And whether or not I'm right about that, there's certainly no evidence—at this time, at least—that she knew anything about his plans. Obviously, under the circumstances, we have to assume both she and the President might have their own motives for wanting to . . . remove Adam from the political equation, and I promise we'll continue to look at that possibility closely. But I can't justify arresting and charging her when there's absolutely no evidence of her complicity."

"Well, the minute you *find* that evidence, I want her locked up. Do you understand me, Mr. Kápička?"

He glared at the Minister for Public Safety furiously for another second or two, then cut the connection with an angry swipe of his hand and wheeled around to Adam Šiml.

"I never imagined those bastards would be idiotic enough to try something like this, Adam!" he said. "It makes me think they probably *were* behind that bomb in your air car."

"I already told you I don't think Cabrnoch and

Žďárská had anything to do with it, Karl-Heinz," Šiml said wearily.

The transstellars' CEO had insisted that both he and Vilušínský be whisked off to Sabatino's penthouse the instant Vilušínský's facial wound had been treated. Frankly, he'd rather be somewhere else—trying to comfort the wife and children of the man who'd just died saving his life, for example. In fact, he'd told Sabatino that rather snappishly when the limo driver pulled up to the penthouse's landing stage, instead. He'd been far too emotionally exhausted to worry about offending the CEO, but almost to his surprise, Sabatino had nodded instead of firing back. He'd also immediately dispatched another limo to collect Alena Špánková Malá and her two daughters and bring them directly to his penthouse. And he'd also already promised to set up a trust fund that would ensure the Malý family never wanted for anything.

"I know you don't think they were behind it," the CEO said now. "And maybe you and Kápička are right. But you could be *wrong*, too, and I'm not taking any chances—any *more* chances—with your life. You and Mr. Vilušínský were incredibly lucky. Lucky he missed with the first shot, lucky that second shot wasn't a single centimeter farther to the left, and lucky that young man was there to die keeping you alive." Sabatino's expression was as serious as Šiml had ever seen it. "I know you think of me as a calculating, ruthless businessman, Adam, and that's fair, because I am. But that doesn't keep me from regarding you as a friend, and it definitely doesn't keep me from appreciating the sacrifice Filip Malý made for you this morning. And I'm sorry if my suspicion of

Cabrnoch and Žďárská bothers you. But you're just going to have to put up with it until Kápička *proves* they didn't order it."

Šiml looked at him for a long moment, and then nodded slowly.

"And, speaking as a calculating, ruthless business-man," Sabatino said with a slight smile that held more than a trace of true sorrow, "I have to say this won't hurt your chances in the special election one bit."

◇　　◇　　◇

"I don't know, Steve," Sinead Terekhov said. She stood on the balcony of the enormous suite on the top floor of the Comstock Hotel, and her expression was unwontedly somber, almost worried. "I just don't know how Aivars will react to this. For that matter, I don't know how *I'm* going to react!"

"Well, can't say I'm real surprised t' hear that," Stephen Westman replied. He stood beside her, gaz-ing out across the capital as the sun settled in the west. "Bound t' be some hard feelin's after how long and how hard y'all fought with each other, Sinead. Don't rightly see how it could be any other way. And I 'spect Admiral Tourville's prob'ly smart enough t' realize the same thing."

Sinead glanced up at his profile and bit her lip. She was, frankly, astonished by how much she'd come to like Stephen Westman in the two T-weeks she'd been on Montana. She could understand exactly how some-one with his personality had taken up arms against the prospect of having his home star system submerged in another star nation, but she had to admire the kind of integrity which could do that, on the one hand, and admit it had been wrong, on the other. And it was obvious Westman not only admired her husband, wasn't simply grateful for what he'd accomplished here on Montana, but actually liked him a great deal. In many ways, he and Aivars were actually quite a lot alike.

But he didn't know about Hyacinth. He didn't know how Aivars' cruiser squadron had fought to the last ship protecting its convoy. Didn't know how savagely Aivars himself had been wounded, or how many of his pitifully few survivors had been tortured and killed in custody of the People's Republic of Haven. Didn't know about the nightmares when he'd waked covered with sweat, trembling, trying not to show his soul-deep wounds—trying not to "burden her" with it! There'd been times she'd almost hated him for not letting her inside, for punishing the man she loved for having survived when so many of his people hadn't.

And now this. Now an entire Havenite fleet, under the command of the man who'd annihilated Sebastian D'Orville's Home Fleet in the First Battle of Manticore, was here in Montana. Not only in Montana, but monumentally senior to Craig Culbertson...which meant he was now in command of all forces in the system. When Aivars returned from Mobius, how was he going to react to that? And how was *she* supposed to react to it?

Well, the one thing you can't *do is create a scene. However Aivars feels, he's going to have to work with Tourville—have to take his orders. If you make that even harder, you won't do anyone any favors. Besides, if anyone should know better than to do that kind of thing, it damned well ought to be* you!

"I hope you're right, Steve," she said after a moment. "But I'd really, really like to be somewhere else this evening!"

"Least you'll have some support, Ma'am," he told her, smiling down at her. "An' I promise t' behave myself an' not spill any gravy down my shirt."

✧   ✧   ✧

"Good evening, Ms. Terekhov," the dark-skinned, blue-eyed, exotically attractive young woman in the mess dress uniform of a Republic of Haven Navy lieutenant said as Sinead stepped into the boat bay of RHNS *Terror*.

The huge superdreadnought swept in orbit around the planet of Montana, and Sinead pictured all the Montanans below gazing up at the sun-reflections of the hundreds of warships orbiting their world.

"I'm Berjouhi Lafontaine, Admiral Tourville's flag lieutenant," the lieutenant continued. "He instructed me to personally meet you—and Mr. Westman, of course," Lafontaine nodded respectfully to Westman, "—and escort you to the dinner."

"Thank you, Lieutenant." Sinead heard the edge of frost in her own voice and wished she hadn't. This young woman was too young, and too junior, to have had anything to do with what had happened to her husband or his people, and the Republic of Haven— the Republic, not the *People's* Republic—and the Star Empire of Manticore were *allies*.

It would've helped if they'd at least changed the color of their uniforms, she thought almost petulantly, then gave herself a stern mental shake. She was an *adult*, damn it. It was time she acted like one.

"That was very thoughtful of the Admiral," she said far more naturally and smiled at Lafontaine. "I appreciate it."

"If you'll come this way, please?" Lafontaine said,

and waved gracefully for Sinead and Westman to precede her to the lifts.

The RHN was unable to match the degree of automation the RMN had embraced, which meant they required much larger crews, on a ton-for-ton basis, yet any SD(P) required substantially fewer personnel than a more conventionally armed ship with the same firepower. As a result, RHNS *Terror*'s builders had found themselves with rather more volume than usual when they designed the ship's crew spaces.

That showed as Lieutenant Lafontaine escorted Sinead and Westman into the spacious mess deck which had been converted for the evening into a formal dining room. The tables and chairs could easily have seated three hundred people, Sinead decided, and it wasn't crowded.

Only a handful of the guests had yet arrived, however, and she felt herself tighten internally as the lieutenant led her across to the tall, broad-shouldered admiral waiting to greet her. She took in Tourville's . . . jubilant mustache and the treecat on his shoulder.

"Ms. Terekhov," he said, extending his hand, and she took it, not entirely willingly. "I'm honored to meet you and grateful to you for coming," he told her. "I've followed your husband's achievements with great admiration."

"Thank you, Admiral," she said coolly. "And please allow me to express my admiration for your part in the defeat of the Solarian attack on Manticore."

My, that sounded properly stiff and formal, Sinead, she scolded herself.

"It was my honor to be there," he said. "And may

I also add," he met her eyes levelly, "that my people and I took great satisfaction from the thought that Manticore and Haven now know who the enemy's truly been for the last several T-years."

"I'm sure you did," she replied. "And, like all Manticorans, I'm deeply grateful for the Republic's assistance."

He nodded and turned to Westman.

"Welcome aboard, Mr. Westman," he said, and smiled rather more naturally than he had at Sinead. "Mr. Van Dort informed me in Spindle that you and I probably have a great deal in common. I'm not sure he meant it as a compliment."

"Bernardus is like that," Westman replied with a matching smile. "And seein's how he knows me as well as he does, it prob'ly wasn't."

◇   ◇   ◇

The evening, Sinead decided some hours later, as the mess attendants began serving dessert, wasn't as dreadful as she'd feared it would be. Of course, that didn't make it the most pleasant banquet she'd ever attended, either. It was readily apparent that their Havenite hosts were doing their best to put their Manticoran guests at ease, but it was also clear she wasn't the only one who felt the edge of tension. To their credit, both Culbertson and Tourville—who'd immediately approved all of Culbertson's decisions since Admiral Gold Peak's departure—appeared to be in the process of establishing a genuine rapport. Whatever their various subordinates might feel, *they* seemed to be completely at ease with one another. Appearances might be deceptive, but the body language of the treecat on Tourville's shoulder suggested otherwise.

Yet, try as she might, her own sense of tension, of being in the wrong place at the wrong time, persisted stubbornly. In fact, it was worse than it had been.

"You don't 'pear t' be enjoyin' yourself," Westman observed quietly in her ear, and she turned to look at her tablemate.

"I know. And I hate it," she admitted, equally quietly. "Admiral Tourville's done everything he could to make me and everyone else genuinely welcome. But I just can't seem to forget he was once a *Peep* admiral." She bit her lip, and her nostrils flared. "I don't know if Aivars ever told you about his time as a POW or what State Security did to the survivors of his crews, but it was...horrible. Just *horrible*, Steve. And on top of that, Tourville's the one whose ships captured Duchess Harrington and handed *her* over to StateSec. Who proceeded to torture and abuse *her*... and would've hanged her if her people hadn't managed to escape! I know it was a different war, and I know the *People's* Republic was a different star nation, and I'm ashamed of myself, but I just...I just can't seem to forget that."

"I didn't know—" Westman began, but then a quiet voice interrupted.

"Excuse me, Ms. Terekhov," Berjouhi Lafontaine said, and Sinead whipped around in her chair, eyes wide and beginning to flush in mingled fury and embarrassment as she realized Tourville's flag lieutenant had been standing behind her the entire time she was speaking.

"Lieutenant!" she snapped. "I don't know what—"

"Ma'am," Lafontaine interrupted, "I'm sorry. I didn't mean to eavesdrop. The Admiral sent me to ask you if you'd join him for drinks and a brief conversation after the banquet. But, if I may, I'd really appreciate it if you'd let me say something to you on a personal level. Something I'm pretty sure the Admiral wouldn't approve of my saying."

"And what would that be, Lieutenant Lafontaine?" Sinead asked coldly.

"Two things, Ma'am," Lafontaine said, meeting her eyes as levelly—and fearlessly—as Sinead knew Helen Zilwicki would have met someone's on her husband's behalf. "First, Admiral Tourville knows what happened to your husband's squadron. In fact, he was one of the officers on the court-martial of the three State Security personnel who were ultimately hanged for what happened to those people, and he deeply regrets that the rest of the perpetrators managed to disappear before Republican forces liberated the planet on which they were held. He's aware of all the reasons Sir Aivars—and you, as his wife—have for hating the *People's* Republic of Haven, and he's impressed that upon his entire staff.

"Second—and this is what I think he wouldn't approve of my telling you—even though *Count Tilly*, his flagship, escorted Cordelia Ransom and *Tepes* when Duchess Harrington was delivered to Cerberus, he loathed every moment of that trip. In fact, it was evident to everyone on his staff that once Ransom— and she was the one who *insisted* Admiral Theisman assign that duty to him—finished at Cerberus, she intended to take the Admiral back to Nouveau Paris to be tried before a People's Court for treason against the Revolution because he'd protested the decision to hang the Duchess as a violation of the Deneb Accords.

And he's the one who allowed her and her people to reach the surface of Cerberus undetected."

"I beg your pardon?" Sinead said with cold skepticism. "And how did he do that?"

"It's never appeared in any official report, Ma'am," Lafontaine said steadily, "and the Admiral's never mentioned it, even to the Duchess. But when the two pinnaces her people stole for their escape separated from *Tepes*, they were tracked...but not reported. In fact, the tracking data was deleted."

"And how did this extraordinary series of events occur?"

"Admiral Tourville personally deleted the data while People's Commissioner Honecker was still staring at the main visual display."

Lafontaine never raised her voice, but her tone was flat, almost hard, and Sinead stared at her in disbelief. Then she gave her head a small shake.

"And exactly why, do you think, the Admiral's never told a soul about this?" she asked. "And, forgive me for asking, Lieutenant, but if he's 'never mentioned it' to anyone, how does it happen *you* know?"

"I can't tell you for certain why he's never mentioned it, Ma'am," the lieutenant replied, still meeting her eyes unwaveringly. "My best guess is that it's because he feels it would seem self-serving and because there's no evidence he actually did it." She shrugged ever so slightly. "It's rather difficult to use erased tracking data to prove a point, Ms. Terekhov."

"All right," Sinead said unwillingly. "I'll admit that's true. But I'd still be very interested to hear how it is *you're* aware of this top-secret good deed of his."

"Admiral Foraker—she was only *Citizen Commander*

Foraker then, of course—was Admiral Tourville's operations officer, Ma'am," Lafontaine said quietly. "She was the one who realized the pinnaces had separated from *Tepes*, and she was about to delete the data from *Count Tilly*'s database when she realized the Admiral was looking at her display over her shoulder. Then he reached past her and erased the data himself. And after he did that, he walked back across to People's Commissioner Honecker and he said—these are his exact words, Ma'am—'Too bad. There can't be any survivors. Too bad . . . Lady Harrington deserved better than that.' And the reason I know he did that, the reason I'll never forget what he said, is that a very young ensign, by the name of Lafontaine, was Admiral Foraker's assistant tracking officer on *Count Tilly*'s flag bridge that day."

The shock of it went through Sinead Terekhov like a splash of ice water, but those bright blue eyes never wavered.

My God, it's the truth, she thought. *I don't have to be a treecat to recognize the truth when I hear it. And he's never told* anyone? *Not even Duchess Harrington herself?*

She turned her head, looking at the smiling Havenite officer with the bushy mustache, laughing at something Admiral Culbertson had just said, and then she looked back at Lafontaine.

"Lieutenant," she said, "please accept my profound apology for any rudeness I've shown you this evening. And thank you for sharing that with me. Should I assume you'd just as soon I didn't tell Admiral Tourville you have?"

"Ms. Terekhov, I think the Admiral would probably

rip my head off if you told him," Lafontaine said wryly. "Mind you, I think he'd hand it back later, and I really, really hope that someday all of this will come out. But if it does, I don't think it'll ever be because *he* told anyone. Personally, I'm hoping Admiral Foraker will be a little less reticent the next time *she* and Duchess Harrington come face-to-face." The lieutenant smiled. "As you may have heard, Admiral Foraker isn't a real stickler for strict military protocol. And she'd probably figure that, as a fellow admiral, she'd have a pretty fair chance of surviving his reaction!"

"I understand." Sinead's smile was far warmer, and she reached out to lay a hand on Lafontaine's forearm. "And I also understand how fortunate Admiral Tourville is to have you, Lieutenant." Her fingers squeezed gently, then she removed her hand and reached for her dessert fork. "And please tell him I'll be delighted—and honored—to meet with him after the banquet."

Chapter Fifty-Seven

KAYLEIGH BLANCHARD SETTLED BACK on her heels beside the dirty, improvised bedroll, leaning her shoulders against the wall behind her. She popped the top off the container of baked beans and the smart can did its job, heating the contents to serving temperature...which she rather wished it hadn't. She'd lost her mess kit in the desperate scramble to evacuate her last command post day before yesterday, and the food was too hot to scoop out with her dirty fingers.

She set the container carefully on the helmet they'd liberated from the Presidential Guard, sitting on the floor beside her. They were running desperately short of food, right along with everything else, and she didn't want an incautious foot knocking it over while it cooled. Then she ran both hands through her short, oily, dirty hair and closed her eyes, and her expression darkened with the despair she would never have let anyone else see.

Not that the confidence she still tried so hard to project was fooling anyone. Not after the last week.

She winced as her hand brushed the cut on her temple and the angry, swollen bruise that covered the right side of her face. Those were souvenirs of the same bitter skirmish which had cost her her mess kit. And it had cost her Carlton Carmichael, too.

Her expression crumbled, tears flowing slowly down her cheeks, as her brain replayed that hideous moment with merciless clarity. The Solarian Gendarmes dropping on them without warning. The breaching charge opening the roof of her cellar command post. The crackle and hiss of pulser darts. The explosion of grenades. She'd killed two of the Gendarmes, punching the darts from her Solarian-built pulse rifle through their body armor at point-blank range as they plummeted through the cellar's shattered roof, but most of her command group had been down already. She'd gotten a third as she turned toward the preplanned escape route, but then the lump of ceramacrete, blown from the wall by enemy fire, hit her in the face. She'd gone down, her face covered in blood, and she'd heard a voice—one with an off-world accent—shouting her name.

"*Alive*, goddamn it! The facial-rec says that's *Blanchard*, and we fucking well want her *alive!*"

The Gendarmes' fire had ceased almost instantly, and she'd fumbled for her sidearm—not to fight, but to disappoint that voice—but she'd been so weak, so dazed. She couldn't seem to find the pulser butt and feet were crunching through the rubble towards her. They were going to—

Then the sound of fresh pulserfire had filled the cellar once more. Someone had charged across her, counterattacking from the escape route. More screams, more explosions. Somebody jerking her up out of the rubble, flinging her over his shoulders in a fireman's carry, and Carlton's voice shouting.

"Get her out of here! *Get her the hell out of here!* Fall back to—"

She would never forget the horrible suddenness with which that voice cut off.

It's over, she thought bleakly. *We're done. We came so frigging* close, *but we're done*.

She covered her face with her hands, eyes closed as she fought the sobs. If they'd only been able to crack Lombroso's final perimeter. If they'd had him—and the goddamned Trifecta execs—in their custody when Yucel and her butchers arrived! But they hadn't. All they'd had was the support of three-quarters of the planetary population. All they'd had was the right of men and women to die for what they believed in. And that hadn't been enough when Yucel's warships started killing towns and cities from orbit.

They'd taken out six of them in a single, tightly sequenced wave of kinetic energy weapons. Close to half a million dead in the space of less than fifteen minutes. There'd been no surrender demands, no warnings to allow the evacuation of noncombatants. There'd been only incandescent lines of fire shrieking down through the nighttime skies and fireballs rising at their kiss, fiery with vaporized human lives and hope. And after the mushroom clouds dissipated, President Lombroso had taken to the air waves to blame their destruction on the MLF and call on every "right-thinking" Mobian to turn upon the terrorists who'd driven the system's lawful government to such draconian tactics as the only way to end their bloody campaign of murder and destruction.

Breitbart had pulled their people out of every other city and town after that, both to disperse them as targets and as the only way he could "defend" Mobius' urban population. He'd even considered surrendering... until Yucel and Yardley changed his mind by publicly hanging two hundred Liberation Front fighters who *had* surrendered. After that, all any of the others had thought about was how many of the bastards on the other side they could kill before *they* died.

At least we're still too frigging close to Trifecta's precious real estate for them to drop any more KEWs on us, she thought. She scrubbed her face fiercely with the heels of her hands, wiping away the tears, then forced them back down, reaching for the cooling can of beans with her right hand. *Michael was right about that. They aren't going to flatten any more of the good side of Landing than they can help. And it's not like they aren't going to finish us off even the hard way in another couple of days.*

The last pockets of resistance here in Landing might last as much as another week. Maybe even ten days. It couldn't be much longer than that. She hoped at least some of the regional cells might be able to go to ground—survive, at least, even if all their hopes for Mobius' future had been crushed. But the writing was on the wall here in the capital. And even if any of the dispersed cells survived, the entire central cadre was gone.

Another tear trickled, and she blotted it angrily with her free hand. Breitbart had made her his field commander because he'd realized how much better at that she was. But he hadn't expected his "field commander" to order *him* out of the city. He'd argued—violently—against "running away," but she'd been adamant. He was the one who'd built the MLF in the first place. He was the only hope of ever *rebuilding* it, and however faint that hope might be, it was all they truly had. And so, finally, manifestly against his will, he'd agreed to get out of the perimeter, contact one of the cells they *thought* was still uncompromised outside Landing.

But he never made it, either, she thought, shoveling some of the still just-too-hot-for-comfort beans into her mouth. *God, I wonder if he's even still alive?*

She chewed methodically, making herself fuel the body she didn't expect to need very much longer. At least—

The door popped open, spilling light into the barren room, and Danny Gibson burst through it.

"Kayleigh! *Kayleigh!*"

"What?" she demanded a bit indistinctly, then swallowed her current mouthful. "What is it?" she asked more clearly.

"There's somebody on the com! Somebody asking for Michael. I think you'd better talk to her."

He held out his hand, and she took the handheld she'd left with the three surviving members of her command group while she snatched a little desperately needed sleep. Breitbart had left that com behind when he set out to wiggle through the Gendarme/Presidential Guard checkpoints because it had been used for too many of the Liberation Front's communiqués before the Sollies arrived. Being caught with it in his possession would have earned an instant pulser dart in the ear, and Blanchard had issued two communiqués of her own—as Commander Alpha—since his capture in the faint hope that it would convince Lombroso and

Yucel that "Commander Alpha" was still in the field, and not in their soccer-stadium prison cage.

Now she crouched over the tiny display and blinked. A young woman looked up out of it. She wore a uniform Blanchard didn't recognize, but it definitely wasn't Solarian.

"Ms. Blanchard?" she said in a crisp accent Blanchard had never heard before.

"Yes," she confirmed warily, wondering what kind of trick Yucel and Yardley had come up with this time. It might be something as simple as triangulating on "Commander Alpha's" com, she thought, but somehow that seemed less alarming than it might have been if there'd been any hope of surviving in the end.

"Please hold a moment," the younger woman said, and disappeared, replaced by a wallpaper that showed some weird golden, bat-winged, scorpion-tailed lion on a five-sided red patch. It looked vaguely familiar, although she wondered what the creature might be. She started trying to chase down the elusive almost-memory, but before her weary brain got very far, another face appeared. This one was male, considerably older, with blond hair, icy blue eyes, and a neatly clipped beard.

"Ms. Blanchard," he said, "I'm Commodore Aivars Alexsovitch Terekhov, Royal Manticoran Navy. We're here in response to Ms. Summers' message."

❖   ❖   ❖

Michael Breitbach sat on the lowest tier of seating, staring out over the squalid, filthy confines of Svein Lombroso Memorial Soccer Stadium. The once immaculate playing fields had long since been trampled into mud by the thousands of civilians confined in it, and the stench was incredible.

It made an excellent prison, he thought...as long as no one cared particularly what happened to the prisoners. The Gendarmerie intervention battalions and what remained of the Presidential Guard didn't. The fact that none of the horde of men, women, and children in the stadium had been proven guilty of supporting the MLF meant nothing. Anyone who *had* been proven guilty—or who even looked like he *might* be guilty—never made it to the stadium in the first place. There were plenty of impromptu firing squads and mass-produced scaffolds to deal with people like *them*. They'd get around to sorting out their other prisoners eventually, and if they lost a few—or a few hundred—to lack of sanitation, disease, or exposure first, that only meant they'd have fewer to sort.

He turned his head, looking up at the towering seats around the stadium's perimeter. The "nosebleed seats," he thought. That was what people always called them, but they were the best ones in the house at the moment. That was where the Solarian Gendarmes stood with their pulse rifles and their tribarrels, gazing contemptuously down on the hapless Mobians below them. It was absurdly easy to guard a prison like this. Just seal all the ground-level entries and exits, and then ring it with guard posts and heavy weapons emplaced all around its rim.

He looked away again. He was astounded, frankly, that he'd made it to the stadium, but he was under no illusions about what would happen ultimately. In fact, he'd considered identifying himself when he was captured—or at least claiming membership in the MLF—as a way to make sure that what he knew about any surviving MLF cells died with him. But if he had, it might have made them wonder why he'd done something so suicidal and led to the very interrogation he needed above all things to avoid. He'd already figured out three different ways to kill himself when they finally got around to emptying the stadium and processing its inmates. In the meantime, though, he was perversely determined to stay alive as long as possible. It probably meant nothing, in the end, but it was the only defiance he had left, and—

The shockwave shattered the enormous HD screens at either end of the main football pitch. People who'd been moving from one seating tier to another were flung from their feet, and Breitbart's teeth jarred together. He jerked to his feet, wheeling towards the incredible thunder of the explosion, and his eyes went huge as the enormous mushroom of fire and smoke erupted over Landing.

He gawked at it, trying to understand. It was hard to be sure from ground level, especially with the stadium's walls blocking his view, but it looked too close to be a KEW strike on any positions Kayleigh might still be holding. Only that was crazy! Why in God's name would Yucel be striking a target in *downtown* Landing? Christianos Frolov would be *furious*, and—

Something shrieked overhead, and he whipped back around, staring up as at least two dozen dagger-winged assault shuttles plummeted from Landing's skies. A golden manticore on a red field adorned their vertical stabilizers, and eight of them swooped directly on the stadium. Breitbart went to his knees, covering his head with his arms, and a cascade of fireballs, born of precision guided missiles and bow-mounted pulse cannon, came down on the Gendarmes manning the weapons emplacements like a fiery hobnailed boot. Screams of shock and terror erupted from the prisoners, but Breitbach lowered his arms, raising his eyes once more, his mind afire with speculation, wonder, and a wild, desperate hope, as still more shuttles streamed across the stadium and scores of battle-armored men and women plunged from them on counter-grav harnesses.

❖   ❖   ❖

"I thought the banquet went well, Sir," Admiral Culbertson said as he crossed to the table, coffee cup in hand, and pulled out a chair.

"I thought so too," Lester Tourville agreed, and beckoned for the mess attendant to go ahead and serve. The breakfast dishes appeared with metronome efficiency, and Lurks in Branches, Tourville's treecat companion, bleeked happily from his highchair as the plate of stewed rabbit arrived in front of him.

"I was especially pleased by my conversation with Ms. Terekhov," the Havenite said. "I know there are still a few rough spots out there, Craig, but overall, I think most of our people are handling it well."

"Yours better than mine, overall, I'm afraid," Culbertson admitted.

"I expected some stiff spines." Tourville shrugged. "And let's be fair—my people've had longer to get used to this entire unnatural notion of 'Peep butchers' and 'Manty Scum' being on the same side." His mustache quivered as he smiled. "Believe me, with Tom Theisman kicking *our* asses and Duchess Harrington kicking *your* people's asses, the notion of coexistence caught on really quickly!"

"I can imagine." Culbertson chuckled.

"I'll admit, I do still have a few worries," Tourville

said. "Not on a professional level, but more of what may happen if, say, some of your Marines encounter some of *my* Marines in some hapless Montana bar."

"That thought had crossed *my* mind, too." It was Culbertson's turn to shrug. "As the home team, I figure we'll take the repairs out of my budget."

"Deal," Tourville snorted as he reached for his silverware. Then his smile faded as he cut the first bite from the medium rare breakfast steak. "Actually, I think the one person in Tenth Fleet I'm most nervous about is Commodore Terekhov. I hugely admire what he's done out here, but, my God. If there's anyone in a Manticoran uniform with a reason to hate 'Peeps,' it's him. I don't know if you're familiar with what happened to his people after the Battle of Hyacinth, but *I* am. That's why I was so pleased—astonished, too, but *delighted*—with how gracious *Ms*. Terekhov was after the banquet last night."

"I'm familiar with what happened in a general sense," Culbertson said. "I've never discussed it with him. As far as I'm aware, he doesn't discuss it with anyone. But I can tell you that Sir Aivars Terekhov is far too professional to let his personal feelings get in the way of working with you and your people, Sir."

"I hope so," Tourville said softly. "I really hope so."

◆   ◆   ◆

"I told you you'd like the cooking," Indiana Graham said cheerfully.

Damien Harahap looked up from his choo chee prawns and mushrooms and smiled in agreement. He was going to miss The Soup Spoon after the destruction of the Seraphim Independence Movement, he thought, and felt his smile try to fade at the reflection.

Because his face was accustomed to doing what he told it to, the smile turned into a grin, instead.

"You were right," he acknowledged. "Although, I have to say I like 'Thai Grandpa's' green curry with duck even better than I do this. Mind you, it's very good, and I'm going to get him to add the recipe to my file before I leave."

"You wouldn't get it if you were staying here," Mackenzie told him, chopsticks busy with her own favorite Pad Thai. He looked at her, and she shrugged. "He doesn't share his recipes with anyone who might leak them to the competition. It took years for Dad to get him to share them with *us*."

Her expression darkened briefly at the mention of her father, and Harahap nodded sympathetically.

And the sympathy, he reflected, was real. He'd spent too much time with these youngsters, and the thought of how he'd manipulated them made him feel something inescapably like guilt. It wasn't the first time that had happened, and it probably wouldn't be the last, but it was . . . sharper this time.

Probably wouldn't have happened if I'd had Факел *available*, he thought. *I'd've been out of here a week ago if all I had to do was whistle up Seong Jin.*

That hadn't been an option this time, though, so he'd left *Факел* and Lieutenant Yong in the Addison System, thirty-eight light-years from Seraphim, and caught one of Krestor's shorthaul transports. He didn't like it, and it had added the better part of a week and a half to his time in-system, but using *Факел* had been . . . contraindicated this time around.

There'd been a lot of tension lately between the Mendoza-Krestor, Interstellar partnership and the

Oginski Group, which had coveted Seraphim for quite some time. Oginski already dominated both the Jubilee and Akron Systems; adding Seraphim would create a three-system, triangular route to anchor this end of a trunk line extending through the Włocławek-Sarduchi Warp Bridge into the heart of the Core. Oginski was also known for a certain bare-knuckles approach which had earned it a reputation as a rogue operation, even for transstellars in the Verge, and at least some of Mendoza's and Krestor's executives believed Oginski might take advantage of the currently unsettled circumstances out here. Exactly what they expected Oginski to *do* was more than Harahap could have predicted, but they were keeping a very close eye on any movement in or out of Seraphim that didn't travel in a Krestor hull. Under the circumstances, it had seemed better not to be flitting around the system in a 'fast personnel transport' which had already visited Seraphim three times . . . operating in this case under cover of its bogus Solarian registry. Unfortunately, no one in Mesa seemed to have considered the minor fact that Oginski and Kalokainos Interstellar were closely allied . . . or that the *Caroline Henegar* was registered as a Kalokainos vessel. Under normal circumstances, that would have been a good thing, given Kalokainos' many reciprocal trade relationships. In this case, however . . .

The inconsiderate bastards could've wrapped this whole thing up years ago, he groused mentally. *And then I wouldn't be stuck here waiting for my return passage!*

Of course, he also wouldn't have had time to add so many of the Saowaluk family's recipes to his personal files, and that would have been a tragedy. Tanawat and

Sirada Saowaluk were both first-generation prolong recipients in their early eighties—although Sirada ferociously warned everyone in sight that they'd better not call her "Thai Grandma!"—and they'd spent seventy-odd years honing their culinary skills, which explained why they were two of the best cooks Harahap had ever encountered. They were also gracious, welcoming, kind, and always friendly . . . and they'd lost their oldest son, Nattaphong, five years ago, when he was caught in the crossfire during a scag raid on "black-marketeers and profiteers." Actually, they'd simply been a group attempting to set up a co-op outside the McCready Administration's circle of cronies, and Nattaphong had only been looking for a less expensive source for bok choy.

His widow, Ning, and his two daughters—Anong, the older, was only twelve—worked in the family restaurant, along with Tanawat and Sirada's surviving son Thanakit, their daughters Kandokwan and Wipada, and their adopted daughter Alecta Yearman, known as "Naak" because of her bright blond hair. Alecta's husband, Josh Ricardo, was a street hand, like Indiana, and it hadn't taken Harahap long to realize how valuable The Soup Spoon truly was to Indy and Mackenzie's organization. He wondered how many of the family and servers were active members of the Independence Movement? He'd bet on quite a few, although probably not Wipada. She was only seventeen, with all the tempestuous passion of her fury over the death of the big brother she'd idolized. She'd have plenty of motivation, but after watching Indy and Mackenzie with her, he very much doubted the Grahams would have recruited someone that young and so . . . impatient.

Not that it would matter much in the end. When the hammer finally came down, the authorities weren't likely to draw any fine distinctions between who had and who hadn't been active members of the opposition.

Stop that, he told himself sharply as he selected another prawn with his chopsticks. *It's part of the job, and you knew it going in. It's your own damned fault for letting yourself get close to these people, start liking* them. *What were you* thinking, "Firebrand"?

"This is really, really good," he said, looking up as Alecta refreshed his hot tea.

"Of course it is," she told him saucily. "We don't allow anything that isn't."

He chuckled and picked up his teacup to sip. But the cup froze midway between table and lips and his head snapped around as the restaurant door flew open and Thanakit Saowaluk burst through it.

"Thanakit!" his wife, Malee, who worked as The Soup Spoon's hostess, looked at him in alarm. "What is it?!"

Thanakit didn't reply. Instead, he grabbed the remote and switched the restaurant's single, ancient HD from its usual sports channel to the Education Channel News. Run by Minister of Education Anderson Bligh, ECN was the official propaganda organ of the Seraphim system government. Unfortunately, it was also the only legal news outlet, so people had a tendency to listen to it, if only in order to know what *wasn't* actually happening.

The face an ECN anchor appeared, and Harahap felt himself tighten inside. The woman was as immaculately groomed as ever, yet something about her expression, her body language, shouted panic and confusion.

"Repeating our breaking news bulletin," she said. "Vice President Tanner has just officially announced the loss of *Seraphim One*, apparently with all on board."

Mackenzie Graham inhaled sharply, her face suddenly pale; Indy muttered an obscenity under his breath; and Harahap felt ice water flow through his veins.

"The ship was approaching Seraphim planetary orbit on its return from a deep-space industrial tour when it suddenly exploded," the news anchor continued. "A spokesperson for Mendoza of Córdoba has confirmed—I repeat, confirmed, that Ms. Helena Hashimoto, Mendoza of Cordoba's Seraphim System Manager, was also on board as President McCready's guest. At least three other members of the President's Cabinet had accompanied her on her inspection of the new freight platform at Mendoza's primary transshipping station, as well. At this time, we have no confirmation, but there are reports Oliver Schonberg, Krestor Interstellar's system manager may also have been on board."

The woman swallowed and looked straight into the camera.

"General Shelton, speaking for the Ministry of Defense, has announced a complete freeze of all system and interstellar traffic in and through the Seraphim System, beginning immediately and lasting until further notice."

The news anchor disappeared, and a gray-haired, stocky man in the uniform of the Seraphim System Army replaced her, standing behind a podium which bore the seal of the Ministry of Defense. A crawl under his image identified him—for the terminally stupid, who hadn't already figured it out—as General Howard Shelton, the Seraphim System Army's chief-of-staff.

"I want to stress to all citizens of Seraphim that the situation is under control," he said. "Unfortunately, Defense Minister Goforth was aboard the President's ship. In his absence, authority for dealing with the current crisis has devolved upon me. And while this has been a terrible tragedy, I assure you we're fully prepared to maintain order while the investigation proceeds."

"Investigation, General?" a voice asked from off camera, and Shelton nodded gravely, exactly as if the question had been spontaneous and unexpected.

"Astro Control sensor techs may—I stress the verb, *may*—have detected a missile trace in the seconds before *Seraphim One* was destroyed. At this time, those records are being very carefully analyzed by Astro Control, the Army's own experts, and the Ministry of Security. Until that analysis has been completed, no ship will enter, leave, or change position within our star system." His jaw tightened resolutely. "If, in fact, this was an *assassination*, and not simply a tragic accident, I assure you that we *will* determine the identity of the guilty party and that punishment will be swift, sure, and severe."

"Oh my God," Mackenzie whispered. Harahap looked at her, his own brain still trying to process the information, and she shook her head. "My God, my God!"

Her reaction puzzled him, since he wouldn't have counted her among the greater admirers of the newly dead, but when he looked at Indiana, her brother's expression was even tauter than her own.

"What?" he asked, and Indiana shook himself.

"If McCready's really gone, this is going to get really ugly really quickly," the young man said harshly.

"McCready picked Tanner because Tanner's got the backbone of one of Thai Grandpa's noodles and the brain of a Pekingese. He's the closest thing to a non-entity you're ever going to meet. And Shelton and O'Sullivan hate each other's guts. Bligh was McCready's man, but if he wasn't on *Seraphim One*, he's going to be backing either Shelton or O'Sullivan. And if Patricia Mansell—she's Minister of the Economy—is still alive, she'll be the third pole of power, because she's tapped in with all of the economic interests. If Hashimoto and Schonberg are both gone, she's in one hell of a position to consolidate control of the entire economic infrastructure. That's a powerbase at least as big as the Army or the Scags, and none of the three of them are going to settle for seeing either of the other two end up in the Presidential Palace. The fact that Shelton's making the announcement may mean Bligh's already decided which way to jump, but it could also mean the real reason that newsy looked so nervous was all the Army troopers with fixed bayonets standing around the set. And O'Sullivan's probably spitting nails because Shelton got in first with the announcement and made himself the face of 'the forces of order' here in Seraphim."

He shook his head, then grimaced at Harahap.

"Sorry, Firebrand. It looks like you're stuck in the middle of a nice, nasty little civil war, but at least this is exactly one of the contingencies we planned for. Never thought it'd happen, of course, but if it *did*, we wanted to be ready. And we are . . . although, with all shipping locked down, it doesn't look like any of us're going to be able to pass word to your friends in Talbott."

He smiled thinly.

"Welcome to the Revolution," he said.

AUGUST 1922 POST DIASPORA

"So I suppose it comes down to a fairly simple question, doesn't it? Are you prepared to comply with my requirements, or do we get messy about this?"

—Captain Amanda Belloc,
RMN,
CO, HMS *Madelyn Hoffman*

Chapter Fifty-Eight

"—AND I DON'T GIVE A single solitary damn what's happening in the capital!" Warden Genevieve Bryant snapped. "Until I hear differently from General O'Sullivan, nothing changes here at Terrabore. *Nothing*, d'you understand me, Sampson?"

"Of course I do, Ma'am." Major Frederick Sampson, the commander of Terrabore Maximum Security Prison's guard force, didn't—quite—snap to attention, but he came close. He also looked more than a little stubborn, however. "I'm only saying the troops are . . . uneasy. There're an awful lot of rumors, Ma'am, and with Shelton saying General O'Sullivan was behind—"

"There's no way in the goddamned world General O'Sullivan shot down *Seraphim One*," Bryant growled. "Even if he'd wanted to—and I can't think of a single reason he would—the SSSP doesn't have anything in inventory heavy enough to take down a ship that size! For that matter, the entire notion that a single missile hit caused the thing to *blow up* with no survivors strikes me as pretty damned suspicious. *Seraphim One* was no starship, but it was still something like a hundred and twenty-five thousand tons. That's a lot of ship to 'vaporize' with a single missile hit. Frankly, it sounds more to me like something went wrong internally, like in its fusion plant."

Sampson looked less than totally convinced, and she suppressed the need to rip off his head and stuff it up a handy bodily orifice. But she knew he wasn't alone in the uncertainty percolating through his brain, and in her calmer moments, she found it hard to blame any of the prison's guards for that.

"Look, Major," she made herself sound as reasonable as she could, "at this moment, Shelton's saying anything he thinks will help his position. But think about this. If anyone in Seraphim *did* have a missile with the capacity to take out a ship that size before it ever got close enough to enter parking orbit, who do you think that would be? *Us* . . . or the Army? And if, by any chance, the Army might have been involved, who do you think the people who really killed all those people would want to blame it on? Some individual crazed gunman? Or the only organized force on Seraphim that could possibly stand in their way?"

Sampson cocked his head for a moment, then nodded slowly.

"I don't say it necessarily was the Army," the warden continued. "All I'm saying is that I know damned well it wasn't us. At the moment, Shelton's not saying it *was* us, either. I know he's implying it as hard as he can, but he hasn't come right out and said it . . . yet. So go back to your people and tell them the Security Police are still in charge of this prison, that we'll *stay* in charge of it until someone with the legal authority to tells us otherwise, and that General O'Sullivan—unlike General Shelton—is a Cabinet minister. That means he's in the *civilian* chain of command, and that means he's Shelton's superior."

"Yes, Ma'am."

This time Sampson did come fully to attention, saluted, then turned smartly and marched out of Bryant's office.

She watched him go with mixed feelings, then stalked around her desk and flopped into her chair with an expression that was far more anxious than she'd allowed the major to see. The truth was that even now, forty-eight hours after *Seraphim One*'s destruction, she still didn't have a clue who'd fired that missile, except that she was *almost* as confident as she told Sampson that it hadn't been Tillman O'Sullivan. For one thing, she was pretty sure he'd have taken her into his confidence if he'd planned anything like this. He hadn't selected someone he didn't trust to command the SSSP's most sensitive prison, and he and Bryant went back a long ways together.

On the other hand, she was nowhere near as confident as she'd tried to imply to Sampson that Howard Shelton had been behind it, either. She'd always known Shelton was ambitious, but she'd never seen any sign he had the sheer nerve to try something like an out-and-out coup. That would take a lot more courage than he'd ever displayed. Now, taking advantage of the confusion created by *someone else*'s coup attempt—*that* she could see him doing. And Anderson Bligh was smart enough to recognize that Shelton's command of the Army's forces in and around Cherubim gave him de facto control of the capital . . . at least for now. That could explain why he appeared to be backing Shelton. Whether he'd *go on* supporting the Army general if the open fighting that was beginning to look inevitable actually broke out was another question, of course.

And then there was Patricia Mansell. She, Bligh, and O'Sullivan were the only surviving members of Jacqueline McCready's Cabinet. Well, Vice President Tanner was also a member and, under the strict letter of the Constitution, he was also McCready's successor. But McCready, who'd had a healthy sense of self preservation, had been very careful about who she chose for that position, and Hussein Tanner was a nonentity. He was, however, smart enough to realize that in any fight to the finish to succeed McCready, the body count was likely to be high...especially on the losing sides. Unless Shelton got hold of him and managed a miraculous infusion of backbone, Tanner was more likely to be looking for a way out of the impending dogfight than a way into the presidency. So the four people with the inside track to power in the Seraphim System were Bligh, O'Sullivan, Mansell, and—if he could manage it—Shelton. And while the Army was more heavily armed than the SSSP, it was also much smaller than the system-wide police force O'Sullivan commanded. That was probably the only reason Shelton was still firing barrages of innuendo in O'Sullivan's direction instead of getting off the centicredit and actually proclaiming martial law with himself as acting head of state.

It was all very complicated, and it was likely to get messy as hell, but Genevieve Bryant couldn't quite rid herself of the suspicion that none of the "usual suspects" had actually been behind what happened to

Seraphim One. The problem was, she didn't have a clue who *else* it might have been.

✧ ✧ ✧

"Are you sure you want to be quite this hands-on, Firebrand?" Indiana Graham asked, Seraphim System Army helmet tucked in his left elbow. "I know you're a daring interstellar secret agent and all that, but there's a really good chance you could get yourself shot."

"Comes with the territory." Damien Harahap shrugged rather more calmly than he actually felt. "Like you said, welcome to the revolution."

Indy grinned and smacked him on the shoulder, and Harahap smiled back at him, wondering how all this was going to end.

Badly, probably, he thought. *On the other hand, I'm sort of like the fellow in that old story about riding the tiger. Nobody's getting out of this system anytime soon, and the SIM is* going *to do this, whether I* participate *or not.*

It was a less than enthralling prospect, but he'd always tried to be a realist about these sorts of things. And one of the realities was that if the SIM mounted a rebellion that *failed*, it was extremely likely one Damien Harahap would find himself enmeshed in the inevitable post-failure investigation and ruthless purge. Somehow he doubted the Swallowan authorities would draw any fine distinctions between an outside agent provocateur who'd intended the uprising to succeed and one who'd only intended for it to fail.

That meant he'd damned well better see that the SIM *succeeded*, and this sort of thing *was* something he was good at.

Besides, I never had anything against *Indy and*

Mackenzie, he reminded himself. *Fine with me if they pull it off. And if they do, I'll get my ass aboard the first ship out of this system before Mendoza and Krestor—or Oginski and Kalokainos—move in and "restore order" under new management.*

Personally, he strongly suspected the destruction of *Seraphim One* hadn't been a *political* assassination in the normal sense at all. There was no evidence of an actual missile strike, aside from Howard Shelton's so far unsubstantiated statements, and that sounded like an inside job to him. That was the way *he* would have handled it, anyway, and for his money, Oginski had been after Hashimoto and Schonberg, with killing McCready and her cabinet officials as no more than a useful side effect. That was a little more bare-knuckled than usual, even for an Oginski op, but no one had ever accused the Oginski Group of shying away from a little bloodshed. It was unfortunate for them that they'd missed Schonberg, but if Harahap had been the Krestor Interstellar system manager, he'd be hiding in a very deep, very well protected hole somewhere while he screamed for help...assuming he could get a ship out of the system. The kind of people prepared to take out a presidential yacht with a thousand people on board, including its crew; the President, three members of her cabinet, and her entire staff; and the security personnel for McCready and Hashimoto, were unlikely to leave the job half done.

In the meantime, however...

"All right," Indy said to the two hundred other men and women gathered in the crowded, dilapidated Rust Belt warehouse. "We're ready. Firebrand, you're number two in the queue. Juggler," he turned to

Thanakit Saowaluk, "you're number three." The other two men nodded, and he looked at the others. "The rest of you get to your own vehicles and be ready to move the instant Magpie or I come up on the com and call you in. I hope we won't need you; if we do, come in balls-to-the-wall and shoot anything in a Scag uniform on sight. But remember, no one else moves until Saratoga and Osiris do, and *you* don't move at all unless one of the two of us tells you to, right?"

Heads nodded, and he nodded back. Then he pulled on his helmet, glanced at Harahap and Saowaluk and twitched his head at the three waiting air lorries.

They were standard *Mastodonte* heavy-lift lorries which had been acquired from Mendoza of Córdoba courtesy of the funds Firebrand's superiors had made available to the Seraphim Independence Movement. By a strange coincidence, the *Mastodonte* had been selected twelve T-years ago—only after a scrupulously honest and open bidding process, of course—as the Seraphim System Army's primary troop transport and cargo vehicle. And by an even stranger coincidence, all three of these *Mastodontes* were painted in the SSA Transport Command's colors . . . and their cargo beds were fully occupied by grim-faced, heavily armed men and women in SSA uniform.

"Time to go," Indy said, and lowered his helmet's visor as he headed for the lead air lorry.

◆   ◆   ◆

Mackenzie Graham checked her chrono and tried very hard to look calm. It wasn't easy, and she tried equally hard not to rip a strip—mentally, at least—off her brother. He was undoubtedly correct that one of them had to man the SIM's communications center, but she knew perfectly well why the "man" in question happened to be female. And if she was reasonable about it—which she *really* didn't want to be—she had to admit he was better at the sort of physical violence his current mission entailed. So it made impeccably logical sense for her to be the one who stayed behind to manage their communications and coordination. It even made her technically the commander in chief of the Seraphim Independence Movement at this historic moment. The fact that it also let him protect her hadn't played any part at all in his thinking. Oh, goodness, no!

She gritted her teeth, then made herself inhale deeply.

"Communications check," she said, and the three men and two women manning the center with her bent over their panels.

That was one thing Mackenzie was profoundly grateful Firebrand's people had gotten to them. Unlike the civilian coms they'd originally planned on using, the military coms the Manties had supplied were capable of setting up secure networks using sophisticated frequency bouncing and encryption. It was entirely possible—probably likely, actually—that the Army would detect those networks' existence. Truth be known, she and Indy were *counting* on the Army's picking them up, but pinning them down or penetrating them, especially with the repeater sites they'd established to throw off triangulation, would be a much greater challenge. This would be the first time they'd brought those networks online anywhere close to the capital, however, and they needed to know if they'd gotten it right.

"Saratoga," she said, "Magpie. Communications and status check."

"Magpie, Saratoga," Leonard Silvowitz replied instantly, and despite her tension she smiled, remembering Silvowitz's reaction when he'd discovered that his old friend and business partner's little boy and girl were the ones who'd organized the Independence Movement. "Communications good. Standing by."

"Copy standing by," she replied, and shifted to the next channel on her list.

"Osiris, Magpie. Communications and status check."

"Magpie, Osiris," Janice Karpov replied. "You sound good. We're ready."

"Copy ready," she replied, and shifted channels again.

"Tannenberg, Magpie. Communications and status check."

"Magpie, Tannenberg," Tanawat Saowaluk answered. "Communications good. Standing by."

"Copy standing by." Another channel shift. "Juggler, Magpie. Communications and status check."

"Magpie, Juggler," Thanakit Saowaluk replied. "Communications good, we are in position."

"Copy in position," she said and shifted channels yet again. "Firebrand, Magpie. Communications and status check."

"Magpie, Firebrand. Communications good. We're ready."

"Copy ready," she said, and shifted channels a final time.

"Talisman, Magpie," she said much more quietly. "Communications and status check."

"Magpie, Talisman," her brother's voice came back over the off-world com which had replaced his helmet's original equipment. "Communications good. We're in position."

"Copy in position," she said. Then, softly, "Be safe."

"Affirm," he said, equally softly, and she drew a deep breath. Then she straightened her spine, squared her shoulders, and pressed the button that dropped her briefly into all of their communications nets.

"All primary strike groups, Magpie," she said, and now her voice was strong and clear. *"Execute!"*

◇   ◇   ◇

The crumpled ball of paper arced across the office and landed neatly in the waste basket against the far wall. Lieutenant Bassett Juneau, Seraphim System Army, made another tick mark on his blotter, then began crumpling another impromptu basketball. So far, his average was up to almost seventy-five percent, which, given his "basketballs'" aerodynamic qualities, was actually pretty good.

And it was nice that *something* seemed to be working out well. The three days since *Seraphim One*'s destruction had seen plenty of gathering tension, but not much in the way of resolution. In theory, Vice President Tanner was in charge, but he'd been conspicuous by his absence. According to General Shelton, Tanner was alive, well, and preparing for an orderly succession of authority. And just this very morning he'd named General Shelton—whose troops just happened to have ringed the Presidential Palace to protect the remaining civilian government—Minister of Defense in place of the recently deceased Simon Goforth.

Exactly who was protecting whom—and *from* whom—remained an open question, however. And in the meantime, tensions between the Army and Tillman

O'Sullivan's scags continued to rise, especially since the Army's move on the Presidential Palace. Even more ominously, from Juneau's perspective, the regular Cherubim Police Department seemed to be inclining towards the SSSP. Probably not too surprising that police would find another police organization less threatening than the Army, he supposed. Especially when the Army appeared to be holding the current legal President hostage in his own palace.

Except, of course, he thought sardonically, *that everyone knows that's a self-serving lie being put out by that arch traitor O'Sullivan. Or something to that effect, anyway.*

In the meantime—

❖   ❖   ❖

"Ready," Leonard Silvowitz, a.k.a. Saratoga, said. His voice was taut, but he forced his body language to remain relaxed as the air van which had acquired the livery of the Seraphim System Security Police came to a halt at the Harris Street Arsenal's security checkpoint. The bored-looking Army corporal in charge of the five-person gate guard stiffened, obviously unhappy at finding a trio of SSSP vans calling on an Army installation—especially one as important as the Harris Street Arsenal—during such a . . . fraught time. She touched the stud on her helmet, clearly checking with higher authority, and listened for several seconds.

❖   ❖   ❖

Lieutenant Juneau's desk com buzzed. He dropped his current wad of paper and punched the acceptance key.

"Juneau," he said, grateful for a distraction from his anxious boredom.

"Wittek, Sir," Staff Sergeant Louisa Wittek, his senior NCO, replied. "Sir, we have a situation at the front gate."

"What kind of situation?"

"Sir, Corporal Terahaute says we've got three six-meter SSSP cargo vans."

"What?!" Juneau sat up suddenly. "What do they want?"

"Terahaute hasn't asked them yet. She commed me for instructions before she talked to them."

"Well, tell her to find out what they want but to keep the gate closed while she does it," Juneau said.

It was only a civilian-grade rolling gate, unlikely to stand up to any serious assault, but at least it was something. And, he reminded himself, there was no reason—yet—to believe these Scags were up to anything the least improper. Somehow the thought didn't keep him from wishing General Shelton had considered augmenting the arsenal's normal guard force at the same time he was moving in to protect Vice President Tanner.

"Yes, Sir," Wittek replied, and Juneau climbed out of his chair and reached for his pistol belt.

❖ ❖ ❖

"Take us in, Ning," Tanawat Saowaluk said flatly.

"Yes, *Pôr*," the young woman in the pilot's seat replied, and Saowaluk's face tightened as she called him "daddy."

He and Sirada had argued ferociously against their widowed daughter-in-law's participation in the actual fighting because they loved her . . . and because they didn't want their granddaughters fully orphaned. But Ning Saowaluk was a determined woman whose hatred for the entire McCready government burned with a white-hot flame. Despite their arguments—despite even Saowaluk's abortive attempt to simply forbid her from joining the fighting—they'd been unable, in the end, to stop her. And so Saowaluk had done the best he could to keep her safe, assigning her to pilot the genuine (if stolen) SSSP *Vencejo* tactical van transporting the first wave of the attack. It was remarkably well armored, despite the *Vencejo*'s original civilian pedigree, it was fast, and once its troops had disembarked, its job was to sit tight and wait to pick them up again.

She'd protested that he was treating her specially because she was his daughter-in-law, and he'd agreed with her. But he'd also pointed out that she was one of the best pilots they had... and told her flatly that it was the only way she was coming.

He was pretty sure she'd forgive him someday.

Now he sat in the front passenger seat, watching through the windscreen as she took them directly down the long, straight approach corridor to Fort Silvano Nagpal, the Swallow System Army's major armor park.

"Here she comes," Silvowitz murmured as the corporal stepped through the small personnel door in the main gate and walked towards the lead van.

A soft chorus of responses came back from the cargo area behind his seat, where eighteen additional men and women in SSSP uniforms and light body armor waited. Silvowitz pressed the button that lowered his pilot-side window and the corporal flipped up the visor of her Army-issue helmet.

"Good morning, Corporal," he said.

"Good morning, Sir," she replied, her expression about as neutral as it could get, as she responded to the major's insignia on his uniform. "Can I ask what brings you here, Major?" she continued.

"Well, Corporal, I'm here to oversee a weapons transfer," he told her.

"Weapons transfer, Sir?" she repeated dubiously, and he nodded. "Sir, I haven't seen any paperwork on that."

"I'm not surprised, Corporal. It came up rather suddenly."

"Major, I'm afraid I'm going to have to see some kind of authorization before I can allow you on to the Arsenal's grounds."

"Of course, Corporal," Silvowitz replied, and nodded to the SSSP lieutenant—or what looked like an SSSP lieutenant—in the passenger seat beside him. "Here it is."

Ginger Terahaute's eyes widened. That was all the reaction she had time for before the pulser dart hit her squarely in the center of her forehead.

The corporal's body tumbled backward, although at least the helmet contained the explosion of gore that would otherwise have covered several square meters of pavement. The instant the "lieutenant" fired, Silvowitz opened the throttle wide, and his air van exploded forward, smashing through the civilian-grade gate as if it hadn't existed.

The other members of Terahaute's guard detail stared in stunned disbelief—disbelief which held them three fatal seconds too long. They were beginning to bring up their weapons as Silvowitz's air van went past them in a howl of turbines and a hurricane of pulse rifle darts exploded from the concealed gun ports in its sides. Two of them had time to scream; neither of the others managed even that much, and the three vans sped into the Arsenal.

"Magpie, Saratoga!" Silvowitz said over his com. "Kickoff!"

✧   ✧   ✧

"Magpie, Teacup," the voice said into Mackenzie Graham's earbug.

"Teacup, Magpie," she replied. "Go."

"Magpie, Fort Silvano's at a higher degree of alert than we thought it was." It was Lieutenant Alfredo Duncan, Seraphim System Army—otherwise known as "Teacup"—and assistant logistics officer, Fort Silvano. "Just got a look at the duty roster. They've doubled the regular watch and issued extra ammo."

Oh, shit, she thought. *Damn it! I was* afraid *of this!*

The possibility that one or more of their targets might go to a higher degree of readiness had always been the greatest risk for this particular operations plan. But Shelton and O'Sullivan had been so careful about denying one another excuses to escalate, and none of their inside people at the other targets had reported anything like this. Yet she wasn't even tempted to dismiss "Teacup's" warning; Alfredo Duncan was one of the most reliable people she knew.

"Teacup, Magpie copies," she said, then punched channels.

"Tannenberg, Magpie," she said harshly. "Teacup says they've doubled the regular duty watch and issued extra ammunition. Abort. I say again, *abort.*"

"Magpie, Tannenberg." Tanawat Saowaluk's voice sounded preposterously calm to her. "I'm afraid we can't. We're coming up on the main gate, and they've already signaled us to stop."

Mackenzie bit her lip, desperately tempted to repeat the order. But she wasn't there; Tanawat was, and it was his mission. She could only hope he had a better feel for the actual situation than she did.

"Understood, Tannenberg," she said, instead. "Good luck."

❖   ❖   ❖

"Sir, we've got several Scag vans at the main gate," Staff Sergeant Martin Rucelli told Captain Salvador Vasilev, the morning duty officer at the Henrietta O'Byrne Arsenal. "They say they're here for some sort of weapons transfer."

"What?" Vasilev frowned. "I haven't heard anything about any weapons transfers—especially to a batch of Scags!"

"Just telling you what the gate detail says, Sir," Rucelli said with a shrug.

"Well, tell them they're just going to have to wait while I clear this!"

"Yes, Sir."

❖   ❖   ❖

"Major," the senior noncom of the gate guard told Janice Karpov, "I'm afraid Captain Vasilev says he'll need to confirm your orders. If you'd park your vans over there—"

He was raising his hand to point when Karpov put three pulser darts into his chest. Her air vans—there were five of them, this time—charged through the gates in a tornado of turbine wash.

"Magpie, Osiris," she said into her com. "Kickoff!"

❖   ❖   ❖

"I need to see some authorization, Major," the Army sergeant told Tanawat Saowaluk rather more coldly than a nonçom should address a field-grade officer.

"Of course, Sergeant," Saowaluk said, and opened the passenger side door.

The sergeant backed a couple of paces as he did, and Saowaluk made himself keep smiling despite the other man's obvious wariness. He kept his hand well away from the butt of his holstered pulser and unsealed his tunic so that he could reach into it.

"And you're right," he continued. "Until we get a better handle on what the hell is going on, it's a lot better to be safe than sorry."

"You've got that right, Sir," the sergeant said, still watching him carefully.

"Wish I didn't," Saowaluk said wryly... and the sergeant's torso exploded.

The other eleven men and women of the reinforced gate guard, just like their sergeant, had been watching the Scag major, not the *Vencejo*'s rear doors. In fairness, they couldn't *see* the rear doors from their position, and so they hadn't noticed the quartet of riflemen who'd silently eased through them. Two of those riflemen had gone prone, crawling forward underneath the air van as it hovered on its counter-grav. The other two waited, hidden behind the vehicle's bulk until their companions suddenly rolled out on either side. Then all four of them opened fire on the gate detail which hadn't been quite suspicious enough.

"First Team, unload here!" Saowaluk barked over the tactical net. "We go in on foot. Second Team, once we clear the gate, you're go for the south vehicle park! Third Team, take the north park! Get those charges placed, and then get the hell out!" Then he drew a deep breath and punched another channel.

"Magpie, Tannenberg," he said crisply. "Kickoff!"

"Talisman," Mackenzie's voice said over Indy's com, "Magpie. We have kickoff. I repeat, we have kickoff."

"Magpie, Talisman copies kickoff," he replied, and nodded to Alecta Yearman, sitting in the pilot's seat.

"Go, Naak," he said, and three *Mastodonte* air lorries, packed with a hundred and twenty armed and armored men and women went racing towards Terrabore Maximum Security Prison.

Tanawat Saowaluk swore viciously and hit the ground behind the barely adequate cover of a parked ground car as the burst of darts hit Jessica Lambert squarely in the chest. Her light body armor—they hadn't dared risk anything heavier than normal SSSP issue—never had a chance. She went down, twitching but already dead, and Saowaluk hosed a burst of fire at the position which had killed her.

It did no good. The improvised strong point wasn't a true bunker or pillbox, only a maintenance shop where the better part of a platoon of SSA troopers had hastily forted up. Unfortunately, its ceramacrete walls were proof against pulse rifle fire, his fire team had no tribarrels, and they'd already used all three of their rocket launchers. And, even more unfortunately, it had his seven survivors pinned.

The rest of the attack seemed to have succeeded in most of its objectives, although casualties had been far higher than they'd hoped. If he'd been willing to poke his head up where it could be shot off, he could've seen the clouds of smoke rising from the primary vehicle parks. He was sure there had to be at least some operable vehicles in the midst of all that smoke, but there couldn't be very many. And if he'd only been able to get inside the maintenance shop, he and his team would have eliminated the possibility of any damaged vehicles being quickly repaired. But they weren't going to get there.

In fact, they weren't going to get *out*, either.

"Team Two and Team Three," he said over the net, "pull out. Head for Rally Point Six."

"What about you?" Anson Tolliver, Team Three's leader, demanded.

"We're not going anywhere," Saowaluk said bleakly. "They got too many people into the shop, and we're pinned on the approach. The rest of you get out." His smile was as bleak as his tone. "We'll hold their attention while you get clear."

"No, *Pôr!*" Ning cried over the com.

"It's not my choice, *kwanjai*," he said more gently. "Go home to the girls. They need you."

"They need you, too! We *all* do!"

"I'm sorry." He leaned around his covering air car and sent another burst screaming towards the maintenance shop. "Go home. And be careful when you lift out. Remember the tribarrels on the western perimeter."

There was silence for a moment, and then—

"I'm coming to get you, *Pôr*," his daughter-in-law said, and his heart spasmed as he recognized her suddenly calm tone.

"No!" he shouted. *"No, Ning!"*

The air van howled in from the west at barely ten

meters, and pulser darts from the maintenance shop shrieked to meet it. Most of them ricocheted madly from the *Vencejo*'s armor. Not all of them did, though, and his heart froze as bits and pieces flew.

"*Noooooo!!*" he screamed, but the air van never hesitated. It swept over the remnants of his team, battering them with turbine wash, absorbing that hurricane of fire. And then, with the unerring accuracy of an arrow and the fury of its pilot's battering-ram rage, it smashed directly into the maintenance shop's main repair bay at over two hundred kilometers per hour.

The explosion shattered every unbroken window within a thousand meters.

Chapter Fifty-Nine

"WELL, THE NEWS JUST GETS better and better, doesn't it?" Agatá Wodoslawski stabbed a disgusted finger at the intelligence summary on the display and glared around the enormous conference table at her companions. "It doesn't look like deciding to investigate Beowulf's 'treason' was such a wonderful idea after all."

Her glare settled on Innokentiy Kolokoltsov, Permanent Senior Undersecretary for Foreign Affairs and the acknowledged senior member of "the Mandarins," the five unelected bureaucrats who truly ran the Solarian League. From the outset, Wodoslawski, the Permanent Senior Undersecretary of the Treasury, and Omosupe Quartermain, the Permanent Senior Undersecretary of Commerce, had tried to warn their fellows of the economic consequences of all-out war with the Star Empire of Manticore. They'd also been the two most in favor of seeking a diplomatic solution to the crisis which had exploded with the death of Josef Byng and the battlecruiser *Jean Bart*. It wasn't that they'd disagreed with their fellows' desire to teach the uppity, arrogant Manties their place; it was simply that they'd had a more realistic appreciation for just how badly Manticore could hurt them in return.

In fact, even their estimates had been dismally overoptimistic, and none of the Mandarins—including the late and extremely unlamented Fleet Admiral Rajampet Rajani—had possessed a shred of realistic appreciation of the Manticorans' war-fighting capability. Despite which, Kolokoltsov thought resentfully, she and Quartermain remained in the best position to be casting stones at this bleak moment in history.

"It's not over yet, Agatá," he said, after a moment. "Whatever the newsies may be screaming, the latest polls show a plurality—over forty-seven percent, in fact—of the Core World population supports the Assembly's condemnation of Beowulf. And over fifty percent believe Beowulf's decision to call in *Manticoran* ships of the wall to back its refusal to allow Admiral Tsang to pass through the Beowulf Terminus constitutes collusion with the enemy."

"That's not exactly a resounding majority," Quartermain observed sourly.

"No," Malachai Abruzzi, Permanent Senior Undersecretary of Information, conceded. "But the percentage is growing, especially on the 'collusion with the enemy' front. When you add in Beowulf's decision to secede from the League—and the totality of Filareta's defeat *after* it denied Tsang passage to reinforce him—the percentage that believes the Beowulfers are colluding with the enemy jumps to almost eighty-three percent. And well over sixty-five percent of the population strongly condemns Manticore's interference with freedom of

astrogation and sees the Star Empire's seizure of warp
termini as blatant, imperialistic aggression. Trust me,
that percentage's going to climb steadily as the economic
consequences begin to bite into the civilian sector."

He did not, Kolokoltsov noted, mention that the
polling data—like all polling data in an interstellar
civilization—was always outdated by the time it could
be collected. The numbers for the Old Terran population were actually quite a bit higher than the ones he
and Abruzzi had just cited, but it hadn't been possible
to gather data from some of the more distant Core
Systems since Beowulf had declared its intention to
leave the Solarian League.

"All that indignation against the Manties is going to be
of limited utility if the Treasury goes dry and the government collapses," Wodoslawski said caustically. Abruzzi
looked at her sharply, and she gave him an abrupt,
jerky shrug. "Service on the debt already costs us about
twenty percent of our *peacetime* budgets, Malachai, and
we're paying almost ten percent on a forty-year bond,"
she told him. "Current revenue projections, adjusted
for the effect of the Manties' seizure of warp termini
and withdrawal from our carrying trade indicate we're
going to be able to cover less than seventy percent of
projected *expenses*. That's a deficit rate of over *thirty*
percent, and we didn't have Admiral Kingsford's new
budget requests while those projections were being
prepared. In other words, the actual numbers are going
to be worse—a *lot* worse—not better."

She paused a moment, her expression grim, then
shrugged again, with a curious mix of glaring anger,
resignation, and something else. An emotion Kolokoltsov
couldn't quite define.

"Within the next six months, barring some sort of miraculous military turn around, our borrowing rate's going to go to at least *fifteen* percent." Her glare circled the conference table again. "Think about that, all of you. The *Solarian League*—the government of the biggest, wealthiest economy in the history of humanity—will have to pay more than *three times* the current interest rate just to borrow money to fight the damned war! I don't care about your damned polls, Innokentiy! Those numbers are the clearest possible indication of how the business and financial communities view our prospects if this thing drags on."

Kolokoltsov managed not to swear. It wasn't easy.

"I didn't know about those numbers," Nathan MacArtney, the Permanent Senior Undersecretary of the Interior, growled. "But assuming they're as accurate as your numbers usually are, Agatá, that only lends added urgency to keeping the Protectorates under control. God knows we can't afford to lose any more of the revenue stream from them! I think these new missiles from Technodyne will probably help, but I'm concerned about our approval of Kingsford's commerce raiding strategy. I agree it's the best way to hurt the Manties, but I don't like the thought of pulling all those platforms out from under Frontier Fleet when we've got these reports about Manty efforts to stir up trouble in the Verge."

"None of those reports have been confirmed," Kolokoltsov pointed out. "I'm not saying there's nothing to them!" he added quickly, raising one hand as MacArtney reopened his mouth. "I'm only saying they haven't been confirmed *yet*. And, frankly, while I agree with you about the economic importance of the Protectorates, especially given what's happened to our usual revenue flow, I'm actually more concerned about the additional secession declarations arriving from the Shell than I am about the Verge."

The mood in the palatial conference room darkened further, and he sat back in his chair, folding his hands on the table in front of him.

"So far, we have four of them," he said. "And, unfortunately, the Manties have followed through on Carmichael's threat. They've distributed recordings of our conversation month before last to the newsies."

His mouth twisted sourly as he recalled that conversation with the Manticoran Ambassador and Lyman Carmichael's blazing contempt. Not to mention his plea for the Mandarins to call off Massimo Filareta's attack on Manticore . . . and his only too accurate prediction of what would happen if Filareta *wasn't* recalled. They didn't have poll numbers back on the public's reaction to that little bombshell, either—not yet—but he was sinkingly certain that it would be disastrous.

"Thanks to the fact that they now control something like eighty percent of all warp termini, those recordings are spreading a hell of a lot faster than any rebuttal from our side," he continued. "We're getting to most of the Core Worlds first, but the Shell and the Verge are getting the Manties' version unchallenged. Personally, I think that's what's really driving these secession declarations, and that's going to get worse."

"*Four* of them," Wodoslawski repeated. "Already?" Kolokoltsov gave her a choppy nod, and she grimaced. "God help us, but that sounds like the first trickle. What happens when the floodgates open?"

"We're not hearing anything like this from the

Core Worlds—aside from the damned Beowulfers, anyway!" he replied. "And most of these declarations are coming from star systems that don't have the military wherewithal of Beowulf."

"Are you suggesting we send task forces to pound them into submission?" Quartermain asked. "Doesn't seem to've worked out very well in Beowulf's case, does it?"

"That's pretty much what *I* just said, Omosupe," Kolokoltsov said sharply. "And, no, I'm not proposing to 'pound' anyone into submission. But the Manties and Havenites can't afford to disperse this Grand Fleet of theirs too widely. As powerful as their weapons are, and whatever they may have done to our economy so far, they're still punching above their weight against the Solarian League. So it's not like they're able to start dispatching task forces of their own to every star system that threatens to secede. I've discussed it with Admiral Kingsford, and he's agreed to send a couple of squadrons of wallers to each of these star systems. What I propose is that we issue no threats, we send professional diplomats along with the admirals commanding the task forces, and our position is simply that at this time, given the deteriorating situation with Manticore, the Assembly and Government can't in good conscience allow these secession efforts to move forward. After the conclusion of hostilities with the Manticoran Alliance, we'll be in a better position to determine the constitutionality of secession and to process secession applications that we know aren't being driven by Manticoran pressure on the system governments. In the meantime, the Battle Fleet forces assigned to each system will protect them—in case

Manticore has been using coercive threats to produce the proclamations—and also protect and conserve League property and installations in those systems. Not to mention collecting the central government's lawful duties and fees."

"And how long d'you think that'll bandage over the situation?" Abruzzi asked caustically.

"I don't know, but if you've got a better suggestion, I'd love to hear it."

Kolokoltsov met Abruzzi's eyes for three or four seconds, until the Information Undersecretary looked away with a frustrated shrug.

"In the meantime," Kolokoltsov continued, "one of Admiral Kingsford's intelligence people, a Captain Gweon, has produced a very interesting analysis of the *real* reason Manticore and Haven were so determined to get Beowulf into their corner. It makes interesting reading, and I'd like you all to consider it between now and tomorrow." He smiled thinly. "If Captain Gweon's right, then it could just be that there's a quicker alternative to Admiral Kingsford's commerce raiding when it comes to bloodying the Manties' nose."

❖   ❖   ❖

"'Scuse me, Floyd," Jason MacGruder said, "but weren't the Manties s'posed to be here today?"

Floyd Allenby scowled at his cousin. Not because MacGruder didn't have a point, but because Allenby didn't have an answer.

The two of them stood on a sixth-floor balcony of the President's House in the heart of Landing. The balcony's previous owner, Ex-President Rosa Schumer, was currently in confinement in one of the VIP prisons formerly operated by her cellmate, Felicia Karaxis.

General Tyrone Matsuhito, unfortunately, hadn't survived to be taken into custody. Allenby found it difficult to regret that particular fatality, although he *had* been looking forward to Matsuhito's trial.

The truth was that the Cripple Mountain Movement's coup had worked almost perfectly. Casualties in the SSA had been heavier than Allenby, MacGruder, or Frugoni had wanted them to be, but casualties in the CMM had been much lighter than predicted. That didn't make losing the six hundred men and women who'd died once the Army recovered from its initial shock any less painful—especially since virtually all of them had been family—but they'd still overthrown the Shuman Administration at a miraculously low cost in blood.

Alton Parkman, Sheila Hampton, and the rest of Tallulah Corporation's personnel in Swallow were all under house arrest. No charges had been preferred against any of them—yet—but on behalf of the provisional government, Allenby had declared a state of emergency and martial law, which gave it an amazingly broad range of powers under the Shuman Constitution and made all of their actions to date—aside from the minor unpleasantness of attacks on places like Fort Golden Eagle, of course—thoroughly legal.

Not everyone was happy with the new state of affairs. A lot of purely Swallowian investors and business owners, not all of them Schuman cronies (although those cronies represented a substantial majority), stood to be badly hurt if Tallulah collapsed. Whatever the future might hold for them, at the moment they still wielded a lot of clout, and there were signs they were getting organized to use it. On the other hand, at least sixty-five or seventy percent of the system's population supported the CMM's accomplishments... so far, at least.

Unfortunately, although Frugoni's strike on the *Donald Ulysses and Rosa Aileen Shuman Space Station*, coupled with the destruction or capture of every sting ship at Fort Golden Eagle, had given the CMM a monopoly on armed spacecraft in the Swallow System, at least one Tallulah Corporation freighter had managed to avoid interception and translate into hyper.

No one doubted what that freighter's skipper intended to do once he reached a handy Frontier Fleet base. And that was what lent Jason MacGruder's question such a sharply honed point.

"All I can tell you is that we sent them our timetable, Jase," Allenby said now. "And I s'pose there's lots of reasons a squadron of destroyers might get themselves delayed en route. So 'pears t' me that 'bout all we can do at this point is dig in and hope the Manties get themselves sorted out—and here—'fore we hear anything back from Frontier Fleet."

"Commodore Terekhov!"

Michael Breitbach rose from his desk chair with a huge smile as General Kayleigh Blanchard, the Mobius System's new Acting Defense Secretary, escorted Sir Aivars Terekhov into his office.

"Mister Acting President," Terekhov responded with a smile of his own as he shook Breitbach's hand.

"I understand you're leaving us," Breitbach continued, waving for Terekhov to accompany him to the enormous windows of the hotel suite. The Templeton Arms Tower in the city of Templeton, Mobius' second-largest city, had been pressed into service as the provisional government's temporary seat.

There wasn't much left of the old Presidential Palace.

"I'm afraid so, Sir," Terekhov replied, standing beside him and gazing out at the peaceful, bustling city. "You seem to have the situation pretty well in hand, and the last thing either of us needs is to lend additional credence to the idea that the Star Empire's been deliberately fomenting rebellions out here."

Breitbach's smile turned into something much less cheerful, and he nodded sharply, tasting once again his elemental rage when he'd discovered how the Mesan Alignment had played him. Not, he reminded himself once again, that the Alignment had created the Mobius Liberation Front or the circumstances which had forced his own hand long before he'd intended to launch his rebellion.

And if they hadn't "played you," you wouldn't've sent Ankenbrandt or Summers for help and you and Kayleigh would both be dead right now. Don't forget that part, either, Michael!

"I'm going to leave my destroyers and a pair of heavy cruisers to keep an eye on you, backed by a couple of squadrons of Captain Weiss' LACs under Captain Laycock's command. Combined with the missile pods we're leaving in orbit, that should be enough to handle anything Frontier Fleet's likely to send this way. In the meantime, we're pretty sure you're not the only system the Alignment's been working on. Admiral Culbertson's probably going to need the rest of my force back in Montana to go play fire brigade somewhere else."

"Well, all I can say—again—is that Mobius will be

eternally grateful to you and to Admiral Gold Peak. Her willingness to help a bunch of revolutionaries she'd never even heard of was remarkable. And the speed and decisiveness of your actions here in Mobius..."

He shook his head, his eyes dark, and Terekhov shrugged.

"Mister Provisional President—Michael," he said, "I don't doubt that Lady Gold Peak's decision was approved the second her report reached Manticore. I can't conceive of my Empress' wanting me to do anything other than exactly what we did here *anywhere* someone takes a stand, trusting in the Star Empire of Manticore's word...whoever actually gave it to them." It was his turn to shake his hand. "The truth is, it's been my honor to assist you, and my only regret is that we didn't get here before Yucel and her butchers."

He and Breitbach stood looking into one another's eyes for several seconds. Then he held out his hand again, and the Provisional President gripped it firmly.

"I hope to come back and see what you've made of your star system, Mister Provisional President," the Manticoran said. "Right now, however, my pinnace is waiting, so I suppose it's time to tell you goodbye."

"Goodbye, Commodore," Breitbach replied. "Godspeed...and I'll hold you to that promise to come back."

Chapter Sixty

"WELL, THANK GOD WE SENT YOU, Pat," the Earl of White Haven said. "These Alignment bastards are pretty ambitious, aren't they?"

"And this comes to you as a surprise because...?" Elizabeth Winton inquired.

"It was more of a rhetorical comment than a deeply freighted analytical insight," Honor Alexander-Harrington's husband told his monarch.

"My own 'analytical insight' is that we need to nip this thing in the bud," Patricia Givens said seriously. The Empress and White Haven looked at her, and she shrugged. "We need to assume they wouldn't have approached just Maya and Kondratii—not way the hell and gone over on our opposite flank. Maya's more than thousand light-years from Talbott, for God's sake! And that means God only knows what kind of snakes' nest is squirming away under the surface."

"Pat has a point, Hamish, Your Majesty," Thomas Caparelli put in. "And I'm inclined to think we need something more...proactive than Lady Gold Peak's initial response. I think she made exactly the right decision, but we're seeing more and more evidence of how widespread this is. I don't think we can afford to wait for requests for assistance to reach us ... especially since the 'Manticorans' talking to Barregos and Rozsak set up a communications channel that sure as hell didn't go to *us*. Unless we're extraordinarily lucky, a lot of people who think they've been promised our support are going to call for it and get no answer when the hammer comes down on them, which is exactly what the Alignment wants."

"So what sort of 'proactive' response did you have in mind, Tom?" Elizabeth tipped back in her high-backed chair and Ariel, her treecat companion, raised his head, watching the two-legs with bright green eyes.

"Well," the First Space Lord said, "from what Barregos and Rozsak said to Pat—and from their messages to you and President Pritchart, for that matter—they're about as pissed off as it's humanly possible to be. It's also obvious they're still too thin on the ground to take an open stand against the League. Erewhon's actually got a lot more firepower currently in commission than they do, but even if their ... partnership's as tight as we think it is, they'd both have to feel nervous about pasting any bull's-eyes on their chests where the League is concerned."

He paused, and Elizabeth nodded, her eyes intent.

"I realize we haven't heard directly from Erewhon about this yet," Caparelli continued, "but I talked to Tony Langtry, and his analysts agree that Walter Imbesi and the Triumvirate won't be any happier than Barregos and Rozsak. He also thinks Erewhon would jump at the opportunity to get back into a ... happier relationship with us. Especially now that Haven's our brand-new ally and trading partner.

"Bearing all that in mind, I think our best response might be exactly what 'Ellingsen' and 'Abernathy' offered Barregos. And I also think we should consider including Erewhon in it."

"Um." Elizabeth frowned, but she clearly wasn't surprised by Caparelli's suggestion. She thought about it for a moment, then looked at White Haven.

"Hamish?"

"I think it's a good idea," he said promptly. "Of course, we need to clear it with Benjamin and with Theisman, now that Pritchart's en route home. We *could* do this unilaterally, but I don't think that would be a very smart idea."

"You've been talking to your wives again, haven't you?" Elizabeth said with a grin. "All that sneaky diplomacy stuff is finally starting to stick, I see!"

"I do my feeble best," White Haven replied, and she chuckled. Then she drew a deep breath.

"How much firepower do you think we'd actually have to divert from Grand Fleet?"

White Haven glanced at Caparelli for a moment, then back at the Empress.

"We could probably cover it with three or four squadrons of SD(P)s," he said. "Especially if we threw in a couple of CLACs and a few munitions ships with Mark 23 pods. For that matter, I don't think it would be inappropriate to offer both Barregos and Imbesi Mycroft for their home systems."

"I'd really prefer not to let Mycroft out of our hands just yet," Caparelli cautioned, and White Haven nodded.

"Agreed. I'm thinking we'd offer them Mycroft on the basis that an Alliance detachment would emplace, operate, and oversee the FTL platforms and control stations." He raised one hand, palm uppermost. "I'm pretty sure they'd jump at the opportunity once we explained what Mycroft and Apollo can do in conjunction with one another."

"That sounds reasonable," Elizabeth said. "Tom, I'd like you and Pat to write up a formal recommendation for me to present to Admiral Theisman and the Protector. Get Sir Anthony involved to be sure it includes the Foreign Office's perspective."

"Yes, Your Majesty," Caparelli said formally.

"How soon do you think you could have something to me?"

"By the strangest coincidence, Your Majesty," the First Space Lord opened his briefcase and extracted a chip folio, "I seem to've brought it along with me."

"Well, imagine that!" Elizabeth said while Ariel bleeked with laughter. The Empress shook her head and held out her hand. "I suppose I should at least go through the motions of reading it," she said. "Would it happen you've already drafted movement orders to go with it?"

"Ah, no, Your Majesty," Caparelli replied after a moment.

"I'm disappointed, Admiral Caparelli," the Empress of Manticore said. "I suggest you return to your lonely office and get started on that immediately."

❖   ❖   ❖

"And so," Adam Šiml said from the steps of Lidový Dům, the traditional home of the Národní Shromáždění, the Chotěbořian National Assembly, gazing out across the packed expanse of Náměstí Žlutých Růží, "the task before us will be neither simple nor quickly accomplished. Some changes will come very soon; other changes will take time, effort, and the sweat of hard work. Fortunately," he allowed himself a quick smile, "anyone who's been associated with Sokol as long as I have understands about sweat."

Laughter rumbled across the vast crowd, despite the overcast skies and a temperature several degrees short of warm. But then his expression sobered.

"The worries, the fears, the hopes which have led to so much unrest here in Velehrad and elsewhere across our system represent the valid aspirations of our people. The violence which cost so many lives here in our capital is not the proper way in which to express those aspirations, however, and I think it only proper that both you, the people, and those within your government, should look at that violence and contemplate both its causes and its consequences. During the riots, many of you listened to me and to other leaders of Sokol, other citizens trying to stem the tide of bloodshed and destruction. Others of you did not, and let us be honest with one another, some among the forces charged to restore order were as guilty of excess and of brutality as any of those disrupting the peace.

"I have instructed Minister for Public Safety Kápička and Chief Justice Dalibor Čáp to begin an immediate investigation of the causes of the disturbances, the steps taken to control them, and their consequences. In order to ensure transparency, that investigation will be conducted in partnership with the Národní Shromáždění, which will impanel a special committee for the purpose. The investigation will take however long it takes, but the special committee will issue public reports every thirty days. Those reports will become part of the public record and the basis for remedial action on my part."

Another sound swept the crowd, but this one was more complex than laughter. It combined astonishment and gratification at the offer, seasoned with more than a trace of skeptical cynicism. The surprising thing, in light of Chotěboř's experience under the Cabrnoch Administration, was that there was so *little* cynicism in it.

"Some of the issues which produced and drove the riots are fundamental, underlying problems," he continued. "Fixing that sort of problem will require that hard work and sweat I mentioned a moment ago, and it will also require an additional ingredient: patience. I can't promise *all* of them will be fixed at all; I can only promise we will fix all of them we can, and that we'll do so as quickly as we can. There's no doubt in my mind that many of you will become impatient in the process, and that's both an inevitable part of human nature and your right as citizens of Chotěboř. But there's also no doubt in my mind that one element which drove the riots was the sense that legitimate expressions of political opinion and the right to petition for redress have been far too . . . circumscribed in our public and civic life. Therefore, I am announcing today the immediate suspension of The Defense of the Republic Act."

This time something very like a gasp rose from the crowd, followed by a total, singing silence, for it would have been impossible to find a single law imposed by the Cabrnoch Administration which had been more universally hated than DORA. Šiml knew that perfectly well, but he went on steadily, his voice clear and calm in the sudden stillness.

"Some provisions of the Act may well be necessary, but from this moment, none of those which constrain freedom of speech, freedom of assembly, or freedom to petition the Národní Shromáždění or the courts will be enforced. Further, I now announce the revocation of the State of Emergency originally proclaimed by President Hruška during the height of the Komár Crisis, and I intend to dissolve the current Národní Shromáždění and call for new elections within the next three months. When the new Deputies are seated, I will formally request that they impanel another special committee charged to review *all* legislation enacted during the previous administration and recommend to me what portions of that legislation require revision, amendment . . . or repeal. And that committee, too, shall report publicly every thirty days."

A thunderous, tumultuous cheer roared up from the crowded square—one that went on and on for at least two full minutes. He waited until it had faded, then looked out across that enormous throng once more.

"And so, my fellow Chotěbořans, I take up the office to which you have elected me. I won't guarantee success in all the pledges I've given you, because sometimes success proves impossible, however powerful and sincere the effort to accomplish it. But I *will* guarantee you that I will work with every scrap of energy, any trace of wisdom I might possess, and every gram of integrity, imagination, and determination within me to honor and redeem every one of them. If

I do not succeed, it will *never* be because I willingly
settled for anything less than total success. I ask you
now to support me in this effort by giving me your
trust, by making your own wishes and desires known,
and by remembering not simply me, not simply the
Národní Shromáždění, but our entire star system and
every man, woman, and child in it in your prayers.

"Thank you, and good day."

The cheers went on for almost fifteen minutes.

"That was a marvelous speech, Adam," Karl-Heinz
Sabatino said that evening, standing on a balcony above
the great ballroom in the Presidential Palace with
the newly inaugurated president of the Chotěbořian
Republika and his vice president.

The Frogmore-Wellington/Iwahara executive had
remained tactfully out of sight, aside from a very
brief—and formal—greeting and exchange of best
wishes following Šiml's inaugural address. Now, at last,
the final guests from the Inaugural Ball had departed,
and the three men stood gazing down on the staff
beginning the monumental cleanup.

"Thank you, Karl-Heinz," Šiml said. "I hope it'll
do the trick."

"So do I," Sabatino said. "I have to admit, though, I
feel a little ... concern over that proposal to review *all*
of Cabrnoch's legislation. Some of its provisions—and
not necessarily the most *popular* ones—are there for
very important and valid reasons."

"I'm aware of that." Šiml turned from watching
the work crews to face Sabatino squarely. "And I'm
aware there are limits in all things. Despite that, I
fully intend to carry out that review. And I intend to

act on any of the special committee's recommendations that *can* be acted upon. You and I both know that what happened in the riots happened because the unrest, the unhappiness with the way in which Cabrnoch tried to silence all dissent, lock anyone who might oppose him completely out of politics, built up a head of pressure that had to vent sooner or later. If the people of Chotěboř decide that all they got out of the special election was a change in faces—that there isn't really any difference between Cabrnoch and Juránek, on the one hand, and me and Zdeněk, on the other—that pressure's going to explode even more violently than it just did.

"I realize that as the custodian of Frogmore-Wellington and Iwahara's interests you have to be concerned about any actions which might impact those interests. But Daniel doesn't really need DORA or the more extreme measures Cabrnoch adopted under the state of emergency to maintain public order and prevent the government's overthrow. *He* doesn't think he does, for that matter—it was part of the reason he argued when Cabrnoch ordered him to use the CPSF against the rioters—and I agree with him. More than that, I firmly believe that providing Chotěboř with a government its citizens believe is truly committed to its civil rights and political freedom is the best way to reduce the pressure that caused the riots in the first place. I'm sure you'll have a great deal of influence on the membership of the new Národní Shromáždění, just as you did in the previous one, and between the Deputies and myself, it should be possible to provide enough real, substantive relief of that internal pressure without having the entire structure fly apart and produce the chaos and death that could destabilize all of Frogmore-Wellington and Iwahara's interests."

He met Sabatino's gaze levelly, and finally—slowly—the off-worlder nodded.

"It's going to be a difficult needle to thread, Adam. But I'm confident that if anyone can do it, it's you."

"Thank you," Šiml said quietly. "I appreciate that. And I promise you, I'll never forget who made it possible for me to hold this office or why I'm here. People who forget their friends have no one but themselves to blame when they come to a bad end, and I have no intention of coming to any bad ends."

Chapter Sixty-One

"I SHOULD BE BACK IN Lądowisko catching up on things," Justyna Pokriefke grumbled as the air car swept across the Wiepolski Ocean. "I don't have time to be gadding around to social occasions!"

"Oh, for God's sake, *Szefie!*" Gabriel Różycki scolded. "You've *always* got something to 'catch up on.' You could spend the next three years in the office and not change that. Besides, it's been months since you stuck your nose outside the capital, and this is the biggest *Dzień Przewodniczącego* since the *Agitacja*! You need a break. And even if you didn't, you *need* to be here."

She looked at him balefully, but she also nodded. Różycki was thirty-seven T-years old, only about half her age, and improbably handsome with his blond hair and gray eyes. She knew there were rumors—very *quiet* rumors, considering who they were about—that he was considerably more than merely her assistant and closest aide. In fact, there was no basis to the rumors at all, although she'd sometimes considered exploring the possibility. Never very seriously, though.

He was too smart—and too valuable—for her to risk destroying his utility to her. Besides, she'd come to think of him as the son she'd never had.

And in this instance, he was right . . . again.

She didn't really like Tomasz Szponder. There was something about him, an air of superiority or possibly . . . disapproval. *Something*. Perhaps it was her sense that he was perfectly prepared to enjoy all his own privileges but sneered judgmentally down his nose at the woman who made sure he had them. Or maybe it was just the prestige his extraordinarily low Party number bestowed upon him. Despite her present position, Pokriefke wasn't one of the *Trzystu*; her party number, unfortunately, was only 1,413—respectably low, but scarcely one of the "Three Hundred"—and perhaps that was what made her feel ill at ease around him. He'd never been anything but courteous to her, and he'd brought her more than a little useful information when his newsies turned up something he thought she should know about. But there was still that *something*.

Yet he was also a very powerful man: one of the foremost members of the *Oligarchia*, a personal friend—virtually an uncle—of the Przewodniczący, and one of the shrinking number of *Trzystu*. With all that behind him, Tomasz Szponder wasn't a man anyone wanted for an enemy. He was considerably more popular with the RON's rank and file than the majority of the current Party leadership, too, and his reputation for philanthropy made him far better liked and admired by lower class Włocławekans than the vast majority of his fellow oligarchs. And on today, especially, the fact that only six people in the entire Włocławek System, none of them still active in Party affairs, had lower Party numbers than his meant declining his invitation would have been . . . contraindicated. Besides, it was a foregone conclusion that with everyone who was anyone in the Ruch Odnowy Narodowej in attendance, all manner of alliance building and tweaking would take place over the vodka and canapés.

Maybe that's why I'm feeling so sour. The truth is that I hate *"social affairs" at the best of times, and this is going to be the grandmother of all social affairs!*

Well, maybe it was, but Gabriel was right. Wherever she wanted to be, this was where she *had* to be, and she gazed out the window as the green and white, reef-fringed dot of Szafirowa Wyspa appeared against the dark blue water far below.

"Welcome, Szymon!" Tomasz Szponder said, shaking the Przewodniczący's hand as the official limousine lifted away from the landing stage, bound for the parking garage at the rear of Prezent do Praksedá's enormous chalet.

That parking garage rose three landscaped stories into the air, with another four levels buried underground, not a minor achievement on an island. Szponder's great-great-great-grandfather had intended his estate for serious entertaining, and the current Szponder sometimes wondered if his ancestor had been inspired to outdo the ancient palace of Versailles on Old Terra. He'd have been certain that was what the old man had in mind if Teodozjusz Szponder had ever been off Włocławek. What mattered right now, however, was that there was room in that garage for literally hundreds of air cars. On the other hand, even its capacity was going to be seriously challenged today, which was one reason he'd convinced his guests to let him consolidate their security needs rather than piling dozens of additional vehicles into the available parking and servicing space.

"I think it's wonderful of you to offer to host this *Dzień Przewodniczącego* celebration here on Szafirowa Wyspa," Szymon Ziomkowski replied, gripping Szponder's hand firmly. "I've always thought this was a remarkably beautiful place, and I know *Wujek* Włodzimierz loved it here. I remember him telling me once that one reason the language in the *Karta Partii* was so beautiful was that it was composed here, looking out over the Wiepolski. And he added that his host's love for the language was another reason."

"I'm honored to hear he said that," Szponder said, and he meant it, despite what was about to happen. "Those were wonderful days, Szymon. We genuinely believed we could change the world."

"And you succeeded, Mr. Szponder!" a bright soprano voice said, and Szponder made himself smile at Klementyna Sokołowska, Ziomkowski's personal aide and assistant.

Sokołowska was thirteen T-years younger than Ziomkowski, red-haired, blue-eyed, and quite attractive. She was also, Szponder suspected, considerably more intelligent than she chose to appear. Not surprisingly, since she'd been personally selected by Agnieszka Krzywicka as Ziomkowski's watchdog. One of her jobs was to keep him convinced the RON was still the strong, forward-looking organization his uncle had intended it to be, and she'd been known to flatter him shamelessly in pursuit of that goal. Szponder was confident she'd have happily used her physical charms as another leash for her nominal boss, but for the fact that Szymon loved his wife dearly and would never dream of betraying her.

"No one succeeds completely, Ms. Sokołowska," he said calmly. "It's an imperfect universe. Włodzimierz understood that when we were drafting the Charter, although it's true we sometimes come closer to success than others."

"You always were a philosopher, Tomasz," Izabela Ziomkowska said, following her husband down the landing stage stairs. He held out his hand to her, too, but she ignored it in favor of a firm hug and a peck on the cheek. "But I think Włodzimierz also said that even if we have to settle for less than perfection at any given moment, we're always free to go right on pursuing it."

"Indeed he did, Izabela," Szponder said warmly. Izabela Ziomkowska was one of his favorite people, and if he suspected Sokołowska was smarter than she chose to appear, he *knew* Izabela was. In fact, he was rather counting on that.

"Szymon, why don't you and Izabela—and Ms. Sokołowska, of course—head down to the Green Salon? That's where the munchies have been laid out, and Grażyna's holding the fort at that end while I manage the greeting line at this end. I'll be along as soon as I finish my 'Welcome to Szafirowa Wyspa' duties."

"Of course," Ziomkowski said. "Try not to get stuck up here too long, though. It would be rude of us to begin the banquet without our host, but I warn you, I haven't eaten a bite since breakfast." He smiled broadly. "I've been saving room. I know what your kitchen staff's capable of!"

"We'll try not to disappoint you," Szponder promised.

❖   ❖   ❖

"Mazur isn't going to make it," Tomek Nowak murmured into Szponder's ear as they started down the sweeping staircase into the Green Salon. Szponder cocked an eyebrow, working hard at keeping any dismay from his expression, and Nowak shrugged. "I think it's legitimate. He was out at *Piłsudski* for some meeting. First it ran over, and now his shuttle's developed engine trouble. He says he's still coming, but he won't get here before the deadline. And neither will Miternowski."

"That's . . . unfortunate," Szponder murmured.

Stacja Kosmiczna Józefa Piłsudskiego was the Włocławek System's primary industrial and freight platform. It was also the site of the Stowarzyszenie Eksporterów Owoców Morza's off-world offices, and Hieronim Mazur spent quite a lot of time there. Szponder had hoped he'd be able to resist the temptation to just run by his *Piłsudski* office today of all days, but the one virtue Mazur possessed was that he was genuinely hard-working.

Damn it.

And to make bad worse, Asystent Pierwszego Sekretarza Partii Tymoteusz Miternowski, Krzywicka's deputy, was traveling with him. Krzywicka had groomed Miternowski as her assistant because she was confident he'd go right on being her *assistant*, without developing any unfortunate notions about taking her *job*, instead. He was not, to say the least, noted for driving ambition or intestinal fortitude. Left to his own devices, having him elsewhere at the critical moment might not be disastrous. Left to *Mazur's prompting*, however . . .

"How late will they actually be?" he asked as they neared the foot of the stairs.

"Sounds like at least several hours. He says he'll *try* to get here before the fireworks, but he can't guarantee it," Nowak replied quietly, and Szponder muttered a quiet, fervent curse. The fireworks display wasn't scheduled until after sundown, another eight hours away.

"Then we'll just have to go ahead on schedule without them, I suppose," he said, and produced a broad smile as he walked out into the crowded vastness of the Green Salon.

His wife, Grażyna, came to meet him, tucking her hand into his elbow as their guests realized he was there and turned to face him. The hand on his arm gripped a bit more tightly than usual, but that was the sole sign of uneasiness she displayed. He waited until the side conversations had faded into near silence, then raised his right hand in welcome.

"Ladies and Gentlemen!" he said. "Thank all of you for coming. I hope you'll find the trip's been worth it. We have quite a few hours yet till sunset, when I trust the fireworks display will be suitably awe-inspiring, as promised. Fortunately, that gives us time for the banquet and the speechifying you all knew you'd have to put up with when you accepted the invitation. And Włocławekans can always use more time to dance!"

Laughter answered, along with a few humorous catcalls, and he smiled even more broadly in acknowledgment.

"So, if you'll all accompany us, the weather's cooperating and we've laid out the tables on the East Terrace. Mister Przewodniczący, if you and the Pierwszy Sekretarz will lead the way?"

"I imagine we can find the East Terrace," Ziomkowski

replied with a chuckle, and turned to Agnieszka Krzywicka.

Izabela Ziomkowska was twenty-seven centimeters shorter than her husband, but she was still forty centimeters *taller* than Krzywicka. Standing between the Ziomkowskis, the First Secretary looked even tinier than usual, but she smiled and took her place on Ziomkowski's other side while Sokołowska brought up the rear, flanked by Ziomkowski's personal security detail. The other guests—a veritable Who's Who of Włocławek's *Oligarchia* and the Ruch Odnowy Narodowej—shook out into order behind them and headed out the French doors to the shaded breeziness of the enormous East Terrace.

Long tables awaited them, covered with snow-white tablecloths, sparkling crystal, hand-glazed flatware, and table silver polished enough to use for mirrors. Discreet name cards marked each guest's place, and live musicians played on the other side of the dance floor which had been erected just beyond the shading canopies.

Szponder watched his guests find their seats while the serving staff began collecting beverage orders, then glanced over his shoulder at Nowak and nodded casually. The younger man returned his nod, turned, and ambled casually back into the villa while Szponder escorted Grażyna to their own places at the center of the high table.

❖   ❖   ❖

Grzegorz Zieliński swallowed another sip of iced mineral water and sternly suppressed an ignoble desire for something a little stronger. The possibility of anything untoward happening here, of all places, was about as minute as it could get, but the members of the Przewodniczący's security detail took nothing for granted. The Departament Ochrony Przewodniczącego was rather strict about little things like drinking on duty.

He chuckled and set the glass back on the portable bar at his elbow. The DOP agents assigned to today's festivities would eat after they were relieved, but at least as the detail's senior agent he got to enjoy the canopies' shade. Of course, that was a bit of a mixed blessing, since he also got to smell the delicious meal everyone else was enjoying.

He nodded to the bartender, then began another discreet sweep around the perimeter, and his smile faded. He knew Szafirowa Wyspa was one of the most secure locations on Włocławek, and he only had to glance upward to see the trio of armed air cars from Torczon Security Services, the security agency which had served the Szponder family for at least three generations. Torczon was the service of choice for at least two thirds of the *Oligarchia*, and Zieliński had felt relieved when Szponder informed the BBP Torczon would be handling security for the gala in order to reduce the vehicle congestion.

Despite that, something nibbled at Grzegorz Zieliński's sense of comfort. He didn't know what it was, yet he had the nagging sense that something wasn't exactly where it was supposed to be. It was foolish, of course, but he couldn't quite seem to shake it.

He was halfway through his sweep when Wincenty Małakowski's voice came over his earbug.

"Grzegorz! There's—"

The voice cut off and Zieliński stiffened.

"Wincenty?" he said sharply into his lapel mic. *"Wincenty?!"*

He was reaching for the panic button on his wrist com when he felt something cold touch the back of his neck. His head whipped around, and his eyes widened as Tomek Nowak smiled at him. There was something bright and glittery in Nowak's hand, and Zieliński blinked, wondering why it was so hard to focus on it. He blinked again, and then his eyes widened. A hypo. That was a hypo gun. But why would Nowak be carrying a . . .

Zieliński's brain stopped working. He stood there, eyes empty, and Nowak touched his shoulder gently.

"Why don't you go have a seat over there by the musicians, Grzegorz?" he suggested, and Zieliński nodded. That sounded like an excellent idea, he decided. He was a little tired and a bit dizzy, and it would be good to get off his feet for a few minutes. He nodded to Nowak again, grateful for the suggestion, and headed off across the dance stage, walking a little carefully.

Tomasz Szponder watched the Przewodniczący's chief bodyguard cross the stage, find a chair, and sit down, smiling at nothing in particular, his head moving gently in time with the music. Then Szponder turned his own head to find Nowak near the portable wet bar, and Nowak raised the glass in his hand.

Szponder drew a deep breath, squeezed Grażyna's suddenly tense hand under the cover of the tablecloth, stood, and tapped his goblet with a spoon. The sweet chiming sound was surprisingly audible through the breeze and the background surf of voices, and faces turned in his direction.

He tapped again, and the side conversations died as all the guests gave him their attention.

"Ladies and Gentlemen," he said, "when I invited you, I promised fireworks and a surprise announcement in honor of this *Dzień Przewodniczącego*. To be honest, I trust the fireworks will be a bit less spectacular than they might be under other circumstances, but it's time for my announcement.

"This is the hundredth anniversary of the birth of my dearest friend and mentor, Włodzimierz Ziomkowski. Forty-two years ago today, here, in this villa, we wrote out and signed the *Karta* of the Ruch Odnowy Narodowej. The RON was Włodzimierz's life's dream, his life's work. *Nothing* was more important to him than its ideals, the need to improve the lives of every Włocławekan man, woman, and child. I can't tell you how honored I was that he chose this island, and this villa, as the place where the words enshrining those ideals, those commitments, were first formally committed to writing."

He paused, and a spatter of applause turned into a rolling ovation. More than half his guests rose, applauding still harder, and he smiled and raised his hands, waving them back into their seats.

"But the truth is," he continued once quiet had returned, "that no task is ever completely finished. There's always more to be done, more to accomplish, and that's true here in Włocławek. And because it is, I invited all of you here on the centenary of Włodzimierz's birth to begin the next step in fully realizing his dream for our star system."

He paused once more. There was another splatter of applause, but one or two of his guests looked a bit confused and he heard a quiet mutter of whispered conversation. He waited another ten seconds, until the unobtrusive earbug in his left ear chimed, then straightened his spine, and his voice was harder when he spoke again, with an edge of steel none of them had heard from him in decades. Not since the violent, street-fighting days of the *Agitacja*.

"Ladies and Gentlemen, please direct your attention to the villa," he said... just as fifty heavily armed men and women came through the French doors and spread rapidly around the perimeter of the terrace.

Shocked silence spread with them, but only for another ten or twenty seconds.

"What's the meaning of this?!" Agnieszka Krzywicka demanded sharply. She half-rose, staring about her, and her face tightened as she realized neither her security detachment nor Ziomkowski's was anywhere to be seen.

"The meaning, Ms. Sekretarz," Szponder said calmly, coldly, turning to face her as Grażyna rose to stand proudly at his side, "is that we're taking back the movement you and your *aparatczycy* hijacked twenty T-years ago. Hopefully, we can accomplish that without bloodshed. However," he met her stunned, furious eyes very, very levelly, "if you insist on watering the tree of liberty, we can do it that way, too."

Chapter Sixty-Two

"ALPHA TRANSLATION IN FIFTEEN MINUTES, Ma'am," Lieutenant Commander Saint-Germain announced.

"Thank you, Ulrich," Captain Amanda Belloc replied, watching her plot as Task Group 10.2.7 approached the alpha wall.

Captain Belloc's task group was twenty-three days out of Montana, and she felt the tension ratcheting up within her. She had no qualms about the capability of the task group Admiral Culbertson had built around the heavy cruiser *Madelyn Hoffman* to perform the *first* part of her mission orders. Backed by Captain Leah Piekarski's division of *Rolands*, the older but still capable light cruiser *Huang Zhen*, and the five *Culverin*-class destroyers of Captain Zachariah Lewis' Destroyer Division 102.1, she had more than enough firepower to deal with anything she couldn't outrun effortlessly.

No, the problem was exactly how she went about executing the *second* part of her orders. Her task group was essentially a commerce raiding force, with the capacity to leave a fairly capable system-defense force in perhaps two of the four star systems on her list, but she had no capacity at all to *occupy* any of them. That meant she couldn't go around, kicking in Frontier Security's doors dirtside or issuing demands to independent governments, however deep in bed with the League they might be. She *could*—as her orders specified—contact any independent (or nominally so) system government *after* removing any Solarian forces in deep space with a message of friendship and a request to establish formal—and friendly—relations with the Star Empire. But even if the aforesaid nominally independent governments *were* in bed with the League, that was about as far as she could go. Unless the Mesan Alignment had been fomenting rebellion against those nominally independent governments and promising Manticoran support, the Star Empire had exactly zero moral justification for demanding their capitulation, at any rate.

She really wished it could be as simple as settling into orbit and posting something like "Hey! Any revolutionaries down there expecting Manticoran assistance? Here we are!" to the planetary boards. Somehow, though, that seemed a little lacking in . . . subtlety. Worse, it might very well spark a rebellion which wouldn't have occurred otherwise. That could get a lot of people killed unnecessarily, not to mention undermining the Star Empire's assertion that someone *else* had been promoting violent rebellion and only pretending to be Manticore. The admiral's orders covered her if something went wrong, but it wasn't the job of a Queen's officer to *let* things go wrong, and Amanda Belloc had no intention of allowing anything of the sort to happen.

Now if the rest of the universe would just cooperate.

❖   ❖   ❖

"Well, I've got some good news, or I've got some *bad* news. The only problem is I don't know which it is."

"Been a bit of that goin' around, Vinnie."

Floyd Allenby's weathered face was as unwaveringly determined as ever, but he'd lost a lot of weight. The promised Manticoran naval support was three weeks overdue, and they hadn't heard a single word from Harvey Eldbrand to explain where it was. By his most optimistic estimate, Frontier Fleet had had plenty of time to respond to the escaped Tallulah freighter's demands for SLN and OFS to restore the situation in Swallow. In fact, by *any* reasonable estimate, Frontier Fleet should have arrived at least five days ago. According to some hints picked up from their "discussions" with Alton Parkman and Sheila Hampton, his chief of staff, Frontier Fleet was in the process of reorganizing its deployments. That might explain the delay, but nothing was going to delay it much *longer*.

"S'pose you'd best tell us what it is so's we can all figure out *which* it is," he continued, twitching his head at the other men and women in the conference room. Jason MacGruder sat at the far end of the long, polished table, flanked by Joyce Allenby and Truman Rodriguez, and his own sister, Gemma, sat at Floyd's right hand.

"Well," Frugoni said, "according to Nathan, *Dumber Ass* has picked up a batch of hyper footprints. They don't have military grade sensors up there, so they can't be certain, but when sixteen ships come over the alpha wall at the same time and head in-system, I think it's probably safe to say they aren't a batch of freighters that all just happened to arrive at the same time."

"S'pose not," Floyd said quietly. He sat back in his chair and looked around the conference table, then returned his gaze to Frugoni. "So why aren't you sure this is *bad* news, seein's how we haven't heard squat out of the Manties?"

"Well, that's the thing," Frugoni replied. "They've been in normal-space for the better part of thirty minutes, and they haven't said a word. I've got to wonder why a Frontier Fleet commander wouldn't be blistering our ears already."

"Might just want us t' have time t' work up a good sweat 'fore they get around t' tellin' us why they're here," MacGruder suggested. Floyd and Frugoni looked at him, and he shrugged. "Think they call that 'psychological warfare,'" he elaborated.

"That could be it," Rodriguez agreed. "And it could be that they want to wait until we know they're in missile range before they start issuing any demands. They might figure we'd be less likely to do anything stupid—like, oh, I don't know...threatening to blow up Tallulah's infrastructure if they don't go home and leave us alone—if we know they're in position to blow the crap out of all the *rest* of our infrastructure."

"Could be you're both right," Floyd said after a moment, "but damned if I'm gonna get on the com t' them any sooner'n I have to." He smiled mirthlessly. "Might be pointless as all hell, but I'm not goin' t' give the bastards as much as the time of day till I have to."

⋄　　⋄　　⋄

"Something strange about this, Ma'am," Commander Frieda Mawhinney said.

She and Commander Lawrence Hillshot, *Madelyn*

Hoffman's XO, stood on either side of Captain Belloc's command chair, watching the main plot. At the moment, it was configured to show the entire inner system, fed by the Ghost Rider drones which had been sent speeding ahead.

"Enlighten me, Frieda," Belloc said, and her tactical officer shrugged.

"We've been in-system over an hour now, and that's long enough for even Sollies to get around to challenging us, Ma'am," she pointed out. "The fact that they haven't is odd enough, but what's really strange is how little *traffic* there is. We're only tracking three impeller signatures bigger than small craft in the entire inner system, and there's no sign of collector ships moving along the asteroid belt, either. According to our intel, Tallulah has at least a hundred asteroid extraction ships, and they're supposed to do a lot of gas mining from Bigsby, the system's gas giant, too. But we don't see any sign of that, and it's not like they all went scurrying for home the instant we turned up, either. For that matter, they couldn't even all have shut down and gone doggo without our having picked up at least some impeller signatures first."

"Guns is right, Ma'am," Hillshot said. "Especially about the challenge side. For that matter, Astro Control should've contacted us a good twenty minutes ago even if they were stupid enough to think we're just a convoy of merchies."

"Agreed."

Belloc tipped back in her chair, fingers of her right hand drumming lightly on the armrest while she considered the situation.

There was no legitimate reason for an entire star

system to decide to turn off its com net, yet that appeared to be exactly what these people had done. Which suggested a reason that was *less* than legitimate, and an unpleasant possibility suggested itself to her. If this was another Saltash, with a Solarian squadron or task force hiding in stealth somewhere, prepared to pounce from ambush, that ambush's commander might have decided to go to com silence. The only reason she wasn't certain that was what was happening was that a Solly naval commander with a clue would have ordered Astro Control to hail them in a normal, routine welcome. She would *not* have opted for a silence which was likely to make her intended victims suspicious.

The only flaw in that analysis, Amanda, is that you're thinking about a Solly naval commander with a clue, *and so far no one's ever met one.*

She smiled sourly at the thought, then let her chair come back upright.

"All right. I think you're onto something. Unfortunately, I'm not sure what 'something' is. Frieda, I want a second shell of Ghost Rider drones, and I want the first shell to sweep all the way to the hyper limit on the far side of the system. If this is another Saltash and there's someone hidden out there, I want her found."

"Aye, aye, Ma'am." Mawhinney started back to her own console, but Belloc's raised hand stopped her. "Ma'am?"

"Just in case there are any unfriendly individuals thinking homicidal thoughts out there, I think it would be a good idea to bring the task group to Condition One. I don't want to deploy any Mark 23s yet, but inform Captain Piekarski that we may be looking at a Mark 16 engagement. And inform Captain Lewis that I want his destroyers to hold here, close to the hyper limit, with *Veerle Vosburgh*. If there's any shooting, I want that freighter over the wall into hyper before any bad guys even *think* of getting close to her. The last thing we need is to lose the pods in her holds. Then I want a launch of decoys prepped."

"Aye, aye, Ma'am."

"And as for you, Aquilino," Belloc continued, turning to *Madelyn Hoffman*'s communications officer, "I'd like you to warm up your little com. I'm sure I'll feel a need to talk to these people ... eventually."

"Not now, Ma'am?" Lieutenant Aquilino Demeter asked, and Belloc shook her head.

"No. If they're not friendly enough to talk to us, I don't see any reason we should be in a rush to talk to *them*." Belloc smiled unpleasantly. "We'll wait until we hit turnover and they know for sure—Sollies can be a little slow on the uptake, I've heard—that we're headed for a zero-zero with the planet. That'll give the TO time to get all her ducks in a row, anyway."

✧   ✧   ✧

Another ninety minutes dragged slowly past. Then Lieutenant Demeter cleared his throat without ever—quite—glancing at his captain.

"I haven't forgotten, Aquilino," Belloc said dryly, and the lieutenant nodded.

"Never thought you had, Ma'am."

"Liars come to bad ends." Belloc smiled briefly, then squared her shoulders. "All right, put me on."

"Live mic, Ma'am," Demeter said promptly, and the captain looked directly into the pickup.

"Astro Control, this is Captain Amanda Belloc, Royal Manticoran Navy, commanding officer, HMS *Madelyn Hoffman*. I request approach instructions."

TG 10.27's units—minus Zachariah Lewis' five *Culverins* and the Mark 23-packed *Veerle Vosburgh*—had maintained a leisurely 2.9 KPS^2 since crossing the alpha wall. *Madelyn Hoffman* was still almost seven light-minutes short of planetary orbit and the improbably named *Donald Ulysses and Rosa Aileen Shuman Space Station* where this system's astro control kept its headquarters, and she sat back to await a response. Fifteen minutes crept by, and then—

"I have a response, Captain," Demeter announced. "It's not from Astro Control, though."

"No?" Belloc raised her eyebrows. "What a surprise. Who *is* it from?"

"It's coming from the planet, Ma'am."

"Not the space station at all?"

"No, Ma'am."

Belloc nodded while she toyed absently with a lock of hair. According to the limited intelligence packet Admiral Culbertson had been able to put together for her, the real power in this system was supposed to be the system manager for a transstellar called the Tallulah Corporation. Tallulah couldn't be a major player by Solarian standards, given that Belloc had never heard of it, but the system manager in question was supposed to have his headquarters aboard the space station. There was no official Solarian presence on the planet, either, so she'd assumed any response would come from someone pretending to be Astro Control or else from whatever force the Sollies had dispatched to ambush her here. In either case, the transmission should be coming from someplace in space, not on the planet.

"Well, I suppose you'd better put them through, Aquilino," she said mildly.

"Yes, Ma'am."

An instant later, a face appeared on Belloc's com display. The stranger was brown-haired and brown-eyed, with a close-cropped beard and an eagle's beak of a nose. His image was motionless until she tapped the key to play the transmission.

"Afternoon, Captain Belloc. My name's Allenby—Floyd Allenby. And I b'lieve what you're looking for is 'Davy Crockett.'"

Davycrockett? Well, that *was certainly unexpected,* Amanda Belloc thought. *What the hell is a "davycrockett"?*

❖   ❖   . ❖

Floyd Allenby sat tautly, watching the com display with Frugoni at one shoulder and Jason MacGruder at the other.

The long, agonizing wait as the silent warships crept closer and closer had almost—*almost*—overcome his determination to wait them out. If they'd been Manties, they should already have contacted him ... or the current commander of the Cripple Mountain Movement, assuming something unpleasant had happened to him. But no one had been able to think of a reason for Frontier Fleet to approach so slowly and wait so long before opening communication, either.

And then this Captain Belloc had finally contacted them ... without asking for him, without asking for *anyone* from the CMM, without the code phrase announcing why she was here, and contacting Astro Control, instead.

Clearly, something was very wrong, yet he'd seen no option but to transmit the peculiar code phrase Eldbrand had given Frugoni and hope for the best.

'Sides, if this here's a fleet of Sollies, ain't gonna make a whole heap o' difference what I say to 'em, now is it?

✧   ✧   ✧

"Excuse me, Mr. . . . Allenby, was it?" Belloc said. "I was expecting to contact Astro Control. Could I ask why I'm speaking to you, instead? And exactly what a 'davycrockett' is?"

✧   ✧   ✧

"Y'know, this here's getting' stranger by th' minute, Floyd," MacGruder observed. "You reckon Mantics could be as just plain dumb as *Sollies*?"

"Doesn't seem likely," Allenby replied, scratching his beard. "Mean, I hear they can count t' ten with their boots on an' everything." He thought about it for a moment, then shrugged. "Might's well be hung for a snow bear as a house cat," he said, and touched the transmit key again.

✧   ✧   ✧

"Don't rightly know what—or who—a 'Davy Crockett' is, Captain," the bearded man on Belloc's display said twelve minutes later. "Wasn't my idea. But your man Eldbrand said you'd recognize th' code phrase when you got here. Course, we expected you 'bout a T-month ago."

Both of Amanda Belloc's eyebrows rose, and then she shook her head wryly.

Well, assuming this isn't some sort of elaborate deception plan after all, it looks like Admiral Culbertson was onto something, doesn't it, Amanda? And you're not going to have to go around looking for them after all!

"I'm sorry we're late, Mr. Allenby," she said aloud, "but I believe there may have been a slight . . . misunderstanding. You see—"

Chapter Sixty-Three

"ANY LAST THOUGHTS?" Captain Gerald Hagan, Solarian League Navy, asked, as he looked around SLNS *Ratnik*'s briefing room.

"Sounds pretty straightforward," Captain Hiram Albani, CO of SLNS *Kriger* and CruDiv 423.1's second-in-command, said from his quadrant of the master com display. "We go in, we...explain things to these people, and we kick ass, if that's what it takes to make them see reason."

He shrugged, and Hagan suppressed a desire to scowl at him.

It wasn't easy, given how much he'd always disliked the other captain. Albani was abrasive, arrogant, and hotheaded, with major family connections in OFS. He wasn't simply a blunt instrument; he was someone who enjoyed *being* a blunt instrument, and sometimes that tended to be...counterproductive.

Hagan himself had no qualms about breaking heads, if that was what it took to convince these neobarbs to mind their manners. That never had bothered him, to be honest. It was what Frontier Fleet was for, when it came down to it. And these days, with the lunatic Manties trying to set the entire galaxy on its ear, he had even less patience than usual with anyone willing to help out by planting daggers in the League's back. Not only that, but Admiral Torricelli had made it abundantly clear to all his senior officers that the government absolutely couldn't afford to lose any more revenue-producing systems now that the Manties had thrown such a monumental spanner into the League's interstellar economy.

So, yes, he was more than prepared to explain, however forcefully was required, to the citizens of Swallow that it would be wise of them to return the Tallulah Corporation's property. Unfortunately, aside from a single Gendarmerie intervention battalion and two companies of Solarian Marines, he was a little short on the means to convince them of the error of their way if they weren't prepared to be overawed by his four *Warrior*-class light cruisers. It was unlikely the situation on-planet was as dire as Captain Romero Shwang, the skipper of *Tallulah Dawn 7*, which had fled the system to seek help, insisted it was. Shwang had been more than a little hysterical in his interviews with Admiral Torricelli. Nonetheless, it seemed likely the rebels against the Shuman Administration really were equipped with modern, military-grade weapons, and even a small planetary population was counted in billions. If any significant portion of those billions supported the insurrectionists, pacifying it would be a bitch with so few warm bodies. Unless he was prepared to resort to KEWs, and he wasn't. Whatever Shwang might've said—and whatever Torricelli might have to say, for that matter—Gerald Hagan had no intention of using KEWs against civilian targets . . . and not just because he objected to killing golden geese.

"There was a military theorist back on old Earth, once upon a time," he said now, looking at Albani. "Well, there were probably a lot of them, actually. But the one I'm thinking about said something along the lines of 'in war everything is very simple, but doing even simple things is very hard.' I'll agree our objective's straightforward, Hiram. But don't make the mistake of thinking it'll be easy to 'kick ass' if the local yokels aren't prepared to see reason."

Albani's mouth tightened ever so slightly as Hagan reiterated what he'd probably said no more than four or five hundred times since Admiral Torricelli sent them off. He also nodded, however, and Hagan decided to settle for that and turned his attention to Commander Trudi Vercesi and Commander Antonia Valakis, who commanded SLNS *Harcos* and SLNS *Guerriera*, respectively.

"Any new thoughts occur to either of you since our last conference?"

Heads shook, and Hagan nodded. That was pretty much what he'd expected.

"All right, then," he said more briskly. "We go in as planned."

❖   ❖   ❖

"Still no response, Sir," Lieutenant Commander Shahrizad Kantor, *Ratnik*'s communications officer, said, and Gerald Hagan frowned.

He'd transmitted his "request" for approach instructions to Swallow Astro Control as soon as his light cruisers and the chartered transport *Priscilla Lane* crossed the alpha wall into normal-space. But that had been thirty minutes ago, and the range to the local space station had been only fourteen light-minutes. There'd been plenty of time for Astro Control to respond.

So the idiots plan to be stubborn, he thought sourly. *Big surprise. Anybody who'd try something like this in the first place isn't blessed with an overabundance of smarts. But they're not going to make things any easier on themselves.*

He glanced at the astrogation display. CruDiv 423.1 was up to an approach velocity of 7,431 KPS and had covered just over 6,672,000 kilometers since crossing the wall. At their current 420 gravities of acceleration they were still over an hour and a half from turnover for a zero-zero rendezvous with the planet. There was plenty of time, he supposed, but it would be best to get a few things clear from the beginning.

"Record for transmission, Shahrizad," he said.

"Live mic, Sir."

"Astro Control," he said into the pickup, "This is Captain Gerald Hagan, Solarian League Navy, commanding officer of the light cruiser *Ratnik* and senior officer of Cruiser Division Four-Two-Three-One. You have not responded to my previous transmission. Be advised that I am in your star system in response to claims that Solarian citizens' lives and property have been threatened by violent extremists. As such, if you do not respond to *this* message, I will have no choice but to assume criminal elements are in control of your com facilities and to construe your continued silence as a hostile act. Under those circumstances, I will feel free to use whatever level of force is necessary to compel you to respond, and I will take whatever measures seem appropriate to safeguard Solarian lives and property in the Swallow System. I intend to maintain my present flight profile, which will bring my vessels to a zero-zero orbital insertion around Swallow in approximately—" he glanced at the maneuvering display "—three hours and fifty minutes. If you fail to respond within the next three hours, I will consider Swallow a hostile world, and adopt the appropriate stance—and tactics—for a force entering contested space. I would advise you, most strenuously, to avoid circumstances liable to result in loss of life and destruction of property. Hagan, clear."

He nodded to the pickup, then look back to Kantor. "Play that back, Shahrizad," he said.

She did, and he watched it through, then nodded again.

"Send it," he said, and leaned back in his command chair once again.

❖   ❖   ❖

"Captain, I have an incoming transmission!"

Hagan looked up sharply from his discussion with Commander Brenda Travada, his executive officer. They'd just passed the turnover point and begun decelerating to kill their 32,000 KPS velocity relative to the planet, which put them better than an hour and a half outside missile range of Swallow orbit, but Hagan believed in thinking ahead and he wanted his attack options nailed down well before time. But now something about Shahrizad Kantor's urgent voice raised his mental hackles.

"From someone in the legitimate government?" he asked, striding back towards his command chair.

"No, Sir," she replied.

"So it's one of the frigging outlaws," he growled as he reached the command chair and swung himself back into it.

"No, Sir, it's not." There was something very peculiar in her tone, he thought. "It's from—" Kantor paused and drew a deep breath. "Sir," she said quietly, "it's from someone who claims to be a Manty officer."

Hagan's nostrils flared, and it was suddenly very quiet on *Ratnik*'s bridge. He felt all eyes snapping to him and commanded his expression to remain calm.

He rather doubted that it had obeyed him.

"Well," he heard his own voice say, "I suppose I'd better view it."

"Sir," Kantor said even more quietly, "it's not a recording. It's a live transmission from a com relay about eighty thousand kilometers from us."

Hagan just looked at her for a moment. Then his eyes whipped back to the tactical display, which showed absolutely no one and nothing within twenty-five million kilometers of his ship.

"Very well," he said after a long, taut moment. "Put it through."

"Yes, Sir."

Kantor touched her panel, and the image of a tallish woman with blue-green eyes and long auburn hair, pulled back in a thick braid, appeared on his display. She was quite attractive, in a stern-faced sort of way, a corner of his mind thought. More immediately, however, she wore the black and gold uniform of the Manticoran Navy with the single-planet collar insignia of a senior grade captain.

"Who are you and what can I do for you?" he

asked tersely, and composed himself to wait out the transmission lag with as confident an air as he could manage. Whoever this was, she had to be at least eighty-four light-seconds away from *Ratnik*, given that blank tactical display. That meant a two-way delay of the next best thing to three minutes, so—

"I'm Captain Amanda Belloc, Royal Manticoran Navy, commanding Her Majesty's Ship *Madelyn Hoffman*. And what you can do for me is to cut your drives, stand down, and prepare to surrender your ship, Captain Hagan," she replied flatly...and barely three *seconds* later.

Hagan twitched upright in astonishment at the nearly instant response. Then the words registered and his face darkened.

"I beg your pardon?" he grated. "How *dare* you issue that sort of demand to the Solarian League Navy?! And what in God's name makes you think I'd do anything of the sort?!"

"Issuing it is no problem at all, Captain. You may not have heard this, given the slowness with which word seems to percolate through Solarian space—and brains—but the Star Empire of Manticore and the Solarian League have been formally at war for over two T-months. Something to do with an unprovoked, undeclared attack on our capital system, I believe. I realize the Solarian League, as the guardian of all proper behavior and moral authority, sees no reason to bother with little things like formal declarations of war before attacking other star nations. We're a bit less sophisticated than that in Manticore and Haven, though. After Duchess Harrington finished blowing half of Admiral Filareta's wallers out of space, it seemed appropriate to my Empress and her allies to go ahead and make it official. So trust me—I'm not especially worried about Solarian sensitivities at this particular moment.

"As to what makes me think you'll comply with my requirements, I continue to hope that eventually we'll find a senior Solarian officer with at least the IQ of a gnat. I don't much like Sollies, but I don't take a lot of pleasure out of slaughtering them in job lots, either."

Belloc's flat, confidently contemptuous tone sent an icy chill through Gerald Hagan.

"That's very generous of you," he replied after a moment, his voice harsh. "And it's also bold talk from a woman who's not even in range of my ships."

"Who says I'm not?"

He frowned, then—

"Sir!"

The half-strangled exclamation came from Lieutenant Commander Gennadi Hudson, his tactical officer, and Hagan's eyes whipped back to the tactical display. A display which was suddenly spangled with dozens of tiny impeller signatures—the signatures of recon drones, he realized sickly, some of them less than ten thousand kilometers clear of *Ratnik*, and—

"Impellers lighting off," Hudson announced. His voice was clearer, but no less tense. "We have five ships, range one-one-point-four light-minutes. Sir," he turned to look at Hagan, "CIC makes it four light cruisers and one possible battlecruiser."

Hagan felt the color drain from his face. Less than twelve light-minutes? And none of his sensor crews had seen a *thing*? How was that *possible*? Then he looked back at those diamond-dust recon drones. If they could get drones with active impellers that close undetected, of course they could hide a starship without any active emissions at twenty thousand times the range! But still...

My God, a numbed corner of his brain thought. *Their stealth's* that *good?!*

"For your information, Captain Hagan," Belloc continued from her display, "you're currently several million kilometers inside my engagement range. I, on the other hand, am at least four million kilometers outside *your* range. So I suppose it comes down to a fairly simple question, doesn't it? Are you prepared to comply with my requirements, or do we get messy about this?"

Chapter Sixty-Four

THE ROOFTOP TRIBARREL BELONGED to either the Army or the Scags; it was hard to know which, these days.

Nor did it matter a great deal as the solid bar of shells—every tenth round a tracer, looking more like an old-fashioned, pre-space idea of a "death ray" than solid projectiles—ripped down at a steep angle. The heavy-caliber weapon was obviously there to interdict movement down the Tyrone Boulevard approach to Landing Memorial Park on the southwestern edge of The Mall, and its gunner appeared to have plenty of ammunition. He was also an unfortunately good shot, and what had once been an Army Víbora APC exploded in a blinding glare of hydrogen. Pieces of wreckage flew skyward, then came crashing down as much as a hundred and fifty meters away, and when the smoke and dust cleared—some, at least—all that remained was a shattered, broken, barely identifiable hulk.

There'd been eighteen men and women aboard that Víbora . . . and its glacis had been repainted with the green "liberty tree" of the Seraphim Independence Movement.

"Shit," Ruben Broadhead said bitterly. "*Now* what the hell do we do?"

"Now we find a way to deal with it," Damien Harahap replied much more calmly. The two of them stood on the roof of an apartment building on the far side of Tyrone and two blocks farther west. Now Broadhead turned his head to glare at him, but Harahap only shrugged. "I know you knew more people aboard that APC than I did, Ruben. But we still have to find a way to deal with it. And—" he bared his teeth briefly "—if we can do it in a way that sends that tribarrel crew straight to hell, so much the better."

Broadhead glared a moment longer, but then his anger—at Harahap, at any rate—faded, and he nodded, hard.

"Absolutely," he agreed. "Any thoughts?"

Actually, Harahap reflected, he had quite a few thoughts, most of which he had no intention of sharing with Broadhead or any other member of the SIM. However . . .

"I can think of a couple of approaches," he said. "Unfortunately, my first choice would entail an orbiting starship and a kinetic energy weapon."

"Just a *little* short on those," Broadhead pointed out with a flicker of genuine amusement, and Harahap grinned back.

"Well, in that case we'll just have to dust off one of the other options."

He raised his electronic binoculars, gazing through the smoke-laden air at the heavily sandbagged tribarrel while distant—and not so distant—explosions and all the other sounds of combat came from what seemed like every direction. Actually, he reflected, the vast majority of that appalling racket came from the east, which was a good sign for the SIM. It meant they were closing in on The Mall, the Presidential Palace, and the Hall of Ministries at the heart of the Government District. Taking that would break Howard Shelton's last redoubt here in the capital. Then all they had to do was clear the five or six square blocks Tillman O'Sullivan's SSSP troopers still held on the southern edge of the city, and all of Cherubim would be in the Independence Movement's hands.

He shook his head mentally, moving the binoculars as he scanned adjacent buildings. They were fortunate so much of Cherubim had been built by a planet without counter-grav. The handful of proper residential towers would have been nightmare propositions from any attackers' viewpoint. If the SIM was forced to fight its way into one of *those*, its manpower would evaporate like spit on one of The Soup Spoon's woks.

Fortunately, three quarters of the Cherubim Police Department had come over to the rebels' side once open fighting broke out between Shelton's Army troops and O'Sullivan's scags, and the local cops had known all about those towers. They'd been the ones with all the detailed floor plans and schematics . . . not to mention the people who'd been responsible for planning—and rehearsing—ways to deal with potential hostage and terrorist threats inside them. They'd known exactly how to secure them before it occurred to the Army or the SSSP that *they* should take them over as forts. That struck Harahap as a serious oversight on Shelton's and O'Sullivan's parts, but he was probably being unfair. They'd never seen anything like *this* coming, and it was clear O'Sullivan, in particular, had never anticipated the CPD's defection to an entirely new player.

He'd obviously known the regular, uniformed police had never been that fond of the SSSP, but, in fairness to him, they'd started deserting to the rebels only when he'd proved he was no better than Shelton by launching his own coup attempt. Of course, what the cops still didn't know was that neither Shelton nor O'Sullivan had intended to launch anything of the sort. Not until one of them had been far more confident of succeeding, at any rate.

His lips quirked as he remembered his initial reaction to Indiana's strategy. Mackenzie had staunchly maintained that the plan was a product of their joint endeavors, not simply a crazed notion of her lunatic brother, and Harahap was prepared to believe she'd spent a lot of time hammering down rough spots. But whatever she might say, the inspiration had to have come from Indy. It was exactly the sort of thing that *would* occur to him, and Harahap had decided that if Indiana Graham had been a bit less inhibited by his unwavering moral compass, he would have made an outstanding covert operator in his own right.

The Independence Movement hadn't been able to acquire as many Army and SSSP uniforms as Indy had really wanted, but it had found enough of them, and Indy's opening strikes had convinced Shelton that O'Sullivan was attacking him at the same instant O'Sullivan concluded Shelton was attacking *him*. The sudden violence had taken both of them by surprise, each had reacted by declaring all-out war against the other, and the attacks on the Army's main arsenals had deprived Shelton of sixty percent of his armored units.

At a cost. Ning Saowaluk was far from the only SIM member to die in those initial strikes, and Harahap knew Indy and Mackenzie found that hard to live with. He'd suspected they might, once the casualties became real—dead and maimed friends, no longer theoretical, faceless strangers. But they were tough, the Grahams. Their grief wasn't about to shake their resolve, although Indy had aged at least ten years in the past three weeks.

Yet the hard, tough core of steel which had driven him to organize the Seraphim Independence Movement out of nothing had been tempered and refined, not broken, and the attack on Terrabore Prison had been a masterstroke.

Indiana and Mackenzie had never tried to pretend the need to break Bruce Graham out of Terrabore hadn't been a major reason they'd created the SIM, and Harahap suspected the opening moves of every single one of their planning options had included an attack on Terrabore. The fact that their hearts had been at least as engaged as their heads hadn't made them wrong, however. Terrabore was more than "just" a prison; it had also been the SSSP's primary HQ and communications node. The attack using "Army" vehicles and the heavy weapons smuggled in from off-world—heavy weapons which *only* the Army would have possessed, here on Swallow—had convinced O'Sullivan that Shelton was attempting to decapitate his own organization outside the capital, even as the "scags'" attack on Shelton's arsenals convinced him that O'Sullivan was trying to destroy the heavy combat equipment which might have given the Army the edge.

Harahap was pretty sure both had begun to suspect, probably within the first few hours, that they'd been duped by yet a third player. But they'd had no idea who that third party might be—or any proof it even existed—and by then their forces had been fully engaged.

The first few days of pitched combat between the Army and the Scags had eliminated much of the remaining heavy equipment on both sides, and Indy and Mackenzie had spent those same days integrating the liberated prisoners from Terrabore into their existing structure. Bruce Graham hadn't been the only reason they'd targeted the prison. McCready and O'Sullivan had collected all of their most visible and potentially dangerous opponents—those they hadn't simply murdered, at any rate—in one place, and Indiana's audacious plan had snatched all of them. Journalists, political opponents, religious clergy, college professors, business people who'd been driven into opposition by the jackals who scavenged in the transstellars' wakes . . .

The SIM had liberated all of them in a single stroke, and in return, they'd provided the public face of the secretly organized group which had made their liberation possible. That had given the Independence Movement a degree of instant legitimacy nothing else could have, which was a huge part of the reason so many municipal and county police forces had come over to the SIM when Indy and Mackenzie finally launched their own offensive against both Shelton and O'Sullivan. Just as importantly, thousands of regular civilian volunteers had flocked to join them, as well. The arms provided by Harahap and the Alignment had run out quickly, but by then they'd begun capturing sizable stockpiles of Army and SSSP weapons. By the time Shelton and O'Sullivan recognized what was happening and attempted to unite against the common threat, it was too late. The SIM was riding the crest of a huge wave of popular support. If they succeeded in taking Cherubim, the rest of the planet—and the star system—would fall into place quickly.

At least until Krestor, or Mendoza, or the Oginski Group, or OFS got around to smashing the rebellion. And before that happened, Damien Harahap was going to requisition one of the dispatch boats in orbit around Seraphim and head out "to tell the Manties the SIM needed fleet support."

His mouth tightened at that thought. Not that he had any other option, of course. But the fact that this part of Operation Janus was about to succeed brilliantly left an undeniably bad taste in his mouth.

You'll get over it, he told himself cynically. *Once you've gotten back into the groove, forgotten how much you wound up liking these people, you'll get over it. And you'd* better. *Because if you don't, the Alignment will make* damned *sure your conscience doesn't bother you for long.*

"I think we can flank out that position if we swing south, up Shimanouchi Street," he told Broadhead. "See that water tower on the roof at Shimanouchi and Vine? If we get one of our own tribarrels up there, we'll have the angle down on these bastards."

"Assuming *they* don't already have someone up there waiting for us, of course."

"Well, of course!" Harahap smiled. "That's what makes life *interesting*, Ruben!"

Broadhead chuckled, and Harahap slung his binoculars and picked up his pulse rifle.

"Let's get over there before anybody else gets hurt over *here*," he said, and led off into the smoke.

❖   ❖   ❖

"Got a call from Talisman, Firebrand," Joyce Albertson said, and Harahap looked up from his thirty-centimeter sub and potato chips.

The vast majority of Seraphim's local business community had come over to the Independence Movement—in many cases, he was sure, from cynical calculation, since the premises of businesses that *didn't* endorse SIM tended to end up especially heavily damaged in the fighting. In a lot of cases, though—probably the majority—those businesspeople had genuinely endorsed the rebellion, and the owners and operators of the Three Hills Sandwiches chain were among those for whom that was true. Despite the disruptions of the fighting, the dozens of Three Hills restaurants managed to feed hundreds SIM fighters every day. It was unlikely they'd be able to keep it up much longer, given the dislocations in their supply chain. On the other hand, now that the Government District was firmly in rebel hands, the fighting here in the capital would probably wrap up in the next couple of days and let something like normalcy reassert itself.

Now Harahap waved one hand at the woman who'd interrupted his lunch as he chewed the current bite of sandwich—astonishingly good; Three Hills was actually still managing to bake fresh bread every day—and swallowed it. Albertson handed him the encrypted com, and he held it to his ear.

"Firebrand," he said.

"Talisman," Indiana replied. "Are you at a point where you could hand over to somebody else for an hour or two?"

"Sure. Why?"

"Magpie and I are over at Tobolinski and we've just found something I think will interest you."

Harahap's eyebrows arched. Tobolinski Field was Cherubim's primary spaceport. There'd been quite a bit of fighting out that way, but it had ended late yesterday. Which was good. As soon as he tied up the loose ends on his side of town and could hand over to Broadhead or one of the others without looking like he was running out on them, he intended to be aboard one of those captured shuttles and headed for a dispatch boat just as quickly as he could.

"What kind of 'something'?" he asked.

"It's a surprise," Indy replied, and chuckled. "In fact, it surprised *us!* I think you'll get a laugh out of it, though, and God knows we can all use as many of those as we can get!"

"You're right about that," Harahap agreed, and glanced at his chrono. "Give me a half hour to hand over here and I'll be there."

"Great! See you then."

It was actually closer to forty-five minutes before the ex-Army ground car deposited Harahap at Tobolinski Field's South Annex. The SIM sentries outside the enormous, crystoplast-walled building recognized him and grinned as they waved him inside. He smiled back at them, and felt another ripple of that bittersweet regret.

"Talisman said they'll be waiting for you in Concourse Five," one of the sentries said, pointing at the right slidewalk.

"Thanks."

Harahap nodded to the woman and stepped onto

the slidewalk. It swept him off through the vast terminal's air-conditioned interior, and he watched the freestanding sculptures and the art decorating the marble walls as they passed. The murals would need extensive remodeling, he reflected as the recently deceased Jacqueline McCready gazed back at him, flanked by radiantly smiling schoolchildren, but the terminal itself was completely undamaged.

The fighting for the north side of Tobolinski had been far fiercer, and the North Annex was going to require complete rebuilding. That was where Tillman O'Sullivan and Anderson Bligh had made their last stand, probably because they'd seen the spaceport as their only way off-world. They hadn't even been able to retreat to the space station, because the cops aboard it had gone over to SIM, as well. By the end, their last real hope had been to hold out in Toblonski long enough for the inevitable response from Krestor, Cordova, or OFS to rescue them.

Unfortunately for them, they'd run out of time. Bligh was in custody; O'Sullivan was in the morgue. Harahap was almost—*almost*—prepared to believe the Scags' commander had chosen to die fighting, but he wouldn't lose any sleep over the possibility that his demise had been less than voluntary.

The slidewalk delivered him to Concourse Five, and he stepped off as Indiana turned and waved to him.

"So, what's this surprise?" Harahap asked, shaking hands with him, and Indy chuckled.

"Oh, believe me, you're gonna love it," he promised. "Come on. Someone you have to meet."

He turned, leading the way to one of the lounges, and Harahap listened to the soft music playing over the terminal's speakers as he followed. Looking out across the shuttle pads he saw at least a half-dozen heavy-lift and passenger shuttles which had been caught on the pads with nowhere to go, and reminded himself—again—that he needed to get started on that trip "to get help" as soon as possible. It couldn't be too much longer until someone turned up from the Sollies' side, after all.

He stepped into the lounge and felt something pluck at his waist. It happened so quickly and smoothly it took even him by surprise—mostly, he realized later, because he'd never seen it coming. His head turned, eyes widening in surprise, and Indy stepped back with the pulser he'd just extracted from Harahap's holster.

"Like I said," the younger man said, his voice suddenly colder than Harahap had ever heard it, "you're gonna love this, Firebrand."

Harahap's brain raced, trying to figure out what that coldness portended. Then it stopped racing and froze in shock as a small, dark-featured man with blue eyes stepped into the lounge through a side door. He was flanked by two much larger, hard-eyed men in black tunics and green trousers, both carrying flechette guns as if they knew what to do with them, but he himself wore a black and gold uniform with four golden cuff bands, a single golden planet on its collar, and a golden, winged beast, rampant, on a five-sided red patch, on its right shoulder.

"Good afternoon, Mr. Firebrand," he said. "I've been looking forward to meeting you for some time now. My name's Zavala—Jacob Zavala." He smiled thinly. "I understand you represent the Star Empire of Manticore . . . too."

Chapter Sixty-Five

"WELL," GLORIA MICHELLE SAMANTHA EVELYN HENKE murmured to herself, "I suppose we're entitled to at least one or two *good* surprises."

The Countess of Gold Peak was tipped back in her favorite chair, her feet—in their fuzzy purple treecat slippers—propped on her desk as she studied the recorded message from Craig Culbertson which had just arrived. It was almost four T-weeks old, but it certainly made . . . interesting viewing.

A million more ground troops? I knew Augustus and I were onto something when we recommended organizing the Quadrant Guard, but I never thought they'd be able to turn up that many fully equipped troops!

She thought about it some more, then snorted.

There are a dozen star systems in the Quadrant, Mike, and their populations average right at two-point-five billion. If only ten percent of that many people are potentially available for military service, that's a pool of over three billion warm bodies. Probably shouldn't

be all that surprising Augustus and Krietzmann could
shoot a measly million *of them your way!*

That was certainly true, she reflected, and her surprise probably said something about the fact that she'd
seen the Quadrant primarily as a military liability—
something to be defended, people to be protected, a
deadly serious responsibility to distract her from taking
the fight to the enemy—rather than as an asset. The
troop numbers in the dispatch which Culbertson had
forwarded to her, however, were a sobering reflection
of how the Talbott Quadrant's annexation had increased
the Star Empire of Manticore's population and hence
its deployable military manpower.

Of course, it also underscored just how hideously
the Solarian League's enormously greater population
and industrial power out-classed that of the entire
Grand Alliance. *That*, however, was a calculation she'd
already fully internalized, she thought grimly.

She sipped from the coffee cup in her right hand
while the fingers of her left hand slowly and rhyth-
mically stroked the belly fur of the enormous Maine
Coon cat draped across her lap. Actually, it would be
more accurate to describe him as draped *along* her
lap . . . and also along her thighs and her shins. The
deep rumble of his purr, absolutely distinct from the
buzzing sound of a treecat, vibrated through her, and
she paused to smile down at him—albeit with a certain degree of resignation—before she returned her
attention to the information in Augustus Khumalo's
dispatch.

The timing, she thought, was ironic.

It was barely three weeks since the Myers System
had surrendered, having shown unusual wisdom—for

Sollies—by not forcing her to fire a shot. And despite a certain vengefulness where Solarians in general were concerned, Michelle Henke was just as happy not killing anyone she didn't have to.

The other star systems of the Madras Sector had taken their cue from the capital, surrendering as soon as a few cruisers or destroyers arrived. In the space of less than a month, she'd taken the entire sector—the first time the Solarian League had ever lost control of even *one* star system to a hostile power. But that success had brought problems of its own.

Here in Meyers, the government of King Lawrence looked like providing a sound basis for a legitimate, local, *independent* constitutional monarchy. Michelle knew she was constitutionally—she winced at her own unintentional double entendre—biased in favor of constitutional monarchies, but she also genuinely believed Lawrence represented the best shot for Meyers.

The sector's other systems were more problematical. Without a good local mechanism for establishing self-government, and without support from the Foreign Office (she felt a fresh pang of regret for Amandine Corvisart's death), she felt highly unqualified to muck around in their internal affairs. So she'd settled for scrapping the handful of light warships and the fixed local defenses which had surrendered to her and left the current civilian administrations on notice that the Star Empire *would* get around to all of them, in the fullness of time. The best she could hope for was that they'd take her at her word and do their very best to avoid any actions to which the Star Empire might object.

She hoped that worked out less disastrously than it

potentially could, but in the meantime, it had freed her hands and she'd intended to move immediately on the Mesa System. In fact, her operational plans called for her to depart Meyers for Mesa less than twelve hours from this very moment.

Plans were always subject to change, of course, she reminded herself dryly.

She never doubted that quite a few people back home had been horrified by her proposal to broaden the Grand Alliance's war against the Solarian League, but sometimes too much caution was more dangerous than too much audacity. Against something the size of the League, the Alliance couldn't afford to "play safe." Besides, Mesa wasn't a member of the League. It would be interesting to see if this Mesan Alignment had sufficient clout with the Mandarins to deploy the League to defend its home star system, but she doubted that was likely to happen. It was always possible, however, which was the reason she'd dictated and sent off her message to Empress Elizabeth. It not only informed her cousin of her intentions—and the reasons for them—but also gave Elizabeth all she would need to disavow the consequences of her decision if that became necessary.

Very noble of me it was, too. Her lips twitched in a wry smile. *I hope Beth properly appreciates me! But I have to admit this changes things a bit.*

The one aspect of attacking Mesa which had most concerned her was her critical shortage of Marines. Her intelligence on the Mesan Navy and the system's fixed defenses was thinner than she'd have liked, but she had at least a general notion of what she'd face there, and she was confident her ships of the wall and range advantage would be more than enough to deal with it. The situation on the ground was quite different, however. She had no qualms about her Marines' ability to take over all of Mesa's spaceborne infrastructure (assuming any of it survived her arrival), but this was a star system which kept two thirds or more of its total population in involuntary servitude. That meant the other third *had* to be heavily militarized. No doubt much of that coercive capacity was concentrated in police and paramilitary forces of one sort or another, but they had to be backed up by a formal military organization with real combat capability, and Tenth Fleet didn't begin to have enough Marines to go down there and take their planet away from them, if they did. Not unless she was prepared to resort to the sort of kinetic bombardment missions it would take to "shoot" them onto their objectives.

Which I can't do without killing several million helpless slaves, she thought grimly. *That would sort of defeat the purpose of liberating them, I suppose.*

But a *million* more ground troops . . . that was the proverbial horse of a different color, indeed.

She sipped more coffee, then set the cup down and poked the cat currently using her for a hammock.

"Hey, you! Time to get up. Somebody's got to go back to work."

Dicey's eyes slitted open. The fact that he'd deigned to lie on his back to graciously permit her to scratch his tummy meant his head was upside down in her lap, and he looked suitably absurd gazing up past his muzzle at her.

"You heard me, monster," she said more firmly, poking a bit harder, and he stretched luxuriantly, briefly accomplishing the impossible feat of being twice his normal hundred and sixteen centimeters of length. Then he rolled onto his side and flowed down onto the decksole with a solid thump.

"Thanks," she told him. "Now go find Chris! He's the one who technically owns you, so mooch something off *him* for a change."

He blinked at her, then yawned, turned and ambled away. She watched him go with a smiling headshake, then let her chair come upright and pulled it closer to her workstation.

All right. Khumalo and Krietzmann's numbers for theoretically available manpower were impressive, and even equipped with only the export versions of Solarian planetary combat equipment, they'd be a formidable force. With her starships to provide fire support, that should be more than enough to deal with any challenge Mesa's military might present. Unfortunately, actually *deploying* those numbers depended on finding transport for them. From the analysis Khumalo and Loretta Shoupe had appended to the dispatch, it looked to her as if they'd probably be able to—it was for damned sure the Admiralty would pull out all the stops to provide it as soon as it found out Khumalo wanted it . . . and digested the fact that she intended to attack Mesa—but there was going to be at least some inevitable delay. And since he clearly hadn't known about her plans to attack Meyers, he intended to send them to her at Montana, which happened to be approximately two hundred and nineteen light-years from her present location.

She began entering notes on her terminal. First, she had to sit down with Cynthia Lecter, her chief of staff, and Dominica Adenauer, her operations officer, and reconsider her original plans. Second, she had to get at least some of the Quadrant Guard's personnel transferred to the Madras Sector to back up the destroyers, LACs, and missile pods she'd earmarked to cover the systems against Solarian nuisance forces... and remind those governments she hadn't displaced of the fact that they were under new management. Third, it would make a lot more sense to hold the reinforcements at Montana, divert her own routing from the straight line course to Mesa, and return to Montana en route to collect them. Fourth, she really ought to...

She went on entering notes, frowning thoughtfully as her mind flitted busily through the possibilities and options.

❖   ❖   ❖

"You know, just the other day I was thinking we were entitled to some *good* surprises for a change," Admiral Gold Peak said whimsically. She stood on HMS *Artemis'* flag bridge, gazing at the detailed three-dimensional map of everything within two hundred and fifty light-years of her flagship. Captain Lecter, Commander Adenauer, and Captain Veronica Armstrong, *Artemis'* chestnut-haired flag captain, stood helping her gaze at it. "I have to admit, though, that some surprises are surprisingly more surprising than other surprises."

"That's a little redundant, Ma'am," Lecter pointed out.

"Saying that something is 'a little' redundant is redundant, Cynthia," Michelle Henke informed her trim, blond chief of staff severely. "It's either redundant, or it's not redundant."

"My point stands," Lecter said respectfully.

"It's known as hyperbole—you know, exaggerating for effect?" Gold Peak shook her head. "And don't tell me you don't *agree* with the sentiment!"

"Oh, I think you can take that as a given, Ma'am." It was the chief of staff's turn to shake her head as she gazed at the side display's impressive list of tonnages. And the even more impressive, to Manticoran eyes, *names* on that list.

"It certainly came as a surprise to me, too, Ma'am," Armstrong said. "To be honest, I was surprised as hell when they offered to help us defend the Binary System. I never expected to see this much of their fleet clear out *here!*"

Gold Peak nodded slowly, her eyes distant as she considered how this was likely to shred her plans for Mesa all over again.

But shred them in a good way, Mike, she reminded herself. *Remember that. And under Lester Tourville, too. That's likely to be...interesting. From all reports, the two of you have quite a bit in common. Now that's a scary thought for the rest of the universe!*

"All right," she said out loud, turning away from the display and shoving her hands into her tunic pockets. It was an inelegant pose, perhaps. Her mother had always told her it was, anyway. But it also helped her think, and she began pacing a slow circle around the freestanding display while she did just that.

"According to Tourville's dispatch, Admiral Khumalo and Governor Medusa are going to dig up enough transport to get at least three quarters of the available planetary forces forward to us. At the moment, they're still planning on sending them to Montana, not here, but that could change."

She paused to glance at the others, and Lecter nodded. Their dispatch direct to Spindle announcing Meyers' capture—and requesting additional ground force support—had gone off to the Quadrant capital three and a half weeks ago. At the moment, it was just under seventy percent of the way there.

"By the same token, though, it might not." Gold Peak resumed her pacing. "The same dispatch will tell them I plan on hitting Mesa, and they'll realize I need all the ground forces I can get for that. In addition, they'll know Tourville went direct to Montana and that he was bound to stay there until he could inform me of his arrival and find out where I needed him. Given all that, Admiral Khumalo's smart enough to realize Montana's still the logical rendezvous point and send his transports there."

She paused again, and this time all three of her subordinates nodded.

Funny, she thought for a moment. *Honor always used to tease me about my "harem" of male bridge officers, and here we are, not a single man amongst us. Ah, those were the days!*

"All right," she said again. "How many dispatch boats do we have left?"

"Counting the one that just brought in Admiral Tourville's messages, I make it eleven," Adenauer replied, and Michelle grimaced. Any admiral who ever thought she had enough dispatch boats should probably be locked up somewhere before she hurt herself. Still, if Tenth Fleet had eleven of them, it was far better off than altogether too many other Manticoran fleets had been.

"One of them goes to Spindle," she said, "but not until we've gotten one off to Tourville."

Adenauer nodded and Gold Peak looked back at Lecter.

"Hitting Mesa with Tourville in support won't just give us more platforms, Cynthia." She shrugged. "We already had more than enough firepower to punch out anything Mesa might put in our way. But his presence should make it crystal clear to the Sollies that this isn't just the Star Empire—or yours truly—going off on a wild hair. I imagine it'll send a message about how serious we are about this, too. And it should emphasize the same message to the Alignment, as well, although it'll be just but more *pointed* in Mesa's case."

"Ma'am," Lecter said feelingly, "the thought of Manticoran and Havenite warships operating together against a sovereign star nation full of genetic slavers and other bottom feeders on the other side of the League should send just about all the messages you'd like to everyone concerned."

"Which won't be a bad thing." Gold Peak smiled coldly. "And God knows, sometimes you have to be just a *little* obvious to make Sollies pay attention."

Her subordinates chuckled and Gold Peak began pacing again.

"I need another new ops plan, Dominica. Assume Admiral Khumalo's going to make his shipping goals and get, say, two thirds of his proposed planetary forces forward to Montana. Also assume he'll meet his proposed timetable."

Adenauer nodded, entering notes on her memo board, and Gold Peak continued.

"We'll direct Tourville to await those forces at Montana. Once they arrive, he's to sortie with them in company and rendezvous with us somewhere en route to Mesa. Get with Sterling Casterlin and pick a nice, deserted red dwarf somewhere in the general vicinity—within, say, ten or twelve light-years of Mesa—as an astrogation mark. Someplace we can join up and possibly conduct some brief training exercises before we move on."

Adenauer nodded again.

"As for timing, figure we'll aim for departure from Meyers by the middle of next month. Call it September fifteenth, although if we can get out a day or so earlier I won't mind a bit."

"Yes, Ma'am."

"As for you, Cynthia," Gold Peak went on, "I think I need to have another talk with Prime Minister Montview. We'll be here longer than I expected, so I'm thinking we could help move King Lawrence's perceived legitimacy along if the Prime Minister 'spontaneously' invites me to address Lawrence's Parliament or a few news conferences." She grimaced, yet she knew how important that was. And as not simply the local Manticoran military commander but also the Empress' first cousin—and fifth in the line of succession for the throne, for that matter—reassurances from *her* carried just a tad more weight than they might have from someone else. "I hate the entire publicity business, but anything we can do to shore up his position before we pull out is worth doing."

"Yes, Ma'am. Gwen and I will get right on that."

"Good! And while you're doing that, and while Dominica's putting that new set of movement orders together, I think Vicki and I should sit down in one of her simulators and start thinking about all the interesting options this—" she pulled one hand from a tunic pocket to gesture at the displayed list of warships "—will make possible."

She jammed the hand back into her pocket and smiled evilly.

"I really, really wish I could see Kolokoltsov's expression when someone tells him Manty and 'Peep' ships of the wall are cooperating to punch out one of his most lucrative corporate sponsors. I know I'm not going to get that, but what I *am* going to get to see is CEO Ward's expression when I send the Mesa System Board of Directors my surrender demand in *both* star nations' names. I am *so* looking forward to that!"

Chapter Sixty-Six

"THIS IS GOING TO END BADLY, Tomasz," the silver-haired man on the display said coldly.

Hieronim Mazur was very fit and—normally—very tanned, a consummate yachtsman who spent every moment he could steal from his busy schedule out on the water. At the moment, his tan was somewhat lighter than usual, however, because for the last month or so he'd been stuck off-planet, concentrating on staying out of Krucjata Wolności Myśli's reach. That was wise of him, Tomasz Szponder thought. For a lot of reasons.

Not least, because it looked like it was working.

"I received word about an hour ago," Mazur continued. "Commissioner Radisson informs me the Office of Frontier Security and Frontier Fleet are prepared to support the restoration of the legitimate government. When they do, things will be even worse for all those little people you claim to care so much about." His smile was even colder than his voice. "I really think you'd do better to release Krzywicka and the others

945

and make the best terms you can with *us* before the Solarians get here. Given how long we've known one another, and how close our families have been, I'll even give you ninety days to liquidate investments here in Włocławek before I kick your ass out of *my* star system forever."

"Interesting choice of pronouns there, Hieronim." Szponder's tone was equally icy. "*Your* star system. I appreciate your generosity, but bastards like you hijacked Włodzimierz's movement once. I don't think we'll do it that way again."

"I imagine your devoted followers will see things differently when the intervention battalions and Marines arrive. And I warn you, if it comes to actual fighting, if lots of people get killed, you won't be going anywhere except on trial for mass murder."

"And I'm sure it'll be a completely fair trial, too." Szponder snorted contemptuously. "And don't try to tell me you're worried about loss of life, Hieronim! What *you're* worried about is the damage the fighting will do to SEOM's infrastructure on the planet. Trust me, it'll be at least as severe as anything you could imagine. Because those 'little people' I'm so concerned about have had a bellyful of the *Oligarchia* and the *Aparatczycy*. I doubt they'd hand their guns back over to me so I could surrender even if I asked them to, and you—and the damned Sollies—will play hell getting them away from them."

"Then I don't suppose there's much point to continuing this conversation, is there?" Mazur sneered at him. "My offer's open until Frontier Fleet actually gets here, but you know how OFS works as well as I do. If there's not a legitimate local government in power when the Sollies arrive, they *will* install a puppet, and after that they'll squeeze every centicredit they can out of this system for the next T-century. Trust me, it'll be a lot worse for your friends and neighbors then."

He flicked the switch contemptuously, cutting the circuit, and Szponder sat back in his chair.

The hell of it is that he's right, *damn him to hell*, he thought bleakly.

If only Mazur and Tymoteusz Miternowski had made it to the *Dzień Przewodniczącego* celebration! With Mazur in his hands, the rest of the *Oligarchia* would have dithered. They *might* have gotten themselves together and sent for the Sollies, anyway, but it would have taken them far longer. And with both Krzywicka and Miternowski in his hands; they'd have had no standing to claim to represent the legitimate system government. Especially not since between his own and Grażyna's and—especially—Izabela Ziomkowski's—efforts Szymon Ziomkowski had agreed to support not simply the Crusade's overthrow of Krzywicka's regime but a new constitution. One which would prohibit the restriction of all public offices to party members which had permitted the *aparatczycy* to usurp power in the first place.

Unfortunately, while that had given them control of the capital and the official organs of government, *Krzywicka* had steadfastly refused to have anything to do with their effort. And with Miternowski available for Mazur to trot out as the only member of the legally constituted government who wasn't in the hands of the "insurrectionists"—and thus the only one those paragons of virtue in the Office of Frontier Security could know wasn't "acting under duress"—it wouldn't matter a damn that Ziomkowski and the Izba Deputowanych—for that matter, the entire *official* government, since the Ruch Odnowy Narodowej's control of anything except the Przewodniczący's position had always been indirect—wanted nothing to do with Solarian intervention. No doubt as soon as OFS finished deposing the current government, they'd hold scrupulously free and open elections to create a new one.

His teeth grated together as he contemplated that... and what would happen to anyone who'd supported his people. But the Manties were over two T-weeks late. Only his innermost advisors knew the schedule to which Dupong Mwenge's superiors had agreed. They, like him, continued to hope the Royal Manticoran Navy had simply been unavoidably delayed. That it was truly coming.

But also like him, they'd begun to face the sickening possibility—indeed, the *probability*—that the Manticorans weren't coming at all. That they'd *never* intended to come... and that he, Tomasz Szponder, had doomed his star system's last hope for freedom by allowing himself to be used as an expendable cat's-paw to divert Solarian attention from the Star Empire.

Another T-week, he thought grimly. *I'll give them another T-week. But then...*

He shook his head, his face grim, and rubbed his eyes wearily.

❖   ❖   ❖

The pinnace settled neatly onto the pad. The hatch opened, and Helen Zilwicki tried not to dance in place as she waited behind Commodore Terekhov and Commander Pope for the boarding ramp to run out. Under normal circumstances the tradition that seniors were the first to exit Navy small craft didn't bother her especially.

Today wasn't normal.

Terekhov glanced over his shoulder, then smiled and shook his head.

"Patience, Helen. He's not going anywhere."

"I don't know what you mean, Sir," she replied as her face heated.

"I suspect there's probably a power tech third-class down in engineering somewhere who doesn't know what I mean, young lady," Terekhov told her with a twinkle. "*You*, however, know *exactly* what I mean. Or was there some other reason you finagled shore leave this morning?"

"It's not nice to pick on people younger than you, Sir," she said, conceding defeat. "And, with all due respect, you seem awfully anxious to get dirtside today, too!"

"Guilty," he acknowledged cheerfully. "However, rank—"

"—hath its privileges," she finished for him. "Yes, Sir. I believe I may have heard that a time or two before."

"I believe you may," he agreed. "But—" He broke off, leaning slightly to the side as he gazed out the hatch, then chuckled. "I see they finally managed to find the ramp. Please remember my advanced years and don't trample me to death going down it."

There were times, Helen thought, when silence was golden.

❖   ❖   ❖

"Oh, stop *vibrating*, Paulo!" Sinead Terekhov scolded. The preposterously good-looking ensign looked up at her. She wasn't an extraordinarily tall woman, but that still made her six centimeters taller than he was. And at the moment, he looked considerably younger than his twenty-five T-years.

"Am I really?" he asked with a smile.

"In a word, yes," she told him. "But it's such a charming, puppyish sort of vibration that no one really minds."

"Ouch." He winced, and she laid a hand on his shoulder.

"I'm only teasing. And the truth is, I think I'm almost as happy for you and Helen as I am for me and Aivars."

"I don't know where Helen and I are going," he said, with the air of someone trying to be scrupulously honest with himself, as well as with her. "I mean, I know where I *want* us to go. But we haven't even seen each other in over nine T-months. And I'm not . . . I mean . . ."

"I know exactly what you mean," she said. "And don't bend yourself out of shape. You're both Navy. You know about long absences, about slow communications, about career pressures." She shook her head. "There are so *many* things that can stress any officer's relationships, but both of you know exactly what they are. And the truth is, you're both fairly levelheaded youngsters. Your relationship will go where it'll go, and you'll both be fine, wherever that is."

"I hope so," he said, and smiled with what might almost have been a trace of bashfulness.

During *Charles Ward*'s voyage from Manticore to Spindle, Sinead Terekhov had made a point of winning Paulo d'Arezzo's confidence. She'd realized early on how important he was to Helen Zilwicki, who was very much a member of her official family now. And Paulo had responded by admitting things to her that she doubted he'd ever admitted to anyone else... except Helen. She knew exactly why he was so nervous.

"You'll do—"

She broke off as a tall, blond-haired, blue-eyed Manticoran commodore came through the lounge door with a long, quick stride.

"*Aivars!*"

She flung her arms wide, and then she was in *his* arms, and any trace of concern she might have felt about his reaction to her arrival here in Montana vanished in the power of his kiss.

Helen watched Ms. Terekhov fly into her husband's embrace and felt a quick surge of happiness for both of them. But her attention wasn't really on them. She was staring at the fair-haired, gray-eyed young man standing just beyond them. Her stride hesitated for just a moment as she saw him with her own eyes for the first time in three-quarters of a year, but then she saw the almost wistful edge to his smile of welcome, and her hesitation vanished.

"Hey, Ensign d'Arezzo," she said with a huge smile of her own, holding out both hands to him. "Long time no see."

"At least I tried to write," he said, gripping her hands in his while his gray eyes devoured her face.

"Yeah. That *does* put you a meter or so up on most people with Y chromosomes," she acknowledged.

They stood for several seconds, still holding hands, looking at each other, and then Paulo gave his head a little twitch.

"You know we're not in the same chain of command anymore," he pointed out.

"No? Really?" Her eyes glinted at him. "Is there some special significance to that?"

"Actually, there is," he said, and her eyes widened as he released her hands and his arms went about her. "I always did hate Article One-Nineteen," he said, his voice much huskier than it had been a moment before, and then his lips met hers.

❖   ❖   ❖

"I don't know whether to be disappointed or relieved," Captain Prescott Tremaine said as HMS *Alistair McKeon* accelerated towards the Golem System's hyper limit.

"Either way, we racked us up some more Sollies, Sir," WO5 Sir Horace Harkness observed. "Didn't have to kill any of 'em, even. Made a nice change."

"No, not this time," Tremaine agreed.

The only SLN presence in Golem had been a pair of hopelessly long-in-the-tooth destroyers, a handful of purely sublight customs vessels, and two squadrons of transatmospheric sting ships. And, as Harkness had just observed, their senior officer had recognized sanity when he saw it.

The truth was, however, that using a formation as powerful as Task Group 10.2.9 to eliminate such a paltry force was a gross underutilization of resources. And despite the analysis which had suggested the possibility of unrest in Golem, no one on the planet had attempted to contact him—or any of the personnel he'd sent dirtside on one pretext or another—to request naval assistance. After three local days in orbit, he'd been forced to the conclusion that the Mesan Alignment hadn't been tilling the soil in Golem after all.

In many ways, that was an enormous relief. But as he'd just implied to Harkness, it was a disappointment, as well.

You know, after so long running around with Lady Harrington, you really ought to begin to grasp the notion of boredom as a good *thing, Scotty,* he told himself.

Well, perhaps he should. But he knew the real reason for his ambivalence. There was no telling what might have been happening in *other* star systems while he'd swung uselessly in orbit around the Golem System's sole inhabited planet.

"All right!" He straightened himself and turned from the visual display's image of the slowly dwindling planet. "I feel the need for some exercises, Horace! Something to keep our people on their toes. Something...*challenging.*"

"Oh, I expect Commander Golbatsi and I will be able to come up with a little something, Sir," his staff electronic warfare officer assured him.

"I knew I could rely on you." Tremaine rested a hand affectionately on Harkness' broad, muscular shoulder. "And go ahead and see if Captain Selleck would like to contribute to the mix. She always has such a nasty, devious streak."

"What I like most in the Flag Captain, Sir," Harkness agreed with a huge smile. "I'll just go get started on that."

"Good," Tremaine said, patting his shoulder.

Then he stood back, watching Harkness cross *Alistair McKeon*'s flag bridge. The warrant officer said something to Adam Golbatsi, and the ops officer looked up, then laughed. He pointed at his console, and Harkness settled into the bridge chair beside him as the two of them began punching numbers.

He could trust them to come up with something... suitable, Tremaine thought cheerfully. He really would ask Mary-Lynne Selleck to give it a little fine tuning after they did, too. And it would give them a chance to kick around the tactic Harkness had christened "Barricade" after Tremaine had suggested it to him. It was unlikely to be useful a lot of times—certainly not once the other side caught onto it—but based on the preliminary reports on Massimo Filareta's fleet at Manticore it might just come as a nasty surprise the *first* time they tried it. Even if the logic behind it didn't pan out when they tried it in the simulators, training was always useful.

Besides, it would help pass the eight days to their next destination.

⋄ ⋄ ⋄

Sir Aivars Terekhov exited the inter-ship car and walked down the passage at the Havenite lieutenant's heels with a hard, purposeful stride. There was no expression at all on his face, but his eyes were blue ice.

He followed the youthful lieutenant with the sword-straight spine and the braided shoulder rope of a flag lieutenant around a final corner and she stopped at a closed door. She glanced over her shoulder once, then reached out and pressed the com key beside the door.

"Yes?" a voice asked.

"Commodore Terekhov is here, Sir," she replied.

"Thank you, Berjouhi," the voice said, then the door slid open, and the dark-skinned, blue-eyed lieutenant stood aside and waved courteously for Terekhov to walk through it.

He started forward with that same, hard stride, then stopped and looked at his guide.

"Thank you, Lieutenant," he said. "I appreciate the guidance . . . and the courtesy."

It would have been grossly inaccurate to call his voice warm, but those blue eyes of hers—darker than his, but just as hard as his had been—softened ever so slightly.

"You're welcome, Sir. It's been my privilege," she replied, and he nodded once and continued through the door.

The compartment beyond it was rather smaller than the day cabin of a Manticoran flag officer with a superdreadnought flagship would have been. It was also simply but comfortably furnished, although very few of those furnishings had the look of permanence which attached itself to a space-going officer's possessions over the course of time. Terekhov was familiar with that sort of absence. He'd experienced exactly the same thing after HMS *Defiant*'s destruction.

His mouth tightened at that thought, but he continued across the decksole to the officer standing to await him, one hand extended. For a heartbeat, Terekhov felt an overwhelming temptation to ignore that hand.

He hadn't truly realized how deep the wounds of Hyacinth still cut, even after all this time, until he'd reached Montana and learned who was now in command of the star system. He'd known then, though. Known when he felt the anger, the *rage*, boil in his blood.

The sheer passion of his emotions had astounded him. He'd known for T-months that the Republic of Haven had become the Star Empire of Manticore's ally. He'd greeted that news with very mixed emotions.

He'd known only too well how desperately Manticore *needed* allies, yet that wounded part of him had cried out in fiery protest at the very thought of *Havenite* allies. In the end, that awareness of need—and, hard though he'd fought to resist it—the matching awareness that Haven had *voluntarily* allied itself with the Star Empire, even in the face of the Solarian League's vast power, had defeated the protest.

Or that was what he'd thought, anyway.

"Commodore Terekhov," the man who awaited him said as their hands met.

"Admiral Tourville," he replied.

The admiral's handshake was strong, firm, and his eyes met Terekhov's steadily. The treecat on Tourville's shoulder studied Terekhov just as carefully, his head tilted to one side, his ears cocked and the very tip of his tail curling and un-curling slowly.

"Thank you for coming," Tourville said, waving Terekhov towards one of the cabin's armchairs. "I know you've only been back in Montana a short while, and I apologize for taking you away from your wife, but I felt it would be best for us to meet privately before we encountered one another in an official setting."

"I see." Terekhov sat in the indicated chair. "Should I take it, Sir, that there was a particular reason for that?"

"Of course you should."

Tourville's voice was level, and Terekhov felt his face heat ever so slightly. The Havenite's even tone recognized the bite he hadn't quite been able to keep out of his own voice. And that recognition, Tourville's refusal to let any matching bite color his reply, was its own reprimand.

Not really from Tourville, he realized, but from *himself* as he recognized the enormous contrast between his own emotions and the admiral's cool lack of discourtesy.

He inhaled deeply.

"I apologize, Sir," he said. "That came out more . . . confrontationally than I intended for it to."

"No apology's necessary."

Tourville sat in a facing chair. The treecat moved from his shoulder to the chair back, and the admiral stroked his mustache with a forefinger.

"I know about your experiences at Hyacinth . . . and afterward. I know what happened to your people." He said in that same, even voice, and shook his head, his expression somber. "Under the circumstances, I can't—and don't—blame you for any anger or hostility, even hatred, you feel. I've lost men and women who were important to me, too, and I was fortunate enough to be fighting the Star Kingdom of Manticore, not the People's Republic of Haven. I knew any of my people who became POWs would be treated compassionately and with respect. And my greatest regret, my deepest shame, was that I also knew any of your people who became POWs wouldn't have that assurance. What your people suffered after Hyacinth was far worse than most. It was not, however, unique. And one of the reasons I wanted to meet with you was to personally apologize to you for it. I know how . . . inadequate that must sound, but it's both the least I can do and the most I can offer."

Terekhov sat gazing at the other man, then flicked a look at the treecat. Lurks in Branches looked back at him with eyes as level as Tourville's own.

"It's my turn to be ashamed, Sir," he said. "Ashamed

that I can't master my own emotions. I know you personally had nothing at all to do with what StateSec did to my people. I know that almost certainly no one currently under your command did, either. But I'd be lying if I pretended there wasn't still a lot of that anger, that hatred rolling around inside me. More than I even realized there was. God knows I've seen enough combat, killed enough other people, to know how it happens, that it's a case of doing your duty and of killing or being killed. But it's still there." He shook his head, offering Tourville the same honesty the other man had just offered him. "It's still there, and I don't know if it'll ever go away."

"It shouldn't," Tourville said simply. "I hope the *pain* may ease someday, but the anger? No." He shook his head. "That shouldn't. You owe that anger to your people, Commodore. You owe it to *yourself*. And in a way, you owe it to the Republic of Haven, too."

Terekhov's surprise showed, and Tourville chuckled. It was a soft sound, one that held very little amusement, and he shook his head again.

"There are going to be some Havenites, for decades to come, who long for the glory days. People who had comfortable niches in the People's Republic. Or who will never get over the fact that your Navy beat the ever loving crap out of ours again and again ... and killed a lot of their sons and daughters, brothers and sisters, along the way. People who look at the number of star systems that took advantage of President Pritchart's guarantee of self-determination and *left* the Republic and feel that that's ... diminished us. Made us less than we were.

"Those people are *dangerous*, Commodore Terekhov. Perhaps not now, not while we're engaged in active operations against the League. But eventually, when the pressure eases, some of them will crawl back out of the shadows. At the very least, they'll deny the People's Republic was as bad as people say it was, and they'll have the guaranteed free speech to say it. They'll whitewash the crimes, the atrocities, and when they do, they'll do their damnedest to reject any lingering responsibility for them.

"The hell of it is that, in some ways, they'll be justified. Not for themselves, not for the criminals who actually committed those atrocities, but for Haven. For my star nation and all the decent men and women who are trying to make Haven what it used to be before the Legislaturalists turned us into the *People's* Republic. But that's the rub, Commodore. If we let them get away with denying the truth, however painful it may be for us, then we *can't* make Haven what it used to be. The rot, the canker, will still be there, and if we don't face it, then we break faith not just with people like you who suffered from those atrocities, but with our own children . . . and ourselves.

"So hold onto that anger. I hope you'll be able to direct it at the people who truly deserve it, but don't ever fault yourself for feeling it."

Terekhov's eyes had widened while Tourville spoke, and he remembered what Sinead had told him. *Tried* to tell him, really, because the anger—the fury—had burned too hot for him to hear her. Just this once, he'd rejected what she'd tried so hard to tell him, and he felt a fresh and very different burn of shame as he admitted that to himself.

"Forgive me for asking this, Sir," he said finally, "but is it true you sat on the Seaburg court-martials?"

Tourville hesitated visibly before he answered, but then his nostrils flared.

"Yes. Yes, I did. And as I told your wife, I deeply regret how long it took us to liberate that system and how many of the people who should have been tried escaped arrest before we got to it."

"I believe you and Admiral Theisman had a few other minor problems to deal with. Something to do with winning a civil war." Terekhov was surprised by the genuine humor that edged his tone, and Tourville quirked a fleeting smile below his mustache. "Seaburg wasn't exactly a strategically vital system, so I imagine it wasn't unreasonable for you to worry about the survival of your star nation first. And at least when you did liberate the system, you didn't let the cockroaches who were still there scurry out of the light."

"We tried not to." Tourville inhaled deeply. "At the same time, I have to admit we couldn't carry the trials as far as Admiral Theisman or I—or President Pritchart— wished we could. There were too many people who could cover themselves by claiming 'I was only following orders' that were—damn them to hell—*legal* when they were given." His expression had turned grim. "I *know* dozens—hundreds—of the bastards who used that defense should've gone to the wall, but we couldn't send them there. If we started hanging or shooting people without absolute proof of wrongdoing—wrongdoing that *wasn't* 'legal' when it was done—we were no better than Saint-Just's State Security or Palmer-Levy's Internal Security, and we *had* to be better than they were. And that means there are people in the Republic today who are just as guilty, just as culpable, as any of the bastards we executed in Seaburg."

"Neat resolutions where goodness and light triumph and all the guilty are punished only happen in bad fiction, Admiral," Terekhov said.

"That, unfortunately, is true. And when you're trying to clean up a cesspool like the People's Republic, there's an awful lot of 'guilty' to go around. I guess it's not too surprising some of them slither down the drain before they can be dealt with, but that doesn't make it any better when it happens."

Terekhov nodded and leaned back in his chair. It was odd. He'd come into this cabin aware only of his anger—and the grief and the pain that still fueled it. He'd come, he realized now, not because he truly expected to deal with it, but almost to . . . embrace it. To *validate* it and prove he was right to go on feeling it. And he did feel it. Not only that, he knew Tourville was right; that he *should* go on feeling it. Yet that anger had changed somehow. It was still there, still just as strong, but it had lost those white-hot fangs of vengeful hatred. And rather than the focused, burning rage he'd felt whenever he thought of serving under Lester Tourville, actually *taking orders* from someone who'd fought so well and so hard for the People's Navy—the admiral who'd completely destroyed Home Fleet—what he felt now was almost a sense of . . . kinship.

It wasn't friendship. Not yet, at any rate, and he didn't know if it ever could be. Yet even that was a monumental shift in the bedrock of his anger, because fifteen minutes earlier he would have known—definitely, beyond any possibility of contradiction—that it *couldn't*, which was very different. And yet . . .

He thought about the young lieutenant who'd escorted him to Tourville's quarters, and about the other thing

Sinead had told him. The thing he'd been flatly certain had to be a falsehood. The thing, he realized now, that the part of him that needed to go on hating had rejected even more fiercely than the knowledge that Tourville had sat on the Seaburg courts-martial.

"I have a question I want to ask you, Sir," he heard himself say. "Before I do, I want you to understand that in asking, I'll be violating a confidence. Secondhand, perhaps, but still violating it. I hope you'll consider the *reason* I asked it when you deal with the possible repercussions of that violation."

He paused, knowing Tourville would recognize what he was truly saying, and the Havenite sat very still, his gaze hooded. Then he drew a deep breath.

"Ask it, Commodore," he said.

"Admiral, I want you to know I believe every word you've told me. I also want you to know that what you've said—and the way you've said it—has . . . unsettled a lot of things I thought I knew. So, what I want to ask you now is what really happened on *Count Tilly*'s flag bridge the day *Tepes* blew up in Cerberus orbit."

Tourville stiffened and his expression turned to stone. He said nothing at all for several seconds, then he laid his forearms very carefully along the armrests of his chair, cocked his head, and said one word.

"Berjouhi."

"Yes, Sir," Terekhov confirmed levelly. "She's obviously devoted to you. I couldn't follow her all the way here from Boat Bay without realizing that. And"—he smiled ever so faintly—"I've had some experience of my own with loyal flag lieutenants. But, yes, she told Sinead, because Sinead's Navy to her toenails . . . and because she loves me. She wasn't about to forgive any Havenite ever born for what happened to my people. Not in Hyacinth itself, but afterward, in Seaburg. Lieutenant Lafontaine recognized that, and because she *is* devoted to you—and probably because she can't serve you as closely as she does without recognizing the feelings and the thoughts you've just shared with me—she violated *your* confidence...exactly the same way, and for a lot of the same reasons, as I'm now violating hers."

"I never actually told her not to tell anyone," Tourville said very, very softly, looking away from Terekhov for the first time since the Manticoran had entered his cabin. "So I don't suppose anyone could actually accuse her of violating any confidences. But I never meant for anyone to find out."

"May I ask why not, Sir?"

"A lot of reasons, some of which I'm sure I don't know myself." Tourville looked back at him. "Because it would seem self-serving, I suppose. And because there's...a history between Duchess Harrington and myself." He shook his head. "We've each hurt the other more times than either of us likes. I don't blame her for that, and I don't *think* she blames me...now. But right after the Battle of Manticore, we both blamed each other a lot. I wasn't about to tell her then, and if I tell her now, it'll sound...I don't know. Boastful? Like someone trying to prove his moral superiority? Besides, there's no proof of what happened. If there had been, StateSec would've made sure I was dead by now!" He twitched another brief smile. "You have to be careful about making statements about your own alleged courage and magnificent morality when they're going to not only seem self-serving but be impossible to prove one way or the other."

"But you *did* erase that tac data, didn't you?" Terekhov's question was even softer than Tourville's voice had been, and his blue eyes were strangely gentle.

"If I hadn't, Shannon Foraker would have," the Havenite said after a handful of seconds. "I couldn't let her do that. It wasn't her responsibility; it was mine. And don't mistake me, Commodore Terekhov. I didn't do it because I'm such a noble, heroic fellow. For that matter, I didn't do it simply because it was the right thing to do. I did it because I was *ashamed*." His strong, confident voice wavered at last, turned husky, and he shook his head sharply. "I was ashamed of my star nation, ashamed of my superiors, ashamed of what was about to happen—what I knew had *already* happened on the way to Cerberus—to an honorable, *innocent* woman, and ashamed of the way the Navy—*my* Navy—had been turned into Cordelia Ransom's executioners. We were *better* than that. We had to be. And so, just that once, I *was*."

The treecat on the back of Tourville's chair moved at last. One long-fingered true-hand reached out and laid itself ever so gently against the admiral's cheek and those grass-green eyes met Sir Aivars Terekhov's. And then, slowly, Lurks in Branches nodded.

But Terekhov hadn't needed that confirmation—not about *that* man—and he pushed up out of his chair and stood facing Tourville.

"No," he said quietly. "Not 'just that once,' Admiral Tourville. You did it because you were *always* better than that. I doubt I'll ever be free of that anger you think I should go on feeling, but if I'm going to be honest, a lot of that anger's strength is probably guilt. Survivor's guilt, because my people didn't just die while I survived. They died fighting under my orders, fighting for *me*, and it's a lot safer to focus on the people who killed them than it is on the man who commanded them when they died in Hyacinth and couldn't even be with them in Seaburg.

"But Sinead was right. No matter what the *People's* Republic of Haven may have been like, and no matter what *some* of the people who served it may have been, some of them were truly extraordinary human beings, even then. And"—he extended his hand once more, his expression very different than the one he'd worn the first time—"I'm honored to have met one of them this afternoon."

Chapter Sixty-Seven

"OH, SHIT," SENSOR TECH 2/C Paige Thuvaradran said very, very quietly. Thuvaradran had the duty on SLNS *Harpist*'s bridge, and as it happened, Lieutenant Commander Franz Stedman, the tactical officer and her direct boss, was the current officer of the watch. Now Stedman, who did not approve of . . . informality on the bridge, turned his command chair to face the tactical section, and his expression was not incredibly happy.

"I don't believe I quite heard that, Thuvaradran," he said frostily, and she looked up from her display quickly.

"Sorry, Sir," she said.

"Perhaps you'd care to share whatever inspired that comment with the rest of us?" Stedman suggested.

"Yes, Sir." Thuvaradran cleared her throat. "Sir, we've just picked up a thirteen-unit hyper footprint at twelve light-minutes, right on the limit."

"Thirteen?" Stedman's eyes widened, and he sounded very much like someone who hoped his normally efficient, highly competent sensor tech was wrong.

"Yes, Sir. Hard to tell anything at this range from just the footprints, but it looks like at least a couple of them are probably in the battlecruiser range."

"I see," Stedman said. "Put it up on the main plot."

"Yes, Sir."

The icons of the incoming starships appeared on the main display, not even crawling, on such an enormous scale, at their low initial velocity. Their hyper footprints had long since dissipated, but the signatures of their impeller wedges burned clear and sharp. Obviously, whoever they were they weren't even trying to hide. That could be a good thing, since this was a Solarian-administered system . . . or it could be—and more probably *was*—a very *bad* thing, indeed.

Just our luck to be passing through, the TAC officer thought glumly. *Three more days and we'd've been out of here. But, no!*

Harpist and the destroyer *Reaper* had only stopped off en route to the Lucas System to pick up their new missiles because Captain Astrid Caspari, the senior officer permanently assigned to the Kumang System, had gone to the Academy with Bretton Ibañez, *Harpist*'s CO. They were an entire week ahead on their scheduled movement orders, so Ibañez had seen no reason not to stop off for a two or three-day visit with his old classmate. But now . . .

Stedman inhaled deeply and pressed the stud on the arm of his chair.

"Abbott," a voice growled in his earbug.

"Sir," Stedman told *Harpist*'s executive officer, "I think you'd better come to the bridge."

❖   ❖   ❖

"So what do you make of it, Chiara?" Captain Aldus O'Brien asked. He and Commander Chiara Marciano, his tactical officer, stood gazing at the master display in HMS *Trebuchet's* CIC.

"Well, if I had to guess from the station-keeping emissions, I'd say this"—she indicated the slightly larger, brighter icon in orbit around the system's inhabited planet—"is a cruiser. Probably a *heavy* cruiser; we'll know more when the optical platforms and active sensors get a better look at her. This other one, though—she's definitely a *War Harvest*."

"Think they have anything else trying to imitate holes in space?"

"Doubt it, Skip." Marciano shook her head. "I think we caught them flat-footed. In fact, I'm willing to bet they didn't even have their impellers at standby. We sure don't see any—"

She broke off for a moment, pressing her earbug with an index finger while she listened, then turned and grinned—positively *grinned*—up at her much taller captain.

"The closest Ghost Rider bird just picked up first-stage initiation. They were sitting there with *cold* nodes."

"Well, wasn't that considerate of them," O'Brien murmured.

He stood gazing at the display, rubbing his chin thoughtfully, for several seconds. Then he looked back at Marciano.

"Let's take this to the bridge," he said.

The two of them headed for the intra-ship car, which delivered them less than a minute later to the *Saganami-C*-class heavy cruiser's bridge.

"Captain is on the bridge!" the quartermaster of the watch announced as the doors slid open, and people popped to their feet.

"As you were," O'Brien said, striding briskly towards the command chair which was currently occupied by Commander Darren Boyd, his executive officer. Boyd rose as O'Brien approached, and the captain settled into the chair.

"I have the ship," he said.

"Aye, Sir. You have the ship," Boyd acknowledged, and O'Brien gave him a brief nod, then looked at Lieutenant Commander Yaeko Yoshihara.

"Run me some numbers, Yaeko. Assume this fellow spotted us the instant we crossed the alpha wall. He's got cold nodes, he's, say, a *Kutuzov*-class heavy cruiser, and his engineers get his nodes online in Book time. Where do we run him down and when do we bring him into missile range?"

"Just a sec, Skipper," the astrogator replied.

She punched in numbers, then looked over her shoulder at her captain.

"Assuming he gets them up forty minutes after we crossed the wall, we'll be up to approximately one-eight-point-seven thousand KPS and one-one-point-six light-minutes from the planet when he does. If we maintain pursuit at our present acceleration for another hundred and thirty-five minutes, we'll have a zero-range intercept. Of course, at that point we'd be traveling at damned near twice his velocity: seven-six-point-six thousand KPS compared to four-three-point-eight. We'd have the range for the Mark 23s in roughly twenty minutes before that, given the velocity differential at launch. And at that point, they'd still be over twenty light-minutes short of the hyper limit."

❖   ❖   ❖

One good thing about starting with cold nodes, Bretton Ibañez reflected grimly. *It gave me time to get back aboard before we started running. Not that running's going to do one damned bit of good in the end.*

In truth, he knew the extra forty-one minutes it had taken to bring up *Harpist*'s impellers wouldn't have made any difference, either. Even if she'd been sitting there at full readiness and started accelerating at maximum military power the instant she'd detected the intruders, they'd still have run her down short of the hyper limit. The delay had only shortened the agony.

By the time she'd started accelerating, six of the newcomers had already attained a closing velocity of over 18,000 KPS; the other seven had been up to only 12,000 KPS, and from the accel curves, it looked like at least one of the potential "battlecruisers" was actually a merchant ship. That was the good news. The *bad* news was that although they hadn't identified themselves, they were obviously Manties, since the six chasing him were pulling an acceleration of over seven hundred and twenty gravities in a ship that had to mass a half million tons. No one else in the galaxy could do *that*. And that acceleration gave them an advantage of almost two KPS^2, so even after *Harpist* got underway, her enemies' velocity advantage had actually *increased* steadily.

So it was only a matter of—

"Captain."

The voice belonged to Lieutenant Addison Faust, his communications officer, and Ibañez felt something tighten inside. Odd. He wouldn't have believed he could get any more tense.

"Yes, Addison?"

Another surprise. His voice actually sounded calm.

"Sir, I have a transmission for you. It's from a Captain O'Brien of the Royal Manticoran Navy."

"What a surprise," Ibañez said dryly. Then he squared his shoulders. "Put it on my display."

"Yes, Sir."

A face appeared on Ibañez's com display. It belonged to a tall, chunky fellow with sandy-brown hair, hazel eyes, and a luxuriant mustache who wore the black and gold of the Star Empire of Manticore.

"I am Captain Aldus O'Brien, Royal Manticoran Navy, commanding Her Majesty's Ship *Trebuchet*," he said coldly. "I'm also the senior officer of Task Group Ten-Two-Eight, and my orders are to take or destroy any Solarian naval units in this star system. Be advised that you are now in range of my missiles."

Despite himself, Ibañez felt his face tighten. It had almost certainly turned pale, as well, he thought. If O'Brien was telling the truth, his missiles had a range of over thirty-six *million* kilometers! It was true the Manties had built their overtake velocity advantage to over 30,000 KPS, which would boost their effective range significantly, but even so—!

"I realize you may doubt whether or not you are, indeed, in my range envelope. Accordingly—"

"Missile launch!" Lieutenant Commander Stedman said suddenly. "One missile closing at an overtake of one-three-six KPS squared!"

Ibañez watched the display as the single missile icon streaked after his ship. It accelerated fiercely, but it also had thirty-six million kilometers to go. The impellers on a Javelin, the SLN's latest missile, would burn out three minutes after launch, which would have given an effective envelope of just under eight million kilometers from that geometry. It could still have caught *Harpist*, assuming no radical course changes on her part, but its overtake velocity when it did would have been down to a mere 5,000 KPS and it would have long since gone ballistic. That would have made it dead meat for point defense, nor would it have been able to execute any terminal attack maneuver to bring its laserhead to bear, which would have made the chance of actually hitting the ship nonexistent. But this wasn't a Solarian missile, and his stomach turned into a hollow, singing void as it went on accelerating at 46,000 KPS^2.

The Javelin's acceleration was actually seven percent higher than that . . . but *this* missile accelerated effortlessly past the hundred eighty second-mark where a Javelin's drive would have failed. Four minutes. Five minutes. Six minutes. *Seven* minutes.

He felt his jaw clamping harder and harder in something very like horror. He felt the tension—the fear—of his bridge crew as that incredible missile just kept *coming* for them. And then, nine impossible minutes after launch, it streaked directly past *Harpist*—still under power, still able to execute its final attack maneuvers—and detonated harmlessly a hundred and fifty thousand kilometers ahead of her.

"You have ten minutes to reverse acceleration at four hundred gravities and prepare to surrender," Aldous

O'Brien said from his com. "In *eleven* minutes, we begin firing for effect."

✧   ✧   ✧

"—and I most strongly protest this naked aggression against the innocent people of the Kumang System!" System Administrator Luis Verner said firmly. "Whatever your quarrel with the Solarian League, there can be no justification for the invasion and subjugation of a neutral star nation."

"Odd," Aldus O'Brien mused, gazing at the man on his com display. "That never seems to bother Frontier Security when *it* invades and subjugates neutral star systems. Of course, we're only interested in liberating them—although, I will admit that swatting any Solarian Navy ships we come across is a worthwhile accomplishment in its own right—whereas OFS specializes in handing them over to one Solly transstellar or another." He pursed his lips and arched an eyebrow. "I'm only an ignorant neobarb, of course, but could you please go back and explain the bit that makes *Solarian* invasions legitimate, highly principled exercises in beneficent nation-building and *our* invasions unjust, imperialistic conquests? Something seems to have gotten lost in transmission."

Trebuchet was 6,723,000 kilometers from Chotěboř, decelerating steadily towards the planet while the ex-SLN prizes *Harpist* and *Reaper* followed at their own best acceleration with four *Roland*-class destroyers to keep them company. Now O'Brien waited out the twenty-second transmission delay and then watched Verner's face darken. The Solarian's jaw tightened visibly, and O'Brien wondered if the man was going to spontaneously combust, explode, or just melt.

"Obviously," the system administrator grated finally, "I'm not going to dignify that farcical, self-serving mischaracterization with a response. But while it's painfully evident you have sufficient brute force to do whatever you wish in this star system, I am serving formal notice that the people of Kumang are under the protection of the Solarian League. I caution you that any outrages, any assaults on person or property in this star system, will lead to the most serious repercussions for you personally and the entire Star Empire of Manticore!"

"I stand cautioned," O'Brien said sardonically. "And I have no intention of assaulting any person or property in Kumang, unless it happens to belong to the Solarian League. In which case, of course, it becomes a legitimate military target, and I suppose it's unbecoming to admit it, but in *that* case I will take intense personal satisfaction in blowing it into very tiny pieces."

He leaned back to let that settle in for several seconds, then continued.

"I'll enter Chotěboř orbit in approximately twenty-three minutes. If I were you, I'd start packing, Mister System Administrator. I think you're likely to be out of a job very shortly." He smiled brightly. "Have a nice day."

❖   ❖   ❖

"Mr. Sabatino is here, Mister President," Květa Tonová said, opening the door to the magnificently furnished *Růžová* Office in the Presidential Mansion. She stood aside, and Karl-Heinz Sabatino walked past her into the office which had once been Jan Cabrnoch's, his expression tense.

"Karl-Heinz." Adam Šiml rose and stepped around his desk to offer his hand. "Thank you for coming so promptly."

"It seems like a good day for doing things promptly," Sabatino replied with a strained smile as Vice President Vilušínský shook his hand as well.

"I know," Šiml said. "Please, sit down." He glanced at the longtime secretary who'd followed him into the Presidential Mansion. "Květa, please have coffee sent in. We may be here a while."

"Of course, Mister President," she murmured, and withdrew.

Sabatino settled into the indicated chair, and Šiml and Vilušínský sat facing him across a stone-topped coffee table.

"I asked you to come to the Mansion today, Karl-Heinz," the President said after a moment, "because of what's happening to the Frontier Security presence here in the system. System Administrator Verner hasn't kept me informed as to his communications with the Manticorans. He probably has a lot on his mind at the moment. They haven't communicated directly with me yet, either, but I'm sure they will, and I'll be very surprised if they permit any official Solarian presence in Kumang going forward."

"Frogmore-Wellington and Iwahara Interstellar are private entities, not affiliated with the League government in any way," Sabatino pointed out.

"Forgive me," Šiml said, "but we both know that's a polite fiction, given their . . . cordial relations with the Office of Frontier Security, not just here but in other star systems, as well. More to the point, the *Manticorans* know that. As I say, however, I'm not privy to their communications with Verner, so as of this moment, I'm in no position to speak to what their intentions may be vis-à-vis Frogmore-Wellington or Iwahara. In fact, that's not why I asked you to come here."

"No?" Sabatino glanced back and forth between the two Chotěbořans. "Then why *did* you invite me?"

"To tell you it's over," Šiml said, and his voice was suddenly, deeply gentle, almost compassionate.

"Over?" Sabatino frowned. "What do you mean 'over'?"

"I mean we're taking back our star system," Šiml continued in that gentle voice. "I mean that as of today, the power to make decisions that affect the people of Chotěboř will be in Chotěbořian hands once again. And that we're not giving it back to Frontier Security, the Solarian League . . . or you."

Sabatino sat back in his chair, his expression suddenly masklike.

"When I first accepted your financial backing, I saw you as only one more leech—one more *komár*—sucking the life out of my star system," Šiml told him. "And in many ways, that's exactly what you are. But I've come to know you better since then, and I saw your reaction during the Velehrad Riots, when Cabrnoch turned the Safeties loose. I pushed the limits with you, deliberately, when I suspended DORA and began reinstituting political freedom here on Chotěboř, and you not only didn't protest but actually seemed to understand that kind of reform was necessary. I never doubted that you'd try to put the brakes on if I started openly threatening the *financial* interests you represent, but I suppose that's your job. And while

I'm not remotely prepared to nominate you for saint-hood, I've come to realize you're a man who takes doing his job seriously."

He paused, and the office was very, very quiet.

"I don't like the avarice and greed you represent, Karl-Heinz, and I find it difficult to excuse the support you gave Cabrnoch—and Verner—when it came to erecting Jan's police state. Or for *maintaining* it, after it was in place. But the truth is that Cabrnoch was homegrown. He was a *Chotěbořian* problem, one which arose out of our own response to a system-wide disaster. Without Frontier Security—and you—he could never have retained power as long as he did or hurt so many people *while* he did, but you didn't create him. You only *used* him, and from what I've seen in the last few T-months, I think you've become steadily—and honestly, I believe—less and less happy about that.

"I have no doubt the Manticorans are going to want to speak to the government of Kumang once they've entered Chotěboř orbit and finished their business with Mr. Verner. Thanks to you, I'm the head of that government, and about fifteen minutes before you arrived at the Mansion, General Siminetti was placed under arrest and I accepted Daniel Kápička's resignation." Šiml smiled briefly. "I have to say, in some ways, Daniel was actually relieved. I think *he's* been having a few qualms since the Velehrad Riots, himself.

"I've also ordered the stand-down of the CPSF, and armed members of Sokol are securing control of Public Safety's equipment depots and nodal offices at this moment. It's my hope that there won't be any violence, whether of Safeties trying to resist our people *or* of our people seeking vengeance on the Safeties outside the law. I assure you that if there are any instances of either of those, they *will* be punished. And when I *do* speak to the Manticoran commander, I intend to inform him that the Kumang System desires cordial relations with the Star Empire, invite him to regard our star system as a friendly neutral in any future operations, suggest that the *independent* system of Kumang would welcome any security detachment he might wish to leave stationed here, *and*"—his eyes narrowed ever so slightly—"inform him that we will gladly welcome future Manticoran investment.

"Which brings me back to you."

"How?" Sabatino asked tersely.

"While you're certainly guilty of bribery, corruption, graft, and any number of other criminal offenses under the letter of Chotěbořian law, and while I strongly suspect you approved of Cabrnoch's tactics for suppressing the Náměstí Žlutých Růží demonstrations, I don't think of you as an *evil* man. For that matter, I think it could be legitimately argued that all your actions were approved—or at least knowingly tolerated—by the closest thing Chotěbor had to a legal government. And the truth is that I've genuinely come to regard you as a friend, which I never expected to happen. Moreover, whatever I may think of the circumstances under which Frogmore-Wellington and Iwahara acquired their leases here in Kumang, they never actually violated the law in doing so. I think you're intelligent enough to admit that even if they acted legally they still acted *immorally*, and we both know laws enacted by corrupt people are themselves corrupt. But the fact remains that those leases were legally granted—and signed—by President

Hruška under the auspices of the Office of Frontier Security and ratified by President Cabrnoch when he assumed office.

"Eventually, though, this war between Manticore and the Solarian League is going to end, one way or the other. Personally, I suspect the Manticorans are going to do far better out of the peace terms and postwar power arrangements than anyone in the League could possibly have expected four or five T-months ago, but the League will still exist. So will many of the transstellars, although I imagine more than a few will go to the wall and that many of those that don't will still be . . . radically, downsized, let's say. I don't know about Iwahara, but Frogmore-Wellington will almost certainly be one of the survivors—cut down to size, reduced in power, but still there. And thanks to the *komáři* and the malfeasance of Cabrnoch and his cronies— and, I'm afraid, your own modest efforts—Chotěboř doesn't—and *won't,* for quite some time—have the domestic capacity to effectively develop the Kumang System's resources.

"So here's what I'm prepared to offer you. The leases your employers currently hold will be . . . amended to assign them to a new legal entity. We'll probably call it something like Kumang Enterprises or Chotěboř, Incorporated, and both Frogmore-Wellington and Iwahara will be represented within it, with shares representing their relative pre-amendment positions in Kumang. *However,*" his gray eyes bored into Sabatino, "the Chotěbořian government will hold a majority shareholder position in the new entity. This time, it will be a genuine *partnership,* Karl-Heinz. One which will provide our extra-system partners a *reasonable* return on their investment but which will also consider the economic interests of Chotěbořans and prevent the sort of slash-and-burn rape Solarian transstellars have practiced in the Verge far too often.

"In effect, I suppose what I'm offering you is a soft landing—a soft landing not just for your employers, but for you personally. I'm sure they're going to be furious about what's about to happen out here. I'm sure their head offices will be incensed about the hit their bottom line's going to take. But in the end, they'll find themselves in a far stronger position than they would if we simply nationalized the leases . . . or transferred them to one of the Manticoran cartels. They'll probably make at least half the profit they would have otherwise, and they'll reap the benefit of goodwill when I announce their *voluntary* acceptance of the new lease terms. And you'll be the man who salvaged so much of their position here in Kumang by recognizing the wisdom of compromising rather than backing some sort of forcible suppression of the legitimate system government which would ultimately backfire disastrously. And it *would* backfire, Karl-Heinz. Unless Manticore is completely defeated, it's not going to permit the imposition—or re-imposition—of League protectorates or client states this close to Talbott, and you know that just as well as I do."

He sat back in his chair with a smile as a liveried staffer wheeled in the coffee cart. Silence hovered while the young man poured cups all around, set out creamer and sugar on the coffee table, then withdrew wordlessly. Šiml picked up his cup and sipped, then lifted an eyebrow at Karl-Heinz Sabatino.

He said nothing, and Sabatino took a long swallow

of his own coffee. Then he sighed, leaned back with the cup and saucer in his lap, and shook his head.

"I should never have decided to bribe you," he said wryly.

"On the contrary, I'm the best investment you ever made," Šiml chided with a broader smile. Then he allowed the smile to fade a bit. "Whoever was sitting in the President's chair, the Manticorans would have been here today anyway," he said seriously. "I expect Cabrnoch would've addressed their arrival a little differently, but as soon as Verner and OFS were removed, Chotěboř would've had a few things to say to him. Judging by his actions three T-months ago, the bloodshed to get rid of him would make the Velehrad Riots look like a children's quarrel in a sandbox, and I don't think you even want to contemplate what would've happened to Frogmore-Wellington and Iwahara down the road from *that*. As it is, you stand to get the credit for helping ease him out of office, you get the credit for all that philanthropic effort you put behind Sokol—for which, by the way, I thank you—*and* you'll get your out-system bosses' credit for salvaging so much of their position in Kumang." The President actually chuckled. "From where I sit, you're likely to make out even better under the new arrangement than the old!"

"Aside from a certain chagrin over how neatly you manipulated me, at least," Sabatino observed.

"Well, yes. Aside from that," Šiml conceded. "I did warn you, though, that I had no intention of coming to any bad ends . . . and"—those gray eyes were on Sabatino's face once again, but this time there was an undeniable warmth in their depths—"I also said I had no intention of forgetting who made this all possible."

Silence fell once again as Sabatino sipped more coffee. Then he leaned forward to set saucer and cup carefully on the table between them.

"Well," he said with a small, whimsical smile, "I suppose you'd better trot out that dotted line you need signed."

Chapter Sixty-Eight

"IT'S GOOD TO SEE YOU, Walter," Luiz Rozsak said as Oravil Barregos escorted the fourth (and very unofficial) member of the triumvirate which governed the Republic of Erewhon into his kitchen. He climbed off his barstool and offered his hand. "How are things back home?"

"Lively," Walter Imbesi said, shaking his hand and smiling. "Your message threw a cat right into the middle of the pigeons, and then Delvecchio delivered Empress Elizabeth's message." He shook his head with a chuckle. "I don't think I've seen Fuentes, Havlicek, and Hall that excited—and scared—over anything since Theisman launched Operation Thunderbolt!"

"I trust they're at least a *little* less worried this time?"

"Well," Imbesi took one of the other stools at the kitchen bar as Barregos settled beside him, "I think it's safe to say they'd rather be back on the Manties' side than on the *other* side, but they're—"

He paused and sniffed.

"That smells delicious, Luiz...as usual. What is it?"

"Pad Thai," Rozsak replied. "Actually, I've been waiting to put it together until we saw the whites of your eyes and all you're smelling right now is the prep work. Wait'll I put it on your plate!"

"With bated breath...and lots of salivation," Imbesi assured him with a smile, then turned back to Barregos and the thread of their conversation.

"The truth is," he said in a much more serious tone, "they know the Manties, they *trust* the Manties—now that Janacek's dead and High Ridge is in prison, anyway—and they know what the Royal Navy can do. But they're still nervous about defying the League—openly, I mean—this early. This much acceleration of the timetable makes them...anxious. And the notion that this Mesan Alignment's taking an interest in our neck of the galaxy doesn't make them any happier." He snorted. "Any Erewhonese gets nervous when he doesn't know who all the players are. Makes it hard to calculate the odds and slip in the dagger—figuratively speaking, of course...these days—at the right moment."

"I can understand that," Barregos said with feeling. "In fact, I worry about exactly the same sort of timing issues. A lot." He shook his head. "But if Elizabeth and Pritchart are ready to provide the levels of support they're talking about, the risks from our side will actually be a lot lower."

"That's my thinking, too," Imbesi agreed. "And Fuentes zeroed in on that aspect like a laser. Hall's a lot less enthusiastic, but then he's always been ambivalent about our 'special relationship' with Maya. Havlicek's the swing vote on this one, and I'm afraid Alessandra's still not one of Manticore's greater admirers. Frankly, I think that's because her family's financial interests got hurt worse than most when they jacked our Wormhole transit fees. She understood why they did it—intellectually—and realized the retaliation could have been one hell of a lot worse, but she's still the sort who takes that kind of thing personally."

"Ms. Havlicek takes a great many things personally," Rozsak put in dryly from the cooktop as his wok began to make interesting sizzling sounds.

"Yes, she does," Imbesi agreed with a chuckle. "That doesn't mean she doesn't have good instincts, though. And although I strongly suspect she may be the only woman in the entire galaxy who can hold a grudge longer than Elizabeth Winton, she also has a very good brain that she uses more often than other people I could mention. As a result of which—" he paused just perceptibly, looking back and forth between his hosts "—she's in favor."

Oravil Barregos had played high-stakes politics for far too many years to exhale a noisy sigh of relief, but his posture relaxed ever so slightly and he smiled. Then he shook himself.

"She's on board with including Torch, as well?"

"That's stickier," Imbesi admitted. "She's never had the emotional investment in Torch—or the opposition to genetic slavery in general, I'm afraid—that Fuentes and I have. We don't have genetic slavery in Erewhon, and I think she and Tomas both think that makes it someone else's problem. What Mesa already tried to do to Torch is a factor in her thinking, too, since we're inclined to think it had to be this 'Alignment' that pulled off the Yawata Strike."

"Jiri and I agree with you on that," Rozsak said, "and so do Brent Stephens and Richard Wise." The admiral shrugged. "It obviously wasn't Haven, there's no way in the galaxy it was the League—not with the tech it took to make it work—and we don't see anyone else sticking knives in the Manties' backs. So she and Hall are worried about Erewhon's getting the same treatment?"

"That's exactly what they're worried about." It was Imbesi's turn to shrug. "Personally, I think Mesa would probably have higher priorities—like hitting Nouveau Paris, for example. Let's be honest here. Impressive as our naval building capacity's become for a single-system star nation—thanks in no small part to your investment, Oravil—we're nowhere near the military threat of someone like the Manties or Haven or even Grayson. If that 'ghost fleet' plans on blowing up any more star systems, I doubt we'd be high on the list, however visible we might make ourselves by breaking their kneecaps locally. They're . . . a little less convinced of that."

"I can understand that, I suppose." Barregos said, and cocked an eyebrow at Rozsak. "Luiz?"

"Something to think about," the admiral agreed through a fragrant cloud of steam as he added the sauce to the noodles, eggs, green onion, bean sprouts, and chicken. "On the other hand, I think the Manties are right about how the—'ghost fleet,' I think you just called it, Walter?—got in to attack them in the first place, and on how to keep it from happening again. That's why they've put together a sensor shell around their inner system—and to cover Nouveau Paris, too—that relies on active systems and pays a lot more attention to non-gravitic *passive* platforms, as well. It's the first stage of what they call 'Mycroft.'"

"Yes." Imbesi nodded vigorously. "I'm not sure I understand Mycroft fully, and I'm damned sure Tomas doesn't. I'm not positive about Alessandra, but I think it's probably what tilted her towards the 'yes' side of the vote."

"They want to keep the hardware tightly held, at least for now, and I can certainly understand that," Rozsak said, stirring the wok's simmering contents. "But they've been pretty good about sharing the system's capabilities, and as I understand them, it should provide pretty good security against another Yawata Strike. Essentially, what they've done is to take the networked system-defense platforms and missile pods Foraker came up with for the Havenites, couple them with God's own holy horde of additional sensor platforms, add FTL transmission to the sensor and fire control net, and replace the regular missile pods with those God-awful FTL-commanded MDMs." He grimaced. "Believe me—nothing their sensors get a whiff of is going to last long enough to launch any missiles, Walter."

"It was my impression that their thinking is that the missiles themselves were deployed quite some distance—possibly several light-minutes—from their actual targets and came in unpowered on ballistic profiles," Imbesi pointed out.

"And that's undoubtedly what happened." Rozsak nodded and removed the wok from the heat. "I don't care how good their super-secret drive technology is, they would *not* have wanted a fleet capable of firing that many missiles swanning around the Manticore Binary System. Way too much chance of something getting picked up, no matter how hard to see their drive is. But one or two small, very stealthy ships with the same sort of drive would be a very different proposition, and they have to've gotten some sort of targeting array in-system. *Something* had to update those birds after that long a ballistic flight. In fact, the Manties detected an encrypted transmission from what was almost certainly exactly that sort of array just before the attack missiles came into attack range. They think—and I agree—that the transmission was most likely from an unmanned platform that self-destructed after serving its purpose, and they've nailed down a pretty firm locus for where it was transmitting *from*. But as I just said—and as Admiral Givens pointed out to me when we discussed this—getting that sort of platform into position required them to penetrate the system in the first place. They may've gotten away with it using one or two ships when no one knew to be watching for them; they won't find it very easy to do a second time."

He began ladling the pad Thai onto the plates laid out on the bar.

"Something else she pointed out to me was that the Yawata Strike was so overwhelmingly successful only because no one saw it coming. They've analyzed the actual number of missiles—including those 'graser torpedoes,' or whatever the hell we decide to call them in the end—and the Alliance could have launched several times that many birds from a single squadron of SD(P)s. If the Manties' defenses had been active, or if they'd even had time to interpose the impeller wedges of their standby tugs to protect the space stations, the way doctrine specified, the damage would've been enormously lighter. So their thinking is that with the additional warning their new, denser short-range sensor shell's likely to provide, and with the higher readiness state they've adopted—permanently—for their antimissile defenses, any future attack using the same technique would be relatively ineffectual. And if the bad guys want to come dance with them in an attack that *doesn't* incorporate that lengthy ballistic flight, they'll be just as delighted as hell to set up the dance floor. Trust me, they *want* these people."

"And they're prepared to supply that—all of it, including the sensor shells—to us?" Imbesi asked.

"They are." Barregos picked up his chopsticks as Rozsak set the wok aside and settled back onto his own stool. "They won't be able to provide it *immediately*. They're still in the process of emplacing it in Beowulf. For that matter, they don't have it *fully* in place even in Manticore. But Beowulf and Haven are churning out the platforms in enormous numbers. Admiral Givens' estimate is that they can have their own capital systems outfitted with the all-up Mycroft within the next sixty T-days or so, and Erewhon, Maya, and Torch could be covered in another couple of T-months, given how their production rate's ramping up. They'll be able to provide similar protection to all of the other star systems in the Maya Sector within an additional four T-months. And, as she pointed out, it's highly unlikely the Alignment has a 'ghost fleet' strike force already organized to go after you or us. It'll take time for them to decide we might be worth hitting, and coupled with the relatively lower priority they'd give to hitting *us* as opposed to the Alliance, the threat to our infrastructure and populations has to be minimal, Walter."

"I don't think anyone in Erewhon's especially happy about even minimal chances of something with the casualty totals the Yawata Strike produced," Imbesi said somberly. "Despite which, I've been authorized to sign on the dotted line if you can convince me the risk is manageable."

He looked back and forth between his hosts for a long, silent moment, then shrugged and reached for a fork.

"I won't say you've completely persuaded me ... yet. But you've definitely made a good start in that direction. I'm going to try to remind myself that I need to be a hard sell specifically because my natural inclination is to get behind this and push, you understand."

"Of course we do," Rozsak said, eyeing the barbarism of Imbesi's chosen eating implement with scant approval. "On the other hand, we're pretty good salesmen. Especially when we genuinely believe all of our selling points."

"Then I'll try to listen with an open—if skeptical!—mind," Imbesi assured them both as he dug his fork into the pad Thai. He chewed, then swallowed.

"Delicious, Luiz!" He grinned. "I see you understand the finer points of negotiating."

"So I'm giving you an opportunity to save your people's lives. You have ten minutes to strike your wedges and surrender. At the end of that time, I will open fire once more. If I do, I doubt there will be many survivors.

"The decision is yours, Admiral."

—Captain Prescott Tremaine,
Royal Manticoran Navy,
CO, Cruiser Division 96.1.

Chapter Sixty-Nine

"I CANNOT *believe* THIS SHIT!" Kevin Haas snarled.

"And what 'shit' would that be?" Janice Marinescu replied, turning her float chair to face him. "Let me rephrase that. What 'shit' are we talking about *this* time?"

"This!" Haas jabbed a furious finger at the display in front of him. "That idiot Charteris is asking questions."

"Crap." Marinescu's expression was one of profound disgust, but she didn't look very surprised. "I *knew* that one was going to be trouble. Something about that bitch's attitude when I collected her and the other bleeding hearts just set my teeth on edge from the get-go. One of those goody-goodies who don't want to know a damned thing about people who do the *real* work. I don't suppose there's any reason he should be any different from her. In fact, that's why I asked you to keep a personal eye on him." She shook her head almost resignedly. "What *kind* of questions is he asking?"

"Well, to be fair—which I damned well don't *want* to be, you understand—it looks like he's at least trying to be discreet. But it's pretty clear he's not completely buying her responses from McClintock." Marinescu raised her eyebrows in a "tell me more" expression, and Haas shrugged. "The surveillance teams caught him contacting Christina McBryde." Marinescu frowned, and he shrugged again. "That's Zachariah McBryde's mother," he reminded her.

"Oh. Right." Marinescu nodded as the name slotted into position. It was an indication of just how harried she was that she'd needed Haas' reminder, but the orderly mental files opened obediently once she'd made the connection, and she frowned. "What's so significant about his contacting her? They've known each other for years. In fact, if I remember, weren't he and his wife dinner guests at the McBrydes a few weeks ago?"

"Almost right," Haas agreed. "Actually, Dr. McBryde took his parents and the Charterises out to dinner about a week before we picked him up. But you're right, they've known each other a long time, and of course he knows Dr. Charteris and Dr. McBryde worked together. There's no sign they ever let their covers slip—Charteris and McBryde's parents obviously still think the two of them worked for Kepagane and Bellini. But he does know they worked together, and he's asking his parents what they know about this conference Charteris and McBryde are at."

"Damn it."

Marinescu's expression could have soured all the milk in Mendel. It was good to know that someone as pablum-brained as Lisa Charteris had at least managed to maintain rudimentary security. Frankly, Marinescu wouldn't have bet a half credit on her doing that, given some of her other decisions over the years.

But if Jules Charteris still bought her cover story, then Marinescu had probably been doing her a disservice . . . in *that* regard, at least. Which didn't make *Jules* Charteris' curiosity bump any better.

Kepagane & Bellini was a diversified scientific think tank and research organization which worked closely with the Mesa System government. It was so enormous a hundred researchers could easily disappear into its personnel files without a trace, and quite a few of the inner onion's technical people had been hidden there. No flesh-and-blood individual at Kepagane & Bellini had ever seen or heard of any of those hidden people, however. The Alignment's hackers had created an entire fictitious division over forty T-years ago, and it just quietly ticked away, establishing the bona fides of the individuals theoretically employed by it. It had a budget, an admittedly somewhat obscure niche on the corporate flowchart, and actually generated several terabytes of more or less useless information every year. It even had a really nice suite of offices in one of the more modest industrial towers on the fringes of Mendel.

That, unfortunately, meant the revised Houdini plan would have to do something about that building. It would never do to have anyone's investigators discover that none of the people who theoretically worked there had ever actually *been* there. And, by the same token, Kepagane & Bellini's executive offices were scheduled to take a nasty hit. The nice thing about computer records was that even the most suspicious investigators tended to accept them as gospel unless something—or some*one*—else suggested there might be something . . . problematical about them. So it would be necessary to remove the human management personnel who had oversight over the department to which the Alignment's fictitious division nominally belonged before anyone looking for disappearing genetic supermen asked them about it. Fortunately, they'd have to kill no more than another seven or eight hundred people—a thousand, at the outside, by Marinescu's current estimate—to get anyone who could have raised red flags about the fictitious division. Of course, the executive offices in question were in Beadle Tower in downtown Miescher, and getting to them would take some doing... and a really *big* bomb. The total death toll would probably be closer to six or seven thousand, by the time the rubble stopped bouncing.

"What kind of questions is he asking them?" she asked after a moment. "Are we going to have to tidy *them* up, too?"

"I don't think so. Not yet, anyway." Haas grimaced. "Whatever else, he seems to've bought the notion that there are real security issues here. He's been really discreet in the way he's phrased his questions. More of a 'Have you heard from Zach?' or 'Boy, I wish Zach and Lisa weren't still stuck out there on the island! Has Zach mentioned when they might be heading back?' That kind of thing. And he hasn't gone near Kepagane and Bellini's corporate offices. Even he probably figures he'd get his wrist slapped—hard—if anyone noticed him doing something *that* stupid! I'd say he may be... concerned, and he's obviously digging at it, but it's pretty clear he's not actively *worried* enough to risk breaking security over it. Yet, at least. So far, he's been careful not to come right out and ask the McBrydes—or anyone else—just exactly what the meeting's supposed to be about, for example. I'm inclined to think he won't as long as he thinks he's still actually talking to her. It's what happens afterward that has me concerned. But like I say, so far he hasn't asked the McBrydes anything that's likely to start them looking for answers of their own."

"Well, that's something, anyway," Marinescu growled. The fewer additional mandatory kills she had to add to her to-do list, the better. Arranging to get all of them into the proper kill zones was proving a royal pain in the ass from a logistics viewpoint. There were only so many of them to whom they could give direct orders, after all, and she and her team would be busy enough without figuring out how to eliminate whole additional families just because some idiot couldn't keep from running his mouth! Not that they hadn't already compiled a sizable list where that was clearly going to be necessary, anyway, including more than six hundred—so far—who'd have to be killed in individual assassinations because there simply wasn't a plausible way to maneuver them into one of the mass-casualty events. And that didn't even count the less important members of the inner onion who'd have to be eliminated because there wasn't enough time or shipping to evacuate them.

It was no wonder Haas was looking a little frazzled, she thought, but he was a good man. A steady subordinate who understood the realities. That was more than she could say for some of her team members. The fact that even more of the personnel originally earmarked to execute Houdini had been out-system and unavailable than she'd thought when Rufino Chernyshev dropped this mess into her lap meant she'd had to pull in entirely too many operatives who'd never been fully briefed on the realities of even the original Houdini plans. Some of them had been less than enthralled when they discovered what the new, revised Houdini entailed. In fact, she'd had to have five of them "retired with extreme prejudice," as the really bad spy HDs liked to put it, for protesting their orders. And over a dozen more who hadn't actively protested had been involuntarily loaded aboard ship and packed off to Darius under Gaul escort lest their obvious qualms endanger operational security, which had been a copper-plated bitch. What she'd really have preferred would have been to simply cull the lot of them and be done with it. Like she'd told Chernevsky, this whole bitched-up mess would have been an ideal filter for identifying and skimming off individuals who'd demonstrated they'd lack the necessary intestinal fortitude in the coming years. Unfortunately, she'd been overruled because some of the weaklings were deemed too important for removal. Like Lisa Charteris herself, for example.

Marinescu snarled a silent mental curse. She'd *known* Charteris was going to be a problem. The mere fact that the woman had been stupid enough to actually marry someone she *knew* would never be brought fully inside the onion should have been a flare-lit tipoff. She should have been eased out of any responsible position and quietly eliminated in a nice, plausible traffic accident or accidental drowning *T-years* ago, because anyone of her seniority who was stupid enough to leave family to wonder what had happened to her if she had to disappear was clearly far too irresponsible to be trusted with anything important. And for *damn* sure she should never have been allowed into a position which made it mandatory to pull her out instead of simply killing her. But had anyone consulted Marinescu about that? No, of course they hadn't! And now it was her job—hers and her people's—to take out the garbage.

"Any idea what it is that's bugging Charteris?" she asked after a moment.

"Not really." Haas twitched one shoulder in an irritated sort of way. "There's no indication from the bugs in his apartment or his office—or on his uni-link, for that matter—that he has any suspicions about the CGI. And Donnie says her people have come up with all the right answers in his com calls . . . so far, at least. But if I had to guess, something just doesn't sound quite 'right' to him. For God's sake, Janice! The two of them were married for over half a T-century. Who knows what could've slipped past us and never made it into the data banks with that much shared history?"

"*We'd* damned well better know, that's who!" Marinescu snapped.

Despite which, she had to admit he had a point.

Donatella Primaticcio was her senior cyberneticist, in charge—among other things—of managing the communications interface for people like Jules Charteris when they tried to contact someone who'd already been shipped out. Every call was taken by a flesh-and-blood operative—always the *same* operative for each evacuated individual—from behind the mask of a computer-generated image of the person the caller *thought* she was talking to. Armed with complete dossiers on the people they were impersonating—files that detailed every moment of their lives, cross indexed the names of every person who knew them, however remotely, and incorporated the most brilliant matching algorithms available to match and identify names, places, and dates—the operatives were responsible for convincing the callers those people were right here on Mesa, doing exactly what they'd told everyone they were doing.

For the most part, it wasn't that difficult. Most of the callers already "knew" where the people they thought they were talking to were and what they were doing, and most of the conversations were brief enough—and sufficiently focused on relatively recent events—that they could be managed easily. Besides, *most* of the critical people on the Houdini list hadn't been as fucking stupid as Lisa Charteris. The people trying to call them were acquaintances—casual lovers, at the worst—and it was simple enough to fob with them off with a "Gee, we've *got* to get together again as soon as this conference"—or workshop, sales trip, or whatever the hell excuse had been used in this particular case—"is over and I get back to Mendel."

But for someone like Charteris, with a goddamned *fifty-T-year* history with the person trying to reach her, there were entirely too many potential potholes. Not even the dossiers Alignment Security assembled could cover every detail of that many years together. And if Jules Charteris wasn't really suspicious yet, if he only had a sort of vague itch he couldn't quite figure out how to scratch, it was for damn sure he'd get suspicious as hell if his beloved wife never turned up again. Even if the Houdini team's plan for covering her disappearance was perfect, someone like him was entirely too likely to start asking himself . . . inconvenient questions if investigators from someplace like, oh, *Manticore*, for example, started hunting for an Alignment whose ultimate goals were rather different from the ones he'd always *thought* the Alignment embraced. Worse, *their* questions were likely to get him to share *his* questions with them, and that could be one hell of a lot worse than simply inconvenient.

"All right," she sighed finally. "Put him on the list to be tidied up before we go and keep an eye on anyone else he talks to about it. I'm half inclined to go ahead and tidy up the daughters, too, just in case. But I guess we'd probably better pass on that, unless you turn up something concrete to suggest he's shared whatever suspicions he might have with them." She ran an irritated hand through her dark hair. "I think Chernevsky's too frigging worried about 'avoidable casualties,' but whether we like it or not, he's in Bardasano's office now. And he'll pitch three kinds of fit if we go ahead and pop them all without at least some fig leaf to justify it."

"Is he really monitoring the kill lists that closely?" Haas sounded skeptical, and Marinescu snorted.

"Personally, I think the man's an idiot—in his present position, at least—however good he may have been in the field. And to be honest, I've got my doubts about that field reputation of his, now that I've had the ineffable joy of working with him. But don't make the mistake of thinking he's stupid. I knew his brother Luka a lot better than I know him, but I can tell you *Luka* was nobody's fool, and I'm not about to assume he's any less sharp than Luka was. I think he should have one hell of a lot of more important things to do than keep looking over our shoulders and joggling our elbows, but if he's decided that's what he's going to do, then he's probably doing a thorough damned job of it."

"If you say so." Haas still sounded less than convinced, but Marinescu didn't worry about that. One thing about Kevin Haas, he understood following orders. "At least it shouldn't be too complicated where Charteris is concerned. The simplest solution's probably to have 'Lisa' invite him to join her at the Bateson conference in Saracen Tower. That's the 'Ballroom strike' scheduled to erase her."

"Works for me," Marinescu agreed. "After so long together, the least we can do is let both of them 'die' together, too." She smiled thinly. "Speaking of Saracen, though, how does the execution queue for Final Flourish look?"

"Pretty good, so far. It's taking a little longer than we'd thought it would to get some of the assets in place, but none of the slippage is critical yet. Just as happy 'the Ballroom's' not carrying out any active operations right this minute, though. We're too short on manpower to do that and get everything for Final Flourish into position."

"Well, even the Ballroom needs a little while to reload between its murderous slaughters," Marinescu pointed out cynically. "And after how busy they were last month, it shouldn't surprise anyone that it's taking a little time for them to get their next wave of attacks organized. Besides, it gives more time for their manifesto and communiqués to sink in."

"Right." Haas chuckled. "You know, I've actually enjoyed drafting those communiqués of theirs. They're so delightfully . . . I don't know . . . Over the top, I suppose. And the frigging newsies just eat them up!"

"That's what newsies do," Marinescu said even more cynically. "One of the things I love about them. Feed them the right raw meat, and you can guarantee exactly what their headlines will be."

"Yeah, and we've fed them plenty of that," Haas agreed.

He was right, too, Marinescu reflected. The "Ballroom terrorists" had announced their fresh campaign of terror by sinking the passenger liner *Magellan*, the Voyages Unlimited Line's deliberately archaic oceanic cruise ship. The Houdini teams had managed to kill the next best thing to three thousand passengers and crew people in their opening salvo *and* extract no fewer than seventy-three of their evacuees in the process, and not a reporter on Mesa had turned a single hair when the Audubon Ballroom claimed responsibility for the attack. Nor had they questioned the Ballroom's responsibility for the shoot-down of the Knight Tours shuttle over Mendel. The Houdini teams had erased almost twenty of the names on their list in that one, and there'd been over a dozen more incidents in August. The total death toll—real and simulated—was well over seventy-five hundred, and the evidence that the murderous psychopaths who'd carried out the Green Pines Atrocity were back had rocked Mesan public opinion. The panic was coming along nicely, Marinescu thought, and there'd already been some really nasty incidents of obvious vengeance attacks against the seccy population. That was good. Haas' "Ballroom" communiqués had picked up on them and added them to the justifications for their murderous attacks. Given how quickly they'd had to organize the entire thing, the revised Houdini was coming along nicely, but giving public opinion several weeks to . . . marinate properly would only make the crescendo of Final Flourish even more effective.

She was rather looking forward to her pièce de résistance, although she supposed someone like Chernyshev would get all teary-eyed thinking about it. She'd never understood that kind of flabby mindedness, but she didn't have to *understand* it to take it into her calculations. And when it came down to it, the fact that so few people would have had the toughness to realize what was necessary and actually do it was the best long-term protection for Houdini's secrecy. Most of the galaxy would have a hard time convincing itself that someone would kill as many people as Final Flourish was going to kill just to hide the disappearance of a far smaller number of *other* people. Even if something leaked, the most likely reaction would be to reject the entire idea as the product of some terminally paranoid conspiracy addict.

Unfortunately, they couldn't afford to *rely* on that, which was why it was her job to make sure nothing *did* leak.

"All right," she said more briskly. "I'll leave Mr. Charteris in your hands. And I'm glad to hear Final Flourish's on schedule. Shoot me a fresh summary of where we are, though. I'd like to be able to go over it and clear any minor concerns with you before we close up shop today." She grimaced. "I'm meeting with Collin and Chernyshev over supper. I don't want to get caught with my pants down if one of them has any questions about where we are."

"Gotcha." Haas nodded. "It'll be in your in folder by four."

"Good. That's good, Kevin," Marinescu said, and gave him a broad smile of thanks. It was important to remind him how much she valued him.

Good help was so hard to find, after all.

Chapter Seventy

"ALPHA TRANSLATION IN SIXTEEN MINUTES, Sir," Captain Shirley Shreeyash announced.

"Thank you, Captain," Admiral Winslet Tamaguchi replied. Tamaguchi was known for his formality at the best of times, which the last several months hadn't been, and he turned from his staff astrogator to his ops officer.

"Any last-minute concerns, Captain Levine?"

"No, Sir." Captain Bradley Levine shook his head. "All units report full readiness."

"Excellent." Tamaguchi's smile was wintry. "Hopefully this will be a simple matter of demonstrating our determination, but if it turns ugly, I want it settled quickly and with as little collateral damage—or casualties—as possible."

"Yes, Sir," Levine acknowledged, and watched Tamaguchi return his gaze to the master astrographic display, reflecting on what the admiral *hadn't* said.

The latest intelligence from home suggested the Manties had found a way to spread the SLN still thinner by fomenting rebellions in the Protectorates. And while the Włocławek System wasn't a protectorate—*It hasn't* been *one, at least*, he thought—its location at one end of the Włocławek-Sarduchi warp bridge made it particularly valuable. A relatively wealthy, prosperous star system in a strategic location and possessing a natural resource in high demand on the luxury foods market was worth a half-dozen typical Verge systems. In the normal course of affairs, Frontier Security would be salivating at the internal crisis which gave them a chance to add Włocławek to the protectorate fold.

Unfortunately, affairs weren't normal at the moment, and if the Manties *were* behind what was happening in Włocławek—and the system's proximity to their new Talbott Quadrant would make installing a suitable puppet government of their own highly valuable to *them*, as well—it was likely they'd have arranged a naval presence to back their cat's-paws' efforts. There was no hard evidence that this was anything but a purely internal neobarb squabble, and it certainly sounded to Levine like one more bunch of neobarbs selling out their fellows for personal benefit. But no one had ever said that sort of situation couldn't be manipulated by outsiders—OFS had proven *that* often enough, for God's sake!—and Tamaguchi would've been more than human if he wasn't worried about possible Manties in the underbrush. Particularly given how poorly things had turned out in every previous confrontation with them.

Except, of course, the ops officer thought sourly, *for that idiot Byng's* first *engagement. Leave it to one of Battle Fleet's finest to screw the pooch for all the rest of us that frigging thoroughly. Pity no one else has managed to catch a handful of Manty destroyers in orbit with their wedges down! At least the Manties made sure he wouldn't screw anyone else over!*

And at least all of Tamaguchi's battlecruisers carried the new Flight Two Cataphract, with almost twenty percent more powered range and marginally improved warheads. Levine had been amazed by the original Cataphract's enormous range...which had made the discovery that *Manticoran* missiles' out-ranged even the Cataphract an even more stunning blow. Fortunately, all available evidence suggested the Manties' truly long-range birds were pod-launched, and they seemed to be really big bastards, too.

He would have been much happier if that evidence had been *conclusive* and not simply the best *available*. Unfortunately, the SLN had a dearth of combat reports from ships which had faced the Manticorans in combat, since none of those ships had returned to base to make the aforesaid reports. They did have Admiral Liam Pyun's report from Zunker, though, and the survivors of the Saltash debacle seemed to back Pyun's account, although no hard sensor data had been available to support their account of events. For that matter, the limited information from Spindle pointed in the same direction. And if Pyun's report *was* accurate, the Manties had launched their "demonstration salvo" at *thirty million* kilometers. That was damned near twice the range even the Flight Two Cataphract could manage in a continuous burn, but the Cataphract was a two-stage weapon. They could delay separation of the second stage for as long as they liked, then send it into the attack at twice the accel reported out of the Manties' weapons. They'd have to accept a lengthy ballistic segment, and targeting would suck at such vast ranges, but they could by God *reach* the bastards.

But only with Spatha-level laserheads, on the tube-launched birds, he reminded himself. *Even with the throughput upgrade, that's not a lot of punch against anything above cruisers or battlecruisers. If we run into one of those damned pod-laying wallers of theirs, we're going to get hammered with one hell of a lot more damage per hit than they are. But against cruisers and destroyers, we should be able to go toe-to-toe if we have a big enough advantage in tubes.*

And then there were the two dozen pods of Flight Two Cataphract-Cs tractored to each of BatCruRon 720's units. *They* carried the same laserhead as the Trebuchet capital ship missile, and any damned Manty that got hit by one of *them* was going to know he'd been nudged.

Bradley Levine smiled thinly as he turned back to his own displays, and steadfastly fought the sense that he was whistling in a graveyard.

✧   ✧   ✧

"Alpha translation in five minutes, Sir."

"Very well."

Captain Ephron Vangelis acknowledged the report. "Anything more from Flag Bridge?"

"No, Sir."

"Thank you."

Vangelis hadn't really expected to hear anything more. Admiral Tamaguchi had explained his intentions, and he wasn't the sort to go back over something he'd already covered. Nor was he the sort to encourage warm, fuzzy relationships with his subordinates. Some flag officers had a close rapport with their flagships' captains; as far as Vangelis could tell, Tamaguchi didn't have a "close rapport" even with his wife. He did have a record as a tough, tenacious commander, however, and that made up for a lot.

So did the improved missiles in SLNS *Triumphant*'s magazines and the tweaks to her point defense software. Vangelis found it difficult to credit the missile velocities which had been reported, although he couldn't quite decide whether that was because they seemed so ridiculous they couldn't be true or because he so desperately *wanted* them not to be. If they *were* true, he was none too confident the software tweaks would be enough, although at least the computers weren't likely to simply reject the solutions because they were so far outside the programmers' assumptions.

According to a friend of his in Fleet Acquisitions, simulations at System Development had confirmed Keeley O'Cleary's contention that the missile-defense systems aboard Sandra Crandall's ships had done just that. And according to the same friend, Admiral Polydorou had carried out those simulations—under protest, since they were so "obviously unnecessary"—only at the direct orders of Fleet Admiral Kingsford when he replaced Rajampet Rajani as CNO.

Vangelis found it difficult to decide which of those reports were more depressing.

"Do you think the Manties are really behind this, Sir?" a quiet voice asked in his earbug, and he smiled thinly.

"I don't know what to think, Lance," he told his executive officer. At the moment, Captain Richardson was on the backup bridge at the far end of *Triumphant*'s core hull. "One thing I *do* know is that it'd make sense from their perspective. In a lot of ways, it'd just be an extension of their shutting down the warp bridges by seizing the wormholes, when you think about it."

"I guess you're right, Sir." Vangelis heard Richardson exhale. "You know," the XO went on after a moment, "I'm sort of torn between hoping it *is* the Manties and hoping it isn't."

"I imagine we're all feeling a bit like that," Vangelis agreed.

And even if it isn't the Manties, Tamaguchi's going to hammer these people flat, if that's what it takes. Partly because Kingsford's emphasizing how much we need every revenue source we can find, but even more importantly because Tamaguchi wants to send a message. If the Manties are behind this, he wants anybody who might think about throwing in with them to . . . reconsider his options. And even if the Manties aren't behind it, it'll be proof Frontier Fleet's still on the job, no matter what's happened to Battle Fleet.

"Alpha translation in one minute, Sir."

❖   ❖   ❖

"I told you this was going to end badly, Tomasz," Hieronim Mazur said coldly. "It turns out I was right."

"I assume you mean your new masters are here?" Tomasz Szponder replied. "How does it feel to fit your own neck for their dog collar, Hieronim?"

"One hell of a lot better than *you're* going to feel shortly!"

"I don't suppose you've pointed out to them that the closest you have to an actual member of the government up there on *Piłsudski* is a single unelected *aparatczyk*?"

"He's close enough," Mazur said cynically. "Admiral Tamaguchi seems to think so, anyway."

"I suppose any Solly knows a serviceable political whore when he sees one," Szponder said, but he also felt an undeniable chill.

The long-dreaded Frontier Fleet task group had made its alpha translation into Włocławek over forty minutes ago, and only thirteen light-minutes from the planet. There'd been plenty of time for its commander to contact the legal government in Lądowisko, and the fact that Mazur knew that commander's name seemed to indicate he'd been talking to *someone* in Włocławek.

The fact that it wasn't Tomasz Szponder or Szymon Ziomkowski indicated he had no intention of discussing his purpose here with the people actually on the planet.

Oh, he'll "discuss" it with us... eventually, Szponder thought bitterly. *When he hands down his surrender demands and tells us exactly what he's going to do to us if we don't cave in. I suppose the only question is how badly he's willing to damage the golden goose to get the Sollies' hands on its eggs.*

He kept his upwelling despair out of his expression as he faced Mazur over the com, but it was hard, and deep inside he cursed the Star Empire of Manticore. No doubt they'd anticipated exactly what was about to happen—an additional diversion of the SLN's strength, something to tie down a little more of the League's combat power. And he'd fallen for it. He'd walked straight into it, and he'd taken his entire planet—his friends and family—right along with him.

He wondered how long they expected the ground fighting to take? How many days or weeks of delay they anticipated out of the torrents of blood his people would shed before they surrendered their weapons and their world?

"Well, Hieronim," he said, "I imagine your new masters will be along to collect their property shortly. You might tell them they'll need quite a few Marines to do it, though. Oh, and by the way, we've placed demolition charges in every SEOM installation on the planet." He smiled thinly. "You might want to think about that, because we've done the same thing for all the rest of the *łowcy trufli* likely to swill at the Sollies' trough with you. Your new friend Admiral Tamaguchi probably won't thank you a lot for handing him a planet that needs to be completely rebuilt before it starts pouring any credits into OFS' pockets."

"You wouldn't dare," Mazur sneered. "And even if *you* would, those proles down there with you wouldn't. They may be stupid, but they're smart enough to realize they'd be blowing up their own livelihoods right along with it!"

"That's the point you've never understood, Hieronim," Szponder told him quietly. "It's not 'their' livelihoods. It never *has* been, because of people like you. People who systematically make sure they'll never have a chance to be more than the 'proles' you keep calling them. People who think all 'proles' care about is licking the hand of someone who treats them like cattle, not human beings who know their lives could be better. People who want to have a voice in how their world's governed. Who want their children's lives to be *better* than theirs—not snuffed out by some stupid fucking *oligarcha* who gets away with mass murder just because she's *your* cousin. Those people you have so much contempt for are *angry*, and they understood the risks when they decided to support me, to support what the Ruch Odnowy Narodowej was always *supposed* to be.

So, yes, they *are* 'stupid' enough to fight—and if the only way they can fight is to destroy everything you plan on taking away from them again, they're 'stupid' enough to do *that*, too. You think about that over the next hour or so…not that it's likely to do you much good now. Those Solly bastards won't rebuild one damned thing for *you*, Hieronim. Your only value was to be the turnkey, to hand over an intact infrastructure, up and running and ready to start producing for its new owners. Only you're not going to be able to, are you? When the dust settles, you won't have a pot to piss in, and Sollies aren't known for generosity to people who can't follow through on what they promised to deliver."

He smiled savagely and cut the connection.

"I believe I understand the situation, Mr. Miternowski," Winslet Tamaguchi said.

The transmission delay was irritating, since his flagship and her consorts were still just over six light-minutes from *Stacja Kosmiczna Józefa Piłsudskiego*. But after a sixty-T-year Frontier Fleet career, Tamaguchi was as accustomed to that as he was to dealing with predictable, corruptible, contemptible neobarbs like the two staring out of his display while they awaited his last transmission. Of the two, he actually felt far less contempt for Tymoteusz Miternowski. At least he clearly grasped that he was a tool. His recognition of that had been apparent from the beginning. Mazur, on the other hand, seemed unaware of just how radically his comfortable little universe was about to change.

The stupid bastards always expect us to come in and fix things for them, give them back all their toys. But it doesn't work that way, Mr. Mazur. And somehow I

*doubt your fellow citizens are going to be especially
fond of you, starting tomorrow morning. Pity about that.*

The truth was that Winslet Tamaguchi had far more
disdain for Verge oligarchs than for the proles they
exploited. The proles might be uneducated, and they
might be unsophisticated, but they were seldom stupid
enough to barter away their worlds for personal gain.

And, as his mother had always told him, ignorance
could be fixed; stupid was forever.

"My ships should enter Włocławek orbit in approximately two hours and ten minutes," he continued. "At
that time, I believe it would probably be appropriate
for you to join me in a com conference with Mr.
Szponder and his hooligans." His smile was frosty. "I
don't want any misunderstandings from his end before
I begin active operations to restore the legitimate
government. At that time—"

"Excuse me, Admiral."

Tamaguchi hit the pause button that brought up
Triumphant's wallpaper and looked away from the
com pickup with a scowl.

"What?" he snapped.

"I apologize for interrupting you, Sir," Vice Admiral
Lorne Yountz said, and Tamaguchi's scowl segued into
a frown as his chief of staff's expression registered.

"What is it, Lorne?" he asked in a rather calmer tone.

"Tracking's just picked up a group hyper footprint.
CIC makes it thirteen point sources. They're almost
directly astern of us at six-point-eight light-minutes."

❖   ❖   ❖

Well, Scotty Tremaine told himself as he studied
CIC's master plot, *at least Włocławek's not going to
be as* boring *as Golem was.*

His lips twitched as he remembered his earlier thought about the positive aspects of boredom.

Alistair McKeon and the rest of his task group had been in Włocławek space for just over three minutes, although he'd been in no hurry to move in-system the instant he arrived. Even now, he was pulling only eighty-three percent of his slowest unit's maximum accel—there was no point showing the Sollies any speed advantages they didn't already know about—and TG 10.2.9's velocity was up to only 1,500 KPS while the Ghost Rider drones sped ahead of them at 10,000 gravities. He wanted those birds up forward to give him as close a look as possible at what CIC was calling eight battlecruisers and eight destroyers, 104,808,572 kilometers ahead of them, headed for the planet of Włocławek at 27,948 KPS and accelerating at 3.83 KPS^2. The Solarians had been *decelerating*, clearly headed for a zero-zero with the planet. They'd changed their minds, however, within less than ninety seconds of detecting his own arrival, and he allowed himself a moment of respect for the prompt decisiveness of that Solly commander.

That has *to be a Frontier Fleet admiral*, he thought. *God knows nobody's seen a* Battle *Fleet flag officer smart enough to run from a force so much lighter than his! That's a major step up from Byng and Crandall, even if all he's doing—for now—is taking out an insurance policy and buying a little more time to think. In fact, I'm surprised even a Frontier Fleet CO's willing to do that.*

Now, how do I convince him to stop being smart?

❖   ❖   ❖

"Tracking's confident of its IDs now, Admiral," Captain Levine said. Tamaguchi only looked at him and curled the fingers of his right hand in a "tell me more" motion, and Levine glanced down at his memo board.

"We've got one of those big-assed heavy cruisers or cut-down battlecruisers of theirs, Sir. Five more look like light cruisers, from their tonnage. They *might* be destroyers—or what the Manties're calling 'destroyers,' anyway, based on the scrubbed tac recordings of New Tuscany they sent with their 'protest note'—but they're all at least a hundred and forty k-tons. There are also four ships that're *definitely* destroyers. Judging from *Jayne's*, I'd estimate they're *Culverin*-class ships."

He grimaced, and Tamaguchi smiled sourly, well aware of how...frustrating Levine found it to be forced to depend on *Jayne's* instead of the hard, reliable data *ONI* was supposed to provide to its tactical officers.

"In addition, there's what looks like a freighter—fairly small, two or three million tons, max, but it must have a milspec compensator to pull that accel, so it's probably a purpose-built collier—and what looks like a pair of them dispatch boats."

"I see. And that acceleration rate's confirmed?"

"Yes, Sir. They started in-system at a fairly low accel, but they kicked it up to five-point-seven KPS squared about four minutes ago."

"Definitely Manties, then," Vice-Admiral Yountz observed.

"Yes, Sir," Levine said again. "And it indicates they aren't pursuing us as hard as they could be if they dropped the freighter back."

"Five hundred and eighty gravities sounds to me like they're pushing it pretty hard," the chief of staff said. "Dropping the freighter probably wouldn't help much."

"Probably not enough for them to overhaul us, no, Sir," Levine agreed. "But if the wilder reports we've had are accurate, they should easily hit six hundred or even six-fifty. In fact, even that would be fairly low for Manties."

"*Low?*" Yountz's eyebrows rose, and Levine shrugged irritably.

"I did say they were 'wilder reports,' Sir. But according to the only Solarian report we have from New Tuscany, their *battlecruisers* were pulling over six-ten before they took out *Jean Bart*. And Admiral O'Cleary's debrief after Spindle suggests the same sort of accelerations."

"The report from New Tuscany's hardly conclusive. And with all due respect," Yountz didn't *sound* particularly respectful, "there's bound to be some CYA in Keeley O'Cleary's debrief. I'd take anything coming out of Spindle with a grain of salt."

"Which, unless the term 'wilder reports' means something different to you than it does to me, is precisely what Bradley just did," Tamaguchi pointed out with an edge of frost. "He also brought it to our attention, however . . . which is precisely what he was supposed to do."

"I know, Sir. And I didn't mean to sound like I was biting your head off, Brad." Yountz smiled crookedly at the ops officer. "I just find it a *teeny* bit hard to accept that a Manty battlecruiser can out-accelerate one of our *destroyers*. I'll grant ONI's badly underestimated their capabilities, but that's still a mighty steep leap in compensator tech."

"Agreed." Tamaguchi nodded, then folded his hands behind himself and stood gazing at the main display while he considered his options.

If CIC's analysis was accurate—and he was confident it was—there were no true capital ships, or even battlecruisers, in that pursuing force. The freighter didn't count once the actual shooting started, and without it, any comparison of tonnage ratios came down in BatCruRon 720's favor by a ludicrous margin. All the Manty warships, together, couldn't mass more than a million and a half tons, whereas his battlecruisers, alone, massed over seven. But as the Manties had demonstrated to Admiral Crandall and Admiral Filareta, simple tonnage was no longer the best meterstick when it came to evaluating relative combat power. The admission left a bitter taste, but Winslet Tamaguchi had no desire to follow in the footsteps of such luminaries as Sandra Crandall or Josef Byng.

His mental jury was still out on Massimo Filareta—as a naval commander, at least. As a human being, Tamaguchi could only be grateful the Manties had eliminated him from the gene pool.

Still, Levine had a point about Manty acceleration rates.

He'd never really expected to be able to outrun Manties in a straight up race. Fortunately—or *un*fortunately, depending upon one's perspective—he didn't have to. If the Manties wanted to bring his far larger force to action, they had to catch him before he raced across the inner system to the farther hyper limit and translated out. The thought of ignominiously fleeing from an opponent one out-massed better than five-to-one was hardly the stuff of derring-do and heroic news stories, and it might well have negative career repercussions when word got back to Old Terra. For that matter, it wasn't a thought Tamaguchi found appealing. Given his enormous velocity advantage, however, the Manties should find it impossible to overhaul him unless he chose to let them.

Should.

It was currently—he checked the astrogation display—687,191,428 kilometers to the limit. At his best acceleration, his force could reach it in roughly three hours and thirty minutes. At their current acceleration, it would take the Manties sixty-one minutes longer than that to reach the same destination. But if they had additional acceleration in reserve—especially if it was the ridiculous sort of acceleration some of Levine's "wilder reports" ascribed to them—his ability to outrun them was far from assured, even if that was what he decided to do. Oh, he could always tweak his own accel, but the absolute best he could do, even cutting his compensator safety margin to zero, was only 4.78 KPS^2... almost a full kilometer per second squared lower than the Manties were demonstrating even with the freighter to slow them. And three of his eight battlecruisers had been overdue for major overhauls well before Josef Byng blew up the League's relations with Manticore and put maintenance schedules on indefinite hold. He frankly doubted their compensators were up to that sort of strain.

The problem, he thought grimly, *is that they didn't send me these up-rated missiles just to run away from the big, bad Manties. I'm sure* someone's *going to point that out when I get home... and they damned well* should. *Sooner or later we* have *to take it to them and actually* win *a frigging battle! But after Saltash, I've got to think twice as many Manty launch platforms could rip the ass off any SLN battlecruiser squadron. All Dubroskaya's survivors insist the Manties only had five of their light cruisers—and* these *people have at least* eleven... *not to mention that damned heavy cruiser. If I let them fight their kind of battle, I'm going to get a lot of people killed, but if I don't fight some kind of battle when I've got this kind of tonnage advantage, when the hell* will *we be able to face these people?*

It was an unhappy thought, and not just because of the potential criticism he'd face if he avoided action. Resuming his acceleration away from the Manties had been an instinct reaction to at least preserve his velocity advantage while he considered his options. And he knew avoiding action was almost certainly the smart tactical move, despite the apparent force imbalance. Yet if they were ever going to pin back a Manty naval force's ears, dealing with *this* one would—

"Excuse me, Sir." It was his com officer, Commander Phanindra Broadmoor.

"Yes, Commander?"

"We have a message from the Manty commander, Sir. It just came in."

"Ah. I wondered when we'd hear from him." Tamaguchi smiled thinly. "Put it up on the display, please."

"Yes, Sir."

The main display shifted to com mode and a remarkably young senior-grade captain in Manticore's black and gold looked out of it with cold blue eyes.

"I'm Captain Prescott Tremaine, Royal Manticoran Navy." His voice was even colder than those eyes. "In the name of my Empress and her allies, I call upon you to drop your wedges and surrender to avoid needless bloodshed. If you choose not to cut your acceleration and surrender, I will engage and destroy your force. Tremaine, clear."

Well, that *was certainly succinct and to the point,* Bradley Levine thought, watching over his admiral's shoulder. *Arrogant as hell, and mighty bold talk from someone with so little tonnage, but definitely to the point.*

Tamaguchi gazed expressionlessly at the display and Tremaine's frozen image, for several seconds. Then he glanced at the com officer again.

"Record for transmission, please, Commander," he told him, and turned his head to face the pickup.

"Live mic, Sir."

"This is Admiral Winslet Tamaguchi, Solarian League Navy," the admiral said in wintry tones. "You apparently have a very high opinion of both yourself and your capabilities, Captain Tremaine. Unfortunately, I don't share it. If you believe you have the capability to engage and destroy my force, I cordially invite you to make the attempt. Tamaguchi, clear."

"Good recording, Sir," Broadmoor said after a moment.

"Then send it."

"Yes, Sir."

Tamaguchi nodded and returned his attention to the display, waiting out the ten-minute communication loop.

❖   ❖   ❖

"For a fellow who's eager to fight, he's running awfully hard," Commander Francine Klusener, Scotty Tremaine's chief of staff, observed dryly.

"Probably, unfortunately, because he's not an idiot," Tremaine replied, his expression thoughtful. "Even assuming he's got the missiles they gave Filareta before he moved on Manticore, anyone with a clue would realize we've still got every advantage in missile combat. And if he's heard about what happened in Saltash, he can't possibly want to take on four times as many Manticoran missile platforms with only twice as many battlecruisers."

He frowned for a moment, then looked at his intelligence officer.

"What, if anything, do we know about this fellow, Adelita?"

"Not a lot, Sir," Lieutenant Adelita Salazar y Menéndez replied, looking up from the data search she'd just completed. "There's a bare-bones bio entry in the ONI files, but very little beyond a list of commands he's held. There *is* a note that he's considered by the Sollies to be a determined sort of man. Apparently he's been handed several sticky jobs here in the Verge and accomplished all of them. There's also a note from SIS, not ONI, that he's viewed as not especially bloodthirsty but perfectly willing to kill however many 'neobarbs' he has to to complete a mission."

"So even if he's willing to run, he's not the sort of fellow who'd *like* to run," Tremaine murmured, rubbing the tip of his nose thoughtfully. None of the other members of his staff noticed Sir Horace Harkness' slight smile as he recognized who that mannerism had been acquired from.

"Sir, excuse me for pointing this out," Klusener said, "but he's got a lot of missile defense over there. Not as good as ours, but a lot. And Filareta had a god-awful number of pods riding his hulls. Tamaguchi may, too."

"Oh, trust me, I'm well aware of that." Tremaine

smiled coldly. "And once the RDs get close enough, I *definitely* want a look at what he might be carrying externally. On the other hand, we've got a bit of missile defense of our own . . . and a lot more accurate birds. I have no intention of trading hit-for-hit with these people, Frannie. But I don't think we have to, given what Horace, Adam and I have been thinking about since we got the intel reports about their new missiles. If they want to use all that range to shoot at us, they'll be very disappointed in the number of hits they manage to score. The problem's convincing them to let *us* get close enough to shoot at *them*."

He rubbed the tip of his nose some more, then turned to his astrogator.

"Tell me about our friend Tamaguchi, Elspeth."

"He's pulling a steady three hundred and ninety gravs, Sir, which is about right for a standard eighty percent margin on a *Nevada*." Lieutenant Dreyfus shrugged. "That means he's got some in reserve, although how much depends on a lot of factors, like his compensators' maintenance state. At the moment, he's up to two-niner-point-two thousand KPS and he's opened the range by just under fifteen million kilometers. Our accel's cutting into his speed advantage—we're up to four-point-niner thousand KPS—but at present rates it'll take us another three-point-six hours just to match velocities."

"And he'll clear the far hyper limit well before that."

"Yes, Sir. About eleven minutes before we equalize."

"And the range at that time?"

"We'll be two-seven-seven-point-seven million kilometers behind him."

"And if we went to maximum acceleration?"

"Our overtake accel—assuming he doesn't change his—would almost double, Sir. We'd match velocities in an hour and three minutes, eighty-seven minutes before he hits the limit. At that point, we'd be roughly two-zero-niner million kilometers behind him and he'd still be the next best thing to three-five-zero million kilometers from the limit. We'd begin making up distance, but he'd still cross the limit about twenty-eight minutes before us, and the range when he did would be one-six-seven million kilometers."

"About what I'd estimated." Tremaine nodded. "So, we can't catch him."

None of his staffers, he noticed, commented that given the disparity in tonnage, his task group was rather like a treecat pursuing a hexapuma.

Except, of course, that in this case the 'cat's packing a pulse rifle, he reminded himself. *But if he can't get the damned thing into range . . .*

"Break back across the limit and micro-jump across to intercept him on the far side, Sir?" Lieutenant Commander Golbatsi suggested.

"Time to do that, Elspeth?"

"Just a second, Sir." Dreyfus bent back over her panel and crunched numbers. Then she looked back up. "Eleven-point-five minutes to decelerate to zero relative to Włocławek, Sir, assuming we detached *Charles Ward* and took only the warships at *McKeon*'s maximum decel. We'd be roughly two-zero-seven million kilometers inside the limit at that point, so we'd need another forty minutes to get back across. Call it an hour and forty-three minutes."

"At which point he'd still be better'n two hours short of the limit," Horace Harkness pointed out.

"Yes, but he'd realize what we're up to the minute we start decelerating," Tremaine said. "What happens if he goes to, say, ninety percent of a *Nevada*'s max acceleration, Elspeth?"

"At ninety percent," Dreyfus said, inputting numbers, "he clears the limit in . . . two hundred minutes. At a hundred percent, he'd do it roughly ten minutes earlier."

"So we'd still have an hour to work with before he could translate out."

"Yes, Sir," Golbatsi agreed. "And pushing his margin to zero's not something a Solly's likely to do. Especially when he's got that much tonnage advantage."

"The fact that he's not already decelerating indicates he's not your typical Solly, Adam," Tremaine pointed out. "If he realizes what we're doing and he's *really* determined not to fight, he splits his force and sends them on diverging courses for different spots on the limit, and he's got more of them than we do. We'd play hell trying to intercept just his battlecruisers. Then there's the problem that astrogation's not exactly precise on such a short micro-jump. We'd almost certainly end up a couple of million kilometers off on our alpha translation, and it could be a lot worse than that. No offense, Elspeth."

He smiled at the astrogator, and she smiled back.

"None taken, Sir," she assured him.

"If we chase them hard, we could still get at least a couple just from compensator failures, Sir," Harkness pointed out. "I could live with that all day long, Sir."

"But I don't want 'a couple of them,'" Tremaine said grimly. "I want *all* of them."

And without killing any more of them than I have

to. After what happened in Saltash, we know how outclassed they are even if they haven't figured it out, and however pissed I may be with Sollies in general, massacring them in job lots isn't real high on my priority list.

Pulling back and micro-jumping across would almost certainly get us into position, despite what I just said, but my options would be limited. Given his closing velocity, I'd have to go for kill shots on all his units to keep them from sliding across the limit and translating out. Even if they went to maximum decel, they'd be well across the limit before they could stop, and no way do I have enough warm bodies to put prize crews on that many ships. Not to mention the fact that my pinnaces couldn't even match accel with them to put people onboard short of the limit! But how do I . . . ?

The hand rubbing his nose stopped suddenly. He stood gazing at the display for another dozen seconds or so. Then he began to smile and turned to Lieutenant Stilson MacDonald, his com officer.

"I think I need to speak to Captain Lewis, Stilson," he said.

Chapter Seventy-One

"COMING UP ON THE MARK, Ma'am," Lieutenant Commander Nakhimov announced, and Ginger Lewis looked up from her smaller maneuvering plot, where she'd been reviewing Scotty Tremaine's proposed movements, and turned her command chair back towards the main display.

"Run away. Run away!" she murmured under her breath.

It was one of her favorite lines from one of the incredibly ancient "movies" to which Duchess Harrington had introduced her (and much of the rest of HMS *Wayfarer*'s crew) on her very first cruise. Fortunately, however, none of her bridge crew heard her. Somehow she doubted it would have comported well with the gravitas of a proper CO.

Charles Ward was just over 136,580,000 kilometers inside the hyper limit, and her velocity relative to Włocławek had risen to 13,908 KPS. Like all the rest of TG 10.2.9, she continued to lose ground on the Sollies, although the *rate* at which they lost it was decreasing steadily. It was going to start *increasing* for *CW* in just another few seconds, however.

It felt . . . odd to be about to run away from the enemy, but Ginger Lewis had been aboard another armed fleet auxiliary which had taken on battlecruisers, and she hadn't enjoyed the experience. True, there was a universe of difference between her present command and *Wayfarer*. There were a few similarities, too, however, and *CW* had a few disadvantages all her own.

The most noteworthy of which, she thought dryly, *is just a* teeny *difference in the command experience of their COs.*

She looked around her bridge. *CW* might be armed, but she'd dispensed with the separate backup command deck of a true warship. There was a secondary tactical station located down in the big ship's CIC, which was currently manned by Lieutenant (JG) Burgulya Gödert, her assistant tactical officer, and Lieutenant Yolanda Cornelisz, *CW*'s electronic warfare officer, while Lieutenant Commander Atkins manned the bridge tac station with Paulo d'Arezzo as his EWO. At the moment—and hopefully for the foreseeable future—none of them had much to do.

Also at the moment, however, Nakhimov had a point. So—

"Initiate separation, Oliver," she said in a rather louder tone.

"Initiating separation, aye, Ma'am," Lieutenant Primikynos replied from his cargo control panel, and she smiled. She might not be a proper tac officer herself, but she could appreciate deviousness when it came along.

Never saw this *one coming*, she thought wryly. *I'm a frigging engineer, not a tac officer! But I really like it. Scotty and Harkness always were a sneaky pair, and the Duchess would be proud of them this time. It's probably a damn good thing my job's as simple as it is, though. And if it all drops into the pot anyway, Creswell can probably bail me out.*

Actually, as she knew full well, if it all "dropped into the pot," she'd do the best she could because she was senior to Commander Henry Creswell, HMS *Feng Meng's* CO. That meant it would be her job, and she'd damned well do it. But she'd never expected to find herself in command, however temporary, of a combat formation, and—

"Clean separation," Primikynos announced.

"Lieutenant Mallard confirms acquisition, Ma'am," Lieutenant Sughavanam said a moment later.

"Very good," she acknowledged both reports and smiled more broadly at Lieutenant Commander Nakhimov. "And now, Mitya, I think we should go elsewhere, so"—she smiled—"let's be about it."

✧　　✧　　✧

"Excuse me, Sir," Bradley Levine said, and Tamaguchi turned from the plot to face him.

"Sir, the freighter's just reversed acceleration and five of the combatants are going with it. It looks like the *Culverins* and one of the light cruisers. We're designating the remaining warships as Sierra One and the group that's decelerating as Sierra Two. Looks like Sierra Two's decel's holding steady at five-point-seven KPS squared."

"Getting the freighter out of harm's way, do you think, Sir?" Yountz asked, crossing to Tamaguchi's shoulder to contemplate the plot.

"It seems a trifle . . . excessive," Tamaguchi replied after a moment. "Especially after this long. The freighter has to be well into its compensator margin to hold that accel; it's already pulling twelve percent or so more than one of ours could even with military nodes and a zero margin. If they just wanted to park it safely somewhere, all they really had to do was have it reduce acceleration and fall astern. That would have to increase its compensator margin, and they could've done that any time after they went in pursuit in the first place."

"And if they're just letting it fall back, there's no need to send almost half their warships to keep an eye on it, either," his chief of staff murmured with a nod of agreement, and Tamaguchi nodded back, his eyes thoughtful.

"Sir, Sierra One's just increased accel," Levine announced. "Looks like they're going to about six hundred gravities, maybe a little higher." The ops officer studied his displays for a moment, then looked up. "Six hundred and five, Sir. Call it five-point-niner KPS squared."

"Thank you, Captain," Tamaguchi acknowledged. He frowned and turned back to the master plot, gazing into its depths. Sierra One's increased acceleration seemed to confirm that the Manties had detached the freighter to free up the warships' acceleration, and an additional twenty-five gravities was impressive. The maximum accel an SLN ship that heavy cruiser's size could have pulled was only five hundred and one gravities, and that was with a zero safety margin on its inertial compensator. Somehow he doubted Captain Tremaine was willing to run his compensators flat out—if that acceleration number from New Tuscany was accurate, he *definitely* wasn't—but he was clearly coming close, or the uptick would be higher than four percent. With that slight an increase . . .

"What does their new accel do to their approach to the hyper limit, Astro?" he asked Captain Shreeyash.

"It cuts their arrival time a little, Sir," Shreeyash said so promptly he knew she'd already worked the figures. "They'll shave off about four minutes, but they'll still be five-one-point-four minutes behind us."

"And at its current deceleration, where will the freighter be when we clear the limit?"

"Just a second, Sir." The astrogator crunched some more numbers, then looked back up. "Assuming all accelerations remain constant, it'll recross its entry hyper limit about eighteen-point seven minutes before we hit the exit limit, Sir."

Tamaguchi nodded and frowned at the master plot some more.

"I wonder . . ." he said softly. Yountz looked at him, and he shrugged. "I'm wondering what's in that freighter's holds," he expanded.

"Logistical support, I imagine, Sir," Yountz said. "Unless it's a transport. I suppose they could be hauling Marines to support what's been going on down on the planet."

"I can't imagine they expected to need much ground combat capability." Tamaguchi's tone was desert dry. "The one thing there *doesn't* seem to be any of dirtside is local opposition to Szponder's coup. No, it's a freighter. I think you're probably right that it's along to provide logistical support . . . and I'll bet you most of that support is ammunition. Cruisers and destroyers can't have huge magazines. Not for weapons the size any sort of multiple-drive missile has to be." He snorted. "That's probably the reason they're building such big damned ships and calling them 'heavy cruisers'!"

"Makes sense, Sir," Yountz agreed.

"Well, it looks like this Tremaine's been able to crank his compensator a bit higher, but even at this rate—" he twitched his head in Shreeyash's direction "—he's not going to catch us. So I'm wondering if he's decided to kill two birds with one stone."

Yountz raised a respectfully inquiring eyebrow, and Tamaguchi turned his back to the plot and clasped his hands behind him.

"Dropping the freighter obviously helps Sierra One's acceleration curve, but not enough to catch us unless we let him. And the fact that it's decelerating so hard—and that he's sending so many combat units with it—seems . . . odd. I suppose it *could* have been to allow Sierra One's *other* warships to increase their acceleration. Correct me if I'm wrong," he smiled thinly, "but doesn't *Jayne's* say their *Culverins* entered service before the turn of the century? That makes some of them at least twenty-two T-years old, and it's always possible they haven't been refitted with these newer, more efficient compensators of theirs. I think it's unlikely *all* of them wouldn't have been, though. The tactical advantages are glaringly obvious, and they'd be even greater for such light units. So it may be *possible* that's why he detached them, but I don't think it is."

"I agree it wouldn't make much sense, Sir," Yountz agreed. "But if that's not why he did it, what *is* he up to?"

"At least one nasty possibility suggests itself to

me, especially since he *hasn't* cranked his own accel more. I mean, if a freighter can pull five-point-seven, a warship eighty percent less massive could sure as hell pull more than that with the same safety margin! But suppose he doesn't have any intention of actually *trying* to catch us with Sierra One and that his freighter's loaded with those god-awful system-defense missile pods they used on Crandall? It'd make sense to send some of them along to help secure the system once Szponder hands it over to them. And suppose he's sent Sierra Two back across the hyper limit so it can micro-jump across the system to the *farther* hyper limit? Eighteen minutes would be enough for our freighter friend to translate into hyper, use the local grav wave to kill its velocity, and make the jump ahead of us. The astrogation might be tricky, but it's doable. And suppose Tremaine intends for that freighter to run ahead of us and deploy a hundred or so of those same missile pods while Sierra One stays close enough on our tail to discourage us from breaking back to avoid them? Somehow I doubt even their military support ships have the fire control to do anything with pods like that, but what if the reason he's splitting his warships. sending along the cruisers and destroyers, is to provide that fire control?"

"That's an ugly thought, Sir," Yountz observed after a moment.

"Indeed. But our Manty may've outsmarted himself, too. He's clearly reacting to the fact that he can't overhaul us before we cross the limit, despite his higher acceleration rates. But he's also—as you just observed, Lorne—sending forty-five percent of his warships off to ambush us six hundred million kilometers from where we are right now. And, if that freighter *is* his ammunition ship, he's also just sent away a bunch of additional pods he might have deployed against us in the inner system."

Yountz was nodding, and Tamaguchi pursed his lips. Then he shrugged.

"He's split his forces, and we've got Flight Two Cataphracts. His birds may still be faster than ours, but we've got just as much range as he does. In fact, we may have *more*; no one's reported any ballistic segments in any of their missile flight profiles, so it's possible they don't have that capability. And along with the freighter's 'escorts,' he's sending away forty-five percent of his *missile defense*."

The admiral smiled coldly at his chief of staff.

"We don't know how big an edge their missiles actually have, but it's not as big as they probably think it is, especially against the Flight Twos. So if they're confident enough—*arrogant* enough—to let us engage half their force in detail, they're giving us the best chance anyone's had yet to collect hard reads on how good their hardware really is. And if they *aren't* confident enough to let us into range, that will tell us a lot about how good they *think* their birds are."

"Looks like they bought it, Sir," Harkness observed, and Tremaine nodded.

Forty-one minutes had passed since his task group had gone in pursuit of the Solarians, and HMS *Charles Ward*, the light cruiser *Feng Meng*, and all four of Commander Jemima Toulouse's *Culverin*-class destroyers had reversed course five minutes earlier.

At ninety percent of military power, *Charles Ward*'s

compensator and impeller nodes could have managed six hundred and thirty-five gravities with no cargo pods riding the racks to slow her, but she hadn't revealed that fact to the Sollies. *Alistair McKeon*, Lieutenant Commander Jansen Slagle's light cruiser *Rama*, and Commodore Priscilla Tanager's four *Rolands*, on the other hand, had increased to eighty-three percent of *McKeon's* maximum . . . which Tremaine devoutly hoped the Sollies would conclude was the best he could do—or was *willing* to do, at any rate—now that he'd detached the auxiliary which had been "slowing" them. At that rate, the range from *McKeon* to Tamaguchi's squadron had increased by 58,644,475 kilometers, but the Sollies' velocity advantage had fallen from the 26,448 KPS it had been immediately following the start of his pursuit to only 21,297 KPS.

And Tamaguchi had just reversed acceleration. Not only that, he'd increased it considerably—to ninety percent of a *Nevada's* maximum military power—which seemed a pretty clear declaration of his resolve to seek battle. He was decelerating back towards Tremaine at four hundred and thirty-nine gravities now, for a closing acceleration of over 10.2 KPS^2. Assuming they maintained current headings and accelerations, they'd overfly one another in just over two hours at a closing velocity of 61,668 KPS.

Now, what I ought *to do, thinking conventionally and assuming I wanted to be smart about this, would be to turn Ginger back around. But the whole object is to convince Tamaguchi I'm* not *smart.* Tremaine smiled mirthlessly. *Now if he just doesn't figure out the* real *reason our accel's been so low . . .*

❖　　❖　　❖

Winslet Tamaguchi sat in his command chair, gazing at the master plot and the bands of overlaid color which showed engagement ranges. At the moment, his ships were enormously far outside the Manties' estimated range envelope, but the crimson sphere representing that envelope expanded steadily as the velocity differential between BatCruRon 720 and Sierra One shrank. Paring his compensators' safety margins so low represented a substantial risk, but if he was going to do this, he wanted the highest closing velocity Tremaine would allow.

The latest estimates from ONI gave the Manties' missiles a sprint acceleration of 92,000 gravities and a sustained acceleration of 46,000 gravities. That was for a reported six-minute burn, which was twice the endurance of any SLN missile drive, even the Cataphract's. Assuming those numbers were accurate, the 30,000,000-kilometer range ascribed to them was probably equally accurate. On the other hand, no one had yet seen—*or no one's* reported *seeing, at any rate*, he reminded himself—a Manty missile which accelerated, stopped accelerating, and then *resumed* accelerating. No one had ever managed to build a missile drive that did that, either, and once a missile's drive burned out and it could no longer maneuver, it had virtually no chance of penetrating alert, active defenses. It didn't matter what its velocity might be; what mattered was that it was an easy, non-evading target for counter-missiles and point defense . . . and that *its* target could maneuver at several hundred gravities to generate a miss. So it was at least possible Manticoran missiles used a *single* drive whose endurance had somehow been hugely increased rather than *separate* drives, like the Cataphract. And if that was the case, it meant they weren't capable of integrating a ballistic phase into their attack profiles... and couldn't reach beyond that admittedly impressive 30,000,000-kilometer range and still attack effectively.

The Cataphract, on the other hand, did have two separate drive systems. Indeed, doctrine—as much of it as the SLN had been able to evolve in the time since the Cataphract had become available—specifically called for using ballistic flight to boost its range to match or even exceed that of the RMN. And at any range, it would still have terminal maneuver time on its clock when it got there.

So far so good, he thought. *The problem is that Filareta had that capability at Manticore, and it doesn't seem to've helped him one damned bit.*

Of course, the fragmentary—*very* fragmentary—information and speculation about what had happened to Massimo Filareta suggested the Manties and their friends had ambushed him well inside their own range, presumably because their frigging stealth technology was better than the League's, too. Unlike Filareta, however, Winslet Tamaguchi had entered this system first and seen his enemies arrive after him, which pretty much made stealth technology a non-issue. He'd discovered the hard way that Manty *counter-missiles* had more range than his, as well, which was depressing and had cost every recon drone Levine had sent closer than four or five light-seconds. He'd have preferred to get them in closer, and Levine was still trying. But the important point was that there was no way BatCruRon 720 was going to lose track of warship impeller wedges even at ranges ten times that great, so ambushes were unlikely to become a factor.

But this Tremaine knows I know that. And the Manties didn't just see Cataphracts in action at Manticore; the bastards must've captured a lot of them, too. That being the case, they have t've tested them enough to be aware of their characteristics. So why is he deliberately courting an engagement?

In light of all those unknowns, he needed to get as close as possible. He had no intention of opening fire before Sierra One did. Given how poor accuracy was bound to be at such ranges, he had no missiles to waste, especially with so much of his heavy punch—the next best thing to two thousand Cataphract-Cs—in the pods riding his battlecruisers' hulls. He needed to make their presence felt...and to avoid exposing them to incoming fire as long as possible. In fact, he'd love to keep right on closing all the way down to a range of zero. He was damned sure he'd have every advantage there was in a short-range energy duel, and until the range dropped to seven million kilometers or so, his escorting destroyers' missile tubes were useless. Admittedly, a *War Harvest* had only six of them, but more to the point, if they kept closing all the way in at their current accelerations, he'd overfly Sierra One with so much velocity advantage his surviving units might well escape across the nearer hyper limit.

The odds of that happening were...remote, since a thirty million-kilometer range gave the Manties a *sixty* million-kilometer engagement envelope. Even assuming Sierra One didn't alter acceleration at all, BatCruRon 720 would still need over fifteen minutes to completely cross a sphere that deep. That didn't mean it *couldn't* happen, though, and so far this Tremaine seemed as eager to close the range as Tamaguchi was.

The Manticoran commander could have avoided that by simply using his higher deceleration rate to hold the range open and use his missiles' greater range against him. Instead, Sierra One had *maintained* acceleration... and the freighter and its escorts had continued to race back towards the hyper limit astern of him. The range between BatCruRon 720 and Sierra One had grown to 171,832,356 kilometers, but Tamaguchi's velocity advantage was down to only 16,709 KPS. As he continued to decelerate and Sierra One continued to accelerate, the rate at which the range was opening would steadily decrease. In fact, BatCruRon 720 would still be a half light-hour from the farther hyper limit when they reached a relative zero velocity, assuming both sides maintained their current accelerations. More importantly, even at his current risky acceleration rate, Tamaguchi would be two hundred and sixty-three minutes' *flight time* from the limit at that point... and Sierra One would be only two hundred and *twenty-seven* minutes from it. If Tamaguchi turned back at that point, Sierra One would run him down in barely two hours and ten minutes at its current acceleration, 49,358,000 kilometers short of the hyper limit.

In short, it would be physically impossible for him to avoid action unless *they* chose to avoid *him*.

Which, given their approach so far, seemed... unlikely.

The question Tamaguchi's mind kept picking at was *why* Tremaine was so stubbornly closing. He had to know at least something about the Cataphracts. He couldn't know whether or not Tamaguchi *had* them, but he had to assume it was possible... and that

Tamaguchi had the reach to engage him. Knowing that, why would such light combatants charge headlong into range of eight battlecruisers?

No, he's not just going to rush all the way in, whatever I'd like him to do. So what the hell is he planning?

"He's up to something," he murmured. "This isn't just a young officer being stupid."

"I beg your pardon, Sir?"

Tamaguchi looked up, eyes narrowing as the question intruded into his thoughts, and realized he'd spoken aloud. That was probably not a good sign, he thought dryly.

"I couldn't quite hear you, if you were speaking to me, Sir," Captain Levine half apologized.

"I wasn't. I was talking to myself. But I wasn't getting any answers back, so I suppose additional input would be welcome." Tamaguchi smiled thinly. "I'm just trying to figure out what this Tremaine has in mind."

"Sometimes it's really as simple as it looks, Sir," Vice-Admiral Yountz said, joining the conversation. "I admit it's usually better to assume it isn't, but it could be he really is just charging in without thinking it through."

"That, unfortunately, sounds more like our friends in Battle Fleet than the Manties," Tamaguchi observed acidly. "And from how many of these oversized heavy cruisers we're seeing, the damned things are obviously their conceptual equivalent of our battlecruisers—'ships of force,' with lots of firepower for their size, sent out to find hot spots and *deal* with them. They aren't likely to hand those over to just anybody any more than we would, and the Manties have a lot of

experienced combat commanders to choose from. So
this fellow may be young, he may be wrong, and he
may be making a serious mistake, but one thing he
isn't is stupid. And if he knows anything about the
Cataphracts' range, he also knows he's coming into
our reach. Why would a terrier—even a really *nasty*
terrier—come into reach of a Great Dane?"

"Well, if he doesn't think he's going to be able to
take us with missiles, why not just run the hell away
in the first place?" Yountz asked reasonably.

"A bluff?" Levine didn't sound like he put much
stock in his own suggestion, but he shrugged when his
superiors looked at him. "If he thinks we're terrified
of his missile advantage, maybe he hopes we'll break
and run and leave him the system without a fight."

He had not, Tamaguchi noted, suggested that Tremaine hoped BatCruRon 720 simply wouldn't *stop*
running. Tactful of him.

"He may've hoped that initially, but it must be
pretty clear by now that we aren't going to," Yountz
pointed out, and Levine nodded.

"That's true, Sir. But he's showing a big enough
acceleration advantage that he can still break back
and avoid us. If he did that any time in the next—"
the ops officer glanced at a display "—in the next
thirty-six minutes, he'd never come within thirty million kilometers of us."

Yountz frowned, and Tamaguchi didn't blame him,
because Levine's logic was impeccable. Of course, if
Tremaine *didn't* break off in Levine's time window, the
range would fall to 8.9 light-minutes, still vastly out
of range, but with a closing velocity of 22,502 KPS.
Even if Tremaine suddenly decided engaging was a

bad idea at that point, Sierra One's current acceleration couldn't overcome that differential without letting Tamaguchi close to within 30,000,000 kilometers. On the other hand, Tamaguchi reminded himself, the Manties almost certainly had at least some acceleration in reserve—*he* definitely wouldn't have shown the other side all he had—so it was probable Tremaine could continue to close a *little* longer than that and still avoid action.

And then, of course, there was the *other* side of Levine's logic. If Tremaine didn't break off within the next thirty-six minutes, BatCruRon wouldn't be able to avoid Sierra One, either.

It was an uncomfortable thought, but Tamaguchi had accepted it from the moment he turned back. And whatever anyone else might think, he hadn't reversed course for fear of the career repercussions if he'd "run away" from such a "vastly inferior" force. He knew those would have happened, but he'd cared one hell of a lot less about that than he had about keeping the men and women under his command *alive* ... something Solarian admirals hadn't been managing too well, lately. Nor was he especially interested in securing the Włocławek System—not now that he knew the Manties truly had been involved in its unrest. Getting that confirmation home would be more valuable than adding one more Verge system to Frontier Security's collection, yet even that was secondary, for Winslet Tamaguchi was no accountant, no credit-cruncher fretting over cash flows and budgets. No, he sought a different sort of information.

However much it galled him to admit it, Manticore had earned the right to the infuriating sense of superiority officers like this prick Tremaine radiated. And—even more galling admission—the SLN's confidence in the inevitability of its tactical and technological superiority had betrayed the League into one disaster after another. But Solarians weren't the only ones who could be betrayed into arrogance by overconfidence, and despite what he'd just said to Yountz, Tremaine *was* obviously young. He might really be as good as he thought he was...but he might not be, too.

And information lag cuts both ways, Tamaguchi reminded himself. *He's one hell of a long way from home, and whatever the Manties may've learned from anything they captured from Filareta, Tremaine may not've gotten the word yet. That could explain a lot. If I were him, and if I didn't know what the Cataphract can do, I'd damned well get as close to the edge of my opponent's envelope as I could, too, to maximize my fire control solutions while still staying just out of his reach.*

He smiled thinly at that thought. It was speculative as hell, and he knew it, but to paraphrase an ancient wet-navy admiral of Old Terra, in a space battle, something had to be left to chance. Warships that couldn't—or wouldn't—engage the enemy might as well not exist...and some things were worth taking quite a lot of chances to obtain.

To the best of his knowledge, this was the first head-on engagement in which an SLN force with a significant tonnage advantage could be certain there were no additional ships hidden in ambush, no missile pods deployed in orbit. And as he'd suggested to Yountz, that made it the best opportunity yet for the Solarian League to actually evaluate Manticore's war-fighting technology. To nail down hard sensor reports on their missiles, on their stealth and electronic warfare capabilities . . . and this time get that information home.

It was always possible, Tamaguchi thought grimly, that Captain Tremaine did have the capacity to defeat his much heavier and larger force. He couldn't really bring himself to believe it, not on any sort of an emotional level, but he'd faced the possibility of his battlecruisers' total destruction at least intellectually.

More probably, his squadron was about to be hurt far more badly than he believed it could be, but not so badly as Tremaine thought it *would* be, and that was entirely acceptable—not desirable, but acceptable under the circumstances. He was prepared to lose virtually his entire force to get even a single ship home with the data he sought. So far, the Manties had been given ample opportunity to examine Solarian technology, to evaluate *Solarian* defensive and offensive systems in action. The SLN needed that same look into Manticoran capabilities, and it needed it *now*—quickly—without the delays inherent in any bloodless way of getting it. Without it, it was impossible to formulate any meaningful doctrine or strategy, and whether it wanted to admit it or not, the Navy desperately needed a *new* doctrine and strategy.

Winslet Tamaguchi was no berserker. Nor, whatever certain of his far distant ancestors might have been, was there any kamikaze in his makeup. But he was quite prepared to die facing his star nation's enemies if that could provide the window into its foes' weapons that might ultimately give it victory.

Chapter Seventy-Two

"COMING UP ON POINT FEARLESS, Sir," Lieutenant Dreyfus announced, and Scotty Tremaine nodded.

"Thank you, Elspeth," he said, then looked at the display which connected him to *Alistair McKeon*'s bridge. "Time to turn around, Mary-Lynne, They're deep enough in they can't outrun us to *either* hyper limit now. I just hope," he added piously, "that they realize in the end this is all for their own good."

"Aye, aye, Sir," Mary-Lynne Selleck, his flag captain, acknowledged with a broad smile. "I'm sure they will—realize what nice people we are, I mean . . . eventually," she added, and Tremaine sat back in his command chair with a much thinner smile of his own.

"What do you figure Tamaguchi's going to do now, Sir," Lieutenant Commander Golbatsi asked quietly.

"Well, that's an interesting question," Tremaine replied. "At the moment, I'm pretty sure he's busy trying to figure out what the hell we think *we're* doing. And I'm equally sure he's going to have some uncomplimentary things to say about us when he finds out."

✧　　✧　　✧

"Well, he's no Admiral Giovanni, Sir," Vice-Admiral Yountz observed as he watched the chronometer, and Tamaguchi snorted. Ysidro Giovanni, victor of the Eridani Campaign, was regarded as the best tactician the Solarian League Navy had ever produced. He'd never failed in a single operational assignment, and he'd been almost as good a teacher as he was tactician and strategist. It was little wonder he'd become the SLN's institutional pattern of operational excellence.

It's a pity Battle Fleet's fallen on such sad times since, he reflected, briefly contemplating what Giovanni would have had to say to officers with names like Byng and Crandall. He doubted it would have been pretty, but Yountz had a point about Tremaine.

Sierra One had passed the thirty-six-minute mark three minutes ago, with no sign of breaking off. The range was still increasing—in fact, it was up to 215,365,000 kilometers—but it was going to start decreasing . . . now.

The range readout froze, then began to edge downward, and he smiled to himself as the plot shifted. Sierra One no longer had the acceleration to keep him out of range. Unless, he conscientiously reminded himself it still had a *lot* of accel in reserve. But their closing velocity was up to 24,687 KPS, and—

"Sierra One's reversed acceleration, Sir!" Levine announced.

Tamaguchi kept his face impassive as he watched the numbers on the display change.

The range continued to fall, and at their current accelerations, BatCruRon 720 would still get into range—*closer* range—of Sierra One. But Tremaine's timing certainly seemed to support the notion that

Manticore's missiles were indeed capable of thirty million kilometers. At their present accelerations, closing velocity would be down to only 11,119 KPS when they reached that range. But that would take over another hour, now ... and it would be impossible for Tamaguchi to cross a 60,000,000-kilometer range basket and get out its farther side. They'd still overfly one another, but unless he destroyed Sierra One in passing, any of its survivors could hold him under fire all the rest of the way back across the system.

Nothing you hadn't already counted on, he reminded himself. *And this could give Tremaine the worst of all worlds. You've got to have more magazine capacity than him, it'll take ninety minutes for velocities to equalize, and you'll be within less than a hundred thousand klicks when that happens—if that happens. And if you can get inside four or five* million *kilometers,* eight *battlecruisers should damned well kick the shit out of any six cruisers ever built!*

He told himself that firmly. He even knew it should be true, but he couldn't quite convince himself it *was* true. And the timing—the decision to let him close *at all*, instead of turning and running early enough to prevent that—suggested at least one man was convinced it wasn't.

He only hoped Tremaine was wrong.

❖   ❖   ❖

"Coming up on Point Nike, Sir," Elspeth Dreyfus announced, and Scotty Tremaine straightened in his command chair.

For the last hour and ten minutes, *Alistair McKeon* and her consorts had decelerated steadily as they approached Admiral Tamaguchi's battlecruisers. Their velocity was now up to 7,187 . . . directly *away* from Tamaguchi's flagship. Of course, *Tamaguchi's* velocity was up to 18,305 KPS, giving him an overtake of over 11,000 KPS, but he was also just over 30,000,000 kilometers astern. Given their current accelerations, he'd continue to gain slowly for the next hundred and sixteen minutes and actually overfly Tremaine by about eight million kilometers.

Oh, yes, he reminded himself. *Given "current accelerations." However . . .*

He watched the time readout spin downward, then looked back at the com link to *Alistair McKeon*'s command deck.

"Show him our next surprise, Mary-Lynne," Prescott Tremaine said.

"Aye, aye, Sir," Captain Selleck replied, and turned to her astrogator. "Turn up the wick, Frannie," she said.

❖   ❖   ❖

"—getting good reads from the drones, Sir," Apumbai Peng said, watching the data scroll across his tactical section's displays. "Not as good as I'd like, in a lot of ways." He shook his head. "I know Captain Levine would really love to get in closer, and those damned counter-missiles—not to mention their ability to even *see* our RDs clearly enough to target them at that range—say things I'd rather not hear about their missile defense. But we've still got hard reads on all of them, and their emission signatures are actually clearer than I'd've expected."

"And *their* drones?" Ephron Vangelis asked with just a hint of gentle malice, and Peng grimaced.

"I know they're out there, but trying to localize them isn't a lot harder than bailing out the Pacific

Ocean with a teacup," he admitted. "I don't *think* they're getting inside a light-second or two, but I'd be lying if I said I could guarantee that, Sir." HMS *Triumphant's* tactical officer's grimace turned into something much more like a scowl. "To be honest, that's one reason I'm a little surprised their ships' emissions are as clear as they are. If they can build that kind of stealth into their remote platforms, why aren't their starships stealthier?"

Vangelis nodded. He enjoyed needling the TO just a bit, but that was because Peng was one of the best tactical officers he'd ever had. He was smart, he was determined, and he *wasn't* one of the idiots who persisted in rejecting the "impossible rumors" about Manty capabilities. In fact, he'd actively sought out every "rumor" he could get his hands on and inserted *all* of them into his worst-case analyses.

"Could be as simple as older tech in the ships," Captain Richardson suggested from Command Two, and Vangelis cocked an eyebrow at his XO's com image. "Recon drones are a lot smaller and a lot cheaper than starships, Sir," Richardson pointed out. "Building new generations of remotes is easier than building ships, and platforms are usually a *hell* of a lot less expensive—or time consuming—than upgrading existing ships!"

Vangelis nodded. Every SLN officer knew about the huge numbers of hulls in the Reserve which—in theory—were ready for instant deployment . . . as soon as they were de-mothballed and technology that might be as much as a couple of T-centuries out of date was updated. Which shouldn't take very long at all, should it? After all, how rapidly did naval technology change?

Hadn't the same basic design and combat philosophy applied for over a hundred and fifty T-years? Of course it had! And it was far cheaper to let the Reserve wait until it was needed than to be constantly fussing with incremental upgrades to ships you wouldn't need anytime soon, anyway. Besides, Battle Feet wallers already in commission had outnumbered all existing fleets by a comfortable margin!

Ephron Vangelis had had his doubts about certain of those comforting assumptions even before the Solarian League started figuring out just how much "updating" any ship expected to live in combat with a Manty was likely to need. Now he strongly suspected it would be both faster *and* cheaper to just build from scratch if they wanted effective (and, hopefully, survivable) ships in an era of Manty-driven missile ranges.

Once we figure out how *to build the damned things, that is*, he thought grimly. *Probably not something I need to be bringing up at the moment.*

"The only problem with that, Lance," he said instead, "is that, according to Apumbai's best estimate, these people appear to be from the Manties' most recent classes. Seems to me they'd be likely to have the most recent generations of ECM and EW fitted." He shook his head. "I've got a nasty feeling he's onto something we aren't going to like."

"At least we're running good firing solutions, Sir," Peng said. "Accuracy would really, really suck at this range, but at least our birds would go hunting for them on a first-name basis!"

"That's nice to know," Vangelis said dryly. "Unfortunately, I can't quite rid my mind of the suspicion that if we're getting good targeting info on them, when we can't get our drones any closer than we are, then they must be—"

"Excuse me, Captain."

Vangelis' expression showed his surprise as Peng's assistant tactical officer interrupted him.

"Yes, Janice?" From some SLN captains, the question would have come out sharply, under the circumstances. From Vangelis, it was simply . . . crisp.

"Sir, I'm sorry to interrupt," Commander Rendova said, "but Sierra One's acceleration's just changed, and, well—"

She pressed a button, throwing the new data onto Vangelis' command chair display. The flag captain looked down at it, and his expression tightened.

❖   ❖   ❖

"Admiral, they've gone to an accel of six-point-four-one KPS squared," Captain Levine said quietly, and Tamaguchi's jaw clenched.

Six-point-four-one KPS^2? A ship the size of that cruiser could pull better than *six hundred and fifty gravities* of acceleration?

He remembered his earlier thoughts, when Sierra One had increased to only 5.9 KPS^2. That heavy cruiser back there didn't have a seventeen percent advantage; it had at least a *thirty* percent edge! And he had to assume Tremaine was still maintaining at least some margin. This was clearly a preplanned maneuver, and he could have tweaked his acceleration rate earlier and used a smaller increase, pushed his compensator limit less severely, if he'd wanted to. So the numbers were almost certainly worse even than that!

My God. That implies a zero-margin acceleration that's at least seven hundred gravities, maybe even seven-twenty, if he's gone to a ten percent margin. That's damned near a forty-five *percent advantage!*

"Projections, Astro?" He felt vaguely surprised by how normal his voice sounded.

"Sir, if they can sustain this acceleration," Captain Shreeyash sounded shaken, despite the qualifier, "velocities will merge at two-niner-point-four thousand kilometers in eighty-nine minutes." She looked up at him. "From that point, we'll lose ground at just over two-point-one KPS squared."

"He timed it well," Tamaguchi observed, "but he's still in trouble."

Yountz and Levine looked at him, and he shrugged.

"We always knew this was a possibility," he pointed out much more calmly than he felt. "And we've got the range to reach them from *here*, if we have to, far less from thirty million kilometers. It doesn't really change anything."

From the look in their eyes, they didn't buy that last sentence any more than he did, but neither of them was about to say so.

"We could increase *our* acceleration a little more, Sir," Yountz suggested in a tentative tone.

"No." Tamaguchi shook his head. "I'm worried enough about *Kronprinz Wilhelm*'s and *Poltava*'s compensators at ninety percent. I'm not about to take them any higher than that."

Yountz looked relieved, despite the fact that he'd been the one to raise the possibility. *Eighty* percent was the SLN's standard "never exceed" compensator setting. Tremaine's most recent little surprise only underscored something which had become unhappily apparent T-months ago; no SLN ship could stay with its Manticoran counterpart without radically reducing safety margins. But compensator failure was one of any spacer's worst nightmares, and unless acceleration rates were very, very low, no one survived when it happened. And what made the nightmare even worse was how little warning compensators typically gave before they failed. Which was also why, given the parlous state of his squadron's maintenance history, Tamaguchi had already pushed his luck much farther than anyone could consider even remotely prudent.

"Besides," he said, clasping his hands behind him once again and turning back to the master plot, "it's obvious Captain Tremaine really does intend to engage us. It looks like he's bringing himself right to the edge of his own missile envelope, and I'll admit he's arranged it very neatly. But the whole time he's been arranging that, he's also been arranging to bring his own ships into *our* range." The admiral smiled thinly. "I suspect he wouldn't have . . . unless he's underestimated our capabilities just a bit."

❖　　❖　　❖

"So according to the recon platforms, each of the battlecruisers has a couple of dozen pods tractored to her hull," Adam Golbatsi said.

Tremaine stood at his elbow, looking down at the detailed profile of Tamaguchi's force displayed on Flag Bridge's primary tactical plot. Eighty-seven minutes had passed since they'd increased their deceleration, and the Ghost Rider platforms had spent that time getting ever better reads on the Sollies. By now, two of them had actually gotten in close enough to read the ships' *names*.

"If they're like the ones Filareta had at Manticore,"

Golbatsi continued, "they'll have ten birds each. So, call it nineteen hundred, maybe two thousand."

"And with a ballistic phase, they've got the range to reach us right now," Horace Harkness pointed out from the ops officer's other elbow.

"Yes, and they've had that ever since we started after them," Tremaine replied, his eyes thoughtful. "That's sort of what we're counting on, isn't it, Horace? What they don't have is anything like our targeting capability at extended ranges. And judging from the *Nevadas* we've been able to strip down and examine, they can't control anywhere near as many birds as we can, either."

"And even without Barricade, we've got a lot more missile defense than they do, Horace," Golbatsi added. "Of course, they probably don't think that."

"No, I imagine they don't," Tremaine agreed.

"Point Wayfarer in two minutes, Sir," Dreyfus said, and Tremaine nodded.

"Tell Lieutenant Marsden he can make his presence known, Stilson."

❖   ❖   ❖

"Thirty million klicks in twenty seconds," Captain Shreeyash announced.

"I don't imagine it'll be much longer," Tamaguchi said. He sat in his command chair and the display in front of him was tied into *Triumphant*'s bridge. "Unless it's a lot heavier salvo than these people ought to be able to throw, I don't see any reason to rush our own launch, Captain Vangelis."

"Understood, Sir," Vangelis replied. "Commander Peng's solutions are better than I anticipated at this range, really, but—"

"Status change!" Levine barked, his voice so sharp Tamaguchi's head jerked up, eyes whipping to the display. "Additional bogeys! Three . . . four . . . *eight* of them, Sir!"

"*What?!*"

The sudden announcement snapped even Tamaguchi's *sang-froid*. They'd been watching Sierra One for over three hours! How the *hell* could anything have hidden from them *this* long?!

But the new icons blinked mockingly, burning sharp and clear in the plot's depths, and they were *between* his flagship and Sierra One, almost thirty thousand kilometers closer to BatCruRon 720.

"They aren't starships, Sir," Levine said, hands flying across his panel as he and his assistants tried to sort out the new data. "The impeller signatures're too small."

"They look pretty damned big to *me*," Yountz said, leaning over a sensor tech's shoulder to study the woman's readouts. "Christ, Bradley! The frigging things're showing almost as much power as a *War Harvest*'s wedge!"

"But they aren't *big* enough," Levine shot back. "The drones're getting good specs on them—not what I'd like, but enough to determine the wedge's physical parameters—and they're too small even for a dispatch boat! It's almost . . . almost like some kind of LAC with a destroyer's nodes shoved up its ass."

Levine's language was an indication of his stress, Tamaguchi thought, but as he pulled up the same readouts in a window on his own display, he realized the ops officer had a point.

"Well, whatever they are," he said as levelly as he could, "we hadn't exactly counted on them, had we?"

❖   ❖   ❖

"I sure would like to be a little birdie on Tamaguchi's flag bridge about now, Skipper," Ensign Jethro Sanders said as Her Majesty's Light Attack Craft *Nożownik* brought her wedge to full power.

"No, you wouldn't, Jethro," Lieutenant Benjamin Marsden, *Nożownik*'s commander and Senior Officer in Command of LAC Detachment-FSV-39, replied with a small. cold smile. "In about ten minutes, that flag bridge's going to be the last place *anyone* wants to be. Trust me."

✧   ✧   ✧

"The Old Lady would've loved this one, Sir," Harkness said quietly, standing beside Tremaine's command chair.

"I like to think we wouldn't've embarrassed her, anyway," Tremaine agreed. "'Surprise—'"

"'—is what happens when you didn't recognize something you saw all along,'" Harkness finished for him, then smiled wickedly. "Of course, in this case, it's something they *didn't* see all along."

Tremaine nodded and watched the icons of the eight LACs *Charles Ward* had left behind. At *Alistair McKeon*'s acceleration—a rather sedate one by the standards of a current-generation *Shrike* or *Katana*—a Manticoran LAC could be a very hard target to find. In this case, he'd cheated and made it even harder, however, by tractoring six of them to his starships and completely concealing them inside the larger ships' impeller wedges. But the other two, under Lieutenant Rhonda Mallard, the skipper of HMLAC *Raven*, had relied solely on their EW systems, their low acceleration, and their greater separation from the rest of his ships. It had helped that the Sollies had tried so persistently to get their recon platforms into range of *McKeon* and her consorts, and Tremaine had deliberately avoided any but the most rudimentary emissions control to keep the Sollies looking at *them* rather than hunting for anything else. It appeared to have worked, too; the Sollies had been so fixated on the targets they knew about but couldn't get close to that they hadn't even tried deploying any of their drones to sweep the vast volume of space between *McKeon* and the rapidly departing *CW*.

Which meant they almost certainly hadn't had a *clue* the LACs were there . . . and that they equally almost certainly hadn't noticed the pair of Mark-17 CUMV(L)s *Charles Ward* had dropped off along with her LACs.

The UMVs weren't huge compared to *CW* herself, but the fleet support vessel had loaded four of them on her external racks before leaving Montana, and the Mark 17 variant had been designed to let ammunition colliers provide reloads to multiple SD(P)s simultaneously. Each of the unmanned, automated vehicles had the capacity to stow up to three hundred Mark 23 flatpack missile pods, and they were equipped with high-speed, high-volume cargo handling equipment to transfer them rapidly to the RMN's SD(P)s pod rails. What they were *not* equipped with were weapons of their own, point defense, anything remotely like an impeller drive . . . or the stealth systems capable of hiding an impeller signature even if it had been physically possible to fit nodes into them. They were intended for only relatively short movements under reaction drive or using the small, equally unmanned towing units normally paired with them. Yet even though they hadn't been designed for concealment, their size and lack of emissions made them *very* hard to detect except on active sensors at very short ranges.

The sort of sensors mounted by the recon drones which hadn't come within ten or twelve millions kilometers of them.

Which was why *Raven* and *Parasol*—which were among the stealthiest vessels ever built—had taken the two CW had dropped off under tow and tagged along behind *Alistair McKeon* and her consorts at a much lower acceleration. Combined with their onboard stealth systems, they'd been almost impossible to detect, and they'd coordinated their acceleration with *McKeon*'s. Now the UMVs lay less than eight thousand kilometers ahead of Tremaine's flag ship with the range closing at less than fifty kilometers per second, although that was climbing at 6.41 KPS². More to the point, the first of them had already used its pressors to eject one hundred and forty pods—each of which contained nine Mark 23 D multidrive missiles—into space.

It was unlikely that many would be required, but the other four hundred and sixty were always available if Tremaine needed them.

Not that I'm going to, he thought coldly. *These people are so screwed, even without Barricade. Welcome to Reality 101, Admiral Tamaguchi. Pay attention— there's going to be a quiz later, and you'd better come up with the right answer.*

"Good solutions, Sir," Adam Golbatsi announced.

"Then I suppose we shouldn't keep them waiting. Execute William Tell."

"Executing, Sir!"

❖ ❖ ❖

Tamaguchi's brain skittered like a ground car on ice, trying to grapple with the sudden appearance of those additional impeller wedges. From their formation, they were intended as some sort of screen—or possibly decoys, he thought—between him and Sierra One's starships.

Maybe they aren't really there at all, he thought. *O'Cleary's report from Spindle talked about how good the Manties' decoys and ECM are. Maybe she had a frigging point! If she did, then it could be that—*

"Missile launch!" Levine snapped. "Multiple launches! Estimate a minimum—repeat, *minimum*—of two hundred inbound at four-five-one KPS squared! Time of flight six minutes!"

Two hundred, Tamaguchi heard his own voice repeating in the back of his mind. *They fired two hundred missiles that frigging big from only six ships, the biggest of them less than* half *my flagship's size.*

All sixteen of his ships combined could have put only two hundred and thirty-six into space from their internal tubes, even at normal missile ranges.

Either they had a hell of a lot more pods on their hulls than we *could've fitted onto ships that size, or they must have God's own number of internal tubes. But how* could *they have limpeted very many pods? Those frigging LACs—or whatever—of theirs had to've sucked up a lot of the volume inside their wedges that might've been available for pods. That's the only way they could've hidden them from our RDs!*

It seemed flatly impossible for anyone to cram two hundred missile tubes—or that many pods, for that matter—into less than two million tons of warships. But Tremaine had already demonstrated quite a few "impossibles" this afternoon, he reminded himself grimly. And if they could fire a second or even a third salvo this heavy, the consequences could be ugly.

They could be uglier, *Winslet*, he corrected himself. *"Ugly" you've already got.*

"Return fire," he said out loud, eyes on the crimson icons howling towards his command with ever mounting speed. Then he looked up, meeting Levine's strained gaze levelly. "Fire Plan Zulu. Flush the pods."

❖   ❖   ❖

Scotty Tremaine watched the missile icons race away from his starships. Well, not from his *ships*, precisely. He could have thickened that salvo considerably by using his ships' tubes, but there was no point. He hadn't even called upon the pods limpeted to his ships' hulls . . . and William Tell had used only sixteen percent of the pods already deployed from *Charles Ward*'s UMVs.

Of course, he had other plans for *some* of those other pods.

"Good telemetry, Sir," Golbatsi reported, and Tremaine nodded.

The range was over a light-minute and a half, but the Ghost Rider platforms keeping watch on Tamaguchi's battlecruisers from as little as eighty thousand kilometers gave Golbatsi exquisitely accurate targeting data . . . in real time. He didn't have the FTL *command* links Apollo made possible, but his command loop was only half as long as the Sollies,' and that mattered in a missile engagement. It mattered a lot—especially when the one ship Tremaine most emphatically did *not* want to kill was the enemy flagship—and so did the quality of the defender's electronic warfare systems.

"Enemy launch," Golbatsi announced a moment later. "Multiple launches. Acceleration rate is five-six-one KPS squared. That's about thirty-five KPS better than Filareta's Cataphracts could turn out, Sir."

And, he did not add, twenty percent better than the Mark 23's maximum acceleration. Of course, the Mark 23 could sustain that acceleration a lot longer.

"Assume the same endurance on the nodes," Tremaine said, never looking away from the plot. "Range at burnout?"

"From rest, assuming a three-minute burn and no change in the final stage's acceleration rate or endurance, about niner-point-one million klicks," the ops officer replied. "Call it roughly a hundred thousand KPS terminal velocity. Assume they've got the same final stage, and we're looking at about one-six-point-four million kilometers total powered envelope. How far they can actually reach depends on how big a ballistic phase they insert into the middle of that."

He looked up from his display.

"Figure they're still going to bring up the final stage around ten million kilometers out to give them the best combination of velocity and time on the clock when they actually come in on us and peg time-of-flight at this range at roughly four-point-niner minutes. Given those numbers, I recommend Barricade in—" He punched a macro, glanced down at a readout, and then looked back up at Tremaine. "—one-zero-zero seconds."

"Approved."

"Second launch, Sir," one of Golbatsi's ratings announced, and the ops officer returned his attention to his plot.

"Looks like they're flushing all of the pods from their battlecruisers, Sir," he said in satisfied tones. "They're firing them in a very tight sequence. They probably want to get all of them off before our launch gets there."

"Salvo density?"

"CIC makes it approximately five hundred per flight."

"*Third* launch."

The rating's professional calm seemed to have ... eroded just a bit, Tremaine reflected.

"Well, Horace," he said almost whimsically, looking away from his own plot for a moment, "that should make Barricade even more effective. Of course, if it falls flat on its face, I suppose we'd better hope you're your usual efficient self when it comes to dealing with this."

"We try to please, Skipper," Harkness replied.

He seemed remarkably unfazed by the possibility.

❖ ❖ ❖

Winslet Tamaguchi watched the destruction of his command race towards him in an avalanche of blood-red icons and realized he'd never truly believed—not deep down inside—how deadly Manty missiles had become.

"Implementing defensive measures," Levine announced. "Halo active."

"Very good," Tamaguchi replied, playing his role to the bitter end.

Battlecruiser Squadron 720 turned sharply, pulling the vulnerable throats of its impeller wedges away from that oncoming torrent and opening its broadsides to clear its offensive telemetry links, counter-missile launchers, and tracking systems. Tamaguchi glanced at the maneuvering display as his ships settled on their new courses, but his attention was on the outgoing traces of each side's missiles.

His own missiles' higher acceleration gave them a shorter time to target, despite the minute and a half of ballistic flight in the middle of their profile. He told himself that was a good thing, but ten seconds had passed between the Manties' launch and his own. That meant the total differential would be less than sixty seconds.

✧   ✧   ✧

"Barricade in thirty seconds," Golbatsi announced. Quite unnecessarily, Tremaine reflected, since his own eyes had been on the readout for the last *ten* seconds. He thought about mentioning that, then decided it would only indicate he was nervous over his own brilliant idea.

"Twenty . . . ten . . . five . . . *now*," Golbatsi said, and a second salvo of Mark 23s launched. There were less than half as many of them this time . . . but their acceleration was twice as high.

✧   ✧   ✧

"Second missile launch! Estimate seventy-two inbound!"

Tamaguchi pressed his lips firmly together. He'd flushed all his own birds in four waves, sequenced so tightly they were *almost* a single extended salvo. Normal doctrine would have called for spacing them out more, giving more time for his tactical sections to update the follow-on waves' targeting profiles as the lead waves's telemetry produced more data. But hopefully his tight sequencing would bring them in closely enough to overload his enemies' point defense to at least some extent. An equally important consideration, however, had been the need to get them off before the Manties started killing the vulnerable, deployed pods...and there'd been no point holding any back for targeted follow-on salvos. Not only did BatCruRon 720 face a "use them or lose them" situation, but it was impossible to individually target missiles at such an enormous range. They'd be totally reliant on their internal seekers—trying to give any kind of precise updates or direction would actually be counterproductive, with a ninety-second-plus transmission lag—and so he'd been forced to accept what amounted to blind fire. Hopefully, with that many laserheads, at least some would find targets despite whatever the Manties' EW could do to confuse them.

He'd hoped Tremaine had done the same thing—that the massive salvo already streaking towards him had represented all the pods available to Sierra One—but it appeared he'd been wrong. Either that, or Manty warships mounted about twenty more tubes per ton—tubes big enough to launch missiles with *that* kind of performance—than any Solarian ship did!

"Well," he said to Yountz, never taking his attention from the tactical display, "at least it would appear they didn't have a *lot* more birds in reser—"

"Third launch!"

Tamaguchi's eyes snapped to the ops officer, and Levine looked up at him.

"Sir, it's another seventy-two-bird launch and both of them are pulling ninety-two thousand gravs acceleration."

He sounded puzzled, and well he should, Tamaguchi reflected. Why fire multiple, smaller salvos rather than clump them into another single, massive pulse, like Sierra

One's *first* salvo, to swamp BatCruRon 720's defenses? And at that acceleration they couldn't possibly have the range to reach Tamaguchi's ships, anyway...could they?

For just a moment, the possibility that they truly could terrified Winslet Tamaguchi, but then he drew a deep breath and shook off his sudden, almost superstitious dread.

No, of course they couldn't! If their impellers had *that* kind of endurance, the *first* wave would've been fired at far higher acceleration! But in that case...?

It seems like a stupid move, he thought, turning back to the tactical display. His first-wave missiles' second stages would activate in less than twenty seconds now, and he felt himself tightening internally. Yet his brain continued to worry at it. *Yes, it* seems *like a stupid move, but Tremaine hasn't done anything* else *stupid all afternoon! So why should he launch in a pattern that—*

He jerked upright in his command chair as he found out why.

❖   ❖   ❖

One hundred fifty seconds and 10,149,210 kilometers after launch, the Mark 23 Ds of Scotty Tremaine's "Barricade launch" adjusted their courses with finicky precision. One might have wondered why they were altering trajectory when they were still well over eighteen million kilometers—and three and a half minutes' flight time, even at that acceleration—short of their targets. But that would have been because their targets weren't what one might have expected.

They spread out, taking station on one another in response to Adam Golbatsi's commands. Those commands were thirty-four seconds old by the time the missiles received them, but it didn't really matter. Their targets had been obligingly stacked in a (relatively) small volume of space, they couldn't change course, and the Ghost Rider platforms midway between *Alistair McKeon* and BatCruRon 720 had plotted their vectors very, very carefully at the moment their first stage impellers burned out.

Those Mark 23s knew *exactly* where to find their prey.

The seventy-two missiles of Tremaine's "Barricade" drove directly through the heart of Tamaguchi's first five hundred-missile salvo. Although a Mark 23's impeller wedge was bigger than any standard missile's, it remained considerably smaller than the outsized wedges counter-missiles used to sweep incoming fire out of existence.

Against non-evading targets unprotected by any wedges of their own, however, it worked just fine.

❖   ❖   ❖

"Those *bastards!*" Apumbai Peng blurted.

Captain Vangelis looked up from his com link to Flag Deck at his tactical officer's totally uncharacteristic outburst. He started to demand an explanation, but Peng had twisted around to face him before he got his mouth fully open.

"Sir," he told Tamaguchi's flag captain, his voice tight and strained, "I don't know how many of them they got, but they just killed a *lot* of our initial launch."

"What?" Vangelis frowned. Maximum counter-missile range was no more than three million kilometers—four million, tops—and their birds were still more than *eleven* million from Sierra One!

"We'll know how *many* they got in another—" Peng flicked a glance at a time display "—eleven seconds, but I already know they got a lot."

"What you talking about?" Vangelis demanded.

"They took advantage of the ballistic phase," Peng said, his own eyes back on the tactical plot. "They must've used recon platforms to get solid reads on them when the first stages shut down, and—"

He broke off as the plot was suddenly dotted with icons which hadn't been there the moment before. At such extended ranges, active sensors were useless, and passive sensors were limited to light-speed. But impeller signatures produced a ripple along hyper-space's alpha wall that was effectively *faster* than light, and that plot should have been liberally dusted with small, powerful impeller signatures as BatCruRon 720's first launch activated its second-stage drives.

It wasn't. Instead of hundreds, there were simply scores of them.

"They knew where they were, Sir," Peng said bitterly. "And we used a standard dispersal pattern."

The ops officer's mouth twisted in disgust, directed at himself, not anyone else, and Vangelis' jaw tightened. SOP for the SLN—and every other Navy, for that matter—had always kept shipkillers in close proximity, relatively speaking, in order to minimize the communication problems. The available window for any ship's broadside com arrays was sharply constricted by the roof and floor of its wedge, which extended for dozens of kilometers on either side of even the smallest warship. That meant keeping missiles in a small enough volume—the smallest wedge fratricide allowed, really—while their mother ships monitored their telemetry and updated their attack instructions. If they strayed much wider than that, they moved out of the launching ship's transmission window.

Attack missiles would normally be preprogrammed

to spread wider as they approached their final attack runs, but even that degree of dispersal was often limited. Maximum tactical effectiveness required them to be brought in on their target as close to simultaneously as possible and to bring their lasers to bear through the narrow aperture of that target's sidewalls, and the extent to which they could be spread and then maneuvered into position to accomplish those two ends depended entirely on how much time was left on their drives for the final attack run. Indeed, in some instances, where particularly heavy counter-missile fire was anticipated, doctrine actually called for bringing them in "in trail," stacking them one behind the next, in lines two or even three deep on exactly the same trajectory, like beads on a string. That deliberately sacrificed the lead missiles and accepted a shorter time window for the following missiles' onboard sensors to directly acquire the target, but it also used the leaders' impeller wedges to take out the counter-missiles which might otherwise have reached the trailers.

And *of course* BatCruRon 720 had seen no reason to disperse their shipkillers during their ballistic phase, because no one could possibly have targeted them at that range, so—

"Their second stages are programmed to light off at least six million klicks short of CM range," the ops officer went on bitterly, completing Vangelis' thoughts for him, "so there'd be plenty of time for them to disperse during their final attack runs. Only we forgot how frigging long the Manties' burn times are . . . and no one's *ever* used attack missiles as CMs. *We* couldn't have done it even with their birds; there wouldn't've been enough time to track, launch, and guide. But they must really have FTL capability with enough bandwidth for *tactical* control, or at least communication. Their frigging RDs tracked our birds *and* had the transmission speed to send their tracking data back in a tight enough window for them to feed it to *their* birds and launch. And it never even occurred to us that anyone might be able to do that. So we handed them a nice, tight target, and they just cut the crap right out of it with their *shipkillers'* wedges!"

Vangelis felt the blood draining out of his face, and the tac officer shook his head slowly, wearily, like a very old man.

"It wasn't very efficient," he said. "From a cost effectiveness perspective, taking them out this way instead of using standard CMs must've cost at least a hundred times as much for each kill, not to mention using up a slew of missiles they *won't* have to use as shipkillers now. But it damned well *worked*, and the cost per kill's going to come down, because they're about to do the same thing to all our *other* launches. The computers say they only lost two of their own birds—must've been to direct collisions, since there wasn't any wedge fratricide, although I'd hate to try to figure the odds of *kinetic* intercepts in that kind of volume—and they're already reorienting. In fact, they've already passed through our second launch, and they're bearing down on number three."

"And there's a second and third wave coming behind this one," Vangelis said grimly as his brain grappled with what had just happened.

"Yes, Sir. They waited to be sure we wouldn't have time to send any new commands to our birds before they interpenetrated. It means they got less of the first wave, but we can't tell any of the others to evade before they've driven all three of their follow-on launches right through them. And if I were them, I'd have more of those frigging FTL platforms sitting out there tracking the survivors from each of our follow on waves so they can tweak the trajectories on *their* follow on waves."

"Shit," Captain Ephron Vangelis, Solarian League Navy, said very quietly and precisely.

❖　　❖　　❖

"Fire Plan Bravo," Scotty Tremaine said.

"Fire Plan Bravo, aye, Sir," Lieutenant Commander Golbatsi acknowledged.

"Wish we had Apollo, Sir," Sir Horace Harkness remarked, never looking away from his own displays, as TG 10.2.9's first Barricade launch slashed through the oncoming Cataphracts. "Be nice to be able to steer them into even better intercepts."

"Don't be greedy," Tremaine admonished. "What we've got is more than enough to piss the Sollies off."

"Yes, Sir. Guess it is."

❖　　❖　　❖

At least now I know why Tremaine's been so god-damned willing to let me close the range . . . some, Tamaguchi thought bitterly.

The Manties' crystal-clear impeller and emission signatures had just become abruptly far less clear. They didn't *disappear*—no EW in the galaxy could have managed that—but they were suddenly far, far weaker. And even as he watched enormously powerful— *impossibly* powerful—decoys came to life, duplicating the full-powered gravitic and electronic signatures of the warships which had deployed them. They might have been less effective against missiles which were still under shipboard control, but Tamaguchi's missiles weren't. They *couldn't* be, at that range, and without that control their internal seekers were all too likely to lock up the strongest signature they could see ... whether it was actually a warship or not.

Only ninety-one of his first-wave missiles had survived the Manties' long-range interception. And, somehow, he suspected that less than a hundred blind-fired missiles were going to be severely overmatched by their defenses.

Tamaguchi's surviving shipkillers streaked towards TG 10.2.9 at an acceleration of 98,000 KPS² and a closing velocity that was already above 102,000 KPS. By the time they reached their targets, it would be well over 170,000 KPS ... assuming they reached them.

Given their velocity and acceleration, the effective launch range for the RMN's Mark 31 counter-missile was in excess of six million kilometers. The first wave of CMs launched thirty-four seconds after the surviving Cataphracts' second-stage impellers activated. The second launched ten seconds after that. The third launched ten seconds after that ... and then, with four hundred and thirty-two Mark 31s headed down range in final acquisition, Tremaine's entire force—aside from the LACs—rolled ship.

Between them, his cruisers and destroyers mounted a total of one hundred and four counter-missile launchers backed up by a hundred and forty-eight laser clusters. That was far more defense than Tamaguchi had allowed for. His own ships mounted only sixty-nine percent more tubes—and fifty-four percent *fewer* laser clusters—on seven times TG 10.2.9's tonnage. With Ginger Lewis' detached LACs, Tremaine actually had only eight fewer launchers and better than three and a half times as many laser clusters.

Of course, he's got seven times the tonnage to absorb damage, *too,* Tremaine reflected. *And if these are like the missiles Filareta had, they've got capital ship laserheads. We can't take many hits from something that heavy.*

Fortunately, they wouldn't have to.

❖   ❖   ❖

Tamaguchi's face was carved from stone as the preposterous—*the* equally *preposterous*, a little voice said in the back of his brain—waves of counter-missiles lashed out from the Manticoran ships.

They have to be firing the things from both broadsides, he thought. *That's* another *thing we can't do. Dubroskaya's survivors said they could launch offbore, but I didn't really believe it. They must have an incredible redundancy in control links, though. Of course, that would make sense, given the kinds of missiles they and the Havenites must've been throwing back and forth out in their isolated little corner of the galaxy.* He snorted in harsh self-reproach that was far more bitter than anything Commander Peng could possibly have felt. *I suppose that's another logical implication I should've taken into consideration.*

❖   ❖   ❖

BatCruRon 720's Cataphracts encountered TG 10.2.9's Lorelei platforms.

Tremaine didn't have many of them. They were a very new system, and they'd been produced in only limited numbers before the Yawata Strike destroyed the Star Empire's military industrial base. Fortunately, Beowulf's industry had proved fully capable of building them, once Manticore provided the specs, and the supply ships which had reached Montana in company with the *Charles Ward* had delivered a few hundred of them. More were in the pipeline behind them, though, and Admiral Culbertson had dipped deep into his initial supply to send seventy-five with each of his task groups on the theory that he'd soon be receiving replacements from home.

Adam Golbatsi had deployed only twelve of them, but the fusion-powered platforms were many times as capable as any previous independently powered decoy. Their power plants also let him deploy them substantially farther from TG 10.2.9's starships than he could have with tethered decoys, dependent upon their mother-ships for the energy needed to successfully imitate a starship's impeller wedge. In fact, Loreleis were capable of independent maneuvers, which let them counterfeit starships even more effectively.

And the Cataphracts' onboard sensors were nowhere near as sophisticated as those of a Mark 23 D.

Thirty-three of the seventy-one survivors of Barricade's ambush fell to Lorelei's seduction. They swung wide, arcing away from *Alistair McKeon* and her consorts.

The first-wave counter-missile launch killed fifteen of the fifty-eight which resisted the decoys' blandishments. The second wave of Mark 31s killed eighteen more. Nine actually made it through all three waves of counter-missiles, but the forward laser clusters of the LACs deployed in the antimissile role ahead of TG 10.2.9's starships nailed eight of them.

The single survivor streaked past, racing to within less than ten thousand kilometers of HMS *Alistair McKeon* . . . and wasted all ten of its powerful X-ray lasers on the roof of the impeller wedge no laser could possibly penetrate.

❖   ❖   ❖

Winslet Tamaguchi felt every muscle in his body tighten as the last of his initial launch vanished. That single missile might—*might*—have actually inflicted damage, but the Manty cruiser's impeller wedge never even flickered.

Only forty-three of his second wave had survived Barricade. There were fourteen in the third...and twenty-one in the fourth. That was it: a total of only one hundred and sixty-nine—less than *nine percent*—had lasted even to reach the Manties' counter-missile perimeter. Somehow he doubted the remaining thread-bare triple handful of shipkillers were going to be any more successful than the first wave had been.

And now two hundred *Manticoran* missiles came hurtling in into *his* defensive envelope.

Counter-missiles streamed to meet them, and he leaned forward in his command chair, pressing against the shock frame as if he could somehow *will* those CMs into greater effectiveness.

❖   ❖   ❖

"Penetration ECM coming up...now," Sir Horace Harkness said.

❖   ❖   ❖

Thirty-six of TG 10.2.9's missiles carried only pen-etration aids, not laserheads, and BatCruRon 720's electronic defenses shuddered as the Dazzlers came to life. They blasted huge, blinding gaps in the intri-cate sensor coverage upon which missile defense absolutely relied, and behind them, taking advantage of the confusion they'd generated, the Dragon's Teeth activated. The number of threat sources ballooned impossibly, more than doubling, then doubling *again*, and missile-defense computers and counter-missiles' onboard sensors, already hammered by the Dazzlers, found themselves hopelessly overloaded.

Counter-missiles killed nine of Scotty Tremaine's attack missiles. Point defense killed ten more. One hundred and forty-five survived . . . and every single one of them drove in on SLNS *Lorraine*.

TG 10.2.9 lacked the Keyhole Two platforms which would have let Adam Golbatsi monitor and update his Mark 23 Ds in real time at that range. But each pod had included one Mark 23 *E*, the most capable and sophisticated forward fire control platform yet built. Each 23 Echo took in the feed from the sensors of every 23 Delta in its pod, then added the shared take of every other Echo in the salvo, and the Solarian decoy platforms were useless against them. In fact, they were *worse* than useless. The Halo system and the manuals detailing the doctrine behind it had been analyzed to a fare-thee-well by the Royal Manticoran Navy and fed into the Echoes' AIs. Instead of mis-leading the attackers, the platforms actually helped define the volume in which their targets must lie! The Echoes took note of that, added it to the rest of their commands, crunched the numbers, and updated their detailed, pre-launch targeting orders.

Golbatsi might not be able to talk to his birds in the final seconds of their lives, but even without that, their accuracy at that enormous distance was better than the SLN could have managed at twenty percent of that range.

One thousand three hundred and five X-ray lasers, each almost twice as powerful as the SLN's Trebuchet capital missile could generate, lashed out at a single battlecruiser. Despite the Mark 23 Es, over a third of those lasers wasted themselves on the roof or floor of *Lorraine*'s impeller wedge.

The rest of them didn't.

Almost eight hundred lasers designed to disembowel not just superdreadnoughts, but *Manticoran* superdreadnoughts, blasted into a mere battlecruiser. *Lorraine* massed barely ten percent of an *Invictus*, and there was literally no comparison between the two ships' armor, their cofferdamming, their framing and their sheer depth of hull. The thickness of a superdreadnought's external armor was measured in meters, and its core hull was at least five times as well protected as a battlecruiser's against any damage that actually penetrated that incredible outer shell. Lasers capable of gouging their way through an *Invictus*' armored sides blasted entirely through *Lorraine*'s hull and then out again—not just through her hull and armor, but through both sets of sidewalls, as well.

One of them struck her almost head on. It ripped a perpendicular path down two thirds of her hull's total length, and her after fusion plant lost containment, but it didn't really matter. All the fireball accomplished was to vaporize a third or so of the broken fragments into which she—and her entire crew—had already been shattered.

Winslet Tamaguchi stared at the plot in horror. The visual display showed the spreading cloud of wreckage which had once been SLNS *Lorraine*, and he wondered—numbly—why Tremaine had targeted only a single ship. That massive degree of overkill made it abundantly clear that his single salvo could have completely destroyed BatCruRon 720. And the shipkillers he'd expended eliminating Tamaguchi's own attack missiles proved he could have fired even more of them at the Solarian ships. So why...?

On the plot, the last survivor of his final wave of pod-launched Cataphracts died 1.3 million kilometers short of Sierra One.

And then there were none, he thought numbly. *And if nineteen hundred missiles with Trebuchet laserheads didn't even leave a scuff mark, what in* hell *do I expect my* internal *tubes to accomplish?*

"Sir." Phanindra Broadmoor's voice was shaken, his face ashen. "Sir, I have a com request. It's apparently originating from a platform at about two hundred thousand kilometers."

Tamaguchi inhaled deeply.

"Put it through," he told his com officer.

"Yes, Sir."

Tamaguchi's display blinked from tactical to com mode, and the Manticoran commander looked out of it at him once more.

"I don't like killing people, Admiral Tamaguchi." Tremaine's voice was flat, his expression grim. "That's why I targeted only one of your ships. Be advised, however, that I have sufficient missiles to do that again several times, although I think you must realize I wouldn't *have* to do it 'several times' to destroy your entire force.

"I don't want to do that, so I'm giving you an opportunity to save your people's lives. You have ten minutes to strike your wedges and surrender. At the end of that time, I will open fire once more. If I do, I doubt there will be many survivors.

"The decision is yours, Admiral."

Chapter Seventy-Three

TOMASZ SZPONDER LOOKED UP as the door to his Wydawnictwo Zielone Wzgórza office opened. He could have relocated to far more prestigious quarters—quarters more "appropriate" to the man who was the effective head of state for an entire star system—after his coup, or counter-coup, or whatever the hell it had been. In fact, Szymon Ziomkowski had almost begged him to use the old pre-*Agitacja* prime minister's residence, but he'd refused all suggestions that he move into it. He'd stayed in the townhouse in which he'd always lived, and he'd worked out of the office from which he'd always worked.

And there was a reason he'd come back to that office from the com center where he'd thrown his last, futile defiance at Hieronim Mazur.

As the hours dragged by with the Solarian commander not deigning to contact *anyone* on the planet, the reality—the final awareness—of what was going to happen had driven in on him. They weren't even going to try to reach any sort of peaceful resolution, he'd realized, and this office was where the Krucjata Wolności Myśli had been born. When the time came, when the intervention battalions closed in, this was where it—and its creator—would die.

But if he'd managed not to move to another address, he hadn't been able to avoid at least *some* concessions to the post-coup realities. Tomek Nowak and Jarosław Kotarski had been just as insistent as Ziomkowski when it came to beefing up his personal security. After all, the vast majority of the *oligarchowie* were still right here on Włocławek, and they still had plenty of money. Some of them were certain to invest some of that money in the assassination of the man who proposed to bring down their privileged kingdom. Not just for the vengeance of it, either—although that would've been more than sufficient for most of them. No, they would have seen his death as a serious blow to his supporters.

Justyna Pokriefke was sitting in one of her own prison cells, and "Mała Justyna's" Biuro Bezpieczeństwa i Prawdy had been summarily disbanded. Her authority had been handed over to Teofil Strenk, whose regular police had spent an enjoyable several days rounding up and disarming every one of the her black jackets. It hadn't been entirely bloodless, either, although the casualties had been distinctly one-sided. He couldn't quite shake the conviction that some of Strenk's policemen hadn't tried very hard to take the *czarne kurtki* alive, either. He hadn't much cared for that, but, realistically, he'd known at least some of it was inevitable.

The one branch of the BBP which hadn't been disbanded—and which the police fully respected—was the Departament Ochrony Przewodniczącego, and Ziomkowski had insisted that the organization responsible for his own security should take over Szponder's protection, as well.

Rather to Szponder's surprise, Grzegorz Zieliński had volunteered to head the team assigned to him. In fact, he'd insisted upon taking the assignment. After the way the DOP agent had been duped at the *Dzień Przewodniczącego* celebration, he'd anticipated that Zieliński would be none too fond of one Tomasz Szponder. Apparently he'd been wrong.

Now Zieliński and Kotarski came bursting through his office door, and he frowned as their expressions registered. Zieliński looked tense, although the aura of anxiety which had grown steadily deeper as he realized something had gone seriously wrong with Szponder's original plans was far less in evidence. But Kotarski—*Kotarski* looked almost . . . jubilant.

"Something's happening, Tomasz!" the older man said even before he was completely through the door.

"What?" Szponder knew he sounded less than excited, even despondent despite his friend's expression, but it was the best he could do.

"We don't know," Kotarski replied. "But we just got confirmation from Astro Control's ground stations that Mazur's yacht and at least four other hyper-capable ships have left *Piłsudski*."

"To rendezvous with the Sollies, no doubt," Szponder said heavily.

"No." Kotarski shook his head sharply. "They wouldn't need hyper-capable ships for *that*, Tomasz. Besides, it looks like they're headed for the hyper limit as fast as they can go!"

"What?" There was more life in the one-word question this time, but not a lot, and Szponder frowned. "That doesn't make any sense! They've won. We're only kicking and scratching on the way to the gallows."

"Maybe not, Sir," Zieliński said. "If things were going according to plan for the *łowcy trufli*, the Sollies would already be in orbit. And if that was the case, then why would Mazur—or anybody else, for that matter—be headed out of the system?" The security agent shook his head sharply. "No, something's gone wrong for them. It's the only explanation."

Kotarski nodded sharply in agreement, and Szponder looked back and forth between the two of them.

"I know we all want to believe the best, or at least not accept the *worst*," his voice was almost gentle, "but what *could* have 'gone wrong' for them? The Sollies are *here*, they just haven't bothered to land any troops yet. I should never have trusted the damned Manties."

"Don't you *dare* say that!" Zieliński snapped, his expression suddenly so angry Szponder blinked in surprise. "You're the only man in this entire star system who remembered what the Ruch Odnowy Narodowej was supposed to be about—the one who *did* something about it! Nobody can ever take that away from you, or from *us*, so don't *you* try to do that."

"I'm sorry, Grzegorz," Szponder said after a moment, standing and reaching out to lay one hand on the bodyguard's forearm. "I don't want to take anything away from anyone, but to use Tomek's colorful phrase, I'm afraid we're all screwed. I just . . . I don't want you clutching at straws, because if you do, it'll hurt even more when it turns out that straws were all they were."

"No," Kotarski disagreed quickly. "No, Grzegorz's

right. If something *hadn't* gone wrong, they'd at least be in orbit trying to scare us into caving in." He grimaced in obvious frustration. "Damn! I *wish* we had control of at least some of the deep-space infrastructure! Even the near-planet sensor net might be able to tell us *something* about what's going on up there if Mazur and his *zdradzieckie szumowiny* hadn't locked us out of it!"

"I'm sure we'll find out entirely too soon," Szponder said grimly. "In fact, it's probably just a matter of—"

His door didn't "open" this time; it *burst* wide, slamming back against the wall so hard the framed old-fashioned landscape painting of the "green hills" from which Wydawnictwo Zielone Wzgórza officially took its name, fell with a crash, and he whipped around to face it as Tomek Nowak erupted into his office.

"What the—?!" he started, but Nowak cut him off.

"Here, *Szefie!*" He thrust a hand in Szponder's direction, waving a handheld com while an enormous smile lit up his face. "It's for you! Trust me, you'll want to take this one!"

Szponder regarded him with the wariness with which one ought to regard an obvious lunatic, but he reached out and accepted the com gingerly. He stood holding it, and Nowak waved both hands wildly, urging him to look down at it.

He obeyed the gesture and frowned as a man he'd never seen before—a youngish man, with sandy hair and blue eyes—looked out of the tiny display.

"Yes?" he said cautiously.

"Mr. Szponder?" the stranger replied, and his stomach tightened as he heard the off-worlder accent.

"Yes," he repeated, his voice harsher.

"I understand you're the man I'm supposed to be talking to," the off-worlder said. "I think there's been a bit of a misunderstanding."

"What sort of 'misunderstanding'?" Szponder asked, wondering if he was the only person in the entire Włocławek System who hadn't gone mad in the last hour or so.

"Well, I'm afraid Admiral Tamaguchi's plans have hit a tiny setback. I apologize for not contacting you sooner. Unfortunately, I hadn't realized there was anyone in-system *to* contact. That's where the misunderstanding comes in."

He paused, and Szponder frowned. None of this made any sense!

"The thing is, Mr. Szponder," the stranger told him, "you haven't actually been talking to the Star Empire of Manticore at all." Szponder's confusion was now complete, but the young man in the uniform—the *black-and-gold* uniform, he noted now—went on. "I suppose what I actually should've said is that you haven't actually talked to the Star Empire *yet*, Sir. As it happens, however, my name's Tremaine—Captain Prescott Tremaine—and I believe you and I have quite a *lot* to talk about going forward."

❖   ❖   ❖

The men and women around the briefing room table rose as Lester Tourville stepped through the hatch, followed by Captain Molly Delaney, his chief of staff, and Berjouhi Lafontaine. He crossed to the head of the table and took the chair awaiting him, then looked around the compartment.

"Be seated, ladies and gentlemen," he said crisply. They obeyed him—except Lieutenant Lafontaine, who parked herself at his shoulder, hands clasped behind her in the position of parade rest. From his slight smile and tiny, almost resigned headshake he knew exactly where she was. But then his smile faded and he leaned forward, planting his forearms on the tabletop.

"I'm sure all of you are aware of the arrival this morning of Admiral Gold Peak's dispatch boat from Meyers," he said, and the corner of his mustache quivered in something that was more grimace than smile. "I sometimes think that when flag officers go to hell, they'll have to wait in purgatory for the dispatch boat with their movement orders to catch up with them."

A chuckle ran around the table, and he sat back in his chair and extracted a cigar from his breast pocket. His eyes gleamed as he slowly and ceremoniously unwrapped it, and Lurks in Branches took one look, hopped off his shoulder, and crossed to the bulkhead-mounted treecat perch located as far away from his chair as was physically possible. The air return directly above Tourville began to hum a little more loudly, and the fragrant smoke wisped almost straight up when he lit it.

Almost.

"Now," he continued, once he had it drawing properly, "about Admiral Gold Peak's dispatches."

His expression sobered.

"I have to say I'm impressed. In fact, I'm looking forward to meeting the Countess even more eagerly now, because it would appear everything I've ever heard about her is accurate. At the time I left Manticore, no one realized she was contemplating a direct attack on the Madras Sector. As a result, no one could have realized how well that attack was going to go. According to her dispatches, however, she's taken or destroyed every Solarian naval unit in the sector and installed a new government—or, rather, strengthened an *existing* system government that has actual popular support—in Meyers itself which she believes has the potential to become a genuine, independent sector-wide government. Whether or not she's right about that, the reinforcements Admiral Culbertson forwarded to her"—he nodded courteously in Culbertson's direction—"materially increased her ability to accomplish all of that."

He paused to blow a smoke ring which rapidly ascended to the air intake.

"In the meantime," he continued, "she's also been informed of the much greater troop strength the Quadrant Guard is forwarding to Montana. She doesn't have the most recent hard numbers we've received, but she's aware the troops are on their way and should be arriving here shortly.

"And with that information in hand," he drew deeply on his cigar, blew another smoke ring, and regarded them all levelly, "she's decided to move directly on Mesa."

For just a moment, it didn't seem to register. Then, as one, the assembled squadron and division commanders straightened in their chairs.

"She's taken that decision on her own authority," Tourville continued. "I realize she's your Empress' first cousin, but even given that proximity to the Throne, I'm deeply impressed by her willingness to make that decision on her own. And, for the official record, I also support it one hundred percent. It's obvious there's an infection out here—and probably in a lot of other places in the galaxy *coming* from here—and I think it's time we lanced its source once and for all. Very, very . . . thoroughly."

A soft sound of agreement ran around the conference table, and he nodded as he heard it.

"Her dispatches include our movement orders," he told them. "We're to wait for the Quadrant Guard to arrive. As soon as it does, we will depart Montana, leaving light forces here to safeguard the system, and move with every other unit to SCY-146-H." He smiled tightly. "I had to look it up in the catalog. It's a red dwarf, with no planets, a perfect place for a rendezvous point. It's also a perfect spot for exercises while the units of an invasion fleet shake down together . . . and less than six light-years from the Mesa System.

"She'll be waiting when we arrive."

"And good evening to *you*, Admiral Tourville. We've been waiting for you."

—Admiral Michelle Henke,
Countess Gold Peak,
CO, Tenth Fleet,
Royal Manticoran Navy

Chapter Seventy-Four

JULES CHARTERIS TOUCHED THE authorization code on his uni-link to pay the air taxi, then watched it lift away from the Saracen Tower traffic platform. He'd considered holding it, but Lisa's bosses at Kepagane & Bellini had laid on luxury limos for all of their personnel who'd be attending today's conference as a sort of apology for keeping them sequestered on McClintock Island for so long.

And they damned well should, *too*, he thought more than a little grumpily as he headed for the grav shaft. *It's ridiculous! Over* two months *"incommunicado" is just outrageous. I know they pay well, and I know that whatever she does for them's at least as important to the Alignment as anything* I *do, but she* does *have a life . . . and so do I!*

At least they'd relaxed the total ban on outside contact that was usually part of the full-immersion study groups they convened once a year or so, usually before one of the big conferences like today's. But even that had been tightly limited. He'd been able to talk to her only once a day, although they'd let them have up to thirty minutes at a time on the com when he did, and he'd been a little worried after some of those conversations.

She'd said she was fine, but she *always* said that. In fact, she'd said it right after she finished falling down the stairs at their second daughter's third birthday party. She'd broken her arm in three places, as Jules recalled, but she'd said she was fine. Yes siree, nothing wrong with *her!* "Go back to the party, honey. I'll be back in a few minutes."

Right, he remembered with a fond snort. *She was back, all right . . . just as soon as the EMTs finished setting the arm and scheduling her first quick-heal appointment!*

At least this time didn't rise to that level, but something was twanging his "something's not right" button. Maybe it was fatigue, maybe she was having a personality clash with one of the other researchers, or maybe it was something else entirely—maybe even his imagination! But he couldn't quite shake the feeling that she was . . . out of sorts, somehow.

Well, if she is, at least she gets to go home this afternoon. He smiled, thinking about the catered candlelit dinner he'd arranged to welcome her home. And the rather more . . . personal welcome he had in mind for her *after* dinner. *I may be pissed off that she's been gone so long, but it's not* all *bad. I know my Lisa. In her case, absence really does make the heart—and certain other body parts—grow fonder!*

He chuckled, restored to a cheerful sense of anticipation, as he stepped into the lift car and punched his destination.

❖   ❖   ❖

"All right! Way to go, *Jamie!"*

Allison Renfrew surged to her feet, waving her orange-and-black striped scarf as her fifteen-year-old son drove past the final defender and punched a sizzling kick straight into the goal with his off foot. More orange and black waved furiously all around her in the bleachers on the home field side of the Dobzhansky Soccer Complex as the students and parents from Matthew Stanley Meselson Academy celebrated the go-ahead goal. It was early in the second half—still plenty of time for the Transformers, MSM's hated rivals from Oswald Avery Prep, to score—but MSM had an outstanding goalie. She'd given up only seven goals so far all season, and three of those had been on penalty kicks!

Allison settled back into her seat, and reached for her uni-link. She punched in her husband's combination and grinned as his face appeared on the wrist unit's small display.

"Jamie just put one in!" she crowed. "It was *beautiful*, Stevie! Just beautiful. I wish you could've been here to see it!"

Colonel Stephen Renfrew of the Mesan Planetary Peaceforce smiled at her from the display.

"Great, honey! Left foot or right?"

"Left!" Her grin grew even broader. "From the look of things, Avery Prep's spies never had a clue he'd been working on that, either."

"That's our boy!" Colonel Renfrew chuckled. "I wish I could've seen it, too."

"I know."

Allison's jubilance faded just a bit as she thought about *why* her husband hadn't seen it. There were many things an officer's spouse had to accept about his or her partner's career, and in Allison's opinion the worst of them were the frequent absences. At least Stephen was in the Peaceforce, not one of the other security agencies, so his absences tended to be . . . less irregular than some. They could usually plan around training exercises, for example. But not this time. Not with those Ballroom lunatics *killing* people right and left! There hadn't been another *major* attack in several weeks, but there'd been dozens of small, seemingly random bomb explosions and assassinations—enough to kill and maim three or four hundred people every week.

That might not be that huge a number out of an entire star system's population. In fact, it was a *tiny* number; one of the newsies trying to reassure people that the government had the situation in hand had pointed out that almost four hundred people died in perfectly ordinary accidents in a city Mendel's size every single week. And Mendel, he'd pointed out, was scarcely the only city on the planet. The largest, perhaps, but it represented less than five percent of the total system population. For the system as a whole, accidents killed almost seven hundred *thousand* every week!

Allison was prepared to accept his numbers, but these people weren't dying in "accidents"—they were being *murdered.* That was more than enough to make anyone nervous, and the Peaceforce had been at a much higher than usual readiness state in case it was needed to back up the Office of Public Safety and the Mesan Internal Security Directorate. Allison didn't much care for the Misties, but this time she was willing to admit that even Internal Security's normal tactics seemed justified. Green Pines had been bad enough, but as stunning and terrifying as it had been, it had also been a one-time event, something so totally outside the normal Mesan experience that it had seemed almost like an earthquake or a forest fire. A *natural* disaster, not something someone had done *deliberately*.

What had happened since, and the horrific, gloating "communiqués" from those Ballroom butchers describing their murders in loving detail and promising still more, was something else entirely. Everybody seemed to know someone who'd been killed, and it was little wonder that the cheers for today's game seemed even louder, more frenetic, than usual. A lot of worried parents were finding the same relief—momentary, perhaps, but genuine—that Allison was.

And Stephen was stuck in a command post somewhere as the duty watch officer. There were times, she thought, when the world didn't exactly run over it with fairness.

"Well," she said with only slightly forced cheerfulness, "it's not like this is the end of the season, sweetheart. Hopefully things will settle down enough for you to make at least some of the games. And whatever else happens, you *know* we're going to be facing Avery in the playoffs. They always make it, just like we do, so—"

Her transmission cut off abruptly, and Colonel Renfrew frowned as the link went dead. He punched the callback function.

"Hi, this is Allison!" a cheerful voice said in his earbug. "I'm sorry I'm occupied right now, but leave a message. I'll get back to you as soon as I can. Thanks!"

His frown deepened, and he began to key a diagnostic into his uni-link. But then he was interrupted.

"Sir," a voice said, and his eyebrows shot upright. That voice belonged to Captain Angela Klauser, his battalion intelligence officer, but he'd never heard it sound quite like that.

"What is it, Angie?" he asked quickly, forgetting the interrupted call as he turned towards the captain with a sudden surge of concern for her. "What's wrong?"

"Sir," Klauser said, and an icicle seemed to run down the back of Renfrew's neck as the harrowed, riven sound of her voice—and the stunned sympathy in the captain's glistening green eyes—registered. "Sir, there's . . . there's been another incident."

"Ma'am, you'd better see this," Colonel Byrum Bartel said, stepping unceremoniously into Lieutenant General Gillian Drescher's office.

Drescher looked up from the contingency plans on her display. The last month or two had been an absolute nightmare. As a general rule, Drescher enjoyed her position as the senior field officer of the Mesan Planetary Peaceforce. The job was interesting and professionally challenging, although the MPP had never fought a war in its entire existence. And unlike certain other people—Internal Security and Public Safety came to mind—*her* people didn't get involved in the kind of routine head breaking involved in keeping the planet's slave and seccy populations in their places. Drescher didn't approve of the Misties or the Safeties, for a lot of reasons. She didn't care for thugs who wore uniforms, because she wore a uniform every day of her life herself, and she had strong opinions on how people who wore them were supposed to behave. She didn't care for organizations whose default setting was brutality. For that matter, she didn't much care for the institution of genetic slavery itself, if only because of all the headaches involved in keeping a servile population under control.

Headaches which, as recent experience demonstrated, could turn into something much worse upon occasion. It was obvious to her and to Bartel, her chief of staff, that something from outside had . . . destabilized the normal planetary equations. She didn't really buy the theory being put about by François McGillicuddy, the system Director of Security, and Bentley Howell, his fair-haired boy at Internal Security, that it was the Manties. Oh, it clearly was the *Ballroom*, and God knew the Manticorans had close associations with the Anti-Slavery League. And while the Star Kingdom had never condoned the Ballroom's excesses, everyone knew it had more tolerance for them than most other star nations would admit. But she couldn't convince herself that people as smart as the Manties would have anything to do with a *nuclear* terrorist event when they were already looking down the barrel of a pulser at a war with the Solarian League. She was pretty sure Manty politicians were at least smart enough to pour piss out of a boot.

But whatever lunatic faction of the Ballroom was behind this—and she was entirely willing to accept that the terrorists behind it truly believed Mesa had been complicit in the attempt to genocide the entire ex-slave population of Torch—the problem was no more than a light-year or two beyond the capabilities of someone like Howell or his "colleague" Selig, over at Public Safety. Well, maybe three light-years, in Howell's case; Selig *knew* she was basically a blunt instrument, whereas Howell had genuine illusions of competence. Sooner or later, Drescher's people were going to be called in to pull the Safeties or Misties' asses out of the fire, and she had to admit the MPP's planning for that contingency had been less thorough than she'd believed it was before she'd had to start thinking about actually implementing it. That was why she'd been working such long hours lately, and under normal circumstances, she would have welcomed an interruption of her thousandth—or was it the *two* thousandth?—perusal of the plan currently gracing her display.

From Bartel's voice and expression, however . . .

"What is it?" she asked.

"Ma'am, we just had a mid-air detonation—looks like maybe seven or eight kilotons."

"Damn," Drescher said, much more mildly than she felt. "Where?"

"That's the really bad part, Ma'am," the colonel said grimly. "It was over Dobzhansky. Not centered on the city, thank God, but Eval's preliminary estimate is at least ten thousand casualties."

"Dobzhansky?" Drescher heard someone repeat with her voice, and wondered if her own face had just turned as ashen as the colonel's when Bartel nodded.

Dobzhansky wasn't that big a city, but it was—or had been—a pleasant place to live. There was no seccy district in Dobzhansky; its population consisted entirely of full citizens. And it also produced, per capita, more members of Mesa's police, security forces, and military than any other town or city on the entire planet.

Drescher stared at her chief of staff for four or five

seconds—an eternity for someone as quick thinking and decisive as she normally was—then shook herself.

"Get on the horn," she said. "First, I need General Alpina. While I'm talking to him, you issue an Alpha One Alert to all units. Then get the entire staff in here and up to speed, because we're about to have a hell of a mess on our hands. The one thing I'll absolutely guarantee you is that Selig and Howell are going to fuck up by the numbers when McGillicuddy orders them to move in on the seccies. And you know that's what exactly he's going to do."

Bartel nodded, his expression as bleak as her own.

"After that," she continued, "I'll need a conference link with all our regimental commanders. McGillicuddy will probably send in the Safeties first, but the Misties will be right behind them, and when Howell screws the pooch—and we both know *that's* going to happen, too—everyone will be screaming for *us* to back them up. So while I'm talking to the regimental COs, I need you to be liaising with—"

❖   ❖   ❖

Jules Charteris turned the last corner in the wide, pleasantly lit corridor and stepped through the open doors into the Kornberg Auditorium on Saracen Tower's fortieth floor. He was running a little behind his original schedule—he'd planned on getting here a good twenty minutes earlier—but the keynote speaker was just beginning his address. He'd wanted to meet Lisa when she arrived, but she must have beaten him by a good five or ten minutes, and he keyed his uni-link to ping her link for its location in the vast audience. There had to be the better part of fifteen hundred people present and she hadn't been able to text him her seating assignment, so it would probably take him a little while to reach her, wherever she was.

He frowned slightly. That was odd. According to his uni-link's software, she wasn't here yet. But surely—

The 1.5-kiloton tactical weapon in the auditorium utility closet was almost exactly twenty-five meters to Jules Charteris' left when it detonated.

"Always nice when a plan comes together," Janice Marinescu remarked as the air car soared above the Nirenberg Mountains en route to the extraction point.

The blast cloud above the Blue Lagoon Amusement Park on the outskirts of Mendel had been visible, towering upward from just beyond the visual horizon, when they took off from their control center in the resort town of Haldane. If the preliminary calculations on that one proved as accurate as the predictions on most of the other attacks, the twelve-kiloton warhead they'd used on Blue Lagoon had killed another thirteen thousand people. Between that one and the Dobzhansky attack, somewhere close to twenty percent of Mesa's security and military personnel had just been directly impacted by the "Ballroom" terrorist campaign.

And then, six minutes ago, the remote they'd left behind had confirmed the largest single detonation of Final Flourish—the forty-five-kiloton blast which had eliminated any physical evidence of the control center...and utterly destroyed the entire city of Haldane and at least five thousand people. That would be the *actual* body count. Given the anonymity the resort had always guaranteed to visiting celebrities, Houdini had been able to erase another nine hundred of its evacuees' names in the same explosion.

"Should I send the code?" Haas asked.

"Might as well key it in." Marinescu shrugged, her attention on the flight controls. "No point making them all sit around and wait for a ride that's not coming any longer than they have to."

"Right," Haas said, and began punching the authorization code into the air car's secure data terminal.

Marinescu left him to it, although she was tempted to enter the final commit code herself. It was the sort of thing a responsible craftsperson did, after all. On the other hand, even her appetite for homicide had been momentarily slaked. And she supposed almost anyone ought to feel at least a *little* guilty about the fact that they were about to kill seventeen thousand—give or take a thousand here, or a thousand there—of the onion's inner membership. She'd never been very good at hypocrisy, though, so she wasn't going to pretend that what *she* felt was anything but a sense of satisfaction for a difficult job achieved on time and under budget.

That asshole Chernevsky would probably be peeing himself about now, if he had to push the button, she thought. *God, I know Collin had to pick somebody to put into Bardasano's place, but why the hell did it have to be* him? *The man doesn't have the stomach for it. Probably a damned good thing we got him out of here over a week ago. Wouldn't put it past him to actually try to abort the operation at the last minute!*

She couldn't understand—literally couldn't—how someone could have reached Chernevsky's seniority and been so . . . so . . . *squeamish*. There wasn't time to get everyone out, so another answer needed to be found. It was that simple—a binary solution, for

God sake—so where did he get off looking at her as if she were something stuck to the bottom of his shoe when she explained how she intended to do it? As if there were something *wrong* with her because, unlike him, she understood what needed to be done and had no qualms about doing it. Maybe if she'd been willing to pretend, to display a little of the unhappiness *he* so obviously felt, he wouldn't have felt so holier than thou.

Probably wouldn't have helped, though—not really, she thought. *He'd still be beating his breast over it, the idiot! Necessity's necessity, so suck it up and then put it behind you. Done is done, and you move on to the next job. Why the hell doesn't he* understand *that?*

Well, there might just be some changes after they got things sorted out again in Darius. Right off the top of her head, Marinescu couldn't think of a single other Alignment operative who'd ever managed an assignment on this one's scale so efficiently, and it wasn't written in stone anywhere that Rufino Chernyshev would have Bardasano's old job forever.

"Keyed in," Haas said.

The announcement broke into her reflections, and she quirked a thoughtful eyebrow for a moment, then smiled.

Screw it. This is my *op, and I think I'll enjoy rubbing Chernyshev's nose in it by telling him who actually pushed the button.*

"My bird, I think," she said, and reached past Haas to depress the last key.

A crimson light blinked obediently on the secure terminal as four more kiloton-range blasts eliminated 17,327 members in good standing of the Mesan Alignment.

Another 42,612 innocent bystanders joined them in their moment of incineration, and Janice Marinescu felt a sense of almost sublime completion flow through her.

Then another light flashed on the terminal, and her earbug pinged with an incoming transmission.

"According to the terminal, you've just completed your part of Houdini, Janice," Rufino Chernyshev's voice said in her earbug. "I suppose congratulations are in order, so consider yourself congratulated. The truth is, I've been deeply impressed by the efficiency and... enthusiasm you brought to the assignment. In fact, I've been *so* impressed that I discussed another assignment for you with Collin just before I left."

Marinescu's eyebrows rose in surprise. Chernevsky had recommended her for *promotion*? She'd never seen that one coming!

"Collin fully approved my recommendation, especially in light of your perfectly correct insistence on operational security and tidying up loose ends," the recorded message continued. "So ten seconds after the end of this message, the peewee one-kiloton charge hidden inside this data terminal will detonate. Consider it your severance package. Ten... nine... eight... seven..."

Janice Marinescu was still screaming curses when the warhead detonated.

✦ Chapter Seventy-Five

"PRETTY AMAZING, ISN'T IT?" Zachariah McBryde asked quietly, standing behind Gail Weiss on the balcony. She was a tall woman, but he was still taller, and he shook his head as he gazed out over the city's lights across her shoulder. "I always figured there had to be some kind of . . . I don't know . . . an arsenal world, I guess, like Haven's Bolthole, out there somewhere, but I never imagined this."

"I knew about it, in a general sense," Gail replied. She stood with both hands on the balcony railing, looking out across the city of Leonard, named for the very first Detweiler to ever set foot on the planet Mesa. "I had to, given the work I do. But I didn't know anything really specific, like its location." She snorted harshly. "For that matter, we *still* don't know its location, do we?"

"No, we don't," Zachariah agreed. "Probably just as well, though, don't you think?"

"I do if the alternative is to fall afoul of a 'security issue,' anyway."

Gail's tone was bitter, and Zachariah reached out quickly to lay one hand on her shoulder. She turned her head and looked up at him, and he shook his own head, quickly but ever so slightly. Her mouth tightened but then she drew a deep breath and nodded.

"I know," she said, reaching up to touch the hand on her shoulder lightly. "Security's important. I understand that. If I didn't before, I damned well do now, and given my specialization, I suppose I've always had to put up with more of it than most, even inside the onion. But while I'm sure Security has every square centimeter of Leonard wired for sound, I'm not going to pretend I enjoyed the trip out here. Or that I think it was all necessary." She looked around the balcony, her gaze challenging, as if seeking the surveillance devices they both knew had to be there somewhere. "Anybody who's read my dossier would know I was pretending if I did, and I've always figured that trying to slink around in the shadows and hide the way you truly feel is the best way to make people wonder what you're really up to."

Zachariah's stomach muscles tightened, but after a moment, he realized she was right. Security had complete and detailed files on both of them, and he never doubted that the psych analysis programs based on those files would notice the instant either of them began displaying "aberrant behavior." In fact, they'd probably pick up on it even faster here in Darius than they would have back home in Mesa. There were fewer people to provide background clutter . . . and everyone on the entire planet of Darius Gamma was part of the Alignment.

That was still taking some getting used to. He and Gail had been on-planet for less than two weeks, and after hiding any hint of his association with the Alignment—and especially with the inner onion—from almost everyone around him, he was surrounded by a system population of almost four billion people, every one of whom was a proud Alignment member. In many ways, it was an incredibly reassuring experience, especially after their harrowing journey to get here. To be able to talk to people openly about the Alignment, about the aspirations of the Detweiler Plan, was heady stuff. And the sense of personal security—of being *safe*—was almost overpowering.

In fact, it *would* have been overpowering . . . if not for that same harrowing journey. Of the five members of their initial party, only he and Gail had arrived alive. He didn't know exactly how Lisa Charteris had died—whether she'd been executed by her Gaul keeper before he blew up the *Luigi Pirandello* in the Balcescu System to prevent its capture by the Royal Torch Navy or if she'd been killed in the actual explosion—but he knew exactly how Stefka Juarez had died aboard the *Prince Sundjata* in the same star system. And he also knew that he and Gail would have died with her . . . if the two of them hadn't killed *their* keeper first.

He was positive Caroline Bogunov, *Prince Sundjata*'s captain, hadn't believed very much of their story about how Anthony Zhilov ended up bleeding all over the deck in her officers' lounge, but he and Gail had been the only witnesses, and they'd stuck doggedly to their story. Juarez had panicked when they saw *Prince Sundjata* blow up on the visual display and attacked Zhilov, and Zhilov—possibly because of the damage Juarez's totally unexpected attack had done to his eye—had lost control of himself. He'd killed Juarez in what was arguably self-defense, but then he'd turned his weapon on Gail and Zachariah, as well. They'd managed to knock the gun out of his hand and, in the ensuing struggle, Zachariah had reached it first and killed *Zhilov* in self-defense.

Whatever Bogunov may have thought, their account matched the blood patterns and the bodies' wounds, and she worked for the Jessyk Combine and Manpower. She'd never heard of the Alignment, but she knew all about not asking awkward questions and her orders about delivering her passengers to the next stage of their journey had been explicit. Unfortunate things could happen to Manpower minions who failed to carry out their orders, and it had been obvious to her—questions or no—that whoever her passengers truly were, she did *not* want to get involved with their superiors. So she'd decided to accept their story at face value...and kept them confined in a single cabin until she could be rid of them.

As it happened, their version of events was pretty much true. Juarez *had* panicked, and Zachariah *had* killed Zhilov in self-defense. And, in some ways, that might have been the best thing that could have happened. Nobody who knew anything about Gauls could find it difficult to believe Zhilov would have reacted exactly that way. If their Alignment superiors were surprised by anything, it was that Gail and Zachariah had managed to overcome him and survive. The fact that they had actually seemed to have improved their standing in Security's eyes. And so had the fact that they'd dutifully continued the trip as planned. That had taken quite a lot of ingenuity on their part, since Zhilov was no longer available to guide them to their contacts at the next stage, and their willingness to risk finding those contacts rather than taking the easy way out and simply trying to disappear had demonstrated loyalty and reliability to go with the ingenuity only to be expected from a pair of alpha-liners.

So if Gail wanted to bitch about the way they'd almost been killed, she'd earned the right. And her argument in favor of being open about it had a great deal to recommend it.

Best to continue the way we started, as Mom used to say, he reflected with a pang of loss which had already become familiar. *And it's not as if it's all bad. I'd never have met Gail without Houdini, and that's damned well worth* almost *being killed. Of course, it's the "almost" bit that's important there.*

He snorted in amusement, and she cocked her head, eyes narrowing in speculation. It was sort of scary, really, the way she'd already learned to read him like a book. He supposed the intensity of the moment which had brought them together might have something to do with that, but most of it was simply that she was possibly the smartest person he'd ever met . . . except for a deplorable taste in men, with himself as Exhibit A.

"Just thinking about everything we went through to get here," he said.

"And that's *funny*?" She shook her head. "You're a very strange man, Zachariah McBryde!"

"Oh, that's not what's funny." He shook his head. "I was thinking about the fact that you somehow managed to avoid being killed only to get stuck with me. Some people—like my sisters, for example—would probably question whether or not that was the best possible outcome."

"Well, I think it's worked out just fine...so far, at least," she said, leaning back against him. He tucked his arms around her and rested his chin on the crown of her head, savoring the sweet, solid strength of her. "Of course, it's still early," she continued thoughtfully. "I usually give my men a six-month tryout, you understand." A chuckle quivered through her. "I'm sorry to say that so far none of them have...stood up to the strain for the entire six months."

"That's why I'm taking vitamin shots and spending extra time in the gym," he told her earnestly. "Trying to build up my endurance, I mean."

"Oh, there are *much* better ways to build up endurance," she purred. "In fact, why don't we work on some of those better ways?"

"Sounds like a wonderful idea to me," he told her, lifting his chin far enough to kiss the top of her head. "On the other hand, there is that little matter of starvation. I believe you told me you were faint with hunger when we placed the order. I wouldn't want to have any unfair advantages in the endurance department because of your low blood sugar."

"Low *blood sugar*, is it?" She squirmed away from him and turned to punch him lightly in the belly. "You are *so* going to pay for that one, Zachariah Thomas McBryde! But not"—she continued loftily—"until after I've eaten. Not because I *need* the sustenance, you understand, but as a way to emphasize my prioritization queue and make it clear which is more important to me. A meal or your pitiful attempts to meet my exacting standards in men."

"Oh, that was a good one!" Zachariah congratulated her with a laugh. "It may have been just a little...

I don't know...wordy, maybe, for a truly first-rate zinger, but it was good. Very good!"

She stuck out her tongue at him and sashayed—veritably *sashayed*—off the balcony and into their sumptuous apartment. He watched her as she rolled her hips, winked at him over one shoulder, and headed for the bedroom suite to change into her version of "something more comfortable." He was rather looking forward to finding out what fitted that label for her tonight.

He turned back to the vista of Leonard, marveling again at the stupendous residential towers, the broad avenues and green belts, the blaze of lights running up and down the flanks of buildings, the colorful lights of the pleasure boats on the lake at the heart of the city. Unlike a great many capital cities in a great many star systems, Leonard had been carefully planned from the outset and built with every advantage of a counter-gravity civilization. There were no older sections built out of native materials, no slums, no tenements. It was a brand-new city in every way—its oldest building was considerably less than a T-century old—but its population already exceeded ten million, and unlike Mesa, there were no seccies...and no slaves in that population.

That was probably the most remarkable thing about the entire Darius System, Zachariah reflected. As he'd told Gail, he'd always realized that something like Darius Gamma had to exist, if only to build the warships towards which so much of their research had been directed. They obviously couldn't build them in Mesa! The last thing they'd needed was for any trace of the Mesan Alignment Navy to intrude into sight before the time came to actually use it. But somehow he'd pictured a grim, gray, teeming hive of industry, with genetic slaves laboring under the harsh eyes of their overseers. A place where everything was geared towards wringing the maximum output out of every worker's every waking hour. Where the human element in the labor force was only one more component to be managed with ruthless efficiency.

What he'd found was a world whose every citizen subscribed enthusiastically to the realization of the Detweiler Plan. More than three quarters of those citizens—well over eighty percent of them, in fact—were clones, produced and decanted with all the expertise Manpower Incorporated had developed over the centuries. The proportion was beginning to drop as the first generations aged and old-fashioned natural childbirths expanded, yet for decades to come, vat-grown, cloned children would continue to hugely outnumber those born naturally. Under Mesan law—which wasn't the same as Dariusan law, to be fair—those clones were the property of whoever had produced them. In that sense, they were genetic slaves at birth just as much as anyone Manpower had ever packaged and sold. But once *these* "slaves" had been decanted, they'd been raised by a human surrogate parents. They'd been educated and nurtured, not brutalized—treated as valued human beings, not so many animate pieces of property. They'd been *encouraged* to think for themselves, to *value* themselves.

Families on Darius Gamma tended to be . . . large. The average family had at least a dozen children at any given moment, and with prolong and modern medicine in the mix, a planetary population grew at an awesome rate when that was the case. And every single one of those people was at least a gamma-liner. Over half were betas and at least fifteen percent were alphas. Huge sections of their genetic code would have been identical to that of any Manpower slave, but that was largely because Manpower was the laboratory in which many of the star line genomes had been evolved.

Of course, there were a few small holes in the average Dariusan's education. They knew about genetic slavery, for example, but they regarded it as a grim, dark and perverted legacy of the way in which the galaxy at large had demonized Leonard Detweiler and his fellow visionaries. They were taught that Leonard would have rejected the terrible cancer which had grown within the society of Mesa as its members gave up the struggle and accepted—*embraced*—the outlaw status the rest of the galaxy had forced upon them, and that the Alignment had arisen in large part as a reaction *against* that institution. The Alignment's great mission was to reclaim Leonard's original, glorious vision. To be its defender, its champion—its standard bearer. That vision must be carried to triumph, and if the benighted parochialism of the rest of the galaxy rejected the brightness of its promise, then the people of Darius were prepared for whatever struggle might be required.

Zachariah could literally *feel* the driving purpose, the enthusiasm and commitment which infused the billions of human beings in the Darius System. He only had to look up, past the sky glow of Leonard, to see the huge space stations gleaming in Darius Gamma orbit. And beyond them, he knew, were the asteroid refineries, the smelters, the fabrication centers churning out more and more infrastructure, more and more of the sinews of war. Much of that construction program was in the throes of modification, courtesy of the Star Empire of Manticore's recently revealed capabilities, but the people of Darius were committed to the construction of Juggernaut, and for the part of Zachariah McBryde which had always been committed to the Alignment, that was an intoxicating brew.

But at least part of it's an enormous lie. The thought went through his brain like a bittersweet strain of music. *They don't know the truth about Manpower, about the way the Alignment's used it for so long. What happens if they ever ask themselves why something like the Alignment, with the resources to colonize Darius—to build all this infrastructure in the first place—was never able to root out genetic slavery on its own homeworld? What happens, once they're allowed out of Darius—when they* storm *out of Darius, manning the Alignment's warships? Do they go right on accepting what they've been taught? Or do they start to ask questions? The kinds of questions* Jack *may have asked himself.*

He inhaled deeply as he allowed himself to think that at last. Before his own experiences with Zhilov, the Gauls, and Janice Marinescu, his position deep inside the onion and his work's importance to the Alignment had buffered him against the realities Marinescu represented. He'd been *aware* of those realities, but that awareness had been an intellectual thing, not something built out of personal experience and raw emotion. He'd always known that Jack's experiences as part of the onion's security force had been very different from his own in that respect, yet until the trip from Mesa to Darius, he'd never been able to truly understand *how* different they must have been.

And now, having seen what the Gauls were like, having traveled through the same pipeline as genetic slaves and seen the brutal dehumanization to which they were subjected every day while the Alignment *used* the institution—having traveled aboard actual slave ships like *Prince Sundjata* and seen the provision to dump living, breathing men, women, and children into space like so much refuse simply to avoid being caught with them onboard—he understood exactly what could have driven a man like his brother—a *good* man—to turn against the cause to which he'd dedicated his life.

That wasn't a thought Zachariah McBryde was prepared to share with anyone, not even—or perhaps *especially* not even—Gail. It was a thought he didn't much want to face himself. A thought which a cowardly part of him hoped would die a natural death as he submerged himself more fully in the vibrant, glorious promise being built here in Darius. Yet as he looked out across that gorgeous vista, smelled the flowering native trees of the green belts, watched the Dariusan equivalent of night birds and bats circling the towers, he felt that thought, there at the heart of him, and he knew it wouldn't be that easy.

"Well, we're here," Rufino Chernyshev sighed as he settled into the chair behind his new desk.

Lucinde Myllyniemi had followed him to the office. Now she perched on the corner of that desk, legs crossed, looking out through the immense wall of crystoplast at the towers of Leonard, gilded in shining gold by the early morning sun. Chernyshev had pulled some strings—he admitted it; rank had its privileges, after all—to be sure Lucinde was evacuated in the same flight he was. He wouldn't have put it past that murderous bitch Marinescu to add Lucinde to the "culled" list... especially if she'd figured out how close Chernyshev and she were. The two of them had spent a great deal of time together during the voyage from Mesa, and she'd settled comfortably into her new role as one of his executive assistants. It wasn't like they were going to need her to manage Vitorino Stangeland any longer, and she was far too good to waste on most field assignments. And if it just so happened that he had a personal reason or two to keep her close to home and away from nasty things like blackjacks, pulser darts, or knives in dark alleys, that was his business.

"The trip wasn't really as long as I'd expected," she said now, and he shrugged.

"One of the advantages of traveling first class with the streak drive." He snorted. "And we came straight here from Mesa, for that matter. Believe me, it would have seemed a *lot* longer if we'd been stuck on one of the slave ships all the way out to the collection points!"

"A point," she agreed.

Unlike Chernyshev, she'd been alerted fairly late for Houdini, and he'd managed to avoid discussing the most... unpleasant aspects of Marinescu's plans with her. The same intelligence and capability that made her so valuable meant that she'd almost certainly figured out what a lot of those unpleasant aspects had been, but at least he'd kept her out of direct contact with the sociopathic bitch and her associates. And during the voyage to Darius, he'd discussed the mechanics of actually moving that many people with her in some detail. Even if she might have been a security risk under other circumstances, she'd hardly been one under the circumstances which applied, after all!

"I wouldn't have liked to take the long route," she went on now, hopping off his desk and crossing to the crystoplast wall. "Traveling aboard a slave ship at all would be bad enough, but being stuck there for *weeks*?" She shook her head.

"Not much choice." Chernyshev climbed out of his chair and crossed to stand beside her. "They're freighters, not passenger liners or dispatch boats, and none of their captains and astrogators have any idea where Darius is. We had to get them all off Mesa and filter them out to the collection points where they could be put aboard actual transports—the kind with individual cabins—for the final leg to Darius. If we'd had more time, we could have arranged something . . . less arduous, but we had to start them moving as quickly as possible."

"Especially the potential problem children," she murmured, and he nodded.

"Especially the potential problem children," he agreed, then shrugged. "By the time you and I left, we were making better progress, but we were lucky to have one of the VIP 'yachts' available when we needed it. At least we've managed to assemble enough personnel lift to pull out the rest of the Houdini evacuees directly here without any doglegs."

"That's good," she said, and he nodded.

Of course, it's not quite as "good" as you think it

is, Lucinde, he thought. *Yes, we got the ships into Mesa—fast transports, equipped with the streak drive and disguised to look like freighters—and by now, all of their passengers are on board and they're headed for Darius. But I hope you're a long time learning about all of the members of the onion we couldn't get on board.*

He stood beside her, gazing out into the golden morning of Leonard and felt the semipermanent lump of ice somewhere under his heart. He'd never wanted an office job, and he especially hadn't wanted this one, but he had it. And he'd by God *do* it. But he didn't have to like it.

It's not your fault, he told himself again. *In fact, it isn't anybody's fault. It's simply the way it worked out. There was no way to move enough additional ships through Mesa—or to smuggle that many "dead people" aboard them—in the time we had. Another couple of months—hell, one more month!—and that might not've been true, but we didn't have another couple of months. And so, as much as you hated her, Marinescu was probably right, damn her black soul to hell.*

Maybe that was true, and maybe he'd shuffled a lot of his own sense of culpability off onto Marinescu, made her the scapegoat for his own blood guilt. In fact, he was perfectly prepared to admit that was exactly what he'd done. But that didn't change his analysis of her fundamental character, and the Alignment was entering a new phase. There'd still be times, lots of them, when they needed people capable of "wet work," but the bare-fanged savagery Marinescu had specialized in under cover of Manpower or the other Solarian transstellars' covert operations was about to become a thing of the past. The Alignment was about to make the transition from a conspiracy into a genuine star nation, whether the rest of the galaxy knew of its existence or not, and the rules were different for star nations. With any luck at all, it would be T-decades at the very least before anyone outside Mesa or the allied star systems of the Renaissance Factor knew a single thing about it, but it was time to begin weaning the Alignment away from the sort of wholesale slaughter Marinescu had orchestrated for Houdini.

That was the argument he'd used with Collin Detweiler, and Collin had bought it. Although Chernyshev suspected—more than suspected—he'd had more than one reason for going along with it.

Ironic, isn't it, Janice? he thought now, gazing out that window at the city Janice Marinescu would never see. *All those arguments you came up with for using Houdini as a "filter" for the undesirables and eliminating people to maintain security . . . Never thought about whether or not someone was ruthless enough to apply them to* you, *did you?*

That was the real reason Collin had gone along with her "severance package." She and Kevin Haas and their Haldane staff were the only people—aside from Chernyshev and Collin himself—who'd known all the details of the revised Houdini schedule. A lot of other operatives had known bits and pieces of it, but most of the men and women involved in its execution had been tightly compartmentalized. A lot of them had been lifted out before Final Flourish. Those who'd remained to execute its final stages hadn't realized that they were among the loose ends that had to be "tidied up," to use Marinescu's favorite phrase. He found it fitting that Marinescu herself had seen to the elimination of virtually all of her Final Flourish operatives. The ones she hadn't shuffled off to the nuclear fireballs of the "evacuation centers" to await the shuttles that would never come would die of a plethora of "natural causes" when their nanotech didn't receive its next reset signal.

She simply hadn't expected to be "tidied up" herself.

Never planted a bomb that gave me a greater sense of satisfaction, Chernyshev admitted in the privacy of his own thoughts, *but I'm not going to lie to myself. Burying what actually happened as deep as possible— even from the rest of the onion, if we can—was just as important.*

It wouldn't stay buried forever, of course. Something on that scale, with so many "serendipitous coincidences" simply couldn't. Eventually, once the Alignment had won, its own scholars and historians would undoubtedly unearth at least some evidence of what had actually happened. But there'd be no *hard* evidence, and most would reject the work of the "paranoid conspiracy theorists" out of hand.

Wouldn't want anything to sully the names of the Founders, now would we? he thought cynically. *But the truth is, you don't succeed in something like the Detweiler Plan without doing some of those things you wish nobody had to do.*

And that, he reflected, was true of every star nation, to one extent or another.

He drew a deep breath and squared his shoulders. He'd be a lot happier, he admitted to himself, when Collin reached Darius. And a lot happier even than that when Albrecht and the final tranche of evacuees arrived. He'd argued against Albrecht's decision to wait until the final wave, despite how relatively new he was to his current position, and he knew that both Collin and Benjamin had done the same. But Albrecht Detweiler could have been used to illustrate the dictionary definition of stubborn.

And whatever the galaxy may someday say about the Alignment, Chernyshev reflected, *no one will ever be able to fault Albrecht's sense of personal responsibility and duty. I think the real reason he stayed was to pressure Marinescu to get the most people out that she possibly could. Oh, he agreed with her arguments, and "ruthless" is right up there with responsibility and duty in his personal pantheon. He's prepared to kill however many people—however many millions of people—he has to, but that's the difference between him and Marinescu. He'll kill however many as he has to; she'll kill as many as are convenient, and he figures his presence will be highly inconvenient for her in that regard. I wonder if Collin told him about her severance package? I hope he did. Albrecht would appreciate the irony . . . and I'm pretty sure he needs a laugh at least as badly as I did.*

Chapter Seventy-Six

THE COM CHIMED SOFTLY, and the very dark-skinned woman sat up in bed. The attention key blinked in the darkened sleeping cabin, but she couldn't reach it immediately. Sitting up was about as far as she could get just at the moment, and the enormous cat who'd been busy anchoring her feet sat up with a querulous sound as his pillow shifted under him.

At least she'd finally convinced him to sleep on her feet instead of her chest, she thought as she rubbed her eyes. Being unable to move beat the hell out of being unable to *breathe*.

"Out of the way, horrid beast," she said sternly, poking hard with a toe, and he rolled to his feet, rose to his full height, and gave her a glare of martyred patience. Then he raised his enormous tail straight up behind him and stalked indignantly away.

Now if only he'd be so offended he'd leave her feet unanchored for a night or two, she thought. Not that she expected any such outcome.

The com chimed again, and she swung her liberated legs over the side of the bed and hit the acceptance key.

Dominica Adenauer's face appeared on it, and she went ahead and tapped a key to accept full visual. Fortunately, unlike certain people she could mention, she wasn't one of those who preferred to sleep in the nude.

Not when she was sleeping alone, anyway, and Dicey didn't count.

Besides, we're all girls here at the moment, she thought dryly. *Damn it. I* knew *there were downsides to commanding a fleet. There's not one single male in the entire damned thing who's not in my direct chain of command as far as Article One-Nineteen's concerned!*

"Yes, Dominica?"

"Hyper footprint, Ma'am. A big one."

"Ah?" She ran a hand through her short, tightly curled hair. "I'm assuming it's on the right bearing?"

"Oh, yes, Ma'am. It definitely is."

"Good! I'll be on Flag Bridge in fifteen. Tell Bill to warm up the com."

❖   ❖   ❖

It was actually closer to ten minutes than fifteen when Admiral Gold Peak strode onto her flag bridge. Despite that, and despite the fact that it was the middle of HMS *Artemis'* shipboard night, its stations were fully manned, and she smiled wryly as she crossed to her own command chair.

"Any word from our visitors?" she asked.

"Not yet, Ma'am," Lieutenant Commander Edwards replied.

"Well, I suppose it would only be polite for us to extend a welcome to the newcomers," she said. "Raise them, Bill."

"Yes, Ma'am."

SCY-146-H was an M9-class star, with a hyper limit which lay only fifteen light-minutes from the primary. At the moment, the thick cluster of incoming impeller signatures was just inside that limit, still six light-minutes from *Artemis'* current position, but the newcomers' com officers had obviously been expecting her to call. Barely ten seconds after Edwards hit the send key, a man with a mustache and what was definitely not Manticoran uniform, despite the treecat perched on his shoulder, appeared on Michelle's display.

"Good evening, Lady Gold Peak," he said.

"And good evening to *you*, Admiral Tourville," she replied. "We've been waiting for you."

"I hope we're not late," he said barely six seconds later, courtesy of the FTL com.

"I didn't really expect you until tomorrow, actually. You must've made a fast passage."

"We tried not to let any grass grow under our feet," he acknowledged. "I understand we have an appointment in Mesa, and my people are looking forward to it with what you might call eager anticipation."

"Odd." Michelle cocked her head. "By the strangest coincidence, so are *my* people." The two of them smiled at each other for a moment. Then Michelle shrugged. "We're eager to get on with it, but it's the middle of the night, our ship time."

"And ours," Tourville told her. "We adjusted our chronos to Landing Standard when they sent us off to reinforce you."

"That's very convenient," she said. "But, in that case, it's the middle of the night for you, too. May I suggest that we both complete a good night's sleep and that you and your people come aboard *Artemis* tomorrow morning, after breakfast, so we can all sit down face-to-face? And I think you'd better plan on staying for lunch, as well, come to that."

"That sounds like an excellent idea," Tourville agreed.

"Until tomorrow, then," Michelle said. "Gold Peak, clear."

"Tourville, clear."

Lester Tourville swung himself from the pinnace's boarding tube into the boat bay gallery of HMS *Artemis*. For a fleet flagship, he reflected, *Artemis* was a little on the small side. As battlecruisers went, she was enormous, far larger than any ship of her class in the RHN, but she was still much smaller than a superdreadnought, and he wasn't certain he approved of keeping fleet command in something that fragile. On the other hand, he remembered his own battlecruiser flagships. There was always something special about them. Heavy enough to fight a rugged round if they needed to, but fast, maneuverable.

And independent, he thought. *The kind of ship that suits a man who doesn't want to be tied to the fleet's apron strings*.

And, a corner of his mind added as he landed on the gallery deck, back in the bad old days, battlecruiser admirals had been junior enough to avoid the sort of scrutiny that had sent so many good officers to the wall under Rob Pierre and Oscar Saint-Just.

The woman waiting for him had probably never had to worry about that, though, he reflected.

He shook that thought aside and saluted the lieutenant with the brassard of the boat bay officer of the deck.

"Permission to come aboard, Ma'am?"

"Permission granted, Admiral," the young woman replied, returning his salute. "And welcome aboard *Artemis*."

"Thank you, Lieutenant Franklin," he said, reading the name from the plate on the breast of her space-black tunic.

"And allow me to repeat the Lieutenant's welcome," a throaty contralto said, and he turned to face Admiral Gloria Michelle Samantha Evelyn Henke.

The name rolled through his mind with a certain sonorous majesty, and he felt his lips trying to twitch in an inappropriate smile. As a citizen of the Republic of Haven, where there were no official titles of nobility, he often found the Manty tendency to hang those titles on everyone in sight more than a little amusing. Given his new commanding officer's full name, however he could see where she might find "Gold Peak" preferable.

And some of the people who get titles hung on them damned well deserve *them, Lester*, he reminded himself as he reached out to shake the extended hand. *She may be Queen Elizabeth's cousin, but she's one of the best they've got, too. You'll need to stay on your toes to keep up with* this *one.*

"Thank you, Milady," he said, and discovered she had dimples when she smiled.

"Don't strain yourself, Admiral Tourville," she advised. "We all know you're a good, egalitarian republican. 'Admiral' is a perfectly acceptable way to avoid all those decadent forms of address."

The smile which had threatened to elude his control a moment earlier broke free, and he shook his head.

"Actually, we simple republicans are more sophisticated than some people seem to think, Milady," he replied. "Why, just last week I finally figured out which fork to use for dessert at a formal dinner!"

He sensed a certain tension from the officers who'd followed him off the shuttle and remembered how the State Department experts had warned all of them against giving offense to possibly prickly Manticoran aristocrats. That warning must have a certain point for them at the moment, giving just how towering this potentially prickly aristocrat's family connections were. But Gold Peak's smile only turned into a grin.

"Really?" she said brightly. "In that case, maybe you can help me figure it out at lunch!"

"I'd consider it an honor," he assured her, and she chuckled.

"Speaking of Honor," she said, "she told me once that she thought I'd really like you if we ever met, and she's generally a pretty good judge of those things. Of course, on the other hand, she does screw up every once in a while. Even with Nimitz to help her along," she added, fingers flickering through the sign for "hello" to the treecat on Tourville's shoulder.

"Well, we'll just have to hope that in this case the Duchess got it right, Milady," he said gravely, and waved the rest of his party forward. "For now, though, allow me to present my task force commanders and my staff."

❖   ❖   ❖

It was a good group, Michelle Henke decided later that day as she and Lester Tourville sat across from one another at the table in her spacious dining cabin. There were, inevitably, some rough edges here and there. For example, Tourville's chief of staff, Captain Molly Delaney, seemed a bit . . . uncomfortable working so closely with Manticorans after so many years of enmity. She was clearly aware of the problem and working hard to overcome it, though, and that was about the best anyone could ask for. From the Manticoran side of the table, it turned out that Joshua Madison, Carrier Division 11.2's CO, had much the same problem where Havenites were concerned. Madison had been detached from the rest of Craig Culbertson's carrier squadron to support Michelle when she moved on Madras. That had deprived him of the opportunity to interact with Second Fleet's officers the way the rest of Culbertson's people had in Montana, and she suspected that even he hadn't realized it was likely to be a problem. Addressing the issue was clearly something of an uphill struggle for him, as a result, but she knew him well enough to be confident he'd get there in the end.

And if I'd had any doubts about Tourville's ability to work with Manticorans, just watching him with Aivars would have knocked them on the head, she reflected with intense satisfaction. She'd expected to like Tourville herself, based on both his dossier and Honor Harrington's description of him, but seeing Terekhov's comfort with him had been one of the day's more gratifying moments.

Overall, she was impressed by the rest of Second Fleet's senior officers, as well. Vice Admiral Bellefeuille, Task Force 21's CO, was another Havenite who'd crossed swords with Honor and lived to tell the tale. In fact, she'd done remarkably well against Eighth Fleet, given the crushing technological inferiority under which she'd labored in the Chantilly System. She was young for her rank, but most Havenite flag officers were. So were Manticoran flag officers, for that matter, but at least Manticoran losses had been from *enemy* fire. They hadn't had to worry about being purged by their own government.

Vice Admiral Oliver Diamato, who commanded Task Force 23, was probably even younger than Bellefeuille, but Michelle liked what she saw. His record was certainly solid—*he'd* survived at Hancock Station against no less an opponent than Alice Truman, as a junior officer on one of the first Peep battleships to ever encounter a *Shrike*-class LAC—and he exuded a calm competence officers twice his age might have envied.

They sent me the Havenite first team, she thought. *They're* solid, *really solid, and they've more than doubled my platforms. The Mesans are going to suffer a very embarrassing sphincter failure when we come over the hyper wall with more than* fifty *wallers*.

She smiled inwardly, feeling in that moment very much like Nimitz must feel as he waited outside a chipmunk's burrow. The only thing Second Fleet was short on was carriers, but even with the detachments she'd been forced to make, *Tenth* Fleet still had twelve of them, which would be more than adequate. And Augustus Khumalo had surpassed his own best estimate; the transports and freighters which had accompanied Tourville from Montana had just over 1.2 million troops—and their planetary combat equipment—embarked.

"I don't think I'd like to be CEO Ward in a few days' time, Milady," Tourville said from his side of the table. Clearly his thoughts had been following the same pattern as hers.

"Somehow," she said thoughtfully, "I can't find it in my heart of hearts to feel too broken up over Mr. Ward's tender sensibilities. I tried, you understand, but apparently I lack sufficient empathy."

Several people chuckled, and Tourville shook his head.

"I understand there's a lot of that going around where Mesans are involved these days," he said. His tone was amused, but it carried a harsh undercurrent, and she nodded more soberly.

"Yes, there is. And if I'm going to be honest, there's a nasty, vindictive part of me that almost regrets the way you've reinforced us."

"I could see where you might want to make it an all-Manticore show, after Oyster Bay and the way they accused the Star Empire of ordering the Green Pines attack," he said.

"Oh, no, Admiral! You misunderstood me. I'm delighted to see you here, and I'd say that given how many people we've killed dancing to their piping over the years, we both have more than sufficient bones to pick with them. No, what I find myself regretting is that even a Mesan fleet commander's going to be smart enough to strike her wedge in a heartbeat when she sees this much weight of metal coming at her." She showed her teeth in a grin which would have done any treecat proud. "Like I said, it's the nasty, vindictive part of me that regrets that. I'd been rather looking forward to . . . convincing Mr. Ward to see reason by blowing his entire damned fleet out of space."

❖   ❖   ❖

Captain Scott Akers paused with his coffee cup in midair as the admittance chime sounded. He glanced at the clock, but it was purely automatic. That chime had sounded at exactly the same time—give or take fifteen seconds—every day for the last six months.

He smiled wryly and keyed the cabin door, then watched as Commander Gerald Ortega stepped through it.

"Good morning, Sir," he said...as he'd said every day for the last half T-year, and—

"Morning, Gerald," Akers replied...as he'd *replied* every day for the last half T-year. He truly liked his executive officer, and Ortega was one of the most reliable and conscientious officers he'd ever known, yet he sometimes suspected that one of the Ortega ancestors had managed to get molycircs inserted into his genome. There were people who were orderly, there were people who were precise, there were people who were meticulous, and then there was Ortega. When Akers had told him at the start of the commission that he liked to start the day with a brief meeting with his XO at around 8:30, he hadn't realized what he was about to unleash.

"Have a seat," Akers continued, pointing at the unoccupied chair on the other side of the small table.

"Thank you, Sir." Ortega settled into the chair and laid his minicomp on the table where it would be handy. As always, Akers offered him a cup of coffee. And, as always, Ortega declined.

"Anything particularly pressing we need to consider today?" the captain asked once that part of the ritual had been faithfully discharged.

"Commander O'Simpson mentioned that the Admiral would like to convene an all-captains com conference this afternoon, Sir. I suggested sixteen hundred hours, if that would be convenient for you."

"The question, Gerald, is whether or not sixteen

hundred would be convenient for *Admiral Siminetti*," Akers pointed out gently. Ortega looked at him for a moment, then nodded. He actually seemed to blush a little.

"Yes, Sir. In my defense, Commander O'Simpson asked me to recommend a time without indicating any preference on the Admiral's part."

"I see," Akers said gravely, sipping coffee to hide the smile he couldn't quite totally suppress. "And in that case," he continued, lowering the cup, "I suppose you can go ahead and tell Jasmine to set it up now."

"Of course, Sir." Ortega made a note on his minicomp, although so far as Akers knew, no one had ever actually seen him need to consult one of his memos.

"Anything else earthshaking we need to deal with?" the captain went on.

"Not really, Sir. I understand that Commander Ushikov and Commander MacKelvey have discovered some issues with the extended range fire control on the new Technodyne missiles. They've scheduled a com conference at eleven hundred hours with Technodyne's local Missile Division to discuss that. Hopefully, they'll have something to report by the time Admiral Siminetti's conference goes online."

Akers nodded. Charlotte MacKelvey was MSNS *Vanguard*'s tactical officer and Jacqueline Ushikov was Josephine Siminetti's ops officer. If there was a problem with the new missiles, he could trust them to get to the bottom of it. And if there *was* one, they'd better do just that, he thought more grimly. Not that the capabilities of the new missiles were likely to help a great deal if the Manties came calling. Assuming the reports from Spindle and Manticore—and Saltash, for that matter—were remotely accurate, the RMN wouldn't even work up a sweat dealing with the Mesa System Navy.

Well, fair's fair, he told himself. *Our grand and glorious navy consists of eighty-five ships, none of them heavier than a battlecruiser. A single squadron of wallers*—anybody's *wallers, not just the Manties'— could polish us off in an afternoon.*

Up until fairly recently, that thought wouldn't have bothered Akers. The only people who had super-dreadnoughts were the Manticorans and Havenites— who were half the galaxy away and busy killing each other—and the Solarian League, which was the Mesa System's de facto protector. By the standards of the galaxy at large, the MSN was actually a very potent fighting force. It was simply Mesa's misfortune that it wasn't "the galaxy at large" it had to worry about.

"Sit in on that conference yourself, Gerald," he said. "Charlotte's good about keeping me in the loop, but I want as many eyes as possible on this one. We need to hunt down any bugs and exterminate them ASAP."

"Yes, Sir."

Akers nodded again, this time in satisfaction. With Gerald Ortega plugged into the problem, he could be positive that *anything* he needed to know would be flagged to his attention. Which brought him to another point.

"And what do we hear from groundside?" he asked in a considerably grimmer tone.

"Nothing's changed from yesterday, really, Sir" Ortega said. "According to the official channels, the Peaceforce is about to launch the final offensive into Neue Rostock."

His eyes met Akers' across the table, and the captain snorted harshly.

Of course the Peacies are "about to launch the final offensive." According to Lackland's talking heads at Culture and Information, they been about to do that since day one! Frigging idiots, the lot of them. What the fuck *did they think they were* doing?!

In some ways, he really would have preferred to blame the nightmare situation in Mendel on Gillian Drescher, but the truth was that she was probably the one person who *wasn't* to blame! Not that he expected that to save her career in the fullness of time. Personally, the two he'd send to the wall were Selig and Howell. And he'd have McGillicuddy standing right between them when the firing squad took aim.

On the one hand, he could actually sympathize with them, at least to some extent. He'd felt the same sense of helplessness as any other member of the Mesa System's police and military forces as the Ballroom lunatics wreaked havoc on their homeworld. He'd also wondered what the hell the Ballroom thought it was doing. For all its gleeful bloodthirstiness where Manpower was concerned, Ballroom operations had always—*always*—sought to minimize civilian collateral damage. Not because they loved Mesan civilians, but because however hard Culture and Information sought to portray them as maniacs, they were actually about as rational as any terrorist ever came.

Of course, that was a pretty low bar, Akers admitted, but they'd always seemed to realize that massacring civilians in job lots would cost them even the limited amount of acceptance they'd achieved. Not only that, he was pretty sure—or he had been, until lately—that they were smart enough to realize what sort of reprisals the Mesan security forces would take against the seccy communities if they thought for an instant *anyone* on the planet was complicit in nuclear attacks on civilian targets.

Hell, the Ballroom must've *realized people like McGillicuddy would turn the Safeties and Misties loose on the seccies to make examples. And I'm sure Snyder was cheering them on the whole way. That bitch . . .*

He made himself draw a deep breath and sipped more coffee. There was no point dwelling on Regan Snyder, however much he would have liked to invite Manpower's representative to the General Board for a short spacewalk. The same sort of spacewalk manpower's captains had arranged for so many slaves over the years. Scott Akers was no bleeding heart, and the institution of genetic slavery per se hadn't cost him very much sleep over the years. But the brutality of it, the way Manpower practiced and promoted it . . . that bothered him. It bothered him a lot, and not just because he could see the way that brutalizing the slaves coarsened and brutalized the people responsible for keeping them in line, as well. That *did* worry him, but even leaving that aside, Mesa's support for Manpower—the fact that the system government didn't simply tolerate Manpower's presence but was largely *controlled* by Manpower and its close allies—was enough to turn the entire star system into a pariah, and deservedly so, and that pariah status had coldly pragmatic, potentially deadly consequences.

Thanks to Manpower, Frontier Security and the SLN would need one hell of a fig leaf to justify intervention on Mesa's behalf to the Solly public at large, even under the best conceivable circumstances. Normally, that might not have mattered a great deal. Most of the time, the bureaucrats who actually ran the League didn't give much more of a damn about public opinion than their transstellar patrons did. But that had been when everyone knew the Solarian League Navy was the most powerful fleet in space and that any reverses it might suffer would be both brief and quickly repaired. Given what had happened to it at places like Spindle and Manticore, it wasn't too surprising the Solarian public was beginning to question the SLN's invincibility. OFS' actions and policies—and the use of naval units to support them—were actually beginning to be openly questioned in the public forums, where negative opinion was growing steadily stronger. And that meant it would be a cold day in hell before a Solarian Battle Fleet task force came sailing over the hyper wall to rescue Mesa from the Manties.

And now this shit. He took another swallow of coffee, his eyes bitter. God only knew how many thousands of people—full citizens, seccies, and even slaves—the tsunami of nuclear attacks had killed. *Scott Akers* certainly didn't know, and neither Culture and Information nor his own uniformed superiors were telling him, either. Which probably meant they'd killed a *lot* of thousands. And however many they'd killed, the Misties had racked up at least twenty or thirty thousand of their own counting "just" dead seccies when that idiot Howell called in a megaton-range KEW in the middle of Mendel to avenge the troopers he'd managed to get ambushed and massacred inside Hancock Tower. Culture and Information could try to pass that off as yet another "Ballroom terrorist event" if it wanted to, but nobody over the age of three was going to believe it.

Well, that's not really true, Scott, and you know it, he told himself. *There really are people out there who are either stupid enough—or desperate enough—to take Lackland's word for it. What's that old saying about a sucker being born every minute? But there's no way that any—and I mean* any—*Navy or Peaceforce officer could look at that hole and think it was anything but a kinetic strike. And the Ballroom might* have been *able to smuggle in or cobble up nuclear devices, but no way in hell could it de-orbit an atmospheric penetrator to hit a* seccy *tower with that kind of precision.*

He set the coffee cup down, cradling it between his hands and gazing down into the murky dregs, as that thought went through him. Because, however little he wanted to admit it even to himself, the authorities' claim that the Ballroom was behind the Hancock Tower strike made him wonder if the *Ballroom* had truly been behind *any* of the recent wave of attacks. He couldn't for the life of him think of anyone else who might have wanted to wreak havoc on that sort of scale, but the argument that the Ballroom had managed to smuggle that many nuclear devices through Mesan security strained his credulity well past the breaking point. And the notion that having smuggled them through they would hit targets which could have been specifically designed to provoke exactly what had happened to Hancock—and what was in the process of happening to Neue Rostock—was even more impossible for him to swallow. In fact, the only thing harder for him to believe was the argument that the Star Empire of Manticore had engineered and supported the strikes as retaliation for the attack on their own home system.

He knew damned well that the Manties' allegations of Mesan involvement were ludicrous, because as the flag captain of Task Force One, he knew exactly what the MSN could and couldn't do. But even if the Manties believed every word of their insane accusations, they didn't need any terrorists planting bombs on the surface of the planet. If *they* wanted Mesa trashed, all they needed to do was to send a couple of squadrons of their damned podnoughts to handle the job. It would be more effective, more efficient, and—above all—it wouldn't make them moral lepers the way supporting mass-casualty terrorist attacks would.

I suppose it really is possible the Ballroom could be sufficiently ruthless to have launched a campaign like this to provoke exactly what's happening now, he thought bitterly. *I don't believe it, but I guess it's possible. And it doesn't really matter who did it, or why, because the consequences are going to be the same either way. And there's not one damned thing I can do about it.*

He didn't doubt Drescher would take Neue Rostock in the end, but according to the rumors he'd heard, she'd already lost somewhere between a quarter and a third of the entire Peaceforce fighting her way into that hulking, labyrinthine mountain of ceramacrete. Frankly, he was surprised her casualties had been that *low*! But what mattered was that after the Hancock Tower strike, and after what was about to happen to Neue Rostock's defenders, Mesa's seccies—and slaves—could have no illusions about what would happen to them if something set Public Safety off again. And—far worse, in oh, so many ways—they'd had proof the Safeties and Misties weren't invincible. That they could be beaten. That they could be *killed*. That knowledge, that awareness, was loose in the seccy and slave communities now, and it was far easier to kill a person than it was to kill an idea.

After spending all these centuries making our own bed, our own frigging security people had to go and kick in the door, he thought despairingly. *And the hell of it is, I absolutely understand why the seccies and the slaves are going to burn the planet down around our ears. I'll fight them every step of the way, because I won't have a choice, but if I were them? I'd do exactly the same damned thing.*

He sighed and shook himself.

Well, that's one way to start the day off in a fog of despair, Scott, he told himself tartly. *Any other gloomy thoughts you want to think? Morning's still young, after all!*

"I'm sure General Drescher will retake Neue Rostock . . . eventually," he said out loud, looking back up to meet Ortega's gaze again. "Is there anything else interesting going on?"

"Well," Ortega actually smiled, "you know that Solarian newsy—O'Hanrahan?"

He raised his eyebrows, and Akers nodded. He did, indeed, know Audrey O'Hanrahan, or her work, at least. In fact, his wife was one of O'Hanrahan's avid followers, although the Solarian newsy's postings were usually at least a couple of months old by the time they got to Mesa. And Akers had to admit O'Hanrahan's reputation for dragging all sorts of dark and squirmy things out into the pitiless light of day appeared to be well deserved. It was remarkable to him, in many ways, that she'd lasted so long without someone's arranging a fatal accident for her, and she hadn't made any new friends in Mesa over the last few weeks.

"What about her?" he asked.

"Well, apparently her mic was live during a brief conversation she had with the public relations idiot assigned to play local guide."

"Oh, crap," Akers said, but his own lips twitched unwillingly. "You mean—?"

"Yes, Sir. He was busy spinning her the official line, and she damned well eviscerated him. It was pitiful, like fighting a duel with an unarmed man." The XO shook his head, eyes gleaming with atypical humor. "It's obvious she didn't know it was going on the chip any more than he did, and I genuinely think she's not the one who leaked it afterward, but it was pretty devastating. Among other things, she told him she'd covered lots of 'police actions' in her time, and she knew when the troops were out of control. And"—the humor disappeared, and Ortega's face tightened—"when the troops *weren't* out of control. When they were doing exactly what they'd been *told* to do."

"Gerald, it's not *our* people," Akers said quietly. He could have counted the number of times he'd used Ortega's first name on his fingers and toes without taking both boots off, but now he reached across the table to lay one hand on the commander's arm. "I don't know where this is going to end any more than you do. I know it's not going to be a good place, though. And when we end up there, our star system will need us. So it's our job to be there when it does. That's what we need to be concentrating on right now, not things down there in Mendel that we can't control or influence."

"I know, Sir. I know." Ortega nodded, then smiled crookedly. "That offer of a cup of coffee still open?" he asked.

"It just so happens it is," Akers agreed, reaching for the carafe. "And there's even cream and—"

His com sounded suddenly. Not with its normal musical chime, but with the strident, ugly buzz of a priority signal guaranteed to awaken even the soundest sleeper. And then, a fraction of a second later, the high-pitched howl of the general quarters alarm sounded over every speaker on the ship.

Akers froze, then slapped the acceptance key.

"Captain!" he said sharply. "Talk to me!"

"MacKelvey, Sir," a strained soprano answered. "Tracking's just picked up a hyper-footprint. A big one."

"*How* big?" Akers snapped when the attack officer paused.

"Sir, so far we make it close to sixty—I repeat, Sir, *sixty*—units in the superdreadnought range. Tracking's still trying to sort out the total number of point sources, but it looks like it's got to be close to three hundred."

Chapter Seventy-Seven

"WELL, THEY KNOW WE'RE HERE NOW," Michelle Henke said. "I imagine there's a certain amount of... consternation at the moment."

"I believe that might be an appropriate noun, Milady," Captain Cynthia Lecter agreed, yet something about her tone drew Michelle's attention from the icons of the flag deck plot.

At the moment, her chief of staff was bent over her own display, and Michelle frowned. At Aivars Terekhov's suggestion, she'd sent HMS *Xiahou Dun* ahead of the massively reinforced Tenth Fleet. If all had gone according to plan, Commander Keith Lodwick, *Xiahou Dun*'s CO, had arrived in-system four days ago, but Mesa was unaware that he'd dropped by. His orders had been to make an excruciatingly slow alpha translation at least ten light-hours from the primary, then approach through normal-space under stealth. Given just how stealthy a *Roland*-class destroyer could be, the odds of anyone noticing *Xiahou Dun*'s presence—unless they got dead lucky and caught a flash of her hyper-footprint as the made her downward translation, despite the enormous distance from the inner system—ranged from slim to none.

Michelle's immediate reaction had been to wave off the suggestion as an unnecessary complication. She was a firm believer in the KISS principle, and offering another possible opening to Murphy had struck her as a bad idea. But then she'd thought about it. Terekhov was right about how unlikely the Mesans were to detect *Xiahou Dun*'s arrival. Very few star systems made the sort of investment Manticore had made in its long-range sensor platforms, and even Manticore's would've had trouble picking up a *Roland*'s low-speed transit at that range. She sincerely doubted Mesa's corporate masters had "wasted" the credits on a system which, in all fairness, they really didn't need under normal circumstances. And once *Xiahou Dun* was back in normal-space, there was no way Mesan or Solarian sensors could hope to defeat her stealth and ECM.

And Terekhov had been right in at least one respect. There was no such thing as too much information on an objective. It was vanishingly unlikely that Commander Lodwick would discover some lethal ambush waiting for them—although, once Michelle had thought about it a little, that might not have been as outlandish a proposition as it seemed, given the Yawata Strike. But anything that increased her "situational awareness" was a good thing.

Besides, she was working conscientiously at overcoming her "cowgirl" reputation.

"Cynthia?" she said after a moment, and Lecter twitched, then looked up from the display with the closest thing to a stunned expression Michelle had ever seen on her face. "Cynthia?" she repeated in a rather different tone, and Lecter shook herself.

"Ma'am, you're not—" She inhaled deeply, nostrils flaring. "Lodwick sent a couple of Ghost Rider drones in-system and tapped into the planetary datanet broadcasts, Milady," she said, "and you're not going to *believe* what he found."

"Are you serious, Admiral?" the distinguished looking man on Admiral Josephine Siminetti's display said.

"Mister Chief Executive, I'm not exactly in the habit of joking about things like this," Siminetti said bitingly.

As the senior uniformed officer of the Mesa System Navy actually in space and the commander of Task Force One, the equivalent of the Royal Manticoran Navy's Home Fleet, Siminetti had to spend entirely too much of her time dancing with politicians. She resented it at the best of times. At the moment, what she wanted more than anything else in the world was to reach through the display, grab Brandon Ward by the throat, and then rip out his tonsils for a bowtie.

And I don't see how it could hurt a thing if I did it, either, she thought. *It's not exactly like I need to be worrying about "political repercussions" at a moment like this!*

"Perimeter Tracking has definitely confirmed a minimum of sixty-two superdreadnought-range impeller wedges," she continued flatly. "There could be at least two or three more." She bared her teeth in something no one would ever have mistaken for a smile. "Tracking's losing some in the clutter, Mister Chief Executive. That sort of thing happens when a half-million tons of capital ships start churning up the EM spectrum."

Ward winced visibly, and Siminetti felt a small flicker of sadistic pleasure as she saw reality leaking into the Mesa System's chief executive's awareness.

"They haven't contacted us yet, so we don't officially know who they are, but I'm pretty sure they aren't Sollies, and that only leaves one real candidate. And if these are Manties, and if our reports are accurate, at least a few of those 'superdreadnoughts' are actually the LAC carriers they've developed," she continued. "Assuming six of them are, that's a minimum of five or six hundred LACs, and our best estimate is that a current-generation Manty light attack craft is at least equivalent in combat power to a Solly *War Harvest*-class destroyer. Of course, that estimate's based on information from the Sollies. Personally, I think it's probably closer to a light cruiser. And, speaking of cruisers, there's a minimum of two hundred of *those* out there, too. Plus at least ten or fifteen of those outsized battlecruisers of their. And I feel it's my duty as Task Force One's commander to point out that we have exactly twenty-five battlecruisers in our entire inventory...and six of them are down for routine overhaul. My point, Mister Chief Executive, is that even without their missile range advantage, they could destroy our entire Navy just with their LACs."

Ward swallowed visibly, and she saw his eyes swivel away from the pickup. She wondered who else was present. Probably that idiot Snyder, but she could always hope Pearson was also in the room. It would be nice to have *one* voice of sanity present when her system government decided whether or not her men and women would be ordered out to die. Not that it mattered very much one way or the other. She was willing to go through channels, but the truth was that she could have cared less about what Ward might tell her to do. Against that much firepower, there was only one thing she could do, and she had no intention of pouring out her people's blood the way Gillian Drescher had been forced to do cleaning up after the Misties screwed the pooch.

"They haven't contacted you yet at all, Admiral?" Ward said after a moment, and Siminetti managed not to roll her eyes.

"That *is* what I just said, Sir," she pointed out. "They're still a good ten light-minutes from Mesa orbit, so they're probably waiting until the com lag drops a bit. And I suppose it's possible they're letting us stew in our own juices worrying about them."

"Could . . . could this be an operation planned to coordinate with the terrorist attacks?" Ward asked, and Siminetti surprised herself with a short, sharp bark of scornful laughter. The CEO's eyes flashed angrily, and she shook her head.

"I'm sorry, Mister Chief Executive," she said, and she actually meant it . . . sort of. It was hard to feel *deeply* apologetic when she knew perfectly well he was speaking for the recorders. Exactly who he thought he might impress with whatever spin they managed to put on this mess was more than she could guess, but he *was* the duly constituted legal commander-in-chief of her own service.

"Sir," she continued, "if these are Manties, and *if* they'd intended to coordinate their arrival with the terrorist attacks on Mesa, they would've been here weeks or months ago. In fact, Mister Chief Executive, the fact that they're here at all seems to me the clearest indication that our intelligence that they were behind the attacks was ... ill-founded. If they've been able to cut loose this much firepower and send it all the way out here, then they never had any need to cripple or destabilize us with *terrorist* attacks."

Ward's jaw tightened. Obviously that hadn't been what he'd wanted to hear, but in Josephine Siminetti's opinion, that was just too damned bad.

"Admiral," the CEO began more sharply, "I don't think you—"

"Excuse me, Ma'am."

Siminetti looked away from her com display.

"Yes, Fred?"

"We have a com request from the ... intruders, Ma'am," Commander Frederick O'Simpson said, and twitched his head at Lieutenant Avery Niranjin, Siminetti's communications officer.

"Avery?" Siminetti switched her attention to him, and the lieutenant shrugged unhappily.

"Definitely the Manties, Ma'am," he said. "But it's a split-screen call."

"Split-screen?"

"Yes, Ma'am. It's Admiral Gold Peak ... and Admiral Tourville."

"Tourville?" Siminetti repeated sharply. "The *Havenite* Tourville?"

"Yes, Ma'am. And they're talking to us over something called a Hermes buoy about twenty thousand kilometers farther out from Mesa. With a com lag of only about ten seconds, as closely as I can calculate."

Oh, joyous day, Siminetti thought bitterly. *Twice as*

many superdreadnoughts as I have battlecruisers, *the Havenites have decided to come along to keep Gold Peak company, and they've just casually confirmed that they really* do *have FTL communications. What* next?

She didn't know the answer to that question—yet—but she damned well knew one thing that *wasn't* going to happen. Whatever Brandon Ward and the clueless idiots who'd landed her star system in this mess wanted, she was *not* going to give Gold Peak any excuse to demonstrate the efficacy of her missiles.

"Then I suppose you'd better put our visitors onto my display," she told Niranjin calmly.

"You may be able to control the planetary orbits, *Admiral*," the man on Michelle Henke's display said. "And Admiral Siminetti may have decided—on her own authority, I might add!—to stand down and surrender her vessels without firing a shot. But I assure you, if you attempt to land Marines on this planet, we *will* resist! This is an outrage—a gross violation of interstellar law!—and we will not stand by idly and see our sovereignty *or* our citizens trampled upon!"

"Mr. Ward, let me make a few things clear to you," she said after a moment. "First, I'm not remotely interested in your posturing.

"Second, I have a very clear notion of the selfless devotion with which you and your kleptocratic colleagues have served the interests of your citizens for so long.

"Third, we've been following your newscasts about recent events on Mesa. I don't suppose I should be too surprised that a gleaming paragon of veracity like Mesa should somehow assign responsibility for the attacks on your population to my star nation. In fact, I imagine the only thing that *should* surprise me would be for you to stumble into accidentally telling the *truth* about something. If the reports of General Palane's involvement in the defense of Neue Rostock are correct, then certainly there is a Torch presence on your planet. Precisely how General Palane is supposed to have smuggled so many nuclear devices through your security in her personal carryon and then scattered them broadcast across the surface of your planet eludes me somehow, though. On the other hand, I can think of several legitimate reasons for my Empress to authorize covert information gathering activities in Mesa, given recent events. So I find it quite plausible that the General is, in fact, the one who's systematically kicked your Peaceforce's ass in Neue Rostock. And having *met* the General, I would expect nothing less out of her than to stand—and die, if necessary—in defense of those *'citizens'* of yours when you unleashed your butchers on the population of your own capital."

Her normally warm brown eyes burned into Brandon Ward's taut face like a pair of augers, and he felt something inside him whimpering under their pitiless hardness.

"Fortunately for you, my forces arrived in the system before *your* forces finally overcame Neue Rostock's defenders. I say fortunately for you, because if we'd arrived too late, to find that you'd added the wholesale massacre of those defenders to what you've already done to your own people, the consequences for you and your colleagues might have been even more . . . unpleasant. As it is, General Drescher's demonstrated that she's as intelligent—and reasonable—as Admiral Siminetti. I am now in contact with someone I believe is, in fact,

General Palane, and she confirms that General Drescher's forces are in the process of withdrawing from Neue Rostock. Which, Mr. Ward, is the *only* reason that you don't already have a hundred thousand or so Manticoran assault troops on your planet, with orbital fire on call as needed. That situation, needless to say, is subject to change if I should decide at any time that conditions warrant it. I trust I am making myself sufficiently clear here?"

"A . . . a hundred thousand?" Ward repeated. Then he shook himself. "Preposterous!" he snorted. "I doubt the entire Manticoran Marine Corps has a hundred thousand assault troops!"

"I don't believe I mentioned Marines," Michelle said coldly. "I invite you to contact Mesa Astro Control. I realize they have only civilian-grade sensors, but I'm reasonably confident that they can tell you how many transports I've brought with me. And if there's anyone left at their desks in your equivalent of Admiralty House, I'm sure they could crunch the numbers for you given the hull sizes of our ships. In round numbers, though, I have approximately one and a quarter million members of the Talbott Quadrant Guard. They may not be quite up to the caliber of the Manticoran Marines, but judging from what a few thousand seccies did to what passes for your military establishment, the phrase that comes to *my* mind when I think about landing them on your sorry-assed excuse for a planet is 'like shit through a goose.'

"So, tell me, Mr. Ward," her voice could have frozen helium, "do you really want to play the part of the goose?"

✧   ✧   ✧

"Is it confirmed, Albrecht?" she asked as he crossed the sandy beach towards her.

"I'm afraid so."

He sighed and settled into the lounger beside hers. They sat silently for the better part of a minute, gazing out across the endless expanse of blue towards the crimson western horizon. It was strange, she thought. She'd never really considered it before, but now, at this moment, for some reason she desperately wanted to know how many times they'd sat in this exact same place, looking out at that same infinite horizon. Two thousand times? Five? More than that?

She took her eyes from the ocean sunset and looked across at the man she'd loved for over sixty years.

"How often do you think we've sat here, Albrecht?" she asked whimsically, her soft voice almost lost in the background murmur of the surf.

"I don't know," he said after a moment. "A lot. I remember the first time we had Benjamin out here, and that was—what? Forty T-years ago? And you and I had been picnicking out here for at least ten or twelve T-years before we even built the house!"

"I know." She reached across to his lounger and patted his forearm gently. "I'm glad we got to sit here together one more time though, dear."

"I'm sorry." His voice was even softer than hers had been, but she heard the sorrow hovering in it like unshed tears. "I'm sorry, sweetheart. I told everyone we were running on a short count, but I truly thought there'd be more time. Long enough to at least get you out."

"And what makes you think you could have sent me anywhere without you?" She shook her head. "I'm trying to remember a single time you *ever* made me to a single thing I didn't *choose* to do. Right off the top of my head, I can't remember one."

"Neither can I," he acknowledged with a small laugh. It was a sad laugh, but genuine, and he reached out and gathered up her hand. "But this time, I'd've had them drag you aboard ship if I'd realized how the window was closing."

"Then I'm just as glad you didn't realize," she said gently, turning to let him see the truth in her eyes. "This has been my cause just as much as it's ever been yours, but however important it's been to me as a cause, you're the one who's been my *life*, Albrecht. If it's time for that life to end here, with you, then so be it. I'm not complaining—look at me, and see that I'm telling you the truth."

He stared into her face for what seemed an eternity, and he did see it.

"I don't know what I did to deserve you," he said very softly, leaning close to her, cupping her face in his hands before he kissed her gently.

"Well, as far as that goes, you couldn't possibly have *deserved* me," she told him with a gurgle of laughter. "I suppose you were just lucky!"

"Yes, right up to the end." He shook his head.

"All luck ends eventually, Albrecht, and the boys and the grandchildren are all out there in Darius. You got *them* out, and you were smart enough to get all of them involved practically from the time they could walk. You and I may not see it, but you *know* they'll keep right on going, exactly the way you would have. And if the end game's not working out exactly as planned, well, your projections always allowed for the possibility that it wouldn't. The main elements are in place, Albrecht. They're out there, building strength. It may take a little longer than we thought it would a few years ago, but the end result's going to be the same, and that's the result of your work. *Yours*, Albrecht."

He listened to the sincerity in her voice, and he knew she was right. Or, at least, he amended scrupulously, she was being completely honest with him. And that was important. They'd always been honest with one another, no matter how many masks they'd been forced to wear with others.

He leaned back in the lounger, listening to wind and wave, to the distant cries of Mesa's seabird analogs, and felt something oddly like . . . contentment. Or relief, possibly. The awareness that his race was run, that the baton had been passed fully to their sons and that he could leave the execution of the final stages in their capable hands.

And he supposed he hadn't done all that badly, here in his final gambit. All but one of the disguised passenger liners in Mesa had departed for Darius well before Gold Peak's arrival. The last one wasn't going to make it, and he regretted that, because there were over four thousand valuable members of the onion aboard it. Some of them were personal friends, although only a handful had ever known his true identity, ever guessed he was Alpha One. Indeed, *none* of them had ever known his and Evelina's true last name. That had been one of the prices of his heritage and the ruthless demands of operational security to which he and his family had sacrificed so much.

At least it would be quick, he thought with bittersweet regret. The Gauls aboard the ship would see to that.

But he'd expected to get at least two more liners into Mesa and out again. Almost six thousand other members of the onion—six thousand who hadn't been on Janice Marinescu's "cull list," who'd been supposed to live...and wouldn't. But at least the evacuation sites were completely isolated from the planetary datanet as a security measure, so it was unlikely anyone had heard about Gold Peak's arrival just yet. That was good. It was better not to know some things.

He thought about the parents who were undoubtedly playing with their kids at this very moment. The lovers, stealing a moment of privacy. The teachers, the doctors. All of them, going about their lives, waiting to be evacuated.

"I really do love you," he said quietly, moving from his lounger to hers. She scooted over, making room for him, and he stretched out with her, wrapping his left arm around her as she rested her head on his shoulder and nestled her cheek against his neck. "So much," he told her, stroking her hair with his left hand. "So very much."

"I know," she said simply. "I've always known."

"I'm glad," he said...and pushed the button on the device in his right hand.

❖   ❖   ❖

"*Admiral Gold Peak!*"

The sheer shock in Dominica Adenauer's voice whipped Michelle Henke around towards her flag deck's tactical section.

"What?" she asked urgently.

"The sensors." For the first time, ever, Dominica Adenauer seemed unable to find the words she wanted. Or *needed*, at any rate. "It's...it's—"

Adenauer made herself stop, made herself draw a deep breath, then squared her shoulders and looked across the top of her display at Michelle.

"We've just picked up a series of nuclear detonations, Ma'am," she said in a voice of flattened iron.

"A *series?*" Michelle heard her own voice repeat.

"Yes, Ma'am. Most of them're on the planet, but we have at least four in-space detonations, as well. One of them—" She stopped for a moment, drew another of those steadying breath. "Three of them were in fairly small installations. One of them was a single ship, really. But the fourth... the fourth took out Lagrange One."

Michelle felt the blood draining from her own face. Lagrange One was one of Mesa's major orbital habitats. According to the information in their databanks, its permanent population was just over two and a half million.

"Sweet Jesus," someone whispered behind her, but her own eyes stayed fixed on Adenauer.

"You said 'most of them' were on the planet," she said steadily. "How many are we talking about?"

"I don't have a hard number yet, Ma'am. At least thirty, though."

"Thirty?" Cynthia Lecter repeated very carefully. Michelle turned her head. The golden haired chief of staff stood at her side, the crown of her head just level with Michelle's shoulder. "*Thirty*, Dominica?"

"At least," Adenauer confirmed grimly.

"Where?" Michelle asked. Adenauer looked at her, and she shrugged. "I mean, is there a pattern? A distribution?"

"Not an immediately obvious one."

Commander Adenauer sounded closer to normal, as if she were coming back on balance, and Michelle felt a pang of sympathy as she realized how what Dominica had just seen must resonate with what had happened to her native Sphinx in the Yawata Strike.

"Quite a few of them seem to be . . . random," the ops officer continued, looking back down at her displays as the uncaring computer steadily massaged the data, looking for patterns and correlations. "This one, for example—the biggest one of all. Looks like it was probably at least a couple of megatons." She tapped the location on her display. "It's an island in the middle of the ocean—a *nature preserve,* completely closed to development or even *camping.* Why in God's name would somebody blow up an *island*?"

"I don't have the least damned idea," Michelle grated, "but if they—whoever the hell *'they'* are— wanted to waste one of their fucking bombs on an empty island, *I'm* sure as hell not going to complain! What about the others?"

"The data's still coming in, Ma'am. I can tell you that at least some of them were in urban centers, though. Not as big as the one on the island, but big enough. I can't even begin to guess what the casualties are going to be like. But there are others scattered across small mountain resorts, or isolated manufacturing complexes in the middle of the prairie. There's even one in what the computers are calling a meteorological research station near Mesa's south pole!" She shook her head. "It just doesn't make any *sense.*"

"You're wrong," Michelle said so flatly Adenauer's eyes snapped back up to her. Michelle shook her head, her expression forged from frozen iron. "It *does* make sense...to someone. I don't know who, and I don't know why, but I know it does. And whoever the hell it is, it's the *same* someone who's been setting off bombs on this frigging planet for the last three months. There was something down there—something where *every single one* of those bombs just went off—that *someone* thought was worth blowing the hell up. And we're going to find out who it was and what the *hell* they thought they were doing. Because I can tell you one thing that's going to happen right now, Dominica."

The ops officer looked at her, and Michelle turned her head, letting her flinty eyes sweep the stunned expressions on her flag bridge.

"Whoever set those things off knew we were in orbit when she did it," she told her staff. "They *waited* until we were in orbit. And if the people on this planet were ready to blame us for having sent 'Ballroom fanatics' to wage nuclear terrorism against them, then who do *you* think they're going to blame for what just happened?"

✦ Epilogue

"IT'S BEEN CONFIRMED," Audrey O'Hanrahan said softly into her microphone, looking directly into the lens. Even her superbly trained, always professional voice cracked and wavered about the edges, and her crystal-clear blue eyes gleamed with unshed tears. "The final numbers, the total casualties, are still unknown. The confirmed Lagrange One death toll alone is already almost three million, however, and that number is expected to climb. Casualty estimates from the rest of the brutal attacks are still very preliminary, but sources in the Mesan government tell me it's virtually certain that they will at least double the Lagrange One total.

"Authorities are baffled by the targets of these savage attacks and their apparently random distribution. So far, no pattern has suggested itself. All we know is that planetary and orbital sensors confirm a total of thirty-nine separate nuclear explosions over the space of less than ninety seconds. *Ninety seconds*, Ladies and Gentlemen—less than one and a half minutes. That's how long it took for what will probably be at least six million human beings to be wantonly murdered. Vaporized as they went about their daily lives."

She shook her head, and those blue eyes had hardened.

"Obviously, I don't know what happened here, or who was ultimately behind it. My regular viewers will be aware that I've always been skeptical about claims of Manticoran responsibility for the Green Pines Atrocity just over a year ago here on Mesa. And those who have followed my coverage of the more recent terrorist campaign here will be aware that I've never subscribed to the theory that somehow, for some reason, the Star Empire of Manticore, which has always championed freedom of thought, conscience, and speech, had decided to support terrorist attacks on such a scale. It was inconceivable to me that Manticore might have been in some way responsible for the violence and the death here on a planet which has known so much tragedy, so much destruction of human lives, for so very long. I am not now and never have been an apologist for Mesa's support of the institution of genetic slavery. There is no conceivable excuse for that unconscionable commerce in human beings. But neither is there any conceivable excuse for what has been done to the people of this planet—citizen, seccy, and slave alike—over the past month. *Nothing* could possibly justify death and violence on such a scale!

"And as I contemplate what's happened, try to find some underlying pattern, some common thread, I find myself thinking the unthinkable. How does it happen that General Thandi Palane, the military commander in chief of the Kingdom of Torch, ally of both Manticore and Haven, was on Mesa, of all the planets in the galaxy, at this particular moment? How is it possible that second-class citizens, with no military training and under the weight of the most intrusive surveillance system in the explored galley, were able to amass the weapons and acquire the discipline which allowed them to stand off the full-fledged assault of the entire Mesan Peaceforce for a full T-month? How is it conceivable that the Audubon Ballroom could have smuggled so *many* nuclear devices through a security fence as tight as Mesa's...without assistance from someone?

"There are rumors—unconfirmed at this time—that the Star Empire has been involved in the deliberate destabilization of system governments across the Verge. I am one of the reporters who have always dismissed the endless stream of similar allegations against the Star Kingdom, but now I am forced to reconsider that dismissal. Countess Gold Peak, the commander of Manticore's Tenth Fleet, and Admiral Lester Tourville, her Havenite second-in-command, have both flatly denied the involvement of any of their ships or their personnel in this disastrous chain of explosions. I *want*, more than I can express, to take their word for that. And up until this week, I would have done so unhesitatingly, because the Star Kingdom of Manticore has always enjoyed a well-deserved reputation among serious journalists for transparency and honesty.

"Yet in a time when the entire galaxy seems hellbent on destroying itself, when allegations and counter allegations, conflicting stories which cannot possibly all be true, obscure all certainty, conceal all truth, where does anyone turn for *answers*?

"I can't tell you that, Ladies and Gentlemen. All I can tell you is that at the moment the explosions ripped through the very heart of this planet, Manticoran and Havenite warships were in orbit around it and they are apparently totally unable to offer *any explanation at all* for how those attacks could have been carried out without any of their sensors observing a single thing.

"I can't answer that question either...but I intend to. I've invested two thirds of my life as a journalist, exposing corruption and always seeking the truth behind the lie, because without truth, there can be no justice. I have no intention of abandoning that search at this time, wherever it may take me, whoever it may lead me to. I truly hope it does not lead me to Manticore, but if it does, so be it.

"I'm Audrey O'Hanrahan, coming to you from Mendel, the capital of the Mesa System, and I ask you to keep the victims of this senseless, savage attack in your hearts and in your prayers.

"Good night."

✦ Wloclawek glossary

Agitacja — the "Agitation"; the movement which brought the RON to power.

Aparatczycy — apparatchik, plural.

Aparatczyk — apparatchik, singular.

Biuro Bezpieczeństwa i Prawdy — Bureau of Security and Truth; BBP; headed by the **Minister Bezpieczeństwa i Prawdy** (Minister of Security).

Czarna kurtka — "black jacket," nickname for an officer of the BBP, based on the black tunics worn by the BBP's uniformed branches.

Czarne kurtki — black jacket, plural.

Gorąca czekolada — hot chocolate.

Izba Deputowanych — Chamber of Deputies; short reference = *Izba*.

Kancelaria Partii — Party Chancellery; HQ of the RON in Lądowisko.

Karta Partii — Party's Charter; the foundation document of the RON.

Komisja Wolności i Sprawiedliwości Społecznej — Commission for Freedom and Social Justice (KWSS); headed by ***Minister Wolności i Sprawiedliwości Społecznej*** (Minister of Freedom and Social Justice).

Krucjata Wolności Myśli — the Free Thought Crusade (KWM).

Lądowisko — Landing in Polish; the capital of Wloclawek.

Łowca trufli — truffle hunter, singular.

Łowcy trufli — truffle hunters, plural.

Oczywiście — Polish for "of course!" or "sure!"

Oligarcha — oligarch, singular.

Oligarchia — oligarchy.

Oligarchowie — oligarchs, plural.

Pierwszy Aparatczyk — First Apparatchik.

Pierwszy Sekretarz Partii — Party First Secretary.

Pierwszy Sekretarz — First Secretary.

Policja Federalna — Federal Police.

Policja Miejska — Municipal Police; collective.

Policja Okręgowa — District Police.

Policja Miejska [city name] — [city name] City Police.

Prezent do Praksedy — "Praksedy's Gift," the Szponder estate on *Szafirowa Wyspa*.

Proszę — Polish for "please."

Republika Włocławek — Republic of Wloclawek.

Ruch Odnowy Narodowej — National Renewal Movement (RON).

Ryba/ryby grzmot — singular/plural for "thunder fish," a very large (twice a tuna's size) fish on Wloclawek which is a major part of its gourmet seafood trade.

Sąd Najwyższy — High Court [of Justice].

Sekretariat Partii — Secretariat of the Party.

Sekretarz — Secretary.

Sędzia Najwyższy — Chief Judge; equivalent of Chief Justice.

Siły Zbrojne Włocławka — Armed Forces of Wloclawek (SZW).

Siostry Ubogich — Sisters of the Poor.

Szafirowa Wyspa — "Sapphire Island." Tomasz Szponder's private island estate.

Szeroka Rzeka — Broad River; the major river flowing through the city of Lądowisko to the ocean.

Trzystu — Three Hundred, referring to the surviving members of the Party's original 300 members.

Wydział Kryminalno-Dochodzeniowy — Criminal Investigation Department.